Also by Julia Brannan

The Highlander's Tale: Alex

A Jacobite Chronicles Story

Julia Brannan

DISCLAIMER

This novel is a work of fiction, and except in the case of historical fact, any resemblance to actual persons, living or dead, is purely coincidental

Formatting by Polgarus Studio

Cover design by najlaqamberdesigns.com

Cover model: Jason Tobias

Cover model photography by VJ Dunraven of www.PeriodImages.com

In memory of Lorraine Mary Macintyre
10th June 1936 – 13th June 2021
A wonderful, warm person, who helped me relax on a
very nerve-racking day, and who made my time in
Australia even more special by making me feel like
part of her family.

ACKNOWLEDGEMENTS

First of all, as ever, I'd like to thank Jason Gardiner and Alyson Cairns, my soulmates and best friends, who put up with me on a day-to-day basis, who are sharing my wonderful life in Scotland, and who understand my need for solitude, but are always there for me. They've both supported me through every stage of my writing, and, indeed, in all my other endeavours, both sensible and madcap!

Thanks to the long-suffering Mary Brady, friend and first critic, who reads the chapters as I write them, critiques them for me and reassures me that I can actually write stuff people will want to read, and to my beta readers Angela, Claire and Susan (as well as Jason and Alyson) for their valued and honest opinions. I can't stress how important you are!

Thanks also go to Mandy Condon, who sends me useful articles, has already determined the cast list for the film of my books, and who has been a wonderful and supportive friend for over twenty years. Long may that continue!

My gratitude also to fellow author Kym Grosso, who has been extremely supportive and has generously given me the benefit of her experience in the minefield of indie publishing. I value her friendship and support enormously!

A big thank you also to Diana Gabaldon, who wrote a fabulous review for my books, and who is a kind, supportive, and very interesting person!

Also a thank you goes to the National Trust for Scotland, who are stocking my books at the gift shop in Culloden Visitor Centre and to the Clan Cameron Museum, which also stocks the Jacobite Chronicles. Both sites are well worth a visit, should you be in the area.

And thanks as always go to Jason at Polgarus Studio for doing an excellent job of formatting my books, to the talented and very patient Najla Qamber, who does all my covers, puts up with my lack of artistic ability, and still manages to somehow understand exactly what I want my covers to look like! Thanks also to Àdhamh Ó Broin, who translated various phrases into Gaelic for me in record time, and to the Highland Folk Museum, one of whose cottages I used on the front cover, and which is a fabulous place to visit if you get the chance.

To all my wonderful readers, who not only buy my books, but take the time and effort to give me feedback, to review them on Amazon, Audible, Goodreads, and Bookbub and recommend me to others, by word of mouth and on social media – thank you so much. You keep me going on those dark days when I'd rather do anything than stare at a blank screen for hours while my brain turns to mush…you are amazing! Without all of you I would be nothing, and I appreciate you more than you know.

Special thanks also to Susan Bluntish (you know why)

And finally, to Bob and Dee. You are wonderful people and I love you.

ABOUT THE AUTHOR

Julia has been a voracious reader since childhood, using books to escape the miseries of a turbulent adolescence. After leaving university with a degree in English Language and Literature, she spent her twenties trying to be a sensible and responsible person, even going so far as to work for the Civil Service for six years.

Then she gave up trying to conform, resigned her well-paid but boring job and resolved to spend the rest of her life living as she wanted to, not as others would like her to. She has since had a variety of jobs, including telesales, Post Office clerk, primary school teacher, and painter and gilder.

In her spare time she is still a voracious reader, and enjoys keeping fit, exploring the beautiful countryside around her home, and travelling the world. Life hasn't always been good, but it has rarely been boring. Until recently she lived in the beautiful Brecon Beacons in Wales, but in June 2019 she moved to Scotland, and now lives in a log cabin in rural Aberdeenshire, a perfect place to write in!

A few years ago she decided that rather than just escape into other people's books, she would quite like to create some of her own and so combined her passion for history and literature to write the Jacobite Chronicles. She's now writing the side stories of some of the minor characters, and is researching for her next series, The Road to Rebellion, which will go back to the start of the whole Jacobite movement.

People seem to enjoy reading her books as much as she enjoys writing them, so now, apart from a tiny amount of editing work, she is a full-time writer. She has plunged into the contemporary genre too, but her first love will always be historical fiction.

A NOTE ABOUT ALEX'S BOOK

I just wanted to let you all know that the Highlander's Tale deals with the earlier part of Alex MacGregor's life. This will be continued in The Baronet's Tale: Sir Anthony, which I'm already planning, and which will (hopefully) be released in 2022.

CHAPTER ONE

Loch Lomond, Scotland, April 1719.

By the time the men had imparted various nuggets of practical advice regarding the livestock and spring planting to patient wives who already knew everything they were being told, it being they who generally tended both the animals and the crops, the sun had already risen behind the mountains. It was now light enough to see the group of MacGregor clansmen waiting in the clearing near the chieftain's house for the stragglers to join them. Every man was armed to the teeth with whatever weapons he possessed. Each had a dirk thrust in his belt, a targe slung over his shoulder, some carried muskets and most had a sword, although Gregor had a Lochaber axe, to the amusement of those around him. Dugald carried bagpipes rather than a musket, which he considered a far more versatile weapon of war. All wore a linen shirt and the *féileadh mór*, so practical for the Highland way of life. In the sporran around their waists was packed everything else they would need for the initial journey, which the chieftain had estimated would take around five or six days.

The chieftain, who was wise enough to know his wife needed no advice on household, arable or pastoral matters, had busied himself instead by loading up a garron with various practical and luxury items which would bring a little comfort to his clansmen on the long march to Eilean Donan castle, where the troops were to meet. After sending up a silent prayer that it would not be needed to carry a wounded man home again, Alexander led the sturdy little horse across the clearing, nodded his approval to the waiting clansmen and then headed towards his house. He had intended to go in and say a private farewell, but was thwarted by his wife Moira coming out of the door, the baby nestled in a fold of her arisaid, the two sons following behind. He handed the reins to the nearest man and walked over to his family group, enfolding his wife in his arms.

"Take care, *a ghràidh*," he said softly. "Pray that this one will be a success, and that the king will grant us the lands we're standing on."

"To say nothing of our names, and our rights in law," Moira added.

"Aye, that too," Alexander agreed. "Dinna work too hard. Ye had a hard time wi' her, and ye need to regain your strength." He leaned down and kissed first his baby daughter and then his wife, who smiled.

"I'll try not to, but things must be done, ye ken that. I'll ask Fiona and Barbara to help wi' the heavy work, the butter-making and such. I can ask Kenneth to fetch the water, and he'll help with anything heavy, he's a good lad." She nodded towards a currently sullen-looking youth, who, in spite of his age, was a head taller than nearly all the assembled fighting men.

"Aye. Keep him busy. He's awfu' sore that he canna come wi' us," Alexander murmured.

"Why will ye no' take him? I ken ye'll no' take anyone under fifteen, but he's only a few weeks short of that, and he's taller and stronger than his brother. And his da, for that matter."

"I'm respecting Gregor's wishes, for now. But only because I dinna generally make exceptions, for that way lies chaos. I mean to have a talk wi' him regarding it, though. Right then," he said, crushing his wife to his chest hard enough to elicit a wail of protest from baby Morag, and then stepping back to address his sons, "you two need take care of your ma and your wee sister. If your ma asks ye to do something, ye do it, and if ye see something that needs doing and ye can do it, dinna wait for her to ask." He bent down and placed one hand on top of each son's head, ruffling their hair.

Alexander hesitated then, wanting to scoop them both up in his arms, but aware that his eldest son, although not yet four, already considered himself a man, albeit a very small one, and might be embarrassed by his father treating him like a wee bairn in front of the whole clan. At two, little Duncan had no such pride, but he couldn't treat them differently. He half-turned as if to leave, then stopped.

To hell with it, he thought. *At best I might not see them for weeks, months even. At worst I might never…* No. That was not a thing to think of, not now at any rate. Even so… he stepped forward again and scooped the pair of them up, one in each arm. By God, but they were bonny wee laddies, bursting with health, eyes bright, limbs sturdy. He was so blessed to have them. He crushed them to him as he had his wife, and his slate-blue eyes filled with sudden tears. He blinked them back quickly, so only Moira saw his uncertainty about the venture, and then he loosened his grip, before gently replacing them on the ground.

"Duncan can do the things," his eldest son said once back on *terra firma*. "I'm coming with ye."

Alexander looked down at his namesake, who stood, legs planted apart, his small forehead furrowed, clearly expecting the refusal he now heard.

"Ye canna come wi' me. No man under fifteen can fight."

"But I *can* fight. *And* I've got a dirk," Alex said, taking out the *sgian dubh* which he'd received a few weeks ago, and of which he was inordinately proud, although he still had to be closely observed to make sure he didn't slice his fingers off whilst trying to cut his meat.

"No' a dirk," Duncan observed accurately, earning such a fierce scowl from his brother that he stepped back, alarmed.

"I can stab a man wi' it," Alex reasoned, looking earnestly up at his father.

"I've tellt ye. No one under fifteen. Ye can count to twenty, so ye ken that three is a lot smaller than fifteen. No. Even Kenneth isna going, because he isna fifteen yet."

Alex glanced at the enormous youth in the distance, then back at his father, who had turned away, his goodbyes said, eager to be on his way now everyone was ready.

"But I'm the chieftain's son!" Alex cried desperately. "I have to kill a man!"

Alexander tore his hand through his hair in sudden impatience, and turned back.

"Aye, ye do, one day. But now ye have to obey your chieftain's orders," he said. "Ye canna come, and there's an end of it."

Alex fought hard, but only succeeded in stopping his face from crumpling completely by biting his lip, hard.

"But I need to—" he persisted. Before he could get any further Alexander reached to his left side and drew his sword in one smooth movement. Alex blanched and stepped back, but then his father turned it so the handle was facing his son.

"Here, then," he said, kneeling down and offering it. "Take it."

Alex glanced at his mother for reassurance, but her face was expressionless. Duncan, now half-hidden in her skirts, looked on with huge grey eyes. Alex licked his lips and then stepped forward, putting both hands tentatively on the hilt of the sword.

"You have to grip it," his father said. Alex did as he was told as best he could, given that his hands were too small to encircle the hilt. Then his father slowly released his own grip so that the blade now rested on the ground. Give him his due though, the boy kept hold of the handle, although he staggered a little at first. "Now," Alexander continued, "lift it off the ground."

He watched as his tiny son put every ounce of strength, will and sheer bloody-mindedness into trying to raise the blade from the ground, his face going almost purple with effort. And then, gently, he leaned across and took the weapon from Alex's hands, raising it into the air with ease.

"When ye can lift this sword wi' one hand, like this," he said. "And ye can swing it like this," he swung it back and forth to demonstrate, "for an hour, and no' be too weary to do it for another hour if I tell ye to, then ye can ask me again to take ye with me, and I might. Until then, laddie, ye do as ye're tellt, and help your ma. Ye're the eldest while I'm away, and I'd no' trust just anyone to look after her." He sheathed the sword, then leaned down and ruffled the glossy red-brown hair of his defeated son. "Ye've courage, and ye'll be a bonny fighter one day," he said. "But no' this day."

Then he nodded to his wife, turned and walked away, leading as his men followed him along the side of the loch, heading north to join the others rising in the second attempt in four years to restore James Stuart, *de jure* King of Great Britain, to his throne.

The rest of the MacGregors watched until they'd disappeared into the morning mist which was rising from the loch and spreading across its banks, and then they turned to the chores of the day, and to the long, worrisome wait for their men to return.

* * *

The men, all in good spirits at the thought of taking part in a fight, and even better, one that might improve their futures, soon settled into a brisk walk, chatting quietly together as the mist cleared and the sun appeared above the mountain, heralding one of the first truly warm days of spring. Alone at the head of them, Alexander remained silent for a time, thinking. The men would march where he told them to, and they would fight when he told them to, and fight well. But the responsibility was on him to decide when, or even if they fought. He was concerned, because not the slightest rumour of unrest had reached him until the weary man carrying the burnt cross signifying an urgent call to arms had run into the settlement, calling out the clan war cry and telling them that Scotland was rising for James, that the clans were gathering at Eilean Donan, that James was on his way with a Spanish army, and that England was rising too.

Isolated as the MacGregors were, Alexander would still have expected to hear earlier news of such a huge rising, which surely must have been months in the planning. No, his instincts told him something was not right, but he didn't know what, and probably wouldn't know until they joined the others, when it would be too late to change his decision without both seeming cowardly and disappointing his clansmen. He sighed, feeling uneasy, but knowing he could not show his feelings to his men.

"So, are we away to join up wi' Rob Roy then?" Gregor, who had moved to Alexander's side unnoticed while he was buried in thought, asked. A few others, hearing the question, moved closer, wanting to hear the chieftain's reply. Seeing this Alexander stopped, letting the men gather round him. He reached into one of the garron's packs and pulled out a leather flask of whisky, which he took a drink from before passing it to his neighbour.

"No," he answered. "I've no intention to join wi' Rob Roy."

Murmurs of surprise passed through the group.

"But he summoned us, did he no'?" Allan asked. "He sent out the fiery cross."

"No, he didna," Alexander replied, then corrected himself.

"Well, that is he did send out the cross, but as far as I'm concerned, all that did was inform us of the matter at hand, for which I'm grateful. And if I'm unfortunate enough to meet the bastard at Eilean Donan, which I doubt, judging by his performance at Sherrifmuir, I shall thank him for the news."

The men glanced uneasily at their leader.

"But we canna ignore the fiery cross," James said.

"He isna my chief. I'm under no obligation to obey him. But I'm no' ignoring it," Alexander replied. "We're here, and we're marching to the rendezvous. What I've no intention of doing is joining wi' Rob Roy before that, which, as he didna give me a meeting point other than Eilean Donan, he canna reproach me for. And I've no intention of fighting under him, and if it comes to it, I shall tell him why."

"Why?" asked Gregor.

"Because I've no wish to repeat the farce of four years ago. Many of you were there then and will no doubt remember what happened. I'm heading north to fight for my king, no' to take a meandering tour of the glens so as to arrive as late as possible, and then stand on the ridge observing the battle rather than charging down into it, because the leader is so far up Argyll's arse that he's no thought to fight against him."

There was silence for a moment as the men took this in. As usual, none of them could fault their chieftain. It was true that in the '15 the Campbell Duke of Argyll had fought for the Elector of Hanover, and it was also true that Rob Roy had been sheltered and protected by Argyll and so owed him a debt, which he paid by deliberately taking too long to arrive at the battlefield, hoping he wouldn't have to fight, while still claiming to support James should he win. Rob Roy wasn't the only man to hedge his bets, but that didn't make Alexander like him any better for it.

"I canna speak for you, but I went to the '15 to fight for James, for his right to be king. My loyalty is to the Stuart cause. Rob Roy's loyalty is to himself, and no other. I'd have had more respect for him if he'd refused to come out, or if he'd declared for the Elector. But he didna. He played both sides by pretending to be for the Stuarts, but ensuring that if Hanover won he could say he'd taken no part in the battle, and stay in their good graces. Which is exactly what happened. I'll no' stand behind a duplicitous traitor, which is what he is in my opinion. If he asks me, I'll tell him that. But I'll no' go seeking him to tell him," he added on seeing the look of alarm on his men's faces as they anticipated having to fight other MacGregors, should the two chieftains argue. "If he's there wi' more MacGregors, I'll fight side by side wi' him, as an equal. But I'll no' take orders from him. And if he stands on a hill to dither, he can watch us showing him how MacGregors of honour behave. Maybe he'll be shamed into joining us."

None of the men who had fought in the last rising four years ago could argue with this, as all of them had felt the same way at the time. So instead they passed the whisky flask around and sent up silent prayers that their fiery chieftain would not clash with the equally fiery Rob Roy and drag them into a fight against their own. If he did though, they would stand with Alexander, because he commanded their loyalty and justifiably so.

Once every man had refreshed himself the group continued, and Alexander, noticing that Gregor remained close to him, took the opportunity to broach part of what he wanted to discuss with the man.

"Why have ye chosen the axe, man?" he asked. "Ye're formidable wi' a sword, after all."

Gregor reddened a little.

"Aye, well, it takes a different skill to use the axe, but I ken how to use both, so thought to let Alpin have the sword. It's his first fight, and I'd see him make a good account of himself."

"I'm sure he will. But I'd rather ye used a sword too. I packed a few, in case any get lost or damaged in the fighting. Ye can have one of those, if ye want."

Gregor nodded his agreement, his look of relief telling Alexander that in spite of his claims, it was necessity rather than choice that had made him bring the effective but somewhat old-fashioned weapon with him.

"I'll gie it to ye when we stop for the night," Alexander said.

The two men walked side by side in companionable silence for a minute.

"Gregor, is that why ye didna want Kenneth to come? Because ye didna have a weapon for him? If so, ye should have tellt me," Alexander asked finally.

"He's no' fifteen yet," Gregor said, somewhat testily. "He kens the rule, as do we all."

"Aye, but I'd have made an exception for him, had ye no' made it so clear ye were against the idea," Alexander said. "After all, he's but three weeks from fifteen, and he's looking to be a giant. No one would think him so young. And he's incredibly powerful."

This was true. No one looking at the slender dark-haired Gregor and Barbara would believe that the enormous red-headed youth could possibly be their son. True, the boy had his father's pale blue eyes and his mother's good-natured temperament, but if it hadn't been the case that half the women of the clan were present at his birth, which had nearly killed his mother, no doubt he would have been thought a changeling, a fairy child put in place of a human baby. But too many of them had seen him emerge from Barbara's womb red-faced and bawling, with a shock of blood-streaked orange hair, looking like a three-month-old rather than a newborn baby, so no rumours had ever spread. Barbara said that he took after her grandfather, both in hair colour and size, and no one had questioned that.

As he'd grown, everyone had expected him to be a little taller than the other children at first, having such a head start, but then maybe slow down as he matured. But at fourteen Kenneth was already taller than every man except Alexander, who was himself considered a giant of a man, being over six feet. And if Kenneth continued growing at this rate he would soon pass his chieftain. Nor was he slender and gawky as other youths of his age, and particularly the taller ones, tended to be. Instead his limbs were solid and well-muscled, and he was already stronger than even Alexander, although the chieftain knew he could still put the boy down if necessary. At the moment. Give him a few years and it might be a different matter.

Emerging from his thoughts, he noticed now that Gregor's face was red as his son's hair. Whatever the reason for him not wanting the boy to join them, it was not for lack of a sword.

"Later, then," Alexander said, and Gregor nodded in relief and moved back to join his older son, whose parentage no one could doubt, so much like his father was he, and now brimming with excitement at the thought of participating in a battle.

They stopped to make camp at sunset. They'd made good progress today, so there was no need to continue walking by moonlight. At this rate they'd arrive in very good time, if the weather continued so fine. They set up camp under an overhang of rock, lighting a fire to cook their oatcakes and heading down to a nearby burn to collect water and wash off the sweat and dust of the day. Alexander produced a piece of mutton from the garron's pack, which earned him a cheer. In no time the men were sitting cosily round the fire, eating and drinking, laughing and joking with each other, making the most of the relaxed atmosphere, as all of them knew how different it would be once they reached their destination and had to maybe dig latrines or trenches, do sentry duty, or join with strangers to become a regiment. They might have to be quiet then, or sleep fully armed in case of a night attack. But now they could just relax, and so they did, the MacGregors being experts at living in the moment and enjoying it to the full.

Not so Alexander, who as chieftain had to think ahead. Having watched Gregor disappear round the side of the overhang, he followed him, keeping at a distance until his clansman had finished relieving himself, before joining him.

"Let's get it over with," he said by way of broaching the subject, "for I'll have a great many things to concern me once we arrive at Eilean Donan. What's wrong wi' the boy? I canna think of anything. I've seen him use a sword, and he's fast and strong. And we need to sort this out if it's no' his age that's worrying ye, because next time he asks I'll say yes, unless your reason is a really good one. I ken Barbara canna have more bairns after him, but that's no' a reason to emasculate the boy."

Gregor made a show of arranging his plaid, and Alexander allowed him the time to think of how to word his reasons.

"I've no issue wi' Kenneth's ability to use weapons. He's a fair shot wi' a musket too. It's just…" Gregor hesitated, clearly struggling either to find the words or to admit whatever it was that was bothering him.

"Is it that he's so big, but untried? You're worried that his size will attract redcoats looking to boast that they killed a giant? Because if that's the case, his size is just as likely to make them keep away from him."

"Aye, part of it's that. But…it's just that he's so…he's so gentle. I've never seen him lose his temper, never seen him even irritated. He's always been that way. Your two bairns are what? Two and three, and I've seen them wrestling. Alex was fierce wi' Duncan over the dirk when we were leaving. It's normal. But Kenneth isna fierce. He's never been fierce. In truth I canna imagine him even hitting anyone, let alone killing them, no' even in battle when his blood's up. I dinna ken if he's capable of the red rage. I think he'd hesitate and be killed. Or worse, run away, and shame himself and me." Gregor's voice cracked on making such a terrible admission, and he looked away. Alexander thought for a minute of how to respond to such a delicate matter.

"Aye, I agree wi' ye in part," he said finally. "He's gentle, wi' bairns and wi' animals too. He's a kind heart. I've always been glad of it, because wi' the size of him, he could have badly hurt others of his own age in play without meaning to. But he never has. He's always been aware that he's different, that he's stronger, and I think that's made him be careful, and rein himself in all the time until it's become his nature. He's a kind, considerate boy. But he's no' the only kind, considerate boy in the clan. It's just more obvious wi' Kenneth because of his size. I think ye might be doing him a disservice, maybe no' in the hesitating, because that's something that every man might do in his first battle. But I dinna think he's a coward. Truly, that never crossed my mind. He can stand up for himself, and I've seen him defend others, too."

"Aye, wi' words. But he's never hit anyone, has never even raised his voice."

"No, because he doesna need to, and kens well he could cause them more damage than they deserve if he did hit them. He kens he's stronger than most, because I've no doubt you and Barbara both have tellt him that, many times. He doesna ken *how* strong, because he willna take the risk of finding out by killing a friend in a petty squabble. I think he'd be different in a battle, when he's supposed to kill everyone who comes at him."

Gregor wiped his hand across his face, and sighed.

"D'ye truly think that, Alexander? Ye're no' just saying it to make me feel better?"

Alexander laughed.

"I'm no' in the habit of doing that, as ye ken well, man. Maybe he'll hesitate, the first time, but that's no reason to stop him fighting. Every boy runs that risk in his first fight. But fighting's what we do, and the next raid or battle we're in, I'm bringing him along, Gregor. If this is a true rising, then it'll go on for a while and he may join us later in this too, if we end up going south to fight and passing by our lands. Ye canna stop him forever, unless ye want him to hate ye for it. And he will."

"Aye, ye're right. I wish he'd lose his temper, just the once. I've tried to make him, but it's no' in him to do so."

"I'll promise ye this. The first time he fights I'll keep him close to me, and protect him as best I can without making it obvious and shaming him. But I'm thinking he'll be a credit to us."

Gregor gave in. He couldn't gainsay his chieftain anyway, and in any case he was right. It was something that had to be faced up to. After all, his oldest son was here, and it was his first battle, yet he wasn't inordinately worried about him. But then Alpin had had his fair share of cuts and bruises in brawls, and was fearsome in weapons practice. Whereas Kenneth, even though he was, as Alexander said, adept, always seemed to be holding back somehow, to be considering every move he made, which you didn't have the luxury of doing in battle.

"Are ye thinking it's no' a true rising, then?" he asked, by way of changing the subject.

"I'll no' ken that until we get there. It's just strange, if the Scots *and* the English are rising, James is on his way and Spain's sending an army, that we havena heard anything about it until now."

"The English fought in the '15 too," Gregor pointed out.

"Aye, for what it was worth. But we heard rumours about that before the call to fight came. And there wasna a Spanish army then. No point in worrying about it now, though. Let's go back and join the others. Focus on Alpin and forget Kenneth for now. He'll no' be fighting yet a while, at least."

The two men made their way back down to the camp, where the others, having eaten their full, were settling in to tell tales of their prowess, to start to ready themselves for whatever awaited them at Eilean Donan.

* * *

Although unaware of his father's concerns about his courage, Kenneth, worried about both his brother and father and, very upset that he wasn't with them, found sleep a stranger that night.

Instead he tossed and turned on his heather-filled mattress for hours, before finally giving up on the effort. He rose just before dawn and crept silently out of the hut, not wanting to wake his mother.

It was so early that the settlement was silent. He filled his lungs with the pure fresh pre-dawn air gratefully, and then made his way quietly down to the lochside, wanting a little time to settle his disturbed thoughts in the hopes that he could then appear indifferent if anyone commented on his not being allowed to fight.

He had no right to be upset at not being included in the war party, after all. Alexander was a stickler for the rules he'd set, and fifteen was the lowest age limit for being allowed to participate in a serious fight of any kind. Even so, he knew well that he was exceptional, both in size and strength, and he had thought he'd given a good account of himself in weapons practice. Maybe not. He needed to try harder.

The loch was calm at this time, misty, dark and inviting. Maybe a swim would settle him. It would certainly wake him up. It would be a rare treat to swim alone, to feel as though he was the only person awake in the world. However, as he reached the water's edge he realised that he was not the only person awake in the world. Another troubled soul had clearly had the same idea as him and was seated on a rock, arms wrapped round his lower legs, chin on his knees, staring intently into the mist.

Kenneth smiled, remembering sitting in a similar way as a child himself, his linen tunic pulled over his knees to keep his legs warm. He watched the boy for a moment, heard him sniff miserably, looked around for the child's constant companion, saw none, and then stepped forward, deliberately snapping a twig underfoot to warn the child he was there, give him time to wipe his tears away.

"Ye couldna sleep either, I take it?" Kenneth said softly.

The boy shook his head, his red-brown hair flying round his face.

"Does your ma ken you're here?"

"No. They're asleep. I want to be alone. Don't go," Alex added with apparent contradiction as Kenneth made to step back. Kenneth smiled. It was as possible to be alone with someone else as it was to be lonely in a crowd. He knew that well. He moved forward again and sat down on the ground.

"Are ye afeart for your da?" Kenneth asked after a while.

"No. He's chief. He'll kill all the bad men," Alex replied with the confidence of extreme youth. "Are ye afeart for your da, and Alpin?"

"No' so much for my da, no. But it's Alpin's first battle, so I'm a wee bit fashed for him," Kenneth said honestly.

"Are ye sad that ye couldna go?" Alex muttered after another silence, during which the sky turned a slightly lighter shade of blue.

"Aye, I am. Are you?"

Alex nodded, then settled his chin back on his knees.

"I canna lift the sword, but I could help. I can fetch wood. And I can sing a lullaby! I could sing to them so they'd sleep well," Alex said fiercely.

"Ye could. Ye've a fine voice."

Alex looked at Kenneth suspiciously.

"How d'ye ken that? I havena sung *you* to sleep."

"Your ma tellt me. Ye sing to Duncan at night, d'ye no'? It's a kind thing to do."

The child relaxed.

"Aye. He's a baby. He's only two. I sing to Morag too, though she sleeps all the time anyway. I dinna need a lullaby now I'm big."

Kenneth grinned, thankful that it was still too dark for the boy to see.

"Why did ye no' go?" Alex asked with the brutal directness of childhood.

"I'm no' fifteen," Kenneth replied.

"Aye, but Da said when I can lift his sword wi' one hand and wave it about for two hours, I can go. You could lift his sword wi' one hand, could ye no'?"

"Aye, I could," Kenneth agreed.

"How long is two hours?" Alex asked.

"A long, long time," Kenneth replied. "In two hours it'll be day and everyone will be awake, your ma will be calling ye, and Duncan'll be looking for ye." He would. The two boys had been inseparable since Duncan had learned to walk a few months ago.

Alex looked up at the sky, where the brighter stars were still clearly visible.

"That *is* a long time," he said despairingly. "But you can do it. So you can go then."

Yes, he should be able to go. He was taller than his brother, stronger than his brother, a faster runner, and in truth, a better fighter than his brother, with weapons at least. It was true Alpin was fearsome with his fists, while Kenneth never used his. He'd walk away before it came to hitting someone. But he wasn't likely to be punching someone in battle. He should be there. But it was the rule.

It was an unfair rule.

Kenneth shook his head. You couldn't think your chief's rule unfair. Alexander was a good chief. He had no right to think like this.

"Are ye wanting to get stronger then, so ye can lift a sword?" Kenneth asked, opting to focus on his tiny companion's problem rather than his own seditious thoughts.

"I am," Alex said. "But I havena got a sword to lift."

"Ye dinna need a sword to lift. Ye need to grow muscles in your arms, here, and here too," he said, running his hand up his own arm and across his shoulder. "Ye can do that by lifting anything heavy. Ye can do it and help your ma too, as your da tellt ye to."

"Can I? How?" Alex asked.

The sky was lightening now, and in the distance sounds of the clanspeople starting to go about their business could be heard. Kenneth abandoned the thought of a solitary swim, and put his mind to making Alex feel better.

* * *

Moira watched in astonishment as Alex, trailed by Duncan, made his way to the loch for the fourth time, holding the biggest pail he could manage to lift. He graciously allowed Duncan to help him carry it on the way to the loch, but then insisted on carrying it alone on the way back, even though he staggered and weaved about under the weight.

She glanced at the large pail outside her door, which she would normally carry down and fill herself. It was a little less than half full. Another four trips to fill it then, before she could wash the dishes and clean the floor. She might as well find something else to do for the hour it would take him.

"Kenneth," she called, as she saw the fiery-haired boy passing, a peat iron slung over his shoulder. "Have you anything to do wi' this?" She waved her hand in the direction of her two tiny sons. "I saw ye come up from the loch together this morning. What did ye say to him? He hates fetching water."

"Aye, well, he kens ye're no' to do heavy work on account of the bairn," Kenneth replied evasively.

"He does. He also kens that you could fetch me a pail of water in a few minutes, no' a few hours as it's taking him," she commented.

"D'ye want him for something else? I can fetch the water, if ye want," he offered.

"No. It's no' urgent, and it's good to see him busy and smiling. He was awfu' sad yesterday, when Alexander left without him."

Kenneth relaxed.

"I tellt him that fetching water is a good way to grow muscles so ye can lift swords," Kenneth said. "I also tellt him that moving stones out of the kale patch is good for strength too. If there's anything else ye'd like him to do for ye, tell me."

Moira laughed.

"Ye're a good laddie, Kenneth," she said. "I'm sad for you that ye didna go wi' the other men, but glad for us. Ye'll be a great help to us all, and no' just wi' the heavy work. Ye've a way wi' the bairns, too."

Kenneth smiled.

"I canna make myself fifteen except wi' time, so there's no point in thinking on it. I'm away off to start cutting the peats wi' Alasdair. I'll be there the next week, but if ye need me send someone up for me, or tell me afore I go of a morning."

"I'll send someone up later wi' food for ye both," Moira said. "I'll no disturb ye at such important work. It's what most of the men would be doing now, had they no' been called."

"The fiery cross canna be ignored, even for the peat," Kenneth said cheerily. "We'll get as much done as we can, for they'll no' be wanting such a hard task after a fight, I'm sure."

"If it's like last time, we'll be lucky to see them back in time for the harvest," Moira told him.

Kenneth whistled.

"Really? Well, at least the ploughing's done. I canna think when I'll get to the harrowing though, once the seed's sown," Kenneth said worriedly. "I didna think they'd be away past the end o' May."

"Ye dinna have to do all the work of the men," Moira said, smiling. "Aye, I canna do the harrowing, Alexander tellt me that. But the other women can. The peat cutting is fearsome hard work though. You're better staying wi' that till it's done. Dinna tell Alex, for God's sake, or he'll be wanting to do that to build his muscles."

"I'm thinking he'll be too tired by the end of the day anyway, wi' all the water he's carrying. I tellt him he needs strong legs so he can march for days, and so walking to collect water and moving the stones is good for that too. I ken how wearying boys of that age can be. I was one myself."

They both laughed.

"Duncan'll be weary too, following him everywhere," she said. "Aye, they'll sleep tonight. Thank you."

Kenneth continued on his way, and Moira watched him for a minute, then looked pensively into the distance for a while as though trying to see what the men were all doing now, from thirty miles or more away. Then she pulled herself back to the present, with an effort.

"I hope it's worth it this time," she murmured to herself. "And that they all come back whole."

She turned and headed back to the house. She might have promised not to do heavy work, but there was still plenty she could occupy herself with. And keeping busy was the key to not driving yourself mad with worry. All the women knew that.

She put the baby gently in her cradle, and then dragged the blankets and chaff-filled mattresses off the two box beds. She would make the most of all the males being busy and it being a warm day, and would give the house a good clean, to start. Wash the bedding, air the mattresses, then clean everything. She could do that while keeping an eye on Morag and putting her to the breast regularly. The baby wasn't suckling well, which was a worry.

Then she'd clean the table, the bedding chest, the shelves on which Alexander's few precious books were stacked, and the floors, once she had enough water. The floors were flagged and a great source of pride to her, because the other cottages all had dirt floors which made it impossible to keep the inside of the house clean. One of the benefits of being the chieftain's wife. Another was having white-painted walls which brightened the interior of the house considerably, and a chimney in the main room rather than a peat fire in the middle of the floor and a hole in the roof for smoke to escape through. As well as not having the house constantly full of smoke, it also meant that when it was raining, which it often was, any water dripping down from leaks in the heather-thatched roof was clear rather than black and oily from the smoke.

It also meant that when the boys were a little older and could climb up and down the ladder safely, they'd be able to sleep upstairs in the loft area without choking to death on the smoke. It would be warmer up there for them, and it would give her and Alexander more privacy than they had now, all sleeping in the same room.

It was true that the box beds they slept in gave *some* privacy, but conversations could still be heard even if the doors were shut, and Alex was remarkably astute for his age, and remarkably curious too. Being bombarded with a plethora of awkward questions had led to Alexander and Moira vetting their bedtime chats, and other noises. It would be nice to be able to relax again.

If he came home.

He *would* come home, she told herself determinedly. As much as she loved the bright, warm house she lived in as the chieftain's wife, she loved the chieftain far more, and knowing he would be leading his men into battle and therefore would be at the front of any action, was worrying. She sighed, and forced her mind back to her work, dragging the mattresses outside to air in the sun then watching as her two sons made the return journey, the one staggering from the weight of the small, but very full pail, the other walking sturdily beside him, clutching a handful of vegetation. When Duncan saw her he smiled and started running slightly unsteadily, holding the bunch of what appeared to be grass, but which when he got closer could be seen to be sparsely dotted with tiny white wood anemones.

"Flowers!" he said, presenting them to her.

"Oh thank you, *a leannain*. They'll look bonny on the table."

Alex had instinctively tried to match the speed of his brother, with the result that when he reached them he was scarlet-faced, puffing, and the front of his tunic was drenched from the water that had spilled over the pail.

"I tellt him they're no' flowers," he gasped, then carried on to the large pail and added the water to its contents.

"There are flowers in here," Moira said, "And the green grass shows them off well. Away in and rest awhile. Ye've worked hard."

"It's no' full yet," Alex said, frowning. "I need to fill it for ye. I'll rest then." And without waiting for an answer, he set off again. Duncan, who had plopped himself down on the grass on hearing his mother's words, stared after his older brother in dismay for a moment, before scrambling back to his feet and plodding doggedly after him.

Yes, they would sleep tonight, certainly.

* * *

In spite of making eight trips to the loch in the morning and moving some rocks from the garden, that evening, as Moira lit a precious candle to supplement the light from the fire, Alex was still awake, constantly going to the door to peer anxiously out at the darkening sky, then returning to the fireside to sit on the child-sized chair that his da had asked Allan to make especially for him, and of which he was extremely proud. He would sit there restlessly for a few minutes, then head back to the door again.

After watching him do this half a dozen times while she settled the baby to sleep in the cradle next to her bed, Moira sat down on the bench seat by the side of the fire, on which Duncan was already lying, half asleep.

"Shut the door, Alex, it's getting cold now," she said softly. "Come and sit down, and I'll brush your hair for ye. It's an awfu' mess."

He did as she bid him, and came to sit down on the floor between her knees. She leaned forward, examining the chestnut nest presented to her. After separating the larger tangles and removing a few pieces of vegetation, she picked up the brush and started to gently and patiently smooth his hair.

He loved having his hair brushed, but she loved it even more.

It was like a magic charm. As she established a rhythm, brushing with one hand and smoothing his hair down with the other, she felt her own worries recede, her mind calmed by the repetitive motion. And her son, this boy so full of boundless energy, restless even in sleep, stilled under the soothing strokes of the brush, becoming boneless and limp as she transformed the knotted mess to beautiful burnished chestnut waves.

They sat there in silence, listening to the sounds of the house settling around them, an owl hooting in the distance outside, until Alex's head began to droop like a wilting flower on its stem. He sighed drowsily and she smiled, knowing that his eyes would be closing. Soon he would slump against the side of her leg, and normally at that point Alexander would carefully scoop him up and place him in the box bed where Duncan would already be sleeping.

Not tonight. Alexander was not here, and Duncan was not in bed but sitting up now next to her, his grey eyes observing her seriously.

"Me too," he said, once he had her attention.

"Aye, but dinna disturb your brother," she whispered. She continued the rhythmic brushing until she felt Alex's weight grow heavy against her leg, and then stopped brushing. Alex remained still, his head turned into her skirt, his arms hanging limp at his side, while Duncan sat next to her, patiently awaiting his turn.

She leaned across then, keeping her lower body still, and scooped her youngest son onto her knee, then set to work on his hair, which was not as tangled as Alex's because he was not as restless as Alex. In fact he was not restless at all, had never been restless, even as a baby. After over a year of rearing a constantly fidgety infant, she had initially found Duncan's stillness disturbing, and had often found herself closely watching for the rise and fall of his chest or placing her hand under his nose to make sure he was breathing, as he lay as still as death in the cradle.

His hair, as glossy and wavy as his brother's, seemed almost black in the dimness, although the firelight picked out sudden dark red lights in it as she brushed. He sat quietly while she worked until he too slumped sideways, his head against her chest, his breathing slow and regular.

She would probably wake at least one of them if she was to

carry them to bed, so for now she just enjoyed the peace, the warm presence of her sons, who she loved with a fierceness she had never imagined she could feel until they were born. She glanced down at the two glossy heads and smiled. Strange how they had both inherited a mixture of her fiery red locks and their father's rich dark brown waves. Alex's hair was more red than brown, which suited his fiery, confident nature. Duncan's was deeper brown, with a hint of the fire that he hadn't shown in his meagre two years of life, but which he surely would, in time.

No one would ever doubt their parentage as they might Kenneth's, who she heard now coming back from his hard day's labouring, whistling tunelessly as he walked past the door, accompanied by the creaking of the peat cart's single wheel. He and Alasdair must have managed a full load then, which was a good start.

Alex and Duncan were a real mix of mother and father in their looks. Both had their father's profile, and Alex had his father's slate-blue eyes too, whereas Duncan's were grey, like hers. Both of them had her mouth, upturned at the edges as though always about to smile. Gently she laid one hand on each of their sleeping heads and sent up a silent prayer to God to keep these two precious beings safe from harm, to grant them long and happy lives. And to allow them to die of old age, peacefully in their beds.

Then she leaned her own head against the back of the bench, taking comfort from the heavy warmth of her small companions. Alex twitched suddenly once against her leg and then lapsed back into slumber. She placed the brush by her side and closed her eyes, just for a moment.

She woke once, suddenly, as an owl hooted right outside the window, momentarily confused because she was not lying down in bed, before realising where she was. The piece of candle had guttered and burnt out, although the peat fire still glowed dully, casting enough light for her to see the room's furnishings. Both boys were still deeply asleep, and although the sensible thing to do would be to get both them and herself to bed, she felt no desire to move, contented for the first time since Alexander had disappeared into the mist the previous day.

She listened intently for a moment, but heard no sound from the cradle. And then she smiled and closed her eyes again.

CHAPTER TWO

June 1719

The wet spring soon became a warm sunny summer, which meant Moira had to spend a good deal of time in the fields along with most of the males who had been either too old or too young to go with their chieftain, pulling up the rapidly growing weeds that competed with the oats which had been planted there. As most of the women were now up at the shielings, there was no one to care for her children while she worked, so baby Morag was firmly harnessed to her back by means of her carefully fastened arisaid, and as her two sons were assisting her in pulling up the weeds she was accomplishing very little. She consoled herself with the fact that the boys were learning valuable lessons, such as no matter where you grasped them, thistles could not be pulled up by hand without causing the puller a good deal of pain, and that nettles, although excellent for adding to soup and for making into a soothing drink, could be neither picked nor brushed impatiently aside by hand.

As a result of the latter gesture, Duncan was currently sitting on the damp soil, eyes full of tears, while Alex made soothing noises and wiped his little brother's stinging hands and arms with a dock leaf.

"It's better if ye roll the leaf between your hands first," Moira said, taking it off him and rubbing it briskly between her palms to crush it before giving it back to him. "It's the juice that stops the pain."

"Does it work wi' thistle pain too?" Alex asked hopefully, smoothing the leaf carefully on his brother's now blotchy arm.

"No, that's a different kind of pain," Moira said. "I'll make ye a wee poultice wi' mint leaves later. Ye'll just have to bear it for the minute." On her back Morag moved suddenly, then started to grizzle. Moira sighed. It was impossible to get any productive work done when you had to look after three small children too.

She straightened up and began to unfasten her arisaid, then froze mid-task, her attention caught by a group of men coming into sight through the trees that grew near the loch. She put her hand up to shield her eyes from the sun, and then she saw who they were, and putting her fingers in her mouth gave a piercing whistle, which caused everyone in the field to stop what they were doing and look first at her, and then in the direction in which she pointed.

A great cheer went up, and the weeds were instantly forgotten as the workers started to make their way across the oatfield.

"Come, quick," Moira said, refastening her arisaid. Morag had already stopped whimpering and had stilled. "Your da's coming home."

It seemed that fathers coming home was a better cure for nettle and thistle rash than any squashed leaf, as both boys clambered immediately to their feet.

"Where?" asked Alex, squinting into the distance, while Duncan, too small to see over the growing oat plants, jumped up and down impatiently.

"Ye'll see him in a minute," she said. "Come on, let's go and meet him."

By the time she got there, the rest of the clan members who'd been weeding, and some others from the settlement who'd also seen the men arriving, were crowded round the chieftain and his retinue. Moira stood back a little, holding Duncan's and Alex's hands firmly to stop them barrelling through the crowd. Better to let Alexander greet them when he could give them his full attention.

She cast a concerned glance across the group of men. Marching a long distance would not cause Highlanders to look as weary as they all did. They had lost, then. The fact that they'd returned less than two months after leaving also told her that whatever this rising had been, it had not involved England,

Scotland, James Stuart himself and a full Spanish army.

Alexander finished answering a question and then looked over the crowd, his face lighting up when he saw her, which made her heart race. He raised his arms, and the MacGregors between their chieftain and his wife took the hint and stepped to the side so she had a clear path to him. She let the boys' hands go then, and by the time she reached him he already held one in each arm. Alex was telling him that his muscles were much bigger now and he might be able to lift the sword, while Duncan was stroking his father's new beard in wonder, and smiling. Alexander pretended to bite Duncan's fingers as they brushed across his mouth, making him laugh, and as Moira reached him he was expressing astonishment at the size of his son's muscles as Alex pushed his grubby sleeve up to display his skinny arms. And then his eyes met hers, sparkling with happiness at being with his family again; but there was sadness too. So they had fought then, and hard. Part of her wanted to count the men, see who was missing, who was responsible for the grief in the depths of his slate-blue eyes, save him having to tell her.

But then he placed the two boys on the ground and crushed her in his arms, burying his face in her hair, and in that moment she didn't care who had died, only that this man she adored, without whom she could never be whole, was back with her, and had missed her as she had missed him. He kissed her neck, murmured "later" into her ear, and then let her go, becoming the chieftain again.

"Are the others up at the shielings?" he asked.

"Aye," Kenneth said. "Shall I away up and fetch them down?"

"No," Alexander replied. "The crops will still be there if left for a few hours. The cattle may no' be. We'll go up there now, so ye can all greet your wives and bairns, and I'll tell everyone together what happened."

That had the desired effect of stopping all questions, and the clan set off to the rough huts that under normal circumstances almost all the women and children, and some of the men, lived in during the summer months, up on the hills away from the crops, where the cattle could graze their fill, raise calves and produce milk and cream, which was turned into butter and cheese to keep the people going through the winter. Everyone looked forward to the shieling time; although the dairy work was hard, the weather was often good, the days were long, and there was always enough time for music and storytelling, and for young single women and men to fall in love. The married men would usually stay in the main settlement and tend the crops and houses. This year of course the mood had not been so happy, as everyone was worried for the safety of their husbands or sweethearts, and the unattached young men had all marched away as well, so there had been no romancing to look forward to. That would all change now.

"Ye didna take the boys up to the shielings, then," Alexander commented as they headed up the hill.

"No. There were plenty of women who kent what they were doing up there, but most of the young boys down wi' the crops needed a wee bit of direction to keep them in order. I have to tell ye, Kenneth's been worth his weight in gold. He's cut the peat for the whole village, along wi' Alasdair, and done a good deal o' the harrowing too."

Alexander whistled through his teeth.

"I kent the boy was strong, but *all* the peat? Christ, I couldna do that myself. I'll no' leave him behind next time, though. If there is a next time," he added softly.

"It didna go well then," she answered in an equally low voice.

He laughed, but there was no humour in it.

"It didna go at all, truth be told," he said.

"But ye fought?"

"Aye, we fought, for what it was worth. I'll tell ye when we're all together," he added. Taking the hint, she fell silent.

"Hamish," he said suddenly, as if reading her thoughts.

She blinked.

"Aye," he said. "I didna want him to come. Tellt him he was too old, he'd done his part, earned his leisure. But he insisted."

"Was it quick?" she asked.

"Aye. Well, quicker than many, anyway. I kept him wi' me, to keep an eye on him, but—"

"It's how he'd have wanted to go," Moira interrupted him, hearing the self-reproach in his tone. "He wanted to die in battle. He always said that. The fighting was everything to him. And at least his bairns are all grown, wi' bairns o' their own. Better him than one of the young men."

He reached across impulsively and pulled her into his side.

"One of the things I love about ye," he said. "Ye always see the good side of everything, even when there isna one."

They continued up the hill arm-in-arm, Kenneth behind them carrying Alex and Duncan effortlessly, Duncan smiling, clearly relieved at not having to toil up the hill on his tiny legs, Alex alternating between complaining that he was too old to be carried and commenting joyously on all the things he could see from such a great height.

"So, then," Alexander began as soon as everyone had been rounded up and were all sitting on the gentle slope of the hill where the cattle were grazing, "we'd no sooner arrived at Eilean Donan than we found out that the so-called Spanish fleet didna even get out of Spanish waters before it was destroyed by storms, and James likewise. Well, he was no' destroyed," Alexander added hastily, seeing the instant look of shock on his clan's faces. "Sorry, I'm a wee bit tired, and no' thinking right. That is to say, he's alive and well, but the ship he was on was forced to put in somewhere in the north of Spain, where he learnt that the invasion fleet was destroyed. So it seems he either didna think it worth coming or the Spanish wouldna bring him. I'm no' sure, but he isna here, and that's the important thing."

He stopped to take a drink of ale from his flask.

"Was there no fight at all then?" Jean asked, who was sitting with her husband Dugald, arms wrapped round his waist as though she feared he'd disappear if she let him go for an instant.

Alexander wiped his mouth, closed the flask and continued.

"Aye, there was a fight. We'd no' have stayed away for two months if that'd been the end of it. Although it might well have been, for all the use it was staying. James didna make it here, but a whole gaggle o' lords came frae France wi' two Spanish ships, and they managed to land on Lewis. No' French lords," he added, anticipating the question. "Seaforth, Tullibardine, Marischal, and of course they all set to wasting time arguing wi' each other about who was the most important, as such bloody noble idiots do… anyway Seaforth went to call out the Mackenzies and came back wi' a few hundred, and Rob Roy actually arrived in time to fight, and no, I didna fight wi' him.

"We had maybe a thousand men, no' near enough to do anything wi', but I think they were hoping to send out and get more and then march on Inverness, because there isna a garrison worth mentioning there. If we could have done that, then we might have been able to gather more men and make something of it, given time. But it didna come to that, because by the start of May the British had ships patrolling the coast looking for rebels. Tullibardine really wanted to give it all up and sail off back tae France, but wi' the navy everywhere he couldna, so we left most of the stores and ammunition in the castle, and set off towards Inverness anyway, because we couldna stay where we were."

"So is the castle on the sea coast then?" Kenneth asked.

"No, it's on a wee island in Loch Alsh, but that's a sea loch, so the ships can sail in. That's how the commanders got there wi' all the ammunition and suchlike," Allan commented.

"Ah, of course. I didna think o' that," Kenneth said, flushing slightly.

"No reason why ye' should, laddie," Alexander said reassuringly. "Moira tellt me ye cut the peat for the whole village. That's a mighty achievement. Well done. We'll be warm this winter, thanks to you."

Kenneth flushed deeply now, but smiled.

"Ah, I didna do it alone. Alasdair was wi' me too," he said.

"I was," Alasdair agreed. "But he did all the cutting himself. I just loaded it on the carts. I canna do such hard work as the cutting is now."

"No more should ye. Ye were sore wounded in your shoulder in the '15," Alexander said. "Ye shouldna really be loading the peats even. But to do all the cutting for the whole clan, laddie. I couldna do that myself, I'm thinking."

This was high praise indeed, and Kenneth dipped his head, his joyful embarrassment making him momentarily shy, while his father clasped his shoulder with pride and the rest of the assembled MacGregors let out a whoop of appreciation. Peat cutting was notoriously heavy and dirty work, and none of the men enjoyed doing it, but it was that or freeze to death come winter.

"Ye'll no' have to do it the next time, Kenneth, if there is a next time," Alexander said when he could be heard again, deciding to bite the bullet now while the whole clan was assembled and there could be no argument against him. "If ye're strong enough to cut that much peat, then ye'll cut through redcoats like butter, I'm thinking. Next time ye come wi' us."

Now there was another roar, which made it clear to Gregor and Barbara, as Alexander intended, that all except them had no doubts that their son would be a valuable addition to the fighting MacGregors. Kenneth looked about to burst with pride now, and was grinning from ear to ear.

"Anyway, where was I?" Alexander continued. "Oh aye, the castle. So, there were a few Spanish soldiers who were going to stay there to defend the castle and our stores if the navy came, because we kent that if they were captured they'd be treated well, as prisoners of war, whereas we'd be treated as traitors, seeing as the Elector thinks he's our king. But then as we were preparing to leave, three ships sailed up the loch and besieged us."

"Is that where ye did your fighting, then?" Ann asked.

"No. It isna possible for land forces to fight ships," Alexander said. "We werena on the wee island where the castle is anyway. We had no choice but to leave the Spaniards who were there to defend it, and head off to take Inverness, under Tullibardine. But of course, most o' the powder and shot and suchlike was in the castle, and we couldna get to that."

He waited a minute while the others took all this information in. It was clear to Moira, looking at his expression, that he'd far rather have headed home at that point instead. But of course he couldn't have done that without effectively deserting, and Alexander MacGregor had never deserted those relying on him, and never would.

"Ye were going to take Inverness wi' only a thousand men and no guns?" Alasdair said. Unlike most of the others, he'd been to Inverness.

"Aye, well, it wasna my decision," Alexander said. "We marched inland for a wee while and waited, hoping the ships'd give up, because the walls were thick and couldna be damaged much by wee cannon, but the British managed to take the castle finally, and they blew all our supplies up, and the castle too, for that matter. So we had to make do wi' what we had, and we headed towards Inverness then.

"What we didna ken was that the redcoat commander,

Wightman, had set off wi' his army, and we didna find out he was on his way until we got to Cluanie. We had a few days, so we got into a good position, dug trenches and waited for him. But when he arrived he had all these wee mortar things wi' him. I havena seen the like before. They were a wee bit like cannon, but small, so they could be moved about quickly by just a couple o' men. Anyway, they blew us out of our positions in the end, because we didna have any way to reply to that, and they just kept coming. The wee mortars made a lot of smoke, so some o' the men ran away in the confusion, and then the redcoats attacked us. It was an awfu' messy fight, because we couldna see what others were doing on account of the smoke and suchlike, and having no notion where the mortars would be fired from next. We just fought as best we could, and then…after…well, when it became clear that we couldna win and there was no point in losing more lives for no reason, I called the retreat."

He stopped then and there was silence for a moment, initially because they were waiting for him to finish the story, and then as they absorbed the implication of what he'd said.

"*More* lives?" Alasdair said. "Ye mean someone was lost? One of us?"

"Hamish," Alexander said immediately, not wanting to prolong the agony. No one had noticed that Hamish was missing until now, not because no one cared about him, but because, as Moira had said, he had no parent, wife or child watching out for his return. His children, all girls, had married and moved to other clans and his wife had died years before. He lived alone in a hut at the edge of the settlement, liking his solitude. But he was liked, always had a cheery word for everyone, and was a great teller of stories, having lived long enough to not only remember the so-called Glorious Revolution that had started the whole Jacobite issue, but to have fought at Killiecrankie with the legendary Viscount Dundee, and had even spoken with the man once.

A ripple of grief ran round the clan and some of the women started to cry, while the small children present stilled, recognising something was wrong, but not quite what it was.

"Da, what happened to—?" Alex piped up, stopping as his mother's hand closed over his mouth.

"Later," she whispered in his ear, and he fell silent.

"It's how he'd have wanted to die," Dugald said after a time, unconsciously echoing Moira's earlier words. "He always said he wanted to die wi' his sword in his hand."

"Aye, well, he did that, anyway," Alexander said. "I made sure of it. He was brave to the end. We took him wi' us a short way, then buried him when it was safe to do so. It wasna practical to have brought him back wi' us, because we had to travel a long way out of our way to avoid coming across anyone looking for us. The redcoats would have loved to come across a party of MacGregors, after all. No need to take us prisoner or give us a trial. We could be executed out of hand."

"Aye. So it's over, then," Iain said. "We'll no' get our names or lands back frae the king this time."

There was a general murmur of agreement, and sadness. Alexander, along with many of the men, was tired and wanted nothing more than to go home and have something to eat then fall into bed, but he couldn't end the reunion on such a sad note.

"It's over this time, aye," Alexander agreed. "But James is a young man yet. There'll be other times. Hopefully he'll learn from this and realise that there's two things sorely lacking that he needs to have before the next campaign."

"What's that?" Gregor asked.

"Better leaders. If James himself canna come, then we need men who will think of the cause rather than their own status and pride. They wasted a lot of time arguing about who should lead. That should all have been settled by James before they even embarked. And we need better spies. If we'd kent that the Spanish fleet wasna coming earlier, where the British ships were, that Wightman was on his way to meet us from Inverness…so many things, we'd have been able to act differently.

"I'm hoping James will realise that, because only he can do something about it. All we can do is make sure we're ready when the next time comes. We lost our name and have been proscribed for a long time, but we're still here, and we're no' going anywhere! This was good practice for all of us, and Alpin here made a good show. Ye've raised a bonny fighter, Barbara and Gregor, and I'll be proud to fight wi' him at my side next time. Ye must tell your brother what ye've learned, laddie, for the next time."

"Aye, I will," Alpin said, although he didn't smile at the

compliment as Alexander had hoped he would. He hadn't lied. As far as he knew the boy had fought well, although he hadn't seen him in action for more than a moment, what with the smoke, trying to lead his men first forward and then in retreat, and coping with Hamish being shot. But he'd stayed to fight and Gregor said he'd killed two men, and that was more than some boys managed in their first engagement. He looked around at his clansfolk, read the mood, at which he was expert, and then stood.

"I'll leave ye all to it then," he said. "It's growing late. Stay up here wi' your wives and sweethearts the night, if ye wish. Ye'll be wanting to celebrate being home and safe. I'm away down to my own house wi' my family. I'll send up, or come up myself when I've seen what work needs to be done on the houses and crops. But I'll no' be asking anyone to work tomorrow. Just milk the cows for they canna wait, and make sure they're no' reived, and I'll be happy."

* * *

"That was cleverly done, wi' Kenneth," Moira said as they walked back down the hill, the two boys walking as well now, in the hope that it would tire them out and they'd sleep so their parents could have some precious time alone. "Gregor and Barbara canna object to ye taking him now."

"No. It's no' fair on the laddie. Gregor tellt me he's worried the boy hasna got a temper to lose, and wouldna be able to kill a man in battle. I agree he's verra good-natured, but no one kens how a boy'll react in his first fight. It's no' a good reason to make a laughing stock of him. Was he awfu' fashed at no' coming?"

"I think so, though he didna show it. He kept himself busy instead," Moira answered.

"Aye, I can tell that. All the peat! I'm amazed at that."

"Da, what's spies?" a voice came from Alexander's knee level. He stopped and looked down at his extraordinarily grubby sons.

"Ye were listening then," he said to Alex.

"I always listen," Alex replied earnestly. "Ye said ye need them. Can I do spies? Do I have to lift your sword to do spies?"

Only the intense desire in his son's face to be useful to his father stopped Alexander laughing out loud at that. He fought to keep his expression as serious as his tiny son's was, with limited success.

"Ye might need to lift a sword to be a spy," he said finally. "It's a dangerous thing to be."

"More dange…russ than fighting in a battle?"

"Aye, but in a different way," Alexander said. "Ye're too young, laddie. I'll tell ye about spies when ye're a wee bit older."

"How old?" Alex asked immediately.

Alexander brushed his fingers through his hair, then lowered his hand to waist height.

"When ye're this big," he said.

Alex observed the hand solemnly, then nodded.

"It's good to be back," Alexander said a minute later, watching as the two boys ran ahead, Alex holding Duncan's hand to help stop him stumbling.

"It's good to have ye back," Moira answered.

"How is she?"

Moira sighed.

"She's suckling a wee bit better, but she's awfu' placid. I'm worried about her."

"Duncan was awfu' placid at her age too," Alexander reminded his wife. "He was quite happy to just watch the world go by. No' like Alex. He was never still," he added, smiling at the memory.

"That's true," she agreed. Even in the womb Alex had kicked like a fiend, whereas Duncan had been so still she'd wondered if he still lived at times. "But I see now that Duncan was just different to Alex, that's all. He still is. He's the still pool, where Alex is the river, always moving. But Duncan fed well and grew, and he was placid, but awake and interested in everything. Morag sleeps all the time. It doesna feel right."

"Shall we be getting a physician for her?" he asked. She thought for a moment. They wouldn't be able to get a medical man to come to them. They'd need to go to Glasgow, Stirling or Edinburgh.

"No," she said. "She isna in pain, isna puking up her milk. I dinna think bleeding her would do much for her. And that's what physicians do."

"Maybe she's just even more of a still pool than Duncan," Alexander said.

"Aye. Maybe. So ye think this fight was a waste of time, then?" she asked.

"I do. We all did. I thought something wasna right before we left. Such a big rising and we hadna heard a thing about it. Normally I'd have sent men out to other clans to see what was really happening before I decided what to do."

"But ye couldna ignore the fiery cross."

"Aye, well, if the hot-headed bastard sends another cross out like that I *will* ignore it. He isna my chief, and nor is Balhaldie, wi' his secret election that I didna ken anything about. I'll no' risk my men again for such a farce as that was."

"Did the Spanish never intend to come then?" Moira asked.

"Aye, the Spanish intended to come, but they only sent two ships to Scotland and the whole of the rest of the fleet was to sail to England, wi' James. It's true a storm wrecked the fleet, as I tellt everyone just now. But what I didna tell everyone and I willna, for it's just my view, is that I dinna think there was ever an intention to make a serious fight of it in Scotland. I'm thinking we were bait, no more."

"Bait? Why?"

Alexander glanced around to make sure no one was in earshot, but they were alone on the hill, the only others their two sons who had stopped a little further down to examine something of interest in the grass.

"Scotland has always come out for the Stuarts, and Parliament kens that well. They ken that many of us have no' accepted the Elector, and that we dinna want the Union either. So they're watching us. It's my opinion that the Spanish sent two ships wi' a few nobles to give the impression Scotland was rising, hoping that the Elector would send his whole army up here to deal wi' it. And then the Spanish army, wi' James at their head, could have marched on London wi' no' opposition."

Moira stopped and looked at her husband in shock.

"Ye mean James was willing to sacrifice you all for the chance to take his throne back? For if that had happened, ye'd have been massacred, only a thousand of ye."

"I'm no' saying that's what James himself intended. But I think that was the Spanish intention, aye. What other reason would they have for sending only two ships here and twenty-seven to England, for that's how many it would have been? I'll no' tell the others that, and I'm trusting ye no' to either. But I'll keep it in mind if there's another rising. I'm concerned for what'll happen now, though."

"Why? It's over, is it no'?"

"Aye, the rising is, if ye could call it that. But Scotland rose four years ago, too. The Elector would be mad to let that lie. The English must be thinking that the Scots, or the clans at least, will rise whenever the Stuarts want us to. We're a constant danger to their precious 'Kingdom of Great Britain' and to the crown, and we've just reminded them of that with this ridiculous wee stramash. I'm worried about what they'll do now."

Rather than utter a soothing platitude, Moira thought about this for a few minutes, as was her way.

"We need some spies, to tell us what's happening in London then," she said eventually. "For ye canna do anything until ye ken what they intend, if they intend anything at all."

"That's true enough. I'll no' worry too much about it, but I will keep my eyes and ears open. I canna go to London, but I will maybe go myself or send others to Edinburgh from time to time to find out the news. We're isolated here. I ken we need to be, being MacGregors, but I dinna want to be in a position of ignorance again, as I was in April. But I'll no' think more on it tonight," he said. "Tonight let's be together, just the two of us. Once the bairns are in bed."

Getting the bairns into bed was not such an easy matter, though. In spite of the long walk back to the village Alex at least was still wide awake, and both he and Duncan were caked in mud, having spent the day in the oatfields and the evening running down the hill. By the time they'd both been washed, Moira had scrutinised Alex's hand for thistle spines then made and applied a mint poultice, after which Alex had tried and failed to lift his father's sword, to his huge disappointment, and then had been firmly put to bed, it was almost dark. Moira sang a lullaby to both boys rather than allowing Alex to sing one to Duncan. In truth Duncan didn't need one, having fallen asleep the moment he landed in bed. It was Alex who was the restless one, Alex who would toss and turn even on uneventful nights, while his brother slumbered on.

So Moira brushed his hair, and then sang softly to him until his eyes closed and his impossibly long lashes rested on his plump pink cheeks, as Duncan's had been doing for half an hour. Then she blew out the candle and tiptoed out of the room to join her husband on the bench outside the house.

It was a beautiful warm night, the moon bathing the settlement in a silvery light, while the stars sparkled like diamonds in the royal blue sky. She sat down next to him and he put his arm around her shoulder, pulling her against him.

"I'm glad to be home," he said simply. "I'm in no rush to go off fighting again."

"I never thought I'd hear ye say that," she said. "I'm glad of it, though. It's hard when ye're away. I wish I could come with ye. It nearly killed me no' to be with ye at Sheriffmuir."

Before she'd become pregnant with Alex she had gone everywhere with him. On raids, on feuds with other clans, on cattle sales to Crieff. They'd been inseparable.

"It nearly killed me to ride off without ye too, and you big wi' child. If I'd kent then I'd no' be back in time to see him born, I wouldna have gone."

"Aye, ye would," she said. "I'd have made you. Ye wanted to fight, and ye wouldna have been any use moping around here."

He laughed then, for she spoke true.

"I canna go now, wi' three of the wee monsters," she said, "so I'm in no hurry to see ye ride out again."

"Well I didna come to blows wi' Rob Roy, the crops are growing and there are a good number of calves this year it seems, so unless someone decides to try and relieve us of those calves, I see no reason to fight again this year, at least. The men'll be happy wi' that, too,"

Unless the Elector did decide to do something about the rebellious clans. But neither of them gave voice to that thought. No need to tempt fate.

"Kenneth will no' be happy, I'm thinking, his brother having proved himself a man now, and only half his size," Moira said.

"Aye, well, he'll be the only one."

They stopped talking then, and just sat together, enjoying the rare peace of having time alone, uninterrupted by children or by other clanspeople in need of advice. It was so quiet they could hear the susurration of the loch against the pebbled shoreline, and the breeze softly whispering through the leaves of the trees. In the distance a baby cried suddenly, followed by a low female murmuring as the mother comforted it.

Alexander sighed blissfully as he felt himself truly relax for the first time in two months. This was more important than any lost crown, than any union. Just the pure, simple joy of being where your heart was, with your wife and children, who you loved dearly and who loved you, surrounded by your people, who, in spite of their problems and disputes, would all stand together, would all be there for each other when it counted.

He was home.

* * *

Two of the subjects of the chieftain's conversation with his wife were currently in their parents' cottage, Alpin sitting on his father's chair, while Kenneth was kneeling in the middle of the floor, blowing gently on a piece of smouldering tinder as he attempted to light the fire.

"Ye dinna need to do that," Alpin said. "I can wait till the morrow to eat."

"It's nae bother," Kenneth replied. "I'm an expert wi' the oatcakes now, with me down here and Ma up at the shielings. And it's good to welcome ye home. Ye're glad to be back?"

"God, aye," said Alpin, with such feeling that Kenneth shot a worried glance his way. His brother looked drawn and pale. But maybe fighting made you thinner. Definitely oatcakes then.

"What was it like? Alexander tellt ye to tell me about it. But it can wait till the morning, if ye want," Kenneth said reluctantly.

"Ye'll be wanting the truth of it?" Alpin asked.

"Aye. Why would I no' want the truth?" Kenneth replied, puzzled now. Alpin was behaving really strangely, not at all his normal cheery self. There was something wrong.

"I'll tell ye now then, for I canna say it to Da, or to anyone else. But I can trust you," Alpin said, turning the chair and leaning forward, his face pale, earnest. "I hated it. No' the marching there, but the battle itself. Every minute of it. It was…it was like being in hell. I canna imagine why men want to fight."

Kenneth was so shocked by this that he forgot the fire and sat down on the floor opposite Alpin.

"But ye often fight," he said. "It's me that doesna hit others, no' you."

"Aye, but that's because ye're feart o' killing them by accident. And going to battle isna fighting like that, where ye hit each other and wrestle a wee bit, and then next day ye're friendly again. It's…different."

"How is it different? Ye can tell me. I'll no' tell a soul. I'll swear on my dirk if ye want," Kenneth added when Alpin stayed silent.

"No, I trust ye no' to tell anyone. Everyone was afeart before we got to the fighting. I didna expect that, but they were all sitting telling tales about battles they'd fought to build up their courage, to remind themselves that they'd been through it and lived to tell the tale. I've heard the stories before, but there was something different in the way they tellt them, a fierceness that isna there normally. And then I realised they were afeart, and needed to make themselves brave, to reassure each other through the stories that they had *all* survived before, that they all loved the fighting that gave them the stories to tell.

"I wasna feart myself then, but I realised that the battle was going to be a different thing to what I was thinking. For I'd been expecting a sort of big fight, I think. Christ, I canna believe how raw I was." He put his head in his hands for a moment, and when he looked up tears were sparkling in his eyes.

"Aye, well, I'm raw myself, so I think I need to hear this," Kenneth said. The fire was bright now in spite of his neglect of it, so he put a stone on it to warm.

"So before the actual fighting there's an awfu' lot o' marching about, this way and that, for no apparent purpose. And when ye stop for the night, ye eat and then ye make sure your weapons are sharp and your powder's dry and suchlike, and then ye sleep wi' them close by, in case of a night attack. And if ye're no' marching about, ye're practising fighting, or digging latrines or trenches to hide in, so ye're busy a lot of the time. As I said, I didna mind that bit."

"I'd expect that. What was the bit ye were no' expecting, then?" Kenneth asked.

"It was the battle. I thought we'd be in lines, and then we'd all run down together and attack the men in front of us."

Kenneth thought that too, had been told that was what you did. Better if you could run down from the high ground, for you were faster then, and a harder target for the enemy's muskets.

"Aye, that's right, and ye all shout '*Ard Choille!*' too."

"But it didna work like that. They had these mortar things that Alexander tellt ye about earlier, so we all had to crouch down in our wee trenches while they fired great balls at us. Some o' them bounced in, and they just went straight through anyone in the way, took off arms and legs like they were nothing. And we couldna rush out and fight like we wanted to, because we hadna been ordered to. So we had to sit there listening to men screaming in pain, and I was sure that it'd be me in a minute. And then I got afeart, and ashamed for it."

Kenneth thought on this for a minute.

"Ye shouldna be ashamed for that. I'm sure everyone was afeart, they just didna show it. I would be too. It'd be different if ye could rush out and attack the bastards," he said in the end.

"Aye, that's what I thought. But it wasna, Kenny, no' for me, anyway. When we finally got the order to charge, I was shaking so much I thought I'd faint and shame myself forever. I dinna ken how I ran, but I did, and I waited for the rage to take me like they said it would. But it didna. It didna," he said again, his voice breaking. "I…just didna want to do it. I didna want to kill a man I had no argument wi'. It was so smoky I couldna see much, and I felt as if I was on my own, and then I saw these other men, just like me but wi' red coats on, and I kent I had to hate them. But they didna look like the enemy. They just looked as frightened as I was, and then I had to kill them, and…it was horrible."

A silence fell then, broken only by the crackling of the fire, incongruously merry in the tense atmosphere. Kenneth stood and scraped some butter from a jar on the press in the corner into a scallop shell, poured some oatmeal and water into a wooden dish, then came back to the centre of the room, putting the shell down near the fire for the butter to melt. Alpin was staring moodily into the flames, his expression dark. Kenneth felt something twist in his heart. He hated to see his brother so anguished.

"But they would have killed you if ye hadna killed them, Alpin," he said reassuringly, sitting back down next to the flames. Alpin looked at his brother as though he were a stranger, then seemed to come back from a long way away.

"Aye, I ken that," he answered. "But they were only trying to kill me for the same reason. No' because they hated me, but because if they didna kill me, I'd kill them. If we'd both decided no' to try to kill each other, nothing would have changed, but we'd all be alive. It just seemed stupid, a waste. I…d'ye think me a coward?"

"No," Kenneth said immediately. "If ye were a coward, ye'd have run away. Ye didna do that, did ye?"

"No," Alpin said. "But I wanted to. I think it'd be different if they'd been trying to kill Ma or Da, or even to steal our cattle, but I just couldna find the rage I needed when I didna even really ken what we were fighting about."

"Ye were fighting to get James Stuart back on the throne, so we'd get our name and our land back," Kenneth said.

"Aye, that's what they tellt us. But James wasna there, and even Alexander couldna see the point in going to Inverness when the clans hadna risen. He only did it because once ye're committed to a fight ye canna just walk away without loss of honour. I ken that. But it didna make me hate the redcoats. For all I ken, they felt the same way. They were just fighting because they were tellt to, because they signed up for the army one night when they were drunk, or thought they'd look good in a red coat."

"Have ye said this to anyone else?" Kenneth asked.

"Christ, no," Alpin answered immediately. "For when I looked around at them, the ones I could see through the smoke, they were all fighting like men possessed. Ye could see the hate on their faces, and it drove them on. I just…I just didna have it. I dinna ken how to get it. I think it'll be worse next time, because I'll ken even before we set off just what it'll be like. But Hamish, he loved it, he couldna wait to kill a redcoat. I saw him fall," he said.

"What happened?"

"Alexander tellt us both to stay near to him, but I lost him as soon as we started running. Hamish didna though, most likely because he's more experienced, and when I saw them again he was right behind Alexander. And then the redcoat in front of them fired, in panic I think, for he ran away directly after. He was so close that the ball went straight through Alexander's targe and killed Hamish."

"So he could have killed our chieftain then," Kenneth remarked, pouring the melted butter into the wooden bowl, then mixing it with the oatmeal and water in his hands to a paste, before putting a lump of it on the heated stone and patting it flat with his palm.

"Aye, if he'd aimed to the right a wee bit. I didna think o' that. It all happened so fast. I tried to see where the wound was, to see if I could stop the bleeding, but Alexander grabbed me, tellt me it was too late, to look at his face. So I did, and his eyes were open staring at the sky, but wi' no expression in them. Then he put the sword in Hamish's hand and pulled me up, said I'd be killed unless I forgot Hamish and fought. So I did."

"He must have been shaken," Kenneth said. "Who'd be the chief, if he was gone?"

"I dinna ken. Wee Alex?"

"He couldna be chief. He's only a wee bairn."

"I didna think of that. Alexander's always been our chieftain. I canna imagine another. Anyway, he didna die."

"So did that make it easier to kill the redcoats, seeing Hamish die?"

"Would it have made it easier for you?"

Kenneth took out his dirk and turned the oatcake over. He thought. Alpin was being brutally honest with him. He had to return the favour.

"Sitting here now, aye, I think it would. I liked Hamish very much. But it's easy to say, when ye've never been in a battle. I take it it didna make it easier for you then?"

Alpin shook his head in despair.

"No. It did for Alexander, though. He fought like a madman. I think…maybe I'm no' cut out for fighting. Afterwards they were all acting like they were drunk, celebrating and dancing and suchlike. I just wanted to be alone. I was so sad, at the waste of it all. It was all pointless."

"Maybe the others feel that way too, but are just better at hiding it?" Kenneth suggested.

"No. I looked for it, but I didna see any sign that anyone felt like I did. I would have been so happy if I had. I canna tell ye how it makes me feel," Alpin said, the tears running freely down his cheeks now. "I canna tell anyone, for they'll hate me. I'll understand if you hate me too, but I had to tell someone."

"Christ, Alpin, I dinna hate ye. Ye're my brother. Everything ye've tellt me makes sense. That's why I'm after thinking there must be others that feel the same way. Have ye thought to talk wi' Alexander about it? He could maybe reassure you. I canna, for I havena been to battle and have no idea how I'd feel in one."

"Alexander saw there was something amiss after the battle. But he thought it was because I'd killed my first man. He came over and tellt me it was normal to feel bad, even to be sick afterwards, because it's a hard thing to do to take a life, but it gets easier wi' time. He said I might dream about it for a while, but that's normal too. Then he tellt me he was proud of me, that I'd done well, and I smiled because he expected me to. Then he went away. So I think that's what other men must feel. I didna feel that."

"Maybe a lot of the men feel like you, though, but are feart of admitting it. Maybe *all* of them feel like that," Kenneth said.

"I dinna think so. If they did they wouldna be so happy when they're tellt to march to battle. I remember when they were called four years ago. They all cheered."

"The men did. The women were no' so happy about it. Nor this time, neither."

Alpin laughed humourlessly.

"Maybe I should have been a woman, then. I find it strange that Da was afeart for you to come because he thinks ye canna feel anger, but he wanted me wi' him, because I can fight. He doesna ken either of us at all, does he?"

No, he didn't. Gregor was a good father, a loving one. But he saw only the surface, not just of his sons, but of everything. Even so...

"In fairness though, we dinna tell him everything, never have," Kenneth said.

"No, we've tellt each other instead. But I'd ken ye were holding back rather than no' wanting to fight just by looking at ye. Ye wouldna need to tell me that," Alpin commented.

"Aye, but that's because ye ken me so well, because we *do* talk to each other. And I'll tell ye now, ye're no' a coward, whatever ye might think. I've seen ye stand up for yourself, and for others too. A coward wouldna do that."

"That's no' what the others would think, though. I'm a MacGregor. We fight for everything. It's what we do. What use am I if I canna fight?"

"Ye *can* fight. I hate cutting peat, but I can do it. Hating something doesna mean ye canna do it. Maybe ye'll no' need to for a long time now."

"I hope not," Alpin said. "Although you'll be disappointed. Ye wanted to fight, to prove yourself, did ye no'?"

Kenneth scooped the oatcake off the stone then broke it in half, throwing one piece to his brother, who caught it deftly then tossed it from hand to hand until it cooled. They ate in companionable silence for a while.

"I did, but there'll be more chances, raids at least. The way you describe it, it doesna sound like something I'd want to do either, in honesty."

"But you think ye could," Alpin said.

"Aye, I think I could. But you did too. Killed two men, did ye no'?"

"I did. Alexander was right about it. I dream about them, can see their faces as they died, feel my sword go through them. I never want to go to battle again. Even the thought of it makes me feel sick."

"For what my opinion's worth, it's my view that the only difference between you and the other men is that ye're thinking it through too much. They're no' thinking about James and crowns, and wee boys thinking they'd look good in red. They're just thinking; I owe Alexander everything, he says fight, the enemy wears a red coat, hate everyone in a red coat until it's over. I think that's why it's easier for them. It's nothing to do wi' cowardice."

Alpin laughed naturally for the first time since he'd come home.

"Aye, maybe ye've the right of it," he said. "So ye're saying I've got to stop thinking, and then I'll be fine."

"Well, something o' the sort. No' all the time, just if ye have to go to war. I'm thinking ye'll be fine if another clan attacks us, because then it'll be personal."

"Ye really think that?" Alpin asked, suddenly earnest again. "Ye're no' just saying it to make me feel a man?"

"Alpin, ye *are* a man. No, I'm no' just saying it. It's no' what I do. Ye ken that. The next time there's a battle, if there is one, I'll be going too, and I'll be happy to have ye fight at my side. I trust ye wi' my life, and I wouldna do that if I thought ye a coward. I like my life, and I want to have a lot of it."

"I do, too. I'm just hoping James'll decide he doesna want his crown back after all."

"Maybe he will. He's no' much good at getting it back so far, is he?" Kenneth said.

Alpin giggled.

"What would I do without you?" he said. "I'm thinking I might have found it easier if ye'd been there with me."

"Aye, well, I will be at the next one. So dinna fash yerself about it now. Let's just eat the oatcakes. I'll no' tell Da what ye said, if ye dinna tell him that I ken where he's hidden his secret store o' claret. I'll away and fetch us a bottle."

"Claret? Will he no' notice there's a bottle missing if ye do?" Alpin said.

"He will, but no' for a long time if I take it from the back o' the press," Kenneth said, winking. "And if he does find out quicker, I'll say I thought he wouldna mind us celebrating your first battle. Hopefully your last."

"I'll drink to that, for certain," Alpin said, smiling again now and relaxing a little, as Kenneth had hoped he would.

CHAPTER THREE

Loch Lomond, Scotland, November 1721

Alex was both overjoyed and a little bit sad, which felt very strange to him. Sometimes the joy bubbled up in his stomach and then through his arms and legs, making it impossible for him to sit still. He just had to run around or jump up and down until the bubbles subsided. Sometimes the joy bubbled up through his mouth and then he just had to shout for joy.

He was overjoyed because it was his birthday (he was six whole years old now) and he had succeeded in lifting his da's sword off the floor. He had asked especially if he could try as his birthday present and his da had said yes and had presented it to him, just as he had before he'd ridden off to the fight to get James Stuart to give them their name back. And as on that day, Alex had wrapped both his hands round it, except his hands were bigger now.

Then he had stood for a moment, breathing in and out as he had seen Kenneth doing last summer before succeeding in lifting the *clach cuid fir* to a massive roar of approval from the whole clan, who had assembled to see him do it. Alex had closed his eyes, imagined he had the strength of Kenneth, and then had braced himself, putting every ounce of his strength and will into it, and in doing so had managed to lift the sword from the floor. Only a few inches, and only for a moment. But he had done it and that was the important thing.

What was even *more* important was that Da then said that now he had proved himself capable of lifting a sword it was time he had his own, a real metal sword instead of the wooden stick all boys began with. Then he could start learning how to use it, providing he promised never to take it out or use it unless an adult was with him. And then Alex had taken out his little *sgian dubh* and had sworn a solemn oath on it as it was said in stories that men did, usually when they were about to take vengeance on someone for a terrible wrong. But an oath was an oath, and if you swore it on iron it was binding. Alex didn't know why iron made it binding, but it did, and that was what mattered. If you broke your oath a terrible thing would happen to you, usually involving a mystical creature like a malevolent fairy, a kelpie or even the Devil.

He couldn't have his sword yet, though. He had to wait for James to forge it for him. James repaired tools and sometimes made nails and such things. He also made small knives, but Da said he was quite able to make a sword, especially as it would be a small one, and then when Alex was older they would maybe go to Stirling or Edinburgh and have a fine one made for him. But he was *going* to get one, and that was what was making the bubbles in his stomach. Or some of the bubbles.

That afternoon his mother had come to him and had said that she had a fine piece of woollen cloth that would be just right for his first *féileadh mór*, and as he was such a big boy now he would certainly look very well in it. It *was* a very fine piece of cloth, possibly the finest piece of cloth ever made, brightly patterned in red and green, and Ma had taken the time to show him how to lay it out properly on the floor on top of a leather belt his da had cut down so it would fit him. Then he'd lain down and she'd showed him how to wrap it round himself, and then how to arrange it once he was standing. Tomorrow he would have to do it all himself, but tomorrow was a long way away. Today he felt like a real man, which he nearly was, because he could lift a sword.

Just when he thought the day could not get any better, Da told him that he was going on a trip up to Inversnaid in a few days to see what the soldiers were doing, and that if Alex promised to behave perfectly he could go too.

"Will I have my sword then?" he'd asked excitedly.

"No, it'll take James a wee while to make it for ye," Alexander said. "But ye willna need a sword anyway. None of us will. We're just away to have a wee look at what they're up to. We willna be going down to see them, or to fight wi' them. It'll just be two or three days, but it's time ye started learning what's outside the village, and how to survive in winter when ye canna get home of a night."

There had never been a better birthday ever in the whole world, and there never would be. Except for the little bit of sad, which he felt when he sat outside on the bench with Duncan later in the afternoon. There was a cold wind blowing, so it was nice to drape the top part of his *féileadh mór* over his head and around his upper body. It made him feel warm and snug. And then he looked at Duncan, who still wore the same blue tunic that they'd both worn for as long as they could remember. All the boys wore them, and that was fine. But Duncan was his brother and it didn't seem right that he should have a man's clothing and be getting a sword and be going on an adventure, when Duncan wasn't getting anything.

"It isna my birthday," Duncan pointed out when Alex voiced his thoughts.

"Aye, but ye didna get anything as bonny as this when it *was* your birthday," Alex said.

Duncan thought about this for a minute.

"What did you get when you were four?" he asked finally.

"Ma made me a cake wi' raisins in! You had some too. D'ye no' remember that?"

Duncan shook his head.

"I canna remember things like you can," he said. "So, maybe when I'm six and big like you I'll get a sword and go away wi' Da too."

He seemed to be quite happy, so Alex relaxed and the sad went away. But a few minutes later, as the sun set over the loch and Duncan watched the gold and crimson blaze of the sky, Alex watched his brother instead and it seemed to him that Duncan *was* sad after all. His mouth looked sad somehow, and his eyes did too. You could never be sure with Duncan, because he didn't say everything he felt, and when he was quiet it didn't always mean he was unhappy, it might just mean he was being Duncan. Duncan liked being quiet, which was very strange. He liked being on his own as well. He would spend hours lying on the ground watching some little bug crawl about, and be quite happy.

Duncan liked fishing too. Iain had taught Duncan to fish, and they would go and sit out in a little boat on the loch for hours and come back happy. Alex had gone out with them once and Iain had showed him how to put the bait on the hook, and then how to cast. And then they had sat there for ever, staring at the water while the sun moved across the sky and nothing happened, and Alex had thought he would die of boredom. He couldn't get up and walk about because he was in a boat. He couldn't even talk or sing in case it scared the fish away. It was horrible. He never went with them again.

When Duncan caught his first reasonable-sized fish, Ma and Da had made a celebration of it, and had cooked it with butter and herbs. Da had said it was fine to know he had a son who could provide for the family, and Duncan had blushed with pleasure.

He wasn't blushing with pleasure now, and that was because he was sad that he didn't have a *féileadh mór* and a sword to come, Alex decided. And that made him sad, because he loved Duncan.

He had to do something about it.

"Da, can James make a sword for Duncan too?" he asked his father later, while Duncan was still outside watching the stars, another thing he liked to do. "Then we could learn to use them together."

"No, laddie, he canna. He's too young yet awhile. When he's six like you, then he can have a sword. No' the now. He might hurt himself. He needs to learn to use his wee blade first, as did you when you were his age."

That made sense, and certainly Duncan would understand that too, but it wouldn't make him happy.

"Ma, have ye any more o' this bonny cloth?" he asked his mother a minute later, rushing his words to get them out before Duncan came in.

"Aye, a wee bit. Why?" she asked.

"Is it enough to make Duncan a *féileadh mór* like mine?" he asked. Moira looked at him.

"Did Duncan tell you he'd like one?" she asked.

"No," Alex admitted. "But he wouldna, because he's Duncan. He's sad though, and I think it's because he wants one. Da said he canna have a sword yet, but he could have a *féileadh mór*, could he no'? Ye canna hurt yourself wi' a piece o' cloth."

"Well, if he wants one, he can have one. But I'm no' sure—"

"Duncan, Ma says she's enough cloth left for ye to have a *fèileadh mór* like mine!" Alex cried excitedly the second the door started to open. Coming into the room Duncan looked at his mother, who was putting wooden bowls on the table.

"But I dinna need one," he said. "I've a sark, and a plaid for when it's cold."

Alex stared at his brother in astonishment.

"But…I thought ye were sad because ye didna have one. Ye canna have a sword yet," he said.

"Aye, I ken that," Duncan told him. "I willna need to kill a man till I'm grown. It's coming on to rain." He turned and closed the door, putting the snib on so it wouldn't blow open and let the rain in.

This was incomprehensible to Alex.

"D'ye no' want to be a man grown?" he asked in confusion.

"No," Duncan replied. "I'm too wee. I've a lot of growing to do yet. You have too."

"Why are ye sad, then? Is it because Da didna ask ye to go to Inversnaid wi' us?"

Now it was Duncan's turn to look puzzled.

"I'm no' sad. I tellt ye that. Why would I be sad? We've crowdie wi' honey to eat before bed!"

This was a good point. Alex had forgotten about the edible treat still to come.

"I just thought ye *looked* sad, outside," he said.

Duncan observed him soberly, his grey eyes solemn.

"I can wait. I'm no' sad. So ye can be happy now."

He went over to the fire then to warm himself, leaving Alex standing with a puzzled look on his face, while Moira ladled the crowdie into the bowls, mixing a generous slug of whisky into her and her husband's portions. Then the five of them sat down to enjoy their special treat, while the rain, which had indeed come on, pattered on the window.

"D'ye need to go?" Moira asked later, when the three children were finally asleep, Alex of course being the last to succumb.

"Aye, I do really," Alexander said. "Inversnaid is too close for us no' to ken what number of soldiers are there, and if I leave it till the snow comes it'll be difficult to get there, maybe for months."

"Aye, but if *you* find it difficult to get there, the redcoats'll no' be stirring from their hearths," Moira pointed out.

"True. But if I find out now how many are there, I'll be reasonably sure the numbers willna change until spring. And it'll do the boy good to learn a wee bit about fending for himself. He'll be having to do it soon enough. He's a clever boy, he learns fast."

"He is. But so is Duncan, just in a different way," she said.

"Aye. He's awfu' like you," Alexander commented. "He doesna see as wide as Alex, but he sees deeper. Alex sees the whole situation, but he canna see the detail. No' yet. Duncan sees the detail."

"Alex doesna sit still enough to see anything beneath the surface. I never kent a bairn wi' so much energy. None of the other boys are that wild. Simon, Alasdair Og, Rory...they canna keep up wi' him," Moira said.

"It's good to see him so interested in everything, so healthy, though," Alexander said, casting a glance at the pallet where their not-so-healthy daughter slept. "Soon he'll need to learn to sit and be still. Some things canna be learned by rushing around, no matter how eager ye are. Or how clever."

Moira made a sceptical sound in her throat.

"Aye, well, good luck wi' that one," she said. "Ye're hatching something. What is it?"

Alexander flushed slightly. Yes, Duncan took after his mother. She saw everything. Because she both cared and took the time to observe, to learn what was beneath the surface. Alex cared, no doubt about that, but...

"He'll be chieftain one day," Alexander said. "He's going to have to keep the energy and ambition he's got, but he needs to learn to read and write, maybe go to university one day. I want him to be a greater man, an educated chieftain. He'll need that I think, for I canna see us getting the proscription lifted by the sword."

"Ye truly dinna think there'll be another rising then?" Moira said. "James has a son now, after all."

"Aye, but the laddie's a babe in arms. He'll no' be doing

anything for many years, and after all that time people will have grown accustomed to Hanover on the throne. They'll no' rise and fight in twenty years like they might now. James is the rightful king, but he doesna seem to have the personality to inspire. Maybe his son Charles willna have either. So Alex canna just learn how to fight wi' weapons. He needs to be able to fight wi' words too. I want him to be able to hold his own wi' any chief, wi' any lord in England too. I want him to have a proper education, to prove that the MacGregors are no' just brawling savages, but men of letters too."

"You're going to teach him yourself, are ye?" Moira said.

"I'll start him on his reading, aye, and the writing too. He's clever enough. It'll be easier to get him to sit still in the winter, after all. By the time the spring comes he'll be accustomed to it."

Moira sat back and stared into the fire for a minute, trying to imagine her boundlessly energetic whirlwind of a son actually sitting still for more than five minutes. And failing.

"Teach Duncan too," she said.

"D'ye think? I was thinking to wait a while, for he's still a wee bairn."

"Aye, he is in his body, but he sees things like an older boy. We saw that tonight. He can see things from another person's point of view. Alex canna do that. He thought Duncan was sad because he would have been if their positions had been reversed.

"Now Duncan's a step ahead of Alex there, because he understands that different people want different things, and that just because he likes doing something it doesna mean everyone likes doing it. And he's happy to be different to his brother. He doesna need to prove himself to anyone. Alex needs to learn the self-confidence that Duncan just has naturally. It's no' just about seeing the detail, it's more than that. He's contented wi' who he is. Alex isna."

"He's a kind laddie though. He wanted Duncan to be happy. And he's awfu' gentle wi' Morag."

"I'm no' criticising him. I'm proud of him, though he drives me daft at times. But he needs approval. The opinion of others matters to him. Ye might remember that, when ye're fighting to make him sit down long enough to learn to read."

* * *

"Da," Alex said the following evening, when the men had stopped for the night in a clump of trees down by the lochside near Inversnaid.

"Aye?" Alexander replied, handing his son a small bowl of oatmeal mixed with water, which was to be his evening meal.

"Am I old enough to learn what spies is now?"

Alexander sat on the ground, his back against a tree, and unhooked his flask from his belt.

"Who's tellt ye about spies?" he asked.

"You did," Alex said. "Ye said that when I was up to here," he put his free hand at his waist, "ye'd tell me. I am now. And I can lift a sword. Ye said a spies has to be able to lift a sword."

Alexander frowned for a minute, then looked at his son in astonishment.

"Ye remember that?" he said. "Ye were just a wee bairn then!"

"Aye. But I'm no' a wee bairn now. So what's spies?"

Alexander took a deep drink of water from the flask then passed it to his waiting son, giving himself time to think.

"Spies is the word if there's more than one," he said finally. "So a spy is someone who finds out information about what the enemy is doing, and then tells his friends about it. He finds out important things that might help his clan win a fight."

"Ye mean like Allan and Dugald are doing now?" Alex asked.

"No, no' really. They're more scouts. A scout is someone who goes to see what's just ahead of us. They have to do it quietly so as no' to warn the enemy or be caught. They do come back to tell the others, though, and spies do that as well. But a spy is different."

"Why?"

"Allan and Dugald are no' going to go and meet the enemy, be friendly wi' them, live wi' them, and gain their trust. Spies have to do that. If Allan was a spy, he'd maybe pretend to be a redcoat, live wi' them at Inversnaid, make them all like him. And then he'd find out all the things that we need to ken, like how many soldiers are there, what weapons they've got, what they're thinking to do next. And then he'd slip away one night and tell us their secrets. Then he might have to go back and pretend to be their friend again, to find out more."

Alex sat and thought about this.

"I dinna think I'd like that. It doesna seem right to pretend to be someone's friend. I dinna think I could do that," he said. "I'd rather fight wi' my sword than be a coward. When I get it," he added.

"Aye, no' everyone can do it," Alexander agreed. "I dinna think you could, laddie. But spies are no' cowards. I'm thinking it's harder to be a spy than to fight wi' your clan."

"Why?"

"If ye look around now. Imagine Allan comes back and says some Campbells are trying to kill Dugald, just away over the hill there. What would we do?"

"We'd all go and kill the Campbells and rescue him," Alex said immediately.

"Aye, that's right. But if Dugald was a spy in Inversnaid barracks and someone found out, no one would be able to help him. He'd have to try to save himself, and if he couldna he'd be tortured to try to make him tell who he was spying for. Torture is a terrible thing, and ye have to be awfu' brave to endure it and no' tell what ye ken. And he'd have to go through that alone, sure that no one would come to save him, and that all the redcoats hated him because he'd betrayed them. It's a very brave thing to be a spy. It's a lonely thing too. Ye canna win renown and glory, because ye canna tell *anyone* what ye're doing. And people dinna think of spies as brave men, though they are."

"I dinna want to be a spy," Alex said with great certainty.

"No more will ye be. Hopefully ye'll one day be the chieftain. But ye've a lot to learn before then," his father reassured him.

"What will you be, when I'm the chieftain?" Alex asked.

"Why, I'll be dead, laddie."

Alex stared at his father with wide eyes. Then he shuddered.

"I dinna want to be chieftain, either," he said.

"I'm hoping it'll be a long time afore ye are," Alexander agreed, smiling. "But ye still need to learn how to be one. Now, normally when we go out in the winter we'd light a wee fire to cook food on, and to keep us warm, if we'd the wood to hand. But we canna do that tonight. Why d'ye think that is?"

Alex finished eating his oatmeal, thinking hard.

"We dinna want the redcoats in Inversnaid to ken we're here, and they might if they see the fire," he said.

"Well done, laddie. Nearly right. They wouldna see the fire, no' even the glow of it, because we're down here in the trees, and they're away over that hill. But they might see the smoke from it, because that rises, and because soldiers post sentries and their job is to look very carefully for signs of an enemy."

"Are we the enemy?" Alex asked. "Are we going to fight them?"

"They are the enemy, aye. I've tellt ye, if ye ever see a redcoat ye must run away, immediately. But we're no' going to fight them, no. There are too many of them, and if we *did* fight them, then they'd bring a lot more redcoats here, and we dinna want that. But it's always good to ken how many enemies ye've got nearby. So we're going to sleep here tonight, and I'll show ye how to wrap your plaid around ye to be warm, and then at first light we'll away up to the top of the hill and watch. Ye'll have to be still and quiet though, maybe for a long time. Can ye do that?"

"Aye," said Alex immediately, hoping that a long time wouldn't be as long as he'd had to sit in the fishing boat with Iain and Duncan.

"Good. Now, what we need to do next—"

Alex never did find out what they needed to do next, because at that minute Dugald and Allan came running back through the trees at such speed that Alexander leapt up, drawing his sword as he did.

"It's no' the redcoats," Allan gasped immediately. "It's Andrew."

"*Andrew?*" Alexander echoed. "Where? I thought he was at Fort William."

"No, he's in chains wi' a party o' redcoats, heading to Stronachlachar," Dugald said. "We met wi' Effie, and she tellt us. Glengyle's are all away raiding so there isna anyone else who can help us. They're taking him to Edinburgh to try him."

"*Iochd!*" said Alexander with feeling. "Did she tell ye how many redcoats are wi' him?"

"She said about twenty, but she hasna seen herself. It was wee Roderick that saw them. What do we do?"

Alexander tore his hands through his hair.

"Da, is that—"

"No' the now, laddie," Alexander snapped. "I need to think."

"Come on, Alex," Kenneth said. "I'll show ye how to make a bed for yourself."

Alex got up reluctantly and followed Kenneth, who took him into the trees.

"Ye can use heather or moss," Kenneth said. "But I prefer moss if ye can find enough, and at this time of year ye usually can."

"Kenneth, is that our Andrew, who killt the redcoat?"

"Aye, I'm thinking so, the loon. He shouldna have done that."

"But I thought he was dead!"

"No, he was arrested and taken to Fort William. That's a big barracks away over there," Kenneth said, waving his hand in a northerly direction. "We couldna rescue him frae there."

"Can we rescue him from Strona…?" Alex said excitedly.

"Stronachlachar. That's for your da to decide, no' me," Kenneth said.

"Would ye rescue him, if it were for you to decide?" Alex asked.

Kenneth looked into the distance for a moment.

"It's complicated," he said finally.

Alex's face fell. 'It's complicated' was adult for 'I'm no' telling ye'.

When they got back, carrying armfuls of moss, everyone was sitting in a circle. Kenneth dropped his moss under a tree, Alex doing likewise, then they joined the others.

"I dinna like it," Alexander said as soon as they were seated. "We're no' armed for such a thing, and we've the boy wi' us too."

"I'll no' be a trouble, Da," Alex said earnestly. Alexander ruffled his son's hair affectionately.

"We're only six, as well. We canna fight twenty redcoats," James pointed out.

"No, we canna. But we dinna ken for sure there *are* twenty. Roderick's only a wee laddie, likely he canna count rightly yet. And this will be the only chance to rescue him," Alexander said. He sighed. "We havena time to go and get the others."

"I dinna think we should go at all," Alpin said suddenly, then flushed as everyone looked at him.

"We have to try," Dugald said. "He's one of us."

"Aye, but he didna need to kill the redcoat. They werena attacking us. They were just marching to Inversnaid, and he decided to dirk the man while he'd stopped to have a piss. He could have brought the whole garrison down on us if they hadna caught the wee shite," Alpin persisted.

"How can ye think like that?" Dugald retorted hotly.

"I can think any way I see fit," Alpin shot back. "It's my thought we're better without him. We could all be dead now, if he hadna been daft enough to stay around long enough to get caught. And it wasna the first time he'd done something stupid."

"Wait," Alexander said, raising his hand to stop the disagreement becoming violent, as it looked about to do, judging by Dugald's face. "Ye havena time to fight, and in truth Alpin's the right of it. Ye've both the right of it, in fact. Andrew's a loon. He canna control his temper, and he doesna think ahead. In many ways he's a liability. But he *is* a MacGregor, and I canna let the chance to rescue him pass. If he gets to Edinburgh, he'll hang for certain. But I'll no' try if there *are* twenty soldiers. We need to go to Stronachlachar, see if we can find out."

The men packed up their things with varying levels of enthusiasm, and were soon heading across country again.

"Is this where ye'd need a spy, Da?" Alex asked as they marched along.

"Aye, one would be useful now. But we havena got one, so we'll have to do our best without. Save your breath, laddie. We need to march fast now."

By the time they arrived at the tiny hamlet at the edge of Loch Katrine, the moon was high in the sky and it had started raining. They dropped down in the scrub at the side of the track to plan.

"It's my thinking that if there *are* twenty soldiers, they'll be at the tacksman's house," Dugald said, "for it's the biggest one there, and none of the others would hold that many men. They're redcoats and thinking to stay the night, so they'll want comfort."

"Aye, but dinna forget, they're Scottish redcoats, most likely," Kenneth pointed out. "No' yon soft Sasannach laddies."

"True, but unless they're Highlanders they'll no' be wanting to sleep outside in November."

Alex was about to say that he didn't want to sleep outside in November either, for the rain was coming down fierce now, but as no one else was paying any attention to the weather, he kept silent.

"Alpin," Alexander said, "ye're the lightest on your feet and the quietest. D'ye think ye could go to Malcolm's and listen outside? If there's redcoats there, ye'll hear them."

Alpin was scrambling to his feet when two figures came into view on the track. All the MacGregors dropped flat on the grass, there being no time to move away without being seen. Just as the men drew close though, the moon came briefly out from behind a cloud, illuminating the face of one, a squat, broad-shouldered man.

"Fergus!" Alexander hissed, and the two men stopped dead, then seeing the others move, came to join them.

"What in God's name are ye doing here?" Fergus asked, taking off his bonnet and wringing the water out, before squashing it back on his head.

Alex assumed these strangers were friends, because his father immediately told them exactly why they were here.

"Aye," Fergus said. "They're at Malcolm's. But there are no' twenty, only twelve. Armed to the teeth though and very aware they're in MacGregor country."

"Do they ken Rob Roy's away?" Alexander asked.

"We havena tellt them that, no. But they may do. They ken Malcolm's no' here, at any rate. His wife Isobel tellt them her maidservant ran off wi' her finest gown, made a good show of it, too, and sent us to catch up wi' her afore she can sell it. Me and Archie were away to see if we could find help for the man. Isobel's spent half the evening trying to get the redcoats drunk, but they'll no' drink a drop. This was her last attempt to save him. He'll hang else."

"Christ," said Alexander. "I canna spare a man to take the boy home, no' if they're on such alert they're no' drinking. I never heard of such a thing."

"I dinna want to go home," Alex piped up now. "I want to help!"

Alexander, clearly torn, scraped his long dark hair back, tying it at the nape of his neck with a lace, and then, kneeling so they were face-to-face, he took his son by the shoulders.

"If ye come wi' us tonight, ye must do *everything* I tell ye, and do it immediately. No argument, no questions. All our lives depend on you obeying me. D'ye understand that?"

"Aye, Da," Alex said. "I promise I'll do as I'm tellt."

Alexander looked up the track for a minute, then at his son again. Then in one smooth movement, he drew his dirk.

"Swear on the iron, laddie, for this is a serious matter," he said, his heart catching as Alex bit his lip, but put his hand on the blade immediately and swore to obey. He was a fine boy, but impulsive. Hopefully this would stop him doing something reckless.

"Good," Alexander said. "Let's go, then."

The party, now eight men with Fergus and Archie, made their way through the trees quietly, heading for the tacksman's house. Once outside it, they stopped again.

"Damn, the shutters are all closed, every one," Alexander whispered.

"Aye, that's the first thing the redcoats did," Archie said. "But when we left, Andrew was in the pantry at the back, for there's no window so he canna be got out. And the redcoats were all in the kitchen, that's at the back of the house, but there's a door in to it from the yard."

"We canna go in that way," Alexander said. "If all twelve of them are there, sober and expecting the whole clan to come down on them, they'll have muskets trained on that door."

"Aye, and we havena even got swords wi' us," Kenneth said.

"We werena expecting to fight. If we'd come upon soldiers near Inversnaid we could have said we were Campbells, collecting wood or suchlike. We could claim the dirks were for cutting branches, but we couldna claim swords were for that, no' since the disarming act came in. I didna ken we'd be trying to besiege a damn troop o' soldiers the next day," Alexander said, frustrated.

"We could go back, knock on the door and pretend we've seen the maid or some such thing, and then ye could all burst in behind us. I'm thinking only one soldier will open the door, or Isobel herself, if we call out from outside," Fergus said.

After some discussion, it was decided this was the best chance they had.

"Before we go in," Alexander said, "I ken that you, Alpin, Kenneth, and maybe others, dinna want him back wi' us. He isna popular wi' anyone, in truth. But he's one of us and if we dinna try to save him now we've a chance to, we'll regret it later, I'm thinking. But we canna hesitate once we start, so I'll say this; if we succeed and get him away, then I'll no' have him back in the clan. We'll gie him his life back, but then I'll banish him. Ye need to give this your all. Will ye do it now?"

All the men nodded, and then Alexander smiled.

"Right then, let's do it. Alex, come wi' me."

For one glorious moment Alex pictured himself charging through the door of the house as his father's right-hand man, but then Alexander led him to the tangled shrubbery at the front of the house, where there was a good-sized rock. He took out his dirk, then pulled and cut away a few of the branches that were growing over it.

"There's a wee space there now, for ye to hide in," Alexander said to his disappointed son. "Ye must stay behind the rock, absolutely silent, until I call ye or come for ye. If ye see us come out and run in another direction, stay here. That'll be difficult, but ye swore to obey. Stay here until one of us comes for ye. D'ye understand that?"

Alex nodded miserably, and to his horror his eyes filled with tears, spilling over and down his cheeks before he could stop them. He sniffed and swiped his hand across his nose. Alexander sighed.

"Remember we talked about spies earlier," he said. "I need ye to be a spy for me. Ye canna fight yet, but ye can do something even more important. If ye lie here, ye can see the house from the side of the rock. No' from above it. Ye must lie down. I need ye to see and remember everything that happens, for then ye can tell the clan when we get back. No one else can do that, for we'll all be fighting, and only see our side. But you can see it all. Can ye do that?"

Alex smiled now, shakily, but no more tears fell. He scrambled into the space his father had hollowed out, and lay down.

"Ye're a good laddie, Alex," Alexander said. "I'll see ye in a while."

And he was gone.

Alex lay in the hollow, which was very wet and cold, there being a puddle of water in the middle of it. The shrubs gave some protection from the rain, but as he was already drenched and lying in icy water, he soon had to open his mouth so that he could stay silent, as his teeth were chattering. He would have preferred to charge in with the others and kill a redcoat, or at least wound one. He'd only used his *sgian dubh* to cut up meat, but he imagined that cutting a man was no different to cutting a piece of mutton.

But it would be a great thing to tell the whole clan of what happened! Maybe they would make a song of it, and mention him as the teller! They probably wouldn't do that if he just cut a redcoat, and he didn't think his little knife was big enough to actually kill one with.

He peeped out from the side of the rock, pushing aside the heather so he could see, and watched as the men approached the house, Fergus at the front because he was going to knock on the door while the others moved to the side out of sight, ready to run in when the door was opened.

But the door suddenly opened before Fergus was close enough to knock, before the MacGregors had moved out of the way, so that the pool of yellow light from the hallway streamed out, lighting up enough of them for the soldier who'd opened the door to realise that whatever this was, it was not friendly.

As quick as a flash James threw his dirk, and the soldier cried out. Alex's view of the hall was now blocked by the bodies of the men charging the door in an attempt to get in and overpower the soldiers before they could react to their comrade's cry, but although he couldn't see a lot he did hear a few new obscenities. The door started to close from inside, but then was pushed open again by the MacGregors.

Then a shot was fired and Alex could see a lot of red cloth, after which the MacGregors broke and ran from the house, some to the left, some to the right, disappearing into the darkness as the red cloth became soldiers, who were clearly intending to run after them, until an order barked from inside stopped them in their tracks and they all went back into the house, closing the door behind them.

It grew quiet then, and the rain got heavier. Briefly a shutter opened and the face of a man could be seen peering out, and then an angry voice spoke and the shutter was closed. Nearby an owl hooted, and there was a little skittering as a small nocturnal creature ran for cover. And then a voice came from right next to Alex, which made him jump, because he'd been so intent on remembering everything that went on in the house he hadn't paid attention to what was going on behind him.

"*Isd*, laddie," Kenneth said, and bending down, scooped the sodden child out of his hiding place before taking off at a dead run.

They regrouped on the outside of the hamlet, Alexander waiting until everyone was in place. Alpin had his right arm cradled in a fold of his plaid, but everyone else seemed fine.

"It's nothing," he said immediately on seeing all eyes go to him. "Just a scratch. The ball hit my arm, but I dinna think it's in there. I'm well."

"We canna do anything about it now. Is it bleeding bad?" Alexander asked.

"No," Alpin answered. Kenneth put Alex down and went to his brother, but Alpin waved him off.

"Are ye all right, laddie?" Alexander said to his son, who was shivering uncontrollably, his teeth chattering audibly now he didn't have to be silent.

"Aye," he managed. "I saw everything, I think."

"Good lad. Did ye see anything after we left?"

"The redcoats went back into the house and shut the door. I heard three sounds like bolts inside being put on. And then the shutter opened a wee bit and a man looked out. He had dark hair and a white shirt on, and a wee jacket wi' no sleeves but I couldna see the colour o' that, and then another voice called 'close the fucking shutter, you idiot,' and so the man pulled the shutter closed wi' his left hand. And then I heard another door open at the back, but I couldna get up to look, for I'd sworn no' to. Then two o' the men rode away down the road going that way." He pointed up the track. "I couldna see a lot then, for it was verra dark, but one o' the horses was grey, or maybe white, for I could see him."

A short silence followed this statement, and Alex was just wondering if he'd missed anything, when James spoke.

"If they've ridden out, they'll have gone to get reinforcements."

"Aye," Alexander said. "Which means they think the whole of the clan must be here. They'd no' risk that if they kent there was only eight of us. Alex, tell us what the man said again, about the shutter."

Alex repeated the words he'd heard.

"Did he say them exactly as ye just said?" Alexander asked.

"Aye, Da. Ye asked me to remember *everything*."

"Jesus Christ," Dugald said softly.

"English," Alexander said. "I thought it was a Scots regiment."

"Maybe it is, but they've an English sergeant."

"Maybe. If so, they're likely no' Highlanders then," Alexander said.

"What do we do now?" Kenneth asked.

"Well, we canna get in the house wi' just dirks, no' now they ken we're here. The only other chance we'd have is to try to take them on the road, ambush them," Alexander said. "But it's my guess that the two men have gone to Inversnaid, for it's no' far away. We canna catch them for we havena any horses wi' us, and if they think the whole of the MacGregor clan's rising to rescue Andrew, they'll likely send the whole damn garrison to take him to Edinburgh."

"Do we give up, then?"

"I'd like to wait, hide out near the Inversnaid road till the morning, and see what they send. We didna get a chance to check the garrison. It could be that there's only a handful of redcoats there, and they canna spare them. We'll no' get another chance to save Andrew. If the redcoats *are* English or even Lowlanders, they'll no' be familiar wi' Highland fighting, and they're more likely to slip into the heather to take a shit. If they do that there'll be one less man, and we'll have a sword and maybe a musket too."

"And when they're gone, we can go back to the house and get our weapons," Archie said. "They're out in the barn, well hidden. We'll come wi' ye."

"Good. Then we'll wait. If they bring the garrison, we'll abandon the whole idea."

The men moved further away from the track and settled down as best they could.

"Da," Alex said. "Can ye show me how to make myself warm wi' my *fèileadh mór*? I'm awfu' cold." He looked down then, ashamed for admitting it. But he was shaking so much that it hurt, and he couldn't feel his feet any more.

"Tonight ye'll sleep wi' me, laddie, and we'll keep each other warm," Alexander said, "for I'm cold, too."

Alex felt a bit better then, and a lot better when his da wrapped his plaid around the both of them.

"I'm awfu' wet," he admitted.

"That's a good thing. We'll be warmer for it," his father said. "Wet wool keeps the heat in. Ye'll see that, once we settle."

He thought his da was joking with him, but it was true! Once they were lying down and their body heat had warmed the plaids, he wasn't cold any more! It was wonderful. What an exciting day! Warm and safe, curled into his father's stomach, he felt suddenly weary. His eyes started to close.

"Ye did well, remembering all that, laddie," his father said suddenly. "And ye did as I tellt ye, though ye were awfu' chilled. I'm proud of ye." Alex smiled. And then his eyes closed, and he drifted away.

* * *

"*Gu sealladh orm!* Ye're bleeding like a stuck pig!" Alexander said as he examined Alpin's injury, which he did as soon as it was light enough to see. Kenneth had torn a piece off his shirt and wrapped it round the wound the previous night, but now it was scarlet, and still bleeding. "Why did ye tell me it was a scratch?"

Alpin looked away.

"I thought it was, then," he said. "I was wet wi' the rain, so I didna realise it was bleeding that bad."

Alexander examined him. His face was pale, he was sweating in spite of the cold, and breathing quickly, although he hadn't done anything other than sit up when Alexander had gone to him.

"How do ye feel? I'll have the truth, now," Alexander said firmly.

"I'm...I just feel a wee bit shaky, as though I'm no' quite here," Alpin admitted under his chieftain's intense blue gaze. "But I'll be fine when we're moving again."

Alexander closed his eyes for a second, then came to a decision.

"Kenneth, can ye carry your brother?" he said, then held his hand up imperiously when Alpin started to object.

"Aye, of course. He weighs nothing," Kenneth said.

"Everything weighs nothing to you, laddie," Dugald commented dryly.

"The *clach cuid fir* didna weigh nothing," Kenneth shot back. "Nearly killed me to lift that."

"Ye did it, though," Dugald said.

"Aye. Are ye wanting me to take him home?" Kenneth said.

"No. We're all going. We canna risk ye coming across a band o' redcoats now. The soldiers will have alerted Inversnaid and they'll be jittery, shooting at anything that moves, for it's my view that most of the men there will be raw recruits. It's a show, to tell the clans that they're watching us. Of course I may be wrong and they're experienced soldiers, but whichever the case is, I'll no' split us now."

"But what about Andrew?" Alpin asked. Alexander focussed on him again.

"That's why ye didna tell us? Because of what ye said last night?"

Alpin bit his lip.

"I didna want to be responsible for Andrew dying," he admitted. "I didna want ye to abandon him because of me."

"I wouldna have done that, ye wee gomerel," Alexander said. "Ye spoke your mind, which I've tellt ye all to do. So here's *my* mind. We havena really a hope in hell of rescuing Andrew now. Maybe if we had good weapons, and if half of Inversnaid was no' on its way here. But once the soldier opened the door unexpectedly last night, it was all up wi' Andrew. And I'll no' risk all our lives to rescue the wee shite. The odds are against us. Your wound has just helped me see that clearly, man. You're no' responsible for my decision. But ye canna walk. We need to bind your arm and get ye home as fast as we can."

"I can carry him, nae problem," Kenneth said. "And Alex too."

"No, I can run fast!" Alex objected.

"Ye can. So ye can run until ye're tired, then I'll carry you. Your legs are shorter than ours, so ye take two steps to one of ours. When we're halfway I'll carry ye, for ye'll have run as far as we will to get home. And then we need to teach ye arithmetic," he added, seeing his son's look of utter confusion.

* * *

"Christ, what happened?" Moira cried when the sodden men appeared through the trees and trooped into the clearing where most of the houses were. "I thought ye'd be another day watching the barracks. Did ye find out how many soldiers are there?" She scanned the group expertly, then looked back at Alexander. "What's amiss wi' Alpin?" she added.

"It didna go quite as planned," Alexander said wearily. "I'll tell ye…no, Alex'll tell ye later."

"I can tell ye now, Ma!" he said excitedly. "I was a spy!"

"No, laddie, tell everyone together. We'll meet in the barn, for this rain isna stopping. If ye can tell everyone to gather there, Moira. I need to see to Alpin."

"What happened to him?"

"He was shot by a redcoat!" Alex said. Moira's eyes widened.

"Aye. In the arm. He said the ball's no' in it still, but he's bled awfu' bad, and he fainted while Kenneth was carrying him back. Have ye anything for it?"

Moira thought.

"Aye, for the cut if it's bleeding still. But will I send for Susan? She kens a lot about the healing now, I'm thinking, and her married to a doctor."

"Susan?" Alexander asked, his face a picture of puzzlement.

"Aye. Sorry, Susan came back yesterday. She's thinking to live in Hamish's hut, says she'd be happy there, needing a wee bit of peace."

"Jesus, Ronald and Màiri's lassie? I didna think to see her again. What's she doing back?"

"She went tae Edinburgh wi' the MacIntyre man after they wed. He was a doctor, and she helped him sometimes. He died earlier this year, so she came back." Seeing the look on her husband's face at this, she added, "Aye, well, there's a lot more to tell, as there is wi' you, but she can tell ye herself, and Alpin'll no' be healing while we blether."

"Aye then, send for the lassie," Alexander said. "And get the wee laddie here warm, and some food in him. He's done well." He pushed Alex towards his mother, then headed off to Gregor and Barbara's house.

By the time Susan arrived, Alexander had been in the house for a few minutes and, having looked at the wound, had determined that Alpin had one thing right; the ball wasn't in it any more. He could tell this because there was a small entry wound in his upper arm at the front and a huge exit wound at the back, which was still seeping blood.

A tall, slim, somewhat eccentrically clothed woman suddenly appeared in the room, nodded perfunctorily at the inhabitants, and then her attention immediately moved to the unconscious man lying half-naked on the table. She felt around the side of his neck with her fingers, then closed her eyes, her mouth moving as she counted silently, after which she opened her eyes and smiled at the anxious onlookers.

"He's alive," she said to the onlookers, "but he's awfu' weak. The ball must have hit the vein, but didna cauterise it. When did it happen?"

"Last night," Alexander said. "Hello, Susan. Ye havena changed. Welcome home."

She looked properly at him then, and smiled again.

"Alexander," she said. "Thank ye. You have. Ye were a wee bairn when I left."

"I wasna a wee bairn," he said. "Ye'd no' recognise me if I'd been a wee bairn the last time ye saw me."

"Twelve was a wee bairn to me then," she said, taking the room's only candle and peering into the injury. "It certainly is now. Have ye hot water? Honey, virgin if you have it? I brought some moss wi' me to stop the bleeding. If I clean it out wi' some hot water as best I can, then pack it wi' honey and the moss on the top...I canna see any wee bits o' bone. Kenneth, could he move his arm after it happened?"

"Aye," Kenneth said, his face nearly as pale as his brother's, but with worry rather than blood loss. "He lifted it while I bound it for him, though it hurt him bad. He didna say it, but I could see by his face."

"That's good, then, if the ball didna hit the bone." She stood up, then thought for a minute. "All I ken of medicine is from helping Rob," she said. "But he was a fair one for the cleaning o' things, wounds, sores, even all his wee instruments. The others laughed at him, but he was a fastidious man anyway. He didna lose so many patients as the others, though. I'll say that for him." Barbara brought the water then, and some napkins.

"I weaved them myself," she said. "And they're verra clean, for I'm proud o' them."

"Ma, ye canna—" Kenneth began, but Barbara hushed him.

"Alpin's more important than a wee bit o' napery," she said, then went to get the honey.

Susan focussed back on the wound, cleaning it as best she could, glad in one sense that the boy was deeply unconscious and did not react to what would have been intensely painful had he been awake. She poured honey in the wound at the back, then saturated the moss with it, packing it into the exit wound before repeating the process on the entrance wound. After that she bound it firmly with another clean napkin.

"Well, I didna expect to be tending an injury on my second day back," she said then, standing up, "but it's good to be useful again."

"Will he survive?" Kenneth asked. She looked up at him, and her face softened.

"I hope so," she said. "He'll need to rest, though. And he's lost a lot of blood. Have ye any meat, liver, blood pudding?"

"We can kill a cow," Alexander said immediately, then seeing Gregor about to object to the killing of a precious cow just as winter was coming on, he added, "One o' my cows, to celebrate Susan coming home after nearly twenty years. And we'll keep the liver and make blood pudding for Alpin here."

"Aye, that'll help him to make more blood," Susan said.

"I thought bloodletting was a good thing," Barbara commented. "That's what the doctors always do, is it no', for everything?"

"Aye, well, Rob wasna a great believer in that, either, for he said Vesalius and Harvey had found out enough for him to think that we shouldna be paying so much attention to Galen, and that bloodletting wasna always a good thing. Certainly losing this much blood isna good. That's why he's so pale, I'm thinking. He needs to drink a lot too. Nettle tea, if ye have it. I might have some dried nettle at the house. I'll look, and bring it tomorrow. He'll need to rest now. Come for me if he gets worse."

After Kenneth had lifted Alpin off the table and put him tenderly to bed, she left, Alexander going with her, telling the others that they were all meeting in the barn in a few minutes.

Outside she stood for a moment, taking in deep breaths.

"It's good to breathe God's pure air again," she said. "The air in Edinburgh was a noxious fume."

"Will he survive?" Alexander asked as they continued.

"In truth, I dinna ken. He's young and Gregor said he's in good health. I hope so, although he's awfu' pale, and his pulse is weak, but steady. I wouldna say it to Gregor and Barbara, but I've seen young, strong men die of less. And live through much worse. No doubt ye have yourself by now. He's in God's hands.

"Kenneth's a sight to see, is he no'?" she continued on a lighter note. "He's Gregor and Barbara's son?"

"Aye, he is. The womenfolk said he near killt Barbara when he was born, for he started as he meant to go on," Alexander said. "Hasna stopped growing yet, I'm thinking, though he must be near it now, at seventeen. Ye're a sight to see yourself," he added.

She looked down at her green silk dress ruefully.

"Aye, well, it didna look strange in Edinburgh," she laughed. "And it's silk, so warmer than some o' the other gowns I've got. I've an arisaid, so if I cover myself wi' that I'll no' look too outlandish. Well, I will, but it doesna signify. People will like me or no'. My clothing shouldna decide them."

"Moira didna have time to tell me, Susan. What happened wi' the MacIntyre man?"

"He died," Susan said bluntly. "In May. We were happy together, and he was a good man. Devoted to his patients, but verra stubborn. He didna make a lot of friends, for he was outspoken wi' his ideas. Didna worship Galen, as I said in there." She nodded back towards the house they'd come from. "And he didna make a lot of money either, for he treated the poor who often couldna pay him. So when he died, in truth I didna have any reason to stay in Edinburgh. I'm no' one for the town. It's noisy and it reeks, and I like to spend time alone. We were never blessed wi' bairns, and when he died I found he owed money. He hadna tellt me, no' wanting me to worry, I'm thinking, but I couldna stay in the rooms we rented, for I couldna pay the arrears. So I thought to just come back and see if there was a place for me here." She looked up at him then, smiling, but there was a question on her face, and the smile was tentative.

"Aye, there's a place for ye here. Would have been anyway,

even if ye hadna just proved your worth, for ye're a MacGregor, though ye'd be better to use the MacIntyre name, I'm thinking. Is Hamish's place sufficient for ye? We can build ye another house closer to the rest of us, if ye want."

"No," she said. "I might be asking for help wi' making it watertight for winter, and it needs cleaning out, but I'll be happy on my own for a wee while. I've been surrounded by people for seventeen years, every minute o' the day. The peace will be wonderful, and I can be wi' ye all in five minutes."

"Good. Well, if ye can bear to be wi' people the night, ye can come to the barn. My eldest is waiting to tell ye all what happened the last days, and if we canna kill the cow and cook it so quickly, at least we can have a wee dram to welcome ye home."

"Thank ye. I've no notion what I'd have done if ye'd all refused me. Or if ye hadna been here any more."

"We'd no' have refused ye. And we're still here because we keep ourselves isolated from the likes o' Rob Roy, who causes so much trouble, and because o' the big cave up the hill that we can all be in quickly, given warning of an enemy we canna fight. It's a good place, and I'll no' leave it unless we've no option."

Susan smiled.

"Let's hope that day never comes then," she said. "For I've a mind to live out my days here, if I can."

CHAPTER FOUR

"And then after Kenneth, Alpin, James and Fergus ran toward the loch, and Archie, Da, Dugald and Iain to the trees, five men came out o' the house, and they looked around, but didna ken who to follow. Three of them had dark hair, one was yellow-haired, and the other had a hat on so I couldna see his hair colour. Two of the dark-haired ones had red coats on, wi' yellow down the front, and black boots, but the others didna have coats on. Are ye wanting me to tell everything they were wearing, Da?" Alex asked. "Like all the buttons, and the pretty things on the coats?"

"No, laddie, ye're painting a fine picture, but ye'll be having to go to bed soon, so if ye tell us what they did now," Alexander said.

Alex nodded happily, his eyes sparkling, flushed with happiness at being allowed to tell the tale to the whole clan.

"So then a voice came from inside – it was the same voice I tellt ye about, Da, that tellt the man to close the shutters, and it said, 'Don't go after them, you bloody fools, that's what the bastards want. We've a prisoner to guard.' And all the men stopped and looked at each other, and then one of them – he had a Brown Bess, but I didna tell ye that just now because ye wanted to know what they did instead o' what they were wearing. Anyway, he had it in his right hand, and he said, 'I got one of the savages, Sergeant. He won't be going far. Shall I send two men after him?' and Sergeant said, 'No, you fucking prick, I told you, that's what they want. If any of you go out you'll not come back, and God knows how many of them are waiting in the bushes. Like shadows, they are. You don't know they're there till you've a knife in your ribs. Come back in and barricade the door'.

"So they all muttered things, but I couldna hear what they said, and then they went back in and closed the door, and…" Alex stopped, having looked around his audience and noticed that they all appeared stunned rather than engrossed. "Did I say something wrong?" he asked uncertainly.

"No," said his mother. "It's no' your fault the soldiers have foul mouths. Your da'll tell ye which words are no' fit for ye to be saying later."

"They're no' the only ones wi' foul mouths, judging by what he tellt us Alpin said," Catriona commented.

"Aye, well, he'd just been shot," Gregor jumped in. "And there wasna anyone who shouldna hear it about. Apart from the laddie here. But how were we to ken he'd remember every word everyone said?"

"But Da tellt me to!" Alex protested. "He said, 'I need ye to see and remember everything that happens, for then ye can tell the clan when we get back'. So I did."

Alexander brushed his hand through his hair.

"Aye, ye did, I'll give ye that."

"Is that what Englishmen sound like? That peculiar way o' speaking?" Allan asked.

"Aye, it is," Alexander said, who'd had more dealings with Englishmen than most of the clan, having been to Edinburgh several times and to Crieff to sell cattle, where he'd met some English dealers.

"They didna both speak the same," Fiona commented.

"That's because the sergeant came from the south of England, near London, maybe, and the man wi' the gun was from the north somewhere," Susan said. "I went to England wi' Rob once, to London, and the people in different towns on the way had different ways o' speaking. You call it dialects."

"I canna believe the laddie recalled so much," Alexander said to Moira later, when they were back at home. "On the way back here just now, I asked him to tell me about the redcoats' trimmings, and he remembered everything it'd be reasonable for him to have seen from where he was, even how many buttons they had on their coats, and how many were actually fastened. It's incredible. And he couldna have made up the way the men spoke, for he's never heard a Sasannach in his life, but Susan could tell where the two soldiers came from!"

"Hopefully he's never heard that foul language before, either," Moira said with mock outrage.

"No' in English, at any rate," Alexander replied. "I need to start him on his book learning. If he can remember what happened in that much detail, he's ready to learn to read. After all, Quintilian said a father should start thinking about his son's education as soon as he's born."

"Quintilian?"

"Aye. He was a Roman, wrote *Instituto Oratoria*. I had to memorise whole passages of it when I was learning. In Latin." He screwed his face up. "I hated Latin. It was about oratory – learning to speak well, to be able to persuade people to your way o' thinking. I learnt Cicero too. They believed that oratory was a really important tool for creating civilisation. And they were right, for powerful men like politicians ken all about how to speak, do they no'?"

"In Latin? You're going to teach him Latin?" Moira said.

"No, I'll teach him to read the Gaelic and English first. And write it. Then we'll start the Latin, next year, maybe. I'm no' sure how well that'll go, for I canna remember much. I havena used it since I was a boy, except for prayers, of course. We must start speaking English in the house too, maybe two days of the week, for he'll need the English, even for the cattle dealing and suchlike. And if I canna remember the Latin, he can learn about oratory from English translations."

"He can already speak English well," Moira said. "Duncan too. Even Morag's learning some words now. How old were you when you were learning the Latin?"

"I was ten," Alexander said. "But I stopped the learning at eleven. Da didna have the money for it, and didna think that Latin and Greek would be any use to me. But that was when we thought that James would succeed when William died, and we'd have no need of fancy learning in the clan. Things are different now. If he can fight *and* debate our case wi' the king or other powerful men, he'll be a fine chieftain. Maybe even chief of *all* the MacGregors one day."

"The money situation isna different though," Moira said practically.

"Aye, but I'll find a way. We've ten years before he'll be ready for university. Longer if I canna find a better person than me to teach him."

"Do you no' think six is a wee bit young for Latin oratory?"

"No' after tonight. I couldna remember half of what happened that night, and I'm thirty-one! In truth, I'm thinking I'm a wee bit late starting him."

Moira was not so sure about this. Although she'd been as surprised as the others by the depth of detail Alex had recalled, she knew he had an excellent memory. If he reminded her of a promise she'd made, he usually used the exact words she'd uttered at the time. And he had memories of when he was a babe in arms, memories so insignificant that no one would have told him about them, such as the blue and red tartan of the arisaid she'd worn when nursing him, an arisaid she'd since given to another woman. And he remembered it as a baby would, being warm, hearing the beating of her heart in his ears, lying on a blue and red hill.

What she was not sure was that he was emotionally mature enough to learn things he saw no immediate purpose in learning. He'd been interested in going on the trip with the other men. He was interested in learning warcraft, fighting, surviving in the wild, hunting, in earning praise from the clan. All his focus was on becoming a great warrior so that his father would be proud of him. She'd had an uphill fight getting him to see the point of learning English, which she'd been tasked to do when Alex was three, because she was with the children all day as Alexander wasn't.

Alex had balked at the idea, especially as not everyone in the clan could speak it. She'd told him that all chieftains' children learnt it, that they could have it as their secret language, to no avail.

He was not a disobedient child – if he was ordered to do something, he'd do it, but do it reluctantly. He was as stubborn as his father; if you wanted him to learn something he had no interest in, then he needed a good reason, one he could understand, to give him the incentive to learn it. Then he'd put the same boundless enthusiasm into it as he did into everything else he did.

She'd finally succeeded by telling him that if you learnt the language of the enemy, then it would be easier to beat them in a battle, because you'd know what they were saying to each other on the battlefield, whereas the English believed Gaelic to be gibberish and didn't learn it, so would have no idea what he was telling his men to do. Having a chieftain who understood the English would give the clan a great advantage. After that his knowledge of the language had progressed at an amazing rate.

He would see no point in learning a foreign language that nobody spoke any more though, or in learning oratory. She doubted this Quintilian man had written about how to persuade Alex MacGregor that Latin oratory was crucial to sword fighting or leading the MacGregors. She doubted her husband could do it either. Alex would not understand his father's reasons for a comprehensive education, valid though they were. She needed to sit and think of persuasive arguments that would seem sensible to their six-year-old bundle of energy.

"I still think Duncan should learn with him," Moira suggested. "It'll be easier if they learn together, surely? Ye can teach them the same thing."

"No' yet. When he's five, maybe. He'll no' be able to learn at the same rate as Alex, being younger. And Alex'll want to show Duncan what he's learnt. That'll help him to remember it, and prepare Duncan for what's to come."

Moira gave up. It was about time that her husband learned just how much like him his son was, not only in appearance, but in obstinacy too. This would be interesting.

* * *

February 1722

"This is an excellent wee book," Alexander said from his chair by the window, placed there so he could read without using a candle. "I wasna sure it would be, but the man had sense."

There had been an uncustomary warm spell in the previous week which had melted much of the winter snow, and Alexander had seized the opportunity to go to Stirling, partly to learn any news and partly to purchase some materials and books in order to begin his son's education. The son in question, blissfully unaware of his father's plans for him, was currently outside with his sister, the two of them trying to catch snowflakes on their tongues.

"What is it you're reading?" asked Moira.

"It's by a man called Locke," Alexander said, looking up. "The bookseller tellt me it had all the advice ye need on how to teach a bairn. Tutors all use it, he said. I wasna sure, but he tellt me that if I bought the Aesop, the Euclid and the paper and ink, he'd give it to me for free, as the spine's broken and there's a few wee marks in it."

"What does yon Locke laddie say then?"

Alexander flicked back a few pages in the book, then read aloud: "'The first thing is that children be not too warmly clad, winter or summer. The face, when we are born, is no less tender than any other part of the body. 'Tis use alone that hardens it and makes it more able to endure the cold'. And then he says that he should have 'his shoes so thin, that they might leak and let in water, whenever he comes near it'. I wouldna have expected a Sasannach gentleman to be so wise," Alexander added.

"Aye. It'd be something if we could make them wear shoes at all, thin or no'," Moira said, glancing out at her brood. Duncan had joined them now. Normally they would no doubt start a snowball fight with the other boys; but not when they were looking after their sister. She was the only one wearing shoes, and the only one wrapped in a woollen plaid. The two boys were dressed in their usual linen tunics, their legs and feet bare. Alex had abandoned his *féileadh mór* today, impatience to be out in the precious daylight overriding his wish to dress like a man. "What's that to do wi' teaching the boy to read and write, though?"

"Well, it seems to be a general book on how to rear a child, to make him want to learn, and to make him into a good man. Of course, it's a book for Sasannach gentlemen, so it says ye shouldna teach him fighting or fencing, for if ye do he'll no doubt get into bad company when he's older, and have duels and suchlike."

"What's fencing?" Moira asked.

"It's a sort o' dancing wi' swords. Teaches a man how to fight wi' all kinds o' silly rules and fighting positions. A Highlander'd take the laddie's head clean off while he was getting intae the right pose to start. They warn each other too, say 'en garde' and such nonsense, instead o' just dirking the man and having done wi' it. And ye canna kick your opponent in the balls or break his nose wi' your targe and suchlike. I dinna think they use a targe in fencing. But some o' the advice here might be good, and I'll adapt it a wee bit. Ye can read it when I've finished, if ye want. I'll start him tomorrow wi' his letters, for the reading."

Moira went to the door and called Morag in. She couldn't stay out too long in the cold without becoming breathless anyway, and it would give Alex a chance to enjoy his last day of freedom.

* * *

Alex sat on a stool at the table, on which was a piece of paper, a bottle of ink, some sand, and a book. On the opposite side of the table sat his father, busily sharpening a quill, which he had said was used for writing, although they would not be writing today. First Alex had to learn to read. Alex fervently hoped that he could learn to read before it got dark, because the other children were outside playing with a ball, which Susan had brought back from Edinburgh for them and which was a treasured possession. He gazed out of the window mournfully. At the moment the children were in a circle, with Jeannie in the centre. They were all cheering because Alasdair Og had thrown the ball to another child, but with a superhuman effort Jeannie had leapt into the air and caught it. She moved to the outside of the circle, shaking her hands which were smarting from catching the heavy leather sphere. Alasdair Og, defeated, went to stand inside the circle, where he would have to stay until he'd intercepted the ball.

Alex sighed.

"Da," he said, "Can I no' learn to read when it's dark? There'll be a while before bedtime. I should be able to do it then."

His father looked up.

"No. Ye'll no' learn to read in just a day, laddie. It takes a long time."

"How long?" Alex asked.

"Months. Ye'll maybe be able to read a wee bit by the summer, if ye work hard every day."

By the summer! That *was* a long time! That was *forever!*

He sighed and looked out of the window again. Jeannie had thrown the ball over the heads of all the others, and now Duncan was running to get it. Alexander finished sharpening the quill and glanced out to see what his son was sighing about.

It was on the tip of his tongue to tell the boy that if he learned five letters today he could go out and join the others, as he so clearly wanted to do. But then he remembered; Locke wrote that on no account should you bribe children to learn by offering them a treat if they did. Instead you should commend them when they did well, and show a cold countenance to them when they did badly, so that esteem from their family was the only reward.

So he stood and went to the door.

"Away and play down by the loch," he called to the group.

"Can Alex come wi' us?" Duncan, who had now returned, asked.

"No. He's learning to read."

"Why does he have to do that?" Alasdair Og asked.

Duncan looked through the window, at the pale globe of his brother's face. He knew Alex would be miserable, which made him feel sad.

"Can I learn to read too, then, Da?" he asked.

"No, laddie, you're too wee. When ye're a bit bigger ye can."

"Kenneth canna read, and he's the biggest person in the clan," Jeannie said pertly. "Why does Alex have to, when Kenneth canna?"

Alexander combed his hand through his hair.

"Because he's the chieftain's son, and the chieftain's son has to be able to read," he explained.

"But I'm the chieftain's son too," Duncan pointed out.

"And because I said so, and I'm the chieftain, so ye'll do as ye're tellt and go play away from here!" Alexander shouted, before going in and slamming the door.

"Dinna say it," he said to Moira, irritated with himself for actually wasting time debating with bairns, and aware of how childish his final sentence to them had sounded. He sat down again. Alex pulled his gaze away from the retreating children reluctantly.

"Now," said his father, picking up the quill, "ye'll be learning to read the English first, for nearly all books are written in it, and in the English there are twenty-six letters to learn, which is called the alphabet. Each letter has a sound. This is the first letter." He dipped the quill in the ink and made a shape on the paper. "This is an 'a'," he said, "and it sounds either like 'ay' or 'ah'."

Alex looked at the shape.

"How d'ye ken which sound it should be?" he asked.

His father thought for a minute.

"When the letters are in groups, they become words, and ye can tell by the other letters what sound the 'a' letter makes."

"But why do they no' just make a different mark for the two sounds?" Alex asked.

"D'ye really want to be learning fifty-two letters?" his father replied. "Fifty-two is twice twenty-six," he added, making a mental note to include some arithmetic in the daily lessons.

"No," Alex answered, in a tone that made it clear he didn't want to learn any letters at all. "But if I've to do it, then it'd be easier to learn fifty-two o' them than have to look at all the other letters every time to know what sound it makes."

Alexander brushed his fingers through his hair, which starting to look distinctly untidy.

"Your name starts with that letter," Moira, who was sweeping the floor, said. "And your da's too."

"Does it?" Alex said, looking at the mark with new interest.

"Aye it does," Alexander said. "But it doesna look like that when it's at the start of your name. Then it looks like this." He took the paper back and wrote a capital A on it.

"So that one is the 'ah' sound, then?" Alex said.

"And the 'ay' too, depending on the letters round it," Alexander said. "It's the same as the 'a'."

"If it's the same as the 'a' then why do ye need to learn two marks for the same thing?" Alex asked.

"It's called a capital A," Alexander said. "But ye dinna need to learn the capital letters yet. I just showed ye that one, for your name starts wi' it."

"Does every letter have two marks?" Alex asked.

"Aye. Every letter has a capital."

"So I've got to learn fifty-two letters after all then?" Alex said, aghast. "And they all have two sounds?"

"They don't *all* have two sounds. But this one's a vowel, and vowels all have more than one sound. But I'll be awfu' proud of ye, when ye have learnt," Alexander said somewhat desperately, seeing the look of mingled confusion and despair on his son's face.

* * *

April 1722

Alexander watched from the bench outside the door as his eldest son cartwheeled ecstatically all the way down to the loch and then, pausing only to unbuckle his belt and let his kilt drop to the ground quickly followed by his tunic, ran into the water. The cheer from the other children as he did reached Alexander's ears as he gathered up the paper and book and went back into the house, where Moira was showing Morag how bannocks were made.

"We'll put a wee bit o' barley flour in wi' the oats," she said. "Now, I'll pour water on it, and ye've to mix it together wi' your fingers. Can ye do that?"

The child nodded, her dark brown hair flying round her face.

"Go on, then," Moira said, glancing up at her husband, who was observing this domestic scene. "Morag's making the bannocks for us today," she explained for the child's benefit.

"I'm sure she'll make wonderful bannocks," Alexander said. "Make an extra one for yon wee whirlwind out there. I've never kent anyone wi' so much energy. Maybe we shouldna feed him anything for a few days, so he'll be too hungry to squirm about all day."

Moira laughed.

"I'm sure you were the same at his age. You're very alike."

"Aye, well if I was I canna remember it."

"Where is he, anyway? I thought ye were teaching him subtraction today."

"So did I, but the sun had a different thought. It's the first truly warm day o' spring, which means we'll be starting the ploughing in a few days. I remember enough about being six to ken desperation when I see it. He wouldna have learnt a thing today anyway. He's away down the loch wi' the others."

"I was thinking about it," Moira said. "That's it, squeeze it together, *a ghràidh*. I'm thinking he might learn better if ye let him run about outside for a time each day, maybe instead of sitting at the table to eat his *brochan*. He'll use up some of his energy, and ye can have a wee rest too. It'll be good for both of ye."

"I'm worried he'd be tired if I let him run around, or that he'd find it harder to settle again," Alexander said.

Moira shot her husband a disbelieving look.

"Tired? The laddie could run frae here to Edinburgh and back and no' be tired. Is it no' a different kind of energy from running about that ye use for the book learning, anyway?"

Alexander hadn't thought of it like that, but it made sense. And it would be good to just be able to sit for an hour and enjoy a pleasant domestic scene like this. Although neither parent voiced it, both were very aware of how delicate their daughter was, and that time with her was all the more precious because it might be cut short. Susan, when asked, had said she thought the child's heart was weak and had given them some syrup of Motherwort, which she said helped with trembling of the heart and with swooning.

But as Morag grew older she remained very frail and lately had a blue tinge to her lips at times, which Susan said was a sign of the heart not working as it should. She told them that Rob had treated patients like her, but he'd said there really was nothing to be done, except encourage them not to exert themselves too much, as that put a strain on the heart.

Alexander and Moira had sat down together one heartbreaking night a few months ago, and had agreed not to make her rest all the time, but to let her be a normal child for however long she was with them. She didn't want to run around like her brothers anyway because it made her breathless, and the two boys considerately spent a lot of time doing gentler things with her. If she wanted to go with them to play or help with a task, they would walk at a pace she could match and would rest whenever she needed to. And her parents realised that watching her anxiously every moment of the day would make all of them miserable and would probably not extend her life. So they had come to an agreement to allow her to enjoy life, and to enjoy it with her, for however long God decided to let her stay with them.

Alexander sat down at the table.

"How many bannocks are ye making?" he asked, looking at the tiny amount of dough the child was mangling.

"Ten," Morag said immediately, surprising him. "That'll be two for each of us, for we're five. But ye can have three, Da, for ye're big and I'm no' sure I can eat two."

"I'll be happy if ye can eat two, *mo chridhe*," he said, then glanced at his wife.

"Aye, well, she heard ye teaching Alex his numbers while we were spinning, and she asked to learn to count, so I taught her. She's an ability for it, I'm thinking," Moira said.

"Have ye taught Duncan, too?" Alexander asked.

"No. Ye willna let him stay indoors when Alex is learning, so he hasna heard to ask. Good, now ye need to press it flat wi' your hand, and I'll cut it in two. Then we'll start the next one. We're making them two at a time," she told Alexander, winking at him, "for they taste better that way."

"They do indeed," he agreed, trying to ignore the pain this little lie caused him. Morag might not even manage to knead five small amounts of dough without tiring, but this way she'd at least be able to proudly identify the ones she'd made unaided.

He sat at the table and smiled at his wife and daughter, his heart aching.

"So what did ye learn the day?" Simon asked. The children had swum and played in the loch until they were too cold to continue and were now lying on a rock near the edge of the water, the sun blissfully warm on their naked bodies.

Alex groaned.

"Da said now I can read all the letters and some words, that he'd teach me to write, but only my name for the now, for I need to read well before I can write more. But I dinna want to think about that today."

"So can ye write your name, then?" Jeannie asked.

"Aye," Alex replied shortly.

"Can ye show us what it looks like?" she persisted.

"No. I havena a quill and ink and suchlike."

"I've a wee stick here," Duncan said helpfully, ignoring the malevolent glare Alex cast him. "Ye could write in the mud."

"Aye, show us!" Simon cried enthusiastically.

Alex sighed, but when the others joined in, he stood up and took the stick from his brother.

"My name starts wi' an 'A'," he told the others, who all gathered round him. He bent over and painstakingly scratched an approximation of the letter in the dirt. "And then this is a 'l' sound, and then an 'e'…" he continued. When he'd finished everyone looked at it with great interest.

"And that says Alex?" Alasdair Og said.

"No. It says Alexander."

"But that's Da's name, no' yours!" Duncan said.

"Aye it is. Da said my real name's Alexander, but I'm called Alex for short."

"So which bit says Alex?" Jeannie asked.

Alex looked at the word for a minute, then drew a line after the 'x'.

"Why's your name small then?" Simon asked.

"I dinna ken. Maybe because I'm smaller than my da," Alex said.

"Will your name grow as ye do, then, and when ye're a man grown like Da you'll be Alexander too?" Duncan asked.

Alex considered this novel idea.

"Aye, I would think so. I'll ask him," he replied finally.

"How do you write Jeannie?" the little girl asked.

"I dinna ken," Alex said. "I havena learnt to write the other letters yet."

"But ye said ye learnt all the letters!" Simon said.

"Aye, but only to read, no' to write them."

"Can ye no' read that, then?" Simon asked, pointing at the dirt.

"Aye, of course I can! I wouldna ken I was writing it the right way if I couldna read it!" Alex stated.

"So if ye can read all the letters, and ken what they look like, why can ye no' write them?"

"Because the marks are different when ye write them from when ye read them," he said. "I'll show ye," he added when he was greeted by universal puzzled looks. He bent over again and wrote four different marks in the dirt. "These are all 'a'," he said. "This one's a capital a, but only when you're reading it, and some words start with it, and some words start with this 'a', a small one, for reading. But when ye're *writing,* ye have to learn it all over again. So that's a capital writing a, and that's a wee writing a, and both of those are in my big name, see?"

"But they dinna look anything like each other!" Alasdair Og said, casting Alex a doubting look.

"I'm no' jestin' wi' ye," Alex, intercepting the glance, replied. "It's awfu' daft, the reading and writing. I canna understand why they dinna have just the one letter for the a. And it's even more stupid because…never mind," he amended, not wanting to have to explain that many letters made two sounds. They'd be convinced he was mocking them if he told them that.

"So how many letters d'ye have to learn?" Rory asked.

"Twenty-six. That's this many," he said, making twenty-six lines in the dirt for the benefit of those who couldn't count that far.

"And there's four of every letter?"

"Aye."

"I'm glad I'm no' the chieftain's son," Simon said with great feeling. "I wouldna want to have to learn all that. I'd like to see what my name looks like, though."

"So would I!" Jeannie said, jumping up and down.

"I would too!" Alasdair Og agreed.

"That's the first letter of your name, Alasdair," Alex said, "For it's the same sound as mine. And the second too, the l."

Alasdair Og broke a twig off the nearest tree and made an attempt at copying it.

"So that's 'Al'?" he said.

"Aye. I think so. I can ask Da. I'm no' good wi' the writing yet."

"What're ye all up to?" Kenneth, who had come to check on them all, said from behind them.

"Alex is showing us how to write our names!" Jeannie told him.

"Is he now? So what's that?" Kenneth asked, joining the children looking down at the line of marks.

"That's my name!" Alasdair Og said excitedly. "Well, part of it."

"It says 'Al'," Alex explained, stunned by how interested everyone was in what until now he'd considered a form of torture. "But I dinna ken how to write the rest of it yet. I think that's the start of Alpin's name too, for that's an 'Al' sound."

Kenneth looked at the squiggles with interest.

"So ye look at they wee lines and curls and ye can make a word of them? Like in the Bible?" he said.

"Aye."

"So when ye ken all the words, ye could read the word of God for yourself? And ye could write your own book one day, if ye want to?"

This was another new idea.

"Aye, I suppose I could. I hadna thought o' that," he said.

"That's a powerful thing to be able to do, I'm thinking," Kenneth said in awe. "How would I write my name, then?"

* * *

"Da, tomorrow, can I learn the other writing letters, instead of reading more words?" Alex said that night as they ate the bannocks Morag had made, slathered with butter.

His father looked at him with surprise.

"Aye, I suppose so, although really ye should be learning the reading well first," he said.

"He's going to show us how to write our names!" Duncan said excitedly.

"Is he now? Who's wanting to ken how to do that, then?"

"Everyone," Alex told him. "Well, all the wee ones do."

"And Kenneth," Duncan added.

"Aye. And I think maybe Alpin would too. Kenneth wants to learn Alpin's name, for Alpin's busy learning the weaving. I said it might be the same as mine at the start, and Alasdair Og's too. Is that right?" Alex asked.

"It is. Well done for seeing that," Alexander replied. "So ye want to teach the others to write their names, do ye?"

"Oh, aye! That'd be more fun than…that would be fun," Alex corrected himself.

"Well, then, I canna see harm in teaching ye, for ye'll have to learn it anyway. And you're coming on well wi' the reading," Alexander said. He reached for a second bannock. "These are awfu' good, the best I've ever tasted," he remarked, watching his daughter flush with pleasure.

"Da, when I've learnt to read all the words, will I be able to read the Bible myself?" Alex asked.

"Ye will. And no' just the Bible, but any book in the world, if it's written in English," Alexander said.

"Will I even be allowed to read the books there, on your shelf?" the boy asked, looking across the room to a small collection of books stacked on a wooden shelf to the side of the fireplace, which were his father's pride.

"Aye, if ye take good care of them, for they cost money and I canna replace them easily," Alexander said. "Though I'm thinking ye're a wee bit young to understand them yet. But there's the Aesop mannie I tellt ye about. Ye'll like that book, I'm thinking. In fact, when ye learn to read well, I'll take ye into Stirling wi' me. There's a shop there that sells hundreds of books. I'll buy ye one, if ye'd like that."

Was that what Locke would call a bribe? To hell with it. If it was it was worth it, for this was the first time his son had shown any enthusiasm for his lessons.

"Oh aye," Alex said breathlessly. "I'd *love* that! Can I choose the book myself?"

"Ye can, but ye must let me help ye so ye make a good choice," Alexander said.

"I canna believe we didna tell him that when he can read, he'll be able to read books," Moira commented later.

"I didna think of it, in truth. I just thought he'd ken that was the purpose o' learning to read. But of course how would he, if no one ever tellt him?" Alexander said. "No surprise he was so miserable, if he couldna see any reason for learning all the wee marks, as he calls them. Christ, it's no' easy, being a tutor. I thought I could do it, but there's a mighty difference between knowing something yourself and teaching it to others."

"Ye do it well enough when ye're teaching them fighting, making fires, or hunting though," Moira said.

"Aye, so do ye wi' the planting and caring for the animals and such things," Alexander said. "But this is different, somehow, the book learning, for wi' the other things, everyone does them, and ye dinna need to tell them why they have to learn to fight."

"No, but only because they're learning about fighting in the stories we tell of an evening," Moira said. "And they ken about why we need to milk the cattle and care for them when they see the butter on their bannock, or eat the cheese."

"It's no' the same wi' the book learning though, for all the other things they learn are a matter o' life and death. This is different. I really hadna thought about it until now."

"Aye. Alex needs a reason he can understand to make him want to learn," Moira said. "He always has done, especially if it's no' an active thing. I remember when he had a cough and couldna go out, for the rain was coming down heavy, so I asked him to help me wind the yarn. He did as I asked him for he's a good boy, but his heart wasna in it, and he was squirming around. So then I tellt him that the sark he was wearing started like this, and that when I'd spun and wound enough yarn, then it went to Gregor, who weaved it into a piece of cloth."

"So then he understood why he was doing it," Alexander said.

"Aye, and it wasna just a pointless task any more. But more than that – he wanted to ken *everything* about the process, and asked me questions I wouldna expect a bairn of his age to think of. I had to tell him about the flax growing, how we soak it to get the fibres, spin it, how it changes colour wi' the dyeing…and he did the task happily then, for he saw a good purpose to it."

"How old was he then?"

Moira thought.

"About four, I think, no more."

"I dinna remember asking so many questions about everything when I was a wee bairn," Alexander said.

"Yon Locke laddie said ye should encourage curiosity in bairns though, did he no'?"

"He did. But answering so many questions is awfu' taxing. As is all the squirming and sighing. I wish I could find a tutor for him," he said with feeling.

"Aye, but ye'll no' need to answer a question twice. I'll wager if ye ask, he'll still remember what I tellt him about the flax and linen."

"So long after? I ken he remembered all about the redcoats at Stronachlachan, but that was just a few days later."

"Ask him," Moira said. She was already reasonably certain that Alex had an unnatural ability to remember everything. But after nine years of marriage she knew that if she told her husband that, he'd most likely dismiss it as a doting mother's fancy. However, if she put the seed in his head, he'd be curious to know how much, if anything, Alex *could* remember. Then it would be down to Alex to prove her right.

They were very much alike.

"So then Barbara dyes the wool afore Gregor weaves it into the cloth, and she has to go and find all the right plants for the colours. She uses yellow-flag roots to make the blue colour like the mountains a long way away, and lichen for the red, but there's different lichens, so ye have to get the right one for the red ye want," Alex said happily. "And then she puts the wool or the spun flax in the tub, and then the plant that makes the colour, then more wool or flax, and more plant. Oh, and the lichen has to be soaked in piss for a few days, and she keeps it warm, and then after that she boils the wool in it, wi' the lichen still in there, and it reeks something awfu', but the wool turns red, like magic. And after that…"

Alexander didn't normally allow his son to just talk for as long as he wanted to about a subject, he now realised. Any other time he would have interrupted him by now, or some clan affair would have interrupted them. But everyone knew not to disturb him when he was teaching the boy unless it was really important, so he'd just spent half the morning telling his father exactly how flax became linen, and how wool became the *féileadh mór*.

"So your ma took ye to see Barbara?" he asked, when Alex paused for a moment.

"Aye, but she waited until the rain stopped, for I wasna feeling well and that was why I hadna been allowed out, but was helping her wind the flax," Alex said.

Holy Mother of God. He remembered absolutely *everything,* even the weather! Moira was right.

"I didna ken ye were so interested in the making o' the clothing," Alexander said.

"I dinna want to make it myself," Alex admitted. "It must be awfu' boring to spin the thread all the time as the women do, and I wouldna want to stink o' piss all day in the dyeing of it, but it's good to ken how it's done. And if I'll be chieftain one day, I'll need to ken everything the clan does, will I no'? For I'll be having to tell people what to do, like you do."

"Aye, that's right, laddie, ye will."

Lesson learnt. To hell with Locke, in this, anyway. Although it was true his son *did* blossom when praised – he'd learned to write the rest of his letters extraordinarily quickly when he knew he could gain the admiration of all his friends by teaching them to write their names – he also needed more than that. He needed a reason that made sense to him in the context of his life as a

Highlander, and as a future chieftain.

Once he had that, it appeared that there would be no limit to what the boy could learn, apart from sitting still for more than two minutes at a time. He seemed incapable of learning that, and it tore Alexander's heart to see him so unhappy. But it was important that he learn the reading and the writing. And the geometry, though he had no idea how he'd make that relevant to a six-year-old. He'd managed to make arithmetic relevant by talking about selling the cattle and telling Alex that he'd take him to a cattle sale soon, where he could see how important the numbers were.

The geometry problem would wait a while, though. First the reading and the writing. And during that time he would pray for God to send a tutor to them, somehow.

* * *

Ten seconds after Alex had exploded out of the house like a cannonball, Alexander plodded out more slowly and threw himself wearily down on the bench next to his wife.

"I'm thinking maybe to go to Stirling, once the crops are in and harrowed and the cattle are up at the shielings," he said.

Moira nodded.

"Ye've no' been for a while, and there may be news we need to ken," she said. "Will ye take the boy with ye' to buy him a book?"

"Aye, I could do, I suppose. It wouldna do him harm to see a town. He's nearly seven now, old enough. And I'll no' be there more than a day or two. Maybe the walking there and back will tire him a wee bit, too."

"The sun's shining, the others are helping wi' the sowing or the weeding, and he's inside. It's no' natural to be indoors all day."

"It is for the gentlemen. It was for me, for that matter, when I was learning the Latin and suchlike. I wasna at home. Da sent me away to MacPherson's house. He was the tutor, and he had six boys staying wi' him. We started at dawn and finished when the sun was low."

"Even in the summer?" Moira asked.

"Aye. Well, no' till it was setting, but late enough. They were long days."

"Ye must have been miserable," Moira said.

"Aye. No' all the time though, for I made some friends wi' the other boys from different clans – some of them still useful today. I missed home something fierce though. We all did."

"At least Alex doesna have that. But he's learning alone. Why do you no' teach one or two o' the other bairns? I ken Duncan's no' five yet, but he wants to learn, and Simon's of an age wi' Alex. Alasdair Og too. And Locke says that 'when he can talk, 'tis time he should begin to learn to read'," Moira quoted. "Duncan's been talking well for two years."

"Christ, no. It's hard enough teaching the one. I've no idea how MacPherson managed us all."

Moira resisted the urge to smack her stubborn husband on the head with her distaff. He stretched his legs out and leaned back on the bench, closing his eyes and soaking up the sun. She looked down toward the loch, sparkling in the sunshine. Alex had halted in his headlong dash for the water he loved and was standing by his siblings, who were crouched on the ground. She nudged Alexander with her elbow.

"Look," she said. He opened his eyes and sat up.

"What's amiss?"

"Just look. Ye saw Alex running for the water, as he always does. Watch him now, wi' Morag and Duncan."

Mother and father watched their children.

"I'm away for a swim," Alex said. "Are ye wanting to come? Morag, I can help ye float in the water, if ye want."

When he got no answer, he hopped impatiently from foot to foot and looked longingly in the direction of the loch for a moment. Then curiosity got the better of him, and he bent over to see what could be more interesting than swimming.

"What're ye doing?" he asked.

"It's ants!" Morag said excitedly.

"Ants? What about them?"

"Look," Duncan said, beckoning him to kneel down. "Ye canna see rightly from up there."

Alex cast another glance at the water, then bent further over. Two lines of ants were marching across the ground between Duncan and Morag, one heading for a small pile of crumbs and the other away from it.

"They live over there," Duncan said, pointing to one side, "and Morag put a wee pile o' bannock crumbs there so we could watch them take them away. It's interesting."

"Why is it interesting?" Alex asked.

"Most wee beasties wouldna take food home," Duncan explained. "They'd eat it where they found it. But ants dinna do that. They take it home, just like we would. But they do other things too, that I havena seen before. See that one? That one found a big crumb, too big for him to carry, so he's asked a friend to help him." He pointed. Alex knelt down now to see closer, because Duncan must be jesting with him. Insects didn't ask each other for help, did they?

The three children observed the two ants, who did seem to be working together, carrying the large crumb back towards their house. A little further along their path was a hole, which the two ants carefully manoeuvred around before continuing on their way.

"We dug that wee hole there, to see what they'd do," Duncan explained. "And the first time they all just went down the hole and then up the other side. But when they came back again, they didna. They stopped and looked around, as though they were planning the best way to go. And then they walked round it, see?"

"They're clever!" Morag said happily.

Alex observed this phenomenon.

"I canna believe ants can think about things like that," he said, suspicion all over his face.

"They can!" Morag said.

Alex reached round and picked up a stick, placing it in the path of the marching ants.

"They're just going over it!" he said.

"Aye, but wait till they come back again," Duncan replied.

Alex settled down to wait.

"What are they looking at?" Alexander asked, somewhat stunned that his eldest was actually being still of his own accord, when a minute earlier he'd been intent on getting into the loch as quickly as possible.

"I dinna ken. But watch him, when he's wi' Duncan and Morag. He's no' the same as when he's wi' the other bairns."

"Aye, that's because Morag canna run about, and he's a good-hearted laddie."

"That's true. But he'd be like this if it was just Duncan. Ye need to watch him if ye dinna believe me."

A little cheer went up from the group, and then Alex scrambled up. Moira's face fell. But he took only a couple of steps, picked up a stone and then knelt down again, placing it carefully then settling to watch.

Alexander's eyes widened.

"It must be awfu' interesting, whatever it is," he said.

"Aye, it's caught his interest. But that's no' the point. Remember when he went fishing wi' Iain and Duncan?"

"Aye. He hated it. He tellt me so."

"He did. But I asked Iain how long it was afore he grew restless and Iain said it was a good while, for Duncan has a calming effect on him. I've watched them together often, and it's true."

Alex certainly looked settled. Far more settled than he did when he was learning his lessons.

"Maybe he just doesna like his lessons," Alexander suggested.

"As we said, it'll help him if he has a reason he can understand. He doesna like doing something that doesna make any sense to him. But it's more than that wi' Duncan. The other boys are calmer round him too. Alex is a natural leader, and thinks o' new games to play, which is why ye'll hear them all shout when he comes out from his lessons. They dinna do that for Duncan. But they dinna fight together so much when Duncan's there."

"Why's that?" Alexander asked uncomfortably. It was unsettling having someone, even their mother, tell you things about your own children that you hadn't noticed before.

"I dinna ken. It's just natural to him, as it is to Alex to lead them in new games, and to remember things. Dinna feel shamed. I'm wi' them all day, or for much of it. You're no'. You've too much else to do."

"Aye. That's another reason why I need a tutor for him," Alexander said.

"You do. But I think ye'll enjoy the lessons more, both of ye will, if ye teach Duncan too."

Alexander watched his offspring. Morag was saying something now, and both boys laughed. Then they sat up, but instead of Alex leaping up now and running for the loch as Alexander expected, he looked around, picked some bits of plant and started to fashion it into something on the ground. They laughed again, and then Alex started telling a tale of some sort, waving his hands about as he did. Duncan pointed at the thing and made a comment, and Alex stopped, adjusted it, and then continued.

"For his part, Alex encourages Duncan to do more adventurous things. Duncan's naturally more cautious, more reluctant to try something new."

"Aye, I remember him teaching Duncan to swim," Alexander said.

"He did. But more important, he made Duncan *want* to learn to swim. Duncan makes Alex *want* to stop and look at things he'd never notice. Such as whatever that is."

"I suppose it would be easier to be teaching them both at the same time," Alexander said, still with his eyes on the three children, who were now adding something to the structure Alex had built.

"It would," Moira said, smiling inwardly and resisting the urge to shout hallelujah.

It was easier for her, in fairness, to understand her eldest. After all, she'd had years of practice learning to understand and carefully influence the much larger version of him who was sitting next to her now.

* * *

"Wee Alex has taught me how to write my name!" Kenneth said as he came through the door of the house. "I'm sorry. I dinna want to distract ye," he added, seeing his brother busy at the loom.

"No, it's a good time. I've finished setting it up. Now I'll have Da make sure I've done it right before I start the weaving," Alpin replied.

"What are ye making?"

"It's my first time at weaving the wool, so it's just a narrow piece o' tartan. It's actually for wee Duncan for when he's five, and as he's a bairn he doesna need a wide piece. It'll be good for me to learn on. Dinna tell him though. It's a surprise."

Kenneth nodded.

"How's your hand dealing wi' it?" he asked. He was the only person in the clan who dared refer to Alpin's disability, for he was so very sensitive about it. But since the night nearly three years ago that he'd admitted his hatred of the fighting, the two brothers had grown even closer than they'd been previously, and told each other all their insecurities and frailties that other members of the clan might see as failings, knowing that the other would not mock them, but would sympathise. And would never tell another soul.

Alpin looked at the offending hand ruefully.

"It's no' too bad," he said. "Though it aches at the end o' the day, from passing it across the loom." Although his arm had healed well since he'd been shot the previous year, it had left him with numbness and weakness in two of his fingers, which had not improved with time.

Having accepted that his eldest son was unlikely to be able to fight again Gregor had decided to teach him to weave, which would give him a useful craft and would still allow him to be a valuable clan member.

"Aye, well, that's no' a surprise when ye can only use the two fingers. I daresay mine would ache too. Will I knead it for ye?"

Alpin looked out of the open door, assessing the time.

"Aye," he said. "It helps, and Da'll be gone a while yet."

The two brothers went into the main room of the house and sat together on the *seise*, where Kenneth began to massage his brother's hand and forearm.

"So, ye said ye can write your name," Alpin said, grimacing as the muscles first cramped, then relaxed. "What are ye wanting to do that for?"

"I dinna ken. But it pleased Alex to show me, and if I ever need to sign my name I'll be able to do it, and people will think I'm a man o' learning!" He grinned. "Maybe in years to come someone will see my name and think o' me, when I'm long dead."

Alpin laughed.

"I asked Alex to show me your name too, in case ye're wanting to learn," Kenneth added.

"I'll no' be able to write it though, will I," Alpin said, "if I canna hold a quill."

"Ye havena ever learned the writing though," Kenneth reasoned, "so I was thinking ye could try it wi' your other hand. I dinna see why ye have to write wi' just the one."

"I didna think o' that. Aye, go on then."

Kenneth finished working on his brother's hand, opening and

closing the useless fingers until they were warm and pink.

"Can ye feel my touch at all?" he asked.

"No, no' till ye get to the palm o' my hand. Strange that the fingers pain me so, when I canna feel anything wi' them at all."

"Let me show ye the writing then, while I remember. We can use a stick as Alex did, and write it in the dirt," Kenneth said eagerly.

Within a few minutes various attempts at their names were scratched out in the dirt floor of the room, and the brothers scrutinised them.

"Your name is no' as wobbly as mine," Alpin observed.

"No, because I'm accustomed to using my right hand for everything. You dinna use your left so much, no' for the finer things."

"I'm having to use it more now, though."

"Aye, but writing needs a lot o' control of the fingers to get it right. Alex tellt me that. Ye'll do it, if ye practice."

Alpin took the stick and had another attempt at writing the letters, then nodded.

"Aye, that's better. I can read it now," Kenneth said. "What's amiss?" he asked, seeing a cloud cross Alpin's face.

"I was wondering, if I can learn to write my name wi' my other hand, could I learn to use the sword wi' it?" he said pensively. "I can use the dirk now. No' as good as I was wi' my right hand, but I'm improving."

Kenneth sat down.

"Maybe. And ye could have the targe on your right arm. But ye couldna hold the dirk wi' the targe, so ye'd be at a disadvantage. Do ye really want to, anyway?" he asked.

Alpin shot him a look then.

"Why would I no' want to?" he replied.

Kenneth looked out of the door and then listened intently for a minute. No one was near.

"Well, it seems to me that in one way being shot was a blessing, for ye dinna need to fight any more. In a battle, I mean. Ye said ye hated it. Now ye've a reason no' to go. Or are ye thinking differently now?"

"No," Alpin said. "I canna imagine ever enjoying a battle, like you all do."

"I dinna ken if I do or no' yet," Kenneth said. "There hasna been one for me to find out."

"I'm sorry for that," Alpin replied.

"I'm no'. I can fight, and that's enough for me for the now. I dinna ken if I'll enjoy the killing or no' but I'm in no hurry to find out."

Alpin stared at his brother in amazement.

"Ye're no' just saying that to make me feel better?"

"No. I dinna need to do such a thing. I'm no' fifteen any more. There isna a man in the clan who can lift the *clach cuid fir* higher than his waist, never mind throw the damn thing. I dinna need to prove my strength, and I'll prove my bravery when the time comes, as did you. Whether I'll enjoy it or no' I've no idea."

"It doesna fash ye that Da thinks ye havena the ferocity to fight?" Alpin asked.

Kenneth shook his head.

"That's Da's problem, no' mine," he said.

Alpin laughed suddenly, which made Kenneth's heart soar. He had a lovely infectious laugh, but it was rarely heard since he'd been injured.

"I wish I could think like you," he said. "I'm thinking that I'll never find a lassie who'll want to marry me, and me no' a full man now."

"Och, away wi' ye, man," Kenneth said. "Ye'll have no trouble finding a lassie, I'm sure of it. Ye're the best looking of us, and it wasna your prick that was shot. Ye can still give her bairns, and ye'll be able to earn your keep wi' your weaving and make her fine clothes as well. And I ken well from last time that the women were awfu' worried when the men were away, though they didna show it when ye came back. It's my thinking that a woman would be glad to ken her husband's no' going to get himself killed for some princeling."

"I hadna thought of it like that," Alpin said.

"No, well, ye dinna think like me, ye just said as much," Kenneth commented. "If ye're after asking wee Flora, ye should do it. She likes ye, I can see that by the way her face lights up when she sees ye."

Alpin blushed scarlet.

"Is it that obvious that I like her?" he asked.

"Only to me, for I look for such things, and I ken ye better than anyone does. I daresay if a girl takes my eye, ye'll see it immediately, for ye ken me too, as no one else does."

That was true. Most of the clan members couldn't help but be influenced in their opinion by the sheer size of Kenneth, who now towered over even Alexander. Even though most of them had known him all his life, they found it impossible not to feel intimidated by someone who dwarfed them, not just in height but breadth, and in strength too, as Kenneth had just admitted. His father could not reconcile the physical strength with the gentle nature of his second son, thinking that he should behave as he looked. Only the children were completely unfazed by his size, probably because *everyone* was taller and stronger than them. They accepted him as he was. As did Alpin.

Which was probably why Kenneth spent so much time either with the children of the clan or with his brother.

"I'll ask her," Alpin said. Then a thought struck him. "Can ye ask Alex how to write her name? I'm thinking it'd be a different way to gain her attention. Different from the other laddies, that is. She's awfu' pretty," he finished wistfully.

"She is that," Kenneth agreed. "And I'll ask Alex. But ye dinna need to impress her, for she likes ye well enough already."

"How d'ye ken that?"

"Last week I was looking for ye and asked if she'd seen ye, and she turned as red as a raspberry – exactly like you just did. She likes ye. Take my word for it."

"Even so, it'll gie me a reason to talk to her, if I can teach her to write her name," he said.

"Aye, and a reason to touch her, to guide her hand," Kenneth said, winking.

Alpin laughed again, joyously, his pale blue eyes sparkling.

"I'll ask the boy tomorrow. His da allows him and Duncan a wee rest from the learning each day now, to run around," Kenneth said, overjoyed to see his brother finally seeming to be freeing himself from the black dog of depression that had subdued him since that night in Stronachlachan.

CHAPTER FIVE

Loch Lomond, July 1723

"'Whilst a lion was asleep one day, a mouse came and ran all over his body'," Alex read. "'This woke the lion, who seized the mouse and was going to eat him. But the mouse begged him to spare his life, saying, 'one day I will repay the favour if you do'. The lion was so am…amused that he let the little mouse go. Soon af-ter-wards, afterwards,'" he continued, "'some hunters caught the lion and tied him to a tree with a rope. The mouse heard him groaning, ran to him and gnawed—'"

"Ye dinna sound the 'g', laddie. It's one o' yon silent letters, like the k in knife," Alexander corrected him. Alex frowned. "Go on, ye're reading well."

"What does gnawed mean?" Morag asked.

"To chew," Alexander said.

"'…'and gnawed through the rope until the lion was free. 'You see now,' squeaked the mouse, 'not long ago you mocked me when I said I would return your favour, and save your life one day!'"

Alex closed the book and put it down on the table round which four of the family members were seated. Moira was washing clothes with the other women by the loch.

"Ye read that very well," Alexander said, trying not to smile at his son's animated rendition. "Now, I said there was a lesson to be learnt from the tale. Can any of ye tell me what it might be?"

Silence fell upon the room for a minute.

"I didna ken that lions and mice, and other animals could speak," Duncan commented.

95

"They make sounds, like we do, so maybe they can," said Morag. "That'll be how the ants asked each other to help them wi' the crumbs."

"Aye, and wi' going round the hole we dug," Duncan said in wonder.

"Do mice really speak wi' a wee squeaky voice, Alex?" Morag asked.

"I dinna ken, but I thought they would, so I used one," Alex said. "And it said the mouse squeaked later in the story, so I think they must. I'm thinking a lion would have a deep voice, though."

"It's just a story," Alexander said before they could all go too far off track. "The man who tellt it lived a long time ago, and his name was Aesop. He used animals to show different people what they should do."

"Why no' just use the people instead?" Alex asked.

"Because ye can use animals to describe certain kinds of people," Alexander said, reminding himself for the hundredth time that Locke said children's curiosity should be encouraged. "So you might say someone was as strong as a lion, or as timid as a mouse, as cunning as a fox."

"So Kenneth is as strong as a lion, that sort of thing?" Alex asked.

"Aye, that's it exactly."

"So if ye wanted to tell Kenneth he was doing something wrong, ye might tell him a story about a lion doing it instead, for him to learn from," Duncan ventured.

"Aye."

"And then he wouldna be angry," Morag added.

"But would it no' be easier to just say, 'Kenneth, that was stupid, ye shouldna have done it'? For he wouldna get angry anyway. Kenneth never gets angry," Alex said.

"Aye, but ye might make him feel sad or silly if ye just tellt him like that. But if ye tell him a lion story, it might be about *any* strong person, but he could go away and think on it alone somewhere. It would be a kinder thing to do," Duncan put in.

"I'd rather someone just tellt me," Alex said.

"Kenneth isna like you though, so he'd maybe rather ye tellt him a story about it," Duncan commented.

"Is Kenneth the lion in this story?" Morag asked.

"No, it's just a story about strong people and weak people," Alexander said. He *really* needed to find a tutor. Soon. "What d'ye think Aesop was trying to tell people?"

"God, but it's tiring," Alexander said to Moira later, the two of them sitting on the bench outside. There were items of clothing, bedding, and table napery draped across every available branch, but the wind was freshening so they were keeping an eye on them in case they blew away.

"Are ye away to Perth to see about it then?" she asked.

"Aye, I'll go next week," he replied. "Although I canna think what manner o' tutor would want to come here, and I canna pay him a great deal. But it's interesting to teach them as well. I just havena the time. I hadna thought so much about it before, just thought bairns were wee adults, but they're no'. They think differently. But ye can still see the adults they'll become. Duncan's much better at seeing the morals in Aesop if it isna clear, because he thinks deeper, whereas Alex is already onto the next thing, because he remembers *everything*, and thinks that's enough. Duncan doesna, but he puts more thought into it, because he has to."

They sat together for a moment, holding hands, enjoying the afternoon.

"Oh, I remember what I wanted to tell ye," Alexander said, grinning. "Alex finished all his wee sums earlier than Duncan and wanted to go out. Duncan says, I need to learn about this adding up more, because I canna remember how to do things as well as you do. So Alex offers to help him, but in no time at all he's spending more time looking out the window and squirming about than helping his brother. Then he says, why do ye no' try a wee bit harder to remember things? Then ye could be outside.

"So I says to the boy, we all have things we find easy and things we find hard to do. No one's good at everything. But the chieftain has to be good at everything, Alex says, and I'll be chieftain one day, will I no'? And I says, aye, maybe, but there'll be things ye dinna find easy to remember, things that Duncan finds easier than you, and if ye're to be good at them too, ye'll need to work harder. As Duncan is now.

"Then Duncan says, ye go out, and I'll follow when I've learnt the wee sums. So Alex leaps off the stool as though it's on fire, and when he gets to the door he says, what d'ye find easier than me, Duncan? And without looking up or pausing, Duncan says, sitting still."

Both parents laughed then.

"I'll never ken how I didna laugh out loud then," Alexander said. "But I managed to wait till I'd sent them out, and then I wanted to share it wi' you. For it sums the both of them up."

"Aye," Moira said. "A pity ye canna have two chieftains, for between the two o' them, ye've a perfect one in the making. I'm glad Morag's taken to the learning too. It's easier to do heavy chores when I dinna have to think of something light for her to do. She needs to feel useful all the time. She's old enough now to ken that she's a wee bit different to the other bairns, and it pains her."

"We'll have to tell her soon, I'm thinking," Alexander said. "Should I take her to Perth wi' me, to see a doctor? If I do, someone else will have to come too to look out for her, for I wouldna have her there when I'm doing business."

"No," Moira said. "Ye've always been in good health, thank God, and so ye havena seen what doctors do. We were staying near Edinburgh when my ma was sick, so Da sent for a man. When he'd finished wi' all his bleeding and purging, Ma was white as snow. I thought she'd die. It was clear that the man hadna a notion how to treat her but wanted to earn his money."

"That could just be a bad doctor though," Alexander said. "Your ma recovered, did she no'?"

"She recovered from the doctor, aye, but she wasna any better of the consumption. I trust Susan more than a doctor. If her man was alive I'd let him see Morag, for I think he was a good and honest man. But she said even he couldna cure a weak heart. I think we're doing the right thing for her. When God wants her he'll take her, and until then I'll treasure every day."

"She's awfu' good wi' the arithmetic," Alexander said. "When she's grown more I'm thinking I'll take her to the cattle dealing, for she's a quick mind. I'll no' be cheated wi' her around."

"I think she'll love that, to be truly useful," Moira said. "I must find a counting task, no' an invented one, but a real one for her, in the meantime."

* * *

Blair Atholl, Perthshire

Alexander was exasperated, not least because of the utter waste of several days in the height of summer when there were so many tasks to be done at home, every one of them more profitable than the one he was engaged in right now.

He tuned out from the voices debating pointlessly around him, thinking instead about the cattle raid he was planning in September, the results of which would be sold at the market in Crieff at Michaelmas. He wondered whether he should take Alex on this raid with him. The boy was nearly eight now, the same age as he'd been when *his* father took him on his first raid. It was time he started learning about such things. After all, cattle reiving was an everyday part of clan life, and the risks were…

The drone of voices around him, which had uttered little of interest for two days, now took on a different tone, rousing Alexander from his contemplation. He looked up.

"So now we've agreed that the Grants are descended from Kenneth MacAlpin's father, as we're descended from Kenneth himself—"

"Aye, and we wear the same *suaicheantas*, the branch o' fir in our bonnets," another man interrupted.

"And they've the crowns in their shield as have we," put in a thin man with an extraordinarily large and crooked nose. Alexander thought that the man should be a Cameron rather than a MacGregor, for was the name Cameron not from *cam-shròn*, which meant crooked nose?

God, he was bored. And frustrated.

"So then," the first man continued assertively, clearly a bit annoyed at having been interrupted, "now we've agreed we're one people, we've to decide if we agree to take the name of the Grants, if we canna have our own name restored to us by the king?"

"He's no king o' mine," Crooked Nose said.

"The Elector then," the first man corrected.

How long were they going to spend repeating the same things?

"Whatever ye think George is, he's the powers of the king, and James shows no sign o' trying to take them back again for the minute," Alexander put in impatiently. "I've no notion why we're even thinking of applying to get the proscription lifted. It's a waste of time, for we all ken what his answer will be."

"Aye, well, maybe it wouldna be if Rob Roy hadna gone to fight last time, for a lost cause," the man opposite Alexander said sourly. "George'll no' be likely to grant the MacGregors anything, wi' some of us rising against him."

"And maybe if *all* the men who claim to be loyal to James had done more than wave a bloody glass over a bowl o' water four years ago, James'd be back on the throne now, and we'd no' be here talking o' giving up our names altogether," Alexander bit back. There was general agreement to this sentiment, except from the man sitting directly opposite Alexander, who leapt to his feet immediately.

"Are ye accusing me o' no' supporting my king?" he cried.

"I was too busy killing redcoats to commit to memory every man at the battle. Were ye there, then?" Alexander said coolly, unobtrusively checking that his dirk was loose in the sheath. "I'm thinking ye werena but wish ye had been, for ye seem awfu' sensitive about it. Your conscience is your own, man. I wasna talking about you, or even the MacGregors in particular, but if ye wish to think I was, that's your concern."

Give it up now, he thought fervently, because that was as far as he was willing to go in conciliation. He had no wish to fight anyone, let alone an over-sensitive member of his own clan. He had only spoken the truth, and would not apologise for that.

"So if we assume that George will say no, for he will, then we've to decide if we want to take the name Grant, and the Grants have to decide if they're willing for us to do that," Alexander continued, hoping the man would sit down.

"Why would they no' be willing? For we're bonny fighters, and it'll make the Grants more powerful," Crooked Nose said.

"Aye, it will. But the MacGregors are no' thought well of by many a clan. Our name is tainted, and we've a reputation for lawlessness and savagery," Alexander pointed out.

"So has every clan in Scotland, if ye ask the English," the first man said, to general laughter. The earlier tension dissipated.

"Aye, that's true," said Alexander, grinning. "But we're thought to love fighting for the sake of it. That's why so many clans ask us to join wi' them in their wee stramashes wi' other clans."

There was a murmur of agreement at this, for it was true.

"Although it's my thinking that often when we're asked, it's so we can be blamed if it goes wrong, for we're a good scapegoat, are we no', having the reputation ye speak of and no recourse to law?" the first man said. "That could change, if we all become Grants."

"That's true as well. But even so, the Grants might no' want such a union. It could lead them into feuds they want no part of," Alexander pointed out.

The man opposite had stayed on his feet, staring unwaveringly at Alexander.

"Will ye sit down, man? We should be talking about growing the clan, no' arguing among ourselves," Alexander said quietly.

"I'm no' happy at being called a coward," the man insisted belligerently. "Ye're quick to insult others, but ye're no' so quick to stand like a man."

"Roddy, he didna call ye a coward, ye loon," one of his companions said.

"Why are ye insisting on making a general comment all about you?" Alexander asked, feeling his temper rise now. "My six-year-old can stand for hours, but it doesna make him a man. Have ye a wife and bairns of your own?" he added casually, just in case. He would not make a woman a widow over such a flimsy dispute, and it seemed this man was intent on challenging him.

"No, but when I do have, I'll no' give them a recreant for a father as you have," the man shot back.

The mood around the campfire darkened instantly at this indisputably personal insult, every man tensing except Alexander, who, apart from drawing his dirk in a move concealed by the folds of his kilt, remained seated, apparently at ease.

"Are ye sure ye're wanting this, laddie?" he asked softly.

By way of answer Roddy moved his hand towards the sheath at his waist, and in a flash Alexander jumped to his feet, leapt the fire in one bound and drove his blade straight into the man's throat. When he drew it out a fountain of blood followed and the man crumpled to the ground, clutching his throat in a futile attempt to stem the flow.

Alexander, covered in blood, remained standing, waiting to see if any of the man's companions would react. A very fraught minute passed in which no one moved, not even to give aid to the injured man, for it was clear nothing could be done for him. The man on the ground gurgled faintly one last time, then stilled. Realising no one was going to come to Roddy's defence, Alexander nodded, wiped his dirk on his bloodied kilt, and sheathed it.

"I apologise for interrupting the discussion," he said politely.

"Ye made it memorable, for certain," Crooked Nose replied.

"And proved your point about the MacGregors fighting for the sake of it," Roddy's companion added. "No' you, I mean him," he added hastily, pointing to the corpse at his feet. "Ye tried to calm things. Will I help ye bury him?" he asked calmly.

By the time the two men had dug a makeshift grave, lowered the man into it, said the prayers they could remember for his soul, and then filled in the hole, they'd become friendly. They made their way down to the River Garry, where Alexander took off his clothes and attempted to wash the blood off them.

"That was a fearsome leap ye made over the fire," the man, whose name was Cormac, said. "Have ye cat's blood in your veins?"

Alexander laughed.

"It was clear the man wanted a fight wi' someone. I've no notion why. He wouldna have let it lie, no matter what I said. My da always tellt me the first blow is worth ten, and I've found it good advice."

"It was tonight, certainly," Cormac agreed. "It wasna your fault. Ye were right about him being a coward. Ranald tellt him the same thing last night in the tavern when they were in their cups, but Roddy didna dare to challenge *him*."

"Why? Which Ranald?"

"Rob Roy's son," Cormac explained.

"Ah." That explained it then. The man was nursing a grudge, but didn't dare attack the son of the ruthless Rob Roy, knowing that the rest of his MacGregors, who were at this gathering, would cut him in pieces if he did.

"Aye. Well, in truth, had I lost, I dinna think my men would have taken kindly to it either," Alexander commented.

"Aye, but your men are no' here wi' ye, are they? He'd have been long gone by then."

"In fairness though, it doesna make him a coward. I'd think twice before attacking the son of a man like Rob Roy, for when he does fight…no matter." It wasn't prudent to accuse the man who might even be Cormac's leader, for all Alexander knew, of subterfuge. "I think he was a fool though. He should have fought Ranald or no one. It's stupid to fight one man because ye're fashed wi' another. He'd no' have lived long anyway, I'm thinking."

Alexander wrung out his shirt and *fèileadh mór,* and put them on again.

"Are ye thinking we'll become Grants, then?" Cormac said as they walked back to the meeting.

"I dinna ken. It's no' up to us alone, but the Grants as well. I'm thinking it'll no' be decided for a while though."

Judging by the snail-like convoluted pace of negotiations so far, Alexander reckoned he could afford to spend a couple of days in Perth without missing anything of significance, apart from any more idiots looking to die. Although he doubted anyone else would challenge him needlessly, as word of the incident would spread like wildfire round the gathering. And he had no intention to pick a fight with anyone himself. He'd head over to Perth tomorrow, then.

He had a priest to see.

* * *

Loch Lomond

It was a glorious day. The bees buzzed in the heather, which was now coming into flower and turning the mountains around the loch a hazy purple, butterflies fluttered everywhere like flying flowers, the barley and oat crops were ripening beautifully in the hot sun, and, to make the world utterly perfect, all this was happening on a Sunday.

Sunday was the Lord's day, so those who had daily tasks to do got them out of the way as quickly as possible, while everyone else relaxed and enjoyed the beautiful weather.

The women were chatting, keeping an eye on the babies and younger children and spinning the flax that had already been retted, wrapping it round a distaff as they did so they could move about whilst still working, although none of them thought of this as work – it was just something they did whenever their hands weren't required for anything else. The men were lying around on the grass talking about the jobs they would have to do soon, repairing the heather thatch on the rooves before the weather turned, harvesting the crops, taking the cheese and butter to market for sale. But none of that needed to be done today.

Most of the older children were down at the lochside, some swimming, some skimming rocks along the water, and some collecting flowers.

Duncan, who had hoped to go fishing, but realised the futility of that exercise upon arriving at the lochside and hearing the noise, was instead sitting on a rock at the waterside helping Morag to pierce the stems of the flowers she'd collected so that she could make a necklace of them. Just picking the flowers had used up all her energy, so she leaned drowsily against her brother, watching him.

Alex was practising sword play with Kenneth, who had good-naturedly agreed to watch the children at the loch in case any of them got into trouble. Parrying inept thrusts and blows from the child was something he could do whilst keeping an eye on the others, who were in the main screaming and splashing each other rather than attempting to swim across the loch, which was the most likely thing to require a rescue.

"That's it, laddie, lean back, but dinna *step* back unless ye need to, for what ye do next is move forward to attack. So I'm attacking ye, like this…" He stopped for a minute and knelt down, so that he could get his sword at the right height for Alex to block it. "Right, I'll no' be moving."

"Ye would move in a real fight though," Alex said.

"Aye, I would, although if ye were fast enough I'd no' have the chance to."

"And in a real fight ye'd no' be fighting a man Kenneth's size, for ye couldna cut him above his legs," Duncan added helpfully. He was expecting to get his own sword soon, for he'd be six this month, so as Morag was dozing at the moment he'd abandoned the flowers and was watching intently, hoping to learn something useful.

Kenneth grinned then, causing Alex to scowl. He took his weapons lessons very seriously, but then it was usually his father teaching him and Alexander took the lessons seriously too, telling him that one false move in a real fight could get him killed, so he must concentrate at all times. But right now Alexander was away, so Kenneth would have to do.

"Now, we'll do it slowly. I'm attacking you," he pointed his sword at Alex's neck, "and this is where ye lean back and then ye twist like I showed ye, and bring your sword down on top of mine. Aye, that's it. Now twist the blade and drive it toward me. Ye'll be aiming for my neck or my head."

Alex stepped forward, lifting his blade off Kenneth's as he aimed.

"No, ye have to keep contact wi' my blade as ye come forward, for if ye dinna, then I could kill ye as ye move in. If ye keep the contact your hilt will push my sword up as ye move in for the kill, so I canna strike ye in the body. Do it slowly, it's no' a real fight, after all."

Some time passed, during which Alex perfected the move doing it very slowly, Morag woke up and Duncan threaded some more flowers for her.

"Good. Now, a wee bit faster," Kenneth said.

Alex repeated the move he'd practised numerous times.

"No, ye're lifting your sword again, laddie. See what I can do if ye do that." Kenneth leaned in and touched Alex's chest gently. "Ye'd be dead."

"It's hard," Alex said. "I have to look at your head to aim right."

"It willna be one day. Touch your nose."

"What?" Alex said.

"Touch your nose wi' your left hand."

Alex's forehead furrowed, but he dutifully touched his nose with his index finger.

"How d'ye ken where your nose is?" Kenneth asked.

"It's on my face, where it always is," Alex replied.

"Aye. My head's on the top of my shoulders, where it always is. Ye dinna need a looking-glass to see where your nose is, and no more d'ye need to look at my head to ken where it is. Ye're no' aiming for a particular part of it. If ye hit me anywhere in the head or neck wi' the point of your sword, I'll no' be doing anything but dying."

Duncan laughed. Kenneth was much more fun to watch than Da, for Da had no humour about the fighting lessons. Alex glanced at him and scowled again, then stepped away and wiped the sweat from his face with his shirt sleeve.

"Are ye wanting a swim to cool off, laddie? Ye seem a wee bit fashed," Kenneth said.

"I'm no' fashed," Alex lied. "Let's try again."

He leaned back, Kenneth lowered his sword, Alex smashed his on to it, then—

"Are ye wanting a wee bracelet too, *a ghràidh*?" Duncan asked Morag. "We've enough flowers for it."

"Ye're doing it again, laddie," Kenneth said at the same time.

"Can ye no' make your wee garlands somewhere else?" Alex shouted at his siblings. Morag looked up, eyes wide with alarm, then leaned away from Duncan, ready to climb down. Duncan regarded his red-faced brother with a cool grey stare, putting his arm round Morag to stop her.

"No, we canna," he said calmly. "There's enough room for the three of us. Four of us," he added, nodding at Kenneth. "Da didna take *any* of us wi' him. No need to still be angry about it."

"I'm no' angry about it! Ye're putting me off wi' your blethering on about flowers!" Alex shouted.

"I'm thinking it'll no' be quiet on the battlefield either," Duncan retorted.

"Your brother's the right of it," Kenneth agreed. "Ye'll need to learn to keep your focus on the enemy, or maybe enemies, but pay no regard to anyone who's no' a threat to ye. It's good practice."

"How do ye ken that? Ye've never been on a battlefield," Alex raged.

Kenneth sheathed his sword and stood up.

"I think that's enough the day, laddie," he said. "Away and play wi' the other wee bairns down the loch, for ye're behaving like one at the minute."

"One day I'll be chieftain, and ye'll have to obey me, like ye obey Da!" Alex shouted at Duncan.

"Ye're no' chieftain yet," Duncan pointed out.

"And ye no' will be, if ye behave like that," Kenneth added.

Alex rounded on him.

"I will! I'm the eldest son of the chieftain! One day I'll be chieftain, and then ye'll all have to do as I say!" he cried. "I want to learn that sword move!"

"I'm no' teaching ye anything more the day," Kenneth said and started to turn, then stopped as Alex hit him on the leg with his little blade. He turned back, and in one fluid movement took the miniature sword off the boy, lifted him up by his shirt and threw him an impressive distance across the heads of the boys playing in the shallows, who all watched as the chieftain's son crashed into the loch in a flurry of flailing arms and legs.

Kenneth looked at his leg, which was reddening, and then to where Alex had landed in the water. A few seconds passed and then Alex surfaced spluttering, pushed his hair back off his face and started swimming back to shore. Kenneth nodded to himself and then turned to Duncan and Morag.

"I'm thinking that'll cool him down a wee bit," Kenneth said calmly. "Ye can tell the wee gomerel I'll no' be teaching him anything again until he learns to control his temper, for he'll be no use to anyone unless he can."

"I dinna think he meant to say about ye no' having been in a battle," Duncan ventured.

"I didna throw him in the loch for that, laddie. Dinna defend him when he's in the wrong. He couldna master the move – it takes time. But it isna your fault, nor mine. He'll do it if he keeps trying, in time."

"Da's been teaching him that for a week," Duncan said. "I think he expects to learn everything quickly, because he's so good at his lessons. He's a gift for the reading and suchlike."

"Aye, well I dinna ken about the reading and suchlike. But I'm sure he doesna behave like that wi' your da, and I'll no' have the wee shit behave like that wi' me, either."

Duncan thought about this for a minute, as was his way.

"Aye, ye've the right of it," he said. Morag had forgotten the flowers and was anxiously watching her sodden eldest brother wade out of the loch. She was very pale.

"Ma's been collecting the first of the honey," Kenneth said casually. "Susan's taking some, for she says the first honey's good for all manner of things, such as wounds and sore throats. Are ye wanting to see if she can make a drink for your cough, Morag?"

"I havena a sore throat," Morag said. "I just hurt, here?" She put her hand on her chest.

"Aye, well, it might soothe that. And there might be some honey to eat too. It's made frae flowers, did ye ken that, *a ghràidh?*"

Morag looked at the flowers, then shook her head.

"Away off to Ma's house then, and tell her I sent ye," Kenneth said.

The two children jumped down off the rock.

Duncan smiled at Kenneth.

"Thank you," he said simply, then taking his sister's hand he set off slowly up the slope to the settlement with her.

Behind them Alex strode out of the loch and walked straight up the same slope in a different direction, neither looking at the other boys, who were all silently watching him, nor at the man who'd thrown him in the loch. Kenneth stuck the little sword in his belt and sat down on the rock that Duncan and Morag had just vacated.

"It's over," he shouted to the boys, who, Alex now out of sight, were watching him instead. They'd never seen Kenneth lose his temper, which they assumed he must have done to throw the chieftain's son into the loch. But he didn't look angry now, and seemed unlikely to throw anyone else in, so after a minute they relaxed and carried on playing.

* * *

Alexander returned home that evening, but even though it was growing late it was still quite light, being summer, and part of his news was urgent, so he called a meeting of the clan.

"I'm aware it's late and ye'll have been working all day, so I'll no' keep ye long," he said. "I'll just tell ye the bones of it the night. Firstly, I've some good news. When I was in Perth I had talks wi' a man who I was hoping would tutor my bairns, and he will, so I'll be more available to ye all now and I'll be taking a full part in the harvest work. I admit it'll feel good to be outside again!"

Everyone cheered.

"But the first thing we need to do is build a wee house for the tutor, who'll arrive in a few days. That isna the good news," he added, seeing the worried looks at this sudden added workload. "The good news is that the man's a priest. Father Gordon is his name. He's agreed to teach Alex, Duncan and Morag, and if any others of ye want your bairns to learn the basics of reading, writing and numbers, he'll teach them too. He'll do that for three days a week, and on Sunday he'll give communion. In the first week, while he's settling in, he's agreed to do baptisms, confirmations and hear any confessions. If any of ye are thinking to marry, then ye can talk wi' him, too." Alexander looked round the group, noting Alpin and Flora exchanging glances. He smiled. That would be a good match.

"I'm thinking it'll be good to have a man of God around, for a time. It'll certainly be better than ye having me reading the Bible to ye, which is all we've had in the past years. In return I tellt him we'd give him shelter and food, and protection. On the days he's no' teaching or bringing us back to God, he'll be away doing God's work wi' others, and will take his own risks. Have I volunteers to help start the wee house tomorrow? He's no' expecting anything grand. He's a Highlander himself, and tellt me he's lived in caves and under brambles before now when doing missionary work."

A sea of hands shot up, and Alexander smiled.

"We'll start at dawn," he said. "Hopefully by the time he arrives we'll have it finished as a welcome for the man."

"How was the clan gathering?" James asked. As glad as they might be to have a priest among them to absolve them of their sins and ensure that both they and their offspring had a better chance of going to Heaven should anything happen, they'd expected Alexander to start by telling them whether they were about to be legal or not, which to all except the most devout was of primary importance. After all, Heaven or Hell was hopefully some time away, but the problems of being proscribed were immediate.

Alexander sighed.

"It was as I feared it might be," he said. "I spent over a week listening to them argue about why we should join, and then if we should take the Grant name or no', for some loons still think the Elector will raise the proscription, but at the end of it we'd agreed that we'd take either Grant or MacAlpin as our name. I had a wee stramash wi' a man, and then I went to Perth to meet wi' Father Gordon for a few days and buy a few wee things, and then back to Blair Atholl after that to see what had transpired."

"I'd be Alpin MacAlpin," Alpin commented in the pause that followed whilst Alexander quenched his thirst.

"Aye, but I'd be Kenneth MacAlpin," Kenneth said, to general laughter.

"It's a fine name," his mother said. "None better, in fact."

"I've the founder o' the clan for my wee brother," Alpin said. "Christ, he'll be unbearable."

"I'm no' calling ye Your Majesty, though," Dugald said. "Ye're still a wee gomerel, whatever your name."

"Ah, man, that's unfair," Gregor jumped in in defence of his son. "He's no' wee."

More laughter greeted this, and Kenneth stood up to show both that he certainly wasn't wee and to bestow his version of a royal blessing on the populace.

"Sorry to disappoint ye, Your Majesty, but it doesna seem the clans will join after all," Alexander announced, to mixed reactions. "In truth I thought the Grants might raise an objection to having a proscribed clan join wi' them, in case they were proscribed as well for doing it. But in the end it was the usual problem, for the MacGregors insisted that a MacGregor should be chief of the united clan, and the Grants said Grant should be the chief as he had influence at Court, which we of course dinna."

"Which MacGregor?" asked James. "Could it be you?"

"No. John McGregor of Glencarnock, for he's the heir of Balhaldie, who considers himself the current chief. And they wouldna move on that point, neither side. It didna help that the Grants sent proxies to act for their chief, which gave the impression that they didna consider the matter that important, so no one would take them seriously, and it made our men more belligerent. But I *did* manage to arrange for some of the other MacGregors to come wi' us on our cattle raid, so we'll have some fun in September and we should be able to take more cattle than we would alone, so make a good profit in Crieff."

There was a general uplifting of spirits at this news, as Alexander had intended, after which he said he'd talk about the meeting in more detail tomorrow, but for now let everyone go to bed and make a good start on the priest's house in the morning. After that he and Moira walked back to their house.

"Are the bairns asleep?" Alexander asked.

"Aye. I've a wee thing to talk to ye about them," Moira said, hesitating as they got to the door.

"I've a wee thing to talk to ye about, too," Alexander echoed.

Of one accord, they sat down on the grass outside. The sky was a royal blue now, the stars sparkling.

"Is it about the wee stramash?" Moira asked.

Alexander looked at her. She knew him so well.

"Aye," he said. "I'll no' tell anyone else, apart from Father Gordon, that is. I killed a man." He went on to explain what had happened.

"Could ye no' have just wounded him instead?" she asked when he'd finished.

"No. He wouldna let it go, even after we all ignored him for a time. I may have just continued to ignore him, but when he called me a coward directly, I couldna let that go. If I had, the whole clan would have kent in a few hours that the Loch Lomond chieftain's gone soft. And if I'd wounded him, I've no doubt he'd have gone on to spread lies about what happened and cause more trouble, for ye could see he was that sort of a man. Killing him stopped that and sent a clear message that ye dinna insult *this* chieftain. I wouldna have done it, otherwise."

Moira nodded.

"No. I'm sorry. I should have kent that ye wouldna take a life lightly."

He reached across and took her hand, squeezing it affectionately.

"Will ye tell the Father by way of confession?" she asked.

"I already did. He didna seem overly shocked, which tellt me that he's accustomed to the ways of the smaller clans."

"The Gordons are fearsome though, are they no'?" Moira said.

"Aye, but they're a mighty clan too, like the Campbells are, wi' Dukes for chiefs and vast undisputed lands, so they willna have the same troubles as many o' the smaller clans do, or as we do, having no lands at all except what we hold by the sword. I'm hoping he'll fit in well here. He suggested teaching some of the other boys as well as ours, the basic subjects at least, for he said it's as easy to teach ten as two, and gives a better atmosphere in the lessons. He wasna too keen on teaching Morag though. He's of the mind that educating girls encourages the evil of original sin to blossom in them."

Moira snorted.

"Aye, that's how I thought ye'd react," Alexander said, smiling. "And that's why I was negotiating wi' the man for two days. I tellt him what Locke and Quintilian said about the value of educating women, and then about Morag's illness, that she's a way wi' the numbers and that it will be good for her to feel equal wi' the other children without wanting to run around, and he understood that, in fairness to the man."

"Ye'll no' keep wee Jeannie away either," Moira pointed out. "And if he's thinking about Eve's problem, he'll no' want Jeannie in there, pretty and pert as she is."

"Are ye thinking she'll be wanting to sit still and learn? She's almost as much energy as Alex!"

"Aye, but she's clever too, and eager, as he is. If the boys are doing it, she'll want to, for she plays wi' them more than she does wi' the girls, when Jean will let her."

"Ah well, that's Father Gordon's problem," said Alexander happily, lying down on the grass. "If he can deal wi' me turning up to see him wi' a bloodstained shirt without blinking, I'm sure he'll cope wi' Jeannie. And Alex," he added.

Moira made no comment on the shirt, knowing where the blood would have come from and her husband's inexperience in laundry matters.

"Alex is the wee thing I need to talk wi' you about," she said. "I was going to deal wi' it myself, but I'm thinking it'll come better from you, as you're back."

He lay there while she told him that just an hour before he'd arrived home, his son had come into the house, his hair damp and clothes soaking wet, and had climbed straight up the ladder into the loft area that he now shared with Duncan as a bedroom, without saying a word or asking if there was anything to eat.

"I was about to go up and ask what was the matter, when Duncan and Morag came in together, carrying a pot of honey that Barbara had given them and some honey cakes she'd made and sent for us. They both said they didna want a cake as Barbara had given them cranachan to eat. So I asked if Alex had eaten too much and felt ill, as he'd just come in and gone straight to bed. Morag said that Kenneth had thrown Alex in the loch, Duncan said '*Isd!*' to her, then they both flushed scarlet. I didna make them tell me more then, for I didna want to put them in a position of choosing between me and Alex for loyalty. Barbara wouldna have given them cranachan if they'd been a part of whatever Alex has done to make Kenneth react in such a way."

Alexander sat up and ran his fingers through his hair.

"I was about to go to Kenneth and find out the truth of it," she told him. "But then ye came back."

"I'm weary now," he said. "And I'm no' in the mood to hear what the wee loon's done to make Kenneth act so out of character. And I'm no' wanting to get Kenneth out of his bed either. I'll find out in the morning. I've wee gifts for ye all. Except Alex, depending on what he's done."

* * *

The next morning Alexander was up early, having slept badly, mainly because he spent the dark hours mentally sourcing materials and organising the building of Father Gordon's house, and once that was done his mind turned to how on earth his son had managed to antagonise Kenneth enough for him to throw him in the loch.

Deciding to get one matter out of the way so he could concentrate on the other, he was up and waiting outside Gregor and Barbara's house for signs of life just as the sun rose below the hills and the sky became a paler blue above them. Alpin at least was an early riser, and soon opened the door dressed only in his shirt and yawning hugely, greatly surprised to see the chieftain sitting there.

"I was thinking to send the bairns up the hill to cut heather for the roof," Alexander said by way of preamble. "It'll keep them busy and useful, and out of the way while the heavy work goes on."

"Aye, good idea," Alpin agreed, not asking although clearly wondering why his chieftain was visiting at the crack of dawn to make such a statement.

"Will ye be asking Father Gordon about marrying, then?" Alexander asked next, focussing on Alpin properly now. Alpin blushed scarlet, looked at his feet like a small child caught out in mischief and mumbled,

"Aye, I'd like to. She's agreed and her parents are happy in spite of… and wi' me learning the weaving, ye ken, for I'll be useful. I'd need to ask yourself if that would be agreeable, though. I was going to come to see you today."

"No need. Aye, it's acceptable to me. She's a bonny lassie, and it's clear ye care for each other. And I'm hoping ye're thinking to stay here, for if ye do we can build ye a loom o' your own. Wi' two accomplished weavers we can all be dressed like lords and maybe ye can trade cloth at the markets too."

Alpin laughed, partly from pure joy at there being no objection to his marriage, and partly at the overblown description of his skills.

"I'm no' accomplished yet," he admitted. "I couldna weave of a quality to sell."

"Duncan was enthralled wi' his *fèileadh mòr,*" Alexander said. "For him ye're the best weaver in the world. For now your da can make the cloth to sell, and you for us to wear. But it'll no' be long afore ye're weaving well enough for strangers to gladly pay ye for your work."

"I'm sorry I couldna be a fighter for ye," Alpin said suddenly, his tongue tripping over his words in a way that told Alexander he'd wanted to say this for a long time, but had never had the opportunity to. Or the courage. No, Alpin did not lack courage. It was Kenneth's courage that people doubted.

"I've plenty of good fighters, Alpin. But I havena plenty of good weavers. Dinna think less of yourself. Ye can still fight well enough to protect the women if we're away, which will give me peace of mind, and ye've a valuable skill. There's more to being a man than using a sword. It wasna your fault that ye were wounded, it could have been any of us. I'm blessed to have ye with me, laddie. I mean that. Blessings on your wedding too. Go and see the Father as soon as he's settled in. It'll be a fine ceremony to start his time here, and we'll have had the practice building his house to build one for you and Flora afterwards."

"Thank you," Alpin said, and his eyes filled with sudden tears. He looked away then, embarrassed by his show of emotion at his chieftain's regard for him.

"I'm here so early though to talk wi' your brother and find out what my eldest did while I was away."

"Ah," replied Alpin, in a way that told Alexander he knew

exactly what his eldest had done. "He'll be awake now, go on in."

Kenneth *was* awake, kneeling on the floor over the fire, blowing on it to rouse the embers.

"Ah," he said, echoing Alpin on seeing the identity of the visitor. "Will ye sit down and have a honey cake? Ma made them."

"I will. Duncan and Morag brought some back yesterday. They're very good."

Kenneth smiled.

"How is he?" he asked.

"I havena seen him yet," Alexander answered. "I wanted to find out the truth of things before I decided how to react. Moira said he came in soaking wet and went straight to the loft to bed. I thought I'd get your side of things first."

Half an hour later, having got Kenneth's side of things, Alexander, his son's confiscated sword stuck through his belt, was on his way back home deep in thought, when his youngest son ran up to him, blue and green kilt inexpertly donned so that it almost exposed one buttock, whilst the other side was trailing to the ground.

"Da!" he cried, laughing as Alexander swept him off the floor and swung him round before setting him down on his feet again. "I've missed ye. Ma tellt me ye're building a house for the Father! Can I help?"

"Ye can, laddie," Alexander said, kneeling down and deftly rearranging his son's clothing. "But I wanted to have a wee blether wi' ye first."

Duncan glanced at his father's belt, and paled.

"Aye," said Alexander. "I'm on my way back from Kenneth's, so I ken what Alex has done. I dinna need to ask ye what happened." The relief on Duncan's face was almost comically touching. "Duncan, laddie, it's a good thing that ye've a loyalty to your brother, for he'll be needing that when he's older, and if he becomes the chieftain one day, ye'll be his right-hand man. That man has to be loyal to him to death, and it's seeming that ye will be, which is a reassurance to me."

Duncan nodded.

"And Morag too," he said. "I'll no' let anyone hurt her."

"I ken that, which is why I trust ye to look after her, for ye're a loving and thoughtful boy," Alexander added, giving the compliment before the criticism, which was his way. But then he realised that those words summed Duncan up perfectly.

Perhaps more thoughtful than Alexander would have liked at that point, for Duncan didn't smile at the praise as he'd expected, but instead waited for the negative part.

Alexander raised his hand to his head, and then realising that Duncan would know exactly how he was feeling should he complete his customary gesture, he dropped it again.

"But until Alex *does* become chieftain, or at least until ye're all grown, ye *must* be loyal to your mother and me first, and Alex and Morag after that. If Alex does wrong and we ask ye what he's done, ye must tell us. Ye canna keep secrets from your parents even if you're asked to, for we love ye and need to ken if something's amiss. Honouring your parents is so important that it's one of God's commandments, that ye mustna break. Ye ken that, aye?"

Duncan nodded, and looked down at the ground, much as Alpin had earlier, but being only six, he didn't even attempt to conceal his feelings. Alexander reached out and put a finger under his son's chin, gently lifting it. The big grey eyes, so like his mother's, were swimming with tears, and as he tried to blink them away they cascaded over his long lashes, spilling down his cheeks.

"I'm sorry, Da," he choked out. "I didna mean..." His voice trailed off then and he swallowed convulsively, his face twisting with misery.

Still kneeling, Alexander pulled the boy against him, unable to bear the intensity of Duncan's grief at disappointing his father. He had forgotten how deeply children felt emotions, both positive and negative. They had no filters. No adult could swing from such utter delight to such utter despair in a moment as this child just had. And he had caused it. He felt terrible.

But it had had to be said.

He held his son for a moment as he sobbed, rubbing his back until he calmed a little, marvelling at the fragility of the bones, at the strength of emotion. He would be a fine man one day.

"*Isd*, laddie," he said finally, when the sobs started to diminish. "I'm no' angry wi' ye. No' disappointed, even. Loyalty is a wonderful thing to feel, and I'm proud of the three of you for the love ye show each other. But it's important ye tell us such things as what Alex did, for ye'll tell us the truth of it, I'm thinking."

He felt Duncan nod against his shoulder and reaching up, stroked his long dark hair, still baby-soft. He was so very young. He was growing with frightening speed.

"Da," he said into Alexander's shoulder, "he didna mean to say what he said to Kenneth. He was awfu' upset that ye didna take him wi' ye, that's all."

Alexander smiled.

"Aye, but he shouldna have behaved like that. Ye wanted to come wi' me too, did ye no'?"

Duncan nodded, and stood back now. The torrent of emotion was subsiding.

"But ye didna insult Kenneth and hit him, did ye?"

Duncan thought for a moment.

"No. But I dinna feel things as Alex does," he said, showing a spectacular lack of self-awareness, judging by his reaction of a few minutes ago. "And he finds remembering easy, so he canna bear it when he doesna learn something quickly. I dinna mind, for I canna learn anything so quick."

"Well, he needs to learn to control himself, which you *have* learnt, laddie, and without me teaching ye. I'm proud of ye. Now, I've a job for ye to do, and ye'll be acting for me."

Alexander explained that he wanted Duncan to go to all the houses and tell the children that their job today (unless their parents needed them) would be to go up the hill and get heather for the priest's house, and that he should bring them all back here once their parents had been told.

He watched affectionately as his younger son ran off to do his job, happy again.

Aye, he thought, *when I die, I'll hopefully leave behind a wonderful chieftain and an excellent deputy.* Which would be which though, he was uncertain at the moment.

He stood, braced himself, and headed to the house to face his eldest.

"I'm sure I dinna need to tell ye that ye shouldna have done that, laddie," Alexander said, after listening to his son's version of events. In fairness the boy hadn't lied, and his story matched Kenneth's in most of the factual particulars. The emotional particulars differed somewhat, however.

"Aye, but I need to learn that move, for it's an important one, and I canna be the chieftain if I canna fight properly! And no one was taking it seriously! Duncan was blethering on about flowers so I couldna concentrate, and then he laughed at me and I did the move wrong again, and then Kenneth said he wouldna teach me any more and so I was a wee bit fashed. I shouldna have hit him, but it was only wi' the flat o' the blade. I didna stick him wi' it, and it was only his leg so I wouldna have killed him anyway!"

He stood there, red-faced, earnest. Defiant. Alexander thrust his hand through his hair, making no attempt to restrain himself this time. Alex was not Duncan.

"Who tellt ye ye couldna kill someone if ye stuck them in the leg?" Alexander asked.

Alex hesitated.

"I…I just thought it. Ye havena any important bits there, like your heart or lungs," he faltered.

"Ye need to talk wi' Alpin, if ye think that limbs are no' important," Alexander said, thinking he might just drag Alex over there, and then realising that Alpin did not talk about his disability with anyone. "And Alpin nearly died of his wound, might well have done had Susan no' chosen that time to come home. Same risk of a sword wound as a musket ball," he added. This wasn't quite true, but now was not the time to get into medical details, about which his knowledge was superficial anyway.

"But I didna stick him wi' the blade!" Alex cried.

"Come here," Alexander said, fighting not to lose his own temper at this show of defiance. It would not set a good example if he were to do the very thing he was chastising his son for. In one quick move he grabbed his son by the shirt, drew the little sword from his belt and hit him smartly on the leg with it.

Alex cried out, as much from shock as pain, and then flushed scarlet and closed his mouth firmly to stifle any further cries.

He was so very aware of his standing with the clan, so very intent on being a perfect man, of making his father and clan proud. Which was good. Up to a point.

"So, it hurt, then," Alexander said, watching as an angry red welt appeared on his son's leg. "Now, imagine if ye'd just done a kind and generous thing for me and I repaid ye by doing that to ye. Would ye think well of me for it? Answer me!"

"No," Alex whispered, resisting the urge to look at his leg, fighting back the tears with more success than his little brother had just managed.

"And if I behaved like that, repaying kindness wi' wounds, shouting at other members o' the clan who were doing kind things for their sisters, and then telling them that I was the chieftain and they had to do everything I said, would ye think well of me for it?"

"No," Alex said. He bit his lip, hard.

"Would ye *want* me to be your chieftain, if I behaved like that?" Alex shook his head.

"I ken ye remember things well. Ye're a good boy, much of the time, Alex. And it's good ye want to learn to fight well. But there's a lot more to being a chieftain than remembering things and fighting well. A big part of being a chieftain is winning the hearts of your clan, for if they dinna love and respect ye, they'll no' follow ye. I'm ashamed of ye for the way ye behaved wi' Kenneth, and I expected you to be ashamed of it too, as ye've had a whole night to think on it. I didna expect ye to defend yourself to me, for there's no defence for what ye did. Ye were wrong. Eldest son or no', ye'll no' be the chieftain if ye canna see what ye did wrong yesterday."

Now the tears did well up, and Alexander was treated to a repeat of earlier events, except this time the eyes were slate-blue, and the lashes over which the tears spilled, though equally long, were reddish rather than black. And Alex managed not to dissolve completely, but it took a herculean effort. Alexander was impressed by that, but had no desire to comfort this son.

"So then, tell me what ye did wrong," he said.

"I shouldna have hit Kenneth," Alex said after a moment.

"Aye. What else?"

"I shouldna have shouted at Duncan and Morag."

Alexander waited.

"I shouldna have tellt them I'd be the chieftain one day."

Alexander waited.

Silence.

"And what made ye do all those nasty, stupid things?" Alexander prompted.

"I lost my temper," Alex said after a minute.

"Aye, ye did."

"I'm sorry," Alex said. "I canna be a chieftain if I lose my temper."

"Ye canna be a *man* if ye canna control your temper."

"I…I couldna help it. It just…happened," Alex said, so sincerely that it was clear he was not trying to justify his behaviour now.

"We all get angry, Alex. That's part of being a human. But we have to learn to control our anger, for if ye canna do that, then it doesna matter how many things ye can remember, ye'll never be a good fighter. Or a good person. Ye need to learn to control all your emotions, for if ye dinna ye'll be a liability as a chieftain, for ye'll lead your people without thinking, and maybe get them all killed."

He looked at his son, saw the puzzled frown and sighed.

"Sit down," he said. "Now, when I was at Blair Atholl I talked wi' a few other men, and we're all thinking to go on a cattle raid, when the harvest's in. Now that's an exciting thing, so imagine if the men said that they kent where there were thousands of cattle for the taking, wi' no one watching them. How would I feel?"

"Ye'd feel very excited?" Alex ventured.

"I would. And if I couldna control my excitement, I'd just agree to raid the thousands o' cattle. So, instead of just being excited and wanting to do it, what should I be thinking about? I ken ye havena been on a raid yet, but just tell me what ye think."

"Why is no one watching the cattle?" Alex said after a minute. "Who do they belong to? Er…are the men telling ye true?"

"Good! Ye're thinking well, because ye're no' feeling excited at the minute. Now if all ye were thinking about was making a great profit from the cattle, ye wouldna think properly. Because when your feelings are very strong, ye dinna think as ye should. There's nothing wrong wi' feeling excited, or angry, or very sad. But ye need to learn to control the feelings sometimes, so ye can think clearly, make the right decision. Anger ye *always* need to control, for it's a dangerous thing."

He did not want to be saying this to his seven-year-old son. One of the things he loved about children was their ability to feel *everything* so intently. But displays of petulant rage were not acceptable.

Alex nodded, clearly thinking.

"So, when ye shouted at Duncan and Morag, hit Kenneth, boasted about being the chieftain, that was all because ye were angry and didna even try to control it. For if ye had, ye wouldna have behaved so badly. I'm no' going to hit ye again, although ye deserve it. But until ye can control your temper, I'll no' teach ye to fight any more, and nor will Kenneth. I'll keep your sword till ye've proved ye can use it wisely, for that's more important than learning all the moves. And if ye canna do that, next time I'll throw your sword in the loch as well as you. Ye can take the time ye'd be practising fighting to think about what ye should do next, to make this right."

"I should apologise to Kenneth. And Duncan and Morag," Alex said immediately.

"Aye. But dinna just run off and do it. Think about what ye'll say when ye do, for that's important too. Now, today we're building a house for the priest who'll be coming to live here, has your ma tellt ye?"

"Aye," Alex said.

"Good. All the children need to go up the mountain there, and cut heather for the roof. Ye'll need a lot of it, so ye can take the sacks and when they're full, drag them down. I sent Duncan to bring the others here. Ye can go wi' them, and use the time well. For if ye dinna learn to control yourself ye'll never be chieftain. That's an honour ye need to prove you're worthy of, no' one ye inherit from your da. I thought ye'd have kent that by now. Away wi' ye. I'm no' proud of ye right now. Ye've shamed me."

Then, seeing his son's face crumple completely at these words, Alexander turned and walked out. He could not give way on this. It was too important.

He was about to build a house for a priest, feed him, provide him with fuel, and above all take on a risk to the whole clan, for it was forbidden for Catholic priests to hold Masses, forbidden for them to do missionary work to strengthen faith and bring converts, and forbidden to shelter such men. Because it was widely believed that all Catholics were Jacobites.

Which was probably true, but only because they were treated so unfairly, brutally even. What was also true was that there were far more Protestant Jacobites, particularly in Scotland where

Episcopalians were treated little better than Catholics. But that did not suit Hanoverian propaganda, so it was widely ignored.

Father Gordon was willing to take the risks of imprisonment and possibly execution for his faith. Alexander was willing to take the risks of protecting him to help his son to be the most capable chieftain possible.

And he would not do that for a petulant brat.

He closed the door and sat on the bench outside, deliberating.

He loved his children, all three of them, fiercely. He loved their soft skin, their snub unformed noses, their malleable limbs. He loved their exuberance, innocence, their utter enthusiasm for everything in life. And their trust that he would keep them safe, that if they treated the world fairly, the world would respond with love.

It would not. Even if they were not MacGregors, it would not.

But they *were* MacGregors, and for them life would be particularly hard, particularly pitiless. They were landless, had no recourse to law. It was not that long ago that MacGregor wives had been branded on the face with a key, that children had been taken away from their parents, to be sent to Ireland. Should they try to run away, they were whipped and branded the first time, hung the second, if they were under fourteen. Over fourteen they were hung for the first offence. The law was no longer enforced, but it had not been repealed and could be revived at any time. To survive as a member of such a clan, and especially as chieftain, you *had* to be hard, ruthless.

He did not want to destroy his sons' innocence, for once gone it would never return. His heart ached even at the thought of it.

Give me a child until he is seven, and I will show you the man. Aristotle had said that, and St Francis Xavier had confirmed it. Alex was closer to eight than seven, and Duncan, although only six, had a stillness and maturity his older brother had not yet learned. Instead Alex had enthusiasm, charisma and that incredible memory.

But all these God-given gifts would be as nothing if they did not start learning the truth of life, that it was hard and brutal, and to survive it you had to know when to be gentle and when to be ruthless.

It was time. The incident with Kenneth had showed him that. It was not enough just to teach him to read and write, to use a sword. He had to start stripping away the childish layers, to reveal the exceptional man he believed his son would one day be. The man who might one day be as adept at Court as he was on the battlefield, who might raise the prohibition against the clan. For James Stuart would not, Alexander was sure of that now.

He sat waiting for the children to arrive, closed his eyes and prayed for the strength to break his sons' innocence, to show them the brutality of the world without putting them in direct danger until they were old enough to defend themselves. It would cost him dear to do it, as he realised now it had cost his father dear to do it to him.

Later he would wonder if his prayer had caused God to send him an event that would do that very thing. It would be a long time before Alexander asked God for anything after that without thinking about the exact wording of his prayer. But for now, having no gift for seeing the future, he crossed himself, opened his eyes, saw the children coming across the clearing, and, putting aside his serious thoughts, placed an appropriate expression on his face and went to meet them, smiling.

CHAPTER SIX

Everyone set to work with enthusiasm, for it was an exciting thing to have a newcomer in the settlement, and a priest even more so. It was a few years since they'd built a completely new house but most remembered how to do it, so by the end of the first day the roof timbers were cut, a good number of stones for the walls had been brought and were lying in a pile at the location of the prospective dwelling, and Allan, who had the most skill with carpentry, had made a number of pegs, had cut planks to make the door and window frames, and was hoping to have those for a table, chairs and box bed ready tomorrow. The women were constructing mattresses and gathering together necessities such as blankets and eating utensils.

Everyone agreed that it had been a good idea of Alexander's to send all but the very smallest children up on the hill to collect heather, for it kept them from getting underfoot and meant the adults didn't have to invent tasks for them to do. Later they'd be able to help with lighter work, but none of them could lift the heavy stones needed for walls.

Up on the hill, the children felt similarly. It was wonderful to be completely free from adult supervision, and even (for the older ones) to be treated with maturity, having been given knives with which to cut the heather and a series of instructions on how to collect it, with no one watching, not even from a distance.

Because of this the older children, aware of the responsibility, behaved very sensibly so as to impress the adults with the fact that they could work well and without mishap, and maybe earn more trust and freedom, with the result that the atmosphere on the hill was a mixture of industriousness and joy.

If they'd expected the natural leader of the group Alex to take control though, they were disappointed. Alexander had given Duncan the task of making sure everyone did as they should, and Duncan took his responsibility very seriously, although he was uncomfortably aware that he was, albeit through no fault of his own, usurping his brother.

It seemed to him at first that Alex was upset about this, because a full hour passed during which he uttered not a word, and in fact kept himself away from the others, heading a little further uphill to cut the heather, which he then left in a pile for those too young to be entrusted with a blade to put in the sacks they'd been given.

After everyone had spent a good portion of that hour glancing concernedly up the hill, Duncan decided to take the bull by the horns and made his way up to his brother, who was hacking at the stems with an unsettling ferocity which made Duncan think twice. However he was here now, and someone had to speak.

"Are ye fashed because Da asked me to lead us today?" he asked directly.

Alex stopped cutting and cast his brother a look of such surprise that Duncan immediately knew that whatever was bothering him, it was not that.

"No," Alex said. "Da had the right of it. I'm just...I've a lot to think about, and I want to be alone for it. I'm no' fashed wi' ye. Or wi' anyone," he added. He looked down to where a sea of faces stared up at him and sighed, then brushed his hand through his hair in unconscious imitation of his father. "I'm just wanting to be alone for a wee while," he shouted down to them. "I've a lesson I need to learn, and I'm thinking on it."

"I'll leave ye to it, then," Duncan said, and turned to go back down the hill. There was no point in offering to help Alex with whatever his lesson was, for Alex was much better with all his book learning than Duncan was.

"Duncan," Alex called when he'd gone just a few steps down the hill. He turned back. "I'm awfu' sorry for shouting at you and Morag yesterday. That was a shameful way I behaved, to you and to Kenneth. I'll say as much to Morag later, but I wanted to at least tell you now."

Duncan nodded then, suddenly knowing what the lesson was.

"Aye," he said. "Think no more on it. No' about me, anyway. Thank ye for saying sorry. It's no' always an easy thing to do."

He headed back to the others then, leaving Alex realising for the first time that his younger brother was, in one way at least, older than him.

He didn't join the others until they all stopped to eat. Moira had entrusted the bannocks and cheese to Morag, who had the task of ensuring everyone had two each, and while they were cutting heather she had to spin some flax, which, if she did it well enough, would be used to make a tablecloth for Father Gordon. The importance of this task had kept Morag focussed and quiet all day, which had been her mother's intention.

She handed the oatcakes out with great gravity, and placed the water flasks in the middle of the group, then sat down again.

"Have ye learnt the lesson, Alex?" Jeannie asked through a mouthful of food.

"No' yet," Alex replied.

Everyone waited for him to elaborate on this as he normally would, but he seemed to be focussing all his attention on his bannock.

"It must be awfu' bonny to learn the reading and the writing though," Jeannie persisted after a silent minute. "Ma tellt me that the Father said he'll teach anyone who wants to learn the reading."

"Aye, and the writing, and numbers," Duncan agreed.

Alex looked up in surprise.

"She tellt me this morning, while ye were still…asleep," Duncan improvised. "He'll be teaching us for three days a week, once he's settled."

"Are ye well, after yesterday?" Jeannie asked. "I wouldna think Kenneth meant to hurt ye."

This time the silence was tense. Everyone had wanted to mention what had happened, but hadn't known how to approach it. But Jeannie had no tact, no boundaries. They all knew that.

"I'm well," Alex replied.

"I couldna believe ye'd challenge Kenneth," Simon said, reassured now by Alex's lack of reaction. "He's the biggest man in the clan! In the world!"

"He could have torn ye in half wi' one hand," Alasdair Og added. "Ye were awfu' brave. I wouldna do it."

"I wager no one would," Rory said. "I wouldna."

His tone was one of awe. Alex looked up from his bannock, saw the expressions of admiration and respect on all the children's faces. All but Duncan's anyway. And Morag's. She looked apprehensive. He closed his eyes for a moment, then stood up.

"I'm no' hungry any more," he said. "I'll away and cut some more."

He turned and walked away, the children staring after him.

"Is he hurting?" Simon asked Duncan.

"Aye, I think maybe he is," Duncan replied. "But I'm thinking he doesna want to talk about it."

"What happened?" Jeannie asked. "What did he say to Kenneth?"

"He hit him wi' his sword," Rory said. "I saw that. I didna hear them, but I was walking down to the loch and saw him. And then Kenneth pulled it off him. I thought he was going to run him through, but then he thought again and picked him up and threw him in the loch."

There was a universal gasp of horror at this.

"I still think it was awfu' brave. I canna imagine hitting Kenneth at all, no mind stabbing him wi' a sword!" Alasdair Og said.

Duncan deliberated for a moment.

"Alex didna stab him," he asserted. Everyone looked at him then, faces eager. "And I dinna want to talk about it either." He got up and walked away, and after a moment Morag, seeing the attention turn to her, picked up her distaff and spindle and followed him.

It seemed the children would have to be content with imagining what had happened, because, gentle as Kenneth was, no one was going to ask him.

Alex remained quiet and apart for the rest of the day, and when they made their way down and Alexander praised the children for the amount of heather they'd collected and brought back, he didn't glow with pleasure as the others did. Back at home he ate his meal in silence, Morag chatting animatedly and even Duncan joining in to hide the fact that their normally garrulous brother hadn't uttered a word.

As soon as the food was gone Alex asked permission to leave, and when it was given went straight to bed. His parents stared after him for a moment and then shared an enigmatic look across the table.

"Have ye anything to tell me?" Alexander asked. Duncan reddened and was clearly uneasy for a moment, then looked at his father.

"No," he said. "He was quiet, said he had a lesson to learn. That's all. He didna say anything about…about anything at all." He glanced at the ladder in the corner of the room. "Can I away to my bed too, Da?"

Alexander nodded.

"Good. Ye've learnt yours then. Aye, ye can go."

"Ye've spun an awfu' lot today, *mo chridhe*," Moira said to her distressed-looking daughter. "I'm thinking if ye carry on this way, ye'll have enough for a napkin, or ye can add it to mine for a tablecloth. Are ye wanting to carry on tomorrow up on the hill wi' the others, or would ye rather be wi' me?"

Morag thought for a minute.

"Will Alex be Alex again tomorrow?" she asked.

"Why, what was he today?" Alexander asked.

"He was sad," Morag said. "I dinna like him sad. It makes me hurt." She put her hand on her chest, because that was where she normally felt pain. "It's no' hurting now," she added, seeing her parents' looks of alarm. "But it feels like this, to see him sad."

"I dinna think he'll be sad for long," Moira said.

"I'll go on the hill then."

The next day they all left Alex alone when he lagged behind on the way up to the heather patch, and when he carried on up to cut higher than the others. It must be a really hard lesson if it was taking him this long to learn it. Several of the children started changing their minds about wanting to learn to read and write, if it was this difficult. Although if their parents wanted them to, or Alexander did, they wouldn't have a choice. They would leave him alone until he learnt whatever it was, they decided, and then he'd be happy again. And then they could ask him why he'd tried to kill Kenneth.

That evening Alex waited until the others had set off before following, dragging a sack of heather behind him. Morag fell back, waiting for him, and then walked beside him. He slowed down to match her pace so she wouldn't tire.

"Are ye still sad?" she asked after a moment. "I dinna want ye to be sad. It hurts me."

He looked across at her. She was frowning, her blue eyes troubled. He glanced down the hill, and then stopped.

"I'm sorry for shouting at ye by the loch," he said. "And at Duncan too."

"I'm sorry we were stopping ye learning the move," she replied. "Is that the lesson ye're needing to learn, that's making ye sad?"

"No. Well, yes, part of it. Ye were no' stopping me learning the move. I behaved shameful. Ye didna do anything wrong at all. It was all me, and I'm sorry for it. I was wanting to do something for ye, to show ye how sorry I was, but I canna think of anything."

"Ye dinna need to do anything," Morag said happily. "Ye can just be happy now then. And then I'll no' be hurting. Duncan neither."

She put her little hand in his, and they walked down the rest of the hill together, Alex struggling to drag the heavy sack with one hand, but preferring to struggle than to relinquish the comfort of his sister's hand.

He had pretty well decided what he needed to do now, but not how to do it. He would have to talk with his father, when he got a chance to. But in the meantime he needed to do another thing.

He needed to be happy. Because he could not have his precious little sister hurting any more than she already did. And Duncan was hurting too, he knew that. There was no point in saying sorry for hurting someone if you carried on doing a different thing to hurt them.

When they got back down with their sacks everyone was gathered round the house. For it was now clear that this was, indeed, a house, not merely a stack of stones and wood as it had been on the previous day. The low stone walls were built, with holes where the windows and door would be, and some of the main roof timbers were in place.

"It'll just be the one room, but I'm thinking the box bed can be as a partition to give the Father a second room for the lessons,"

Alexander was saying as the children arrived.

"Aye, or we could build another wee wall wi' turf inside, just so high," Dugald said, holding his hand at chest height.

"I didna think to ask the man," Alexander commented. "He just tellt me he'd be grateful for a dry shelter and a heather mattress to lie down on. But I'm thinking if he's a room for the lessons then he willna need to be moving the teaching things about to write his sermons or rest of an evening. It'll be a kind gesture. And if the man moves on, then it'll be a fine home for the next couple that marry when he's gone."

"Are ye expecting him to stay a long time?" Catriona asked.

"I've no' idea. I'm hoping he'll stay long enough to give the bairns a solid learning, but it's for the man himself to decide. We've done well today though, and ye've enough for maybe half the roof," he added, looking at the sacks of heather. "And we've the turf for under it now too. We'll be finished before he arrives, I'm thinking, which gladdens me."

"Aye, another two days should finish it," Alasdair said, who was the eldest of them all and had participated in the building of many a dwelling, including his own, "but for the doors, that is, and the furnishings."

Alexander smiled.

"Well, then," he said. "I ken there's a harvest to bring in, but I'm thinking that on the day we finish, we'll have a wee ceilidh wi' as much ale and whisky as ye can drink, and the women'll make food for us all. Ye deserve it, for ye've worked hard. You too," he added to the gathered children. "And we can discuss how we're going to help the Father settle in. Before we start the drinking," he added, smiling.

For the first time since he'd landed unexpectedly in the loch, Alex smiled. Not because he'd decided to be happy again, for Morag's sake at least, and Duncan's, but because his father had unwittingly just solved one of his problems.

* * *

Alpin and Flora walked the first part of the way back to their parents' houses together, hand-in-hand, both of them tired from the day's work.

When they arrived outside her house they stopped for a

moment, as had become their custom. Alpin looked around. There was no one within earshot. He resisted the urge to massage the fingers and wrist of his right hand which were throbbing unbearably, and instead focussed on her.

"I was thinking…" he began hesitantly, "and Alexander approves…if you do, of course, that…er…" he faltered, blushed scarlet, then continued, his last sentence coming out in a rush. "When the Father arrives, I was thinking to ask him about marrying us?"

He watched her intently. If she looked uncomfortable he would say he understood, and leave. If she laughed at him he would die on the spot.

She did neither of those things. True, she did laugh, not at him but with joy, because this was what she'd been hoping for, but hadn't known how to suggest it without seeming brash. Her eyes lit up with happiness, and he had his answer. Impulsively he pulled her into his arms and embraced her. They clung together for a moment laughing like children, and then she stepped back.

"When?" she asked.

"I wanted to ask him straight away, but the chieftain said I should wait until he's settled in," Alpin replied.

"No, I meant when shall we marry?"

"I'd marry ye tomorrow, if it were possible," he said. "But we've things to do. The chieftain said building the Father's house would give everyone the practice to build one for us. We could live at your parents or mine though, until the house is built and we've furniture for it."

"No," she said. "I dinna want to start our life together by having our brothers and sisters giggling like loons every time we look at each other."

"I dinna think Kenneth'd be doing that. He's no' one for giggling like a loon."

She hit him lightly on the shoulder.

"Ye ken what I mean," she said. "Ye havena the room at yours anyway, wi' the loom in there, and your brother being a giant. No, let's wait, and do it right. When Allan's finished wi' the furniture for the Father, we can ask him to make some for us, and then maybe once the harvest is in the clan can build us a wee house."

"Aye. We could be married by autumn," Alpin said, his eyes alight.

Of one accord they moved together again, not caring now if anyone saw them and commented. For was this not the happiest day of their lives so far, with another one to look forward to in a couple of months? And then a whole life together!

"I dinna want to wait, though," he admitted. "I want to be with ye all the time."

"Me too," Flora agreed. "But I want to be with ye alone, no' wi' people watching us. We'll go to see the Father together, once he's settled. A week after, maybe? That should be long enough."

"Aye. Will we tell the others first?" he asked. "I dinna mean our parents, but the whole clan?"

"No," she replied. "Let's keep it just between us, a wonderful secret, until the day before we see the Father."

"Can I tell Kenneth?" Alpin asked. "For I'll burst if I dinna tell *someone*. And he'll no' tell a soul if I ask him no' to. Ye can tell one o' your siblings, if ye want."

"Christ, and have the whole clan ken we were marrying five minutes after?" she said. "No, you tell Kenneth, and I'll keep it to myself. It's different for me, being ten years older than all the rest o' them. Kenneth and you are near in age. Go," she said. "I'll slip away and come and see you tomorrow."

"I'll be at the house," Alpin said. "Da's asked me to do some weaving, and wee Morag wants to show me her flax that she's spinning for a napkin for the Father. I'll keep her wi' me, show her what I do so she willna be running around."

"I'll bring something wi' me for her too, then. Some food," Flora said. "She's a bonny wee thing," she added sadly. Everyone knew how delicate Morag was. Everyone looked out for her. And everyone dreaded the day that no one would speak of. Even though she did not cause death but merely foretold it, it did not do to draw the attention of the *ban sìth* to a fragile life. God would decide when it was Morag's time, as he decided everything, Flora thought.

"Let's hope He decides we can wed early in the autumn," she said.

"Aye. I'm hoping he's a kind man," Alpin replied, mistaking the reference. "For the children are to be educated by him, Alex and Duncan at least for a good while. I dinna think Alex will take kindly to a harsh teacher."

"Hmm," Flora said. "From what I'm hearing, Alex needs bringing down a peg. Is it true he stabbed Kenneth and tried to kill him?"

"What? Where did ye hear that?"

"Wee Simon tellt me. All the bairns are talking about it. They think Alex is some kind of hero for taking on the giant Kenneth."

"Did Alex say he'd done that?"

"No," Flora replied. "Rory said Alex hasna been speaking to anyone. He's got some reading lesson to learn that he needs to think about, he tellt them."

"So give it another few days and I've no doubt Alex will have actually thrown Kenneth into the loch rather than the other way round, after decapitating him, maybe," Alpin said.

Flora laughed.

"Aye, likely," she said. "Bairns."

Not just bairns, Alpin thought. Better they did keep the marriage secret, for now. As close as the clan was, that would not stop anyone who thought him a bad catch from trying to dissuade Flora. He was sure she wouldn't be dissuaded, but better safe than sorry.

"When I tell Kenneth our good news, I'll tell him that too," Alpin laughed. "It'll amuse him to be thought of as Goliath to Alex's David. I'll see ye tomorrow, *mo chridhe.*"

He walked back to his house, his feet barely touching the ground, the throbbing in his hand forgotten. He was going to be married to the most beautiful girl in the world. And he had a trade. And although he'd almost certainly have to fight again, being a MacGregor, he would never have to hack at young, frightened men against whom he held no grudge, in pitched battle. Let the others do that.

Life was wonderful.

* * *

"So then," Alexander said loudly when everyone was assembled in the cave halfway up the mountain, the place where the MacGregors could conceal themselves if in danger, provided they had a little warning of the enemy's approach. In fact, even if they had no warning it was still a good place to retreat to because the entrance, concealed with foliage, was almost invisible, and the cave started with several feet of very narrow passage before turning to the right and opening up into a huge cavern capable of holding the whole clan. Two armed men could defend it against an army if necessary. It had its own spring for water, and the MacGregors stored food here, partly because it was cool and partly in case of siege.

Today it was full of happy people rather than besieged ones though, and in one part of it the men had set up a table, which was covered with a snow-white linen cloth and which would serve as an altar. Fir candles burnt around the cave, giving a good amount of light. With one exception the mood of the people was buoyant. After this meeting to discuss the arrival of the priest, they were all going to head downhill and get drunk. Because of this there was much laughing and chatting, until Alexander spoke, upon which the clamour died down.

"So then," he repeated, "I've called ye here because I was thinking that this would be a good place for the Father to hold Mass, partly because the weather willna signify in here, and partly because no one happening to pass by will see us celebrating a forbidden service. Do ye all agree, or has anyone a better idea?"

"I was thinking in the barn, maybe," Fiona said. "It isna dark in there, so we could save the fir candles for winter. And it's closer to the houses."

Alexander thought for a moment.

"Aye, we could, but we canna have it there in the winter, when the animals will be in, or after harvest, when there's threshing to do," he said.

"And anyone passing, no' that many do, but even so, they might hear the Mass if we have it in the barn," James added.

"We dinna need to have this many fir candles burning for Mass, do we?" Dugald said, looking around. "If we've candles on the altar, we can see the Father and the Eucharist, and he can see to read the gospel and his sermon."

"No, I just wanted to make it a wee bit festive today," Alexander admitted. "For we've much to celebrate. We've a goodly house built, the harvest started, and it's looking to be a bumper crop, so we'll be godly *and* no' starve this year."

The cheer at these words gave a good demonstration of the excellent acoustics of the proposed church.

"I have a thought," Susan said. "No one kens about the cave, do they?"

"No one except the MacGregors, no," Iain agreed.

"So if he's to do services here, Father Gordon will need to ken where it is. And if he'll be spending four days a week out spreading God's word and is arrested, are ye no' feart he might give away the location?"

A gasp of shock greeted this comment.

"A priest wouldna do such a thing," Fiona said, aghast.

Susan looked at her neighbour sceptically.

"In my experience, priests are men. They *might* be the intermediaries between God and us, but they're human beings. If he's caught and tortured, he's as likely as any other man to tell his secrets. Whether he does or no' will depend on his courage, no' his calling."

"Did he seem a courageous man to you, Alexander?" Gregor asked.

"Aye, he did. I think any man doing what he does must be courageous. But I only spoke to him for a few hours, so I canna be sure. It takes more than courage to withstand torture. But I dinna think he'd give away secrets he wasna expected to ken." He glanced around then, saw the number of shocked glances being cast at Susan, and her indifference to them. Seeming indifference to them. "Susan makes a very good point. We've lived here for as long as we have because of the cave. If it's ever discovered, then we'll struggle to find another place as good as this. We've survived as long as we have by being cautious.

"Here's what I'm thinking now. Let the man settle in. We'll have the Mass for the first few weeks in the barn, while we get the measure of him. And then we'll meet again, share opinions, and decide whether it's safe to tell him of the cave or no'. In the meantime we'll no' mention it exists, unless we've an urgent need to use it. So let's move on to other things. Allan's making a table, bed and chairs for the Father. What else have we collected together for him?"

The conversation carried on, people saying what they'd already delivered to the new house, or what they were in the process of making, after which it was decided to let Father Gordon decide whether he wanted to visit each family in turn to get to know them, have a meeting with everyone together, or whether Alexander should just tell him a little about each family, and him get to know them gradually.

Alex, the only one who was *not* of buoyant mood, sat silently near the pile of fir candles, moving to replenish them as they burnt down. He'd volunteered for this job, hoping it would keep his mind off what he was determined to do tonight, when the moment was right.

It wasn't working. Replenishing fir candles was a boring task which left his imagination free to dissect all the possible things that could go wrong. He had to do this right, or he would never be able to look anyone in the face again. If he made a mess of it he would have to leave the clan, wander the world alone, without friend or family, like *The Wanderer* had. The wanderer was a character in a very old poem his da had read to him, telling him that the Anglo-Saxons of long ago seemed to have a lot more in common with the clans than their descendants the English did.

He would faint. Or maybe he would just stand there, frozen. Or he would say something to make things even worse than they already were, and shame his father even more than he already had.

This was not helping. His heart was hammering in his chest, and he felt sick. He realised that it would have been better to sit with everyone else and focus on what they were saying. But here near the wall of the cave the sounds echoed somewhat, and he couldn't make out all the words, especially if more than one person spoke at a time.

"Well, then," Alexander was saying. "I think that's about everything. We'll be expecting him any day this week, so there's no' much more to do than to wait. And there's absolutely nothing more to do the night, except eat and drink, and maybe have a wee dance. Dugald'll play the pipes, and I think we could persuade Alasdair to gie us a wee tune on the fiddle." Everyone laughed at that, for Alasdair loved music and was always ready to play for any occasion, or just for the joy of it. "Let's away down, then," Alexander finished, and everyone prepared to move.

Alex stood, his legs shaking.

"I'd just like to say something to everyone," he called out as loud as he could, his high boyish voice cutting through the adult chatter that had started. Everyone stopped what they were doing and looked at him, curiosity in their eyes. He saw his ma exchange a puzzled look with his da, who shook his head.

He hadn't told anyone of what he'd decided to do, in case he found himself unable to. But now he had to do it, because everyone was looking at him, waiting. His tongue cleaved to the roof of his mouth in terror, and he closed his eyes for a second, taking an enormous breath to calm himself.

"Last week I did a shameful thing," he began shakily. "I shamed my da and I shamed the clan. Ye'll all ken by now that Kenneth threw me in the loch, and I heard that it's said I challenged him to a fight because I'm very brave. I've heard some of ye saying that I nearly killed him, and such things." He paused for a moment and took another deep breath to try to calm himself.

"So I need to tell everyone that Kenneth was right to throw me in, because I wasna brave at all. I behaved like a wee bairn. I was in a bad temper and I shouted at my wee brother and sister for no reason, and then I hit Kenneth wi' my sword because I couldna get my own way. I canna tell ye all how shamed I am by what I did, and I dinna want anyone to think I'm brave, for I'm no'.

"I've said I'm sorry to Duncan and Morag, for I am, and I willna be so nasty again to them. But I wanted to say sorry to Kenneth in front of all of ye, for there's people saying he was cruel to me, or maybe that he's a coward and I was brave for challenging him, and it isna true. Kenneth, I'm awfu' sorry for behaving so to ye, and I dinna blame ye if ye never speak to me again, for it was a shameful thing I did to ye. I'm thinking Duncan will be a better chieftain than I will when we're grown, for he's a better man and he's learning to fight well wi' a sword already, though he's only had it a week."

He stopped then, and looked at the sea of faces staring at him. He couldn't see their expressions, for his eyes were full of tears, and he was shaking so badly from fear that he thought he'd die. They would all laugh at him now. Or maybe they would jeer. Or maybe they would all leave in silence, and he would stay here forever, until he died and turned to bones. Because he could never face them again.

Kenneth stood up then and actually bowed to him, not mockingly, but seriously.

"I accept your apology, Alex," he said formally. "Ye didna behave well that day, but it's over, for ye've behaved very well indeed now. It takes a brave man to admit he was wrong, and in front of his whole clan too. Let's forget it now. I daresay we've all learnt something from it, or should have."

And then everyone made approving sounds, one or two cheering or clapping, before standing up and starting to make their way out of the cave. Some of the children, who had spread the gossip, looked embarrassed.

How Alex managed to stop himself from bursting into a flood of tears from sheer relief, he would never know. But he did, and instead smiled shakily. Kenneth came over and clapped him gently on the shoulder, which made Alex stagger slightly.

"Did your da give you your sword back?" he asked.

Alex shook his head.

"I'm thinking he will, after what ye've just done. If ye're wanting me to teach ye again, I'll be proud to. Let's away down to the dancing, for ye've no reason to feel shamed now."

They made their way to the entrance of the cave, then blinked as they stepped out into the bright sunlight of the late afternoon. The others were making their way across the saucer-shaped hollow outside the cave and down the hill to the settlement.

"Does it hurt a lot?" Alex asked, glancing at the bruise on Kenneth's brawny calf, now turning yellow and green. "I canna believe I did it."

"No, it's no' so bad. I couldna believe ye'd do it either, for ye're no' one for tantrums. But we all do stupid things at times. Dinna fash yerself about it now. It's over," Kenneth said.

Alex smiled again, a genuine smile this time. Suddenly the world looked bright and beautiful again, instead of dark and gloomy as it had for the last week. And he was hungry, really hungry for the first time too. His stomach rumbled.

"Alex," his father called from behind him, and the hunger was instantly replaced by the churning misery and dread that had quenched his appetite for the last days. He stopped and let his father catch up with him, while Kenneth continued down the hill.

"That was very well done, laddie," his da said quietly when he reached him. "I ken what that cost ye, and it was a brave thing ye did." He reached out and hugged his son, and then held him at arm's length, looking down at him. "Ye dinna become a good man, or a chieftain even, by never making a mistake," he said. "Ye become one by learning from your mistakes, no' doing the same thing again, and by acknowledging when ye're in the wrong. I'm thinking ye've done that, aye?"

Alex nodded.

"Well then. I'll give ye your sword back, and ye can start practising wi' Duncan, show him the moves ye've mastered. And be as kind to him as ye'd want others to be to you. I'm proud of ye tonight, laddie."

They walked the rest of the way down the hill, or Alexander walked. Alex walked for a few steps and then skipped the rest of the way, his natural exuberance and joy of life rekindled. His father was proud of him. Kenneth thought he was brave. The clan had cheered his action.

It had been the right thing to do, after all.

"I've no idea how I didna just go and hold him, when he stood up like that," Moira said later, when the rest of the MacGregors were either drunk, dancing or singing, and she wouldn't be overheard. "He was absolutely terrified."

"He was," Alexander said. "By God, that took courage. I'm no' sure I could have done that at his age. For to him it wasna just an apology, but a matter of life and death. Ye could see it in his face."

"Aye. My heart was aching, watching him shaking like that. I've never seen him so white," Moira agreed. "It was a matter of honour to him. In his eyes he'd dishonoured the clan, speaking so to Kenneth. He's acting as though his actions already have the weight of a chieftain's though, and some might think he's too high an opinion of himself. After all, it was really just a bairn throwing a tantrum, no more."

"Are *you* thinking he's too high an opinion of himself?" Alexander asked. His wife was very observant and her opinion was worth listening to.

"No," she answered immediately. "He's seven. All bairns have an inflated sense of themselves and their importance at that age. His outburst wi' Kenneth wasna in character. He did it because he's desperate to do everything well, so he can be a worthy successor to you. I truly think it's just who he is. He's driven, has a need to be as good as he can be in whatever he tries to do. There's nothing wrong in that, as long as he can accept that there'll be things he canna do so well, no matter how he tries, for no man is perfect. No' even you," she finished, grinning up at him.

He leaned across then and kissed her.

"Well, he's learnt that he makes mistakes, and he's learnt to think about them and to apologise, and to mean his apology, for he certainly did," Alexander said once the kiss was over, somewhat breathlessly, for he'd been drinking, the mood of the evening was joyous and his wife looked very beautiful, her red hair flaming in the light from the setting sun.

"He did. I'm thinking he'll maybe no' leap to his own defence quite so quickly next time, but might think a wee bit more first, as Duncan does," Moira said.

Alexander squirmed a little as his thoughts manifested themselves in physical form, as it were.

"Ye seem restless. Are ye wanting to dance?" Moira asked innocently.

He looked at her, saw the sparkle of humour in her eye, and grinned.

"Aye, in a manner o' speaking. No' in public though," he said.

As one, they both looked round the clearing. Morag was sitting on Alpin's knee, explaining something to both him and Flora with expressive hand gestures. Alex and Duncan were with a group of other boys (and Jeannie, of course), playing some sort of engrossing game with small stones and a stick. They looked at each other, then quietly stood, clasped hands, and made their way back to the house, unnoticed by anyone except Kenneth, who, having a break from dancing, was eating a bannock with cheese and drinking a flask of ale. He smiled to himself, deciding to intercept any of the chieftain's brood should they decide to seek their parents out. Alexander and Moira deserved a little time alone, and Kenneth was sure they seldom got it, having as they did one child with boundless energy and another with so very little, who was a constant concern to them.

But the children were happy, Alex enjoying the pure relief of being once more part of the clan, all worry behind him, Duncan being Duncan, and Morag slowly wilting and falling asleep on Alpin's lap. As Alpin seemed quite happy just to sit there with Flora pressed close to his side, Kenneth relaxed, returning to the dancing once he'd eaten, and casting just an occasional glance at the increasingly boisterous game in the corner.

The chieftain and his wife enjoyed a good two precious hours of uninterrupted lovemaking before there came a loud knock on the door, after which Alex could be sleepily heard asking why Kenneth didn't just open it so they could go in, Kenneth replying that it wasn't polite to walk into someone else's house without being invited to.

Alex must have been really tired, for by the time he'd thought to comment that it wasn't someone else's house, it was his, Alexander and Moira had become Ma and Da again. Da opened the door to retrieve his sleeping daughter from Kenneth's arms, him having relieved Alpin of her earlier to allow him to dance with his betrothed. Duncan and Alex stood on either side of Kenneth, swaying with fatigue.

"Thank ye, laddie," he said and Kenneth nodded, then headed home.

Alexander placed his daughter gently in her bed in the room she shared with her parents, watched as his sons clambered sleepily up the ladder to their loft bed, then snuggled back in the box bed with his wife.

Or rather, with his wife and the brand new next member of the family, conceived just an hour before.

CHAPTER SEVEN

Kenneth was in the barn threshing the barley when his mother leaned round the door, her face flushed with excitement.

"There ye are! That's one of ye at least. Father Gordon is nearly here! Wee Simon was set to watch for him the day and just ran in to say he's no more than a couple of miles away."

Kenneth put down the flail he was using and wiped his hand across his forehead. He was sweating freely, for it was a warm day and threshing was hard work if you'd been doing it all morning as he had.

"Is he walking or riding?" Kenneth asked.

"Walking. He's on the path along the lochside. He has a garron wi' him, but it's loaded wi' his possessions."

"I'll away down the loch then and wash, for I canna face a priest covered wi' chaff as I am," he said. "I'll be quick," he added, seeing Barbara's frown.

"Can ye look out for Alpin, too?" she asked. "I canna find him at all. I've been out calling him, but no answer. Everyone's going over to the Father's house to welcome him. Alexander's going on ahead to meet him on the path."

"Aye. He mentioned something about going fishing. He might be out on the water. If so, I'll bring him back wi' me."

Kenneth headed in the direction of the loch. It was a good day for the priest to arrive, he thought, for the weather looked to stay dry, which would give plenty of time for the man to unload his goods, and time to sit and talk a little outside, if he'd a mind to. Kenneth didn't have any knowledge of priests, but he assumed that if you were preaching to people all day and then speaking to God after that, you must have a liking for the talking.

When he arrived at the loch there was no sign of Alpin, but there was a little pile of clothes on a rock and Duncan and Alex were swimming about close to shore, giggling and splashing each other. The guilty looks on their faces as they saw him told him immediately that they'd been sent down to wash, not to play. He grinned at them by way of reassurance, unbuckled his belt and in less than a minute was striding into the water, as naked as they were.

"Dinna fash yerselves," he said. "My ma sent me down to clean myself for the Father too. No faster way to do it than by swimming."

Alex and Duncan laughed, and the next few minutes were spent with the three of them splashing each other and generally being silly, although in fairness they were also getting rid of the sweat and dirt of the morning. Then they went back to shore, where Kenneth, having dressed himself in record time, helped the two boys to put on their clothes and arrange them nicely, pinning the surplus material of their kilts over their left shoulders for them. Then he wrung out his hair, pulled a wooden comb out of his sporran, and deftly ran it through the auburn waves.

"Ye've no' seen Alpin about, have ye?" he asked them then, belatedly remembering he was supposed to find his brother. "He tellt me he was going fishing."

"No," Alex answered. "But I saw the boat when I was swimming out a wee bit. It's up that way, in the birches," he added, pointing north a little.

"You go away hame, then," Kenneth said. "If ye see my ma, tell her I've gone to see if he's there, and I'll be back to welcome Father Gordon in a wee while, with or without Alpin. "Here," he added, tossing the comb to them, "put that through your hair, and your ma'll be proud of ye when ye arrive looking as the chieftain's sons should."

He headed off in the direction of the woodland then, leaving the boys to untangle their hair as best they could. When he got there he could see the boat pulled up on the shore, although unusually for Alpin, who was very tidy by nature, one oar was in the boat but the other was some distance away at the treeline. He went to get it, but as he bent to pick it up he saw the man lying at the foot of a tree a few feet away.

Instantly Kenneth was on full alert, every sense acute. He noticed the blood on one end of the oar, then made his way silently across to the prone man. His face was covered in blood, which was starting to coagulate at the edges. So Alpin, if he *had* been fishing, had presumably hit the man in the face with the oar, breaking his nose and knocking him out.

Kenneth quickly assessed the man. A stranger, clothes ragged and filthy even by Highlander standards. He had an unkempt beard and long dark hair which had seen neither water nor a comb for a long time. A broken man, most likely. He was just about to shout Alpin's name, concerned in case the stranger had managed to wound his brother before he'd been rendered unconscious, when he heard it. Laughter.

He froze again, listening, and when he heard someone speak, assessed where the voices were coming from, then, carrying the oar like a halberd in his left hand, his dirk in his right, he headed in that direction, slowly, stealthily, taking great care not to make any sound at all, not even one fellow Highlanders would hear, until he saw a flash of blue cloth through the trees. Then he crouched down, for he had no idea how many men there were, whether Alpin had attacked the man near the tree or if the broken men had just come upon the boat and fought over it for some reason. If there were just a couple of wastrels, he'd head back to the boat and row it away, take it into shore next to the settlement, where it could not be stolen.

He'd tell Alexander of course, but no need to make anything of it if the men just continued on their way. There was enough for the chieftain to think on today, with the Father about to head into the settlement.

He crept closer, until he could see them properly. There were four of them and they were completely oblivious to him, or to anything in fact except the game they were at, which was a source of much amusement, judging by their laughter. They had their swords out and it seemed they'd caught an animal, maybe a deer, although Kenneth couldn't see it from where he was. It must be a large one, for one of the men stabbed at whatever it was from waist height, and then stepped back as the other slashed sideways and upwards at it.

"See, I tellt ye it was sharp!" the man said laughingly.

And then the thing they were slashing at swung out from behind the trunk of the tree in which it had been suspended, Kenneth saw what it was, and his world turned red as, for the first time in his life, the blind killing rage took him.

He stood, and with a bone-chilling roar that set all the birds to flight, charged full tilt at the men, forgetting everything he'd ever been taught about fighting. In fact he ran so quickly that he was among the group before they'd had time to do any more than register the sound and turn towards it.

He hit the man nearest to him with the oar, snapping it in the process and felling his victim like a stone, before running straight at the second man, smashing his raised sword out of the way with the broken oar then ramming his dirk into the man's chest with such force that it would not pull out.

Letting it go and dropping the piece of oar, he charged at the last two men, who stood next to each other, swords up, their expressions registering their terror at his size and ferocity but preparing to make a fight of it. They did not, however, take account of the fact that their now unarmed attacker had no fear of swords, of being wounded, of death, of anything in fact. Kenneth ran past the first man, leaping sideways to avoid the attempted sword thrust, then seizing his victim's hair pulled him backward as he hit him hard in the lower back with his clenched fist, breaking the man's spine.

"Look, I didna—" the remaining man started to say, holding his left hand up, palm forward in a placatory gesture, his sword shaking in his right hand.

He never knew whether Kenneth heard him or not. The sword was knocked from his hand by a paralysing blow, and the last thing he was aware of was the rapidly approaching silvery bark of the birch tree into which his face was smashed so hard he was rendered instantly unrecognisable, as well as dead. A shower of leaves fell from its branches onto Kenneth and his victim.

Kenneth stopped then, just for a second, and took a great sobbing breath. Then he bent, picked up one of the men's swords from the ground and reaching up hacked through the rope that had been tied around his brother's leg before being thrown over a branch and then hauled up. He caught his brother as he dropped, then laid him gently down on the ground under the tree.

To anyone else it would have been obvious that Alpin was dead. One arm was lying a few feet away, having been severed by the final blow, his torso had been stabbed and slashed multiple times, and his body, along with the ground under the tree, was drenched in blood.

But Kenneth was not thinking rationally. Frantically he held his hand under Alpin's nose and felt at the side of the neck for the pulsing which would tell him that his brother lived. Then with a desperate effort he tried to calm his own ragged breathing, tried to ignore the beating of his own heart which was like a drum banging in his chest, praying that he would hear something, just the faintest beat, that he would feel the lightest touch of air on the hand under the nostrils.

Nothing.

And then the truth hit him, a blow against which he had no defences, the worst pain he would know for the next twenty years. The person he loved more than anyone in the world, the only person who truly understood him, to whom he could tell anything, was gone.

No. He could not be dead. He was young, not even twenty-one, full of life, his wedding only weeks away to a beautiful girl who he loved, and who loved him. His future was glorious, and he would die peacefully of old age, surrounded by his children and his grandchildren as he wished to, and not in pointless battle.

He could not be dead. It wasn't possible. Kenneth shook him gently, begged him to wake up. But he did not wake up. Instead he just stared over Kenneth's shoulder at nothing, until, able to bear that empty gaze no longer, Kenneth gently brushed his hand across Alpin's eyelids, closing them forever.

He picked his brother up and sat down with his back against the tree, cradling him in his arms like a small child. And then something broke in him, something that would never wholly mend, and he clutched Alpin to his chest, rocking back and forth and keening in a way that set the birds to flight again and struck terror into the hearts of the two small boys who had just arrived at the edge of the treeline, having heard the roar of anguish Kenneth had uttered earlier and running to see if they could help.

Kenneth was unaware of them, unaware of the effect he was having on them, of the bodies sprawled around him. If a whole army of enemies had charged through the trees he would not have noticed, or cared. He cared only about his brother, who was still warm, who should just be sleeping, but who could never be woken from this sleep.

Alexander, having set out along the path to meet Father Gordon, had been the closest to the birch copse apart from his sons, and arrived on the scene a couple of minutes after Duncan and Alex. They were still standing like statues, white-faced, not knowing what to do, staring at the carnage, in the midst of which the strongest man in the clan sat weeping and moaning like a distressed child.

Alexander took in the scene with lightning speed.

"Holy Mother of God," he said, crossing himself. Both his sons jumped violently at their father's voice, and he put a hand on their shoulders to calm them, then knelt down and took them in his arms, turning them away from the terrible sight.

"Did ye see what happened?" he asked urgently. "Are there any more men?"

Duncan swallowed then tried to speak, but his voice didn't seem to be working, so he shook his head.

"No," Alex, who seemed to be similarly afflicted, croaked. "We didna see," he added by way of clarification. "I…we heard him, so we came to help." His eyes swam with tears and he swallowed hard, then suddenly bent over and retched, bringing up a stream of bile.

"*Isd,* laddie, it's normal to feel so," Alexander said, knowing this son would feel ashamed of his weak moment.

"He…he was looking for Alpin, to go and meet the Father," Duncan whispered, turning his head to look back over his shoulder. His father's hand moved, keeping his son's gaze away from it. They were too young to witness such a thing.

Christ, *he* was too young to witness such a thing as this. This was not battle, where you expected death. This was…

He didn't know what this was. Yet. First things first.

"Ye must go," he said to them. "Stay together. Hold hands, look after each other. Run and tell your ma to come here now. Wi' Susan, if she's there. No' a word to anyone else at all. Can ye do that?"

They nodded, wide-eyed, pale, clammy with the sweat of

horror, but both of them being brave. He had never loved them as much as he did at that minute.

"My bonny laddies," he murmured. And then he let them go, and they took off running like the wind. He watched until they were out of sight, and then turned his mind back to the situation before him.

So, Kenneth was looking for Alpin, and had found him dead? Dying? Had Alpin or Kenneth or both killed the others? He looked at the tree Kenneth was sitting under, saw the cut rope hanging from it, the severed arm nearby, the blood sprayed across the trunk of the tree.

Thinking fast, he weighed up the priorities. The men were all dead or incapable. Any others would certainly have fled. There was a priest coming. He would pass by in a minute. If Alpin was still alive, he could receive extreme unction. That was the most important thing now.

Alexander walked over to his clansman and knelt on the ground in front of him.

"Kenneth," he said, "Kenneth, man. Does he live?"

A moment passed, during which time the red-haired giant stopped rocking, and lifting his head, gazed blankly at Alexander.

"If he lives, Father Gordon can give him extreme unction, ease his passage to Heaven, Kenneth." He watched as Kenneth struggled to pull himself back to sanity, his breathing laboured, the veins in his neck like ropes. Then his eyes focussed on his chieftain, he opened his mouth as if to speak, then shook his head.

Alexander caught a movement to his side and leapt to his feet, drawing his sword then lowering it again as he saw who it was.

"What happened?" Father Gordon said, dropping the reins of the garron and unstrapping one of the panniers. He reached in and pulled out a bundle.

"I dinna ken," Alexander said. "This is my clansman and his brother. Can ye do the rites for him?"

"Are they both injured?" Father Gordon said, his voice remarkably calm considering the scene before him.

Alexander knelt down in front of Kenneth again.

"Kenneth," he said. "This is Father Gordon. He can help Alpin to...find peace. Are ye injured?"

Kenneth still clutched his brother convulsively to his chest, but his eyes were rational now.

"No," he said. "No' me. But he…" His voice broke then, and he closed his eyes for a moment.

"Father," said Alexander, praying the man was as intelligent as he'd appeared to be when they'd met in Perth, "Kenneth is Alpin's brother. He's no' injured, but ye need to do what must be done to send Alpin to Christ. He's…he was a good man."

Father Gordon looked conflicted. Alexander stood up again and moved over to him.

"I canna perform extreme unction," he whispered to Alexander. "If the man's dead and unshriven, it's too late for that. He'll be in Purgatory, unless his sins are mortal ones. We can pray for him, and I'll say masses, but I canna do last rites."

"Ye must do something, to comfort the living if no' the dead. The man's insane wi' grief. I need to calm him, to get his brother away and make him presentable before his ma and da see him," Alexander said. "He hasna the Latin. Say anything. Alpin was a good man. He'll no' be in Hell, at least."

The priest came to a decision, and nodding, unwrapped the bundle and took out a purple stole which he put round his shoulders, and a small jar of oil. Then he went over to Kenneth and knelt down next to him. Behind him Moira and Susan appeared through the trees, then stopped.

"Kenneth," Father Gordon said, "ye must release your brother so I can anoint him, please. This is the only way ye can help him now. He's gone, ye ken that?"

Kenneth nodded, tears spilling down his cheeks. Bending his head, he kissed his brother's blood-soaked hair and then opened his arms so that Alpin was lying across his knees.

"Thank you," the priest said. He opened the bottle of oil, and dipping his finger in, made the sign of the cross on Alpin's forehead. "*De profundis clamavi ad te, Domine; Domine, exaudi vocem meam. Fiant aures tuæ intendentes in vocem deprecationis meæ,*" he began, reciting the prayer for the dead.

Alexander went over to the two women.

"Dear God Almighty," Moira said softly, crossing herself. "What happened?"

"I'm no' sure yet," Alexander said. "Kenneth's in no state to tell me. But Alpin's dead, and we need to wash him and wrap him before Gregor and Barbara or any o' the bairns…the other bairns see him, for he's awfu' badly cut up. Susan, I asked for ye because I didna ken if the boy was alive. He isna, but Kenneth might be wounded. I dinna care about the others," he said brutally as he saw her take in the scene.

"I left Alex and Duncan wi' Allan and Fiona, for they havena bairns old enough to ask the boys what happened. I tellt them no' to say anything to Morag. Did they see everything?" Moira asked.

"No. I think they only saw what we're seeing, but that's more than I'd want," Alexander said.

The priest finished his prayer, and Alexander turned back.

"Kenneth," he said. "Ye must let the women wash your brother now, and wrap him as best we can, for your ma and da canna see him like this. It's a kindness for them. Will ye let them do that for him?"

"Aye," Kenneth said. "I wouldna…I would want him respectable for them. And Flora. Oh Christ," he said brokenly. He brought his knees up then and bracing his back against the tree, he stood, still holding Alpin in his arms.

"We'll away down the loch and wash him there," Kenneth said, walking away without waiting to see if this idea was approved of. The women followed behind, Moira grasping Alexander's arm as she passed.

"We'll see to this now," she said. "Go and tell the others, for they have to ken."

Alexander nodded, then reached up and undid the brooch at his shoulder, before unbuckling his belt. His rich red and black *féileadh mór,* that he wore only for occasions, fell to the ground, and he bent to pick it up.

"Shroud him in this," he said. "The boy deserves it. I canna grieve him yet, for I must think on the others, but my heart is sore wounded."

Moira nodded, and folding the tartan plaid, went after Kenneth.

Alexander turned back to the wide-eyed priest.

"Ye can see now why ye had to do something to comfort the boy," Alexander said. "In spite of his size he's a gentle soul, has never harmed anyone to this day. But he'd the rage on him, and he wasna thinking right. Had he done anything I couldna control him short of killing him, and I wouldna do that. He's as powerful as he looks."

"Aye, I can see that, if he killed these men," Father Gordon said, looking down at the pulped face of the man whose head had clearly been rammed into a tree with incredible force.

Alexander went round the prostrate bodies, confirming that they were all dead.

"I dinna ken if he did, but I'm thinking so. It doesna signify. They're no' from any clan I ken. I'm thinking they're broken men, and unless some ran away, then Kenneth's avenged his brother, and there's no more to do on that matter. I'll bury the bastards, Father, but I'll no' have ye say a prayer over them, for I'm thinking they dinna deserve it. Alpin wouldna have provoked them."

Father Gordon hesitated a moment, then nodded.

"They're likely already in Hell," he said. "No' much I can do for them there anyway."

The half-dressed chieftain and priest set off for the settlement, preparing themselves for the horrendous task to follow.

"Christ, I'm sorry, Father," Alexander said. "This wasna the welcome we'd hoped to give ye. The man was to be married. I'm thinking he'd have been asking you this week about it."

The priest uttered a most unpriestly word in Gaelic.

"I'd have been much happier to have my first Mass a nuptial one," he admitted, "but at least I can give the poor man a proper requiem Mass. There'll be some comfort in that for ye all, I hope."

Down at the loch, Kenneth tenderly undressed his brother, dropped the bloodstained garments on the ground, and then walked into the water holding him, before gently washing him himself, while the two women stood there, watching with tears in their eyes. They could see by his whole demeanour how much effort it was costing him to function on any level at all.

Once Alpin was clean Kenneth brought him back, and let the women untangle his hair and wrap him in Alexander's plaid. He was soaking wet and shaking like a leaf, but otherwise seemed in control of himself now.

"I gave my comb to Alex and Duncan," Kenneth said, "to make themselves presentable for the Father. But I'll make his hair right later. Wait. His arm," he added incongruously, and started to walk back to the trees.

Susan and Moira watched him, concerned, as he suddenly veered away from the path and bent over something lying on the ground, then stood, lifting what at first they thought was a bundle of clothing. And then it moaned, and instantly Moira was on her feet. She took perhaps three steps before Kenneth rammed the man's head into the nearby tree, as he had his companion's earlier. This time he did not let the man drop, but instead kept hold of his hair, smashing his head against the trunk over and over again, while making a deep primal sound in his throat.

It seemed like hours before he stopped, although it could only have been a minute or so. Kenneth held the mangled remains of the man by his hair as though he was weightless for a moment, and then dropping him on the ground he made his way back into the copse.

Moira returned to Susan, who had spread Alexander's plaid out on the grass, and the two women rolled Alpin's body on to it.

"Alpin's arm," Susan said. Moira looked at her. "He's gone for Alpin's arm. It's missing. We'll have to wait until he comes back. I thought to wrap him completely except for the face, for he's cut so badly but his face is unmarked, now the blood's been washed away." She reached down and ripped at the bottom of her dress.

"Ye canna ruin your dress," Moira said. "It's silk!"

"It's useless here," Susan told her. "I wore it only for the priest, although I didna think that he might no' approve of a scarlet dress. It'll no' stand out against the plaid, though. We need to wrap him well, so Barbara willna want to look at him."

"She'll want to anyway, I'm thinking," Moira said.

"Aye, well, Kenneth can tell Gregor why she mustna, and they can stop her, for she'll no' recover from it if she does."

"She'll no' recover from it anyway. None of them will. And Flora..."

"That's the lassie he was courting?" Susan asked.

"Aye. Alexander tellt me. Alpin was going to ask the Father about marrying them this week. They wanted to keep it quiet until it was settled, but they tellt Alexander as he's chieftain, and he said he'd build a house for them."

Susan breathed out through her teeth.

"This is hard," she said. "It's easier to see them die in battle or after an illness, somehow. This…this is pointless. Ye canna prepare yourself for such a thing."

"Aye, well, it willna be the first time, no' for the MacGregors," Moira said. "I dinna ken why they killt him and I guess we never will, as Kenneth's just finished the only living witness. But it isna a crime to kill MacGregors. Two of my ma's brothers were murdered on their way back from the peat cutting when I was a wee girl – Duncan's age. Whoever killt them took their heads, for at one time the Council in Edinburgh offered a hundred merks to anyone who cut the head off a MacGregor. I dinna ken if they got their reward or no'."

"I didna ken that. I'd no idea ye were a MacGregor before ye married Alexander. I'm sorry, Moira."

"Aye, I was, on my mother's side. My da was a Lowlander, a Hay. We lived by Loch Katrine for a time, but my da hated it there, so we moved to Edinburgh. I met Alexander there when I was seventeen. Anyway, I didna rightly understand what had happened to my uncles. Ma tellt me they'd gone to Heaven, and the clansmen were out hunting for vermin. They were, although no' the furry kind I thought she meant. We never found out which clan did it. Maybe just as well, for there'd have been a terrible bloodshed if they had. For we couldna go to law, no matter what the evidence. We still canna."

"I'm thinking I've forgotten a lot in my years in Edinburgh," Susan said.

"Are ye sorry ye've come back?"

"No. This is my home. Is there still a reward for a head?"

"No. I dinna ken if there was then. But it's no' a crime to kill one of us, no matter the reason. Alex and Duncan need to learn that, all the bairns do. But I wouldna have had them learn it in such a way as they just have. And they canna tell the other bairns, for if Morag learns how he died…she's awfu' fond o' Alpin. He was showing her the weaving. Christ," she finished, looking down at the partially wrapped corpse at her feet.

When Kenneth returned a few minutes later with Alpin's arm, Moira and Susan were both crying. He walked straight past them into the loch and washed the final part of his brother, before coming back to the women, who were wiping their eyes and blowing their noses.

"I'm sorry," he said, looking a little shamefaced. "I canna comfort ye. I care, but I canna, for if I do…I'm feart I'll no' be able to come back this time. And I need to be there for Ma and Da, for they'll take this very badly. I mustna give way now."

He was right. Now was not the time to give way to grief. Now was the time to think of others.

"No," said Susan, holding the plaid so Kenneth could reunite Alpin with his limb, and then securing the material round the corpse as best she could with the red silk strips she'd torn from the bottom of her gown. "Ye can do this, for ye've the courage to match your strength. But when it's too much for ye, ye can come to me if ye want, for I've no bairns, and I live away from the others so they willna ken. Ye must promise me that, laddie, for this is a terrible burden for ye to suffer alone."

Kenneth looked at her for a minute. Then he nodded.

"Did any get away?" Moira asked.

He shook his head.

"No. They had no reason to run before I arrived, and I didna give them time after. I'm thinking Alpin took that one," he said, pointing to the mashed body near the tree. "I finished the rest."

"Ye avenged him, then," she said. "That should be a comfort to ye, in time."

"In time," he repeated, as though that time, whenever it came, would be an unimaginable distance away.

Then he bent, put his arm under his brother's shoulders and knees, and lifting him, turned to walk back to the settlement, the two women following.

* * *

What had started as a joyous day had turned out to be one of the most horrendous days the MacGregors had experienced for many a year.

Alexander had gone back to the waiting MacGregors with Father Gordon, and had gently taken Gregor and Barbara back to their home, where he explained to them what had happened, missing out the more gory details. He would tell Gregor later if he asked, or maybe Kenneth would, but Barbara did not need to know exactly how Alpin had died. He gave them the only comfort he could; that he would receive a true Christian burial, and that his death had been avenged.

Then he had left them together to comfort each other and had gone out to make practical arrangements, to find that Father Gordon had already told the other clan members that Alpin was dead, and was in the process of leading a prayer for his salvation, that God would welcome him into His kingdom. Ordinarily Alexander might have felt discomfited by the priest taking on a duty without asking that was, strictly speaking, the chieftain's task, but on a day that would be filled with horrific tasks, he was grateful to be relieved of one.

Instead he said the burial would take place tomorrow, and in the meantime arranged for people to watch over Alpin's body all night, partly to ensure that no evil spirits could enter the body and partly to make sure that his parents did not unwrap him and see the horrific injuries he'd suffered. Alexander said he would supply all the food and drink needed for the wake.

Normally while watching over a body people would get drunk, tell stories, play games and sometimes even get to dancing, but this death was very different from the norm. Any of the younger members who might have thought to become boisterous later had been silenced by the sight of Kenneth, making no attempt to hide his grief, carrying his brother in his arms as though he was a sleeping child. He walked straight through the congregated clan as though unaware they were there, and crouching at the low doorway, entered his parents' cottage. Moments later a wail of such anguish came from the building that almost all the women and many of the men began to cry.

"Let us kneel, and together say the rosary, to comfort the family and to speed Alpin to the arms of Christ," Father Gordon said, taking out his rosary beads then motioning with his head to Alexander to do what he needed to do. Everyone dropped to their knees instantly, and Alexander, after murmuring in the ear of three of his men, set off back to his house, where he gave instructions for getting rid of the bodies of the murderers.

If anyone apart from Gregor had harboured the slightest notion that Kenneth was too gentle or too cowardly to fight in battle, that notion was banished once it was known just how he had disposed of his brother's fully armed killers, using only his dirk and an oar.

Not that Kenneth ever spoke of what he'd done; but the men who tied stones to the bodies, rowed them up to the north of the loch and then threw them overboard would never forget the condition of the corpses, would not forget how hard it was to pull the dirk from the one man's chest, so deeply was it embedded, that Kenneth had obliterated the faces of two of the men, and had killed all but one without any weapon other than his hands, in spite of the fact that his opponents had wielded drawn swords.

Once home Alexander took his two sons, still dressed in their crisp clean outfits, up to their loft bedroom, where he told them how proud he was of them for answering a clansman's cry, for behaving so courageously. He answered their questions about Alpin and Kenneth with as much honesty as he could, taking their youth and how shocked they clearly were into consideration. He added that Kenneth had avenged his brother's death, which was a good thing, but that they should not ask him any questions about what he'd done, ever, unless he told them they could.

And then he told them that their mother was downstairs explaining to Morag that Alpin had gone to Heaven, but that they must never tell her anything of how he'd died, or what had happened in the birch copse, because Morag had a weak heart and a big shock might stop it beating, which would kill her. And she was very fond of Alpin.

It was the first time he had told his sons so honestly what ailed their sister, and as he looked at their expressions he realised that they were more perceptive than he'd given them credit for, because while they both showed concern, neither of them showed the slightest surprise at this news.

Downstairs Moira was also being surprised, by her daughter. Morag listened quietly as her mother told her that Alpin had gone to Heaven, which was very lovely because Heaven was a wonderful place, but that everyone would be very sad for a while now, because they would miss him.

"So, is he dead?" Morag asked bluntly.

"Er…yes, he is, *mo chridhe*. He died very quickly and is at peace now," she confirmed.

Morag contemplated this in silence for a moment.

"He didna say goodbye to me," she said then. "Did he say goodbye to Flora?"

"No. I'm sure he would have done, but he didna have time. If God calls you to Him, you must go."

"I wish God had tellt him he could come and say goodbye to everyone, because we canna go to Heaven to see him unless we're dead, can we?"

"No, we canna," Moira agreed. "But we can say prayers for him, and we can talk to him too and he might be able to hear us. I'm sure he's sorry he couldna say goodbye, but he kens we'll understand."

Morag nodded.

"Aye. And it'll be nice to have someone waiting in Heaven for me when I go," she said. "I love Alpin. I'm no' feart to go if he's there. He's kind, and he's showing me how to weave. Will he be able to weave in Heaven?"

Moira closed her eyes for a second and pulled herself together.

"I dinna ken. He might be able to."

"He can show me when I go then. Will ye talk to me when I'm in Heaven as well?"

"Ye'll no' be going to Heaven for a good while yet, lassie," Alexander, who was coming down the steps now and had heard the last statement, said.

Morag looked at her father and smiled.

"When I go, I'll wait for ye, for all of ye," she said. "Like Alpin's waiting for me now."

* * *

"Christ," said Alexander when they were finally in bed, Morag snoring gently in her bed on the other side of the room, and the murmurings of the two boys in the loft above them stilled. "If I never live another day like this in my life, I'll be happy."

"It's worse because we were looking forward to it so much," Moira said. "I canna even imagine how Gregor and Barbara must feel. We're having the funeral tomorrow?"

"Aye. Father Gordon said he'll be ready to. He'd have been willing today, but Gregor and Barbara need a wake, some time to say goodbye to the laddie."

"To accept it."

"Aye, although I'm no' sure they'll do that for a while. Gregor insisted on seeing the men who killed his son. I didna think he should, but he insisted, and now I'm thinking it was maybe a good thing," Alexander admitted.

"Why?"

"He kens now that it really happened, and that Alpin was avenged. And he'll no' be thinking that Kenneth hasna got the courage to fight any more. No one will."

"He's gentle because he kens how easily he could hurt people," Moira said. "We all understand that."

"Gregor didna. But he does now."

"We underestimate our bairns," Moira said.

"Aye, we do. I tellt Alex and Duncan why they mustna tell Morag what they saw, and I'm thinking they already ken that her heart's weak and she could go so easily. Until now I believed they just thought she was a wee bit weaker than the other bairns."

"And Morag kens it too," Moira said, her voice faltering a little as she did. "Ye heard her, talking about Alpin and Heaven?"

"The last part, at least."

"She just accepted it, that he was dead," she said. "And I thought it was because I tellt her gently, and that she didna understand it rightly. But the way she looked at me when she said she's no' feart to go, because he'll be there waiting for her…she was relieved. And now I realise that she kens she's dying, and that she's expecting to go soon. And…" Moira stopped and took a deep breath.

"And…" Alexander prompted after a minute.

"When she looked at me then, she was sad, no' for herself, but for us, because she kens we'll be grieving when she's gone. I wouldna have expected a bairn to be so wise. Wiser than her parents, for she accepts it and I canna." And then she did cry, in a desperate but restrained way, because she didn't want to wake her children, and Alexander took her in his arms and held her until her sobbing subsided, tears burning in his own eyes.

"I'm sorry," she mumbled into his chest.

"No, a ghràidh," he murmured, stroking her hair. "I feel the same."

"I canna get it out of my mind that I sent Alex and Duncan down to the loch to clean themselves for the Father coming," she said.

"What's wrong wi' that?"

"It was just the two of them. If Alpin hadna been there, we could have been burying our sons tomorrow instead of theirs."

Alexander tensed.

"What d'ye mean?"

"The men, whoever they were, they were heading south along the path. I'm thinking that when they saw Alpin bringing the boat in, they thought to steal it, maybe. Kenneth tellt me that Alpin hit the man near the boat, which he wouldna have done if they hadna made a threat of some kind. If Alpin hadna been there, had been out in the loch fishing, they'd surely have carried on, and the next thing they'd have seen was Alex and Duncan."

Alexander exhaled sharply through his teeth.

"Two wee bairns couldna have been a threat to them though. And they had nothing to steal. They'd likely have been left alone," he said, more to reassure her than anything, while he ran over the day's events in his mind.

"Dinna patronise me," she replied. "It's no' your way, no' wi' me. They were evil men. No normal men would have done what they did to Alpin, torturing him like that, and laughing. Kenneth tellt me," she added, seeing the question on her husband's face in the light of the single candle still burning.

"He'd killed their friend, though," Alexander said.

"No, he hadna," Moira answered. "Alpin hit him wi' the oar, almost certainly. But they were so intent on stringing him up and torturing him that they didna check their friend to see if he was dead or no'. The man was alive. He recovered consciousness while we were laying Alpin out. Kenneth killed him. No, they were evil. Who's to say what they'd have done to two young laddies?"

"They didna, though. Enough has happened the day. We canna be thinking on worse things that might have happened, but didna," Alexander told her.

"No, that's no' my point," Moira said. "I've been thinking on it all afternoon. We have to tell them."

"Tell them what?"

"The truth. What life's really like. For Highlanders in general, but especially for MacGregors."

"We dinna ken the men knew Alpin was a MacGregor."

"Even so. They're old enough now. Well, they're no', but they have to be, I'm thinking."

Alexander laughed then, a bitter laugh, causing her to look at him in surprise.

"I always thought it would be me persuading you to start making them men, no' the other way," he said. "But you've the right of it. I think it's the teaching them that's made me soft. I'll miss it when Father Gordon becomes their tutor."

She looked at him askance then.

"Aye, well, it was frustrating at times, for I'm no' a tutor, and I was very aware that I was neglecting the other clansfolk. But I enjoyed it too. I love the way bairns think about things, the wonder about matters I take for granted. Their innocence. It's a beautiful thing. I expect all mothers see that more than fathers do, as ye spend more time wi' them when they're wee," he observed.

"That's true. And ye'll maybe understand now why women are so reluctant to have that innocence stripped away, to watch the wonder of life disappear. But I'd rather that than go through what Gregor and Barbara are going through now. If the men had come upon Alex and Duncan instead of Alpin they'd have maybe talked wi' them, and if they'd seemed like decent men in need of help, our boys would have offered it, because they're kind, and until today I've been glad of that. But we must learn from this. We have to start teaching them to be MacGregors instead of bairns. That's more important than the Latin and Greek ye're wanting them to learn, in my view. I ken why ye want that. But if we dinna teach them no' to trust *anyone*, and to ken when to run and when to fight, whatever way's best to protect themselves, then they'll no' get to an age where they can debate wi' the Elector about our name or whatever it is ye're wanting them to do."

Whatever Alexander was about to reply to that was prevented by the subjects of the conversation appearing round the side of the box bed.

"What is it?" Moira asked. "Can ye no' sleep?"

Both of them looked embarrassed, uncertain.

"Did ye have a bad dream?" Alexander asked then, "about today?"

Duncan nodded.

"We both did," Alex said. "And now we're feart…we canna go back to sleep."

They looked at their father a little apprehensively, clearly having thought their parents would be asleep, hoping to take comfort from just being in the same room as them for a time. They had never looked younger than they did at that moment, clad only in their little shirts, hair loose and tumbling over their thin shoulders, eyes huge and fearful.

"Ye've the right of it," Alexander whispered to his wife. "But no' the night."

She nodded.

"It's no' something to be ashamed of," he said to them. "Ye saw terrible things today. We all have nightmares about such things."

"Even you?" Alex asked.

"Aye, even me. Are ye wanting to sleep wi' us tonight?"

They had never slept with their parents, that they could remember. Even Alex, who remembered everything, could not remember that. In the same room, yes, but never in the same bed. It had always been discouraged, even on the coldest winter nights.

"We've all seen terrible things today," Moira added, seeing the desperate need for comfort on their faces warring with the knowledge that their parents' bed was forbidden territory. "I'm thinking that we're all in need of comfort tonight."

"We are. Come on then," Alexander agreed then pulled back the covers, and their two sons climbed in between them, relaxing now they knew that their parents needed comforting as much as they did.

Moira and Alexander had said it merely to reassure them, but in fact, once they were all settled, they did get a great deal of comfort from their sons. It was wonderful to know they were alive, strong and healthy, to feel their small warm bodies curled against them trustingly, and then their deep regular breathing as, reassured by the presence of their parents, who would protect them from anything, even nightmares, Alex and Duncan slipped gently into sleep.

Tomorrow they would start learning to be MacGregors. Tonight let them be just children, innocent and perfect as God made them.

By unspoken accord Moira and Alexander left the candle burning, and although they were very tired, for a long time they stayed awake, silently watching their two infinitely precious sons as they slept, skin petal-soft and unmarked by lines or scars, long lashes resting on cheeks that were rosy and childishly plump, noses still snub, hair still baby-soft, inhaling the unique and glorious scent of sleeping child.

In the end it was not until the candle guttered that they finally closed their eyes, soothed by the presence of their children into a restful, dreamless sleep, from which they all woke, if not healed then at least ready to face the difficult days ahead, grateful that they had each other, two of them at least aware that things might so easily have been very different.

CHAPTER EIGHT

August, 1723

Alpin was buried on Inchcailloch, a beautiful peaceful island on the loch. Some of his ancestors were already there, and one day, hopefully many years from now, his mother, father and brother would join him. Often MacGregor funerals, particularly those of old people or warriors who'd died heroically in battle, were noisy drunken affairs, and on one memorable occasion the mourners had been so drunk that whilst trying to row the deceased the short distance to the island they'd managed to capsize the boat, giving the unfortunate MacGregor an impromptu watery burial.

There was none of this jollity around Alpin's death, however. Not because of the priest's sobering presence, but because of Alpin's age and the manner of his death. After Mass had been said and Alpin had been laid to rest, the subdued clan had repaired to their homes, while Gregor, Barbara, Kenneth and Flora had stayed on the island, wanting to be alone with their loved one for a time.

Alexander had walked Susan back to her house, wanting to thank her for calming Kenneth on the previous day and for helping to prepare Alpin's body for burial.

"No need to thank me," Susan replied to him. "I've done that task many times, because as good a doctor as Rob was, he couldna save all of his cases. He'd often take me wi' him to help him, and that would include reassuring the relatives, calming them, or consoling them if their loved one couldna be saved. Everyone reacts differently to death. Ye can see it now, wi' Alpin's family. Barbara seems to be taking it the worst, but the opposite's true.

She's taking it badly because she's already accepted Alpin's dead and she's grieving. Gregor seems to be doing well, but that's because he's pretending it hasna happened, and Kenneth's blaming himself for his brother's death. It's the men who will need help in my opinion, in time. Is that what ye were wanting to ask me? How I thought they were dealing wi' it?"

Alexander laughed, although there was no humour in it.

"No," he said. "I've seen enough death to ken how strangely the bereaved can react to it. But it's good to hear your view, for I wouldna have thought that Kenneth was blaming himself. How could he be? Alpin was already dead when he arrived, and he killed all the men involved. He's nothing to reproach himself for. I ken he's a kindly laddie though, and I'm thinking he's just shocked by what happened. We all are. No, that wasna my question, although ye're right in that I wanted to ask ye something," he finished.

"What is it then?"

"I wanted to ask how ye're settling here now. I've spent so much time teaching the boys in the last months that I havena been doing my duties as chieftain rightly."

"Aye, well, that'll change now, wi' the Father here," Susan pointed out.

"I hope so. And he'll teach all the bairns, although he's a wee bit reluctant to take on the girls."

Susan made a very Scottish scornful sound in the back of her throat, then intercepted the shocked look this earned her.

"He's a man, no more than that," she said. "Aye, I ken he's God's intermediary, but he's still a man. He'll make some good choices, as he did anointing Alpin yesterday. And he'll make some bad choices, I'm sure. I ken ye're disposed to have a good opinion of him because he's a man of God, but dinna let that blind ye to his faults. And dinna let him use his priesthood to try to persuade ye against something ye're set on."

"I dinna think he'll do that," Alexander said.

"I hope not. I dinna ken the man yet, but I've seen many so-called men of God in my years in Edinburgh; Catholic, Episcopal and Presbyterian, and for some of them the priesthood isna about faith, but power. Father Gordon *may* be a good man, but I'm *sure* that you are. Dinna let him use your faith as a weapon against you. Is he taking the girls on?"

"Aye, he is," Alexander said. "I persuaded him of the right of it, wi' the help of Quintilian and Locke."

Susan smiled.

"Ye clearly dinna need my advice then," she said.

"I'm no' sure he'll agree wi' me when he meets wee Jeannie. I assume ye ken the lassie?"

"The pretty one, wi' all the curly black hair?"

"Aye. Pert wee thing she is, no' afraid of anyone. Very endearing. I'm thinking she'll confirm all his fears about women," Alexander said, laughing.

"I'm thinking Alex'll challenge him too," Susan pointed out. "He's a mind of his own."

"That he has. This is a wonderful opportunity for him to get a good education. I hope he appreciates that. What?" he added, on seeing her sceptical look.

"Ye're forgetting I lived here when ye were Alex's age. I remember ye well, all the more because I didna see ye grow to be the man ye are now. Ye'd no more have wanted to spend endless days in a room learning Latin and geometry than he does. He's very like you were at that age."

Alexander ran his fingers through his hair.

"Aye, well, maybe ye've the right of it, but *now* I ken what a blessing an education is. My da would have done the same for me, had he had the chance."

"Did he teach ye to read and write?" Susan asked.

"No. He wasna one for the book-learning. My ma taught me the reading and writing, and I learnt the Latin when I was ten, but only for a year, so I didna get past the basics. And ye're right, I hated it. But Alex is quicker than I am. Ye heard him gie the tale of the fight when Alpin was wounded. He remembered *everything*. He's a fearsome memory. If he puts himself to it, he'll learn fast. I'm hoping the Father can inspire him."

"Or put the fear of God in him?" Susan said.

"Aye, well, as long as he learns, although I've tellt the Father no' to beat him without telling me first. I'd rather he enjoyed his lessons, but ye're right about that too. He's a mind of his own. I'm sure the Father will have no problem. As long as Alex isna disrespectful though. I'll tan his hide if he is. Is that why ye felt he might reveal the location of the cave? Because ye see him as a man first, no' a priest?" Alexander added, changing the subject.

"Aye, maybe. I've seen a lot, living in the town. But then so have you, living here, and being a MacGregor."

"I have. But it doesna go amiss to be reminded of things sometimes. It's the first time we've had another man of authority living wi' us. As long as we both remember our roles here, all will be well."

"And if he doesna?" Susan asked.

"Then I'll take your advice. As I did about the cave. He might think women shouldna be educated, but my da didna think that, and nor do I. And nor will my sons, if I've anything to say about it."

They had reached her door now.

"I'm glad ye decided to come back, Susan," he said. "It's a better place wi' you in it."

To her embarrassment her eyes filled with tears on hearing this. She brushed them away impatiently.

"Pay no heed," she said. "It's been an emotional day. But thank ye. That's good to hear, for I've every intention to live out my life here."

By way of answer he squeezed her shoulder, then turned and walked away down the track. Susan watched him go, remembering him when he was a child, and how much like his son he'd been then, both in looks and personality. And then she felt the tears prick her eyes again, as she wondered for the thousandth time what a child of her own would have looked like, followed by the desolation that she would never know. She turned back to the door, lifted the latch, and went in.

* * *

September, 1723

Once the harvest was in and the livestock and much of the clan had come down from the summer shielings, Alexander started to plan the cattle raid and sale in earnest. He intended to take a number of the clan's cattle along, because it had been a good year weather-wise, so the beasts were healthy and most of the calves had survived. There would not be enough fodder for them all to survive the winter though, so it made sense to sell them and buy alternative provisions, keeping only enough cattle to live off if necessary and to breed from next year.

In addition to his own cows he hoped to acquire considerably more along the way, a risky but potentially profitable venture, and one which, although considered a crime by the authorities, was thought to be a traditional duty by Highlanders. That didn't mean to say they would not fight to the death to prevent their cows being stolen though. The trick was to steal them without being seen, and be far away by the time the theft was discovered. And that involved planning.

Although Alexander missed spending time with his children, in other ways it was a relief to have the task of teaching them delegated to someone else, someone who was far more educated than he was. He would have really struggled to teach his sons Latin, or French for that matter, both of which Father Gordon had already begun them on, to Alex's horror and Duncan's resignation.

The rest of the children were learning basic reading and mathematics, and so far they were all behaving well. Or at least Alexander *assumed* they were behaving well. He had heard no rumours to the contrary, and Father Gordon had made no complaints about them. Alexander knew he probably should have asked how they were coming along, but he'd spent the last month busily clearing the backlog of neglected tasks. Also he thought it wise to give Father Gordon and his pupils time to adjust to each other, so apart from asking his children what they'd learnt that day, he had kept his distance.

There would be more time available in the winter, when the weather stopped most of the outdoor activities. It was a time for repairing tools, coming together, telling stories. Surviving. And in order to survive winter the clan had to spend the other three seasons ensuring there would be enough food for everyone and that homes were in good repair.

After the cattle raid he'd pay more attention to their learning. But for now he had work to do, and because he intended to take both his sons with him, he needed to make the trip as safe as possible. It was true that they needed to learn the brutal facts of life as a MacGregor, but not by being traumatised again so soon after the last time.

Alex's and Duncan's nightmares had stopped now, and they seemed to be putting the event behind them. Morag talked of Alpin occasionally, but in a matter-of-fact way, as though he'd gone to live in a pleasant town a short way away and she expected to visit him soon. Children were so resilient.

Unlike Gregor and Barbara, who had drawn in on themselves, spending a lot more time at home and not interacting a great deal with the rest of the clan. They still did all their tasks, Barbara collecting the honey and dyeing the wool and flax for Gregor to weave, while Flora, having declared that she would never marry now, had asked Gregor to teach her the weaving, saying that if she didn't have something to occupy both her hands and her mind she would go mad.

Kenneth still did everything he'd done before Alpin's death, all the tasks that could use an enormously tall strong man, of which there were many. It had been agreed that someone would always keep an eye on the bairns when they were swimming or playing, just in case, and as Kenneth, who loved children, had often watched out for them anyway, he continued to do it whenever he wasn't needed elsewhere. To those who were not very observant, he seemed to be coping well with his brother's death. He politely refused all sympathy or offers of comfort, and those who *were* observant took heart in the fact that he was still taking part in everything, and that he was young and therefore resilient.

So it was that whilst Alexander, Dugald and Allan were up at the top of the loch strategically planning the raid, Kenneth was sitting on a rock at the water's edge, watching the children enjoying the last few days of the water being warm enough to be enjoyable rather than merely endurable. Every so often he'd look along the rough track which wound along the edge of the lochside, watching for any signs of intruders, and then would return to gazing morosely across the water at the blue and purple heather-clad mountains on the other side.

He was so absorbed in his thoughts that he didn't notice Jeannie had come out of the water, dressed and walked across to him until she plopped down on the rock next to him. Realising that half a dozen broken men could be heading towards them with him none the wiser, he berated himself, and determined to be more attentive in future.

"Are ye cold, lassie?" he asked the small figure sitting next to him, who was currently pulling her fingers through her wet hair to untangle it a little.

"No," she said. "I wanted to sit with ye. Ye look lonely. Ye're missing him dreadful, are ye no'?"

He glanced down at her, both surprised and touched by her perceptiveness. Jeannie was not renowned for her sensitivity.

"Aye," he said shortly, hoping she would now let it drop. He had not talked about Alpin since that dreadful day six weeks ago, and had no wish to do so now, least of all with a small child.

"It makes me sad that ye're so unhappy," she said. "Ye shouldna be. Alpin's in Heaven now, and that's a wonderful place, wi' flowers all the time, and the water's always warm because it's sunny every day. He's happy there. Morag tellt me so. She talks wi' him, she said. I thought if I tellt ye he was happy, maybe you'd be, too."

Kenneth smiled. It was lovely to be a child. Life was so simple. If only it stayed that way.

"That's kind of ye, Jeannie."

"Will ye be happy now, then?" she asked.

He glanced along the track, then down at her again. She had abandoned the hopeless task of her hair now, and was looking up at him, her grey eyes serious.

"I'll try, but it's no' so easy as that," he said. Young as she was, he would not lie to her.

She nodded, seemingly satisfied.

"Alpin wouldna want ye to be unhappy," she commented. "He loved ye. I love ye too. Ye're the kindest man in the clan, and when I'm grown I'm going to marry ye."

She said this last so matter-of-factly that he didn't register the meaning of the words straight away. When he did he swallowed back his laugh, for she was still looking at him, still deadly serious.

"That's sweet, lassie, but ye canna marry me. Ye're still a bairn and I'm a man grown," he said.

"I'll no' always be a bairn though. I'm eight now, my ma tells me, and I'll be grown soon."

"Ye'll no' be grown for a wee while yet," Kenneth said, almost hearing the omitted end of her mother's despairing sentence; *and it's time ye learned to knit, sew, bake....* "and by the time ye are, I'll be an old man."

"No ye willna," she replied. "I dinna care anyway, for ye're kind, and when I marry ye, ye'll protect me, and never let any bad men hurt me, ever."

Kenneth closed his eyes for a moment.

"Ye dinna need to marry me for that, Jeannie," he said.

"No, but I want to. Dinna be sad," she said.

They sat in silence for a minute, watching the other children playing in the loch, then she wriggled her bottom to get more comfortable on the rock and reaching across grasped his thumb, curling her slender fingers round it.

He looked down at it, marvelling at how tiny her hand was, how fragile, and how comforted he was by that innocent, trusting gesture. They sat like that for a while longer, staring out across the sun-sparkled waters of the loch, each wrapped in their own thoughts.

* * *

"I dinna think Kenneth has forgiven me for the bad thing I did to him," Alex announced later to his mother as she was making dinner. She stopped stirring the broth for a minute and looked across at him sitting at the table opposite his brother, both with an open book in front of them. Duncan was frowning, his mouth moving as he read the words silently to himself.

"Are ye no' supposed to be learning a poem or some such thing, for the Father tomorrow?" Moira asked.

"I've learnt it," Alex replied.

"As quickly as that? Ye've only been at it a few minutes."

"He's only to read it the once," Duncan said. "I canna do that. I'll need to be learning it the whole night. Twenty lines!"

"I've got thirty lines, because I'm older," Alex added.

"I'm sure Kenneth has forgiven ye, Alex," Moira said, deciding to reassure her son now before Alexander came home. Later she would help Duncan to learn. "He said as much when ye apologised, and he isna a man to hold a grudge."

"Hmmph," said Alex doubtfully. Duncan looked up.

"He's still grieving, Alex," he said. "He doesna speak to anyone."

"He was speaking wi' Jeannie!" Alex countered. "I wouldna have asked him otherwise."

"What happened?" Moira asked.

"Kenneth was talking wi' Jeannie, and he laughed, too. So I thought he wasna sad any more, and I asked him if he'd help me learn a sword move I'm no' sure of. And he said no' the now, and I asked him when then, because I ken he can teach me for he's a fearsome fighter and I want to be too, and then he tellt me to go away."

Moira wiped her hand across her face, contemplating then rejecting telling her son just why Kenneth might not have taken this sentence well, knowing it would cause a barrage of questions if she did. She had a lot to do and Alexander would be home momentarily, hungry.

"Alex, Duncan's the right of it. He's still grieving. I dinna ken what Jeannie said to make him laugh, but ye dinna stop being sad just in a moment. No' when ye're an adult. He's forgiven ye, I'm sure of it," she said. "Give him time. More time," she added, realising that six weeks was an eternity to a child.

"Ye reminded him of Alpin when ye tellt him he was a fearsome fighter," Duncan put in, more blunt than his mother. "For that's the only time he's been a fearsome fighter until now."

Alex stared at his brother in horror.

"Ye mean I might have *made* him sad again?" he said, aghast.

"No," Moira jumped in. "Duncan's right, but ye didna make him sad. He's already sad. When ye're sad ye dinna want to do things sometimes, for the sadness makes ye tired. He's forgiven ye. Just be kind, but give him the space he needs to grieve. I'm sure your da'll teach ye the sword move. Now come and help me, and let Duncan learn the poem."

Alex closed the book and did as he was asked, but his face showed that he was still concerned he might have upset Kenneth.

"Are ye taking Kenneth wi' ye on the raid?" Moira asked her husband that evening. Alex and Duncan were in the loft space, lying on the floor with the book between them, Alex helping Duncan to learn the last part of the lines from *The Odyssey*. Morag was already in bed asleep.

"I wasna going to. I could certainly use him, for he's good wi' cattle and a fearsome fighter," Alexander said, unconsciously echoing his son. "No' that I'm intending to fight, but there's always the possibility. I didna want to take him from Gregor and Barbara, for we'll be gone a few weeks and they need him, I'm thinking."

"They've got each other, and Flora now, too," Moira pointed out. "But Kenneth's struggling. He's doing everything he's asked to, but there's no life in him. Maybe if he's taken away from where it happened for a wee while, he'll be able to see more clearly."

Alexander thought on this for a minute, then nodded.

"Aye. And even if he doesna, he'll be too busy to have time for brooding. Good idea. I'll take him then."

* * *

The man and two boys, all three of them dressed in dark green and mustard yellow plaids, which blended beautifully with the autumn grass, lay on their stomachs at the edge of the ridge, looking down on the scene below.

"Now, the drovers from Oban will come from that direction," said Alexander, pointing at a thin ribbon of track which snaked across the hills in the distance. "As ye see, some of them are here already, but a lot more will arrive in the next days."

"More?" said Alex. "But there are thousands now! I've never seen so many cattle in my life."

There *were* a lot of cattle, grazing all across the hills at the head of Loch Lomond. There were a lot of men too, sitting in groups on the hillsides, some around small fires, for at this time of year it grew chilly when the sun went behind the clouds or night fell.

"This is no' so many. There'll be many more than that at Crieff," Alexander said. "Which is one reason ye must do as I tell ye, or as Kenneth tells ye, for when I'm busy, he'll be your chieftain, so to speak."

"As I did when we went to Inversnaid," Alex said.

"Aye. Ye were very well behaved, which is one reason ye're here. And Duncan, ye're old enough to be sensible now too. When I came here two weeks ago it was to look at the land, look for the best place for us to camp for the time we're here. It's the same if ye're planning a battle. If ye can, ye go and assess the land first, see where the best position would be for your army."

"So this is like a battle?" Duncan asked.

"Aye, in a manner of speaking. Ye have to plan it as though it is, try to plan for anything that might happen. Except the aim of *this* battle is no' to fight at all. We sneak in and out without being noticed. But we *will* have to act a wee bit like the spies I tellt ye about last time, Alex. When we've taken the cattle down, we'll wander about, be friendly, talk to people, for we need to find things out."

"What things?" Alex asked.

"Ye'll see, for I've decided to take both of ye with me. I can tell people it's your first drive and I'm showing ye everything, so they'll no' be suspicious that I'm wandering about looking at their stock. But when we're doing that, ye must remember that we're Campbells, no' MacGregors. We'll no' be MacGregors again now till we see home."

"But I'm proud of being a MacGregor!" Alex protested. "Why do we have to be Campbells?"

Alexander sighed.

"I havena the time to tell ye all the reasons now," he said. "But I want ye to think for yourself about why we shouldna be MacGregors for now. I'll ask ye later. We'll be here for a couple of days, I'm thinking. There'll be plenty of time for the talking. We're Campbells, from near Glen Orchy," he repeated firmly. "Unless we come across other men wi' bog myrtle in their bonnets, and then I'll ask them where they're from first."

"In case they really are from Glen Orchy?" Alex asked.

"Aye. Well done," his father replied.

"Who will we be then, if they are?" Duncan asked.

"We'll be Campbells from another glen, a long way from Glen Orchy," Alexander said. "Let's away and join the others."

They shuffled backwards on their stomachs until they were below the ridge, before standing and walking briskly back down to the rest of the clansmen.

"There's a perfect wee spot partway up the hills to the east," Alexander told them. "If we camp just below the forest we'll be at the edge of the meeting, and we can drive the cattle straight into the trees then keep west until we're out of danger, before heading down towards Crieff."

The other men nodded, and then, pausing only to tuck a sprig of bog myrtle, the Clan Campbell plant, into their bonnets, they set off to the spot Alexander had mentioned. Once there Kenneth and James set up camp and got a small fire going, while the cattle were allowed to graze in the vicinity under the scrutiny of the rest of the clansmen.

"Now," said Alexander once they were all sitting round the fire, eating the bannocks and cheese their women had provided for them, "I'm wanting us all to stay sober, for if a chance arises we need to be able to take it directly. My thought is to watch, see who's closely marking their cattle, and who's closely marking the whisky, for they're the ones we're more likely to take from without being noticed. If we can, I'd like to take about twenty or thirty from several drovers, rather than a whole herd from just one."

"That'll make them a lot harder to drive though," Dugald commented.

"Aye, I ken that. But my thinking is that if we take a whole herd, then the drovers *will* come after us, and I'm no' wanting bloodshed unless we've no alternative. But if we take a few from each, then they'll no' want to be leaving the rest of their cattle to chase us, and as they're here because they're going south to Dunfermline or Falkirk they'll probably just carry on, for they'll likely lose more money chasing us than continuing down the loch."

That made sense. If it could be done.

"Why will it make them harder to drive?" Alex asked.

"Cows have a homing instinct, and they're more comfortable when they ken each other, just as we humans are," Dugald said. "So if they're suddenly wi' a lot of strange cows they'll be harder to keep together at first, for they're wanting to go back to their friends."

"But if we're no' likely to be followed, then we willna need to drive them so far before we can stop to let them graze," said Allan.

"We'll relax tonight, let the cattle rest, take it in turns to watch them, and try to sleep as much as we can," Alexander said. "For if we take the cattle tomorrow we'll be driving them through the night, so we'll no' be able to sleep then," he added for his sons' benefit, for the other men already knew, having participated in many raids before.

Once it grew dark the men who were not on watch wrapped

themselves in their plaids and settled down on the hillside to sleep. Duncan and Alex curled up together, partly to share body heat, partly because they normally slept together in the box bed at home, and partly because, too excited to sleep, they could whisper together without being overheard and told to be quiet.

"D'ye think we canna be MacGregors because we're proscribed?" Duncan whispered, once they were snugly covered in tartan wool. "That means we canna use our name, does it no'?"

"Aye. Until King James comes back and says we can," Alex murmured. "Maybe if we do we'll have our heads cut off, like the MacGregors in that story James tellt last year."

"What story?" Duncan asked.

"He tellt us that Campbell of Argyll sent for a MacGregor chieftain, Glenstrae, under a truce, to talk wi' him, and said he'd let him go free if they couldna agree. So Glenstrae went, and when he got there, Argyll tellt him that the king had ordered him to make him prisoner and take him to England, for that was where the king lived. He said he kent that Glenstrae would be pardoned, for his offence was a small one, and if he came without a fight he'd be treated well on the way to England, no' put in chains. Argyll made an oath on that, so Glenstrae trusted him because oaths are sacred. D'ye remember the tale now? Ye were there."

"No," Duncan said. "Maybe I was asleep, if it was late. I canna stay awake like you can."

"Aye, maybe. So then, Glenstrae and the guards went down to England, all friendly together, and none o' the MacGregors came to rescue him, which they would have done had he been a prisoner. As soon as they got to Berwick, just over the border, Argyll had Glenstrae put in chains and brought back to Edinburgh, where he had him hung, wi' eleven other MacGregors. It shows that ye canna trust a Campbell, when even the chief will do such a thing."

"Why did he take him to England then? Why no' just take him to Edinburgh directly?" Duncan asked.

"If he had everyone would have said that he'd broken his oath, because he tellt Glenstrae he'd take him to England and treat him well on the way there, but he didna say he'd actually take him to the king. That was what Glenstrae believed, because the king wanted to see him and the king lived in England. So Argyll kept the word of his oath," Alex said.

"That's awfu' crafty. And evil," Duncan said, shocked. "Is it a true story?"

"Aye. James said it was, and Da agreed. He said that when people promise ye things, ye must always listen carefully to the words they say, so as not to end up like Glenstrae."

"I *really* dinna want to be a Campbell now," Duncan said bitterly. "I ken we canna be MacGregors, but could we no' be someone else? Like MacDonalds or Camerons?"

"Or Gordons, like Father Gordon," Alex said. "We can ask Da. The morrow."

"Right, laddies, are ye ready for our wee stroll?" Alexander said the next morning, when they'd finished their breakfast. "We'll be looking for men who are still asleep, or who look like they had a wee drop too much to drink last night."

"Like you did after Ma tellt ye she thinks we'll be having a wee sister or brother in the spring?" Alex asked. "Men wi' red eyes, who're trying no' to move their heads?"

"An' awfu' bad tempered, too," Duncan added. "Should we say good morning to them and if they say '*falbh romhaibh!*' then we ken they've been drinking?"

Those who overheard this laughed. Alexander flushed.

"Aye, men like that. Dinna let yer ma hear ye say such words though," he replied.

They set off down the slope, casually. Kenneth and Dugald, who were watching their cattle, waved as they passed.

"Da," Duncan ventured, "Instead of being Campbells today could we no' be someone wi' honour, like Camerons, or MacDonalds maybe?"

"Or Gordons," Alex added.

"Have ye thought of the reasons why we canna be MacGregors?" Alexander answered their question with another one.

"We think it's because we're proscribed, so we canna use our name," Alex said.

"Aye, that's one reason. A very important one. We can never be MacGregors when we're wi' other clans. But there's another reason today. And it's the same reason we're Campbells."

Alexander waited until it became clear they weren't going to answer before they reached other drovers. He stopped.

"What are we here to do?" he asked instead.

"Sell cattle," Duncan replied.

"No. We'll be doing that in Crieff. Before that."

"Reive cattle," Alex said.

"Aye. So if we go all around the men telling them we're Camerons or MacDonalds, and then we make off wi' their cattle in the night, what will they think of the Camerons and MacDonalds, who are our allies? Usually," he added. Clan allegiances could be very fluid at times.

Alexander looked at his sons. He loved that moment when light dawned on their faces, as it did on Alex's now.

"So the men we take the cattle from will think the Campbells took them," he said.

"Aye. Either that or they'll think we were lying about being Campbells. It doesna signify, as long as they dinna ken we're MacGregors, and they dinna blame a friendly clan."

Both boys grinned, suddenly happy to be Campbells.

"Ye're awfu' clever, Da," Duncan said as they carried on.

"Ye're both clever too. I'm just older, and I've got more experience in things, because I've done more. That's why ye're both here, to learn like I did. It's experience of life that makes ye men."

"Did ye go wi' your da on a cattle raid?" Alex asked.

"Aye. And I watched everything he did, and then I asked questions. But no' till later when we were back wi' our own and no one else to listen. Ye can do the same. But now's the time to watch, for I need your eyes and ears as well as my own. That way ye'll be learning *and* helping me."

They continued walking down the hillside, but in a circuitous way that ensured they passed by a number of groups of men huddled round fires, either eating or, in one or two cases, still wrapped in their plaids. Alexander smiled and wished them good morning, then stopped to exchange a casual word or two, a joke, comments on the route to Falkirk. He introduced his sons, said it was their first cattle fair and he wanted to show them about, for one day they'd be doing this themselves. He was very warm, friendly, but the boys noted that he asked those he talked with where they'd come from early in the conversation, but didn't give his name unless they asked specifically.

After a while Alex and Duncan started saying hello as well, and would answer innocent questions about how old they were or what they thought of the cattle, and if they were enjoying the walk to Falkirk. They'd been briefed not to say anything about where they lived, how long they'd been walking already, or anything that might give them away. No one said *falbh romhaibh* to them, but even so it was clear who'd been indulging. A good number of men had red eyes and pale faces, and a few were drinking already, early as it was. Alex made a note of where they were sitting, as he thought his da might find that useful.

"Ye're doing very well, I'm proud of ye," Alexander said softly after a good while of this. "I'm thinking to head down to the loch now. We can wash there, and I'm wanting to see what yon woman's selling from the cart." He pointed, and the boys looked down to the lochside, where a crowd of men were gathered round a covered cart on which a woman stood, doing a brisk trade in something.

"Are ye going to buy something from her, Da?" Duncan asked.

Alexander glanced round. No one was in earshot.

"No. We've enough food for the journey. I'll be buying a good deal in Crieff, hopefully, which is why we've got the garrons wi' us. And for you to ride when we take the cattle, for we'll be moving too fast for ye to walk."

"Are we taking them tonight then?" Alex said.

"Aye, I'm thinking so. If the cart's selling what I think, then definitely."

The cart was selling what he thought. Alexander sent his sons down to the loch to wash their hands and faces, during which time he engaged in a goodly amount of very coarse ribaldry with the other customers and did in fact buy from the cart, after which he collected his sons and headed back to the fire, where he took the stopper from one of the flasks he'd bought, sniffed and then tasted the contents.

"*Iochd!*" he said, screwing up his face and then passing the flask to Alasdair, who was sitting to his right. "If they're drinking that, we'll be able to leave the hills bare without anyone being any the wiser."

Alasdair took a sip and then spat it out.

"And they were paying good money for this rot?" he said incredulously.

"Aye. Well, some of them were. If ye look behind me down the hill, I'll tell ye who I'm thinking we can take from." They all looked casually over their chieftain's head as he pointed out a few landmarks to identify the men and the cattle they were thinking to take.

"Can ye see to the left there's a mighty grey stone, and the men near it, they're all wearing the same colour of *fèileadh mòr,* a kind o' purple and brown?"

"Aye. Elderberry and beet," Kenneth commented, then reddened. "My ma taught me. I help her find the plants for dyeing sometimes."

"I spoke to one o' them at the whisky wagon," Alexander said. "They're Campbells, from Loch Awe. He tellt me that I didna need to worry about my men drinking, for no one in their right mind would dare to steal from a Campbell. I agreed wi' him. He bought a few flasks, but offered me a bottle of claret, as I'm a Campbell too."

"Did ye take it?" Dugald asked.

"Aye, of course I did. It would have been rude no' to. I thought we could have a wee drink tomorrow to celebrate getting his cattle safely through the trees."

Everyone laughed.

"I'm assuming we're taking more from that herd than the others, then," Alasdair said.

"They've got more, so aye, if we can. In a few hours ye can all head down to the loch to wash or swim, and make sure ye pass them by, but no' close enough to talk wi' em. If they're drinking what they've bought, then we'll be riding through the night tonight. And I think they will be, as they're feeling so safe here. Let's get our heads down and sleep a while, if we can."

Alex and Duncan, unable to sleep for excitement, talked in whispers and watched as the sun stole across the sky with agonising slowness. And then finally it was directly above them and the men who weren't watching the cattle woke up and headed down to the loch in small groups, to wash.

"And to spy," Alex said to his da, who was cutting up a few rabbits that they'd caught. "I thought that spies had to *live* wi' the enemy. I dinna think I could do that. But this is fun!"

"Aye, well, we're no' really spies. We're doing the same sort of thing, pretending to be who we're no', but it isna the same as being a proper spy," Alexander said, cracking the bones to release the marrow and dropping them in the pot of steaming water over the fire. "Now this afternoon we'll all head off wi' our cattle and take them into the trees and onward for a while. Then we'll come back, but ye'll stay wi' Alasdair and Kenneth and wait for us to come. Remember ye must obey Kenneth, whatever he tells ye to do."

"But are we no' going to help ye take the cattle?" Alex cried.

"No' this time. Ye've done well, and learnt a lot. Ye'll learn a lot more in the next weeks too. In fact ye'll learn more tonight, for Kenneth and Alasdair will tell ye why we're doing things as we are. But tonight it's work for men wi' experience. One wrong move could have us all killed. Ye're no' ready for that yet."

At four, Alex would have objected, argued, sulked. At nearly eight, he accepted it. He wasn't happy, but he accepted it. At six Duncan accepted it too, but Duncan always would have, because he didn't need to be at the centre of everything as Alex did.

* * *

Alex, Duncan, Alasdair and Kenneth sat on the hillside watching their cattle grazing and the sun setting in a blaze of crimson and gold. They had made good time, and were now several miles away from the meeting place. The rest of the men had gone with them for the first few miles, and then had headed back to the meeting. If all went well they'd rejoin their clansmen at some point during the night.

"Ye should try to get some sleep," Alasdair said to the boys. "For the others'll likely no' arrive until near dawn, but when they do we'll be moving."

"So the others'll get no sleep at all?" Duncan asked.

"No. None of us will, for we're watching the cattle, and waiting. But there's no reason why you canna sleep."

"It doesna seem right," Alex said.

"Och away wi' ye," Alasdair replied. "I still remember when I was a bairn, curling up in my *féileadh mór* and listening to the men talking round the fire, or whistling the owl calls across the hills to say all was well."

"Nothing changes," Kenneth said. "I remember that too, just twelve years ago when I came wi' my da for the first time."

"It's nearer to fifty that I was here my first time," Alasdair said. "Good memories. Ye've the best of it to come, laddies, when ye do the reiving wi' the men. I'm too old now, canna move fast enough, but ye've got it all to come."

"Do you want to be reiving too, Kenneth?" Alex asked.

"No, I've had enough of…I'm happy to be here, minding the cows, and you two. Hopefully no one'll come upon us here."

Alasdair reached across and squeezed Kenneth's shoulder. Duncan, seeing this, shook his head quickly to Alex, who had his mouth open to ask what Kenneth had had enough of. Alex closed his mouth again. Everyone looked at the sunset, which was really worth watching, for it was glorious.

"Ye've your sword wi' ye, have ye no'?" Kenneth said suddenly.

"Aye, we both have," Alex replied.

"Well then, we've a wee while o' the gloaming yet. Shall I teach ye that move ye canna master? Duncan too, if ye want."

Alex beamed.

"So ye're no' still angry wi' me then?" he said, leaping up immediately and drawing his sword. Duncan ran to the garron to fetch his small sword, which he'd put in the baggage as he was sick of it banging against his leg as he walked. Unlike Alex, Duncan had realistically assessed that he was more likely to be an impediment to any fighting, and had opted for comfort before the unlikely heroic defence of his clan that Alex dreamed of.

"No. I tellt ye I'd accepted your apology, and I meant it," Kenneth said. "I just wasna in the mind for teaching ye until now. Come on then." He stood and drew his own formidable sword, then thought again, and sheathing it, took out his dirk and knelt down in an attempt to be at the same height as they were.

A pleasant hour passed during which Alex and Duncan both learned, or partially learned a new move, with Alasdair observing and passing helpful comments. At one point he stood and demonstrated the move with Kenneth, first slowly and then at close to real speed.

"It's awfu' fast," Alex said with dismay. "I dinna think I'll ever be that fast."

"Ye will," Alasdair said. "We've all been your age. The secret is to learn it over and over, until ye dinna have to think of it. Then when you're in a battle and your life depends on it, ye'll do it automatically."

"Ye think faster too," Kenneth said, who had on that awful day. "So it seems as though everyone else is moving slowly, but they're no'. And ye dinna look around ye, like you did just now, Alex, to see where the noise was coming from over the hill. If ye did that in a real fight ye'd be dead."

"Aye, but in a real fight, when your life's at stake, ye'll focus only on the important things," Alasdair added.

"The person who's trying to kill ye," Alex said.

"Aye, but sometimes ye might have two people trying to kill ye, so ye need to focus on both."

"Like you did on…sorry," Alex trailed off, flushing scarlet.

"Aye, like I did," Kenneth said. "But I'm no' wanting to talk about that, ever."

There was a finality in his tone that put a stop to all conversation for a minute.

"It's getting awfu' dark now," Alasdair commented. "We dinna want to hurt each other accidentally because we canna see."

The males all sheathed their weapons, and sat down.

"What if ye're fighting at night?" Alex asked.

"Most battles finish before nightfall," Alasdair, who had seen many in his time, said. "If ye're fighting at night it's usually a surprise ambush of some sort, and that's a wee bit different. But if ye learn all the moves until they're as natural to ye as eating, then ye'll be fine. Lie down now, and try to sleep."

"D'ye think Da'll be needing to fight tonight?" Duncan asked as both boys lay down obediently.

"No. I doubt it. Your da's the wisest chieftain I've seen. He'll have thought everything through."

"Thinking's more important than the actual fighting, or can be," Kenneth added. "Go to sleep now. We'll wake ye when they come."

They rolled up in their plaids, both convinced that they wouldn't get a wink of sleep, and woke up when the noise of a large number of cattle roused them. It felt as though they'd only slept a few minutes, and yet the moon had passed across the sky and dawn was not far away.

* * *

They drove the cows through the dawn until the early mist rose and the sun was high, while Allan, who was the fastest runner in the clan, lagged a few miles behind. If there were signs of anyone following, he would run forward and warn the MacGregors.

Alexander didn't call a halt until late afternoon, by which time not only the cows but the men were all exhausted. It was hard work to drive unfamiliar cattle, and even harder when they were tired and hungry and kept trying to stop and graze along the way. The benefit of this was that when they finally *did* stop, the cattle showed no inclination to wander off, which meant that the bulk of the men could get their heads down for some sleep, while a few, Alexander included, stayed awake to watch. Alex and Duncan, being the only ones who'd slept during the night, watched with their father, sitting leaning against a rock which protected them from the rising wind.

"How many did ye take, Da?" Alex asked once they were settled.

"I'm no' exactly sure at the minute, for I havena had time to count them all, and because we took from different herds, we walked a wee bit apart. But we took fifty from the Campbells who thought they were safe," Alexander answered. "I'll count them tomorrow when we mark them."

"But what if they're already marked?" Duncan asked.

"Oh, they are. Some are marked on the horn, some have part of their hair clipped – they're the best to steal, for when their hair grows back it's like they havena been marked at all, and some mark like we do, wi' Archangel Tar. We'll stop tomorrow in a woodland about five miles from here and mark them all wi' our mark then. Ye can help us do it."

"But when we sell them, will the buyers no' see both marks?" Alex asked.

"Aye, except for the ones we can mark over the top o' the existing one. But it doesna signify. None of the men we took the cattle from are going to Crieff, so I'll tell the buyers that I bought them at the meeting. When ye buy cattle you put your own mark over the one that's there, so no one'll be any the wiser for it. If the price is good the buyer'll no' be inclined to ask questions anyway. It's the way of things, laddie. They call us thieves and bandits in England, or even in the Lowlands, but I'll tell ye, we've done the Campbells and the others a good turn, for they've lost a few cows they can afford to lose, but they've learnt no' to get drunk, for if they'd been sober we'd no' have been able to walk away wi' their cattle.

"The true thieves are the men who go to poor farmers who only have a few cows, and give them bills of exchange then take the beasts away, promising to sell them and return wi' the money. Then they never go back. That's a cruel thing to do, for it can leave a family to starve."

"Why do the farmers no' take the cows to market themselves, as we do?" Alex asked.

"No' everyone belongs to a clan. Many farmers canna afford to be away from their farms for weeks. It isna worth it for the money they'd make. And then there's a skill to droving, which ye'll learn, for this is how we get money for food if the harvest fails, or to buy things we canna make ourselves. Some of what we earn from this raid will be put aside for your education, I'm thinking," Alexander finished.

"I didna ken ye were paying Father Gordon for teaching us," Alex said.

"No more am I. No' in money. I'm feeding him and giving him protection and shelter. No, I'm thinking for when ye go to university, Alex."

"University?" Alex repeated, shocked.

"Father Gordon went to university," Duncan said. "He tellt us about it. It was in France, he said."

"Aye, he'll have gone to learn to be a priest," Alexander commented.

"But I dinna want to be a priest!" Alex cried in horror.

"Ye go to university for a lot of reasons, no' just if ye want to be a man of God," Alexander said. "Father says ye're doing well at your lessons and ye've a quick mind. I'm thinking ye could go. No' for a good while yet, mind."

"Did you go to university, Da?" Alex asked.

"No. Times were different when I was a boy."

"But ye became chieftain anyway. And Kenneth said ye're a wonderful chieftain."

"Did he now? Well, that's kind of him."

"I think ye're a wonderful chieftain too, Da," Duncan agreed.

Alexander rubbed his hair affectionately.

"Am I no' going to be chieftain one day?" Alex asked quietly.

"Aye, I'm hoping so. Ye're growing out of your foolishness now a wee bit. If ye carry on as well as ye are, I'm thinking ye'll be a fine chieftain. And Duncan, ye'll be a good right-hand man, for ye've qualities that Alex doesna have, and ye do well together."

"I dinna need to go to university to be a chieftain, if you didna!" Alex protested.

"I tellt ye, times were different when I was a boy," Alexander said.

"How?"

Alexander ran his fingers through his hair. He'd been driving cattle all day, constantly tense, and was now tired. The last thing he wanted to do was have a difficult discussion with his eldest son. He contemplated ending it, but had known for some time that he would have to broach the subject at some point, as Alex was growing increasingly restless and unhappy in his lessons, seeing no reason to learn most of the things he was being forced to spend hours on each day. Father Gordon had spoken to him about it only a few days ago, telling him that the boy was industrious when he saw a reason for what he was learning, but careless and distracted when he didn't.

"I dinna want to whip the boy to make him learn, for ye tellt me ye're against it," the priest had said to Alexander. "And I'm no' sure it'd have the effect I want, for he's awfu' stubborn."

Alexander had known then that he would have to explain to his son why a chieftain living in the Highlands might need to learn Latin. And French. And oratory. He had put it off, hoping to wait until his son was old enough to truly comprehend his father's reasoning.

On the other hand, apart from watching over hungry cows who were unlikely to do anything but munch vegetation for the next hours, they were less likely to be interrupted now than when they were at home. He thought for a minute.

"Ye'll remember no doubt when ye were three and wanted to come wi' us to fight for King James," Alexander began. Alex nodded his head. "Well then, that was over four years ago, and James has shown no sign of wanting to make another attempt to take his crown back. To tell the truth the attempt in '19 was a waste o' time, badly organised and we didna have a chance of winning. I'm no' alone in thinking that James has given up."

"Ye mean he doesna want to be king any more?" Alex said incredulously.

"Oh, I'm sure he'd love to be king, if Georgie said he was sick of living in London and offered the crown to him, aye. But Georgie isna going to do that, and James doesna seem to want it enough to fight for it any more. And every year that passes, the Elector and his kin are accepted more by the people. Are ye understanding me?"

"Aye, I think so," Alex said. "But I canna understand why James doesna want to fight. If you were king and someone stole it from you, ye'd fight to get it back, would ye no'?"

"Aye, I would, and so did James's da," Alexander said. He hadn't fought as he should have done, in Alexander's view, and had finally given up, just as it seemed his son was doing, but he was not about to get into that with Alex now.

"So would I!" Alex cried.

"I would too," Duncan added firmly, surprising and heartening his father. He thought of his younger son as a peacemaker, not a warrior. But it was possible to be both.

"I'm glad to hear that. But James is no' like you two."

"But he has a son now, has he no'?"

"Aye, he has. Charles."

"Will he no' fight, as we would?" Duncan asked.

This then was the bones of it.

"Maybe he will," Alexander said. "But he's just a wee bairn now, and he canna fight until he's a man grown. By that time most of the people who remember the Stuarts as kings will be dead, or very old, and willna care about who's the rightful king any more. People dinna like change, and they'll no' fight for Charles if they dinna see a good reason to. I'm thinking that the Stuarts'll no' be kings of Scotland again."

Silence fell for a moment while his sons absorbed this terrible idea, broken only by the sound of the wind through the grass, men snoring, and cows chewing the cud. There was a scent of rain in the air but no shelter to hand, so Alexander stayed where he was.

"But…why does that mean I need to go to university, if you didna?" Alex asked finally.

He really was growing up. A couple of years ago he'd have forgotten the original point of the conversation by now.

"Because when I was a boy we thought we could get the proscription on the clan lifted by fighting for the Stuarts, fighting so well that they felt they owed us that for our loyalty. There are other clan leaders who have influence wi' those in power, whether Stuart or Hanover."

"Like the Campbells," Duncan said.

"Aye, but no' just the Campbells. Many o' the clan chiefs. Gordons, Frasers, Mackenzies, MacDonalds, Camerons, and others too. Now we count a clan's strength by its fighting men, in the main. But to have a lot of fighting men ye have to have land for them, where they can rear families, grow crops. All the clans I just tellt ye about have lands, and those lands were given to them at one point by kings. They might have stolen other clans' lands, too, but they still have the right to *some* land of their own. And they still have the right to go to law, for what it's worth. Now, if ye're friendly wi' the king and his ministers and he likes ye, and then another clan steals your land, what do ye think the king's likely to do?"

"Help ye get your land back?" Alex suggested uncertainly.

"Aye. But even if he likes ye it's going to cost him money to get your land back for ye, and kings dinna spend money unless there's something in it for them, so ye need to be able to persuade him to do it. Which is why ye need to learn oratory. The same if ye're trying to persuade him to lift the proscription on the MacGregors. And ye need to learn Latin, for it's the language of educated men all over Europe. The chiefs of the powerful clans all have the Latin. And the French too, especially if you're a supporter o' the Stuarts, for the French king is their ally. They'll no' pay heed to anyone who hasna a good education, who canna think and speak as they do."

Alex looked into the distance for a minute, trying to take this in, to make sense of it.

"So ye mean that ye think Alex will need to go to university to make the Elector lift the proscription?" Duncan asked. "Because he canna do it by fighting?"

"Aye, that's it exactly. Well done, laddie."

"I hate the Elector. I dinna want to meet him, ever!" Alex said.

"Ye might need to though, if the Stuarts give up all claim to the throne. And if they dinna, then ye might still need the Latin and French and the oratory, to help Charles by talking to King Louis, by being a man of influence." Alexander stopped, seeing that his son was overwhelmed by this prospect of a future he could not imagine. "Ye've the intelligence for it, Alex, and ye've the ability to be chieftain, Duncan, while Alex is away talking wi' other clan leaders and kings. I'm mighty proud of the two of ye, although I dinna tell ye that as often as I should."

"Can I no' just live by the loch, as you do?" Alex asked in a small voice. "I want to fight for the clan, or for the Stuarts, but I dinna want to go away, to talk wi' kings and suchlike. I dinna think I can do that."

"Maybe ye can live a life like that," Alexander said. "And ye're learning to fight and to grow the crops, to reive the cattle, and in a few days to sell them. Soon ye'll need to learn how to persuade the clan to do as ye want when ye're older. Aye, they'll do as I tell them anyway, for I'm the chieftain, and it'll be the same wi' you, or wi' Duncan when the time comes, but they'll do it wi' a good mind and heart if they agree wi' it. And the oratory can help ye wi' that too. I learnt that, and it's been a help to me. But I'm wanting the both of ye to have a good education, for it's a powerful weapon in its own way. More powerful than swords and muskets. If ye ken how to use that weapon as well as the sword, that gives ye more power to defend your clan and your way of life. And that's what a chieftain does."

"And that's what the other chiefs do?" Alex said softly. "The powerful chiefs?"

"Aye, it is."

"And they've been to the university too?"

"They have, most of them anyway," said Alexander, who had no idea who had and who had not actually been to university. But if it would help his son reconcile himself to the possibility of a university education, it would be a white lie. They were all educated, that he did know.

"I'll do it, then, if it helps the clan," Alex said sadly.

"I will too," said Duncan, "for it'll help Alex too. And I dinna mind the sitting, as he does."

Alexander grinned and impulsively wrapped his arms round

his two sons, crushing them to him. It was the way of parents. They always wanted their children to do better than they had, if possible. But it was increasingly likely that in order to even maintain their fragile foothold on the lands his sons would need skills he'd never even imagined when he was a child.

The fort at Inversnaid was established, and barracks had also been constructed at Kilwhimen, Bernera and Ruthven. At the moment the roads between them were mere muddy tracks, but it would surely not be long before the Hanoverians built proper roads to link them, along which artillery could be moved. Which would allow them to penetrate the Highlands.

One of the strengths of the clans had always been that the Highlands of Scotland were impenetrable to all but those who had been born and reared in them, who knew every inch of their hostile territory and how to traverse it, who could survive the inhospitable climate without shelter if necessary and could do it on rations that would leave any other man weak with hunger. The Highlanders were renowned for their almost superhuman abilities to not only survive, but thrive in such conditions. The redcoats feared them for that, and with good reason.

But if you drove roads through the mountains and bogs and mapped the lands, then the clan territories would be more accessible and the influence of the English would creep in as it had in the Lowlands, softening the people into believing luxuries were necessities, and that freedom was a price worth paying for such things.

Change was coming, and if that change was not a successful Stuart invasion and a breaking of the Union between England and Scotland, then his sons would need every weapon available to survive, and to adapt and thrive in the new world.

It did not bear thinking about. But Alexander *had* to think about it. And so did his children. He had hoped not to have to broach the subject with them until they were older, but better now than have them fail to take the importance of their education seriously, as Alex at least was clearly doing.

"Dinna think any more on it for now, though," he said. "Ye'll be learning a lot the next days, useful learning that's no' from books. I'll wake Alasdair and Dugald, then we can lie down together and sleep awhile."

CHAPTER NINE

Once the men were sure that they had got clean away with the cattle and that no one was following them, they relaxed noticeably. It was true that there was still a lot of work to do, not least keeping a constant eye on their acquisitions, night and day, to make sure none roamed, and that no one decided to do as they had and steal them.

For their part, Alex and Duncan were having a wonderful time. The food was somewhat meagre, it rained often, and one morning they woke up with a coating of frost on their plaids, faces and hair. But being Highlanders, cold, hunger and hard work were the norm, so such trivial matters didn't inconvenience them at all, and the days were full of new and interesting learning experiences, none of which featured Latin, numbers or grammar.

"Now," said James, who was walking through the stolen cattle armed with a brush and a pot of pungent-smelling brown liquid, "ye said your da tellt ye about marking the cattle, aye?"

"Aye, he did, said we should put our mark over the top of the existing one, if we can," Alex said.

"Good. So we can do that wi' all the cows who are branded, marked already or have their hair cut," James explained. "The ones wi' the marks on their horns we canna change, so we just add our mark to the cow. We put a solid triangle, wi' a wavy line under it."

"Why do we do that? Why no' have a G for Gregor?" Alex asked.

"I dinna ken why we have the wavy line," James answered. "But the solid triangle is sure to cover up any mark underneath it. I'm no' sure who decided it had to be a triangle instead of another shape, but that's why we dinna use a letter, for letters have holes in and cover nothing. And we wouldna want a G, for we're no' MacGregors when we're dealing. Watch, for ye'll be doing this today."

They watched intently as he deftly marked the cow nearest to them.

"Now we're lucky wi' that one, for she's a placid wee thing, but they're no' all that way, and if any are particularly troublesome I'll have to lay them down, as ye do if ye're shoeing them. The quicker ye can mark them the better, for it's hard to hold them down."

"Shoeing them?" Duncan said. "I didna ken ye shoe cattle."

"We dinna, in truth, no need, for we dinna walk on roads here in the Highlands. If ye take them across country, ye shouldna have a problem. But I've driven down to the south a time or two, and if they're walking on roads they often have to be shod or they'll go lame. Then ye have to tie the legs, but we dinna do that for the marking."

After a while the boys felt confident, so James handed them the pot and brush and watched them for a while.

"Good," he said then. "Now while ye do that I'll look out for any injuries, for the Archangel tar there is good for those too. If ye wipe it over the wound it keeps the flies off and stops it going bad. And if ye see any cows limping, tell me."

They continued working their way through the herd.

"Kenneth was talking about the fighting, on the night ye were reiving," Alex said conversationally, "and he said ye have to focus on who's attacking ye but also be aware of what's going on around ye. I'm thinking that this is a wee bit like that. Ye have to focus on the marking, that ye do it right, but also be aware that ye dinna get kicked, and what the other cattle are doing."

"Aye, well, it becomes as natural as breathing in time," James replied. "If ye're a Highlander, ye have to always have your wits about ye, for ye never ken when there's danger coming for ye, whether it's the weather, animals or an enemy. Ye need to ken all about animal behaviour and their calls too. That can save your life." Seeing the boys' mutually puzzled expressions, he paused.

"Say we were all sitting by the fire tonight and we heard the screaming and barking sound of foxes mating. What would ye think?"

"We willna, for foxes dinna mate in September," Alex said immediately.

"Ye're right. What else would ye think?"

"That it might be someone trying to reive our cattle?" Duncan added. "Alasdair said when he was a bairn the men used to make owl calls in the night to say all was well."

"Now ye're thinking!" James said approvingly. "Or an enemy giving a signal to others to attack us. Now if ye didna ken when foxes mate, ye'd no' be ready when they attacked you or the livestock. So it's no' just watching and listening; ye need to ken what doesna look or sound right. And then ye need to ken how to deal wi' it. Ye canna learn that from a book, which is why your da brought ye along."

"This is a lot more fun than book learning," Alex said wistfully.

"I dinna ken about the book things," James said, "but it seems to me that if ye ken both the things, then ye could be at home anywhere."

"I dinna want to be at home anywhere else but here," Duncan said.

"Nor do I," Alex agreed, carefully marking another cow while James held its horns to stop it moving away.

"There's no better place to be than wi' your own clan," James agreed. "But if ye have the opportunity, then it's good to learn the skills ye might need for other places. So ye have to be alert all the time, especially when ye're travelling alone or wi' strangers, or in battle. When ye're wi' yer clan ye can relax a wee bit, for ye take it in turns to watch and listen. But we willna get drunk until we're safely home."

"Like the Campbells did," Alex said.

"Aye, exactly like that. They thought everyone was afeart of them because the Campbells are a mighty clan. They forgot that they were still only a few men, and their clan isna mighty if it's five days travel away, and if they dinna ken who ye are or where ye come from."

"Which is why we didna tell anyone we're MacGregors," Duncan said.

"Aye, one reason. Now, that cow's limping, so I'm thinking to look at her and put a wee bit of leather round her foot to protect her hoof. So ye can learn another new thing."

This was fantastic. Alex and Duncan were in their element; learning how to drove and care for cattle by day, having sword or wrestling lessons in the early evening from Kenneth or Alexander, with other men passing helpful or friendly comments, and then sitting round the fire when it was dark, listening to a tale about past battles or magical doings.

Tonight's tale was about a cattle reiving that had taken place a long time ago.

"So, tonight," began Alexander, when everyone was sitting comfortably around the fire, apart from the few men out watching the cattle, "I thought I'd tell ye about how the MacGregors came to be proscribed in the first place. It's fitting to do it here, for it was the stealing of livestock over a hundred years ago that began the whole thing. I ken some of ye have heard it already."

"Aye, but it doesna get worse wi' repetition," Alasdair said. Others agreed, and settled down. It was a pleasant evening; that is to say it was not raining, and the fierce winds of earlier in the day had died down to a cool breeze, which fanned the fire nicely.

"As ye all ken, we havena had lands of our own from the crown since the Bruce's time when our ancestor chose the wrong man to support, so we've had to live off our wits ever since, and ye canna do that without stealing from your neighbours to survive occasionally. We got by though, for we were bonny fighters, and because a good number of clans had sympathy for us. Still do, in fact.

"Anyway, the MacGregors of Glengyle had had a few wee disagreements wi' the Colquhouns, but one night when two MacGregor pedlars of Dunan were benighted in Colquhoun country, they asked for hospitality and were refused by Luss, the chief of Colquhoun."

"But I thought ye *had* to give shelter and food, even to your enemy, in such cases," Kenneth, who also hadn't heard the story, said.

"Aye, ye do. And in return your enemy willna harm a hair of your head, nor you theirs, which is why the Glencoe killing was such a mighty thing. But even so, Luss tellt the men to go away, which is a poor way to behave. The pedlars, being stranded out on the moor for the night, decided that they were right to take what had been unjustly refused, so they lit a fire in a wee ruined shieling and killed a sheep to eat. In the morning they went on their way. They may have got home wi' no one the wiser, but the sheep they'd eaten was the only one wi' a black body and a white tail, so the Colquhoun shepherds noticed as soon as it was day that it was missing, and the MacGregors were chased down, caught and hung by the Colquhouns."

"That's no' right!" cried Alex. "They didna have a choice, if the chief refused them hospitality."

"Aye, well, that's what the MacGregors thought too. They were a wee bit fashed, so they had a few stramashes wi' the Colquhouns, after which Luss went to Edinburgh to the king to complain about us, and the king gave him permission to have the clan carry arms so they could defend themselves against us."

"There was an Act of Parliament against carrying arms then," Alasdair added. "For the Highlanders were always a thorn in the king's side, as they obeyed their chiefs first rather than the monarch, and James didna like it."

"That's right," agreed Alexander. "Luss thought the MacGregors would be afeart that the Colquhouns could now carry weapons, and would run away. D'ye think that's what they did?"

"No!" cried Alex and Duncan together. Several of the men smiled.

"Ye have it exactly. Instead they took a band of men, headed by a Duncan MacGregor," he tipped his head towards Duncan, who grinned, "and they raided the Colquhouns in the December, taking sheep and cattle, and killing two men. So Luss, seeing that the MacGregors were no' intimidated, and because he kent well what manner of man the king was, went back to Edinburgh, and he took wi' him eleven shirts all covered wi' blood, and eleven women, and when they saw the king the women wailed in grief and distress and showed His Majesty the bloody shirts of their men."

"But ye said there were only two killed!" Kenneth pointed out.

"Aye, I did. I didna say that Luss was an honest man, though. So the king, who was a man affected deeply by such dramatic shows, as Luss well knew, was incensed against the MacGregors and he gave Luss a commission allowing him to take vengeance on us, wi' the blessing of the king himself. What do ye think happened then?" Alexander asked his sons.

"Is this King James's da, who ye fought for when I was three?" Alex asked.

"Not his da, no, but his great-grandfather," Alexander said.

"So why are we fighting to put him on the throne again, if his ancestor did such a thing to us?" Alex asked.

"Aye, well, it wasna the king's fault, *a leannain,*" Alexander said. "Kings canna ken what everyone in the country's doing, so they have to rely on their advisers. A clever adviser can make a king do as he wants, which is what Luss did."

"So that's why I'm needing to learn Latin and French? And oratory?" Alex said. "So I can make the king do as I want?"

"Aye. Maybe. It's an example," Alexander said.

"So if the MacGregor had kent the king, he could have gone there first and tellt him that the Colquhouns had broken the law of hospitality, and then the king would have been on our side?" Duncan asked.

"Maybe. But he'd have had to explain the law of hospitality and why it's so sacred, for ye're no' likely to freeze to death if ye're in a town for the night as ye are in the mountains. The king wasna a Highlander, but likely he'd have understood."

"If the king liked bloody shirts, maybe the MacGregor should have taken the clothes of the hung pedlars, or their heads, along wi' their wives and bairns if they had any," Alex said. "That's what I'd do."

"Good. Aye, such an action might have changed the whole fortune of our clan."

"It's that important?" Duncan asked.

"Listen to what happened next and then ye can decide," Alexander said. "So then Luss came back to Lennox wi' his commission, and he raised all his men and armed them all, as the king said he could. He had about eight hundred, three hundred horse and five hundred foot. After that he set off, intending to go to Glengyle and wipe out the MacGregors entirely. But—"

Alexander stopped abruptly as a buzzard's call echoed across the glen. Every man leapt to his feet, his hand on his sword, and turned in the direction of the call.

"Wait," said Alexander. "Allan, ye're the fastest. Go to Dugald, quietly, see what's amiss. If ye see anything before ye get there, ye make the male tawny owl hoot, twice, and we'll all come. Female if it's no' a problem."

Allan shot off into the darkness silently, and Alexander turned to his sons.

"Now," he began, "ye must go across—"

He never finished what he'd been about to say, for at that moment the tawny owl hooted twice and at the same time the sound of men running towards them could be heard. Every man picked up his targe, drew his weapons and readied himself.

Alexander grabbed Alex and Duncan by an arm and pushed them towards a nearby copse of trees. "Run, hide," he said urgently, then drawing his sword he turned away from them to face the enemy.

"*Cruachan!*" he yelled as the band of men became visible, remembering even at this moment that they were Campbells, not MacGregors, and using the Campbell war cry. Then he charged, along with the others, headlong at the enemy.

Duncan and Alex did as they were told initially, but on reaching a large rock before the trees Alex crouched down behind it, Duncan skidding in next to him a second later.

"I'm thinking Da wanted us to hide further away than this," he whispered to his older brother, who was peeping over the top of the rock, his dirk clutched in his fist.

Alex, intent on the battle and trembling with excitement, hardly heard Duncan.

"There are more of them than us," he whispered. "Have ye got your dirk, in case?"

Duncan glanced at the trees once, then sighed. It was clear Alex was going no further, and Duncan would not abandon him.

"Aye. But our swords are in the pack," he pointed out.

"Our dirks are sharper," Alex muttered.

"Alex, ye canna fight," Duncan said.

"I ken that. But if anyone finds us, then we must," he said, crouching down for a moment.

"Should we no' try for the trees?" Duncan suggested. "There are more places to hide there."

"Da said hide. He didna say 'go to the trees'," Alex replied. This was technically true, but in any case it was not the time for an argument. Duncan gave in, squatting down behind the rock and listening to the sounds of men grunting and the sharp clash of metal on metal, or duller sound of metal on the wood and leather of a targe. Alex stood again to peep over it.

"I can see part of it by the moonlight," he murmured, "but there's a lot of shadows and I canna see who's winning. I think Kenneth just killt a man," he added, identifying him by his height and the fact that the man attacking him had just been thrown into the fire and was making no attempt to get out of it.

Duncan suddenly gripped his arm and dragged him down to the ground, muttering "*Isd!*" as he did. Then he pointed straight ahead, to where a small group of shadows, bent low, was scurrying across the heather, clearly intending to take the MacGregors unawares from behind.

The two boys exchanged a glance, and then Alex opened his mouth and the call of a male tawny owl came from behind the rock, twice in quick succession. Duncan had dropped flat to the ground, shuffling out from behind the boulder so he could see without being seen, for he was too small to see over it as Alex could.

"They've heard ye," he whispered. "Some of them have turned this way."

Then Alex kicked him urgently, and Duncan turned his head to see one of the men heading straight for them, no doubt alerted by Alex's call.

"Ye wee shite," the man cried as Alex stood and the man saw him. "It's just a bairn. I'll deal wi' him," he called to the others. "You go on."

And then Alex shot from behind the rock, running toward the man, his dirk clasped tightly in his fist, and Duncan realised two things; his brother was about to be killed, and the man had not seen him lying in the heather. Whether deliberately or not, Alex had run in a curve, ensuring that the man was now facing away from the rock, which meant that Duncan, who would later be amazed by how calm he felt, ran straight at the man without being seen. Without hesitation he plunged his dirk into the man's back as soon as he was close enough, feeling the impact jar his arm to the shoulder as the blade hit bone and then continued into the flesh.

The man, whose whole attention had been focussed on Alex, screeched like a *ban-sìth* and turned, swinging his sword at chest height, no doubt assuming that the assailant behind him was a man. Duncan ducked, although he didn't need to, for the blade sailed over his head, and then Alex stabbed the enemy in the side, while Duncan, whose dirk was still buried in the man's back, pulled his *sgian dubh* from his belt and stabbed him repeatedly, frenziedly, anywhere he could reach, desperate to bring him down before he could swing the sword again and kill both of them. One of their blows wounded the man badly enough to drop him to his knees, and then Alex stabbed him in the neck from behind. He fell forward onto his face, made a terrible gurgling noise for a moment, then stilled.

The two boys looked down at the man, then at each other, but before they could do more than that Alasdair arrived, his sword dripping blood. He glanced at the still figure, kicked the sword out of reach, then looked at the boys.

"Are ye hurt?" he asked breathlessly, his voice harsh.

"No," Alex said. "I think we killed him," he added softly, disbelievingly.

Alasdair turned the man over with his foot, sword ready if needed, then nodded.

"Aye," he said. "I think ye did." He looked back then, assessing the situation near the fire, then nodded to himself and turned back to the boys. "Your da's coming. Was it you who made the call?" he asked.

"It was Alex," Duncan said when his brother didn't answer. The clouds had cleared completely now, and in the full moonlight Duncan saw Alex's face suddenly drain of all colour. Knowing what was about to happen, and that if it did Alex would be mortified, Duncan leapt forward, dragging his brother to the ground then pulling his upper body up with a strength he didn't know he possessed and pushing Alex's head between his legs.

"Breathe," he whispered urgently. "Da's coming."

Alex pulled in a few desperate shallow breaths, and then squeezed Duncan's arm. Duncan let him sit up then, sitting next to him while Alex pulled in huge drafts of the cool night air. For a few moments time stood still and there was just the two of them sitting together, both of them trembling with reaction at the enormity of what they'd done, both of them drawing comfort and strength from each other.

And then Alexander came across the grass at a dead run,

skidding to a halt in front of them.

"They're no' hurt," Alasdair said immediately.

"Thank God," Alexander gasped, then bent over, hands braced on his legs while he got his breath back. "Ye got here in time then," he said after a moment. "I canna thank ye enough, man."

"Dinna thank me," Alasdair told him. "I didna kill the bastard. Your sons have maybe no' learnt all the sword moves yet, but they ken what to do when it matters."

"Ye mean...did ye kill the man?" Alexander asked his two sons, who were now looking up at him a little apprehensively.

"Aye," said Alex a little hoarsely, his throat burning from the bile he'd frantically swallowed back just before he'd started to faint. "Both of us. We didna have time to get to the trees. I'm sorry."

"I dinna think ye need to apologise, laddie. He made the owl call too," Alasdair added to his stunned chieftain.

Alexander looked at his sons for a moment, then sheathed his sword and knelt down in front of them.

"Come here," he said simply and pulled them into his arms, embracing them fiercely. Alex and Duncan wrapped their thin arms round their father's back, burying their faces in his neck. After a moment the two boys began to cry, but it was not until he heard Alexander draw in a sobbing breath that Alasdair felt like an intruder on an intensely private moment. Forgotten, he walked silently away.

No one slept that night. Instead they took anything of worth from their attackers, examined them to discover any signs of their identity, found nothing, and then buried them in very shallow graves, having neither the time nor inclination to afford them any more respect. Then they relit the fire away from the original one, around which still lingered the smell of roasted corpse, and sat together, weapons at the ready, on full alert.

"My intention is to leave at first light," Alexander said when everyone was seated, only Allan lying on the ground, as he'd suffered a leg wound, now roughly bound. He looked up at the sky for a moment, then nodded to himself. "That's about four hours from now, so we should try to get some sleep. Allan, I think you should, and Duncan and Alex too, at the least. Half of the rest of us need to keep watch."

"I dinna think I can sleep," Alex said. His father ruffled his hair.

"Ye'd be surprised, laddie. Ye did well tonight, the both of ye. Ye may well have saved our lives wi' your warning about the men coming up behind us. I'm awfu' proud of ye both, and I'll talk to ye more about it when there's time. My worry now is that I dinna ken which clan those men are from, for they've no sign of any about them."

"They're no' anyone we reived from, that's for sure," Alasdair said, who'd checked every face, apart from one whose manner of death had rendered him unrecognisable.

"Were they no' just cattle reivers like ourselves?" Duncan asked.

"No, for if they were they'd have waited until we were asleep for one thing, or would have tried to take the cattle that were at a distance. But they didna pay any attention to the cattle at all. Whoever they were, they were out to kill us, no' to reive cows, and that's why I want to move on as quickly as we can. One reason anyway. Crieff is two days away, and we can have a surgeon look at that wound for ye, Allan."

"It's no' a worry," Allan said.

"Aye, it is," replied Alexander, who had seen wounds like that fester and kill a man. And Allan was the fastest runner in the clan. He wouldn't have him a cripple if he could avoid it.

"If they're no' the men we stole cattle from, why would they want to kill us?" Alex asked.

"Whose lands are we on now?" asked James at the same time.

"I'm no' certain. Maclaren, or maybe Stewart."

"There's no love lost between us and the Maclarens, is there?" Allan said. "Did we no' steal their lands and leave them landless?"

"Aye, we did. But no one kens we're MacGregors. And it was the Campbells that caused that, and they did nothing to help…ah…" Alexander tailed off.

"Did they attack us because they think we're Campbells, Da?" Alex asked.

"Aye. Well done, laddie. That could be it. And it would explain why they werena wearing a clan sprig, or anything to show who they were, for they wouldna want the Campbells to ken they'd killed some of their men," Alexander said.

"Christ!" Kenneth exclaimed. "So we canna be MacGregors *or* Campbells here?"

"No. All the more reason to be gone, fast," Alexander said. "Allan, when we leave you're riding one of the garrons, Alex and Duncan the other. We need to move fast, and ye'll slow us down otherwise. You get some sleep," he added, sweeping his arm round half the group, "but keep your weapons at hand. We'll wake ye in a couple of hours."

Everyone settled down, in a tense, alert sort of way. Whether they slept was another matter; certainly no one was difficult to rouse at the changeover. The moment the sky lightened everyone was moving.

Duncan and Alex sat together on the small horse, Alex in front because he was taller, trotting across the rough grass and heather. They'd both prefer to have walked, but accepted that the men were setting a fearsome pace which they could not have matched for long without tiring.

"Thank ye," Alex said after a time, when he judged they were out of earshot, "for no' letting me faint."

Duncan smiled.

"I thought ye'd have felt like a coward if ye'd fainted, but ye're the bravest person I ken. I couldna let that happen," he said.

"I didna feel brave," Alex admitted.

"Nor did I. But Da says we are. I'm thinking you were, for if ye hadna called to warn the others, the men wouldna have kent we were there."

"Aye, but I couldna have let that happen. If I hadna made the call, ye would have done it," Alex said.

"No I wouldna. I canna make the bird calls yet. I need to learn them."

"I'll teach ye. But even so, ye'd have done something."

Duncan was reassured by Alex's confidence in him, although in truth he hadn't even thought to make a call when it was all happening. He'd had no idea what to do until Alex had acted. After that everything had happened too quickly for him to think about it at the time. He thought about it now, though.

"When ye ran for the man, ye didna run straight for him, but round him a wee bit," Duncan commented.

"Aye, well, I kent when he said, 'it's just a bairn. I'll deal wi' him,' that he hadna seen ye, so I thought if I ran so that he had to turn away from the stone to kill me, ye could get away at least. I couldna in any case, for if I'd run away he'd have caught me and killed me anyway, I'm thinking."

Duncan wrapped his arms round his brother's waist and hugged him, hard.

"So ye thought ye were going to die?" he said shakily.

"Aye. No. I didna really think at all. I just didna want him to kill ye."

"I didna want him to kill you. That's why I ran after ye."

"Thank ye for that as well. Ye saved my life, for I dinna think I could have killed him alone. He was awfu' big," Alex said. "If ye hadna stabbed him in the back he'd have cut my head off for sure."

"We saved each other."

"Aye."

"That's a good feeling."

"Aye, it is," Alex agreed. "I'm glad ye're my brother. I canna imagine no' having ye wi' me."

"Ye dinna need to. I'm no' going anywhere."

They rode on in warm companionable silence for a minute.

"Ye were awfu' calm," Alex said then. "Did ye no' feel dizzy at all?"

Duncan shook his head against his brother's shoulder.

"No' dizzy. I felt awfu' sick when I stuck the man wi' my dirk, when I felt it go in him. But I didna have time to be sick then, for I had to stop him killing ye, so I made myself no' think about it. And after that everything was...slow."

"Ye remember Kenneth saying that? Ye think faster, so it seems as though everyone else is moving slowly," Alex said.

"Aye. I'd forgotten. He's right."

"I didna feel sick at all. I felt...excited. It felt good to be killing the enemy," Alex admitted. "I didna think it could feel good to kill a man, for taking a life is a terrible thing. I'm glad he wasna one of the men we stole from, for I wouldna feel right killing him if he had been."

"We didna have a choice, though," Duncan said.

"No. But I'm glad we hadna stolen his cows. I didna think I'd want to kill him so fierce. And then when he was dead and ye were safe, all the excitement went away and that's when I felt sick, like I was empty. I'm no' sure I should be feeling like that. Happy about killing, I mean. I need to ask about it, if it's right."

"Dinna ask the Father," Duncan said in a surprisingly bitter tone. He never talked about Father Gordon, had never expressed an opinion about him. But then Duncan was not one for talking about others, not one for talking unnecessarily at all. "He'll gie ye a lecture about the fifth commandment and about everything every saint ever said about it."

Alex laughed, for that was *exactly* what Father Gordon would do.

"I'll ask Da," Alex said.

He didn't need to wait long to ask his da, because shortly afterwards Alexander jogged up to the garron they were on. Duncan, who had rested his head on Alex's shoulder and fallen into a doze, woke up on hearing his father's voice.

"Are ye both well?" Alexander asked. "I ken ye're tired. We all are. We'll stop later and ye can sleep. Did ye no' sleep for fear o' nightmares?"

"No," Alex said. "I wasna tired."

"Me neither. I didna think about nightmares. It wasna like—" Duncan stopped and glanced round, but there was no sign of Kenneth, "last time, wi' Kenneth," he finished.

"That's good. But if ye do have nightmares, or anything that fashes ye, ye must tell me. Ye were awfu' brave, the pair of ye, and if ye feel bad, or sick, or get horrors, that isna wrong. That's a natural thing. It isna natural to kill a man, and it hurts us inside, even when we're right to have done it."

"Da," Alex began tentatively, "is it a natural thing to feel good about it? When ye're doing it, I mean? And then no' sorry after?"

"Why d'ye think ye felt good about it?" Alexander asked, in the way both Alex and Duncan had become used to since their 'learning years' had begun.

"I…I think because he wanted to kill all of ye, and then he was going to kill me and Duncan too, so I hated him for that, and it felt good to kill him. And I'm no' sorry, for if I hadna he'd have killed us."

"That's a good way to think about it, in such a case," Alexander said. "For ye didna have a choice whether to kill the man or no'. Did ye feel the same way?" he asked his younger son.

"I dinna ken. I didna think about it like that. He was trying to kill Alex and I couldna let him. That was all. I didna think of him as a man until I stuck my dirk in him, and then I felt sick. But no, I didna feel good, or bad. It was a wee bit like fetching water from the loch. I dinna like doing it, but I like helping Ma. I didna like killing the man, but I liked helping Alex," Duncan said.

Jesus Christ! The boy was six and was thinking that deeply? Alexander revised his opinion of Alex as the brighter one of the two. They were equally bright, he realised, just in different ways.

"Alex made the call to warn ye," Duncan added, oblivious to the reason for his da's stunned silence.

"Aye, but only because Duncan canna do an owl call yet. I'm after teaching him, when we're home," Alex said generously.

"And then he ran at the man in a way so he wouldna see me if I ran away, for I was lying down and he didna ken I was there," Duncan added.

"But he didna run away. He saved my life instead," Alex put in.

If Alexander had thought he could not be more proud of his two sons than he was right now, he had been wrong.

"I'm proud of ye, the both of ye. I canna tell ye how proud I am. No' because ye killed the man, but because ye put the clan before yourself, Alex, in making the call, as a chieftain should. And Duncan, I've no doubt ye'd have done the same if ye'd been able to. And then ye protected each other and stood side by side in battle. There's many men who vow to do that, but when the time comes the fear takes them and they dinna. I'm hoping to live a long time yet, but I'll tell ye both now, after this day, whenever God takes me I ken I'll be leaving the clan in good hands wi' you two, if ye carry on as ye are doing."

He moved away then to check on everyone else, leaving his two sons utterly speechless with pride and delight.

"How are ye doing, man? Ye fought well, there," Alexander asked Kenneth a few minutes later. "Dinna fash yourself," he added as he saw Kenneth redden and glance round to see who was watching, "I've spoken to everyone, as is my way in such matters. But I'll admit I wanted to speak to ye in particular. Part of the reason I brought ye wi' me was because ye're so good with my bairns and they love ye, and part of it was because ye're grieving sore, and both myself and Moira thought the distraction might help wi' that. I didna imagine ye'd have to fight again so soon. I wouldna have had that. It's no' a normal occurrence."

"It's why ye sent me on wi' the boys and Alasdair when ye were taking the cattle. So if there was any fighting, I wouldna be in it," Kenneth replied. It was not a question.

"Aye," Alexander said. "That's the only reason. I ken ye can fight, and well, and Christ, ye proved it again last night. Ye tore through those bastards like they were wee bairns. I'll be glad to have ye by my side in any fight, laddie. But such a fight as this, and the last one ye were in, they're no' the same as when ye go out wi' the intention of fighting. Ye havena done that yet, but it's different, no' just in the way of the fight, but in the way it affects ye later. And that's why I've spoken to everyone, but you and my sons in particular. I'm sorry ye had to go through it, for this unexpected killing affects ye worse and I'm here if ye're wanting to talk to me about it."

Kenneth nodded by way of thanks.

"I was sitting by the loch a few days ago," he said, "watching the bairns swimming, as we do now. Wee Jeannie came over and sat wi' me. She tellt me that when she's grown, she's going to marry me, for I'm the kindest man in the clan."

Alexander took this as a request not to pursue the subject.

"Aye, well, she's a forward wee lassie and no mistake. I dinna envy Father Gordon teaching her. How old is she now? Eight?" He laughed.

"Aye, I think so," Kenneth replied.

"Well, she'll be a bonny woman I'm thinking, but no' a biddable one! Did ye tell her you're the one who's supposed to do the asking?"

"That wouldna mean anything to Jeannie," Kenneth said. "She doesna care what she's supposed to do. She does as she likes." He laughed. It was a start, Alexander thought. Moira had been right to suggest he came along. "She tellt me that when she married me

I'd protect her, and never let any bad men hurt her, ever," Kenneth continued. "And that fair killed me, for I couldna protect my brother. I didna—" He stopped, made a strange strangled sound in his throat, and then suddenly started to cry, great racking sobs that shook his whole body.

Alexander seized him then and dragged him off the track behind a clump of gorse bushes, realising he was about to collapse completely, and knowing that later he would be ashamed to have done so in front of the other men. Once there, Alexander released him and Kenneth fell to his hands and knees on the ground, sobbing and choking. The chieftain knelt down next to him, putting an arm round the huge shuddering shoulders, his heart aching.

"Let it out, man, there's no one to see," he said. It was clear Kenneth had been holding this in for a long time; now he'd let go he couldn't stop. Alexander sat there stroking the giant's back while he bawled like a small child, hiccupping and gasping for breath. At one point Alasdair's head appeared round the gorse, and Alexander waved him away urgently, placing one finger on his lips to let him know not to say anything. Alasdair nodded and disappeared, and they were left alone.

After a time Kenneth managed to regain control of himself, finally sitting with his head between his knees, taking in great sobbing breaths, and then blowing his nose and wiping his face. Alexander offered him the flask of whisky he had on his belt, and Kenneth took a great draught of it.

"Christ, man, I'm sorry," he rasped, his voice hoarse from crying. "I dinna ken what came over me."

"Ye're grieving, man. Ye canna keep such pain inside forever. It'll come out, and I'm glad it did here, wi' no one but me to see it. Ye're a brave man, Kenneth, and a bonny fighter, and ye're sore worried for your ma and da, I'm sure, but ye canna take the burden of Alpin's death on ye too, for it wasna your doing."

"I canna stop thinking that I wasted time playing in the loch wi' Alex and Duncan. If I'd gone straight to where he was, maybe—"

"Alex tellt me ye asked if he'd seen him, and he tellt ye where the boat was. So if ye hadna stopped then, ye might no' have found him until after the bastards had gone. Ye did the only thing ye could do. Ye avenged him, and ye did it magnificently. He's resting peacefully now because ye did. No one could ask more of ye."

"But if I'd agreed to go fishing wi' him when he asked me, then—"

"Kenneth," Alexander interrupted firmly. "No one can live like that. We canna all spend every minute in each other's company for fear that something like that might happen. We canna plan for everything that could happen. Nobody can."

"Would ye no' feel the same, if last night Alex and Duncan hadna fought so well?" Kenneth asked brutally.

"Ah," Alexander said. "Aye, I would. Right now I'd be feeling the same as you about it. I'd be thinking it my fault, that I shouldna have brought them, that I should have made sure they were safe. I'd think that I'd killed my own sons. For a time I'd think that. But when the first pain cleared I'd realise that it isna possible to protect those ye love from everything. Ye dinna help them survive by doing that. I brought my sons on this raid to teach them so when they're older they'll ken what to do, in any situation. They'll need that. Your da did the same for you, and so will you do one day for your own sons. That's the only way ye can protect them, by teaching them how to live as Highlanders, as MacGregors." He sat down next to Kenneth, companionably.

"The night Alpin died, Moira said to me that if Alpin hadna been there, the broken men would probably have carried on along the track, and the next people they met would have been Alex and Duncan in the loch," he continued.

"Christ, I didna think of that," Kenneth said.

"Neither did I. But if Alpin hadna been there, and it had been Alex and Duncan, would it have been my fault, or Moira's fault for telling them to go and wash, to do something we all do?"

"No, of course it wouldna," Kenneth said.

"Well, then, no more is it yours because Alpin was doing something he did often. Grieve him, laddie, but dinna blame yourself. That's no' your burden to carry."

They sat for a time together in silence, Kenneth staring off into the distance, his eyes red and puffy. Then he nodded to himself.

"I'm ready now," he said.

They got to their feet and set off to join the others, who were now some way ahead.

"Ye should talk to Morag one day," Alexander said suddenly.

"Morag?"

"Aye. She talks about Alpin often."

"So do Ma and Da, Flora no' so much," Kenneth replied.

"No, I mean she talks about him now, that he's happy, that he wouldna want us to be sad. She loved him, and we were worried about telling her he was dead, because…but when Moira tellt her, she just accepted it and said she wasna feart now, for he'd be there for her. We thought it just that she didna rightly understand, but now we're no' so sure. She talks about him so matter-of-fact. Ye might find it a comfort. Or maybe no'."

"I'm no' one for the talking, no' about such things," Kenneth admitted. "But I'm glad she took it well. Alpin loved her too. We all do, for she's a bonny wee thing, always happy. Thank ye. Ye've helped me, I think, for I see ye've the right of it. I've no' been thinking rightly."

"No one does at such times," Alexander said, as the rest of the clansmen came into view. "Let's forget it now, unless ye need to talk more at any time. I'll no' tell anyone, including Moira."

Kenneth smiled, and they separated then, rejoining the others in their own time.

* * *

Once they got to Crieff they relaxed, in as far as they no longer had to worry about any clan attacking them. As Alexander explained to his sons while he was dressing outside their canvas tent the following morning, not being able to stand upright inside it, there would be other Campbells at the Highland Fair – in fact there would be many clans there, as well as a lot of English people, wanting to buy the cattle.

"No clan is going to come to Crieff to declare war on another," he said. "I'm thinking they were just fashed that we were on their land. Although they'll no' be happy that we killed their men, but that doesna signify. We're no' Campbells any more, and we'll go home by a different route."

"Can we be MacGregors now, then?" Duncan asked.

"No, for if we were, then we couldna carry weapons. And the

English wouldna be so eager to buy cattle from us if we were, for there are all manner of stories told about us being bandits, and savages. And we'll be wanting to carry weapons," he added, seeing the next question in Alex's eyes, "for although there'll no' be a clan war here, there could still be disagreements. And cattle theft. I'm wanting to sell the cattle as quickly as possible, buy what I need and head out."

"Ye dinna look like our da," Alex said, eyeing his father's strange garb. "Why are ye no' wearing the *féileadh mór?*"

"Did ye see the English, wi' their breeches and stockings?" Alexander replied.

Alex nodded.

"Well, then, we're wanting to sell them our cattle. And we're wanting to get the best price for them. They think the kilt to be indecent."

"I think their breeches and stockings look awfu' silly. And uncomfortable," Alex replied. "Why does it matter what the English think?"

"D'ye think if I go to meet them half-naked, they'll be inclined to trust me? I dinna care a farthing what the English think of me. I *do* care that the clan dinna starve this winter, that I can buy what we need and put away a wee bit for the future. If the English see me as they want to, then that's more likely to happen. There's a time to stand out, to be an individual, and there's a time to blend in." He slipped his feet into his shoes and reached for his swordbelt.

"But ye willna blend in, Da," Duncan said. "The English dinna wear the tartan, and your breeches are no' like theirs."

"No. It's called a trousing, wi' the breeches and stockings all in one. And they're tartan so that the dealers can see at a glance I'm the chieftain, and the one they need to deal wi'. The others will all wear their normal clothes. Including yourselves. Now, enough of the questions. Today I'm wanting ye to watch what I do, for one day ye'll both be doing it yourselves, and it's fearsome work for the mind. If ye've questions remember them, and ye can ask me later when we're back here."

He looked around then, and beckoned to James, Allan, Alasdair and Dugald, who were to accompany them to the tryst. The rest were staying with the cattle, to make sure that the merchandise would still be there when the buyers came to collect it.

* * *

By the end of the day Alex was exhausted just from *watching* the cattle sale. He had no idea what his father must be feeling like. This was like nothing he had ever seen before, and he wasn't sure he would ever be able to do it. He wasn't sure he *wanted* to do it.

His da had talked, non-stop, the whole day, to a vast number of people, some of them friendly, some of them condescending, one or two of them downright insulting, and all of them trying to buy his cattle (well, the cattle they'd taken from the Campbells and others) for less than they were worth. And in all that time he hadn't shown the slightest trace of impatience or anger. Sometimes he'd carried on three or four conversations at once, and had kept track of all of them. It was remarkable. And during all of that he'd known exactly where every clansman was, and exactly what was going on in the surrounding area.

But what was even *more* remarkable was that whilst doing all that, he'd added and subtracted prices, multiplied them by whatever amount of cattle the buyer wanted, calculated percentages of profit, and then reassessed the calculations time and time again while bargaining.

At the end of the day he bought a whole basket of meat pies from a dealer, and carrying them on his head, to the amusement of passers-by, headed back to the tents which were their accommodation for the night, and where the remaining clan members were watching the diminishing number of cattle.

"What did the physician say about your leg, Allan?" he asked as they walked, slower than normal to accommodate their injured member.

"He said it doesna look as though it'll fester, and he washed it in wine then sewed it together. He tellt me to visit him again in two weeks to take the stitches out, but I'm thinking one of the women can do that. It canna be different to unpicking a sark."

There was a general murmur of agreement.

"He washed it wi' *wine*?" Dugald said.

"Aye. He said it stops the wound going bad. When I asked him how, he said it just does. So I dinna think he kens why, for he got a wee bit fashed wi' me for asking."

"As long as he's right, I suppose it doesna matter why. Ye must ride a garron home though, Allan, let it heal," Alexander said.

"But ye'll need them for the provisions!" Allan objected.

"Kenneth offered to carry ye," Alexander responded. "So ye can either ride and Kenneth carry some provisions, or the horse can carry the provisions and Kenneth carry you. They're your only choices."

Hearing his chieftain's tone Allan capitulated, opting to ride, stating that the horse would probably smell better than Kenneth, to the amusement of the others.

"So then, questions?" Alexander asked his sons round a mouthful of still warm meat pie when they were back inside their tent. It was amusing watching their delight at being under canvas, a great novelty for them as Highlanders rarely used tents, finding the *fèileadh mór* a more practical covering when sleeping in the open. Alexander had explained to his sons that they'd brought a tent because he'd known there would be no accommodation in the town, and he would not make a good impression with the dealers if he turned up to the tryst soaking wet and dirty.

"It doesna matter what ye look like if ye're fighting, reiving or hunting," he'd explained. "But it *does* matter how fast ye can move. So a tent's a liability in such cases. But no' when ye're wanting to look respectable to town-bred Sasannachs. Dinna get used to such things, though."

Even so, there was something comforting about being sheltered. It felt cosy, especially if it started to rain. He would never admit that though, not even under torture. A chieftain could not be thought to be going soft.

"I dinna think I'll ever be able to do the numbers like ye could," Alex said forlornly. "How d'ye do it all, with everyone talking to ye at the same time?"

"Ye'll learn. It takes practice, like everything," Alexander said. "Ye're doing well wi' your numbers, Father Gordon tells me."

"Aye," Alex replied, colouring a little with pleasure, as that was not what the priest told him. "I can remember the numbers but I have to be quiet to think how to add them, if I havena got a slate. And it takes a long time."

"Then I'll have to make ye add and subtract at speed, so ye'll learn. It's important, for if ye make a mistake and give a wrong price that's lower, the dealer willna tell ye, he'll just agree. And once ye clasp hands on it, ye canna go back. It's like an oath."

"I dinna like the mathematics," Alex admitted. "I like learning about history, and the poems. We're reading Virgil now. There are lots of battles in it. But no' the Latin. I wish we could read them in Gaelic."

"Aye. But Virgil will no' feed ye through the winter if ye've sold the cattle for a silly price and canna afford to buy food for the clan, will it?" his father said.

Alex coloured again, for a different reason this time.

"I'll try harder wi' the number work," he promised.

Duncan, sensing his brother's discomfort, decided to deflect their father's attention from him.

"I've a question," he said. "Ye tellt us that ye wore the—" he pointed to his father's clothes, having forgotten what they were called.

"Trousing," Alex, who forgot nothing, supplied.

"Trousing," Duncan continued, "so the English would think ye respectable. But ye werena our da today, and I was wondering if wearing yon clothes helped ye be someone else."

Whatever questions Alexander had been expecting, this was not one of them.

"What do ye mean?" he asked. "Why was I no' your da?"

"I havena seen ye be like ye were today before. That's what I mean. But I was looking round the market while ye were dealing and I saw these soldiers wi' their red coats, and all that silly lace and coloured ropes on them—"

"Frogging," Alexander said, smiling at his son's obvious contempt for military trappings.

"Frogging," Duncan repeated, trying to commit this second new word to memory. "I was watching them, and they all looked very proud and as though they were better than everyone else. There didna seem any reason why they were better than everyone else, so then I thought that maybe that was why they had all that stupid…frogging, because it made them feel important and better than they really are. And then in the corner of the market there was a wee man dressed in clothes in lots of colours, who was juggling and making people laugh, and it seemed to me that people thought he was funny because he *looked* funny, and so maybe his clothes helped him to be funny too. And that made me think that maybe your clothes helped ye to be a chieftain selling cattle to Sasannachs instead of our da or the clan chief, which is what ye usually are." He stopped then, as this had been a very long speech for him. And besides, his da was looking at him very strangely, so he wasn't sure if he'd said something to upset him.

A short silence ensued while Alexander took this new idea in.

"I'm no' angry wi' ye," he said after a second, seeing Duncan's wary expression. "I just hadna thought of it like that before, but I'm thinking maybe ye've the right of it. I ken ye havena been to see a play yet. But when ye watch a play, the actors wear costumes, and the costumes help them to play their part, and the audience to see who they're supposed to be, whether it's a king, or a beggar. And aye, I suppose it's the same in real life too. It's true that when I put yon clothes on I feel like a cattle dealer, so it must help me play the part. What d'ye think, Alex?"

"I didna think of that, but ye werena like our da at all," Alex said. "Ye were someone else. Even the way ye spoke, no' the English, but the way ye spoke the English was different to when ye speak it wi' me, when ye're helping me learn. I didna think about the clothes. I was listening to what ye were saying, how ye talked to the dealers. But it makes sense, now Duncan's said it. It was strange, seeing ye be so different, someone I didna ken."

Duncan nodded agreement, and Alexander took a moment to think, washing down the last of his pie with a drink of water.

"When ye grow older, ye'll learn to be what ye need to be, to suit the situation," he said finally.

"Ye mean ye have to be someone ye're no'?" Alex asked.

"No. Ye're still the same person, inside. But ye have to show a different face on the outside sometimes. When I'm at home wi' your ma and wi' you, then I can be the real me, for you have my heart and I can trust ye completely. When I'm wi' the rest of the clan it's mostly the same, for I'm the clan father to them, as I'm the blood father to you. If I've to punish a clan member, it's much the same as when I'm punishing one of you for something ye've done wrong. Just a wee bit different. But when I'm leading the clan to battle, or if I've to execute a clan member, then I canna be the same man I am in the house playing wi' Morag, for instance."

"Ye have to execute members of the clan?" Alex asked in shock.

"Only the once, and it was a long time ago. I hope never to have to do it again, and I'm hoping you never have to. But if ye do, ye have to call on parts of ye that are darker, parts that are no' the husband and father. Same when ye ride into battle wi' the killing rage on ye, for the lives of your men are on your shoulders, and ye must be aware of that, for a wrong decision can get them killed. So ye have to think like a general, *be* a general. I dinna need special clothes for that though, wi' yon frogging and lace," he said, grinning at Duncan, who smiled back. "The more responsibility ye have in life, the more faces ye have to be able to show to others. And ye need to learn that, but ye'll no' learn it in a classroom or a university. Ye learn it through living, and watching others, as ye've both done today. Well done, Duncan, for ye watched very closely.

"It's important though, whoever ye *have* to be in a situation, to stay the same person inside. The real person."

"And your real person is who ye are wi' Ma and wi' us," Alex said.

"Aye. Always."

Christ, this was not what he'd expected to spend his evening doing. He'd thought to talk about how prices were determined, how deals were struck, how to haggle and make sure you won. He had not thought to have a deep psychological discussion with his two small sons. *God help me when they grow older,* he thought tiredly, even as he glowed with pleasure at the promise they both showed, in their different ways.

"Right," he said. "Let's sleep. For we've the whole thing to do again tomorrow. I'm hoping to finish selling the cattle, and if it goes as well as today, then on Thursday we can buy our provisions, and maybe see yon colourful acrobat ye were taken wi', Duncan."

"And a play?" Alex asked.

"Aye, I would imagine there'll be a play of some sort. If we've the time. I canna promise, though."

He hoped there would be. He wanted to reward them for their bravery in attacking and killing a heavily armed man. For standing by each other, and putting the safety of the clan before their own.

The three of them slept together that night, Alex and Duncan curled against their father's chest like puppies, covered with his plaid, snug and cosy under the canvas tent. In spite of his fatigue Alexander stayed awake for a while, feeling a love so fierce, for them and for the two female members of the family at home, that he knew losing them was the only thing in the world that could break him utterly.

He had come so close to losing two of them a couple of days ago. Even the thought of that made him feel sick. He could not keep them from danger; that wasn't possible. But he could teach them how to deal with it, and seemed to be doing a good job so far.

By God, but him and Moira were rearing some fine children, and another one on the way. He must have done something right in his life, to be so blessed.

He closed his eyes, and let the soft regular breathing of his sons lull him to sleep.

CHAPTER TEN

They arrived home a week later, having spent a day in Crieff buying various provisions and watching the street entertainers. Alexander had initially wanted to head back as soon as they'd bought what they needed to get through the winter, plus some little luxuries. But as everyone, especially the boys and Kenneth, had had a difficult experience on the way here and would have a prolonged and tense journey home, Alexander hoped that staying to watch the acrobats and a Punch and Joan show would replace some of the nastier memories with more pleasant ones.

He'd never seen a puppet show before, and had assumed it would be a light-hearted comedy. Certainly the clansmen roared with laughter at the coarse and satirical jokes against the rich, and Alex had been entranced by the marionettes, although he'd probably not understood much of the topical dialogue. Duncan on the other hand had spent his time watching the people in the audience rather than the production, and had later admitted to his father that he didn't like the puppets, finding them frightening with their big staring eyes and strange, jerky but lifelike movements.

The next morning they'd headed off early, the mood of the men upbeat, showing that the combination of the show plus the money he'd given to them all to spend on fripperies had worked. Even so, they had remained permanently vigilant, because although they no longer had cattle to worry about they did have enough provisions to keep a small clan from starving this winter, which would certainly be at least as tempting to thieves as the cows had been.

Therefore it was with great relief that they reached home without incident to find that nothing of importance had happened while they'd been away. After unloading the provisions the men had all headed home to see their families, Alexander and his sons doing the same.

Alexander had expected that the first thing his sons did would be to regale Moira and Morag with the tale of how they'd killed a man, but instead they were more excited about giving their presents and showing what they'd bought.

Alex and Duncan had pooled their money and bought books and ribbons for Moira and Morag, and, to Alexander's surprise, a book for him too.

"They spent most of the morning in the book shop," Alexander said, leafing through his copy of *Pilgrim's Progress* with delight. Perhaps not one to show Father Gordon though. "Now I ken why."

"Your book was written by a lady, Ma," Duncan said. "I forgot her name. It's strange."

"Aphra Behn," Alex supplied. "We thought maybe you could write a book too, in the winter when there's no' so much work to do."

"I've still a lot to do, even in the winter! I didna ken there were women writers," Moira remarked.

"Why would there no' be?" Alex asked.

"Women dinna have the learning like men do, for the most part," she said. "And I didna think a publisher would consider a woman author."

"You have the learning though, Ma. Ye taught me the letters. And the English," Duncan said. "I'm sure ye could write a lovely book. This one's about someone who travels a long way away. Alex's is too."

"Mine's about a man who goes to an island with no one on it. *Robinson Crusoe*. Ye can read it too, if ye want," Alex offered.

"What did you buy for yourself, Duncan?" Moira asked, after kissing them both and tying the emerald green ribbon they'd bought into her hair immediately.

"A book about animals. By Aristotle. But it's no' in Greek," he said happily.

"Father Gordon tellt us about it," Alex explained. "But he said that Duncan canna read it till he's learnt the Greek."

"Is it in the English, then?" Moira asked.

"No. It's in Latin. There isna one in English or Gaelic either. I asked the man in the bookshop," Duncan said. "But I'm learning a wee bit of the Latin now, so I'll be able to read it soon. I dinna mind to wait a year. But no' four."

"We're no' learning Greek until we're ten," Alex explained.

Alexander frowned.

"Why could ye no' read it in Latin wi' the Father, if ye want to?" he asked, knowing his younger son's passion for animals and insects. This would be exactly the sort of book to encourage him to learn Latin, a language neither of his sons were enchanted by.

"I dinna ken," Duncan said. "Maybe he thinks I'll learn Greek so I can read it. But I dinna want to. Ye have to learn all new letters for that. It took me long enough to learn the English ones. I dinna want to learn Latin either, but at least it uses the same letters as English."

Maybe I should have a word wi' the Father, Alexander thought.

For Morag they'd bought *A Little Book For Little Children* and *Euclid's Geometry.*

"The wee book'll help ye learn the letters quicker," Duncan said. "It's got pictures in it for every letter, see? 'Peacocks are proud, and deck'd with richest plume'," he read. "That's to help ye remember 'P', and that's a peacock. They've got big tails wi' feathers of all colours that look like eyes," he added. "I saw a picture of one in the bookshop, better than this one. It was awfu' bonny, but I didna have enough money to buy the book it was in."

"And we got ye *Euclid* for we ken ye're wondrous good with the numbers, and when ye've learnt the reading a wee bit better, ye can learn all the things about numbers and shapes ye want to ken," Alex said.

"Father Gordon's got a copy of Euclid," Moira said. "I've seen it."

"Aye, but that's no' for Morag, for she's only four and she's a girl too. The Father said it's no' a book for girls," Alex informed his mother.

"Is it no'? Why have ye bought it for her then, and her a girl?" Moira asked mischievously.

Alex flushed slightly.

"When I asked the Father why she couldna read it, he wouldna tell me. He said 'it just is', which means he doesna ken. So when I saw it in the shop I read it, and I couldna see anything wrong wi' it, although it's awfu' boring."

"I dinna think it's boring!" Morag said gleefully. "It tells ye how to use numbers to do lots of things!"

"Ye should have heard Da selling the cattle, Morag," Alex told her. "Ye'd have loved it. He can do all the numbers in his head, like you can!"

"Can ye, Da?" Morag asked.

"Aye. Ye have to, at the cattle market."

"He should take you next time, and ye could do all the cattle sums for him so he could talk to the English instead and make them pay more!" Duncan suggested. "And maybe we'll have the time to see a play, too!"

Morag's face lit up with a joy that tore at Alexander's heart.

"Could I come next time, Da?" she asked eagerly.

No, she could not. He could never take her to Crieff. Even if they weren't attacked on the way, the rigours of the journey alone would almost certainly kill her.

"I'll no' be going again for a year, lassie. D'ye think you'd be able to do your sums by then?" he answered evasively.

"She can do them now," Alex said. "Ask her."

Alexander looked at his small daughter, who had abandoned Euclid and was trying unsuccessfully to tie the ribbon in a bow in her hair. Her tongue was stuck out at the side of her mouth, something she always did when concentrating, a trait Duncan shared. It was very endearing.

"Well then…if I've ten cows, and I sell them for £3 each, what d'ye think that would be?" he asked, smiling and leaning over to tie the satin ribbon for her.

"£30," she answered instantly, surprising him. "That's easy. Did ye sell the cows for that, Da?"

"Er, no," he said. "I sold thirty of them for a guinea each. That was the best price I could get," he added to Moira. "The others sold for a wee bit less."

"A guinea is £1.1s English, so that's £31.10s," Morag said.

"Oh, well done. Ye're right!"

"Or £378 Scots," she added after a few seconds, to his utter astonishment.

"How d'ye ken that?" he asked.

"Father Gordon tellt Alex that the English pound is worth twelve times more than the Scots one," she said. "So I did the multip…"

"Multiplication," Alex supplied helpfully.

"Aye, that."

"How did ye do it?" Alex asked, beating Alexander by a millisecond. "I canna do it in my head at all."

"Aye, but that's because the Father willna let ye," Duncan said. "It's no' your fault."

"But I canna think how to do it anyway, and I'll have to if I'm to sell cattle one day," Alex said despairingly.

Morag was deep in thought.

"I dinna think about how I do it," she said. "It just happens. But 10 times 1 is 10, so that's £10, and then it's 10 shillings too. And then I multi… it by three, which is £30, and 30 shillings. And there's 20 shillings in a pound so the 30 shillings makes £1.10s. And then to get the Scots I multi… do that to the pounds by 10 again, so that's 310, and then by 2, so that's another 62. And then I did the same with the shillings, which is 120, which is £6. And then I added the numbers together – 310 plus 62 plus 6."

While Alex, frowning in concentration, repeated this slowly to try to make sense of it in his head, and Duncan started looking through his book about animals, which thankfully had woodcut illustrations in it, because his Latin wasn't good enough to read more than a few words, Alexander and Moira exchanged a glance of utter disbelief.

Morag was not yet five and she could do mental arithmetic faster than he could, at thirty-three. Alex, at eight, could remember just about *everything* he experienced or read, and repeat it back, word for word. Duncan at six could make insightful observations about the psychological impact of fashion on the wearer.

"What the hell are we raising?" Alexander murmured, not realising he'd actually said the words aloud until Duncan looked up from his book quizzically. "Never mind," he added. "Morag, *a ghràidh,* I canna promise to take ye to Crieff, for it's a long way away, and ye canna sleep out in the cold. But in the spring, after your Ma's had the wee bairn that's growing in her, we'll all go to

Edinburgh for a few days and see a play. And ye can buy another book each, for ye'll have read those by then."

And I will definitely have a word wi' the Father, he thought. He wanted his children to achieve their best, not be held back by the priest's prejudices.

* * *

He was still a little stunned as he went to bed that night, following the clan meeting at which they'd discussed what had happened on the way to Crieff, and then about the success of the sale. Alexander had also bought a great quantity of spun wool, which needed to be dyed and woven. He had multiple reasons for doing this; firstly he needed to replace his formal *féileadh mór*, which was now buried with Alpin; secondly, as it had been an extremely profitable sale he wanted to provide everyone in the clan with another set of warm clothing; and thirdly, it would keep Gregor and Barbara extremely busy through the dark cold winter, hopefully helping them to ward off the melancholia which afflicted everyone to some extent, but would surely overwhelm them, being that they were still grieving so badly.

"I canna believe the lassie can do the sums like that," he said as they snuggled under the covers together. There was a distinct bite in the air tonight. It would not be long before the first snow fell. "She tellt me that the Father willna teach her, either. He said she's too young to learn more than just counting. She's learnt by listening to Alex and Duncan's lessons, while he tellt her to draw a wee picture of a flower."

"I canna believe he's a Highlander, if he thinks it'll be more useful for Morag to draw flowers than no' to be cheated by a pedlar," Moira said scornfully. "I'm thinking he's been wi' the Duke of Gordon or whoever for too long. I'm sure if ye live in a castle wi' hundreds of servants and suchlike ye can spend your days drawing wee flowers."

"Ye dinna like the priest overmuch, I take it?" Alexander said.

"He was awfu' good when Alpin was killed. And he gives a fine sermon of a Sunday," she replied. "But I dinna think he likes females. It seems he feels that if he has the lassies in the classroom wi' him, that's enough to satisfy ye. For ye're the one who said he had to, aye?"

"Aye. I vanquished him wi' Locke and Quintilian," he said. "Or I thought I had. I'll have a wee chat wi' him tomorrow."

"Duncan tellt me he's the stupid one, for he canna learn quickly like Alex. I asked him who tellt him that, thinking if it was Alex I'd gie him a skelping. But it was Father Gordon. He said that God seemed to have given Alex Duncan's memory as well as his own."

"Did he now? Duncan didna tell me that. He must have been awfu' upset."

"Duncan? No. He doesna much care what anyone thinks of him, unless he likes them. He just mentioned it in passing when I was helping him learn some Bible verses. I'm wondering where the Father thinks Morag's ability wi' numbers came from, and her an evil wee lassie."

"Hmmm. I thought to allow him to settle in. In truth I havena had a lot of time the last months to ask about the learning. Maybe he thinks I'm no' interested in how he's teaching them. I'll remedy that when I see him."

He felt Moira's head nod in affirmation against his shoulder.

"I'm more shocked that Alex and Duncan killed a man," she said, shuddering. "I kent they'd have to one day, but…Christ, they're just bairns."

"I'm awfu' proud of them. I wouldna have had them go through that so young, but they behaved better than many a grown man would in such a situation. I thought they'd have nightmares as they did after seeing Alpin, but they havena. They seem to have accepted that they had no choice."

"D'ye ken which one of them killt the bastard?" Moira asked. Alexander bent his head and kissed the top of her head. His wife never used bad language, and the fact that she had now showed the depth of her feeling about the matter.

"I'm thinking it was probably Alex, for he stabbed the man in the neck. But Duncan's dirk was still in his back and that wound would surely have killed him, but no' quickly enough. He had other wounds too, but they two were the killing blows, I'm thinking. Alex asked me, and I tellt him they did it together, for I didna want one of them to carry the burden alone."

"Ye were right in that," Moira said. "It's probably a reason why they're dealing wi' it so well, for they can share the horror and the guilt. And the glory. The clan made a lot of them tonight. That was well done."

"Aye, well, I wasna exaggerating when I said Alex may have saved us all by warning us as he did," Alexander confirmed. "We're rearing some mighty bairns. I'm thinking that I *have* to send Alex to the university, for he's got a formidable memory. If he can learn to slow down and look deeply at things as Duncan does, he'll be able to do anything in life. I'd love to see the chieftain he'll be one day, although that isna possible."

"Would ye no' send Duncan instead? Or as well, when the time comes?" Moira asked. "Or are ye of the Father's opinion?" she added, smiling.

"Hmmph!" Alexander replied. "Anyone who blethers wi' the boy for more than a few minutes can see he's a thinker. No, it isna that. I've saved something from the cattle sale and I'll make more raids when I can, but they canna go to university in Britain, for they're Catholic. I couldna ever afford to send the both of them, and I dinna think Duncan would be happy to go alone. I watched them in Crieff. Alex was exhilarated, looking at everything, commenting on all the exciting things – he really enjoyed the crowds of people, all the new experiences. Duncan didna. He curled into himself, as he does when he's unhappy. He tellt me later that he liked buying the books, seeing the acrobats and watching some of the people, but there was too much noise and too many people, and he couldna breathe properly for the smells. He watched the people in the same way he watches yon wee bugs in the grass," he finished, and Moira laughed.

"Will he want to go to Edinburgh next year then? And should ye be spending money on such fripperies?"

"Aye, I should. Duncan will enjoy being wi' us, and I couldna bear Morag's disappointment when I tellt her she couldna go to Crieff. It's too dangerous. She'd no' survive sleeping out in the open, let alone in October. I'll find a way to take her to Edinburgh. Maybe build a wee cart wi' a cover she can ride in, and ye can sleep in it, wi' her and the next wee genius ye're growing." He stroked her stomach, which was still flat, with tenderness. "Are ye sure?" he asked.

"Aye. I wasna absolutely certain before ye went on the raid, but I am now."

"Can ye feel it?" he asked. He always loved putting his hand on her stomach and feeling the little kicks of the growing baby. He had done it with all the others and had a childlike sense of wonder about the whole process, which was incredibly endearing. Most men were not that interested until the child actually appeared.

And with this child, the others were old enough to share in it too. She hoped for a girl, a sister for Morag. But mostly she hoped for a healthy child and a safe birth, although she did not confide that to her husband. Loving her as he did he would worry, and there was nothing he could do regarding the birth. That was not a man's job.

"And we'll go to a play? Really?" she asked.

"Aye. It's been too long since I took ye to one. That was a wondrous night," he said.

"It was the night ye asked me to marry you," she answered.

"I ken. I may no' have Alex's memory, but I'll never forget that. I was so nervous. That's why I asked ye before we went into the theatre. I was going to wait until after the play, for I thought ye'd be feeling that wonder that comes on ye if the play's a good one, and be more likely to say aye. But I wouldna have enjoyed it at all, wondering what ye were going to answer, and it felt dishonest somehow to ask ye in a weak mood, if ye like. I'd no' have kent if ye'd said aye because of the romantic mood and regretted it later."

"Ye loon. I'd have said aye if ye'd asked me in front o' the night soil cart," she said. "It was always you for me, from the first minute I saw ye."

He smiled and wrapped his arms round her, sliding down in the bed and pulling her on top of him.

"Really?" he said. "Ye mean I could have saved the price of the tickets? It was awfu' costly, getting a box and all."

She slapped at his chest playfully, and he caught her hand. After that neither of them spoke for a while. They made love tenderly, carefully, because of the growing baby and because, fierce as Alexander could be when it was needed, he was and always had been gentle with her, not just in lovemaking, but in everything.

Genius or not, if Duncan and Alex grew up to be half the man Alexander was, she'd be satisfied. She had never regretted agreeing to marry him that warm summer night in Edinburgh over ten years ago, even though it had resulted in her parents rejecting her, horrified that she wanted to marry an outlawed MacGregor. They had hoped she would marry a clan chief, but not *such* a one as that! In all the years since she'd walked out of their lives and into his, in spite of the dangers, the privations, the unique difficulties of being part of a proscribed clan, she had never regretted her decision. How could she, when she had a husband who both loved and respected her, who confided in her and consulted her before he made many of his decisions? Theirs was a true and equal partnership, and such things were rare jewels indeed.

Afterwards he reached across and snuffed the candle out with his fingers, and they settled to sleep, still entwined with each other.

"I'll get us a box at the theatre next spring, too," he murmured. "Ye all deserve it. Ye all deserve the best I can give, for I'd be nothing without ye."

"We'd be nothing without you either," she replied. "I dinna need a box at the theatre. I've got everything I want right here in this house."

They kissed again tenderly, and then Morag moaned softly in her sleep and turned over in her bed on the other side of the room. They both fell silent then, listening for any sounds of pain or distress. And then, when they heard nothing, they relaxed and drifted into sleep.

* * *

Father Gordon returned from his missionary work several days late due to a sudden heavy snowfall which had left him stranded in an isolated and rundown bothy for a few deeply unpleasant days.

To say he was not in the best of moods for the conversation Alexander insisted on having with him that evening was an understatement, but nevertheless the conversation was had, because as well as being chieftain Alexander MacGregor was a frightening man when annoyed, and one with the authority to carry out any threats. That, coupled with the fact that the priest was still shivering from his recent experience of homelessness, made the result of the conversation a foregone conclusion.

The priest, to keep his dignity, made a token protest; but the result was that regardless of age or gender, Morag would now start learning arithmetic, along with any other girl who wished to, Alex would be allowed to calculate sums in his head at times, and any more comments on Duncan's ability to remember would result in unpleasant consequences for the person uttering them.

Alexander had then strode back through the snow, his expression still fierce and resolute, and had placed himself next to the fire, into which he stared for a while whilst his body warmed and his temper cooled. Once this was accomplished, he turned to his children, who were all sitting at the table.

Alex and Morag were playing with a series of wooden letter dice that Allan had made for them. Each child threw a handful of dice and then had to make a word from the letters showing. Duncan was reading his new book.

"Aye, that's well done," Alexander remarked to them. "Father Gordon will start teaching ye the sums tomorrow, Morag, but he tells me ye must work hard to learn your letters."

"Alex is helping me, Da, for I want to read the books he bought me," Morag replied, beaming with happiness at the news. "Will I learn wi' Alex?"

"Aye. I tellt the man that ye're as good wi' the numbers in your head as Alex is on paper, and that ye must both learn the other skill. He'll teach ye together."

Morag clapped her hands together with joy, and Duncan looked up from the book he was frowning over, smiling at her.

"I dinna think the Father will be happy to do that, though," Alex observed. "He doesna like lassies overmuch."

"He doesna like bairns overmuch," Duncan added bluntly. "But lassies especially."

"I didna hire him to *like* ye all, just to teach ye," Alexander said. "Ye'll behave to him as ye should, and he'll behave to ye as *he* should. Are ye finding your book hard to understand?"

"Aye," Duncan admitted somewhat hopelessly. "I dinna think I'll *ever* be able to read it. It's awfu' difficult."

"Here," Alexander offered, "sit wi' me on the *seise*, and I'll see how much of my Latin I can remember. I'll translate a wee bit of it for ye, until your ma gets back from Fiona's."

So it was that an hour later when Moira returned from consoling Fiona and Allan over their third miscarried baby, she opened the door to see her own husband and children in a tableau of domestic bliss, two of them playing a game at the table, while the third child was curled next to his father by the fire, engrossed in a book.

This heartwarming sight was marred only by the ferocious scowl on Alexander's face, matched by the words that greeted her as she stepped over the threshold.

"In the great majority of animals there are some...er...psychical qualities or...um...attitudes," Alexander read aloud, translating very hesitantly, "which qualities are more markedly...er...Christ, laddie, what possessed ye to buy this book? Ye'll no' be able to read it for years yet, I'm thinking!"

"The man in the shop tellt me it was about animals," Duncan replied disconsolately. "He tellt me it was the only one he had."

"It *is* about animals, but it's awfu' trying even for me to read. It's full of difficult words. Did ye tell him it was for you?"

"Aye. He said he thought a clever wee laddie like myself would master it."

Alexander muttered a word under his breath that Moira fervently hoped the children hadn't heard. She would not like to be that bookseller if her husband saw him at the next cattle fair.

"What's psychical?" Duncan asked, proving his father's earlier point.

"It's what happens in the mind, rather than the body," Moira put in, taking off her cloak. "Allan's got a book about animals that he might let ye borrow, if ye take care of it. I think you'd like it. It's in the English, which ye can read passably, the words are no' so difficult and it's got pictures of all the animals too. He canna read, but he uses the pictures to help him carve wee animals in his spare time."

Duncan's face lit up.

"Can I ask him?" he said.

"Aye. And if ye like it, I'll see if I can buy a copy for you, when we go to Edinburgh," Alexander said. "How is she?"

"She'll be well. She just needs time, they both do. They're awfu' disappointed, for she carried this one a wee bit longer so they hoped it'd stay there. Susan was there too, said she canna see any reason why they shouldna try again, but I think they'll wait a wee while."

All three children were listening to this cryptic conversation with interest, but when neither Alexander nor Moira offered to translate, they accepted it as 'adult'.

"Da, have ye to go out again tonight?" Alex asked.

"No. Why?"

"Can ye tell us the rest of yon story? Ye didna finish it."

"What story?"

"The one about the MacGregors ye were telling us the night the other clan came to kill us thinking we were Campbells."

"Ah! The one about how we became proscribed," Alexander said by way of explanation to Moira. "Aye, I dinna see why no' if ye all want to hear it?"

They did.

"Can I away and fetch Kenneth?" Alex asked. "For he hadna heard it before either, and he'll want to ken how it ended."

Food was eaten and then while Alex took an extraordinarily long time to fetch Kenneth, Moira lit a candle and settled to knitting a bonnet. Morag sat next to her watching, as she was to learn how to knit this winter. When Alex finally returned the reason for his delay became evident, for he brought a crowd with him.

"I was thinking to bring all those who hadna heard the tale before, for it was a good one," Kenneth said, somewhat apologetically on seeing the look of surprise on his chieftain's face. "I'll take all the bairns home myself afterwards. Or now, if ye want," he added.

"That was a kind thought, Kenneth," Moira said before Alexander could comment. It was the first social thing Kenneth had done by himself since Alpin's death, and after a moment Alexander too realised that.

"No, ye've the right of it. It's a perfect night for a story. I'll need to tell the whole tale from the start, though. Come in and sit down." A good many people who *had* heard the story had come along too, and Alexander resigned himself to the fact that his planned cosy evening with the family was not to be. Once they were all settled, he started to tell the story from the beginning.

"So, then Luss, wi' his commission from the king, set off wi' his eight hundred men, intending to go to Glengyle and wipe out the MacGregors entirely," he said after a time.

"That's where ye were when we heard the buzzard," Alex interrupted excitedly.

"The buzzard?" Catriona asked.

"Aye, the raiders made a buzzard call before they attacked," Kenneth said.

"After dark? The loons," Fiona commented.

"Aye. It was awfu' kind of them, for it tellt us they were there," Kenneth agreed.

"I've tellt ye all the most of what happened that night," Alexander put in, seeing the eager faces, and still hoping to have at least a short time alone with his family. "Tonight it's the MacGregor one. Ye can all come here again in a few days if ye want another tale, and we'll have food for ye too. Maybe Alasdair can play the fiddle for us, for I think the snow's here for a time now, so we'll no' be doing a lot outdoors."

Everyone settled again then, and after taking a gulp of his wine Alexander continued.

"But the MacGregor heard that Luss was coming down the glen to attack him, and…"

"Was it a spy who tellt him, Da?" Alex interrupted eagerly.

"I dinna ken in truth, laddie. Maybe. Or maybe the MacGregors had sentries out, fearing that the Colquhouns might be planning something. At any rate, Alasdair MacGregor, for that was the chief's name, he assembled all his clan, and some others too, for there were Camerons and Anverichs wi' him. Now he didna have as many men as Luss, so he did what yon raiders did to us near Crieff, and split his men. Half of them went wi' his brother round behind Luss, but quietly, and no' making stupid buzzard calls at night."

Everyone laughed at this, and Alexander took the opportunity to have another drink, while Moira put another turf of peat on the fire. It was warming up nicely in the room now, assisted by the mass of bodies sitting on the stools and the floor. Outside the wind howled round the settlement, but it was snug and cosy in the chieftain's house.

"So, then, Glenfruin, where the battle was, had hills on both sides, and the trail along the bottom was awfu' boggy, wi' a wee river running there in the wet weather, and this was February, ye ken. Alasdair went partway up the hill on one side of the glen, and his brother John went up the other, a wee bit further along the glen, and then when the Colquhouns came down and were between the two, on the boggy trail, the MacGregors opened fire wi' their muskets."

"Did they do a Highland charge, Da?" Duncan asked, who had been told about this famous tactic a few days previously.

"No' at that time. I wouldna have done either if I was Alasdair, for the ground was very bad for the Colquhoun horse, and the men couldna get up the hill on either side anyway without being shot. There wasna any need for the charge, for such a manoeuvre always kills some of your own as well as the enemy. If ye can kill them without dying yourself, that's a better way."

"Did they kill all the Colquhouns?" Kenneth asked.

"No, but they killed or wounded a good number, and then the Colquhouns retreated, to a place called *Toman an Fhòlaich,* which was a wee crater they could hide from Alasdair's men. They thought they could put up a defence from there, but they didna ken that John Dubh was on the other side of the glen and could see them all down there, hiding. So the MacGregors just carried on shooting them."

"Why did the Colquhouns no' shoot back, Da?" Alex asked. "Did they no' have any guns?"

"Aye, but they were shooting uphill, where the MacGregors were shooting down, so their musket balls carried further," Alasdair put in.

Alex frowned.

"I ken ye havena learnt to fire a musket yet, but ye've fired an arrow," Alexander explained. "Ye ken that if ye fire an arrow uphill it doesna go as far, but if ye fire it downhill, it goes further because gravity helps it. Ask Father Gordon about gravity," he added on seeing Alex's mouth open to ask the question. "The Colquhouns, seeing that the crater didna help them, retreated as best they could down the glen until they got to Strone, and at that point the MacGregors *did* charge, as they were on more level ground now, and because of that two of them were killed and some others wounded. But they won the day. It was a bonny fight. But the MacGregor didna ken about the king's commission, of course."

"What difference did that make, if the Colquhouns were killed?" Kenneth asked.

"Ah, they werena *all* killed, though. And Luss went back to

Edinburgh and said that the MacGregors invaded his lands wi' no provocation, so the king wasna very happy about that. So when Alasdair was arrested by Argyll, who gave an oath telling him he wouldna be harmed, and broke it…"

"Was he called Glenstrae?" Alex interrupted.

"Aye. Who tellt ye that?" Alexander asked.

"James tellt me that story, and I tellt it to Duncan. Argyll tellt Glenstrae that he had to go to England, but wouldna be harmed, and then brought him back to Edinburgh to be hung."

"Aye, that's right," Alexander said.

"Why did he have to go to England, if the king was in Edinburgh?" Catriona asked.

"Because when the battle took place, James was still in Scotland, but shortly after that yon Elizabeth woman died, and James became King of England too, and went to live in London. So by the time Alasdair was arrested the king was in London," Alexander explained. "Anyway the MacGregors said that they didna invade Luss's lands but had been called to a meeting to try to make peace, and that it was when they were on their way home that Luss treacherously attacked them. Alasdair said he'd suspected he might, which was why he'd sent his brother to hide in the hills, but that he wouldna have attacked the Colquhouns otherwise, for they were under truce. But they hung him and a lot of other MacGregors anyway."

"That isna right!" Alex said. "Did the jury no' listen to him?"

"Aye, I daresay they listened, but it didna signify. They were always going to hang him, for the jury was full of Luss's and Argyll's friends. And by then the whole of Clan Gregor was proscribed by the king, who believed the worst of us."

"Because Luss kent the king well, and how to make him sympathetic," Alex said.

"Aye, and not only Luss, but Argyll too."

"It still doesna seem right though, for the king to just condemn us without finding out what really happened," Alex persisted.

"There's no justice for the MacGregors in law, laddie. We make our own, wi' the sword," Alasdair said, to a chorus of agreement.

"Alex, if your da tellt ye tomorrow that some men were coming along the loch, and that they were our enemies and wanted to kill us, would ye say 'I dinna believe ye, Da. I'll go and talk to them myself and find out why they're coming to see us'?" Moira asked.

"No, of course I wouldna!" Alex replied, shocked.

"Why no'?"

"Because he's my da, and he wouldna tell me a lie!" Alex cried.

"Exactly," Moira finished.

"So ye mean that the king trusted Luss and Argyll like we trust Da," Duncan said after a moment. "Because they were friends."

"Aye, or seemed to be. Men in power always have a lot of 'friends' who seek to make themselves more powerful," Moira said. "It's no' easy to tell the difference, if the man's clever. The secret is to be cleverer than the man you're deceiving."

"Is the king no' the cleverest man in the country, then?" Duncan asked.

"Christ, no, laddie," his da replied. "There's been all manner of loons that have worn a crown. Ye're the king because your da was and you're his eldest son, usually. But it's no' for us to question God's will as to who He wants to be king. We just have to live wi' the consequences."

"That's why we fight for James," Alasdair added.

"Aye. For he's the rightful king, according to God. And because we want him to lift the proscription too," Alexander agreed.

"So if the MacGregor had been a friend to the king instead of Luss, then the Colquhouns might be proscribed instead of us?" Kenneth asked.

"Aye, maybe," Alexander replied. He waited a moment, but Alex didn't ask anything else, and by the expression on his face was pondering his mother's and brother's words. "Right, then," he said, standing. "If ye away to your beds, and come back here in two nights. Alasdair, bring your fiddle, and we'll have a wee dance. Tomorrow we're needing to repair Allan and Fiona's roof, for it's leaking, and I dinna want to wait till the snow clears, for that could be a while, and the woman isna well right now. Allan canna do it for his leg's still healing, and it'll cheer them both to ken we all care. Maybe we can persuade them to come to the dancing, just to take their mind off their loss for a while."

* * *

December 1723

"Aye, they're learning well, all of them, in their own ways," Father Gordon answered in reply to the chieftain's question about the children's education. Since his 'chat' with the priest, Alexander had dropped in every two or three weeks for an update, partly because he was interested and partly to keep the priest on his toes.

"Morag's awfu' happy to be learning the mathematics now, and the rest of us take time to help her wi' her letters too. She doesna find them as easy as the numbers, but it keeps her quiet and that's important. The laddies werena happy wi' the oratorical task ye set them, though. Alex in particular," Alexander commented.

Father Gordon eyed him intently before answering, trying to ascertain his mood.

"Aye, well, I dinna ken what ye said to him, but since ye've been back from Crieff, he's taken to the learning something fierce, instead of squirming on his chair, sighing, and looking out of the window. He's an unnatural gift for remembering, but wouldna put his mind to learning if he wasna interested in the subject."

"Ye mean the Latin."

"No' just the Latin, but that's an example. He didna much like the numbers either, or learning French. If he didna see a reason for it, it was hard to make him focus. Especially as ye tellt me I couldna beat him."

"Ye could have tellt me, though, and I'd have had words wi' him myself," Alexander said.

Father Gordon forebore from saying that the MacGregor chieftain had frightened him so much at their last talk that it would be a cold day in Hell before he'd volunteer to discuss any educational problems with him.

"Aye, well, there's no need now, as I said. He's a powerful mind on him when he sets himself to learn, as he has now. But he only sees his side of any argument, and canna see any validity in an opposite view."

"Well, he is only eight. I daresay I was the same at that age," Alexander replied, honestly rather than defensively. "He's stubborn if he canna see a reason why he should learn something. If ye explain it to him so he can understand it, he'll put in the effort then."

Father Gordon couldn't understand why the MacGregor seemed to think having a wilful disobedient son was a good thing. Children should do as they were told by adults, whether they agreed with them or not. But he was not about to air this view, which might be quite literally suicidal, given the bitter weather right now, his inability to travel anywhere at the moment, and the slim chance of being welcomed elsewhere even if he could.

"Duncan's over a year younger, but he can see more than one side of things," Father Gordon commented instead. "Ye were right about him. He hasna the recall of his brother, I was right in that. I thought he was slow, because if I ask a question he takes a good time before he answers it. But I realise now that's because he's thinking about all the different aspects of it."

"Whereas Alex just says the first thing that comes into his head."

"Aye," said the priest, relaxing a little. "And it's an intelligent comment, usually. But I thought giving them both that exercise would make him think more."

It certainly had.

The task they were talking about was one that would have been more suitable for university students than for two young boys, although Father Gordon explained that he hadn't expected either of them to come up with more than one or two simple arguments.

"I ken that the MacGregors have strong views about why the proscription should be lifted, and that ye'd likely discussed it in front of the boys," the priest said. "So I kent they'd be able to think of a few things to say. I didna much care if they presented their arguments persuasively or no', just that they thought about them."

"Or rather Alex thought about them," Alexander said wryly, grinning.

His son had been horrified by the task Father Gordon had given them. Or rather not the task exactly, but his part of it. Because they had to give opposing views about the same topic – the proscription of Clan Gregor, and why it should be lifted. Or not. And Alex's task had been to say why it should *not* be lifted, Duncan's why it should.

"It's no' fair," Alex had grumbled. "There are no reasons why it shouldna be lifted, are there, Da? I canna do this. I think the Father hates me."

Duncan had looked up from his slate, where he was painstakingly writing a few points down. Alex's, after half an hour, was still blank.

"Ye'll no' think of reasons by being fashed about it," he remarked, earning himself a scowl. He grinned and continued writing.

"D'ye think the king proscribed us for no reason, then?" Moira asked from the corner of the room, where her and Morag were sitting, Morag learning to knit.

"No, he proscribed us because his friends tellt him lies about us," Alex replied.

"Aye. But King James wasna an idiot. He might have been inclined to believe his friends, but they'd still have to give him what *seemed* to be good reasons, even if they were lies," Moira pointed out.

"What d'ye think they'd have tellt him, Ma?" Alex asked.

"Ah, no. It's your job, no' mine. Ye've to think for yourself," Moira said.

Alex sighed.

"How many reasons have you got?" he asked Duncan.

"Three. I'm no' telling ye," he added, because he knew his brother well. "I'll tell ye tomorrow, at the Father's."

"Have ye to argue your points, too?" Alexander asked. Both his sons looked at him quizzically, which gave him his answer. "When ye're older, as well as giving the reasons for whatever it is ye're debating, ye'll need to defend them too. I learnt that in Cicero. He was one of the greatest orators of all time, and he wrote books about how to win arguments. When ye go to university, Alex, others will attack your reasons, and ye have to defend them. Like in a battle, but wi' words instead of swords."

"I dinna want to go to university," Alex said sulkily, "I'd rather learn to fight wi' swords than words."

"So ye're going to kill everyone who doesna agree wi' ye, are ye?" Alexander said. "Ye'll no' live long, if ye do that. Ye'll no' have many friends, either."

"They'll all be dead," Duncan added, earning himself another scowl.

"Part of being a chieftain is to tell people what ye want them to do, and then to persuade them that it's the right thing," Alexander continued, taking pity on his eldest son.

"I ken. But I'm no' going to tell them to do something I dinna believe in, and then persuade them it's right!" Alex cried.

"Ye might have to. And even if you dinna, if ye can think like your enemies, that gives ye an advantage."

"Why?"

"Because ye ken what they might say to attack ye before they say it, so ye can think how to defend yourself in advance."

"Like learning all the different sword moves," Duncan said, still writing furiously.

"Aye, that's right. Ye dinna wait until someone comes at ye wi' a sword and then start thinking about how to defend yourself. Instead ye learn all the ways they might attack you, and how to defend yourself against them," Alexander said. "It's the same wi' this. If ye can think like your enemy, then ye'll be able to anticipate what he does. Be able to ken what he's going to do before he does it," he added, realising from their expressions that the word 'anticipate' was new to them. "So if ye're fighting him, the minute he moves his sword to the right, ye'll already ken all the things he could do, which gives ye a much better chance to kill him than if ye wait until he's made the move. Wi' words, if ye can think like your enemy, ye can prepare a good argument to beat him. And that could save your life or the lives of your clansmen, just as a sword can."

"Because it's no' a good idea to go and kill the king, whether ye've the right of it or no'," Duncan added.

Alexander bit his lip to stop himself from laughing out loud at the expression this comment earned. Duncan was clearly enjoying the novelty of finding a learning task much easier than his precocious brother was.

In fact he finished the task long before Alex, who was still sitting frowning over his slate at bedtime, although he had succeeded in writing a few points down at least.

That was another useful lesson this assignment had taught his eldest son, Alexander thought now, although he did not share it with the priest. Alex was an excellent speaker, with a comprehensive vocabulary for his age, but this had shown him that he would not always excel, even at the subjects he was good in.

"How well did they perform their oratorical task?" Alexander asked now.

"They did well. Duncan had more arguments on his side, which I expected because I'm certain ye dinna discuss wi' the clan why ye *should* be proscribed. Alex said that the king was showing how powerful he was by being able to proscribe a whole clan, and that he thought it would stop the MacGregors fighting his friends."

"Both good points."

"Aye, but after they'd spoken we all talked about it wi' the other bairns too. Duncan added that the king maybe did it as an example, because he believed his friends when they said the MacGregors did all those terrible things, and maybe he thought that if he proscribed the one clan, it'd stop any others thinking of attacking his friends as well, in case they were proscribed too."

"Duncan thought of that by himself?" Alexander asked.

"Aye, he did. And it made me realise that the laddie's brain is every bit as powerful as Alex's. Just in a different way. If he were an ancient Greek he'd have been a philosopher, maybe."

"And Morag?" Alexander couldn't resist adding, watching with interest as the priest managed to hide a look of distaste. Not quickly enough though.

"Ye ken I think learning is a risky thing for females. They havena the strength of personality of men, and are easily tempted by Satan. It's no' just me who thinks that. Saint—" He changed tack on seeing the MacGregor chieftain's expression. "But I can see that learning the numbers would maybe be good for her, because if she can do accounts she'll be useful in a quiet way, for she'll never be able to do the heavier work that clanswomen do, due to her health. Is she learning other, womanly things, the sewing and the knitting, for example?" he added.

"Aye. But the boys learn those too. And the cooking," Alexander replied. "No' to the extent the women do, but even so. And the women learn to defend themselves, in case they're attacked while the men are away. No' wi' swords and targes, but wi' dirks and pistols. I canna believe the Gordons do differently.

Or maybe they do, being as powerful as they are."

Father Gordon did not answer this.

"I'm teaching the lassies everything I teach the laddies, as ye want," he said instead, a little tersely. "I'll leave it to you to deal wi' the consequences."

"Ye do that. I've no concerns in that matter. I'll leave ye to your sermon writing," Alexander said, waving a hand at the table on which were a number of papers and books. "I'll come again to see how they're getting along. I'd no' be unhappy if ye were to set Alex a few more such tasks as yon oratory. He'll need to learn to see things from more sides than just his own. That was well done, Father."

It was always worth unsettling your adversary by unexpectedly complimenting him, Alexander thought as he walked back through the snow to his house, from which smoke was curling invitingly from the chimney. Something else Alex would need to learn. Not yet though. The poor laddie *was* only eight, after all.

CHAPTER ELEVEN

April 1724

"I liked today's lesson," Morag said happily as the three children made their way along the track which led to their house. Father Gordon lived at the other end of the settlement from the chieftain, so they had the longest walk of all the children to get home.

"It was very long," Alex commented, looking at the sky. It would be dark soon, although the heavy black clouds obscuring the mountains and threatening to drop their load of rain any moment made it seem darker than it would normally be at the end of a day of lessons.

"Do ye no' like Pythagoras?" Morag asked.

"I dinna ken the man," Alex replied, pulling the top part of his *fèileadh mór* over his head. The wind was blowing strongly in their faces now, making every step twice as hard as normal.

Morag laughed.

"That's no' what I meant," she gasped. Duncan looked at her.

"Ye're awfu' pale," he said. "Are ye hurting?"

"A wee bit," she admitted. "The wind's stealing my breath."

"I could walk in front of ye, and Duncan behind," Alex suggested, stopping and bending down to look for the familiar signs that she wasn't well. He adjusted her arisaid to disguise what he was doing, for she was old enough now to realise that she was different and was sensitive about it, because she didn't want to be. He stood straight again and tapped his lips, which told Duncan that hers were blue. It could just be the cold, but…

"We could practice that lift Da taught us last week," Alex said, making his voice sound eager. "D'ye remember it, Duncan? The one wi' two of us?"

"Aye. That's a good idea."

"What lift?" Morag asked suspiciously.

"Da was teaching us ways to carry a wounded clansman from the battlefield," Duncan said.

"I saw that. I dinna want to be thrown across your shoulder. Ye might drop me," Morag replied.

"No, that's no' the one I meant. This one, we make our arms like a chair. We'll show you."

The two boys stood either side of their sister, linked arms behind her back, then bending down a little, reached across behind her knees and clasped wrists.

"Now, you put your arms over our shoulders then sit down on our arms, as though ye're on Da's chair," Alex said.

She did as he said, a little uncertainly, and then Duncan and Alex stood, lifting her feet from the ground.

"Ooh! It is like a chair!" she cried.

"Then we walk together, like this," Alex continued, and they began to walk across the grass. Alex's plaid blew off his head, his hair flying wildly round his face, but he paid it no heed.

"Am I too heavy?" Morag asked after a minute. "I can walk, if we go a wee bit slower."

"No, ye're light as a feather," Duncan assured her, although in fact his hand was going numb with the effort of gripping Alex's arm, as being smaller than Alex their 'chair' was on a slant, which meant he was taking the bulk of his sister's weight.

"Aye, and we can walk faster this way and get home before the rain comes," Alex added, glancing back over his shoulder to see, between the tangles of his hair, the rain slanting down over the distant mountains.

"When ye're good at it, ye can run wi' your clansman," Duncan added a little breathlessly. "But no' the day."

"Is it no' easier to carry him across your shoulder though?" Morag asked, swinging her legs.

"Aye, but Da said if he's wounded in the guts ye canna do that, for it'll be awfu' painful and might even kill him."

"It isna very comfortable when ye're no' wounded in the guts," put in Duncan, who had been carried up and down the hill by his brother during this lesson and had vomited afterwards, to his shame.

The trio continued, making it home moments before the rain started. The boys bent their knees in the doorway so that Morag could stand. Moira, who was making up the fire, turned to look at them.

"Close the door, quickly," she said as the wind gusted in, swirling smoke around the room. She'd already lit a candle, which was burning on the table under the window, bowls and spoons laid out around it.

"Morag was feeling a wee bit sore," Duncan said, massaging his hand surreptitiously before examining Alex's finger-shaped marks on his arm, which would be bruises tomorrow. He looked at Alex, who was similarly rubbing his arm. Morag was heavier than she looked. But it had been worth it, for she was not as pasty-looking as she had been, although her lips were still a purply-blue.

"It was the wind in my face," Morag put in by way of reassuring her mother. "I couldna breathe."

"Is it hurting here?" Moira asked, touching her chest. "The truth," she added.

"Aye, a wee bit," Morag admitted reluctantly, then, knowing the next question, lifted her skirt to show the lower part of her legs.

"They're a wee bit swollen, *m'eudail,*" Moira said. "Why no' go to bed until your da gets home? Have a wee sleep?"

Morag glanced into the other room, then shook her head.

"I dinna want to be alone," she said. Everyone looked at her then, for like Duncan she was not a child who was afraid to be on her own. It was Alex who was the gregarious one, who loved to be with people all the time. "Can I sleep next to you, on the *seise?*"

"Aye, if ye're wanting to," Moira said. "Alex, fetch me the brush and I'll smooth your hair. Both of you," she added, as Duncan moved into the light. "It's awful windy and ye both look like wild things!" She settled down on the high-backed bench seat and Morag lay down next to her, using her knee as a pillow.

"There'll no' be enough room for my head soon!" Morag observed laughingly, reaching up to place her hand on her mother's swollen stomach.

"He'll no' be in here much longer," Moira told her. "He's nearly ready to see the world now."

"Or she," Alex said.

"Aye. Ye're wanting a wee sister, are ye?"

"Aye, I'm thinking it would be nice for Morag to have a wee sister, as I've a wee brother," he replied.

"I can feel her, or him," Morag said, sitting up again.

"She's practising walking. Come on then," Moira said to her sons, seeing their eager faces.

The three children stood or sat with their hands on their mother's stomach, while their unborn sibling moved restlessly, as though impatient to join them.

"It must be awfu' strange for you," Duncan commented. "We can feel it, but it must be different for you, for it's inside ye. Does it hurt?"

"Aye, sometimes," Moira said. "No' the now, though. Ye were the same when ye were in there, all three of ye. Alex, you were the liveliest one. I thought ye were playing shinty near the end! This one's kicking fierce too though."

"He's still the same," Duncan said. "Awfu' restless in bed sometimes."

"She must be awfu' cramped in there. How does she breathe?" Alex asked.

"I think you're right. When she gets too cramped she'll come out. I dinna think she needs to breathe, no' till she's out in the air," Moira said uncertainly. Her sons asked the strangest questions sometimes.

Morag yawned and lay down again, the back of her head leaning against Moira's swollen womb. Alex and Duncan sat down, Alex between his mother's legs to have his hair brushed, Duncan on the stool opposite. All of them loved these times, and this one seemed special somehow with the fourth child of the family making its presence felt. The wind and rain battered at the door and windows and that, accompanied by the increasing darkness and warmth of the fire, made the room seem cosy and almost womblike itself.

"I can feel her patting my head," Morag murmured sleepily, her eyes drooping.

Then they were silent for a while, Moira concentrating on smoothing the tangles from her eldest's hair without hurting him, while Duncan watched. Although it was Alex who was famous for his incredible memory, at times like this Moira, watching the intensity of her younger son's expression, always felt that he was somehow recording every tiny aspect of what he saw, and that if asked to paint a picture he would be able to reproduce the scene in intricate detail.

"Is Father Gordon teaching ye the drawing?" she asked impulsively. Duncan startled, and came back from wherever he was in his mind.

"No," Alex answered before him. "Art is a trivial pursuit, more suited to girls or to young gentlemen of equally weak mind with nothing better to occupy their time," he continued in an uncannily accurate copy of the priest's voice, except at a higher pitch, Alex still being some years away from his voice breaking.

Duncan giggled involuntarily, then looked at his mother nervously.

Having automatically laughed herself, Moira could hardly be severe with her sons now.

"Did he actually say those words?" she asked instead.

"Aye. Today," Alex told her. "I tellt him that Morag doesna have a weak mind, for she can grasp the mathematics better than all the boys, myself included. He wasna pleased wi' me."

"I like the mathematics," Morag said from her supine position. "We learnt the five postulates today."

"Did you?" Moira said, seizing the opportunity not to have to comment on her son's lack of respect for the priest, not least because she agreed with Alex. Weak minds indeed! "What are they? I havena learnt them, only the adding and subtraction and suchlike."

"It's for learning about shapes, so it *is* drawing, for ye learn to draw circles and triangles. We didna today, but we will," Morag said. "And then we'll learn Pythagoras."

"It's all about points and drawing lines on them, and rules about it. I canna see the reason why we have to learn them," Alex added glumly.

"Ye canna see the reason why we have to learn Latin, either," Duncan said.

"Da tellt me that all the old books are written in it and there's a lot of wisdom in them, and that if ye're speaking wi' a king or a duke from another country, and he canna speak the Gaelic and ye canna speak the Spanish or whatever language he speaks, ye'll both be able to speak the Latin together, for all rich people ken the Latin."

"Well, that seems a good reason to learn Latin, then," Moira commented.

"Maybe, though I dinna think kings and dukes will come here, and there werena any at Crieff either. Can ye ask Da to tell us why we need to learn to draw a straight line from any point to any point?" Alex asked.

"And why all right angles are equal to one another. Why we need to learn it at all," Duncan added.

"It's to draw shapes properly," Morag said sleepily. "Father Gordon's going to show us his goniometer tomorrow."

"Is he?" Moira asked, having no idea whether she should be pleased or horrified at this prospect.

"Aye. It's a wee thing that ye can use to measure an angle, so ye ken if your triangle or square is right," Morag added. "She's sleeping now, I think."

"She is," Moira agreed. "You join her for a wee while till your da comes home, then we'll eat."

"Will ye say goodnight to Da for me, when he does?" Morag asked, yawning.

"Ye can tell him yourself, *m'eudail,* for I'll wake ye when he comes so ye can eat. He'll no' be long. And ye can ask him why ye need to draw lines from points, but I'm sure there's a good reason." If there *was* a reason to do with battles and clan affairs, Alexander would certainly know it, and once he'd explained it Alex would want to learn it. Moira was sure of that.

Morag yawned again, and sighed.

"He's coming now," she murmured, and then her eyes closed.

Duncan stood and went to the window, looked out, then shook his head and came to sit down again.

"I canna see Da," he said softly so as not to wake his sister.

Silence fell again, punctuated only by the sound of the brush and the rain battering against the window. Moira finished Alex's hair and the two boys changed places. While they were doing so, Moira took the opportunity to stretch, taking care not to disturb her daughter, who was now fast asleep.

Morag murmured something in her sleep, sighed and then

flung her hand out, before settling back into slumber. Alex stood up and moving across, tenderly slid her arm back under her arisaid, which was tucked around her like a blanket. She smiled in her sleep, then relaxed. He sat down.

"Shall I stir the broth?" he murmured.

Moira, focussing on Duncan's dark locks, nodded her head and Alex moved across to the fire, stirring the contents of the pot, which released a savoury aroma into the room. Duncan's stomach grumbled loudly and they all giggled quietly, so as not to wake Morag.

"I'm sure your da'll no' be long now," Moira whispered. Apart from the hunger though, she'd be happy to sit here all evening with her beloved children. As much as she loved Alexander, when he came home, smelling of the rain and wind, hungry and eager to tell his news of the day, the whole mood of the evening would change. She loved his vitality, his eagerness to share everything with her, but there was something infinitely precious about these quiet, thoughtful moments with her children, something that they shared exclusively.

Morag flung her hand out again and her face twisted in a rictus of pain, then relaxed instantly into complete slackness. Duncan jumped, and Moira, thinking she'd caught a tangle with the brush, murmured an apology, then continued.

Alex, sitting where Duncan had been previously, was, uncharacteristically, watching Morag intently. He shivered suddenly, the hair rising at the nape of his neck, the unsettling feeling strong enough to make him first of all glance behind him and then stand and step over to his sister, grasping her shoulder and shaking her gently.

"Let her sleep, Alex," Moira said, then looked up and saw the expression on his face. "What is it?" she asked.

"I dinna ken, but..." Alex replied, shivering again. His sister's shoulder felt boneless somehow, and she did not respond to his gentle shaking of her. She always slept deeply, so that should not have surprised him, but it did.

Duncan, sitting between his mother's knees, turned, a worried expression on his face. His head was on a level with Morag's and he peered at her, then reached up and stroked the hair back from her face.

"She's awfu' pale, Ma," he said, "And she's sweating."

Moira put the brush down next to her, alarmed now. She reached across, lifting her daughter's head from her lap. Morag's hair was soaking wet.

"Morag," Moira said urgently, reaching under her and lifting her into a sitting position. The child's head lolled forward, completely limp. "Get me the candle, now," she said, fighting to hold back the panic that rose in her chest.

Duncan shot to his feet and brought the candle over, shining it on Morag's face as Moira asked him to. The child's lips were blue, her skin clammy.

Alex rubbed his sister's hand frantically.

"Wake up, wake up, wake up," he repeated over and over.

Moira looked at Duncan, and they exchanged a look.

"I'll fetch him," he said before she could speak, and putting the candle down on the table he ran out of the room into the storm, leaving the door swinging wildly.

Moira exhaled sharply. She had to stay calm, she had to.

"Will ye close the door, *a ghràidh?*" she said. While Alex did, she put her hand on Morag's neck as Susan had shown her to. Nothing. No weak, rapid pulse. No slow irregular beat. She moved her fingers, praying that she just hadn't found the right spot. Nothing.

She had known this moment would come, had told herself that she was prepared for it, that she would accept it when it did, as God's will. But now it was here, she did not, could not.

"Ma," Alex said uncertainly. Instinctively she reached out and pulled him into her right side, cradling Morag's upper body to her left.

"We must be strong, *a leannain,*" she said gently, trying and failing to stop the tears spilling down her cheeks, and felt rather than saw him accept that his sister was gone. He wrapped his arms around her neck, burying his face in her shoulder, and she tried to use the moment to calm herself. In this minute she could do nothing for Morag, and she had to think of her unborn child, keep herself calm, for a shock could kill it, and that she could not bear. She could not bear this, but more than this would be…no.

And then the door flew open and Alexander, carrying Duncan, ran into the room, putting his son down clumsily and then dropping to his knees next to his wife and daughter, the rain pouring from his clothes and hair. Duncan moved to the door, closing it quietly.

Alexander looked at his wife, who shook her head.

"I'll go and get Susan," he said, leaping to his feet again, desperate to do something about this thing against which nothing could be done, "and Father Gordon."

"No," Moira said firmly, stopping him in his tracks. "No," she repeated. "She's beyond Susan's help now, and doesna need the priest. She's baptised, and too young for other sin. Please. Let's sit with her, and pray together for her as she goes to Heaven. I dinna want anyone else to be here."

"Alpin's wi' her," Duncan, still at the door, said. They all looked at him, and he flushed. "Alex saw him too, did ye no'? Ye looked back at him."

"No," Alex said. "But I thought there was someone in the room. That's why…" His voice trailed off.

"It was Alpin," Duncan said. "She talked of him often wi' me. Tellt me he was waiting for her. I didna believe her, but—" he choked back a sob, "I should have believed her," he finished sadly.

Alexander stood and went to the window, opening it a little to allow his daughter's spirit to go free, letting the scent of rain and wind into the room. Then returning to his family he beckoned his younger son to him, wrapped his arm round the soaking wet trembling boy, knelt down again, and stroked his daughter's hair.

"Aye," he said. "Just us. And Alpin, if you're still here. Take care of her for us."

They sat like that for a long time, silently drawing strength from each other, while the rain battered on the window and the wind howled around the house, and Morag slept her final sleep of peace, free of pain at last.

* * *

She was buried two days later on Inchcailloch, next to Alpin. Alexander had taken Gregor and Barbara to one side and asked their permission to do so, explaining that the boys had seen him come for Morag as she died. He asked them out of respect, as being the chieftain he could bury his daughter anywhere he wanted, and they were touched that he did so. His words also helped them to cope with the loss of their son, knowing that he was still watching over them, and now had company. They also reasoned that Morag had surely gone to Heaven, and if Alpin had been allowed to escort her, then he must also be in Heaven, which was a great comfort. They did not say this to the chieftain, knowing no way to do so without it appearing as though they were glad that Morag had died.

The funeral was sombre and quiet, and there was no gathering afterwards because the chieftain and his family had expressed an intention to stay on the island overnight, to say their goodbyes. The rest of the clan returned to their homes or fields. The death of a child, though not uncommon, was always a time of great sadness, and the older the child the more tragic it was. Of course, when the new bairn arrived, they told each other, that would bring joy to the family again and make the grief for the lassie more bearable.

Although Morag had been a delightful child, everyone had known that it was unlikely she would survive to reach adulthood. Perhaps it was a blessing that God had taken her, for young and innocent as she was she was sure to be in Heaven. The chieftain and his family would realise that when the intensity of their loss waned a little.

The chieftain and his family *did* already realise that, in their heads, but it did not stop their hearts breaking. With every day that Morag had survived, hope had grown that she would become stronger, that whatever was wrong with her heart would somehow heal itself. Now that hope and their precious daughter were gone.

Alexander, aware how close Moira was to giving birth and how anxious she was about it, as all women were at such times, tried to hide his grief so as not to burden her. Moira, aware of how worried Alexander was about the imminent birth, both for her and the baby, and how a mother's moods affected the welfare of the unborn child, tried to hide her grief, so as not to burden him.

And the two boys, aware that something odd was going on between their normally affectionate and communicative parents, but assuming it was what grief did to adults, discussed their feelings together in bed, in whispers, so as not to make Ma and Da even more unhappy.

The house seemed empty somehow, even with the four of them in it. It was as though the small and fragile Morag had taken up most of the space, and now she was gone there was a huge void which could not be filled. Alex imagined that if he shouted into the house from the door his voice would echo back at him, as it did in caves. He wanted to try it, but could hardly explain why, so didn't.

"Susan tellt me it was her heart," Duncan said once they were settled in bed the night after they got back from the island.

"Ye asked her?"

"Aye, at the funeral. I'd wanted to ask her before, but it seemed that if I did, I'd make whatever was wrong more *real*, somehow, by speaking about it. She said her husband taught her that the heart is like a wee pump, and it pushes all the blood around your body. Ye've got these veins and things that look like tree branches, and the heart works very hard all the time to make sure the blood goes into all the wee branches. Morag's heart had something wrong with it, so it didna pump the blood as well, which is why her lips went blue sometimes and her ankles swelled. And then it wore out much quicker than ours will, and when it did, it stopped working. She tellt me that it wouldna have hurt her. She just went to Heaven in her dreams and then when she woke up she was really there."

"D'ye think that's true?" Alex asked. Duncan thought for a minute.

"Aye, I think it could be. Jesus must have kent she was coming, for He let Alpin come back for her, and He let me see him, so we'd ken she wasna alone. That was kind of Him. And Jesus loves bairns. It says so in the Bible."

"Ye truly saw him," Alex said reverently.

"I didna see Jesus," Duncan replied.

"No, I mean Alpin. What did he look like?"

"He looked like he did when he was alive. I only saw him for a moment, no' long enough to *really* see him. But he was smiling, and he reached out to her. Wi' the arm the broken men cut off."

Silence fell for a minute.

"D'ye think Morag's heart is pumping the blood properly now, then?" Alex asked, just as Duncan's eyes were closing. He opened them, blinking the sleep away.

"I think it must be, if Alpin has his arm back. God can do anything, can He no'?"

"Aye, I suppose so."

Silence fell again, and this time when Alex spoke, although Duncan heard the words he was too far gone to stop himself plummeting into sleep.

"I wish ye'd made her heart pump properly without her having to die, if ye can do anything, Lord," he murmured sadly. He put his fingers against his neck for a minute as he'd seen his mother do so many times to Morag, equally soothed and distressed by his own strong, regular pulse. Then he reached across and did the same to Duncan, gently so as not to wake him.

Then he turned over, closed his eyes and waited for sleep to take him.

* * *

It was the first truly fine sunny day of April, and Moira, along with many of the other women, had taken the opportunity to clean the house thoroughly. Alex and Duncan had dragged the mattresses and bedding outside before going to their lessons, and Catriona had whisked the sheets away to the loch, telling Moira to go and rest, that she would deal with the washing, as it seemed likely the bairn would be putting in an appearance in a few days.

Moira had acquiesced to having the sheets washed for her, but then rather than resting had attacked the cleaning with a vengeance, Alexander returning a couple of hours later to find his wife sweating, standing with her arms braced on the table, head bent, grimacing.

After assuring him that she was fine she had enlisted him to help, with the result that by the early afternoon the house was immaculate and Alexander was sitting on the *seise* reading his book while Moira finished the final task of sweeping the floor.

"What are ye reading?" Moira asked. "It doesna seem that ye're enjoying it."

Alexander turned the book over, as though unsure what it was.

"It's the Platonic dialogues. Plato was a Greek, but this is a Latin translation. The boys are learning fast now, and trying to translate that Aristotle book for Duncan made me realise how much I've forgotten. I canna convince the boys Latin's important for them to ken, if I canna read it myself! I thought to refresh myself. Are ye well?" he asked, seeing Moira's sudden grimace. She didn't answer for a moment, focussing on her breathing instead. "That's the second time."

"Aye," she said once the spasm had passed, not telling him that it was not the second pain, just the second one he'd noticed. She'd been having mild contractions for much of the morning. "I'm thinking it was a good thing that I cleaned the house today."

"Is the bairn coming?" Alexander cried, jumping up.

"I think so," she replied. "But it'll be a good while yet. No need to bother the women, let them finish their cleaning. That was the first wee pain. The second," she amended, seeing the expression on his face.

"Sit down," he said in his chieftain tone, taking the brush off her and finishing the sweeping, brushing the dirt out of the front door with a flourish, then turning back to her. "Will I make ye a hot drink?" he asked. "D'ye want some o' that tea Susan brought ye?"

"The raspberry leaf. Aye, that'd be good."

He bustled about and she watched him, amused as she realised that her incredibly capable husband was more anxious than she was. It was strange, but with every child, even Alex, her first, no matter how anxious she *had* been, a sense of calm and acceptance had descended on her as soon as she'd felt the first labour pains. It was no different now, although she'd worried it might be, with losing Morag only a week ago. He brought her the tea and then looked around for something else to do.

"Sit down," she said. "Tell me about the Plato book. It'll help to take my mind off it. Yours too."

He picked the book up then sat down and she leaned into him, sipping the tea.

"I've been reading *The Republic,*" he said. "They're debating what justice is, and then end up talking about the perfect State. Socrates says that philosophers make the best rulers, because they're no' interested in wealth or power, so they wouldna go to war with each other to win more land, and because they're learned and wise."

"Ye tell me the Father said Duncan would have been a philosopher, for he sees things deeply and thinks before he answers a question," Moira commented.

"Aye, he did. I dinna ken if he'd be the best ruler though. Alex wants it and Duncan doesna, for one thing. In *The Republic* Socrates says ye'd have to force the philosophers to rule, for they wouldna want to. It isna that interesting. Well, it might be, if my Latin was better and I could read it easily."

"I thought ye said it was a book by Plato. Who's Socrates?" Moira asked, before grimacing again.

"Will I go for Susan?" Alexander said immediately.

"No. Tell me about Socrates."

He made an intense but only partially successful attempt to relax next to her, and sighed.

"He was Plato's teacher, but he didna leave any writings of his own behind. Plato wrote a lot about him, and Aristotle too, if I remember rightly. Socrates was a brave warrior, inured to hunger and cold, and could drink an awfu' lot of wine without becoming drunk."

"Good qualities for a clansman then!" Moira said, smiling.

"Aye. But he was a philosopher too, spent his life trying to find out what made a man good. He thought that once a man kent what virtue was, for instance, that he couldna then be anything *but* virtuous. Or just, or pious…so he looked for answers to the questions."

"And that's what yon book is about?"

"Aye, mostly. It tells about the death of Socrates too. He was accused unfairly by his enemies, and could have saved his life if he'd gone against his principles, but he wouldna. He had too much honour for that. I'm thinking he was a great man. I'd quite like to call the bairn Socrates, if it's a boy," Alexander added, to Moira's surprise. "No' as his first name," he added, "but somewhere in there. If he grew up to have some of his namesake's qualities, it wouldna be a bad thing."

"Aye, as long as he doesna end up being hung. I'm assuming that's what happened, if he wouldna abandon his principles?" Moira said.

"Aye. No' hung. They made him drink poison. But I think the name MacGregor is enough to get any man hung unfairly. Calling him Socrates willna make a difference there."

She didn't answer this. After a minute or so of silence he was just about to ask if she was having another pain, when she spoke again.

"Is it helping?" she asked, and did not need to elaborate, for she knew him well, as he did her.

"No," he admitted, putting the book down. He pulled her into his side and kissed the top of her head. "I hoped it would, for I really canna remember a lot of Latin, so I have to concentrate to read it, but she's there all the time. I ken we expected it, but that doesna help, does it?"

"No," she agreed. "I hoped it would too. The only comfort is that Alpin came for her. I wouldna have wanted her to go alone."

"Ye really believe that Duncan did see him?" Alexander asked. She twisted so she could look up into his face, saw the grief, the yearning to believe.

"Aye. I thought about it and I do, for a few reasons. Duncan isna one for flights of fancy, and Alex sensed him as well, although I didna. And at that time we all thought she was just sleeping. I think Morag saw him too - I think she kent what was happening, for when I asked her if she wanted to go to bed she tellt me she didna want to be alone. And then she asked me to say goodnight to ye when ye came home, and a minute later, just as she went to sleep, she said 'he's coming now'. Duncan looked out of the window, for we all thought she must have heard ye coming. It was only today that I realised she wasna talking of you, but of Alpin. She said he'd come for her, ye ken that. And she wasna feart, which is a comfort to me too. Ah, I'm sorry, *mo chridhe,*" she said, observing the tear trickle down his cheek.

"No," Alexander replied, wiping the tear away with his hand, "I needed to ken that, for it *is* a comfort. Did ye tell the Father about it?"

"No, I didna," Moira said in a completely different tone of voice. "It's between us. And he'd only tell me that when ye die ye go to Heaven, Hell or Purgatory, and that spirits are demons sent from Hell to tempt us."

"Your opinion of the priest hasna improved then, I take it?"

"He hasna done anything to improve it. Oh!"

"What is it?" Alexander asked, instantly on full alert.

"I'm thinking ye might want to fetch Barbara. And Susan," she said. "Dinna fash, there's nothing amiss. My waters have broken, that's all. It means the bairn's certainly coming, but no' for a wee while yet."

Even so, Alexander shot out of the house at such speed that within a few minutes the whole clan knew the chieftain's next bairn was on the way without him telling them. So it was, that by the time he returned with Susan a short while later he had no need to fetch Barbara, as she was already in the house along with several other women who were making up the bed with clean bedding, the newly washed bedclothes still being wet outside. Barbara was tearing up cloths and Catriona was heating water by the fire.

"So your pains have started then," Susan said, pulling a gold instrument out of her skirt.

"Aye, but they're far apart as yet, and no' so bad," Moira said. "What's that?"

"It's my husband's pocket watch," Susan told the women. "Have ye no' seen one before? Ah, well," she continued on noting the universal curiosity which gave her her answer, "I havena used it since I've been here, but in the cities, ye ken, time is important. I thought it might be easier to time how close the contractions are wi' a watch. My husband used one when he attended a birth. I'll show ye all how it works when we've prepared everything. There'll be time, I'm thinking."

Alexander stood uselessly, suddenly an alien in his own house, which was very unsettling.

"Away and tell the laddies," Barbara said. "They can go to our house. Ye can too, if ye want. Flora's making the meal, and the boys can help her wi' the dyeing, or Gregor wi' the weaving. Take their minds off their ma. Ye can sleep there too, if the bairn hasna come by nightfall."

Everyone except Alexander recognised this as the dismissal it was. He looked around uncertainly.

"Are ye needing more water?" he asked. "I can fetch—"

"Ye canna do anything here," Moira interrupted. "I'm in good hands. Take care of the boys, that's the best thing to do, and let us take care of this one. Someone'll come and tell ye when it's born."

He went over to her and kissed her fiercely, to the amusement of everyone and the embarrassed pleasure of his wife.

"I love ye," he whispered in her ear. "Ye're my life. If there's anything I can do, ye fetch me." He turned to the others. "Ye take good care of her," he said. "And send someone to tell me about *everything*, no' just when it's born."

And then he turned and was gone, leaving the women to get on with their business.

Susan waited until he was well out of earshot before speaking.

"Alexander tellt me ye've helped birth all his other bairns," she said to Barbara.

"Aye," Barbara said, tearing a cloth with her teeth. "Most of the clan's bairns for that matter. But I'm thinking ye'll maybe ken things I dinna, and ye a doctor's wife. Like yon watch thing."

"Alexander thought that too, and I didna have the heart to tell him otherwise, for he's so nervous. But I've no bairns of my own, and my husband didna deliver babies, unless…it was the wives who did that."

"So ye've never even *seen* a birth?" Catriona asked in wonder.

"Aye, I've seen them, wi' Rob, but only when…never mind. And I couldna see much, for they put all these sheets around the woman because he was a man. Even he couldna see what he was doing, had to feel what was amiss. He hated that."

"So ye've only seen births where something's been amiss?" Moira asked, coming to the point Susan was tactfully evading.

"Aye. But I'm no' sure how much use I'd be even then, for I saw even less than he did. Rob tellt me what he did and I passed him cloths and suchlike, that was all," Susan admitted.

"Well, let's hope we dinna need ye, then!" Barbara said. "I dinna think we will, for the first three came wi' no real problems."

"Morag took a long time to come, but when she finally did, she just slipped out. Ye were right no' to tell Alexander, though," Moira said, gasping a little as the next pain hit. "He puts a lot of faith in ye, where medical matters are concerned. He'll be comforted to ken ye're here."

"Birthing's no' a medical matter though. It's like women's courses, just natural," Barbara said firmly. "But ye can still be useful, Susan, for ye've a cool head, and that's worth a lot. And if Alexander has faith in ye, he'll keep away, and that's worth even more. Now, tell us about yon watch."

The women gathered round, while Moira sipped her tea and breathed through the pains, and Susan showed them the magic of the pocket watch, and how you could use it to time the pains. This provoked a discussion of how strange city folk were to spend money on a wee machine to tell them what time it was, when they could look up at the sky for free.

"Or count," Catriona said. "I can see it's easier wi' the wee watch, for it willna lose count between the pains, but I canna see much need for it other than for births."

"The city people make appointments for certain things, though. And events, like Mass and concerts, start at fixed times. Life is very different there," Susan added.

"But ye prefer it here?" Barbara asked.

"Aye, once Rob was gone. It's more…real, somehow."

"I havena ever been to the city myself," Barbara said.

"I met Alexander when I was staying in Edinburgh wi' my ma and da," Moira put in. "They took me there hoping I'd meet an important man, maybe a lord, for it's awfu' crowded and so much easier to meet people of different social standing than in other places. I was very pretty then, so my da hoped I'd catch the eye of a clan chief, maybe, or a Lowland laird."

"Ye're still very pretty," Fiona said with complete honesty, for she was.

"I dinna feel so, at the minute," Moira said, colouring with pleasure at the compliment.

"They must have been pleased, then, for it worked, if ye met Alexander there," Susan said.

Moira laughed.

"They didna consider a MacGregor chieftain to be good enough for their daughter. They were horrified. Tellt me I couldna marry him. So I walked out, for as soon as I met Alexander I kent it was him or nobody. We married a few days later, and then he brought me home."

"Have ye no' seen them since?" Susan asked.

"My parents? No. I'm sorry for that, but no' sorry I married Alexander. I wrote to them, several times, but they never answered me, so I stopped. He was going to take me back, when the bairn's born. Morag so wanted to go to Crieff in October, but of course she wouldna have been able to…so Alexander was going to take us all to Edinburgh to see a play, once this one's born. I dinna ken if I want to go now."

"It might be a good thing for ye all," Barbara said. "Get ye away from the memories. It helped Kenneth to move on from Alpin, when he went to Crieff."

"Aye, maybe. But we've to get this one out first. I'm hoping it's a girl," Moira said, "for Alexander wants to call it Socrates if it's a boy!"

The exclamations of horror and laughter at this ludicrous suggestion lightened the atmosphere, and no one mentioned Morag after that.

* * *

Alexander sat brooding by the fire in Gregor's house, while Gregor finished the piece of weaving he was doing before it went dark, and Alex and Duncan sat on the floor, watching their father worriedly. In the corner Flora was finishing dyeing the wool that Barbara had abandoned to become a midwife.

"Is she well, Da?" Duncan asked uncertainly, after examining his father's face.

Alexander pulled himself out of his gloomy train of thought, and looked at his son.

"Aye, laddie. She's well. But this is no' a time for men," he said. "What did ye learn in the lesson today?"

"We learnt the Pythagoras theorem," Duncan told him, aware that right now his father couldn't care less what they'd learnt, but was just saying something to avoid talking about their mother. "Ye can use it to work out the length of one of the sides on a triangle."

"It's awfu' difficult and ye can just measure it wi' a ruler instead o' doing yon stupid sum, wi' squares and roots and all. And it's faster wi' a ruler," Alex said scathingly.

Alexander, with a great effort, forced himself to focus properly on his sons.

"Aye, but ye canna do that in battle," he ventured.

"Why would I want to measure a triangle in the middle of a battle?" Alex asked incredulously.

"Well, let's say ye're besieging a castle," Alexander said, drawing his dirk and scratching out a rudimentary castle in the dirt floor of the room. "If ye ken how far away the castle wall is, and how high it is, which ye will if ye've reconnoitred the situation, then ye can calculate how far the cannonballs need to travel to hit it at a certain part o' the wall, and make sure your artillery's in the right place. Or if ye're in range of muskets or arrows." The boys gathered round the drawing, watching as he constructed a tiny cannon and then the triangle between them.

"So ye dinna have to waste cannonballs or shot finding out if ye're close enough?" Duncan said.

"That's right. If ye're building a fancy stone house, no' like this one, but like the big ones ye saw in Crieff, which some of the clan chieftains have, it helps ye wi' the slope of the roof, which is a triangle. And sailors use it when they're navigating too, I've been tellt, although I havena been over the sea."

Alex did not look convinced.

"But I'm no' likely to besiege a castle, am I, Da?" he said.

"I've done many things in my life that I didna think I'd ever do when I was your age," Alexander said. *Including trying to explain the uses of Greek theorums while worrying about my wife,* he thought.

"Morag would have loved it," Alex added. "She was looking forward to…" He reddened and stopped talking. An uncomfortable silence fell on the room.

"Are ye wanting to practice a few wee sword moves while it's light?" Kenneth asked, who had just come in from tending the cattle.

"We havena got our swords," Duncan said, looking longingly at the door.

"Wrestling moves then. Come on."

The boys were out of the door in a flash, Kenneth following, while Gregor appeared in the doorway of the weaving room.

"She'll be well," he said. "She's the hips for birthing, and the others all came easily. And Barbara kens what she's doing. She's helped all the MacGregor bairns into the world. And many of the sheep and cows too, for that matter," he added. "Ye can help me wi' the last part of this, and then Kenneth'll go and get the other men and we'll have a wee *ceilidh* to pass the time and take your mind off it."

Alexander smiled, and stood. Gregor was right. By the time the *ceilidh* was over, the bairn would most likely be born. Although Morag had taken a day and night. By the morning, then. He could do that. Moira was strong. It would all be all right.

"Is that right? Ye can measure for the cannon shot wi' a wee number sum?" Gregor asked as the two men went into the weaving room.

"I havena a notion. I ken it's used for house building and sailing, though I dinna ken how. But it seems it might be used in a siege, so I made it up. Alex willna set his mind to learn something unless he thinks it might be useful to him when he's chieftain. He'll learn it now."

"Will he no' find out if it doesna work for battering castles?"

"Aye, I daresay he will, one day. But by then he'll have learnt it. And once the boy learns something, he never forgets it. So it willna matter then."

Gregor laughed.

"He's a bonny laddie. Looks a lot like you when ye were his age. Duncan takes more after his mother in looks. She'll be well," he added, reaching across and squeezing Alexander's shoulder. "Barbara's no' lost a mother yet, and this is your fourth. She tellt me the first is usually the most dangerous, for ye canna tell if the woman's hips are wide enough to get the bairn out. After that, it's generally easier."

"She tellt ye that?" Alexander asked.

Gregor smiled.

"Aye. She's my wife, we talk! She doesna say a lot about the birthing, for it's no' a man's business, but she talks of it a wee bit. Like we talk about battles wi' the women, but no' the details."

This seemed reasonable. Giving birth was the female equivalent of going to battle. Except men went to battle to take life, and women did it to bring life into the world.

Dear God, let her be safe, he prayed silently. *Let them both be safe, strong and healthy.*

Then he turned his attention to helping Gregor, in a vain attempt to put his wife's imminent battle to the back of his mind for a while.

* * *

By the evening of the following day, while it was certain that Moira was strong and healthy, although tired, the battle was not going well. At first everything had gone smoothly, but then although the contractions had continued and Moira had kept pushing down, no baby appeared. Initially she had been squatting, supported by one of the women, but as time went on and she grew more tired, she lay on the bed, where she now was, exhausted and in considerable pain.

"I canna keep pushing," she said. "I need to rest for a wee while. Can ye no' see it?"

"No' yet. But ye have to keep going, lassie, for it canna stay in there," Barbara said logically. "Susan and I'll just go for a minute of fresh air, and we'll be back. You rest, and then when we come back, ye can try again."

She nodded to the door with her head and the two women went outside.

"Ye said ye'd attended births wi' your husband if something was amiss," Barbara said as soon as the door was closed. "D'ye think the bairn's breech?"

"God, I hope it isna," Susan said.

"Me too, but there's a reason it's taking so long. Did your husband attend such a birth?"

"A breech? Aye, he did. He had to put his hand in and turn the baby."

Barbara grimaced.

"I've done it wi' lambs, but ye can reach in and grip the legs and pull. There's more room in a sheep's womb too. I canna do that wi' a bairn!" she said.

"Have ye never seen a breech birth before?" Susan asked.

"Aye, just the once when I was a wee lassie, and I never want to again. The bairn wouldna come at all. My ma, who delivered the bairns as I do now, finally reached in and pulled the first part she could reach out, which was an arm, and then she cut it off wi' a knife." Barbara wiped her face with her hands. "Then she remembered I was there and sent me out. She tellt me later that she couldna have saved the mother *and* the bairn, so she had to make that decision. We could hear the mother's screams all over the village as my ma pulled the baby out piece by piece."

"Did she live?"

"Aye, but she wasna ever the same again. Nor was my ma for that matter. I dinna think I can do that. I've delivered a few difficult births, and a few that were stillborn, but never a breech."

Susan thought of her husband, of the caesarean operation he'd done, cutting frantically at the body of the dead woman in a desperate attempt to at least save the baby. But Moira was not dead, and chopping her baby up to get it out of her could only be a last resort.

"I'll try," she said. "My hands are smaller than yours, so it willna hurt her so much." This was true, but she was giving Barbara a way to save face, which the older woman took, gratefully. "I've some opium too. I'll give her a few drops to help ease the pain before I do it."

They went back in, smiling happily as though they'd been discussing the spring planting rather than the desperate situation in the house.

"We've decided that we need to find out how the bairn's lying," Susan said. "I've got some wee drops that'll take away the pain for ye, so it'll be easier for ye to push later, and it willna hurt ye. My husband did that once, and the bairn was born wi' no problem later." She dipped into the bag she'd brought and produced a brown glass bottle.

"Ye canna give her anything to take away the pain!" Fiona said with alarm.

"Why no'?"

"Father Gordon willna allow it! He tellt us that God gave women pain in childbirth because Eve was tempted by the Devil in Eden. It's the price we all have to pay for her trans…um…for what she did wrong."

Susan muttered an extremely rude and unladylike word under her breath. "Is it now?" she said. "Well, there's no reason the Father will find out, is there?"

"But God will ken what we're doing!" Fiona insisted. "And the Father will find out when ye confess!"

"I'll worry about that," Susan replied, who had no intention of confessing something she did not consider a sin. "What d'ye think Alexander would say about me helping her wi' the pain?"

"Alexander would say 'do it', and so do I," Moira put in from the bed. "To hell wi' the priest. When he's been through the pains of childbirth himself he can tell me what I should be doing, and no' before."

Everyone except the devout Fiona laughed at this, and, comprehensively overridden, she made no more objections as

Susan carefully measured out the opium and gave it to her patient. Then, when Moira relaxed, she washed her hands in the hot water, rubbed oil into them and then gently eased her fingers in.

"I can feel it," she said to Barbara. She closed her eyes, so as to be able to concentrate. "I think it's the nose. Aye, I can feel under the nose. I'm thinking the bairn's so eager to see the world, it's looking up. That's why it's stuck."

"Can ye get your hand round the head and move it?" Barbara asked. "That should be easier than turning the whole bairn, if the rest of it's in the right way of it."

There followed the longest few minutes of Susan's life, as she desperately tried to remember everything her husband had ever told her and put it into practice, very aware that everyone was watching her intently and that if she failed, mother and baby would die and Alexander would never forgive her. She would never forgive herself, for that matter. As gently as possible she tried to turn the head, to push the chin down, and when she thought she'd succeeded she removed her hand, very carefully. Sweat was running down her back and chest, and she felt sick.

"I think I've done it," she said, "but I canna be sure. What do we do now?"

"We wait," Barbara said, looking anxiously at Moira, who was now ghastly pale, her face contorted with pain in spite of the opium. "I think we should tell Alexander what's happened," she added, effectively informing everyone in the room that she at least thought Moira's life was hanging by a thread.

Before anyone could say anything, Fiona got up and left the room.

"I've no intention of dying yet, Barbara," Moira informed her.

"I'm glad to hear it, for ye've to push again," Barbara said, smiling. "The bairn's in the right way of it now, so it should come, but ye need to help. Are ye wanting to squat down again?"

"I canna," Moira admitted. "I ken it might be easier, but I havena the energy. I'm so tired. But I'm no' giving up."

Several torturous minutes passed, during which Fiona came back and whispered in Barbara's ear. Barbara nodded.

"Aye, if it comes to that, and we can," she said.

"Is he coming?" Moira asked.

"No. He was going to, but I said we didna want him here, for we all had to look to you and he'd be in the way. He said he wouldna as yet. But I think he will anyway, if the bairn takes much longer. Kenneth's off wi' the laddies, doing something to get them out of Alexander's way, for he's beside himself."

A communal sigh passed round the room.

"Well I'll just have to try harder then, will I no'? We canna have him trying to take over," Moira said wryly, making everyone laugh. The tension in the room dissipated slightly.

Half an hour later, and just as Alexander was striding across the grass in the direction of his house, regardless of Gregor and Kenneth's entreaties to him not to, Angus Malcolm Socrates MacGregor, complete with misshapen head and badly bruised face, finally arrived into the world, to the utter relief of every female present.

Having been so desperate to see this new world, enough to have almost killed himself and his mother, now he was in it Angus appeared to change his mind, and set up an indignant howl that carried halfway across the settlement. Alexander's stride turned into a sprint, which came to an abrupt halt as he neared the house to see Susan coming out of it. She shut the door behind her in an obvious gesture that they were not yet ready for him, then walked across the grass to intercept him.

"She's well," she said, before he could ask, "or she will be, but it was a hard labour for her, and she'll need to rest for a while. And as ye can hear, the baby's well too. Ye can go in soon, we just need a wee minute to finish everything and wash her."

Alexander looked toward the house, clearly undecided whether to listen to Susan or just go in. She could not stop him if he wanted to.

"She'll no' want ye to see her as she looks right now. Give her a minute to recover, man. Giving birth is always hard, but this was particularly difficult," she continued gently.

"Is the bairn well? Ye said it was difficult. Is it—"

Susan smiled, touched by the fact that his first question was not the one almost every other new father she'd ever spoken to had asked; is it a boy?

"No, it's no' like Morag was. She had a weak heart. It was just something that can happen, nothing to do with the birth. As far as we can tell, this one's fine. And Moira too," she continued, seeing his mouth open to ask.

And then the door opened and Barbara appeared, holding a loudly squalling bundle in her arms.

"Come in then and see if you can calm your son, for we canna, and he willna feed yet," she shouted, to be heard over the racket.

Susan forgotten, Alexander strode over to his son, looking down at the screaming bundle as though it was a chest of diamonds.

"A boy," he breathed, expertly taking him from Barbara's arms. She reached down to pull back the cloth that was currently obscuring the baby's face.

"Did ye tell him?" she said.

"No, I was about to," Susan replied.

"Mother of God!" Alexander cried. "What happened to him?"

"*Ísd,* laddie," Barbara hissed, looking back into the house.

"He was coming out face-first," Susan said bluntly. On seeing Alexander's confused expression, she sighed. "Bairns normally come out head first – the top of the head," she explained. "But his head was tilted back, like this," she demonstrated, "so he couldna come out. That's why he's so bruised."

"Susan had to reach inside and move his head so he could be born," Barbara said. "So Moira's hurting. But she'll heal, and so will this one. He just looks as though he's been in a wee stramash."

He did. His little face was rapidly purpling with bruising, and his head was slightly squashed-looking. Alexander bent his head and kissed his son's brow, the only part of the face that seemed undamaged. Miraculously the baby quieted, whether because of the unfamiliar touch or because of the huge face looming into his vision, no one knew.

"*Fàilte don t-saoghal, a laoich,*" he said, and beamed at the two women. "Thank you," he added simply. And then he turned and walked into his house.

Moira was lying in bed, looking very pale and utterly exhausted. Catriona was wrapping something bloody up in a cloth, which she now picked up.

"I'll leave you for now, then," she said, and left the house, taking the bundle with her.

Alexander hardly noticed her, all his attention focussed on his wife.

"I'm sorry, *mo chridhe*," he said, sitting carefully on the edge of the bed. "This was hard for ye, Susan tellt me."

"Aye. But he's well, and I will be soon. I just need to sleep," she said, trying and failing to lever herself into a sitting position.

"No, you stay lying, and sleep. I'll take care of him."

"I need to see if he'll feed, first," Moira said. "Barbara said he's probably no' interested yet because his mouth hurts."

"Aye, Susan tellt me how he was born. I would think that's the case," Alexander said. "He looks awfu' battered, poor wee thing."

Neither of them said what both of them were thinking; the first sign that there was something amiss with Morag had been that she was not interested in feeding, had had to be coaxed in numerous ways, and then had only suckled for a moment before falling asleep. If they said it, it might be true, so instead Alexander placed the baby on the bed, then leaned across and gently lifted his wife into a semi-sitting position, taking note of her grimace of pain. The baby was placed against her breast, where he made a soft murmuring sound but showed no sign of wanting to feed.

"Does he ken what to do?" Alexander asked, who had never been present for the first feeding of his previous babies.

"Aye, he should. It's an instinct with them, as it is wi' calves and lambs," Moira said. She repositioned the baby, bringing her nipple close to his mouth, and both parents watched intently as the tiny mouth puckered and then latched on.

After a moment he did indeed start to suckle, and both parents smiled proudly at each other, as though their new son had just won a great battle, although Moira's smile was more of a grimace as her face contorted, and Alexander, on the alert, instantly reacted.

"Is he hurting ye? Shall I move him?" he said.

"No," she replied, although tears of pain welled in her eyes. "It was the same wi' Morag, and wi' Duncan. It's worse wi' each bairn. It's normal," she added, seeing her husband's look of alarm. "It causes...cramps. It'll lessen in time. But he needs to feed, painful or no'. Are ye still wanting to call the poor laddie Socrates?" she asked.

"Aye, I think so. No' as his first name though. We're agreed on Angus Malcolm, aye?"

"Aye. Socrates is a lot to live up to, from what ye tellt me of the man."

"So is Angus, from what ye tellt me of your grandfather," Alexander shot back.

Moira smiled.

"He was an old reprobate, but he was always kind to me. I was his favourite grandchild, he said, for I was the only one of them with the red hair of my granny. She died before I was born, but he tellt me about her."

"Maybe we should have named Alex after him, then. He's the one wi' the most red in his hair," Alexander replied, eyeing the fuzz of blond on his latest son's head.

"No. He was to be named after his da. Hopefully he'll be as good a chieftain to his clan as his namesake one day. One day many, many years from now."

Alexander laughed and reaching across his suckling baby, kissed his wife tenderly. She smiled and her eyes started to close. He watched as she gave up the fight to stay awake, as her face settled into sleep. And then he waited until the baby was full, noting when his eyes closed and his arms and legs relaxed. He would call Alex and Duncan in to meet their brother later. They were safe enough with Kenneth. Right now he wanted his wife to have some undisturbed sleep, and to spend some precious time alone with this beautiful new member of the family.

Very tenderly he picked his son up, pulled the blanket over his wife, and went across to the chair, where he sat cradling his newborn child and thanking God that both of them had survived the birth, and that the women had not had to choose to save his wife over his baby, as he had told them to, should it come to it.

CHAPTER TWELVE

Alex and Duncan looked at their new brother for some time without enthusiasm, before exchanging a glance with each other. Then Duncan turned his gaze from the crib towards the bed his mother was lying in, although it was early afternoon. She *never* stayed in bed in the daytime. She always had too much to do, particularly at this time of year.

"Are ye sick, Ma?" he asked.

"Aye, she's sick. It's a mighty trial, having a bairn. Ye canna just leap out of bed and run around as normal after such a thing," Alexander informed them. "What d'ye think of your new brother then?"

The boys exchanged another uncertain look.

"He's awfu' ugly, is he no'? Is all that black a birthmark?" Alex asked bluntly.

Duncan closed his eyes in horror. He was thinking the same thing, but would never have actually spoken his thoughts aloud.

"No, it isna a birthmark, ye wee gomerel!" Alexander replied angrily.

"He had a hard time of it too," Moira called from the bed before Alexander could say any more. "They dinna ken, Alexander. How could they?" she added to her husband. "He's swollen and bruised, that's all. Give him a few days and he'll be as bonny as ye both were when ye were born."

"Is that why ye're in bed, Ma?" Alex asked. "Did he hurt ye?"

"Aye, but it wasna his fault. Some bairns are born easy, and some are no'. I'm just a wee bit tired, that's all. Ye'll have to help your da with the cooking, and do some cleaning too after your lessons, just for a wee while."

"Susan said she'd come in and help us," Alexander said. "She said she's happy to, and she hasna any man or bairns of her own, so I accepted."

Moira nodded.

"It'll no' be for long, just a day or two," she said, and yawned. "I'm just sleepy all the time, is all."

"Sleep as much as ye need to, *a ghràidh,*" Alexander said. "We'll no' disturb ye."

He cast a glance at his sons, who interpreted it correctly. They would not disturb her.

* * *

Two weeks went by, and although after a few days Moira started getting out of bed in the mornings, she spent most of the day sitting on the *seise,* feeding or holding the baby and staring into the flames. When she became tired, which was frequent, she'd put Angus in the crib that all the children had slept in as babies and go back to bed. She slept a lot.

"Is she still hurting from birthing him?" Duncan asked Susan at the beginning of May. It was a beautiful day. Alex and Duncan were helping with the planting, along with most of the clan. Duncan had cut his hand on an unexpectedly sharp rock, and his father had sent him home for Susan to look at it. She'd washed it and put some salve on, and now they were both sitting on the bench outside sharing an oatcake and a flask of water before he went back.

"Aye, she is," Susan said.

"I thought that when Angus was healed, she would be too," he said. He liked Susan. If you asked her a question, she usually told you the truth, and if she didn't it wasn't because she thought you were stupid, but because there was something in the truth that was only for adults. "He's still a bit yellow, but his head isna squashed now. He looks like a real baby."

"The yellow is just the end of the bruising, that's all," Susan told him.

"So if Ma's still sick, does that mean that birthing is harder for women than it is for bairns?" Duncan asked.

Susan looked down at him. He was a thoughtful laddie.

"Birthing is always hard for a woman," she said. "Even the

easy births, like yours was, are hard. For ye've been growing inside her for nine months, and that takes a lot of work, and then when it's time for ye to come out, it's a lot more work. And sometimes it's an awfu' lot more work."

"Like with Morag, and Angus," Duncan said.

"Aye. D'ye remember Morag being born?"

Duncan shook his head.

"Alex does. He tellt me Ma looked like she does now, but he doesna think she stayed in bed as much."

"I think Morag is part of the reason your ma's staying in bed," Susan said, then cursed herself. It was easy to forget how young Duncan was, for he was wise beyond his years. She saw his expression of curiosity and realised she couldn't leave it at that.

"She's grieving for your sister as well. Ye all are, but it's worse for her, because having a bairn takes a lot out of your spirit as well as your body, so it's harder for her to cope wi' the grief as well."

Duncan thought for a minute, as was his way.

"Can we help her?" he asked.

"Ye're caring anyway, laddie," she said. "Just keep caring, and be patient. And tell Alex to be patient too, for it's no' a strong point wi' him."

Duncan laughed then, and stood up.

"I'll tell him," he said, "but I dinna ken if he'll listen to me. He doesna always."

She watched him as he ran back to the fields, though her thoughts were with the sleeping woman inside. She'd seen this before, the post-natal melancholia. It came without warning, and could lay the strongest woman low. Rob had told her that a lot of men believed it was something only rich and pampered women suffered from, but they were wrong. He'd seen it in women of all classes, because he'd treated everyone who needed him, rich or poor, whether they could pay or not.

God, she missed him. She was happy here, and had a good and useful life. But she still thought of him every day. She could not imagine what it must feel like to lose a child, even one as delicate as Morag had been. It was hard on both of them, but as chieftain Alexander had a lot to distract him. Moira had Angus, although he must remind her of the last baby she'd fed and cared for. But at least she *was* caring for him. Some women rejected their babies when they were afflicted with melancholy.

I'll give her another week, and then I'll start pushing her to do more, she thought. Then she stood, brushed the oat crumbs off her dress and went in.

* * *

In the end she didn't need to, because a week later Moira broached the subject herself.

"I canna think what's wrong with me," she said one day, after it had taken all her energy and will just to get out of bed, get dressed and sit in the *seise.* "I feel as though I've lost myself somehow."

"Ye've been through a lot, losing Morag and then having such a hard time wi' Angus. Are ye still sore?"

"Aye, but I'm healing now, and Alexander's a good man, thank God. He'll wait until I'm ready before he…well, ye ken. It isna that. I just feel as though I'm in a thick fog. I canna see my way through. I'm feart, for I dinna care about…about anything," she finished sadly.

Susan came and sat down on the chair opposite her.

"Have ye no' felt like this before, wi' the others?" she asked.

"No," Moira answered. "I've been sore, aye, but I've always been happy to have had them."

"But ye're feeding Angus and doing everything for him, and that's a good thing."

"Aye, but I dinna *feel* it, in here," Moira said, putting her hand over her heart. "I'm so afeart that I'll always be like this."

"You willna. I've seen it before, and so did my husband. It's a kind of melancholy that comes over some women, a lot of women, when they've had a baby. And wi' losing Morag too, it's no' surprising. It passes. It always passes. But ye must force yourself to do more. If ye're sore, then ye should stop. But ye should come outside, talk to people."

"I canna think of what to say," Moira admitted. "It just seems like a great burden that I canna carry."

"Ye must think of what ye liked to do before, and then do it, even if ye dinna enjoy it. One day ye'll find ye *have* enjoyed it, just a wee bit, and then ye'll start to find yourself again. Ye owe it to yourself, and to Alexander and the bairns too, for they're all worried about ye. They miss ye."

"I miss me, too," Moira admitted.

"I'll help ye all I can. I've never had the melancholy, but I've grieved, so I ken about that part at least."

"Well then, I must brush my hair. And then I'll sit outside for a wee while. And take my spindle."

Susan smiled.

"I'll make some porridge for ye. Ye're no eating enough either."

"I havena the hunger. But ye're right." Susan handed her the hairbrush, and she attacked her hair with a ferocity born of despair and determination, brushing it until it cascaded down her back like a sheet of flame. Then she coiled it up, covered it with a clean curtch, sighed, and stood, as though going into battle. Which in a manner of speaking she was.

* * *

Over the next weeks Moira made a Herculean effort to shake off the melancholy that threatened to wrap her in a dark blanket and drop her down a deep well. At least that was how it felt to her, as though something had sucked all the joy of life out of her. She sat outside spinning or sewing, and once physically healed she started to do the housework and cooking again, although Susan still came in every day, partly because Moira still tired very quickly and needed help to accomplish her daily tasks, and partly because she would often burst into tears or become angry about the slightest thing, which told Susan that she was still struggling and needed emotional support as well.

Moira didn't want to talk about how she felt with the other clanswomen, because as the chieftain's wife she was the person they all came to with their problems. They expected her to be strong, as Alexander was, and she felt ashamed of what she thought they'd perceive as weakness. After all, most of the other women had had babies, and none that she knew of had lost the love of life. So she manufactured a happy and capable persona for all the women except Susan. When she became too tired to maintain it, she used having to tend the baby or herself as an excuse and repaired to the house to sleep or cry.

Or confide in Susan. In fact over the next months both Alexander and his wife confided in Susan regarding their worries about Moira's health. It was not something Alexander would normally do, but it was clear to him that his wife was leaning on Susan a great deal and trusted her implicitly. And Moira was an excellent judge of people. In addition, Susan had at least a little medical experience, and although she was of the clan she was also separate from it in a sense, having been away in Edinburgh for much of her life. And she was easy to talk to.

Alex and Duncan confided in each other. Moira adopted the same attitude to her sons as she did to the clansfolk, forgetting that both of them knew her well, were extremely intelligent, and one of them at least was both observant and deeply sensitive. For once Alex paid heed to his brother's advice, and both of them played along with their parents' pretence that all was well.

All of which led to a forced and artificial jollity pervading the house and replacing the happy relaxed atmosphere that had always reigned there before.

The only member of the family who was completely relaxed was Angus, who did what babies do; he ate, slept, waved his limbs about, made strange noises, and grew.

"It's because he doesna ken what it was like before he was born," Alex said to Duncan one evening. They'd made the excuse that they were going to wash down by the loch, for they'd had a long day of weeding and were sweaty and tired. But in reality they just wanted to get out of the house for a while. Pretending to be happy when you weren't was hard work, as was watching your parents pretending to be happy when *they* weren't.

"I'm thinking he's a wee bit young to ken anything as yet," Duncan commented. "D'ye remember anything from when ye were that wee?" If anyone did, it would be Alex.

Alex stared across the loch for a while, thinking.

"The first thing I remember is lying on a big hill," he said after a time, "and it was soft, red and blue, and there was a steady drumming noise. When I tellt Ma about it, she said I couldna possibly remember that, for it was when I was still suckling, like Angus is now. She said she had a red and blue checked arisaid that she used to wrap me in, and the beating would be her heart. But I canna remember anything else, people speaking or what they were doing."

"I canna remember anything that early. I remember Da sitting on a horse going away somewhere, and I was a wee bit feart of him, but you were arguing wi' him about something."

"Ah. That's when he went to war. I tellt him I wanted to go with him and he said I couldna. Ye'd have been about two then, I think."

"Even if Angus *did* ken that Ma and Pa are pretending to be happy when they're no', he wouldna realise that it wasna normal, for they've been like that since he was born," Duncan mused.

"Aye, that's true. D'ye think they dinna want him?" Alex asked.

"No. He's awfu' bonny, after all."

"He is now his face isna swollen and black, aye."

"I canna think why they wouldna want him, for they wanted us, and Morag," Duncan said. "Should we ask them?"

"They willna tell ye," Alex said firmly. "I asked Da – no' about wanting Angus, but about what was wrong, and he tellt me I was imagining things, that it was just a busy time, wi' the oats and barley to grow, and the cattle to go to the shielings."

Duncan's face creased.

"But it's the same every year, and they dinna act like that normally. Did ye say that?"

"No, for he did that thing adults do and asked me to away and do my school work that the Father gave me, and when I tellt him I'd done it all, he tellt me to go and fetch some water, even though I dinna think he needed it. So I did, for I feared he'd find me a harder task if I kept asking the question he wasna going to answer."

Both boys sat in silence, looking across the loch for a while. It was hard being a child sometimes. Adults told you to ask a question if you wanted to know the answer, but sometimes it seemed that whenever you asked something you *really* wanted to know the answer to, they wouldn't tell you, for some unknown reason.

"Well, if they willna tell us, we'll just have to wait until they're well again," Duncan said finally.

"Or until they tell us anyway," Alex said hopefully.

Duncan made a sound in his throat which conveyed how unlikely he thought that to be, and they both fell silent again. Adults were strange. He would not be like that when he was an adult, Alex decided.

* * *

December 1724

By December Angus was crawling everywhere, which meant that someone had to watch him continuously to make sure he didn't burn himself, as he had an insatiable interest in the pretty orange and red flames of the fire and would make a beeline for the hearth if allowed. He could also make sounds, some of which were recognisable, such as 'Ma' and 'Da', which always made the adults smile.

This, however, still seemed to be the only thing that could bring a genuine smile to Alexander's and Moira's faces. Apart from Angus's development and the passing of the seasons, little else seemed to have changed. Perhaps Moira slept a little less and worked a little more, which meant that although Susan still called every day if Alexander was out, she didn't stay as long as she had when Angus was born. Other clan members would call in too with small gifts, but would tactfully make excuses and leave after a short time, as it was generally known now that Moira had not completely regained her health after the birth, and tired easily.

But the atmosphere in the house was the same. To a stranger it might seem to be a happy home, or at least a contented one. But to all the family members except the youngest, there was still an awkwardness between them. True, it was not as bad as it had been, or perhaps it was just that they were slowly becoming accustomed to it as the new normal.

Or at least the adults were, and Angus because it was all he'd ever known. But the boys were not, although they played their part when in the house. They tried to be outside as much as possible though, which had been easy in the summer and autumn when the weather was fine and there was a lot to do. But now, as the nights drew in, snow began to fall and the wind grew bitingly cold, there were few jobs to be done that entailed leaving the house, and no one ventured outside unless they needed to. It was a time to make small repairs around the home, to conserve energy, watch the food stocks carefully to ensure they'd last until the following summer, and to chat, tell stories, and come together.

Which would normally be pleasant. But not this year, when rather than coming together the adults were measuring every word before they spoke it, when conversations faltered and died due to lack of motivation, and much time was spent sitting silently looking morosely into the fire.

Today the boys had had their lessons with Father Gordon, which they now looked forward to, not because he had grown to be a more interesting teacher or Latin had become a more interesting subject, but because in the break between lessons they felt they could behave naturally, could laugh and relax with Jeannie, Alasdair Og, Simon, Janet, and the newest pupil Dougal, who was just learning his letters.

They all walked home through driving snow, huddled together as the wind blowing down from the mountain was particularly bitter today, and it was already dark.

"If it carries on we should be able to have a war in a day or two," Alex observed. Everyone stopped as one, looking around. Being covered in snow, the ground was visible, even though it was too cloudy for moonlight. He was right; there were already a good few inches on the ground, enough to make a cache of ammunition, and due to the wind there was a number of deepening drifts which could be easily turned into fortifications to attack or defend.

The mood of the group soared immediately.

"Grandda said it's going to snow for weeks," his namesake Alasdair Og informed them. "He tellt us we needna fear any redcoats coming from Inversnaid, for they canna march in winter wi' yon stupid boots they wear."

"What stupid boots?" asked Jeannie.

"Ye mean yon knee-high shiny ones?" Alex asked. "I saw them when I went wi' Da to try to rescue Andrew. They were all wearing them."

"Aye. Grandda says they've got these hard soles made of leather, no' like the soft ones we wear, and the soles are smooth, so they canna walk in this weather without sliding everywhere, as they canna use their toes to grip the stones. And they're no' like us, for they die if they have to sleep outside wi' no tent or fire. So they willna bother us, at least till the spring."

"They didna bother us last spring, or summer," Jeannie observed.

"No, but there's more of them there now. There's talk that

they're going to build roads for the redcoats to move along quicker, for they canna go across the heather as we can. Did your da no' tell ye?" Alasdair Og asked Alex and Duncan. "He went wi' Grandda and Da to see what they were doing."

"No, he didna," Alex said. An awkward pause followed

"Is that because of their leather boots?" Duncan asked, to break the silence.

"I suppose so," Alasdair Og replied.

"Would it no' be easier to make new soles for their boots, than to build roads?" Jeannie asked.

"I dinna ken. But I'm thinking we could have our war here," Alex put in, pointing to an area on the edge of the copse of trees. "Ask the others, and when we ken how many we've got, we can do a wee bit of planning tomorrow, on the way home. Da says it's important to survey the battlefield."

"What battlefield?" a deep voice came from behind them, making them all jump. Kenneth appeared a moment later, his hair covered in snow as he was using the top part of his *féileadh mór* to carry a large quantity of sticks.

"We're thinking to have a battle in a day or two, if the snow stays," Alex told him. "When the Father's away."

"He'll no' be going anywhere in this weather, I'm thinking," Kenneth said. "He doesna normally go out spreading God's word in the winter, does he?"

An air of gloom descended on the group of children.

"Ye said it's a battle, though, and ye're surveying the battlefield?" Kenneth continued. "Can ye no' have a word wi' your da, tell him it's a lesson in fighting? And ye can use that triangle thing your da tellt us about, to measure laying siege to a castle. Father Gordon couldna object if it's a lesson and the chieftain says ye can do it, can he?"

All the children looked eagerly at Alex and Duncan.

"Aye, we can ask him," Alex agreed, without much enthusiasm.

"D'ye think he'll agree?" Alex asked a few minutes later, when he and Duncan had peeled off from the rest of the children to go home, Kenneth still accompanying the others.

"Aye, I think so. I'm no' sure if he'll come and tell the Father though, so he might stop us. I'm thinking Da maybe caught the malady Ma got from having Angus, for he isna interested in anything really. Neither of them are."

"I wonder why he didna tell us about the roads? Why he didna take us? He tellt me he wanted us to go wi' him where possible now, to learn about being a chieftain," Alex said dejectedly.

"He must have had a reason," Duncan answered, although both of them knew he might not. He just didn't discuss things in depth any more, hadn't taken them anywhere at all since April when everything had changed. When they'd asked if they could go on cattle raids with him, he'd said that he couldn't risk them, not after last time. Which had been an excuse. All of them had known it, and all of them had pretended they didn't. It was exhausting.

"I wish Angus—" Alex stopped abruptly. "It doesna matter."

"It wouldna have made a difference if he hadna been born," Duncan said. "Maybe if Morag hadna died. They dinna talk about her at all. Kenneth tellt me that his Ma and Da were like that about Alpin, and it was only when they talked about him that they started healing."

"Ye asked him?" Alex said, aghast.

"Aye. I wanted to ken if we could help Ma and Da. Kenneth didna mind me asking."

"Did he tell ye what we could do?"

"No. He said it's a thing adults have to do themselves."

"I thought that they'd give Morag's love to Angus, and it would be…no' the same, but no' too different," Alex said.

"I dinna think it happens like that. I think Morag took their love with her when she died, and now Angus needs it more than we do because he's so wee, so they're giving what they've got left to him instead of us. It's no' his fault."

They walked in silence for the rest of the way home, while Alex thought about what Duncan had said. Duncan thought in a strange way sometimes, but Alex was old enough now to know that his brother often saw things that he didn't, and that he was worth listening to.

What he'd said about love could be true. But it didn't make it any easier to bear.

When they went in Moira was sitting by the fire and Angus was playing with something at her feet. As the door opened he looked up, his face lighting up at the sight of his siblings.

"Al!" he cried, abandoning his plaything and crawling across the floor at an incredible speed towards his eldest brother, who smiled and scooped him up into the air, making Angus crow with laughter. Then he settled him in the crook of his arm, Angus gripping him round the neck.

"He's growing heavy now," Alex observed. "I willna be able to do that soon."

"I wouldna ken," Duncan said with mock rancour. "He thinks he's only got the one brother. He doesna even ken my name." Whether that was true or not, Angus certainly seemed to have a fixation with his oldest brother, ignoring everyone else entirely if Alex was in the room.

"I'm sure he does," Moira said tiredly, standing up. "He canna make the sounds of your name yet, Duncan, no' even the first part. He will soon. Sit down and I'll get your meal."

"Susan's been here the day," Alex said, looking round before moving over to the table, where he sat down, placing Angus on his knee and ruffling his silky blond hair.

"How d'ye ken that?" Moira asked, ladling broth into a bowl.

Alex flushed. He could hardly say the truth, which was that the house was clean. He exchanged a look with Duncan.

"Are we no' waiting for Da?" Duncan asked, coming to Alex's rescue.

"No. He tellt us to eat without him. He'll be late home, for part of James and Catriona's roof fell in, and the men are all fixing it." She put the bowls in front of the boys, then scooped Angus off Alex's knee before sitting down and putting him to her breast.

In the past Moira would have asked them a multitude of questions about what they'd learnt, or they would have asked questions about the damaged roof, but instead the now habitual silence closed in on them like a shroud, broken only by the sound of Angus suckling and the clatter of spoons against the wooden bowls. Moira yawned.

"We were thinking to have a battle in a few days, if the snow keeps falling," Alex said somewhat desperately.

Moira looked out of the window, as though unaware that it had been snowing all day. Maybe she was: maybe she'd been sitting next to the fire all day, and hadn't looked outside at all.

"That sounds like fun," she said indifferently, moving Angus to her other breast.

A great weight of despair settled on Alex, although he did not recognise it as that. He just knew that the air was suddenly thicker and hard to breathe. An almost overwhelming urge to smash things, or to run out of the house and keep on running came over him. He shook his head to clear it, focussing on his broth, mentally reciting the Homer he'd learned today with the Father, anything to quell the strange urge to do something violent that was sweeping over him.

Lurching up, he lunged out with his hands toward my men
And snatching two at once, rapping them on the ground
He knocked them dead like pups-
Their brains gushed out all over, soaked the floor…

Homer was not helping. He looked at Duncan, who, aware that Alex was having some sort of crisis, reached across the table and touched his hand comfortingly, shaking his head by way of warning.

Alex swallowed, closed his eyes for a moment and pulled himself together. The silent meal continued.

Once Angus had finished, Moira busied herself readying him for bed, knowing he would slip into sleep easily with his stomach full and with luck would sleep through the night. She stood, rocking him in her arms, and took him into the bedroom. After a few minutes the sound of her singing softly drifted through to the boys, who, their broth finished, were sharing a bannock.

"Ged tha mi gun chaoraich agam
'S caoraich uil' aig càch
Ged tha mi gun chaoraich agam
Dèan a leanabh an ba ba.

Eudail mhòir a shluaigh an dòmhain
Dhòirt iad d'fhuil an dé
'Schuir iad do cheann air stob daraich
Tacan beag bho do chré."

When he'd settled into sleep, she came back into the main room, holding a hairbrush in one hand and taking off her curtch with the other.

"Would ye sing us a lullaby too, Ma, when we go to bed?" Alex asked impulsively.

Moira froze in the act of unpinning her hair, the flippant comment on her lips about them being too old for such things stifled by the open, unguarded look of pure longing on her eldest son's face. The son who wanted so much to be a man. The son who blushed scarlet if she tried to embrace him when other clansfolk might see.

Something inside her shifted and then settled, differently from before.

She continued over to the *seise*, where she sat, reaching up and unpinning her hair, which fell around her shoulders in a fiery cascade.

"Are ye wanting your hair brushed as well?" she asked softly. This time the longing was reflected on both her son's faces, and for a moment she felt the tears rise, but swallowed them back, knowing that if she gave way to them Alex and Duncan would misunderstand and this vital moment would be lost, perhaps forever.

"We need to clear the dishes," Duncan said.

"No. We can do that later. They'll no' go anywhere. Come. Alex, you first," she said, recognising that his need was the greater, that there was some great emotional torrent in him which he was struggling to hold back. He had always been calmed by having his hair brushed. "No," she added, when Duncan made to sit opposite, "sit beside me." She patted the seat next to her, and Duncan changed course, sitting next to her, at first keeping a slight distance between them, but after a few moments, realising that she was not going to change her mind, moving closer, so their bodies were touching from shoulder to thigh. She felt him relax into her and smiled, realising now that both brothers had been racked with emotion; Duncan was just more accomplished at concealing it.

"Tell me about the battle then," she said, using her fingers to untangle the worst of the knots in Alex's hair before she started brushing it.

"It was Alex's idea," Duncan said.

"I thought we could have a wee battle, for there's enough snow, and drifts too, that we could make into castles – or walls at least. We'll no' be able to go out at all if it keeps snowing, so we need to do it soon. And then Kenneth came and tellt us that Father Gordon willna be going away now as he does, so we'll be having the lessons every day," Alex explained.

"We ken that he'll no' want us to be having fun," Duncan added unguardedly. "But then Kenneth said that we could say it was a lesson and we were using Pythagoras's theorem, and if we talked to Da and he said aye, then the Father couldna speak against it."

"Are ye wanting me to talk to your da then, when he comes home?" she asked.

"Would ye?" Alex asked, twisting his body so he could look up at her.

"Aye. It seems a matter of urgency, as ye said."

Alex grinned, his face alive for the first time in…oh, so long. Then he turned away again, so she could finish untangling the knots, and Duncan slipped his arm round her waist and squeezed it.

"Dear God," she murmured, speaking aloud without intending to. "I should have done this before."

"We wouldna ask ye," Duncan replied, "because we didna want to remind ye…and make ye sad. More sad," he added.

"That was kind of ye both. It does remind me of her, but no' in a sad way, though I thought it would," Moira told them. "Ye ken how sick she was. It would have been harder for her as she grew. It was a peaceful way for her to go. The best way. I see that now." She said it to reassure them, but realised now that it was true. She was also realising just how desperately she'd needed this time with her sons, this time that was not just calming Alex and reassuring Duncan, but was thawing something deep inside her, something she had thought could never be thawed.

She smiled, and felt the smile warm her inside, crinkle the skin around her eyes, and knew that for the first time in months her eyes were smiling too, because her heart was smiling.

She continued then in silence, and after a while Duncan and Alex changed places. But the silence that before had been suffocating was now comforting, as it had been when Morag was alive.

Finally when both boys' hair was smooth and soft as silk, she started to brush her own.

"Can we do it?" Alex asked. She looked at him.

"Aye, that would be bonny," she said. "Will I sit on the floor then, and you behind me?"

"Aye, both of us, and we can take turns wi' the brush," Alex said.

It was strange having her hair brushed inexpertly by her sons. Listening to them alternately murmuring apologies for pulling her hair and giggling behind her as they wielded the brush was deeply healing. And now she let the tears come, silently, for they could not see her face, and she could not hold them back any more.

Later she got up and went to check on Angus, who was fast asleep, lying on his side, one arm outside the blanket. It was cold in the room, so very gently she pulled the blanket back up over him. Then she went back to the living room, where Duncan was piling the dirty dishes together and Alex was stirring the fire into a blaze with a poker.

"I'm thinking your da will be very late," she commented. "Come on, then, and I'll sing you that lullaby. Are ye wanting the same one I sang for Angus?" she added as she followed them up the steps to the loft where they slept. She sat on the edge of the box bed while they undressed.

"Aye, although it sounded different when I didna ken what the words meant," Alex commented dryly.

"Ye remember me singing that to ye?" she asked.

"I remember ye singing to me when I was a wee bairn, but I canna remember the words from then. But ye sang it for Duncan too."

"Aye, well, it's a MacGregor lullaby, so it's fitting that it's about a man being executed and his head put on a stick," she said, laughing. "But as ye said, when ye're a bairn the words dinna matter, it's the sound of the tune."

"Who was the man?" Duncan asked, pulling his shirt over his head and moving to the side of her to climb into bed.

"Wait," she said, then swung her legs up and climbed in. "Now then, let's all lie together. Alex'll no doubt remember me doing this wi' ye both, when your da was away."

"Aye, I do," Alex said, smiling and climbing carefully over her to lie at her left side. "The bed was always warmer too, wi' three of us in it."

"The man was Glenstrae. He was executed in 1570 and his widow was griefstricken, so she wrote this song, and she sang it to her baby," Moira told them. "That was a way for them to grow wi' the understanding that they needed to avenge their da, when the chance came for them to."

"And did they?" Alex asked.

"I dinna ken, *a chàirdean*. If they were good sons I think they would have done, aye."

"We would," Alex said with conviction.

"Let's hope ye never need to. They were bloody times, bloodier than now, even. I'm sure ye'll learn some useful tactics at the snow battle, though. Wi' Pythagoras's theorem, ye'll be invincible!"

They all laughed, and then snuggled in together. It was lovely and warm in the box bed. Even with the bed door open to let in the light from the single candle on the floor at its side it was warm, for there was no draught up here in the roofspace, as there was downstairs.

After a time she began to sing, sweetly and softly, the Gaelic words haunting and melancholy in the room. She felt the small, strong bodies of her two precious sons relax and then grow heavy as they slid gently into sleep. She lay for a while watching the shadows flickering on the beams of the roof, knowing that something magical had happened this evening.

And then she closed her eyes, and joined her sons in slumber.

Which was how Alexander found them when he came home two hours later, soaked to the skin and frozen to the bone, although being a Highlander he noticed that only because his hands were clumsy on the latch as his fingers were too frozen to feel it. Once in he made straight for the fire, after noticing that the dishes were unwashed and the fire had not been smoored for the night, although the room was empty. At one time he would have been alarmed, but Moira forgot a lot of things now, and would often leave jobs half done. The house was silent.

Once he could feel his hands again he unbuckled his belt, letting his wet *fèileadh mór* fall to the ground. Then he spread it to dry by the hearth before picking up the candle burning on the table and going through to the bedroom. Angus was fast asleep, mouth slightly open, long lashes resting on his plump cheeks. Alexander smiled, then approached the bed and stopped.

It was empty. He felt his heart speed up suddenly, and told himself to be calm. She was unwell, but she would not go out in this weather, and would never leave the baby alone. Maybe one of the boys was sick.

Taking the candle he climbed the steps, seeing them as soon as his head poked through the hole in the floor. He slowed then, so as not to make a noise and wake them, and was soon standing, watching them.

Moira lay on her back, one arm round each of the children, who were curled into her, all of them deeply asleep, their mouths slightly open, their long lashes resting on their cheeks like Angus. All the children had inherited Moira's ridiculously long eyelashes, and his heart caught as he remembered that Morag had too. And then he watched them some more, and felt his pulse slow and his mind and body relax as he realised instinctively that while he'd been out fighting to repair a roof in howling winds and driving snow, inventing curses when he ran out of stock ones to use, something gentle but miraculous seemed to have taken place in his home.

He wanted to climb in with them, share in the intimacy, but knew that if he did he would spoil it, not only because there was not enough room for four of them in the bed, but because they were warm and cosy, and he was still very cold. So he did the next best thing. He tiptoed back downstairs, smoored the fire, checked on Angus, kissing him on his rosy cheek, then went back upstairs and settled down on the floor next to the bed.

He was asleep in moments, lulled by a combination of physical fatigue, the warmth of the room, and a happiness that he had not felt in months.

CHAPTER THIRTEEN

In the end Father Gordon could not object to the snow battle because the whole clan, including the chieftain and his wife, joined in. The snow continued for another two days and showed no sign of slowing down after that, so Alexander called a meeting of the clan at his house. The priest also attended the meeting, shaking his head at the immaturity of the MacGregors, who, once the reason for the meeting had been explained to them, attacked the project with the same enthusiasm as they would have had they been planning to wipe out an enemy clan.

A lively and detailed discussion took place, helped by a large quantity of alcohol (in the case of the adults, at least), at the end of which two teams had been picked, only Kenneth abstaining, saying that otherwise the teams would not be fairly matched; he would look after the children who were too small to participate so their mothers could join in if they wanted to, or assist either team should they need help with anything particularly heavy. This was agreed to be fair, as Kenneth was worth at least two of any other man, in physical strength at any rate.

By the end of the jolly and raucous meeting, a few simple rules had been set: firstly the children were the officers, and it was they who chose the general of their army, organised the plan of attack and commanded their forces. The adults would be the soldiers and would obey their officers, although they would be allowed to make suggestions, and to interfere if anyone was either hurt or seemed likely to be.

Alex was elected general of one army and Duncan of the other, and a headquarters for each force was assigned, after which the meeting ended with some drunken singing and dancing, upon which the priest left, having refused to give a blessing to all the warriors before the battle as was done on real battlefields, saying it was making a mockery of the Lord.

"I canna think what's happened to Father Gordon," Alexander confided to his wife that night, when everything had been tidied away and the two over-excited generals of the opposing forces had been sent to bed together. "When he first came here he seemed to be a reasonable man, one who didna take himself too seriously. Now it's as though he's got a stick up...er..."

"His arse," Moira finished for him. "Aye. I'm thinking he was desperate for a home when he arrived, and was willing to be whatever he had to be to find one. Now he's feeling safe enough to show who he really is. Remember though, he gathered everyone together and tellt them Alpin had been killed on the day he arrived. I ken ye had enough to think of on the day, but even so it wasna his job to do that."

"Aye, that's true. I'll bear that in mind. Are ye wanting to fight on the day?"

Moira thought for a minute.

"I am. I feel as though I've been dead for months, and have just come back to life. It's a strange feeling, but I want to prove I'm alive, to do something silly for the pure joy of it. Of course, the problem now is that our two sons are on opposing sides, so I canna really choose a team without betraying the other one."

"Go wi' Duncan and watch him," Alexander said. "If ye do that, then I'll join Alex, and that'll be fair."

"I thought ye were going to stay neutral," she teased.

"I am on the day of battle, but I want to see how they plan."

"Why Alex?"

"Because Alex and Duncan are learning to work together, to combine their abilities to be stronger, which is what I'm wanting. Alex takes more after me, and Duncan after you in character, so if ye go wi' Duncan and me wi' Alex, we'll see better what they do when they're separate."

"I'm thinking we should act more as observers during the planning, unless they're after doing something dangerous. I'll just take part in the fight."

"Aye, then we can report back to each other. It'll be interesting to see how differently each of them prepares. For God willing they'll both grow to manhood, but they'll no' always be together, and I'd like to ken what they'd do alone. That gives me time to fill in any gaps in their education, as it were."

"I'm wondering who that wee one'll take after," Moira said, nodding her head in the direction of the crib, where Angus, who due to the meeting had been awake much later than normal, was dead to the world.

"I dinna ken. But I *do* ken one thing for certain," Alexander said.

"What's that?"

"I am so happy to have ye back wi' us. I'm supposed to ken how to fix anything, but I had no idea what to do to help ye, at all."

"Ye couldna fix it. Susan tellt me that many women are like this after a baby's born, and it passes with time. I couldna fix it either. I just had to hold on somehow, no' let it take me over completely, and wait. Ye did the right thing, I'm thinking, for ye didna get angry with me, didna leave me."

"I couldna be angry with ye. I put the bairn in there, after all. And I could never leave ye. I'm nothing without ye. I thought that before, but I ken it for certain now. I've been doing like you, waiting, and feeling helpless. And in the end it was Alex that brought ye back to us."

"It was both of them. And I was ready, I think, just needed a spark to light the fire, to bring me back to life. Thank you for being patient, *mo chridhe*. I ken that's no' something ye find easy, but ye were *very* patient wi' me."

He pulled her closer to him, kissed the end of her nose.

"Some things are worth being patient for," he said softly. "Some things are worth *everything*."

* * *

To Father Gordon's disgust there were no lessons for two days before the battle as well as on the battle day, as it was necessary, the chieftain had told him with great seriousness, for a good deal of planning and preparation to take place.

"Have ye ever been to battle, Father?" Alexander asked.

"Aye. I was at the '15 and the '19, ministering to the Catholic soldiers in James's army," Father Gordon replied.

"Ah, well, ye'll ken then, that a good commander always takes time to choose the best spot, and to build whatever defences he can before the enemy comes. Now this is a wee bit different, for the enemies' castles are closer to each other than would be normal, but they'll each be easier to attack, no' being made of stone, ye ken," the chieftain had informed him. "No' as easy to defend though, I'm thinking," he'd added, gazing off in the general direction of the 'battlefield', where much frenzied preparation was underway. In the distance Kenneth was drawing up outside one of the encampments with the peat cart piled high with snow. A great cheer at this drifted across to the two men.

Really, thought the priest, the man was insane. They were all insane. No wonder the MacGregors were proscribed. No doubt it was the foolish actions of their equally soft-headed ancestors who'd got them in their current predicament. He gave up and abandoned his flock to their freezing endeavour, repairing to his warm and cosy house to write a good sermon, and maybe work a little more on the book he was writing about the life of Saint Sebastian.

Over at the battlefield Duncan was watching the opposing side building their defences, using the cartload of snow that Kenneth had just delivered. When it was all unloaded, he would head off and collect another load for Duncan's side.

"It was good that we lost the coin toss for who had the first cart of snow," Duncan admitted to his mother and fellow officers, "for it means we can watch what they do, and gives us more time to plan." He fell silent for a few minutes, watching intently while the other children grew increasingly impatient.

"So, if ye look at what they're doing," he said suddenly, making everyone jump, "they're building a wee wall by piling up the snow, like this." He scooped a little snow together and compacted it into a tiny wall on the ground.

"Aye, we'll need a wall, too, to hide behind," Simon said.

"We will. When we make snowballs," Duncan added, pointing to the growing pile of ammunition being constructed and assembled behind them by one group of children and adults, "why do we make them into balls? Why no' make wee cubes?"

"It's easier to roll them into balls in your hands," Jeannie answered.

"Aye, that's true. But you make a cube of snow now, and then a ball, and throw them, and see what happens," Duncan said. "We've the time for it, Kenneth'll no' be back for a while yet."

The experiment was tried.

"The ball goes further," Peigi said.

"Aye, but which one hurt the most when it hit ye?" Duncan asked Allan, who had been the experimental target.

"The ball, for the wee cube was too soft. It just fell apart."

Duncan grinned.

"We need to build our wall from balls of snow," he said.

"That'll take us a long time," Allan pointed out.

"No' if we roll them down the hill," Duncan suggested. "If we make a lot of balls, about this big," he held a hand up to his shoulder, "we can roll them together, and fill the gaps wi' snow. Then we can kneel behind them, and stand up to throw the snowballs. That'll no' be as much work as they're doing, and the snow will be pushed together as it rolls down the hill, so it'll be harder."

"Or we could make more snowballs and lift them on top of the first ones, leaving wee gaps to throw balls through," Iain said.

Duncan nodded.

"How will we do that?"

"Kenneth can lift them. He's helping whoever asks," Allan said, grinning.

"Will they no' fall off though, being round?" Jeannie asked.

"We could use a peat shovel to make the top of the big balls flat," Duncan said after a minute, "and the same wi' the ones Kenneth lifts up. And if we do it all today, and pack snow round where they join, it'll freeze overnight, and be more solid."

Moira smiled as everyone scattered up the hill to make big snowballs. Her son really didn't need her. But it was wonderful watching him come into his own, away from his charismatic, gregarious brother. On the other side of the clearing, Alex's group were forming their snow into a wall with their hands, feet and spades, laughing and practising singing war songs to boost morale. They sounded as though they were having a lot more fun than Duncan's group.

Even so, Moira thought, when the fight started the day after tomorrow, she would much rather be behind Duncan's frozen snowball wall than Alex's.

* * *

The next day, the walls inspected and modified a little, and the stack of ammunition added to, the two groups repaired to their respective headquarters to make a battle plan.

"Da, ye tellt me that in a battle our greatest strength is the Highland charge, which is a ferocious sight to see, for it terrifies the redcoats and makes them run away," Alex told his group.

"Aye, that's true," his da agreed.

"But we canna do that at the start at least, no' until the time is right to attack their wall full on," Alex said.

"Aye, and they'll no' be terrified when we do, for they're Highlanders, no' redcoats," Alasdair pointed out.

Alex thought.

"Ye said that the redcoats do a wee drill wi' the musket, all together," he said to Alasdair.

"Aye, they come to the front and fire, then fall back to reload so the men in front can fire then fall back, by which time the first line has reloaded. It means that they can keep firing steadily without a pause when they're all reloading. But ye have to stay calm to do it, if the other side is firing at ye too," Alasdair said.

"Aye, which is why the Highland charge is good," Dugald said, "for it makes them afeart, and ye canna load quickly or aim well if ye're shaking or shitting yourself wi' fear."

Everyone laughed.

"The musket drill doesna work so well wi' the matchlocks though, for the men have to be at least a yard apart from each other, or the match fuse can set off the powder in their bandoliers. That means the men shooting have to be two yards apart for the others to pass between them safely," Alasdair added.

"I'm thinking that's no' a danger wi' snowballs though," Alex said, which made everyone laugh again. "But if we do the same thing, then we'll be able to keep up a steady fire of snowballs, and Duncan's men willna be able to stand up without being hit. And the rule is that if ye're hit three times, ye're dead."

"Or if your walls are breached," James pointed out.

"Aye, but if we can kill most of their men before we do our charge, then we'll be able to breach their walls, for there'll be no one left to fight us," Alex said. "And it'll be awfu' good fun to do a charge. We can shout, 'àrd choille!' like Da did when we fought the Maclarens!"

"Well, I shouted 'cruachan!' that time," Alexander said, "for we were Campbells then."

More laughter.

"Ah, it'll be wonderful to do a Highland charge!" Dougal cried. A chorus of agreement arose from the other children, and Alex smiled.

"I ken it's the chieftain that shouts the war cry, but I think we can all shout it this time," he said. "We need to practise our throwing drill."

"Can we practise the charge as well?" Dougal asked eagerly.

"Aye, we must! Come on then," Alex said.

With a great cheer, everyone dashed out into the afternoon snowstorm, and practised until it grew dark.

* * *

The day of the battle dawned, and while the snow wasn't falling as heavily as it had in the last days, the sky was still grey and heavy with cloud, promising a further fall later in the day.

Alex, carrying Angus, carefully walked the distance between the two fortifications, while Duncan counted carefully.

"How many?" he asked when they reached the edge of Duncan's wall.

"Twenty-five," Duncan replied, surreptitiously feeling the area where the lower and upper big snowballs of his team's wall met. Nicely frozen.

Alex looked up at the top of the wall.

"I'm thinking about five feet?" he said.

"Aye. But unless ye've built a cannon out of snow that works, Pythagoras's theorem isna going to help ye in this case," Duncan pointed out.

"That's true. But I tellt the Father that we'd be practising our mathematics, so at least I'll no' be lying to him if he asks us about it later."

"He will," Duncan said, "for he thinks we'll be too excited to remember."

The two of them smiled conspiratorially at each other.

"Now we've the numbers, we can do the sums later," Alex continued. "Although if we do it now, it'll tell us how close we have to be to reach each other when we're throwing."

"I've already—" Duncan stopped abruptly.

"Ye've already what?" Alex prompted.

"It doesna signify." In spite of them being brothers and unified against their tutor, later today they would be enemies. And enemy generals do not give away their knowledge to each other, no matter how amicable they might be outside of battle. Duncan had already made everyone throw a snowball, then had measured the distance they could throw in strides.

Obviously the adults could throw further, so the children had been delegated to making more snowballs for the adults to throw, to their extreme disappointment. To which Duncan had paid no heed, his mind focussing on one thing only; winning. If Alex hadn't done such an experiment, it was not his brother's place to tell him.

They walked back, Alex bouncing Angus up and down with each step and counting, "One, two, three…" making his little brother giggle.

"He'll be wanting to be on your team," Duncan said.

"Aye, but he's too young. Kenneth is awfu' good wi' bairns though. He'll keep him happy. I thought we could have a wee snowball fight with him tomorrow, just wi' soft handfuls of snow, so they dinna hurt."

"Aye, that's a bonny idea," Duncan said, feeling even more guilty for not advising his brother, as he was being so kind to Angus. "Good luck today, *mo bhrathair*," he said by way of alleviating the pangs of guilt.

It's just like chess, he told himself fiercely. Their father was teaching them the game at the moment, and when they played together they were both utterly ruthless and determined to win, which made for an exciting challenge. This was the same.

He did not advise his brother.

* * *

The battle began at noon, because Alexander calculated that it wouldn't take more than a couple of hours, after which everyone could come straight to his house, warm up, get dry and eat. To that end the women who were not taking part in the battle had been baking bannocks and apple pastries to use up the apples that had started to rot, the bad bits being cut out before being enfolded in pastry with honey, a recipe Susan had brought back from Edinburgh.

By the time they finished eating it would be dark and the storytelling and music could begin, but it would still be early enough for the children to all join in for a good while before they grew sleepy. They deserved it; they'd worked really hard in the last days, and Alex and Duncan had been fine leaders in their own very different ways. Their own very different *interesting* ways. Father Gordon would not be impressed, because Alexander intended to keep his sons at home tomorrow to dissect the battle with them, so that important lessons could be learned while everything was still very fresh in their minds.

As the chieftain, he waited until both 'armies' were safely ensconced behind their walls, then shot a pistol into the air, signalling the start of hostilities. Then he went to sit out of range to observe. All of the children who were old enough and almost all the adults had chosen to join in, which told him how restless everyone was already, even though winter had not started to really bite yet. He would have to think of some other active things for them all to do, if the winter was as hard as it was promising to be.

He watched as Kenneth came over, Angus cradled in one arm.

"I was in the way at home," he said by way of explanation. "Most of the women are there, for Ma's got the store of honey for the pastries, and Susan's got a good fire going at yours and is cleaning, so I thought to bring this wee one out, for he's been crying for Alex. He kens something's going on."

Angus clearly did. He turned now to face the battle, Kenneth keeping a hold on him as he squirmed, cheeks rosy with the cold, blue eyes shining, his little arms waving with excitement.

"Al!" he shouted. By way of reply a snowball came from the direction of Alex's castle, and Angus reached forward to catch it, although the snowball landed a good way short of them. Kenneth put one enormous hand on the baby's chest to stop him falling forward, and grinned.

Alexander reached forward and ruffled his son's fuzz of blond hair.

"Aye, he's at the age where he kens when someone's gone," he said.

"Why, did he no' ken that before?" Kenneth asked.

"Well, he kent they werena with him, but he didna realise that they were somewhere else. He does now. That'll be why he was crying for Alex. He's very taken wi' him."

"I didna ken that – ye mean that when someone's no' there, wee bairns think they've disappeared entirely?" Kenneth said, intrigued.

"Aye. He takes after Alex too. He's developing fast, already trying to stand up."

"He looks awfu' like him. And like you."

"Aye. I couldna deny any of them. Duncan favours Moira, but there's still enough of me in his face."

"They're good lads."

"They've worked hard for this. And if ye look now, ye'll see the difference in their tactics," Alexander said.

Both men watched, Angus crowing and wriggling about with excitement.

At first glance it seemed that Alex's group had the advantage. Initially Duncan's side had thrown snowballs at irregular intervals, although they were all travelling a good distance, either hitting the walls of the enemy fortification or going over the top of them. Meanwhile, after a few false starts, Alex's group had set up a ferocious and steady barrage of snowballs, although many of them landed ineffectually in the middle ground. Even so, every time one of Duncan's group showed themselves to throw a ball, they were immediately hit.

This continued for a couple of minutes, and then no more snowballs came from Duncan's side. Alexander smiled.

"Three hits and ye're dead?" Kenneth asked.

Alexander nodded.

"Duncan must have lost a good few men, then," Kenneth observed. "How are they doing it?" he added, watching the unceasing flow of balls coming from Alex's castle.

"He's reassessing, I'm thinking," Alexander said, still watching his younger son's wall. As Alexander had chosen to leave Alex's group to watch from outside, Moira had agreed to make no suggestions to Duncan, although she was taking part in the actual throwing. "They've got a drill – Alex had them practising it yesterday, like the redcoats do. Sorry," he added, remembering that although Kenneth had been taught about the musket drill, he'd never actually faced one, which was the thing that seared it into your memory. Quickly he explained the tactic, and Kenneth whistled through his teeth.

"They're doing awfu' well," he said in awe.

Alexander, still watching Duncan's side, laughed suddenly, then put his hand over his mouth to stifle it.

"Look," he said. Kenneth looked.

"Ah, they'll all be dead soon, if they keep coming up like that," he said, "And they've lost the power in their throws as well."

That seemed to be true. The snowballs from Duncan's team, instead of hitting the walls of the enemy castle as they had been earlier, were now coming in a high arc and landing pointlessly several feet short of it.

"He'll be counting," Alexander murmured, then started doing so himself.

"Counting what?" Kenneth asked.

"The hits. When he thinks enough of Duncan's men are dead, then he'll storm the wall. He's promised them a Highland charge."

"Oh, but that's a bonny tactic," Kenneth said in admiration.

Alexander grinned.

"Watch," he said, and then spoke no more.

"Keep making the snowballs," Duncan said once all the adults had stopped throwing on his command, and had hunkered down behind the wall to confer.

"But we dinna need to, if ye're no' throwing them!" Jeannie said crossly, blowing on her hands, which were frozen. There was a chorus of mutinous agreement from the other children, who were all annoyed at not being allowed to throw.

"We will, if I'm right in what I'm thinking," Duncan told them. "Ye'll see. Keep making them. Ye'll be throwing them soon." He turned to the adults, and, dismissed, the children continued making ammunition, but slowly. "Alex wants to do something big, like in a real battle," he continued. "He's wanting to kill a lot of us, and then he'll come out. He's always blethering on about the Highland charge, since Alasdair tellt him about it at Killiecrankie.

When he thinks he's killed enough of us, he'll charge, like the soldiers do in battle."

"But he canna kill us unless we show ourselves. So do we just sit here, then?" Allan asked.

Duncan thought. How long could they just sit here before Alex lost patience and charged anyway? A couple of years ago Alex would already have been coming out from behind his walls, but he was learning patience now. Was learning, but had not *learnt* it yet.

Duncan looked across at the other children, who all looked sullen and resentful, and suddenly realised that unless he did something it would be a contest between Alex's patience and theirs, and they looked ready to mutiny now. He thought, quickly.

"Stop making snowballs," he said. "Can ye go over to yon trees without the others seeing ye, and break off some wee branches, about as tall as you are?"

"Why, what are ye going to do?" Jeannie asked.

"When they think they've hit enough of us, they'll come out," Duncan said, unsure as to whether he should be explaining himself, as the general. Should he not just give commands, and they obey? Regardless, it wouldn't work if he did. "And when they do, we'll *all* be throwing balls, for we need to kill all of them before they breach the walls," he explained. "So we need to make them think we've been hit. Get the sticks, quickly, and I'll show ye what I mean."

Energised by the promise that they'd be throwing snowballs, the children scuttered off, keeping an eye out for any snowballs that came over the wall, so they weren't hit.

"Oh, great shot, Alasdair!" Alex cried, jumping up and down with excitement. "Ye're awfu' accurate," he added with envy as he watched the snowball land on the unfortunate victim's bonnet. That counted as a hit.

"Aye, when ye've fought as many battles as I have, ye learn to use anything that comes to hand as a weapon. A well-aimed stone can knock a man out, kill him even, if ye're lucky," Alasdair replied, throwing another, which hit the next person from Duncan's side who'd shown themselves to aim a snowball. As a result of this, their snowballs were now going all over the place, none of them even reaching Alex's castle, let alone coming over the walls. The moment someone appeared so they could aim properly, they were hit.

"How many kills now?" Dougal asked.

"Forty-one, I think," Alex answered. "Which means there's no' many left alive."

"We're running low on ammunition," Alasdair pointed out.

Alex glanced back at the dwindling pile of snowballs, and anticipation flared in him. He knew he should calculate the odds of how many of his soldiers could be killed by their survivors in the time it would take to run across the space between and breach their walls, but then he felt the adrenaline tear through his veins, setting his mind and body on fire, and everything except the overwhelming desire to scream the battle cry and run vanished from his mind.

"Right, then," he shouted. "This is it. Are ye ready?"

A great cheer from his followers fanned the flames in him, and he grinned.

"*Àrd choille!*" he roared, and they all repeated it.

Then they scrambled over their wall and charged full tilt towards the enemy.

Angus, bouncing up and down on his father's knee now, screamed with joy as his eldest brother appeared, followed by all his army, and began to charge across the snowy clearing in the direction of Duncan's camp.

"Ah, it seems they'll win then, for there canna be many left over there," Kenneth said, nodding in Duncan's direction, "although Duncan's castle is awfu' strong."

Kenneth never found out whether Alexander intended to answer or not, for at that moment an explosion of activity came from the seemingly decimated population of Duncan's army, as the children were hoisted up to sit on top of the walls and the adults, standing now, alternated between handing snowballs to the young ones to throw, and throwing snowballs themselves, hitting the charging force with deadly accuracy.

Alex, at the front of his army, as was fitting, was one of the first to die, but the others were not far behind him, as it was virtually impossible for Duncan's soldiers to miss. Within minutes it was over, and a great roar of victory came from the other side, after which Duncan's army emerged to celebrate wildly, while Alex came disconsolately over to his father and Angus, who lunged toward him, laughing. Alex scooped him up from their father's knee and turned back to look at the battlefield.

"I canna understand it," he mused. "I counted myself. I was sure they were all dead, or nearly all."

Alexander was gratified to note that Alex had not immediately jumped to the conclusion that they'd cheated and carried on taking part after being hit three times. Such a thing was unthinkable to him, as they'd all sworn to obey that rule.

"Ye'll have to ask Duncan later," he said, standing, intending to go across and congratulate the winners. "Ye did very well, though, laddie," he added, and then stopped as a snowball flew across the space between the victorious and defeated armies, hitting Alex square in the face, upon which all the dead soldiers on Alex's side were miraculously resurrected and leapt to their feet, grabbing handfuls of snow from the ground as they did. A furious snow battle ensued in which at first everyone participated, but which, as it grew more boisterous, some of the women left, dragging the younger children with them.

Alex, still holding Angus and wiping snow off his face, stood for a moment, frozen with bemusement, in which time his father and Kenneth exchanged a look over his head and then both charged eagerly into the fray, leaving Alex looking around for a willing adult who would take Angus from him. After a few minutes, when no candidate appeared, he sat down on the stone his father had vacated, wrapped the top part of his *féileadh mór* round Angus and himself, then settled to watch his clan engage in a good-natured but hair-raisingly ferocious brawl.

* * *

"I canna believe I'm having to treat so many injuries, after a *bairns'* game," Susan said in disgust, putting great emphasis on the word bairn before casting a scathing look around the chieftain's house, to which, as agreed, both armies had repaired once the extended fight was over.

The house was lovely and warm as a result of the fire which had been burning all day, and the table was piled with food, which both looked and smelled delicious, but over which Barbara now stood guard, arms folded and a determined expression on her face. It was clear that no one was going to be allowed to eat until the women said so. The men sighed and accepted their temporary role as naughty children, which, in fairness, they had been.

But it had been worth it. That had been a great battle, both the one that involved castles and snowballs, and the energy-burning aftermath. They were ready now to relax, to eat, drink, tell stories and dance. To forget the bleakness of the dark icy months to be endured before spring. But first they would have to accept the superior good sense of women, and act suitably chastised.

Or would have had to but for the one exception, who now came forward to be treated, red-faced, nose bleeding and cradling one hand in the other. Susan ignored the nosebleed entirely as it was already subsiding, although the victim would have black eyes tomorrow, and focussed on the hand instead.

"Ye've broken your finger, I'm thinking," she said. "It isna twisted though, so if I splint it and bind it, it should heal."

"Ah, ye've let us down, Moira," Barbara said from the corner, "for how can we berate the men all night, when ye were as bad as they were, and ye the chieftain's wife, too?"

Moira looked up from her hand to Barbara and grinned, then winced at the resulting pain from her nose.

"I'm sorry," she said insincerely. "But it was worth it. I havena felt so alive since…for a good while," she amended.

Barbara returned the grin, in spite of her attempt to stay severe. God, but it was good to see Moira enjoying herself again. Many of them had wondered if she would ever recover from the death of the one child and the difficult birth of the other, but it was clear now that she was back with them.

Observing the smile, several of the men made a move toward the table, stopping as the frown returned.

"When everyone's treated, and no' before," Barbara said. "What sort of example is this to show wee bairns?"

"A damn good one, if ye ask me," Alasdair said. "It'll teach them that ye canna assume a battle's over just because one side seems to have lost, or because someone in command thinks it is." Everyone laughed, and Alex reddened.

"He's no' talking about you," Alexander whispered into his

son's ear. He wasn't waiting to be treated, although he'd have an enormous bruise on his leg in the morning from where Kenneth had hit him by mistake. Christ, the man had fists like sledgehammers! "He's talking about real battles, when the communication's lost between the officers and the men. We'll talk about it tomorrow." He watched as his wife's finger was splinted with a stick and bound, and then moved forward to put his arm round her shoulders.

"As chieftain of the clan, I'd like to say a thank you to both generals for the fight they organised. I watched the whole thing, and it was a damn good battle on both sides!"

A great cheer arose from the men, and now Alex reddened with pleasure instead of humiliation, as he and Duncan were hoisted up onto the uninjured men's shoulders and carried in a little impromptu honour parade out of the house and around the clearing.

By the time they returned, liberally sprinkled with snow, Susan had finished treating those who needed it, or rather who'd admitted they needed it, and the celebrations commenced.

* * *

The next morning after breakfast, Alexander sat at the table with his two eldest sons, not because they particularly needed the use of the table, or the dull winter's light from the window it was next to, but merely due to force of habit.

"Let's talk about the battle yesterday, while we remember all the details of it. Aye, I ken ye'll remember them all until your dying day," he added, seeing Alex open his mouth, "But I havena got your memory."

"Nor have I," admitted Duncan.

Alexander nodded.

"Now I ken I only tellt the Father that it was a practical lesson so he wouldna complain about ye missing your Latin or rhetoric to have a bit of fun, but in truth it turned out to be an excellent opportunity for learning after all, especially because the other bairns chose the two of ye to be their leaders. Why do ye think they did that?"

"Because we're your sons, and you're the chieftain," Alex said.

"No. If the adults had chosen ye I'd have said that was the

case, but the bairns wouldna think that way," their father replied.

Clearly surprised, they both thought for a moment.

"They chose Alex because he always has ideas for games when we've time, and they're usually good ideas," Duncan said.

"And they chose you because you think about everything, so they thought ye'd think of the things to win. Which ye did," Alex finished a little ruefully.

"So that should tell ye that the people who'll be following ye when ye're men grown, the young ones at least, already think both of ye make good leaders," Alexander added.

Both boys smiled at this.

"Now, Alex can go first. I want ye to think of what Duncan did that was good," Alexander continued. Duncan was staring across the room, but he often looked away when he was thinking, so Alexander thought nothing of it until he stood.

"Are ye needing some help there, Ma?" he asked, crossing over to the *seise*, where Moira was clumsily trying to switch Angus from one breast to the other. Deftly he plucked his little brother from her and repositioned him, while Moira adjusted her clothing. "It looks awfu' sore," he commented, looking at her hand. Susan had put a stick between two fingers and had then bound them both to it, so he couldn't see them, but the whole hand was swollen and black with bruising.

"It's more awkward, having the two fingers stuck straight out like that. I'm catching them on everything, and then it's sore, for certain. Thank you, laddie, that's better," she added as Angus settled.

"Ye must rest it, no' go banging it on everything," Alexander said. "I'm going nowhere the day, and Susan will be here soon to do the cleaning. Ye must tell me though, for I dinna ken what ye need me to do. I'm no' usually here to see what ye get up to."

"And we can help too, for we've no lessons today!" Alex said.

"We've to have a wee snowball fight wi' Angus, that's all," Duncan added, returning to the table.

"Duncan led the group that won the fight," Alex said once his brother was seated, having remembered the question from earlier. "That was the most important thing. He kent what we were going to do, and he planned for it. That was awfu' clever."

"I didna ken what ye were going to do until ye did it," Duncan replied. "It's like when ye play chess. I shouldna tell ye this, but when I beat ye it's because ye always make the same moves. Once I see which pawn ye move first, I ken ye're going to do one of three or four things, so I try to stop all of them."

"But we havena had a snowball battle like that before," Alex said, "so ye couldna ken the moves I'd make."

"No. But when I realised ye were throwing snowballs much faster than we could, I kent ye had some sort of a routine, and then I thought about everything we've learnt about real battles, and I remembered that the thing ye want to see most is a Highland charge. So then it was easy, for I kent that ye'd want to do a Highland charge, but wouldna have any hope of winning unless we were all dead. I just had to think of a way that ye'd think we were all dead, so I had the others put their bonnets on top of sticks and show them, so ye'd hit them and think we were all killt."

This was an extraordinarily long speech from the normally taciturn Duncan, and Alex sat back and thought about it, waiting for his father to comment. When he didn't, Alex leaned forward again.

"Do I always make the same moves?" he asked.

"In chess? Aye. Ye learn fast, but ye grow bored quickly," Duncan replied. "So once ye ken enough to be sure of winning, ye stop learning that and move on to something else. Ye're the same in your lessons. Ye learn enough to please the Father, but ye dinna look any deeper than that. If it's something ye're *really* interested in, then ye learn more than ye need to."

He stopped suddenly, blushing as he remembered that both their parents were in the room and listening intently, his father with one raised eyebrow at this news. "Ah, I'm sorry," Duncan murmured to his brother, cursing himself for his accidental disloyalty.

"I didna think of it like that," Alex said, focussing completely on the battle tactics, oblivious to his brother's discomfiture or his father's expression on hearing that his eldest son was coasting in his education. "That's why ye won then. Because I had one plan, and ye could anticipate it because ye ken me well, and could think of a way to beat me. But I couldna see what you were doing, because I dinna ken ye as well."

"Ye do. Ye ken as much about me as I do about you. But once

ye've fixed an idea in your head, ye're awfu' stubborn about it, and ye just focus on that. So ye dinna look for the ways it might no' work, and what to do if it doesna. Ye put all of yerself into that one thing, whether it's a game, learning a new sword move, or a poem. That's one reason why ye learn things so quickly. But ye dinna learn things if ye think ye'll no' need them, even though ye could." Seeing his brother's puzzled look, he continued. "Like wi' Homer…no, it doesna matter," he added, glancing at his father and blushing again.

"No, this is important," Alexander said, speaking now it was obvious both sons had become painfully aware of his presence. "I'll no' use whatever ye say now against ye, I swear it. Tell me about Homer."

There was a moment's awkward silence, and then Alex nodded to Duncan, giving him permission.

"Homer, then," Duncan said. "When the Father gives us a piece of *The Odyssey* to learn or to talk about, ye learn it much faster than I do, for ye only need to read it the once. And then ye can talk all about it, and answer all the Father's questions, much better than I can. And after the lesson, a few days later, I can remember just some of the lines we've learnt, but ye'll remember every one, and all the things about it ye learnt in the lesson."

Alex smiled at this compliment.

"But have ye read the rest of the poem?" Duncan added.

"No. Why would I do that? There are too many other things to do," Alex admitted to his father.

"I have, though."

"Ye've read *all* of it?" Alex said, stunned.

"Aye. The parts the Father gives us to learn are no' the interesting ones. It's very good, and there's a lot of useful information in it."

"Is there? What sort of useful information?"

"That's something ye'll need to find out for yourself, by reading the poem," Alexander cut in, to stop the conversation going off track. "What did Alex do well, Duncan?"

"I didna do anything well, for I lost," Alex said.

"Aye, ye did," Duncan insisted. "Ye all had a lot of fun. I could hear ye singing and laughing, and cheering when something went well. I'm thinking, as it wasna a *real* battle but a game, that having fun was the most important thing."

"Did ye no' have fun, then?" Alex asked. "Ye won, so ye must have had."

Alexander noticed that Moira had stopped feeding Angus now, who, stomach full, had fallen asleep in her lap. She was listening, fascinated by her sons' views on this battle, looking into the future as was he, seeing the adult Alex and Duncan sitting together to plan a battle and winning. Or, God forbid, sitting separately and losing, for different reasons.

Unless he could help *both* his sons combat their weaknesses. He'd thought he'd have to point out their strengths and weaknesses to them, but at the moment they were doing a fine job of it themselves. He would let them run with the conversation for now.

"Aye, it was fun when we won," Duncan agreed, both of them oblivious to their parents' fascination. "But I think your army would have done whatever ye tellt them."

"Why, did yours no' do that?" Alex asked.

"Aye, they did, but they werena happy about it. Or some of them werena. I was like you are now," Duncan said, thinking hard. "I thought winning was the only important thing."

"It was."

"No, it wasna. I can see that now. The important thing was to have fun. Ye only think it was the most important thing now because ye lost, so ye're forgetting everything else. I didna care whether everyone was happy or no', I just wanted to beat you. The other bairns werena happy, because I wouldna let them throw snowballs, for I kent they couldna throw them as far as the adults. So I made them make the snowballs for the adults to throw."

"But ye were right," Alex said. "I wish I'd done that. If I had, we might have killed more of ye before we ran out of snowballs."

"Ye might. But ye wouldna do that," Duncan said.

"I would now ye've tellt me."

Duncan shook his head.

"Ye say that now, and I ken ye remember everything, but if we have another snowball battle next year, ye'll forget it once ye're leading your men," Duncan said.

Seeing Alex reddening with irritation, Alexander cut in.

"Why would he forget it?" he asked.

"Because the excitement of it will make him. And because he

wants everyone to love him. He wants the glory of it. That's why he did a Highland charge, because he kent that if he won, everyone would remember that and love him for it. Even though he lost, his army'll remember that charge, and what fun it was. I wanted to win, and my army'll remember that we did, but they'll no' laugh about it," Duncan said with brutal honesty. "So he willna make the bairns do things they dinna want to do, because he wants them to love him. I didna care about that. But I should," he added softly.

"Why?" Alexander asked, seeing the realisation dawn on Duncan's face.

"Because in a real battle, or if I'm to be chieftain if Alex isna there, I'll need the clan to *want* to follow me. If they dinna, then I'll no' be able to rely on them and that could have us all killed. Jeannie and Simon and the others, I dinna think they'd have continued making snowballs forever. They were awfu' miserable. In a real battle, that would be a terrible thing. Alex wouldna have that problem. He doesna have it now, wi' games, because he always makes them fun, and makes everyone *want* to do what he suggests. I canna do that."

"Why no'?" Alexander asked.

"It's a gift from God," Duncan said. "I havena got it."

Alexander waited.

"I dinna really care what everyone thinks of me," Duncan admitted. "No, I do care about what the people I love think of me. But Alex cares what *everyone* thinks of him."

"Do ye really no' care what everyone thinks of ye?" Alex said, clearly finding this incomprehensible.

"No. As long as they leave me alone to do what I want, why would I? Apart from if I was the chieftain, of course," he added.

Alexander waited, hoping Alex would attempt the same self-analysis Duncan had just performed so remarkably about himself. Silence fell and then Moira, who was not as optimistic as her husband, broke it.

"So Duncan doesna care what everyone thinks of him, but sees that he might need to learn to when he's older, sometimes at least, if he wants them to follow him. Alex, ye do care what everyone thinks of ye. Think now, when might that be a bad thing? No, ye dinna need Duncan to tell ye, or your da," she added, seeing him glance between the two others at the table. "Think yourself for a minute."

Now the silence stretched, and no one broke it.

"I lost because I was thinking more about the glory of it all, about making everyone admire me, than I was about how to win the battle," Alex admitted finally, a little uncertainly. "I thought that was what makes a good chieftain."

"Aye, well, it is part of it," Moira said.

"But I need to think more about it, like Duncan does," Alex continued. "Because if I lost a real battle because I hadna planned it well, then they wouldna like me anyway. And I'd get them all killed, which isna at all what makes a good chieftain. But if I work wi' Duncan when I'm the chieftain, then he can help me plan, for he's better at it than I am."

"Aye, and Alex is better at making everyone want to do things," Duncan said.

"That's true. But ye need to be able to act alone too, if one of you is elsewhere," their father said. "And ye can both do it. Ye just need to learn how, while ye're young enough to. If ye do that, then no clan in the land will have better leaders.

"Let me tell ye about Dundee. Ye ken he led the army for James at Killiecrankie because Alasdair's tellt us all about it, being there as he was. He was a fearsome leader, and he could plan well too. And he won the battle of Killiecrankie. But here we are, wi' the Elector on the throne instead of James. Why?"

"Because Dundee was killed," Alex said.

"He was. And there was no one else who could inspire the men like he could. Ye can learn from him."

"So I need to learn to inspire men like Alex does, so I can take over from him if I need to?" Duncan said.

"Aye, that's one thing to learn. What can you learn from Dundee, Alex? Has Alasdair tellt ye why he was killed?"

"He was shot, was he no'?" Alex said.

"Ah. I'll tell ye, then. His men begged him no' to lead the charge, for they kent, even if he didna, just how important he was. He believed that if he didna lead the men they wouldna respect him later, might think him a coward, even. And he was a Lowlander, so maybe he felt even more that he had to prove himself, for it was a Highland army in the main. So he ignored his officers and was killed. The Highland charge was a good idea," Alexander added to help his eldest think in the right way, "for it won the day. That isna what ye can learn."

"So ye mean I shouldna care so much what everyone thinks of me. I should be a wee bit more like Duncan, and plan on how to win."

"Aye, but ye've got to keep your army happy as well, which ye did, and I didna," Duncan added.

"I'm thinking it was the fight *after* the battle that made them happiest though, and that wasna my doing," Alex pointed out.

"Ah, I meant to talk a wee bit about that," Alexander said. "In real battles such things as that often happen. It's always the victors who do it, for in a real battle the dead canna get up and fight back. But ye need to ken about it. Men dinna stop fighting just because some general tells them to."

"Why no'?" asked Duncan. "Are they no' supposed to obey their generals?"

"Aye, they are. Sometimes they dinna hear the order, for battles are awfu' messy, no' the way ye see them drawn on a wee picture. But more often it's because their blood's up, and they canna just switch off the bloodlust. So when one side starts to retreat, or is obviously losing, the victors will often break discipline and charge after them. That's often when everything becomes very brutal and bloody. It's also why sometimes one side will *pretend* to retreat, because they want that to happen, and soldiers who're overcome wi' bloodlust dinna think right and can be separated from the main army and then slaughtered. I'll teach ye more about that another time, for it's an important tactic to ken. And also important to stop your men falling for it."

"It's no' going to be easy, being chieftain," Alex said glumly.

Alexander just managed to stop himself from laughing out loud at his sons' despondent faces. He gave in. They'd thought very hard today, showing more insight about themselves and each other than many adults did.

"Ye've done awfu' well, dissecting the battle," he told them. "And ye've a lot to think on. So I'll tell ye what ye can learn from Dundee. Ye're partly right. He shouldna have cared what the Highlanders thought of him to the point of risking his life, when he was crucial to the success or failure of James's cause. But there's something else. If ye're a battle commander, ye need to ken what your men *do* think of ye. No' what ye *want* them to think. Ye also need to ken your place in the battle. Dundee didna truly realise just how much the Highlanders loved and respected him. He'd proved time and again that he wasna a coward and didna need to do it again, in such a dramatic way. Nor did he realise how gifted a commander he was, and how unique. If he had, then he surely wouldna have thrown his life away as he did.

"Now, I dinna ken if ye'll ever be as great as he was. But if ye can learn from his mistake, then ye'll no end by dying pointlessly. For there's no glory in throwing your life away without purpose. Ye have to look at the whole picture in such a case, as Duncan said. Dundee could only see Killiecrankie, when he should have seen how essential he would be *after* that. Ye've the right of it, Alex. It isna easy to be a chieftain. Or rather it isna easy to be a *good* chieftain. Ye've both got the ability to do it, though, which is why I push ye so hard. Ye might hate me now, but I'm hoping that one day ye'll thank me for it."

"We dinna hate ye," Alex said, Duncan echoing him.

"I'm no' so fond of Father Gordon though," Duncan admitted.

Alexander heard Moira strangle her laughter, and realised that her middle son was even more like her than he'd thought.

"Aye, ye dinna have to like the man, as long as ye learn from him. And that ye're doing," he said. "But no' the day. Yesterday was a fine day, and much of that was due to the both of ye. Ye made a huge effort, and so I'm no' going to give ye any jobs to do. Ye can do as ye wish, the whole day."

"But Ma needs—" Duncan started.

"Your Ma's got me and Susan to help her. Ye said ye were going to have a wee snowball fight wi' Angus though?"

Everyone looked at the comatose baby lying in Moira's arms.

"Aye, well, maybe no' the now. Away and do what ye're wanting. I'll call ye when he wakes."

* * *

Alexander and Moira watched from the window as their three sons had a snowball fight, a couple of hours later.

Alex had laid a blanket from their bed on the snow for Angus to sit on, so he wouldn't get too wet and cold, while Duncan carefully made some very small, soft snowballs. Then they sat on the ground, just a few inches from their excited baby brother, and put a snowball in his outstretched hand.

After several attempts at this, with Angus trying to eat one, dropping several and crushing his fingers through some more, they threw a few at each other, hoping to give him the idea of what to do, which little Angus found incredibly exciting, although he learnt nothing about throwing snowballs from it.

"He's too young, yet," Moira said in a low voice. "He'll no' be able to throw or catch for a while."

"No, but he's enjoying himself," Alexander pointed out, pulling his wife into his side. God, it was so good to have her back with them. She still had her moments, when she would stare into the fire or sit back and close her eyes, her unguarded expression showing the effort she was making to throw off the remains of the melancholy. And then she would shake her head and stand up, do something, anything to stop the dark mood enveloping her. And it was working, Alexander could see that.

He did not know how to help her, so he did the only thing he could, which was to be patient and tender with her.

"He's the happiest of all of them," she said now, watching him scream with laughter as a snowball hit the tree he was leaning against, the powdery snow cascading over him. He put his hand down suddenly and grasped a tiny fistful of snow, then jerked his arm forward, copying his brothers in an attempt to throw it. Moira and Alexander exchanged a look of amazement.

"Are ye thinking we're raising yet another wee genius?" Alexander asked.

"I think it's a bit early to make such assumptions," Moira said. "I think we're raising a very happy wee laddie, and two other wonderful, loving sons. We're so blessed."

"I'm so glad ye're feeling well again, *mo chridhe* and can see that. I canna imagine life without you. I need you as Alex and Duncan need each other."

"Aye, they do. I ken that worries ye, but they'll learn from each other. They havena fought wi' each other since they were wee. I havena seen the like before. All the other women wi' sons tell me they fight all the time, and it's exhausting."

"That's true. I fought wi' my brother when we were bairns. I wish I hadna now, for the fights were all over trivial things."

She squeezed his waist.

"They didna seem trivial then, just as yesterday's battle doesna seem trivial to them," Moira said. "Ye loved each other, though. Ye tellt me that."

"Aye, we did, but no' in the way these two do. It's a joy to see, but I'm hoping wee Angus can fit wi' them somehow, for sometimes they feel like two halves of a whole."

"They were today, certainly. I've never heard them talk like that together before. It was incredible," Moira said.

"I'm thinking they normally do it when they're alone, for Duncan was mortified when he spoke openly, then remembered I was there." He laughed. "They're like us," he added. "Two halves of a whole."

She smiled and kissed his shoulder, which was the closest body part to her lips. Then they stood and watched their three sons sharing a tender, caring moment, while they shared their own, happy that all was well with them again, or nearly so.

CHAPTER FOURTEEN

Late September 1725

"I'm no' sure why ye're hesitating," Moira said. "It makes sense for ye to go after the cattle sale. Ye can take the boys with ye, take them to that play ye promised them."

She watched with interest as Alexander coloured, started to speak, then changed his mind.

"I promised we'd *all* go," he said finally, when she showed no sign of filling in the awkward silence that had fallen on the room. She smiled then, and putting down her sewing stood up and went over to the window where he was standing, now with his back to her, hoping she wouldn't have seen the conflict written on his face. Too late. She wrapped her arms round his waist.

"A promise made to yourself is one that can be broken, *mo chridhe*," she said softly. "Ye mentioned it, but ye didna promise. And a lot has happened since then."

"Aye. All the more reason for me to take ye," he answered. She squeezed him, pressing her face against his back.

"It makes the most sense to go straight from Crieff," she told him. "The other men can bring back the goods and money ye get there, and ye can go on to Edinburgh wi' the boys. It's overdue, for there's news ye need to ken and ye'll no' hear it staying here."

"If I come back straight after the sale, we could go to Edinburgh together," he suggested.

She made a derisory noise in the back of her throat.

"If ye do that, there's every likelihood we'll be trapped in Edinburgh for the winter," she said, "and even if we're no', ye'll be on edge, checking the skies every day and peering into the distance, wishing ye could see if the snow's started here yet."

He laughed then, and turned in her arms, enfolding her in a warm embrace.

"Ye ken me too well, woman," he said, kissing the top of her head.

Before ye suggest it, I've no' wish to go to Crieff wi' ye. I'd no' take that wee devil on such a journey," she added, nodding her head in the direction of the crib. They both looked across to where their eighteen-month-old son was sleeping peacefully, currently resembling a small angel rather than a devil, with his shock of pale blond hair, rosebud lips, and petal-soft cheeks. "But I wouldna leave him for such a time, either," she finished.

"I'd a mind to treat ye, go to a fine eating house, stay in a better lodging than The White Hart," he admitted.

"I dinna need ye to do that for me," she said, smiling.

"Aye. Even so."

"Take the boys. It'll be good for them. Take them to the play. They deserve it, after all they've done in the past weeks."

That was true. Over the past month Alexander had taken them on numerous night time cattle raids, in which they'd walked for miles over mountains and through bogs, slept in the open in pouring rain, and had comprehensively learnt the art of stealing cattle surreptitiously in the middle of the night. On each raid they'd taken no more than twenty cows, using the foul weather to their advantage and ensuring that by the time the previous owners of the cattle awoke they were far away across the mist and rain-drenched mountains. After over twenty raids they now had a good number of cattle, all re-branded, all ready to make the journey to Crieff.

And in all that time Alex and Duncan had not complained once, though they'd been soaked to the skin for much of the time, living on meagre rations even by Highlander standards, and spending a good deal of time either crawling through the mud and heather, or sitting for hours with nothing to do. These raids had been very different to the previous one they'd been on, which had been full of camaraderie, stories by the fire and better food, to say nothing of the excitement of the ambush by the Maclarens. These raids had been grim, silent, focussed. Any mistake which led to them being discovered might bring the whole of the clan they were stealing from down on their heads, so there was no levity, only alternating tension, action, relief and tedium. There had been no fires, no amusing tales…but at least the incessant rain and wind had kept the plagues of midges that normally infested the Highlands at this time of the year away. That had been a blessing indeed.

It had been a successful month in more than one respect though, Alexander thought. The boys had worked well together, and with the men. They'd improved their stamina and endurance. And they'd effectively learnt a lot of the techniques needed for conducting ambushes and irregular warfare, except that instead of attacking people they'd silently herded cows away, a vital skill in itself, useful both when stealing cows from others and when stopping others stealing cows from you.

"Go," Moira injected into his thoughtful silence. "Learn what this General Wade's about with his road-building, see if there's news from over the water. Then next spring, before the planting, I'll go to Edinburgh with ye. I'll no' mind leaving Angus for a few days then, when he's just a wee bit older. Susan can look after him. She'll love that, for if ever a woman should have been a mother, she should. And Alex and Duncan can stay here too, which will make me happier about leaving Angus, for ye ken he dotes on Alex. We'll have a few days together then, just the two of us."

He looked down at her, his eyes sparkling at the thought of a few days alone with his wife. No children interrupting, no clan problems to be addressed…

"Oh, that would be bliss," he said aloud, then reddened, for he hadn't meant to actually *utter* the words. "I mean—"

"I ken ye love being a chieftain, and I ken ye love the bairns," she interrupted. "But that doesna mean they're no' a nuisance at times! So then, forget your other promise, and let's make this one instead. And we'll keep it, unless something urgent happens."

"We'll keep it," he said. "And to hell with everything else."

He bent his head then and kissed her, tenderly at first and then with increasing passion, and was on the point of carrying her off to bed when the door opened and Alex and Duncan ran in, eager to tell them about some boyish trick they'd played on Kenneth.

At that moment next spring seemed a lifetime away.

* * *

October 1725

When the others finally left, Alexander stood on the track leading from Crieff, watching the rest of his clansmen until they disappeared from view. Then he stood for a while longer, as though he expected them to come back. Duncan and Alex exchanged a look.

"We dinna have to go to Edinburgh, Da, if ye'd rather go home now," Alex ventured, breaking Alexander's thoughts. He looked down at his sons, then smiled and picked up the reins of the garron they'd kept to carry the things they needed to spend a few days in the city, and headed south, the boys walking beside him.

"No," he replied. "I'm no' just going to show ye a play. There's news I need to learn too. And it'll be a good thing for ye to see a real city, for it's very different to anything ye've seen before."

"Susan's tellt us about it," Duncan said unenthusiastically.

"Aye, but ye must never form an opinion about anything until ye've seen it yourself. For people can only tell ye things from their own viewpoint, and yours might be different. Take Crieff, now. Alex, ye loved it, aye?"

"I did!" Alex said. "Although the selling of the cattle was awfu' difficult. I didna love that part."

Alexander had allowed Alex to take on his role in the market, haggling with the buyers to get the best price, intervening only when necessary. Alex, white with fear at the start, had slowly warmed to the task, and once he'd relaxed a little he'd clearly enjoyed the bartering part of it at least, and had done well for a first attempt.

"Ye did well, the both of ye," Alexander said.

"I didna do anything," Duncan pointed out.

"Aye, ye did. I was watching you. Ye looked at the men who came to see the cattle, watched their faces, their attitude when they were looking at the goods."

"And ye tellt me about them, which was really useful, because my head was full of sums, and I canna judge a man as quick as you anyway," Alex added. "I need to practice my mental arithmetic."

"That's a very useful skill ye've got, Duncan," Alexander said, causing his younger son to blush with pride. "For if ye can tell what manner of man ye're dealing with, ye can change the way of the bargaining to suit him. Ye both did well, and ye deserve a reward. And it'll do ye both good to see the city, for ye'll need to come here as adults, and ye need to have your wits about ye in other ways in the town than ye do in the countryside."

It took them two days to get to Edinburgh, walking at a steady but constant pace throughout the day, sleeping out in the open wrapped in their kilts at night. They still lit no fire to warm them, although being mid-October it was frosty at night.

"A wee bit of frost willna kill us," Alexander said, "but a band of men attracted by the firelight could, and I'll no' take that risk wi' just the three of us." He had been going to say 'alone' but had amended his words just before they were uttered, and knew he'd done right when he saw his sons' faces light up at being effectively classed as warriors by their father and chieftain. He smiled. It was only fair; they *were* warriors, for young as they were they had killed a man between them. They would be children for a time yet, but in Alex at least you could now see glimpses of the man he would become, in his long straight limbs. He was losing the softer curves of childhood now, the snub nose becoming long and straight like his father's, sinewy muscle developing on his arms and legs from the exercise and physical work he, as all clan children, had to do.

He's going to be tall, Alexander thought, *judging by how fast he's growing. Maybe taller than me.* It would feel strange to have a taller, and possibly broader, son than himself.

At eight Duncan still had a child's body and profile, although he too had some muscular definition from physical toil, and in attitude at least was mature beyond his years. More so than Alex, at the moment anyway.

They had slept soundly on both nights, brushing the frost from their hair in the early morning without complaint, rubbing their arms and legs briskly with their hands to get the blood flowing. Then they had eaten a little oatmeal mixed with river water and had set off.

"We'll reach Edinburgh the day," Alexander told them as they walked along, the garron between them and him, "and when we do I'll buy coal to make a fire, and we'll have a hot pie, or a mutton chop maybe for our supper."

"Like the one we had at Crieff?" Alex asked. "That was awfu' good," he added, licking his lips in memory of it.

"Better than that," Alexander said, "for we'll have a hot drink to go with it, and a warm room to eat it in. Ye can get all manner of food in Edinburgh. Ye deserve a good meal, the pair of ye."

It was the afternoon when they finally reached Edinburgh, the castle being the first building that came into view, situated as it was on the top of the hill to their right. The boys stopped and looked at their father questioningly.

"Aye, that's it," he said. "That's the castle, and then there's a road, ye canna see it, but ye'll see the houses along it directly. The road goes all the way down the hill to Holyrood Palace, which is where the king lived before he moved to England. We'll see our play there, if there's one on at the minute. And then there's all these wee roads," he added, "that run off either side of the high road, and we'll stay in a room there."

"It's beautiful," Alex said, looking at the castle with awe, and then at the rooves of the buildings along the road down the hill, which came into view as they continued. "Why did the king no' live in the castle?"

"I dinna ken," Alexander said, caught off guard by the unexpected question. "Maybe he did, sometimes. But castles can be awfu' cold and dark to live in, I'd think. I suppose he only went there if he thought he might be attacked, for it's very easy to defend, where the palace isna."

"It's very big," Duncan contributed as more and more buildings came into view, his tone one more of dread than awe.

"It's no' big enough for the people who live there," Alexander replied. "I was tellt there are sixty thousand souls in the place. So the buildings are high, for there isna the space to spread out, although there's talk of doing so. Ye'll see when we go through the gate. But first we need to change our clothes," he added, stopping and rummaging in one of the bags the garron was loaded with. After a moment he produced a brown paper package in which the seller at Crieff had wrapped his purchases.

They changed, and while the boys were donning the unaccustomed apparel, Alexander folded and packed their dirty shirts and kilts back into the paper. Then he looked at them both critically, before producing a comb from his own coat pocket.

"Here, let me tidy ye both a wee bit," he said, setting to work with a clumsy attempt at finesse that would have set the clanswomen roaring with laughter, had they been there to witness it.

He combed through their hair, tied it at the nape of their necks with a piece of blue ribbon, and then adjusted their clothing, pulling their shirts into place, fastening up the waistcoats that both boys had left undone, then kneeling down to garter their stockings correctly.

"There," he said, looking at them both with satisfaction and trying not to grin at their uneasy expressions. "Ye'll pass. Come on then."

They carried on in silence now, both boys' attention occupied by the increasing detail they could see of the city in which they were to spend the next days, and the strange feeling of their new clothes.

Finally they passed through a gate and then the Netherbow Port, Alexander paying some coins to the guard there to gain admittance while the boys gazed at the port's impressive conical towers, and then they emerged onto the High Street, where the full sensory impact of the city hit them.

There were people *everywhere,* standing in groups talking, laughing, singing, walking up and down, buying and selling a multitude of goods, begging, leaning precariously out of the windows of the impossibly tall buildings which loomed over the street, shouting and gesticulating to the people below in the street. And it seemed, by the smell that assailed their nostrils and the filth in the streets, that no one ever bathed and all of them used the street as an open privy.

"Holy Mother of God," Duncan breathed, and his father let that go, but made a mental note to remind his sons later that they were neither MacGregors nor Catholics whilst here.

"The people call this area World's End," he told them, "for everyone has to pay to come through the port, so those who havena the money to come back in darena go out. Some people spend their whole lives here because of it."

Duncan looked back at the port apprehensively.

"Have ye the money to go out again, Da?" he asked urgently.

"Ye dinna need coin to leave, laddie, only to enter," he said.

Duncan breathed a great sigh of relief, telling Alexander all he needed to know about his middle son's initial opinion of the great city. Alex was looking everywhere, blue eyes sparkling, trying to absorb as much as possible.

"When they hang an important person, they sometimes put the head up on the Netherbow Port, to deter people from committing the same crime," Alexander continued. "There are no' any there at the minute, though. Come on, we're staying down here," he added, turning down a narrow alley flanked on both sides by more imposingly tall buildings, which meant that they had to squelch their way through unidentifiable stinking refuse until their eyes became accustomed to the permanent gloom imposed by the height of the houses and the narrowness of the wynd.

Alexander stopped at one building for a minute, unloading the garron and distributing the packages between the three of them, before giving a stableboy some money and addressing him in rapid soft-voiced Gaelic for a minute, after which the boy paled and swore to take wonderful care of their fine mount.

They continued down the dark and oppressive alley until they reached another door, which Alexander opened, then, the boys following, set off up a circular stairway, stopping at the seventh landing they reached, which had two doors, one of which he knocked on. After a minute a filthy woman opened the door, wiping her flour-covered hands on an even filthier cloth.

This turned out to be Mrs Grant, their landlady, who showed them to an icy cold room furnished with a closet bed, a rickety table, four chairs and an empty fireplace. In one corner was an equally rickety chest, underneath a grimy window.

"Ye'll be staying four nights?" she asked. "Will ye be wanting meals?"

"No. But ye can send for some coal, for we'll be wanting a fire while we're here," Alexander said, producing a coin from his pocket when this request received no response. "Is there a play on at the Tennis Court Hall?" he added.

"Aye, I'm thinking there is," she said with disgust, as though he'd asked for a pail of shit. "Ye're wanting a ticket, I assume?"

"Three," he said. "What manner of play is it?"

"I havena a notion what manner of heathenish spectacle it is," she replied, holding out her hand. "It's no' my soul ye're putting in jeopardy," she added when more money had been passed over.

They were then left alone to enjoy their accommodation.

Alex crossed immediately to the window, wiping a pane of glass with his sleeve so that he could look out of it.

"Oh!" he said in a disappointed tone. "We're awfu' high, so I thought to see across the whole city, but I canna see anything except a wall! Ah, I'm sorry, Da," he added, turning back to the room. Duncan was sitting on a chair flexing his toes and rubbing his heel, having kicked off his shoes.

"Why are ye sorry?" Alexander asked, looking up from the chest where he was storing the parcels they'd carried up.

"I didna want to sound ungrateful by being disappointed wi' anything," Alex admitted. "Ye brought us here to see a play, which is a mighty thing."

"I'm looking forward to the play," Duncan said. "Although the lady doesna seem to think a deal of it."

"The lady is of the Presbyterian faith," Alexander told him. "Pay her no heed. Although, mind, ye mustna tell anyone we're MacGregors, or that we're Catholics, no' while we're here. As for the disappointment, if ye're unhappy wi' things ye must tell me. I brought ye for the play, that's true, but the other things we'll be doing are part of your learning to be chieftain. So I'll no' think ye're ungrateful if ye dinna like the place. I'll no' be surprised in truth, for Edinburgh's no' a place I'd come to if it wasna necessary from time to time. Ye must be honest. Ye tell me at home when ye dinna like something. There's no reason to be different here."

There was a moment's silence while both boys assessed this, and decided he was genuine.

"I wouldna want to live here, but I like it. It's awfu' interesting, for there's so much to see that I havena ever seen before," Alex said. "I'm no' liking the stupid clothes they wear here though."

"I dinna like them either," Duncan said. "These breeches chafe my legs horrible, and the shoes hurt. I canna think why people choose to wear clothes that hurt them."

"Ah, well, I agree with ye there too, but we canna wear the *féileadh mór* in the city, for if we do everyone will ken we're Highlanders, and we dinna want that attention, no' wi' the men we'll be meeting."

"We'll?" Alex asked.

"Aye. I'm thinking to take ye to the meeting tomorrow where I'll find out what's happening over the water. But it's a time for listening, and ye mustna speak a word unless I tell ye ye can. When ye're older ye'll be doing this yourselves, so it'll be good for ye to see what it's like and how to behave, for it's no' like anything else ye've done. And I can trust ye both well enough now to say nothing of what ye see and hear."

"Nothing is like anything else here," Duncan said. "Does it always smell so bad, Da? I canna breathe rightly."

"No," Alexander replied. "In the summer when it's hot it smells far worse than this!" Seeing his son's saucer-like eyes, he laughed. "Ye grow accustomed to the smells in time. And the constant noise. Ye'll see. Ye willna notice it so much in a few days. Now, let's away and get ourselves a hot pie and a drink, and then we can come back here, take these damn breeches off, warm ourselves by the fire, and sleep without frost the night. And I'll tell ye what we're doing while here, which will include bookshops and money for ye to spend on two books each."

"As well as the play?" Duncan asked, looking happy for the first time since he'd passed under the Netherbow Port.

"Aye. Ye deserve it. Ye've done well these last weeks and I've no doubt ye'll do well here too. We'll no' have to walk too far, but I've some sheep's wool in one of yon packages for such an occurrence, for it happens to me too when I wear these stupid shoes wi' the heels. Put that in the heel of your stocking and wrap some round your toes and your feet'll no' be blistered, for we canna have ye limping all the way home. It's a long walk back."

* * *

In spite of the strange noises and the smells, all three of the MacGregors slept well that night, partly because their stomachs were full of hot and tasty food for the first time in weeks, partly because by the time they went to bed (which was miraculously vermin-free) the room was lovely and warm, and partly because Alexander bolted the door *and* wedged a chair under the doorknob, so all of them felt safe and could relax.

As a result of this they slept late, although that didn't really matter as their meeting was not until noon. Refreshed and much more optimistic due to the undisturbed slumber, they descended the stairs to the street in search of breakfast.

"Why are the stairs like this?" Alex asked as his father grabbed his arm to stop him toppling down them when he stumbled. "It's hard to go up and down them wi' the steps being so wee at one side. Is it to save room for all the people who live here?"

"I was thinking that," Duncan said. "But if it was that, they could just use ladders like we do at home to go to bed."

"Castles have stairs like these as well," Alexander replied. "It's because they're easier to defend if ye're being attacked by an intruder."

"Aye, I suppose so. Ye could just give him a wee push and he'd go all the way to the bottom," Alex said, focussing much more closely on placing his feet on the wide part of the step now.

"No, it isna that," his da said. "Here, let me go past ye, and I'll show ye."

After a few moments of precarious manoeuvring on the narrow stairway, Alexander succeeded in placing himself a few steps down from his sons.

"Right then," he said, turning to face them. "Draw your swords."

"We havena got them," Alex pointed out. "Ye said we canna wear them here."

"Aye, well, *pretend* to draw your swords," Alexander amended. "So ye see, if ye have your sword in your right hand then ye have the room to use it, and to attack me as I come up the stair at ye, while ye're standing on the wide part of the steps. But I canna attack round the curve of the stair wi' my right hand and if I try to hide round the bend of the stair, then I'm on the narrow part of the step and off-balance, so it makes it easy for you and awfu' hard for me. Only one person at a time can attack *and* if ye do kick or push me and I fall, then I'll take everyone behind me down the stairs too. It's a clever thing. Ye might need to ken that, if ye ever besiege a castle."

"But we're no' in a castle," Alex said.

"No. But we're in a city, and one that's been attacked many times. The people here havena got a hidden cave up the mountain to go to if they're attacked as we have, so their houses were built this way to help them defend themselves."

They stood on the stair for a minute, Alexander giving the

stick he was carrying for defence if necessary to each of his sons in turn so they could see how the spiral stair idea worked, while he held onto the filthy rope that was looped through iron rings in the wall by way of a banister, so as not to topple down the stairs if one of his sons hit him.

"If intruders come in the people living here can cut the rope from the top, so they canna use it as I am," Alexander said, flattening himself against the wall to dodge a well-aimed blow from Duncan.

"Good Lord, what on earth are you doing, sir?" an astonished voice asked from below them. Alex and Duncan both looked down at the man who had appeared on the stairway behind their father. Alexander turned, immediately understanding the stunned expressions on his sons' faces as he saw the stranger.

"I'm sorry, sir, were ye wanting to pass us?" Alexander asked.

"Oh no. I never go above my floor. I was in the process of descending to perambulate the thoroughfare, when I heard the commotion above and became curious. Are you all quite well?" he finished, only the slightest trace of a Scottish brogue betraying him as a native.

"Aye. Malcolm Drummond at your service, sir. These are my sons. I was teaching them about castle warfare, and how to fight on such stairs as these. We had no wish to disturb ye."

"Oh no, I assure you, I am fascinated rather than disturbed, my dear sir," the gentleman said. "Ah, but I have not introduced myself. Sir David Armstrong. Baronet. Delighted to make your acquaintance. Are you the good lady's new tenants?"

"No, we're staying only a few days," Alexander said. "I've brought my sons to show them the attractions of this great city." Of which it seemed the baronet was one, judging by the stifled giggles that were coming from behind him.

"Of which there are many!" the baronet cried, stepping back onto the landing. "Well, I will not keep you. I wish you luck in besieging your castle, young men," he said merrily as they passed him.

As soon as they reached the street and were out of earshot of the strange first-floor tenant, both boys burst out laughing.

"What on earth was he wearing, sir?" Alex asked in a perfect imitation of the baronet's squeaky voice. Even Alexander couldn't stop himself laughing at that.

"He's a baronet, and a new one, I'd say, for ye would normally just use your title, no' tell others your rank as well. And by his dress, he's what people call a fop."

"He was very colourful," Duncan said tactfully, referring to the man's bright green breeches and coat, coupled with a red silk waistcoat, yellow stockings and heavily powdered wig.

"What was wrong wi' his face?" Alex asked, eyes still wide.

"He was wearing paint. And rouge. Ye'll see others, men and women, wearing such ridiculous stuff when we're out, and wigs, although nearly everyone wears one of those if they can afford to. Terrible things, much worse than breeches to wear," he added. "Ye'll no' see so many wearing clothes like his though. He's a man of fashion. Fashion is when ye have to wear what the king and queen tell ye is the 'right thing' for the moment, which changes all the time. The nobles pay heed to 'fashion', for they can afford to buy stupid clothes and keep changing them. It tells everyone how rich they are."

"If he's rich, why is he living here? Ye said ours wasna a good room but was warm and dry," Alex asked.

"And cheap. The man likely spends all his money on his clothes, and hasna enough for a grand house as well. But ye see that often in Edinburgh. The wealthier people live on the ground floor, and then the poorer ones live higher up in the same building. He'll no doubt have the whole of the ground floor for himself, no' one wee room as we have. And some good furnishings too. Ye dinna find that in other cities, though, where the nobles have their own houses, wi' gardens too. It's because everyone wants to live here, but there isna the room to build outward. That's why the houses here are so tall."

"I dinna want to live here," Duncan said fervently.

"No more do you need to." Alexander assured his son. "A baronet is the lowest title ye can have. When ye travel to Paris, Alex, ye'll no doubt see many more such creatures," he finished, his tone one of disgust.

"I dinna want to travel to Paris," Alex said.

"I canna imagine the MacGregors besieging a castle," Duncan leapt in, changing the subject to avoid any disagreement between his brother and father regarding the topic of university. "We've only about fifty men."

"Yon baronet couldna besiege a kitten," Alex said. "The wig was slipping over his forehead. He'd be dead in a minute in a swordfight, for he'd no' be able to see, or grip his sword, wi' all that lace he was wearing, and he couldna move rightly, for his breeches were so tight I could see everything."

"No' much to see, though," Duncan added coolly, having seen many to compare the baronet's with. One of the side-effects of the *fèileadh mór* was that men's private parts were often on display, especially on windy days. "Is that what wearing breeches does to ye, Da?" he asked, turning to face Alexander with genuine interest.

Alexander committed this to memory. Moira would be convulsed when he told her.

"I dinna ken. I dinna intend to wear the damn things long enough to find out. Come on, let's eat. It's growing late."

"Fifty-three," Alex supplied, "men we've got," he added when he saw his father's puzzled expression. That's no' enough, is it, Da?"

"Ah. No. But if we're going to besiege a castle, it'll likely be wi' a number of other clans, fighting for the king."

"Are we really going to do that?" Alex asked eagerly.

"I havena a notion. That's why we're going to the meeting today. After we've eaten."

"It's a good thing that there's a second prince now, that's true," said a tall, thin-featured man, who had introduced himself only as Aeneas, once everyone was settled in one of the small rooms at Jenny Ha's tavern on the Canongate.

As Alexander had introduced himself as Malcolm and not named his sons at all, it was likely that Aeneas was not the thin-featured man's real name either. This, from the boys' point of view, lent an air of intrigue and mystery to the proceeding, which was enhanced by the gloom of the room, lit only by a single candle placed on the wooden table round which the men all sat, having passed their glasses over a basin of water in the centre in a toast to the 'King over the Water', before the meeting started. Alex and Duncan, comprehensively ignored, sat in the corner of the room near the small brazier, absorbing everything.

"Aye, and the first one, Charles, seems to be thriving. Five now, so past the most dangerous age, at least," another man with a Lowland Scottish accent added.

"We must be realistic, though. It doesna matter how healthy the princes are, things are no' going well for James right now. The French are no' particularly enthusiastic about supporting us, and the Tsar's death was a great blow," a red-haired man put in.

There were murmurs of agreement at this, for the Tsar of Russia, Peter the Great, had promised James that he would send an expedition to England to restore the Stuarts to the throne, but his death shortly after the birth of James's second son Henry had put an end to that hope.

"James isna going to rise without a good deal of help," Aeneas said, "for in truth he hasna the personality to rally his subjects in Scotland and England. Both the '15 and the '19 tellt us that. I'm thinking the French are no' likely to finance an expedition either at the minute."

"Is it true that there's a scandal with the King and Queen?" another man put in.

"Scandal?" Alexander asked.

"No, no' a scandal," Aeneas said. "James decided to take the older laddie away from the women's influence and put him wi' tutors, and Clementina isna happy. I think she thought to keep the boy a good while longer by her side. It'll all blow over, I'm sure. It's normal for a boy to go to male tutors at his age."

"So what ye seem to be saying is that no one of any importance is supporting the Stuarts, James doesna have the ability or money to rise alone, and the two princes willna be old enough to rise on his behalf for many years yet?" Alexander ventured.

There was a silence as they all realised that that was actually what they *were* saying.

"Christ," the red-haired man groaned.

"So even if the princes *want* to claim the throne, we have to wait. And his direct line hasna been on the throne for nearly forty years already!" Alexander said.

"Aye, and no Stuarts at all for over ten years now. Once Hanover's been settled there for twenty-five years, which they will have been by the time Charles is eighteen, no one will even remember the Stuarts, let alone want to fight for them!" the red-haired man said.

"I will!" Alex exclaimed from the corner, then flushed scarlet, remembering what his father had said about not speaking.

"That's good to hear, laddie," Aeneas said, "but I'm doubting enough men will still feel that way by then. No' enough to risk everything for them, at least."

As this was all both logical and deeply pessimistic, a gloomy silence now fell on the group, broken only by the sounds of the men's throats working as they drank.

"Well, there seems no point in talking about the weakness of the castle's defences then, if we'll no' be needing to take it," another man commented.

"Which castle?" Alexander asked.

"This one. Edinburgh. Yon Wade mannie that's been sent by the Elector was here, and he did a wee survey of the castle. He made four armed soldiers scale the rock face to it and they were in within a few minutes, he found."

"Aye, well, any citizen could have tellt him that, for the soldiers regularly appear in the taverns after the gates are shut. They climb down from the parapet. How the hell some of them make it back up there at the end of the night, the state of them, is anyone's guess," Aeneas said.

"Has anyone more information on the roads that Wade's building?" Alexander asked, seeing no point in discussing Edinburgh Castle any further. If Wade had surveyed it, then he had fifteen years at least to shore up the defences. Better to look at more immediate issues that could impact the clans. He would have preferred to interject with a happier question, but in truth he couldn't think of anything happy about Jacobite prospects at the moment.

"Aye, we've an informant on his survey team, so we've good information on that," Aeneas said. "It was yon bastard Lovat that started it all off, for he sent a report to the Elector telling him that the clans were ready to rise at a moment's notice, and that the defences were inadequate to stop them. He was wanting to be made commander in Scotland, but it seems even London kens what a duplicitous shite Lovat is, so they sent Wade instead."

"Even the Frasers must be ashamed o' the man," the red-haired man put in.

"They've sworn allegiance to him, though, as their chief," an older man called Rory stated.

"Aye, but he's no allegiance to anyone except himself. A chief's job is to protect his clan, but he'd sell the whole of the Frasers into slavery if there was enough money or power in it for him," Alexander said in disgust. A general tone of agreement greeted this remark.

"Well, Wade canna be bribed to turn, so it's as well we've a man in there," Aeneas said. "He decided that the forts the government's built are no use as they are, for ye canna station enough men at each one to be of any use in the event of a rising, and they canna travel fast enough to send men, arms or provisions from one fort to another to be of any use. Which is why he's building the roads, for the redcoats canna travel as we do. They need all manner of comforts to do so, and their horses canna go over bogs and mountains as ours can. So he's building roads to link the forts, wide enough to move artillery, and he's started the first one, from Fort William to Kilwhimen Barracks. It's a wide road too. He'll be building every year from April to October, and the men are working at a ferocious pace. For now they've built a wee ship that's sailing down Loch Ness to take supplies from Inverness to Fort William, until the road's finished."

"Could we no' slow them in the building?" Rory asked.

"I suppose we could, but if we do we'll prove Lovat right and they'll likely send the whole army up to wipe us out. If they do the Campbells will join them to gain more land and most likely Lovat will too, to show the Elector how reliable he is," Aeneas said.

"I'm thinking it'll be easier to attack the redcoats on the roads than in wee ships, for we havena the artillery to attack boats," Alexander said. "But we can always ambush men on land, for we can move across country *and* on roads. If they dispose of the ships once they've got the roads, then we have another advantage, for we'll always ken exactly which way they're coming but they willna have a notion where we are."

"There's talk of them building wee houses along the way, every ten miles or so, to guard the road," Aeneas said.

"Even better, for that'll split their men, and no matter how good their road is a few Highlanders could wipe out a wee house and be far away before the laddies from the next house heard about it and arrived."

This was an interesting thought, and the first uplifting

comment of the whole meeting so far.

"Wade also talked about enlisting companies of locals to enforce the Disarming Act," Aeneas said. "It seems the Elector's finally realised that a law passed in England doesna mean anything to the Jacobite clans. All the Hanoverian clans dutifully handed their weapons in, it seems, and we didna, of course, because we dinna find his Act good enough even to wipe our arses on."

"Oh, we did," said Rory. "I handed in a good many swords myself. Of course they were rusted through or so bent they couldna be straightened, but that's a triviality."

Everyone laughed at this, for they'd all done the same, hiding their useful weapons in all manner of places where it was unlikely they'd be found.

"Are ye thinking they'll set these companies up?" the red-haired man asked.

"Only if there's a good number o' men who are after dying, or idiots. For who's going to walk into clan territory and tell the Camerons, the MacDonalds, the Gordons to give up their weapons?" Aeneas pointed out.

"They did it to Glencoe though," Rory said.

"That was treachery, and a different matter. And one reason why they'll no' do it again. For we dinna need to have a lesson twice to learn it. No Highland hospitality for redcoats, whether Scots or English," Aeneas said grimly.

The answer to this was more sounds of agreement followed by a toast to all the loyal clans, and to the King over the Water again, to which Alex and Duncan, much to their pleasure, were invited to join, the raw whisky burning their throats, for their father would not shame them by watering it down in front of these strangers as he did at home.

They left the tavern a short time later, after more drinks and ribaldry, which ensured that even if the contents of the meeting had been unremittingly pessimistic, the mood of the participants as they went their separate ways was not.

Alexander had intended to take his sons straight to the booksellers' stalls around St Giles's church, where he'd be able to leave them browsing happily for their two books while he went round the jewellers' stalls, for he wanted to buy his wife something that would complement the gift he'd already sent back with the other clansmen for her. He smiled at the thought, but on observing the somewhat unsteady gait of both his small charges realised that this pleasure might be better delayed.

"I'm feeling a wee bit hungry myself," he said, although in fact he wasn't, as one of the valuable qualities of whisky for clansmen was that it dulled the appetite. "Why do we no' buy another three of those fine pies we had last night and go back to the room to eat them?"

This suggestion was instantly agreed with, as active and excited boys always have an appetite, which cannot be dulled even by strong spirit, and so he managed to get both his sons home, fed and then sleeping off the effects of the whisky without offending their pride, and hopefully without them even realising that he'd noticed how intoxicated they'd been by the unaccustomed quantity of liquor they'd drunk in a short time.

While they slept he sat by the fire and thought. His sons were good boys and trustworthy, but even normally trustworthy *men* could utter indiscretions when in their cups. And the meeting they'd just been to was a dangerous one, for the men attending had all been clan chiefs and the authorities would have given a good deal to catch any one of them alone and outside their territory, with a reasonable excuse for arresting them. They would have given as much to know there was an informant in Wade's team too. No, better they sleep all afternoon than let something slip in public.

It was depressing news though. All Alexander could do now, all any of the Jacobite clans could do was keep in readiness for when young Charles and baby Henry, now the sole hopes of the Stuart cause, were old enough to decide if the British crown was worth fighting for.

Now more than ever it was important to have a son who could, if opportunity arose, fight for the proscription of the MacGregors to be lifted by peaceful means rather than by the sword. Or perhaps to persuade a prince of the blood to fight for the crown of Scotland at least, so they could free themselves of the tyrannical Union with England.

Both Alex and Duncan were coming on well, and even at eighteen months Angus was showing potential. That at least was a cheering thought. There was hope for the MacGregors at least, and hopefully for Scotland.

He smiled. The room was warm, the cacophony of street noise dulled by the seven floors between it and him. He had time to rest, and his sons looked so comfortable curled up in the bed that he decided to enjoy the pure luxury of an afternoon nap. Moving to the bed he pulled back the covers and climbed in carefully, although he could probably have shot a cannon off in the room without waking them at the moment. Then he snuggled in next to them, yawned, and closed his eyes.

If only Moira was here now, life would be perfect. Present life at least. The future would take care of itself, with preparation.

* * *

As their chieftain and his sons were passing through the Netherbow Port in Edinburgh, his clansmen arrived home, laden with provisions for the winter, money, and presents for their wives and children. They were welcomed back with joy and relief, for everyone knew that on a raid there was always a possibility of them having to fight at some point, as they had last time. Or even choosing to fight, for they were MacGregors after all.

When all the provisions had been stored away and the men had gone to their homes to rest and eat, Kenneth made his way across to his chieftain's house, where Moira was returning from fetching water at a snail's pace, Angus walking with her.

"Kennet!" Angus cried, rushing over to him on unsteady legs and gripping him round the calf, which almost caused Kenneth to fall, burdened with parcels as he was. Moira put down the pail she was carrying and looked at the pair, laughing.

"He hasna let me out of his sight since the menfolk left," she said. "Thank God Susan's here, for I canna get anything done wi' him hanging on me."

Kenneth moved to the bench outside their house, still hampered by Angus, who had now decided to stand on Kenneth's foot and so have a ride home. He put the parcels down, then prised the yellow-haired toddler off his leg and raised him high up in the air, making Angus scream with laughter.

"Ah, but he's a bonny wee laddie," Kenneth said, "and growing fast. He looks exactly as Alex did at his age, except for the hair of course."

"Aye, and he's as lively as Alex was too," Moira said. "We're having a wee war at the minute," she added, looking at the parcels with interest.

"They're for you," Kenneth told her, tucking the child under his arm like another parcel. "Alexander asked me to deliver them to you especially, said ye'll maybe have time to start on it while they're away."

Moira's face creased in puzzlement.

"I've no' time for anything, wi' the monster there," she said. "When Alex is home Angus follows him everywhere, so I can get more done. Come away in," she added, picking up the parcels and going into the house, where Susan was busy making a meal, which smelled wonderful.

"What's the wee war about?" Kenneth asked, sitting down on a stool and hoisting the boy onto his knee.

"He's decided that he doesna want to sleep at the time I'm putting him down, and wakes up in the middle of the night crying for me. Even Alex didna do that, restless as he was. I'm still putting him down at nightfall and ignoring him when he wakes, but I'm no' sleeping well because of it."

"Will I tan your hide for ye, keeping your ma awake?" Kenneth asked the boy, who giggled and reached to grab for a strand of his long auburn hair. Kenneth pulled his head back sharply to whisk the hair out of reach. "I could take him to ours for a couple of nights, let ye sleep," he suggested.

"I've said the same, but she willna have it. The bairn gets his stubbornness from her," Susan commented from the hearth.

"He's upset enough that the others have gone. I couldna go too, and that's how he'd think of it," Moira said, looking at her youngest fondly. "It's true that I'm awfu' tired, but that'll pass when he accepts the inevitable and I can sleep again."

"Well, open your presents in peace at least. I'll keep him here while ye do," Kenneth offered, looking hopefully in Susan's direction.

"Aye, there's enough for ye too, laddie. Sit yourself down at the table," Susan said. Kenneth obeyed with alacrity. He was starving, having lived on oatmeal mixed with water for days, with a few late blaeberries when they could be found.

"Oh!" Moira said in absolute wonder from the corner of the room, having carefully undone the twine wrapped round the largest parcel and folded it for re-use, after which she'd unfolded the paper with equal care. The other three looked across at her, intrigued.

"What is it?" Kenneth asked. "I havena seen it, for he gave it to me wrapped."

She turned to them then, holding a length of purple silk which shimmered in the pale autumnal sunlight coming through the open door. Susan abandoned the meal and went across to Moira to get a closer look.

"Oh, but that's beautiful!" she said with awe, for it was. "Ye must come outside so we can see the colour rightly."

The two women went out, holding the length of material between them to admire it.

"It's a good weight," Susan said. "It must have cost him a pretty penny."

"Well, I ken he did a deal of fierce bargaining at a dressmaker's shop. He was there for a good time. I'm thinking he must have been buying that for ye then," Kenneth said from the doorway, holding Angus in the crook of his arm.

"I canna think what possessed him," Moira said. "I canna think of a situation when I'd use such fragile material."

"Are ye no' going to Edinburgh wi' him next year, just the two of you?" Susan asked.

"Aye, but we'll only be away for a few days. He wouldna spend so much money just for that!" Moira said.

"It seems he would," Kenneth put in. "For everyone kens how much he loves ye. It's no' exactly a secret. I'd do it for my wife, if I had one," he added.

"I canna imagine wee Jeannie wearing a silk dress for more than a minute without ruining it entirely," Barbara put in, who was passing and had come over to look at it.

"I'm no' marrying wee Jeannie," Kenneth protested. He heartily wished he hadn't mentioned Jeannie's childish declaration of a few years ago, as it had now become a clan joke. "She's a bairn."

"Oh, that *is* bonny! Is that all of it?" she asked, ignoring her son.

"No, there's more, and other wee parcels too," Moira said.

"And what else? I'm hoping there's the thread for it, and

trimmings, and suchlike," Barbara added. The women went back into the house, and the rest of the parcels were unpacked, which included ribbon in a darker purple and lace in a lighter shade, as well as the thread and other sundries.

"It makes your eyes look purple too," Susan commented. "Hold it up against your neck."

Moira, grey eyes sparkling, complied.

"Aye, it does," Barbara said. "Gives them a lavender hue. Lovely wi' your hair, too."

"Ye willna need to cover your hair when you go out in Edinburgh," Susan said. "I've some paste hair clips ye can borrow that sparkle in the candlelight. What manner of dress are ye wanting to make?"

Moira's forehead creased.

"I havena a notion what women are wearing in the towns now," she said. "I havena been there since before Alex was born."

"I've an idea," Susan said. "Wait there while I fetch something from home. I'll no' be long."

"I'll go as well, for I'm thinking I can maybe dye some wool to make a shawl for ye," Barbara said. "And that at least ye could use here at home, too."

"Are we no' going to eat first?" Kenneth interjected hopefully. The women looked across at him, sitting at the table again, Angus squirming on his knee. Moira sighed.

"Ye've eaten at home," Barbara said, turning back from the door to look at her son, who reddened.

"Aye, well, it was a hungry journey we had," he mumbled, embarrassed.

"I dinna mind feeding him again, for Angus loves him," Moira said. "We'll eat first, and then maybe that wee *peasan* will sleep."

After the meal Kenneth beat a hasty retreat, bored senseless by the incessant discussion about frills and mantuas and *robes volante* and other feminine mysteries, after which Susan went home, returning half an hour later with a russet-coloured gown over her arm.

"I was thinking the mantua might be the best because they've been worn for a long time, and they've become court wear in England, whereas the sack dress is more informal wear," she said.

"So ye'll no' be out of fashion in Edinburgh if ye wear one, for certain. This is a mantua, one of the stupid gowns I brought with me that are no use whatsoever. I brought a wee mirror too. If ye try this on, ye can see if ye like it."

Moira tried it on, whereupon Susan produced a handful of pins, and kneeling down, pinned up the hemline.

"You're a good bit shorter than I am," she commented.

"You're a good bit slimmer in the waist though," Moira retorted.

"Aye well, I havena had any bairns. And ye've a lovely shape to ye," Susan said, standing and memorising where it was too tight around the waist. The bosom was perfect though. It would work. "Right then," she said. "Take it off and we can make a start tonight."

"I wouldna ken where to start making such a dress as this," Moira said, moving backwards as Susan held up the mirror, in an attempt to see as much of herself as possible. "I feel like a duchess!"

"We'll start by unpicking the seams on this one, and then we can use it as a pattern for yours," Susan said.

"What? No, ye canna cut up such a lovely gown!" Moira cried.

"I can. I'll never wear it, for I've no intention to go to the city again in my life, if I can avoid it. I've no notion what possessed me to bring it wi' me."

That was a lie. She had brought it with her because it had been her favourite dress, in her favourite colour. Because Rob had bought it for her, for her birthday. And because they'd visited the theatre at the Tennis Court Hall of Holyrood Palace, just as Alexander intended to do with Moira. And she had felt like a princess that night. It had been a night she would never forget, all the more so because it had been the last night out they'd had together before her husband had died.

But cutting up the dress would not cut up the wonderful memories. Clan life was hard, brutal at times, and any pleasure, however small, was cherished. Luxuries were few and far between. And Alexander and Moira shared a love every bit as deep as her's and Rob's had been, and had gone through hell in the last years. Watching Moira bubble with happiness as they carefully unpicked the seams, anticipating a weekend alone with her handsome husband in the capital city, Susan knew that she would cut up a lot more than a beloved dress to see this kind and gentle woman come into her own again.

* * *

The following afternoon, having cut out the pattern of the dress in the morning on the table, Susan and Moira sat outside on the bench to take advantage of the natural light as they started pinning the pieces together.

"Once we've pinned the basic gown, ye can try it on carefully, and then we'll make adjustments before we sew it," Susan said. "But when we do the train for it I think we should ask Barbara, for there's a special way to do it. Ye have to join the wrong side of one piece to the right side of another, and I'm no' sure of how it's done. I've altered and repaired my own gowns, but I havena made one from the start."

"I dinna think Barbara's ever made a gown such as this," Moira said.

"No, but she makes a lot of the clothing for the clan, and she's a good eye for such things," Susan replied.

"That's true. And she's been to Edinburgh too, so may have seen mantuas," Moira added. She stopped for a minute, blinked several times, then shook her right arm, flexing the fingers.

"What's amiss?"

"Nothing," Moira answered automatically, and then, remembering it was Susan she was talking to, sighed. "I'm very tired the day," she admitted, "and my eyes keep going a wee bit blurry."

"Hmmph. Why are ye shaking your arm then?"

"It's just tingling a wee bit, as though I've slept on it. My neck's a bit stiff too. I'm thinking it's just that I need some sleep."

"Did the wee gomerel keep ye awake last night again?" Susan asked.

"Aye. I went to sleep but he woke me up, it felt like minutes later. Maybe I will ask Kenneth to take him for one night after all. He loves Kenneth, so maybe he'll no' be fashed if I leave him there."

"All the bairns love Kenneth," Susan observed. "He's natural wi' them, has endless patience. He'll make a fine da one day. I'll fetch some lavender oil for ye later. If ye put a few drops in some hot water and breathe the steam in, that might help relax ye, ease the stiffness in your neck. And it'll help ye sleep, too."

Moira laughed.

"I'm thinking I'll no' need help to sleep, if Angus isna here," she said. "I'll be fine after a night's rest."

They continued working in silence for a while, Susan casting covert glances at her companion from time to time. Moira looked pale, but she would if she hadn't slept properly for days. Hopefully a night without her son would do her good.

"Shall we go in?" she suggested a short time later. "It's awfu' cold now and the light will start to fade soon. We've about finished pinning the pieces, so if ye try it on we can see what it looks like. Then I'll go and fetch some lavender oil, and on the way back I'll call in and ask Kenneth if he can keep Angus overnight and if Barbara can come to give us her thoughts. Then we can start the sewing tomorrow."

They gathered all the material together, and went inside.

"We should have pinned this together on you, instead of doing it first," Susan said, after it took them nearly an hour to get Moira into what would be the gown and then out of it again, although there'd been a lot of laughter in the process which seemed to have done Moira good, for although she kept blinking her eyes, they were sparkling with humour, and her face had a little colour in it.

"Aye, I'm thinking we certainly need Barbara, for the common sense if nothing else," Moira agreed. "You away and fetch her while I make up the fire and light the candles. I'm having so much fun though. I canna wait to see Alexander's face when it's finished."

"Ye'll be a wonderful sight to see, for you're a lovely-looking woman," Susan said, making Moira giggle girlishly with a mixture of delight and embarrassment. "I'll no' be long."

Once home, she picked up the lavender oil, found the hair clips she intended to lend to Moira, and then headed back by way of Barbara's. Angus and Kenneth were sitting opposite each other on the dirt floor having a fine game of roll the ball to each other.

"Aye, he can stay, of course," Kenneth said, when Susan asked. "He can sleep in my bed if he wants," he added, pointing to a heather-filled mattress in the corner of the room.

"Kenneth sleeps so heavy that he wouldna wake if Angus

screamed down his ear all night," Barbara said dryly. "Here, I'll come with ye now. Flora can finish the bannocks. They've only to cook. I'll no' be too long," she said to them.

The two women set off to the chieftain's house, looking at the sky as they did.

"There's rain coming in," Barbara said, sniffing the air. "And soon, too."

"Aye. We can work as well indoors, if we sit at the window," Susan said, "and in truth I'm thinking she'll sleep for most of the day if she can."

"Aye, bairns are a blessing, no doubt, but they can be a curse at times too," Barbara said. "Oh, Christ, I'm sorry."

"Why are ye sorry?" Susan asked, puzzled.

"Ah. Well, we all ken ye havena any of your own and yet ye clearly love them, so we thought…" Her voice trailed off.

"That's kind of ye, but I'm over that, have been a long time. Rob and I accepted that we werena going to have bairns many years ago. I'm at peace with it now. Oh, that's odd," Susan added, looking at the house, which was still in darkness. "She said she'd light the candles."

When they opened the door and went in it was immediately clear why Moira had not lit the candles, although she had made up the fire. By its glow they could see her, sitting on the *seise,* leaning forward, her hands gripping her head convulsively. She was moaning, a low, almost primeval sound of pure agony that Susan had never heard before and which would intermittently haunt her dreams for the rest of her life.

Barbara, who had entered the room first, ran to Moira, dropping to her knees in front of her.

"What's wrong, *a ghràidh?*" she asked urgently.

Moira looked up vaguely, as though responding to the sound rather than the sight of Barbara, still gripping her head fiercely.

"I..uh…sh…" she stammered, and then, jerking suddenly, she collapsed forward, knocking Barbara backwards as she fell, landing on top of her.

Susan ran forward then, lifting Moira off the older woman and lying her on the floor, where she convulsed and moaned.

"Holy Mother of God, what's wrong wi' her?" Barbara cried, crossing herself.

"I dinna ken," Susan replied. "We need to get her to bed, and I need some light to see what she looks like."

Barbara ran to the door and out of it, shouting for help in a voice loud enough to bring several people to the room in moments. Iain and Allan gently lifted the chieftain's wife off the floor and laid her in the box bed she normally shared with Alexander, still convulsing, although her movements were less violent now. Barbara lit every candle she could find, and by the light of them Susan examined Moira as best she could. She was pale, and when Susan held the candle close to her face she saw that the pupil of one eye was dilated, making it look almost black instead of grey. She surmised from the rigid neck muscles and the unearthly moaning sound that Moira was suffering from terrible head pains, judging by the way she'd been holding it when they arrived. But she had no idea as to the cause.

She looked up at what was now a crowd of worried clanspeople in the room, wanting to reassure them, but knowing that she could not.

"I havena ever seen anything like this before," she said honestly. "I havena a notion what's causing her pain. But we ken Moira isna one to complain without cause."

"Is it something very terrible?" Fiona asked fearfully, watching Moira's twitching limbs. "Is she possessed of a demon?"

"No, she isna!" Susan said sharply, seeing several people immediately cross themselves. The last thing she needed was the priest being called to pontificate about God's will and try to exclude her from the room, for she did not like the man, and he knew it and reciprocated the dislike. "I'm thinking it's some sort of a megrim, maybe, for she was holding her head when we came in, and she tellt me earlier that her vision was blurred."

"Aye, I canna see rightly before the megrim comes," Catriona, who also suffered from them, put in. "I get wee sparkles in my eyes. Is that what she had?"

"She just said that her vision was blurry."

"I'm thinking she's a fearful headache, from when we came in on her," Barbara agreed. Everyone relaxed a little. Megrims were horrible, but they were not of the Devil and they were not fatal. Even so…

"I never heard anyone moan like that though," Catriona said, voicing Susan's thoughts. "I'm thinking it's a fearful bad one, if it is. And she hasna had them before."

Could it be an apoplexy? Susan wondered. If it was, that would explain the tingling in the arm she'd complained of. And if it was, and this severe, it could certainly be fatal. She closed her eyes, trying to ignore the anxious weight of the clanspeople all looking to her for reassurance, for she was by now established as the official physician of the MacGregors. Until now she had relished it, for it made her a valuable member of the clan. And if Alexander had been here she would not have been torn, would have done what she could, admitted she wasn't sure what was wrong. But Alexander was not here to take charge. Alexander was in Edinburgh.

Edinburgh.

Suddenly she was certain what she had to do, what *she* would have wanted had Rob been stricken while she was far away. And *he* was in Edinburgh, which made her other decision easier too. Susan looked at Moira, who had stopped shaking and was now lying still, although her face was twisted with pain. Then she looked at the crowd of people gathered round.

She stood.

"Do ye ken where Alexander stays when he's in Edinburgh?" she asked.

"Aye, I do," Alasdair replied. "He tellt me he'd written to Mrs Grant. She's a room in the area near Dickson's Close. No' so clean, but she's reliable. I dinna ken the name o' the wynd, but I ken how to get there."

"Ye're thinking we should send for Alexander, then? Is it grievous, what ails her?" Barbara asked.

"I'm no' certain, but I think it might be. And he'll never forgive us if we dinna send for him, if it is. Allan, ye're the fastest. How long will it take ye to get to Edinburgh?" Susan asked.

"If I go now, I could be there tomorrow," he said. "I'll need ye to tell me how to get to this Mrs Grant, once I'm there," he added to Alasdair.

"Ye'll kill yourself, running that fast for so far," Alasdair remarked.

Allan glanced at Moira.

"It's for Alexander," he said simply, and no one objected any further. He moved toward the door then, clearly intending to prepare to set off immediately.

"Wait," Susan said, and ran into the living area, where she laid out a piece of paper, and grabbing a quill and ink wrote quickly across it, her mind racing, as she had to word this correctly. "There," she said, when she'd dried the ink, after folding it and passing it to Allan. "I've written the address on the top. Ye must give it to Francis Ogilvy."

"I canna read the words," Allan said.

"Who's Francis Ogilvy?" Alasdair said at the same time.

"He's a physician. He's the best physician I ken, now my man's gone," Susan said. "And he lives on Niddry's Row, which isna far from Dickson's Close. Ye must show him the letter, bring him back with ye. I'll go now and fetch ye some coin, for ye'll need it to go through the gate."

"I've coin of my own for that, I'm thinking, but no' to pay a fancy physician," Allan said.

"No physician will come here, at any price," Gregor put in. "No' to MacGregors, and no' so far."

"If anyone will, Francis will," Susan said. "I'd wager my life on it. He's a good man. If the paper is spoiled by the rain, then tell him Susan needs him to come and he'll ken that it's no' a trivial matter."

Allan looked at her and nodded.

"He'll come regardless, if he can save her," Allan said grimly, nodding at Moira.

"I dinna ken if he can save her, but if anyone could, it would be him. I'm praying when they arrive she'll be well, but I canna take a chance on that," Susan said, uncertainty in her voice now.

"If ye bring Alexander back and she's well, he'll forgive ye," Barbara said. "But if ye dinna and she dies, then he willna. Ye're doing the right thing."

"Oh, thank you. I needed to hear that," Susan replied gratefully. Then she turned back to her patient, to do what she could for her.

Allan, having listened to rapid instructions from Alasdair, left the house, stopping only for a few minutes at his home to grab whatever he could find that was edible and arm himself, for if he was to run alone he would be armed, and to hell with any damn laws telling him otherwise.

Then he went outside, swore fluently at the icy drenching rain that had now started to fall, and set off, vanishing into the inky darkness of the night in moments.

All everyone could do now was wait and pray that Moira recovered, for they all loved her and could not imagine Alexander without her by his side.

CHAPTER FIFTEEN

For the first part of the walk home after the play the boys were quiet, still lost in the magical world the theatre had created. *The Gentle Shepherd* had been a good play for them to see as their first, Alexander thought. It had been a gentle play indeed, set in rural surroundings they were familiar with, and without the crudity that would render an audience unruly, heckling or throwing things at the actors, although they had all joined in singing the songs that were scattered throughout the performance. Alexander and his sons were exceptions, as if most of the tunes were well-known in Edinburgh, they were not in Loch Lomond.

"That was an awfu' good play," Duncan said eventually. "I liked it much more than the puppets at Crieff."

"Aye, well that was a different thing entirely," Alexander commented. "The playwright owns the wee shop ye bought your books from earlier today, Alex."

"The man who wrote the play lives in Edinburgh? I'd like to meet him," Alex said.

"Aye. It's said he's a good man too. He runs a thing called a 'circulating library' from his shop. I dinna ken rightly how it works, but ye can have a book to read and then take it back to him and get another one."

"So he lends books to people?" Duncan asked.

"Aye, but he lends them to strangers, to people who canna afford to buy a book themselves. I think they maybe pay something, but then when they bring the book back he returns the money. I'm no' sure though. I never heard of such a thing before."

"It sounds like a wondrous thing!" Duncan said dreamily.

"Are ye wanting to stay in Edinburgh then, and read books?" Alexander asked, smiling. Duncan woke up instantly.

"No," he said with resolve. "Nothing would ever make me want to live here."

"It would be lovely to see a play again, though," Alex said. "Did ye see that baronet mannie in the audience, waving his arms about and talking through the play?"

"No," replied Alexander, who had been too busy watching for pickpockets and other dangers to pay attention to the audience members, having not warned his sons about them as he'd wanted them to relax and enjoy the play.

"Aye, I did," Duncan said. "He looked even worse than he did yesterday, wi' his pink coat wi' all the pictures on."

"His waistcoat was purple," Alex giggled, "I thought everyone would laugh at the man, but no one seemed to notice what he was wearing at all."

"Oh, they'll have noticed, but if he's a man worth being on the right side of, no one will say anything about him. No' to his face, anyway," Alexander said. "What did ye like about the play, then?" he asked as they walked along the Canongate in the direction of the Netherbow Port.

"I liked that it had a happy ending," Duncan said. "And the songs were lovely. I wasna expecting there to be songs. Ye tellt us it was like a story, but wi' people acting it out."

"Most plays are like that. I didna ken this one would have songs," Alexander admitted.

"Everyone kent the songs, but I havena heard any of them before," Alex commented.

"Some people go to the play every night, to meet other people. And ye can buy the words to the plays, in wee books," Alexander explained. "And the notes of music too, I think."

"Could we buy the wee song book, Da?" Alex asked. "Maybe Alasdair could play the tunes then and we could all sing them."

"Ah, I dinna think Alasdair can read music," Alexander said sadly. "He learns the tunes by listening to them."

"*The yellow-haired laddie sat down on yon brae,*

Cried, milk the yowes, lassie let nane of them gae;" Alex sang. "I want to learn that one, for Angus'll like it. It's a fine song, and about a yellow-haired laddie like him. I ken the words now."

"Ye havena the tune, though," Duncan told him. "It's like this."

He started humming it, and after a minute Alex joined in singing the words, while Alexander walked behind them committing this wonderful moment to memory, as two of his sons occupied themselves learning a song for the third son at home. He was such a lucky man. If only Moira were walking with them now, sharing this moment with him, life would be utterly perfect. He told her everything, always had since they'd married, but nothing compared to actually sharing such perfect moments as this. Suddenly a wave of longing to hold her washed over him.

Still, they had done everything they needed to in Edinburgh now, and could set off for home tomorrow. Hopefully *The Gentle Shepherd* would be playing again when he came back with Moira next spring. It was the sort of play she'd love.

They arrived back at the lodgings, and as it had been a long day full of new and exciting events, the boys at least were yawning and needed no persuading to get into bed.

"Da, what does it mean to rack?" Alex asked as they all settled under the covers.

"To rack?" Alexander repeated.

"Aye. In the play, yon man who keeps Sir William's secret and brings Patie up, says, '*The laird wha in riches an honour wad thrive, should be kindly an free, nor rack his puir tenants wha labour to rise abuin poverty*,'" Alex said.

Christ, the boy's no doubt memorised the whole of the play, Alexander thought.

"Ah. A laird is a man who owns an estate, so this Sir William in the play must own lands and houses, and he rents them out to his tenants. Some lairds, if they see that their tenants appear to be doing well from their labour, will raise the rent by a goodly sum, even if they dinna need the money themselves, so their tenants do all the work, but are always poor."

"So a laird is a kind of chief?" Duncan asked.

"No, it's an entirely different thing. For he hasna the blood or loyalty ties to his tenants as chiefs have to the clansfolk, and he canna rely on his men to come out for him in battle. A clan chief owns his land, either from the crown or by the sword, but a good one willna rack the rent, for he's the father of his clan, and although he might have more than his clansmen, he willna have them starving while he lives in a palace. And the people who are doing well will share with others of the clan in need anyway. Racking the rent isna the way of the clans. Most of the clans," he amended, because in fairness some clan chiefs cared little for their people except when they were useful to them. "So we have a bigger house, wi' a chimney and maybe a wee bit more food when there's enough for all. But if our people starve we starve too, for we'll share everything. And my house is always open to the clan for they're my children, as it were. As their father they obey me, and I protect them. One day you'll be the father, and will feel the same, I'm hoping. Now, enough questions," he added, seeing Alex was about to ask another one. "Let's sleep, and tomorrow before we leave we'll walk up to the castle, and see the inside of St Giles', which is a fine church. We only saw the outside today when we were at the Luckenbooths."

He blew out the candle and they settled down, allowing the muted noise from the streets to lull them to sleep.

* * *

When the banging on the door came a few hours later all three of the sleeping inhabitants were instantly awake and alert. Alexander leapt out of bed dressed only in his shirt, grabbing his dirk from where he'd placed it under his pillow.

"Stay there and quiet, but keep your weapons ready," he said to the boys, passing them their own dirks from the chair next to the bed. From outside came the querulous tone of their landlady, who it seemed had also been woken by the sudden racket.

"Who is it?" Alexander shouted, as there was no point in being quiet any more. Half the building was probably awake and listening.

"Allan," came the reply. "I've a message for ye." Clearly Allan was of the same opinion as his chieftain, for he volunteered no more information which could be passed about the town.

Alexander pulled the chair from under the door handle, then unlocked and opened it to let Allan in. Then he stood in the doorway so that Mrs Grant, holding a candle which lit up the landing, could not follow him as she showed signs of wanting to do.

"I'm truly very sorry for disturbing ye, Mistress," he said. "It must be an urgent message from home. We'll no' make any more noise at all. Ye'll no doubt be wanting to go back to your bed directly. I'll no' keep ye standing on the stair in the cold. Good night to ye." Then he stepped back and closed the door before she could say anything else, locking it once more.

He turned then, saw the state of his clansman by the dull light of the fire, and put one finger on his lip, shaking his head while pointing with the other hand at the door to indicate that the landlady would almost certainly not be wanting to go back to her bed directly, but would be listening at the door, hoping for some juicy gossip. Once the identity of the visitor was known Alex and Duncan had jumped out of bed, and Alex was now busy coaxing the embers of the fire back into life while Duncan lit a candle.

By its light the state of the clansman could be seen much more clearly. His legs and feet were covered with mud, his shirt and kilt soaking wet, and he looked completely spent, his legs shaking uncontrollably, breathing still laboured. He looked as though one more movement of any kind would kill him.

Alexander moved to him, quickly unbuckling Allan's swordbelt to allow the sodden kilt to fall to the floor. Then he pulled the man's shirt over his head and grabbed a dry one of his own from the chest.

"Put this on, man, and then get yourself in the bed," he said. "It's still warm."

Allan shook his head.

"If I do, I'll sleep. I canna sleep," he said. "I must tell ye—"

"*Isd,*" Alexander hissed, then turned and opened the door quickly.

"I've just been down to make sure the outer door was locked, and am away to my bed now," Mrs Grant said, flushing scarlet, as it was blatantly clear that she was doing no such thing, but had been standing next to their door.

"I'll wish ye good night then," Alexander said, then watched as she reluctantly went into her room, closing the door behind her. He went back in then, closing and locking the door once more. "Her door creaks dreadfully, so we'll hear if she opens it again. But speak softly. And sit down by the fire if ye willna lie, and warm yourself. I'll wake ye if ye sleep."

Allan did as told, and Alexander pulled another chair up to sit close to him, while the boys sat on the floor.

"Susan sent me," Allan said immediately. "She said to tell ye that Moira's very sick and ye must come home directly. She tellt us it might be some kind of megrim, but I'm thinking it's more than that, for Moira was moaning awfu' bad and jerking like one possessed."

A wave of panic washed through Alexander, and he closed his eyes for a moment, fighting to pull himself together. Susan would not send for him to come home for a megrim. She must be sure it was something much worse to make Allan run all the way here. He fought back the urge to run blindly out of the room now and head back. He had the boys to think of, and a clansman who was completely spent.

"When was this?" he asked.

"Yesterday," Allan replied. "I left at nightfall."

"Jesus Christ, man!" Alexander replied. "Ye ran the whole way without stopping?"

"I stopped to drink and eat, but otherwise, aye. It was raining when I left, but it stopped soon after, and started again as I entered Edinburgh. I wanted to get here quickly, for I thought...she looked awfu' sick to me, and it came on very sudden. Oh, Susan gave me a paper and tellt me to take it to a man, Francis Ogilvy, a physician." He made a move to stand, looking at his clothes which were still lying on the floor, but Alexander lifted his hand then stood and went over to them, separating the shirt and kilt and bringing them over to the fire. Alex and Duncan spread them out to dry while Alexander pulled the folded paper out of Allan's sporran and held it up to the candle to read. Then he sat again, rubbing his hand fiercely through his hair before leaping up and going to the window to look out.

"It's harder to ken the time in a place like this," he said after a minute. "But I'm thinking it'll be dawn very soon, for the sky is lightening a wee bit and there are a few people about below."

In fact there were always a few people about in Edinburgh, but Alexander was verbally justifying what he was about to do. He turned back to the others, who were all watching him closely.

"Go to bed, man, and get some sleep. We'll go and fetch this Ogilvy man and the garron, and some food for ye. When ye've slept enough, ye can come after us. Dress yourselves, I'm wanting ye to come with me to this physician," he said to Alex and Duncan, who jumped up immediately, while Alexander pushed Allan into the bed.

A few minutes later they had dressed, combed and tied their hair, and were outside in the cold grey light of early dawn.

"The man lives in Niddry's Row, it's no' far," he said. "Then we'll get some food and eat, for I'm thinking the doctor willna be ready as quickly as we can be."

"What did the letter say, Da?" Alex asked as they hurried along beside their father.

"It said your Ma's awfu' sick and Susan wants him to go to her." He stopped then outside a building that looked a good deal more respectable than the one they were staying in, and rang the brass bell hanging outside. "Try to look grieved," he added unnecessarily, for Alex and Duncan were already very worried. Like their father, they knew Susan would not ask a doctor to travel all the way from Edinburgh if their mother was not desperately ill.

"Will he come? It's a very long way," Duncan asked.

"Aye. He'll come," Alexander said, his tone making them shudder and hope that this Ogilvy man did not try to refuse. And then the door was opened by a sleepy-looking maid who observed them carefully for a moment, clearly assessing their criminal potential.

"Is this the home of Francis Ogilvy?" Alexander asked impatiently.

"It's very early," she said. "What's amiss?"

"My wife is desperate sick and needs the physician."

"He's asleep," she said. "Can it no' wait?"

"No," Alexander told her. "I've a note here for him. Ye must wake him and give it to him directly. I'm sorry to wake him, but it canna wait."

She took the note, told them to wait and then shut the door in their faces, which informed Alexander if not his sons that she considered them too disreputable to allow inside.

They stood on the step, Alexander taking deep steady breaths to try to calm himself, because every fibre of his being wanted to break down the door and drag the man out of bed, but he knew that he really needed this Ogilvy man to come willingly, for that would be quicker and easier. Violence had to be the last option in this case.

"Da, do they no' give hospitality in Edinburgh?" Alex asked, bringing Alexander back into the present.

"No, laddie. That's a Highland custom," Alexander replied. "They dinna ken it here, and in truth it isna needed as it is in the Highlands, for in Edinburgh ye can always shelter from the weather in a doorway, and ye willna fall in a bog or off a cliff and die if ye're a stranger to the area, as ye can in our country."

Alex absorbed this.

"And then if they dinna ken it here, I suppose if ye invite a man in he wouldna ken that he mustna steal from you or kill you, even if he's your enemy, as we do," Alex commented.

"Aye, ye've the right of it. It isna safe here, for the city people are no' like us and can be awfu' primitive," Alexander said.

Then the door opened again, revealing a very handsome, but tousled-looking middle-aged man in a green silk banyan patterned with flowers and tied at the waist with a sash.

"I'm sorry to keep you outside," the man said in a soft Scottish accent. "Emily was being cautious, which is, I'm afraid, necessary in this town. Please, do come in. Is Mistress MacIntyre with the patient?"

"She is, and I'm most sorry to disturb ye, but she tellt my man that if anyone could save my wife it will be yourself. I'll pay ye handsomely, but ye must come urgently," Alexander said.

"Of course. I must dress and fetch my instruments. Would you care for some refreshment while you wait, or do you wish to return to your wife? If so, tell me the address and I'll be with you directly," Dr Ogilvy said.

"Did ye no' ken that Susan…Mistress MacIntyre had returned to her clan, sir?" Alexander asked.

"Of course. Most tragic, her husband dying like that. I had no idea she was back in Edinburgh though. Please, we must not waste time, and I must dress."

Alexander scrubbed one hand through his hair, placing the other on the man's arm as he turned to leave.

"Sir, she is not in Edinburgh, and neither is my wife. But ye must come regardless. I will pay ye whatever ye ask, but ye must come," he said desperately.

Francis Ogilvy turned back then, his face a mask of shock.

"You mean she is in the Highlands, MacGregor country?" he said.

"She is. But ye'll come to no harm, I swear it on my life. I am the chieftain of my clan. No man over whom I have power will touch ye, and no other except over my dead body. I will protect ye with my life, but ye must come."

"We'll protect ye as well!" cried Alex. "We can fight."

Francis looked at the two boys.

"You are her sons," he said.

They both nodded, and Duncan's eyes misted with tears. He swallowed quickly and looked away, hoping the man hadn't seen his weakness.

Francis sighed, then came to a decision.

"Susan's husband and I were close friends," he said. "And she is a woman I respect above all others. I will come, for her and for you, for you clearly love your wife and mother most dearly. But I will need time to prepare – I will make it as short as possible. How far is it to your home?"

"Two…three days, for the boys canna run as fast as Allan," Alexander said, raising his hand as Alex made to object. "Is your horse a city animal, sir, accustomed to paved roads?"

"Aye, he is, but he's a good mount."

"We'll be faster if ye ride the mount I brought wi' me, for the kind of horse I'm sure ye have will no' be surefooted in the terrain we'll be crossing. I would ask ye to trust me on this. We'll escort ye home, or to a place where ye can take a coach if that pleases ye. But we must go directly there, for we havena time to waste."

"Well, this will be an adventure. Tell me where you're staying and I'll be with you within the hour," the physician said.

Alexander breathed a great sigh of relief.

"Thank ye, sir. In truth I didna expect ye to agree so easily. But I'm thinking Susan wouldna send for ye on a fool's errand, and Moira is the dearest thing in the world to me."

Francis smiled then, his green eyes warm.

"She would not, although I suspect my staff will think me a fool indeed. No matter. I will see you in an hour."

And then he turned and ran quickly back up the stairs, leaving his visitors to see their own way out.

* * *

"Sir, I would beg you not to do this," Elspeth Ferguson said, wringing her hands as she watched her master stuff items of clothing willy-nilly into a bag. Francis stopped momentarily and smiled at her.

"Elspeth, you are a fine woman, and the best housekeeper I've ever had. I know that you will keep the place in perfect order while I am gone, but you know I must do this. I will never forgive myself if I do not."

"But you have no knowledge of these men, and said yourself they are Highlandmen! They are not like us! They're savages. They could murder you in your bed! Please think on this before you rush into danger," she cried.

"Well, if they are civilised enough to own a bed, then I need have no worries," he replied lightheartedly.

"But how do you know they speak the truth? They could murder you directly you leave the city!"

"Why?" he asked.

"Why what?"

"Why would a stranger bring two children to my house, make Susan write a letter to me, allow my servants to see them clearly, then tell me a lie to get me out of the city, only to murder me? It makes no sense. If they wished to rob me they would have wanted me to bring Samson, for he's a valuable stallion, but they told me not to for he'll not manage the terrain. They're genuine, I'm sure of it. And it will be an adventure."

He reached into the chest, pulled out a shirt, then shook his head and threw it on the bed, rummaging for another, warmer one. Mrs Ferguson thought fiercely for a minute.

"Perhaps one of the patients you couldn't save was a relative, and they want revenge, sir! The Highlandmen are very vengeful people!" she persisted desperately.

He straightened then, and moving across to her, cupped her face gently with the palms of his hands.

"Elspeth. You are only thinking of my safety, and I am very grateful to you for it. But I am going. They are in real need of my services, I am sure of it. The youngest boy told me that," he said, seeing again the tears misting the earnest grey eyes, and the attempt to conceal them. "And Susan sent for me."

"Ah. Then there's no point in reasoning with you, sir, for

you've never seen reason regarding that situation," she said, deflating suddenly. "Here, you fetch your instruments, for you're making a terrible mess of packing your clothes. I'll do that."

"You're a wonderful woman, and I'm blessed to have you," Francis said, then kissed her on the nose, making her giggle like a young girl rather than the sixty-year-old matron she was.

"Away with you," she said. "I just hope you don't regret it, that's all."

"I won't," he said with absolute conviction. Then he was out of the door and running down the stairs to his surgery.

* * *

Francis Ogilvy remembered that conversation two days later as he lay on the wet ground, sheltered from the pouring rain only by an overhanging rock and the chieftain's plaid, which Alexander had kindly given him, telling him to wrap it round himself.

"Ye'll be warm soon, sir, for the wool keeps your body heat in when wet," he'd told the shivering doctor before going to sit with his sons in the heavy rain, for the overhang was not large enough to shelter more than one man. Francis knew he should offer his slightly sheltered place to the boys, but at the moment he was too tired even to speak, let alone get up and move. The offer would not be accepted even if he made it, he was sure of that.

He watched as his three companions sat, the man in his shirt, the boys in their tartan kilts, eating a mess of oatmeal mixed with rainwater from a wooden bowl with their fingers, talking together softly in their language, which he understood nothing of, and he realised that his housekeeper had been right in one thing at least.

The Highlandmen were not like him. He had met Highlanders before, but always in Edinburgh. He had never experienced them in their own environment, although he was not regretting his decision, for he kept his mind on the sick and possibly dying woman who needed him, and the living one who *he* needed. This had kept him astride the ridiculously short but very sturdy garron for endless hours as he rode through heather and bogs, across rivers, up insanely steep hillsides and along impossibly narrow paths with sheer drops at the side that made him queasy if he looked at anything other than the garron's neck. Every muscle in his body was screaming with pain and fatigue and his stomach was griping with hunger, even though they'd given him the lion's share of the watery oatmeal they lived on.

And for all that time the man Alexander and his two sons, aged ten and eight, as they'd told him on one of their short rest stops, had alternately walked and run by the side of the garron through all that brutal terrain without a word of complaint, lying down on the ground in the torrential rain and falling asleep instantly when they stopped, leaping up again fresh as a daisy a couple of hours later, ready to run again. Because Alexander was focussing solely on reaching Moira, he allowed them no more rest than was absolutely essential.

For them, but not for him, a mere mortal. Francis had to admire them. They were formidable. If they *had* had nefarious ideas, he would not have stood a chance.

A few hours ago another man had joined them, causing them all to make an impromptu stop for a few minutes while Alexander briefed him. While that went on the younger boy Duncan had come over to Francis, who was slumped over the horse's neck, and had held out his hand, revealing a number of small dark berries.

"I thought ye might like these, sir," the boy had said. "For I think ye're used to living on finer food than we are. I found them growing on the hillside earlier and picked them for ye."

Instinct told Francis not to refuse this kind gesture, which might offend the boy, so he accepted them gratefully, biting into one gingerly. It was tangy, sour even, but after two days of watery gruel it tasted like manna from Heaven.

"What are they?" he asked.

"Blaeberries. They taste awfu' good in hot porridge, for they burst and are sweeter then. But they're still good," Duncan told him. He looked ahead across the heather-clad misty hills, assessing. "We should be home tomorrow, and then there'll be better food, and ye can get warm and dry too. Barbara's honey is a wondrous thing." He smiled up at Francis, looking very young in that moment. "Da isna a hard man," he added suddenly. "He's just awfu' feart for Ma, so he canna think of anything else. I'm sorry for your pains."

"I understand that," Francis said. "I'm not accustomed to travelling in this way, that's all. But it's interesting to see another part of the country, for I've lived in Edinburgh my whole life."

Duncan, who had been about to leave, stopped then, and looked up at the physician in shock.

"Ye mean ye've never been out of Edinburgh?" he asked.

"No, not since I was an adult, no further than Arthur's Seat, anyway."

"Is that because ye canna pay to go through the Netherbow Port?" Duncan asked. "Da tellt me that there are people who never leave the city, for they canna afford to return. That must be a terrible thing. I'm sure Da will pay ye back through the Port, sir, when ye return."

Francis fought not to laugh then, for it was clear that the boy equated Edinburgh with some deepest layer of Hell.

"Arthur's Seat is outside the Netherbow Port," he said. "It's the hill overlooking Holyrood Palace. If you walk up there, you can see the whole city spread out beneath you."

"Ah. We went to see a play at the Tennis Court Hall, near to the palace," Duncan replied. "Da was going to show us some of the other places, the castle and St Giles' before we left, but…" His voice trailed off for a moment, then he pulled himself back. "He tellt us that there was a dragon once, who used to fly around the city and eat all the cows and the sheep, and that one day it ate too much, lay down and fell asleep, and that's what made the hill. Is that Arthur's Seat?"

"Aye, that's it," Francis said, warming to this strange boy, who seemed mature beyond his years in some ways, but still believed utterly that a sleeping dragon could form a hill. "On May Day all the young women go up on the hill at dawn and wash their faces in the dew, for it's said to keep them young and beautiful forever."

"And does it?" Duncan asked.

"I'm not sure. But there are some beautiful women in Edinburgh, so I think it must do," Francis replied.

"I didna see any," Duncan commented with brutal honesty. "But I'll tell Jeannie. It's the sort of tale she'd like."

And then the man who'd caught up with them finished talking with Alexander, and came across to them.

"I'm fashed wi' myself, for I slept the day through," Allan said. "But I'm fresh now, so I'll keep on and tell the clan ye're coming. That'll cheer them all and maybe give Moira the will to stay with us, if she's no' already well. Thank ye, sir, for coming. This canna be easy for ye, we ken that. Ye're an honourable man, Dr Ogilvy."

"I'm just doing my duty, sir," Francis replied.

"Och, no. Ye're doing far more than that. And ye ken we're MacGregors too, Alexander tellt me. We'll no' forget that. I'll see ye tomorrow."

"Allan, if Ma's still bad when ye get home, will ye tell her I love her?" Duncan pleaded, suddenly a small child again.

"I'll tell her ye all love her, laddie, though she kens that well enough already," Allan said. Then he turned and set off again, running as nimbly as a deer through the heather.

Francis watched him go, a wave of unexpected affection for this outlawed clan washing over him.

For the first time he had an inkling of why Susan might have chosen to abandon the attractions of the city, its comforts and entertainments for what he had always thought of as a primitive, barbaric existence.

He was a man who had been born and reared in wealth and comfort, whose greatest eccentricity so far had been to decide not only to become a physician, but to treat the poor, along with his closest friend, the intense and earnest Robert MacIntyre. If his family considered the poor of Edinburgh to be vermin, he could not imagine what they would think about their precious son riding off into the wilderness with Highlanders. And not only Highlanders, but possibly the most dangerous Highlanders of all; the outlawed MacGregors.

He smiled to himself. He had made the comment to his housekeeper in jest; but this was turning out to be an adventure after all. And most definitely a learning experience.

* * *

When they saw Loch Lomond ahead of them, its waters sparkling in the afternoon sunlight, the clouds having briefly cleared, the MacGregor boys' spirits lifted immediately, for although they would never have either admitted or shown it, both Alex and Duncan were bone-weary from the pace their father had set, which had been close to the maximum the two boys were able to endure.

Alexander had been aware of how much his sons could

manage, but looking at the physician slumping over the horse, pain etched deep on his face, he realised that he had not been aware of just how different a creature a city man was from a Highlander. And yet to his credit the man had not complained once. Feeling guilty for being too intent on getting home, Alexander made his way over to the man.

"I'm sorry, sir, for I see I've driven ye too hard," he said. Francis raised his head, eyes heavy with fatigue, and attempted a smile.

"I understand, Mr MacGregor. Your concern for your wife is commendable, and all else is irrelevant at such times. No need to apologise, although I confess I will be most relieved to arrive at your abode, for several reasons," Francis admitted.

"That water there, sir, is Loch Lomond," Alexander told him, pointing. "And we live just a wee walk along its banks. We'll be there directly. Will ye be able to see my wife immediately, or are ye too spent?"

"God, no. I am never too tired to see a patient!" Francis said, although in truth he had never been as tired as he was now. As he had been many hours ago, for that matter. But Alexander's eyes lit up, which was the important thing. "But I do think I will sleep for a long time once my head hits a pillow."

"We'll give ye the finest bed we have, sir, and the finest food too, although it'll no' match what ye're used to, I'm thinking."

"This is a beautiful place," Francis said as they arrived at the edge of the loch.

"Truly? I think it is, for it's home, but most Lowlanders think the Highlands to be a dark and gloomy hell," Alexander said, his mood lifting a little now they were nearly home. She was alive. She *must* be alive, for if she was not the sun would not shine, the birds would not sing, and he would know it. He was sure he would. She was alive.

"I daresay they think of it much as your son thinks of Edinburgh," Francis replied, making Alexander laugh. "He was not so impolite as to tell me so directly, I must add. I will admit that I've thought it dark and gloomy at times in the last days, but I realise now that was the weather, for with the sun shining it's beautiful, in a dramatic, awe-inspiring way."

Much like its inhabitants, he thought, but did not say.

A few minutes later the first houses came into view, although they were almost among them before Francis realised that was what they were. He had thought them to be naturally occurring mounds of turf and heather until they were close enough for him to see doors in the sides and smoke seeping through the rooves.

And then they came to a clearing in which a number of people were standing, the men all dressed in the same outlandish clothing as the chieftain and his sons, albeit in different patterns of tartan, the women in plain ankle-length dresses, a shawl of the same tartan patterns as the men's dress wrapped round their upper body and head. Most of them were barefoot; all of them looked very anxious. At the edge of the clearing was a building, this one unmistakably a house, although a very primitive one from a city viewpoint. But it did have a window and a chimney as well as a door.

As they arrived at it the door opened and Susan came out, nodding to both Alexander and Francis, which made both men's hearts soar, although for entirely different reasons. And then Alexander and his two sons dashed past him into the house, Susan following them, while Allan came forward and took the reins of the garron, which had come to a stop.

"She's alive, sir, but only just, Susan says," Allan commented.

On hearing this Francis's aches, pains and fatigue faded into the background, and he dismounted stiffly, reaching into one of the bags and pulling out his medical case. Allan led the way to the house, and Francis walked inside, stopping for a moment to let his eyes become accustomed to the relative darkness.

"She's through here, sir," Allan said, pointing to a partitioned area at the right, allowing Francis to go ahead of him.

"...and Father Gordon has given her the last rites, Alexander, so ye mustna think her soul's in jeopardy," a woman's voice was saying. "But she couldna—"

"Ye can go now, Fiona," Susan said abruptly, cutting the other woman off mid-flow. "He doesna want to hear that now," she added in a softer voice. "He wants to be with Moira, nothing else. Go."

She had not lost her ability to manage people, Francis thought, and then she came into the living area to him, speaking very quietly but urgently.

"She's desperate sick, Francis. I think you're too late, in truth," she said by way of introduction.

"What are the symptoms?" he asked.

"Started with tingling in her arm and blurred vision, then terrible head pains, convulsions, vomiting. She was talking nonsense for a good while, but has been unconscious since this morning. One pupil is very enlarged. I havena seen it before, but thought if anyone had it would be you. I think she's been holding on for Alexander and the boys to return. They're devoted."

He nodded.

"Let me see her," he said, and she stood to the side to let him through into the bedroom.

Alexander was sitting on the edge of the box-bed, and had lifted his wife onto his lap, her head resting against his shoulder, her beautiful auburn hair spilling over his arm. Even though Francis understood no Gaelic, he knew that the man was desperately begging her to stay with him, tears spilling down his cheeks unheeded.

The older boy, Alex, was holding his mother's hand in both of his as though he could infuse his life force into her by doing so, while Duncan sat at the foot of the bed, his hand on her leg. Although he knew he was intruding, Francis moved across to them, reaching past Alex to feel for the pulse at her neck. It was there, but very weak and erratic, and in that moment he knew that she was past any help he could give. Her fate was in God's hands now.

Alexander looked at him then, his blue eyes dark with grief, and Francis found tears welling up in his own eyes as he shook his head. The other man closed his eyes tightly for a second, then opened them again and bent his head, kissing his wife on the forehead.

"Da, she kens we're here," Alex said suddenly, urgently. "She squeezed my hand!" Francis looked at the hand enfolded in the boy's own, thinking he was deluding himself, for the woman was unconscious and on the brink of death, there was no doubt about that. But as he did he saw her fingers twitch against her son's, very slightly but unmistakeably. And then they relaxed completely, and he knew in that minute that her spirit had passed.

Unable to state this to her family, instead he left them to take what comfort they could before they realised that she was gone from them, going back into the living area and passing his hand across his face, which was wet from his own tears.

"Ah, Christ," Susan said simply on seeing his expression. "Does he ken?"

Francis shook his head, incapable of speech at that moment. Later he would attribute his unprofessional emotional reaction to fatigue, but in truth there had been something about the chieftain's single-minded determination to get home, coupled with the tableau in the other room and the presence of the only woman in the world who could induce such emotion in himself, that had torn at Francis's heart.

"I'll no' tell the clan until he does, then. I canna imagine what he'll do, for they're completely devoted to each other," she said softly. "Thank ye for coming, Francis. I'll stay until...but ye can go to my house and rest, if ye want. Ye look awfu tired."

"No, I'll stay as well. I couldn't sleep at the minute, in any case," he said wearily.

And then an unearthly roar of pure agony came from the other room, which, if he lived to be a hundred Francis would never forget, and would pray never to hear again. It made his blood run cold, and froze the clan members standing outside, who understanding the meaning of the sound, instantly dropped to their knees in the mud to pray for God to take the soul of the woman who they all loved dearly to His side.

Francis looked at Susan, whose face had suddenly paled. Then he made a move toward the room, but she gripped his arm fiercely to stop him.

"No," she said. "I dinna think—"

Alexander staggered from the bedroom, breathing heavily, trembling as though he had the ague. He walked to the door, fumbling for the handle, oblivious to anything except his need to escape the unbearable truth. His hand brushed the silk of the partly made gown which was hanging on the back of the door, and he stared blindly at it for a moment before drawing his dirk and slashing at it frenziedly, moaning incoherently. Then he tore open the door and staggered out, charging headlong through his kneeling clan unheeding, across the clearing and into the trees. Kenneth jumped to his feet and set off after his chieftain. No one tried to stop him, knowing that Alexander was beyond reason and the only person with the slightest chance of preventing him doing anything rash, should he try to, was the giant of the clan.

In the house Susan and Francis stood among the ruins of the gown, which swirled around their feet in the breeze from the door. And then she went into the bedroom and gathered the two boys to her. They did not resist, not even Alex, being too heartbroken by their mother's death and shocked by their father's reaction to care about behaving as a warrior should.

Francis stood for a moment in the doorway, suddenly unutterably weary, and then he moved towards the bed, laying Moira down neatly, closing her eyes, and pulling the cover up around her. And then he clasped his hands and said a prayer for this woman he had never known, but who must have been incredible indeed to inspire such love, such indescribable grief from the grim MacGregor chieftain. They were Catholic and he was Episcopalian, but he did not think that would make any difference to Christ.

After a few minutes Barbara came into the room, crossing herself as she looked at Moira, and nodding to acknowledge Francis. Then she looked at the group sitting huddled together on the floor.

"Will ye be taking the boys to ours?" she asked Susan. "Angus is there with Flora, and Gregor too. Kenneth has gone after Alexander, to…watch him," she said, aware that the boys might be listening, although they seemed oblivious to everything at the moment. "We'll take good care of her," she added.

With a good deal of tender persuasion, Susan and Barbara managed to get the boys out of the room, Francis following as they made their way across the clearing to another, less impressive hut. It didn't seem right to go in uninvited, so he sat outside on a rock, feeling useless and lonely, and waited until Susan came out again, still pale, her eyes red from weeping. She looked at him and smiled sadly.

"You're a good man, Francis," she said. "I kent ye'd come. No one else would have done such a thing. I'm sorry it was all for nothing."

"So am I, very much. I'd give a lot to have been able to help the poor woman," he replied. "But it was not all for nothing, Susan. You know that, I think."

"Well, come then. I'll feed ye, and then ye must sleep," she said, not responding to his last remark.

He stood and followed her across the muddy clearing and along a track, leaving the rest of the clan still kneeling in the mud, some of them holding rosaries, all of them praying to God both to receive Moira's soul and to give Alexander the strength to bear his loss.

* * *

Alex sat next to his brother on a stool, staring into the orange flames of the central fire, trying to make sense of what had happened. His mother had just died and his father seemed to have gone mad, both of which were impossible. His da was the strongest man in the world and could cope with anything, anything at all. And his ma could not be dead, because he needed her. They all needed her, the whole clan, and Angus especially, who was not even two yet.

Angus.

"Where's Angus?" he asked Gregor, who was coming into the room with two cups of mulled ale, which he gave to the boys.

"Drink that," he said. "Ye're shocked and ye're cold, and that'll help in both cases. Angus is asleep in Kenneth's bed. Kenneth had him helping wi' collecting heather to repair the rooves before the winter comes. No' that he did much, but he had him running around all day so he'd be tired before ye arrived. Allan tellt us ye'd be here today."

"How will I tell him?" Alex murmured. Duncan reached out and clasped his brother's hand.

"We'll tell him together," he said.

"He's very young," Flora added, passing the boys a bannock smothered in honey each. "He'll no' understand rightly, no' at that age. Dinna fash yourselves about that now. Eat those."

The two boys looked at the great treat in their hands, which at any other time they would have devoured immediately, but right now could not even imagine eating. Flora sat down opposite them, her eyes full of pity. And understanding.

"Ye need strength to deal wi' this," she said gently, "and ye're already at the end of it just getting home. Your da canna help ye right now, for he's grieving too fierce. So ye must find your own strength, and we'll help ye, as you both helped us wi' Alpin. Eat."

Had they both helped with Alpin? At that moment they couldn't remember, but maybe they had without knowing it. It was fair to say though, that if anyone knew about loss and grief, it was this household.

Still clasping hands, they took a small bite of their bannocks, a wave of guilt washing through them at the pleasure of the taste of the sweet honey. And then they took another bite and ate ravenously, for they were young boys and very hungry.

"Drink the ale too, and are ye wanting to sleep?" Gregor asked. Both boys shook their heads, even though they were very tired. If they slept now there would be dreams, which might be even worse than staying awake. "Kenneth's watching over your da," Gregor continued. "He'll make sure no harm comes to him. Ye can sleep if ye want, for like wi' the food and drink, sleep will make ye stronger for the days to come. Warriors always sleep whenever they can, for they ken that."

Alex and Duncan exchanged a look.

"We could lie down, maybe, just for a few minutes," Duncan ventured. "For we didna rest much on the way back from Edinburgh."

"That's a fine idea," Gregor said, smiling. "There's a wee mattress in the weaving room. Ye can lie on that for a few minutes."

They went into the next room and lay down on the mattress together, still fully clothed, still gripping each other's hands fiercely. Gregor laid a blanket carefully over them, then watched them for a minute, by which time they were both already fast asleep. Then he moved silently out of the room and sat down opposite Flora.

"Poor wee bairns," he said, "to lose their ma at such an age. And her still young too. I hope Alexander doesna do anything rash. She was his life. He's never even glanced at another woman, and there have been plenty who've tried over the years, and him such a handsome man."

"Kenneth will stop him if he tries to. I'm more afeart that the grief will break him. It nearly broke us, after Alpin," Flora commented, tears sparkling on her eyelashes. She blinked them away.

"He'll come round, in time," Gregor said, "just as we did. We must support him, and the boys, until he does, that's all."

* * *

At Susan's a similar situation had occurred, in that Francis had drunk a cup of mulled ale, eaten a bannock with cheese and then had gone to sleep in Susan's bed, although he had needed no persuasion to do so.

While he was asleep she'd gone to help Barbara with the task of laying Moira out, and, because no one else would, had told the priest in no uncertain terms that regardless of his views of women and of Moira in particular, he would write a wonderful sermon for her funeral, if he valued his life.

"For Alexander is out of his mind wi' grief, and ye'll no' be wanting to anger him wi' any comments about original sin or the weakness of women. It'll no' take much to do so, I'm thinking," she said. At that Father Gordon had flushed scarlet and had blustered that he had no such thoughts, held Moira in high regard, and that the requiem service would reflect that. Which, judging by the expression on his face, told Susan that he'd had every intention of getting in a few sly remarks about females and God's judgement.

Hopefully he would think again now, although Susan would shed no tears if Alexander carved the man into pieces, for she had no time at all for him and thought the clan would be better off without him, even at the cost of foregoing the sacrament. But if Alexander acted in rage whilst his mind was unbalanced with grief he would never forgive himself, and that Susan did *not* want.

After that she headed over to Gregor's, was told that all three boys were fast asleep and then returned home, busying herself with indoor tasks, including cooking a good meal, while she waited for Francis to awaken.

"My God, but that was good!" Francis said, having ploughed his way through two large bowls of broth and three bannocks slathered with butter. Susan smiled, and poured a good measure of claret into a glass before handing it to him.

"Anything would have tasted good to you after three days of riding a garron, I think," she said.

"Anything except watery oatmeal," Francis confirmed. "Although in honesty, the broth *was* very tasty. Thank you."

"Thank you for coming. That was very kind of you, and took a lot of courage."

"You didn't doubt I would, surely?" Francis asked, looking across the table at her.

"I wasna sure, and it didna seem right to ask, but I was desperate to save Moira's life and you were the only person I kent who might be able to, and who was insane enough to ride into the savage Highlands to do it," she admitted.

He laughed then, and took a sip of his wine.

"My feelings for you haven't changed, and never will. You must know that, Susan. I would ride into Hell for you without a second thought. And this place, whilst alien to me, is far from that."

"Aye, well, I'm sorry it was all for nothing, Francis, truly I am."

"I'm very sorry that Mistress MacGregor died, all the more so when I saw how desperate her husband was to save her. I think he would have brought me by force if I hadn't agreed to come. But it was not all for nothing. Or I hope it was not."

"Do ye ken what ailed her?" Susan asked. Francis sighed. Susan had always been one to tackle issues head on, and the fact that she was not doing so now told him a lot. Of course, he could be wrong. Hopefully…

"I'm no' sure, but I've seen something similar the once. It was a man, and he was drinking in a tavern with some friends when he suddenly screamed with the pain in his head, talked gibberish and then collapsed on the floor, convulsing as you said Mistress MacGregor did. But he died almost immediately. By the time I arrived he was dead and the landlord had carried him into a back room, worried about losing custom if it became widely known that a man had died while drinking his ale."

Susan snorted. This was typical city behaviour.

"Of course it did become widely known, in a matter of minutes," she said.

"Aye, it did. There were the inevitable rumours about poison, because he was a young man in the prime of his health and had shown no signs of being unwell until then, so I was asked to do an autopsy. When I did, I discovered that he had had a massive bleed in his brain, for a part of his brain was very congested with blood, which is not normal. I have no notion of what could cause such a thing, but I didn't believe he was poisoned, and said as much to the authorities."

"So you believe that's what Moira died of?" Susan asked.

"It would be my guess, but I couldn't be sure without doing an autopsy. Maybe she lived longer because the bleed was not as great as that of the man in Edinburgh. But there is no suspicion of poison, surely? Everyone seems to be devastated by her death!"

"God, no. I wish you'd kent her. She was a wonderful woman, kind, intelligent, loving…everyone adored her, myself included. I canna think of anyone who would wish her dead. No, I think it must be as ye say. No autopsy. Alexander couldna cope wi' that, I'm sure."

"What time is it?" Francis asked, realising that it was very dark and that he had no idea how long he'd slept.

"Time? I havena a notion. It's been dark for a good while, though. Why d'ye ask?"

Francis suddenly became very aware that although still in Scotland, he might as well be in India or America, so foreign was everything to him. Clock time was meaningless here.

"Has Alexander come home? He was in a terrible way."

"I dinna ken, in truth. But Kenneth followed him, and Kenneth wouldna let him do anything desperate," Susan explained.

Francis was about to ask what manner of man could stop the tall, muscular chieftain doing anything he wanted, and then realised that there were more important things to talk about. For it was clear that Susan was now a central figure in the clan, and, in view of what had happened, this might be one of the rare moments he would have alone with her.

"Was it all for nothing, then Susan?" he asked gently. Now she met his eyes for the first time since he had said the words earlier and he knew that his hope was forlorn.

"Francis, you are a very dear friend, and I hope you always will be," she said. "But there was only ever one man for me. I thought ye kent that."

"I did. But he has been gone for years now, and would want you to move on with your life, not to mourn him forever."

"I have moved on with my life," Susan said. "And I'm no' still mourning him, no' in the way you're thinking. But Rob was the only man I'll ever love in that way. I have no desire to marry again. Ye must let that wish go, Francis. When I asked ye to come here I was desperate, but I hesitated because I feared ye might think I did it because I'd changed my mind and was ready to accept ye. And then I thought that couldna be, for we havena seen each other in years, and there are a great many women in Edinburgh."

"Not for me. There is only one woman for me, and always will be," he said passionately.

"Then I'm sorry for it. For I love ye dearly as a friend, Francis, and I always will. Ye're a good man, a brave and kind one, and any woman would be fortunate to have you as her husband. But I'm no' that woman, for I canna love another man as I loved Rob, and I wouldna marry for less than that."

He felt the tears well up then, and looked down at his bowl, willing them to go away, as he would never try to make a woman accept him from pity, not even this one. Even so one tear escaped to roll down his cheek, and she saw it glittering in the candlelight.

"Ah, I'm so sorry, Francis. I wouldna hurt ye for the world. But I canna marry ye, for we'd both be miserable in time if I did. Ye need a woman who loves you in the way of a wife. Ye deserve that."

He sniffed, then drew out his handkerchief and wiped his face, as there was no longer any point in pretending he had not been tearful.

"Then we are in a dilemma," he said sadly, "for just as there is no other man for you after Rob, there is no other woman for me, has not been since the day I met you. Would you not consider living with me as a friend? We would have to marry to prevent scandal, but we could at least have a platonic relationship! I would be very happy with that, and you could do anything you wished, have complete freedom to treat people if you liked. You would want for nothing, I promise you! That would be—"

"Francis, stop," Susan interrupted. "Could you be happy living here? Look around you."

Obediently he looked around him, taking in the rough walls, the heather thatch through which the smoke from the central fire slowly made its way, the dirt floor and the meagre furniture.

"The last three days, which ye'll have found a great adventure, are nothing out of the way for the clansfolk, excepting the speed at which ye travelled," she added. "Ye'd hate it, Francis. It would kill ye, for ye're no' accustomed to such poor food, such hard physical labour and such hardship as the people here take for granted, for they were born to it. They ken nothing else, and are content for the most part."

"But you *do* know something else," Francis argued. "You lived in Edinburgh for twenty years!"

"I did. And I hated it," Susan said. "I hated the constant noise, the stench, the dark, suffocating wynds, and the people, so many people everywhere. It was impossible to get away from them, and if ye tried to ye didna ken whether some footpad or worse would attack ye when ye were alone. I hated the fact that ye could spend a pleasant evening wi' a group of people and then discover they'd been spreading lies behind your back, because they didna have the courage to tell ye the truth to your face."

"I didn't know you felt that way about Edinburgh," Francis said.

"No. Neither did Rob. He kent that I needed time alone, and that I needed to be busy, which was one reason why I went with him to his patients, and which was the reason for much of the gossip about me. And he would ride out wi' me at times into the fields so that I could breathe. He was a good man. But he never kent how much I hated living in the city."

"You stayed because you loved him," Francis said.

"Aye. And I'd do it again, for Rob. But no' for anyone else. Never. This is my home. I was born here. And I'll die here. So we do indeed have a dilemma. For I love ye dearly as a friend, Francis, and I always will. But I will never live in the city again, and you couldna live in the country. Nor should ye. Ye must move on with your life, as I have since Rob died. Nothing would make me happier than for ye to write and tell me that ye've met a lovely woman and have married. And I canna tell ye how it grieves me to see ye as unhappy as I've just made ye."

He sat back in the chair then, and let out a long, deep breath. She had told him the truth. She always told the truth, which was one of the reasons why he loved her. And she was right, although it broke his heart to admit it, even to himself.

"You haven't made me unhappy, Susan," he said. "You could

never do that. I've made myself unhappy. I can see that now. I cannot imagine marrying anyone else, and I can't say I will stop loving you, for you would know it to be a lie. But I will try, for I realise now that there is no hope for us, for you are right. I could not live here, and you could not be happy in Edinburgh, and I would die before I did anything to make you unhappy. I ask only one thing of you, if I may."

She waited for him to say what it was, and he smiled. Anyone else would say 'anything' or some such word, but not Susan, who would not make a promise she could not keep.

"I would ask that we remain friends. That I can write to you from time to time, and that you will write to me, tell me how you are, and how Alexander and his sons fare, for I confess I have grown fond of them, even in three days. And I would ask that if you ever need my help again, in anything, you do not hesitate, but ask immediately. And in return I promise to take it only as a confirmation of the deep friendship between us and nothing more."

She smiled then, and reaching across the table, took his hand.

"I agree. And I would ask the same of you, for although I could never live in Edinburgh again, I would visit there, if you needed me. And I will remain your friend for life, for your friendship is very precious to me."

He squeezed her hand then and she returned the gesture, then stood and moved to the press in the corner, from which she retrieved a flask.

"I'm thinking we should confirm this wi' whisky as well as wine," she said. "Or have ye already had whisky on the journey?"

"No," Francis replied. "Although Alexander mentioned a few times that he wished he had a dram to offer me for it warmed the body like nothing else and took away the hunger pangs."

"Then ye must taste it, for Alexander is right. It's the taste o' the Highlands, in my opinion, the taste of home, although I wouldna say that to the clan. They'd think me maudlin if I did for they've never been away from home and missed it as I did, and wouldna understand."

He would remember that evening for the rest of his life, and the taste of the spirit, which was harsh, an almost brutal assault on his tastebuds at first and which seared his throat as he swallowed it. But then the burning faded, leaving his body feeling pleasantly warm and invigorated, the assault on his tastebuds forgotten as the sweet smoky aftertaste of the whisky caressed his mouth, leaving him wanting more.

And that, he thought, as he rode away a few days later accompanied by Allan, who would see him safely home, summed up the Highlands and the Highlanders perfectly.

As he'd prepared to leave, Susan had given him a flask of whisky, or *uisge-beatha*, as she called it, telling him it would keep him warm on the way home. He had not drunk it on the way home, although he had been very cold for much of the journey. Instead he had stored it away, and treated it as one of his most precious possessions.

In years to come, whenever he felt lonely, when missing her became almost intolerable, or when he received a letter from her, he would pour himself a small glass and sip it, shuddering at first and then smiling as the warm smoky peatiness soothed him. And he would remember again, as clearly as if he was still in the cottage, the soft warmth of Susan's hand in his, the sadness in her brown eyes as she'd destroyed his hopes of marriage with her but affirmed her eternal friendship, which, he realised later, was more important, as that was genuine and abiding, whilst marriage would have been false and transitory.

And he would find himself, in thought at least, back on the banks of Loch Lomond, watching as the clansfolk tried in vain to comfort their broken chieftain after the funeral of his beloved wife, watching the genuine love and loyalty that the MacGregors shared, that they took for granted. Any one of them would kill or die for any other, without hesitation. He had breathed deeply of the crisp clean air, which had caressed his lungs as the whisky now caressed his tongue and his mind.

He had understood then why Susan had returned to the place of her birth, and why she would never leave it. And at times when he had drunk enough of the spirit to become a little tipsy, he wondered if he had made the wrong decision in riding away from that dramatic, beautiful place.

But then he would sober up, in his warm cosy study, surrounded by every comfort money could buy. Except love. And he knew that had he stayed, he could not have survived there. He would never have been fully accepted as part of the clan, and would never have been accepted in the way he wished to be by the only woman he would ever love.

And then he would drain the last of the whisky from his glass, put the flask away and go to bed, his nose full of the scent, his mouth full of the taste of the Highland spirit, and would live in dreams the life that he would never live in reality.

It was some comfort, at least.

CHAPTER SIXTEEN

February 1728

Kenneth made his way down to the loch, intending to have a cleansing if brief dip to wash off the sweat he'd been lathered in for most of the day. The MacGregors had recently made an almost suicidal raid on a neighbouring clan, which had resulted in them capturing some cattle and foodstuff along with a good number of weapons, which James was now repairing, altering, or making into something else entirely, depending on their condition.

In the last two years the clan had undertaken a number of these raids, in which various members were growing increasingly reluctant to take part, in spite of the MacGregors being renowned for their ferocity and eagerness to fight at the slightest excuse. Although at the moment no one was actually willing to openly speak against the chieftain regarding this.

At the moment. But it would have to come soon, Kenneth thought glumly as he walked through the trees, because the advantages of the raids were far outweighed by the disadvantages, in that they were making enemies of clans with whom they'd previously had no real problems, and the items captured were not worth the risk to life, especially as Alexander's skill in organising well-planned attacks seemed to have deserted him recently. How half of them hadn't been killed in this last raid, Kenneth had no idea. God must have been looking after them, for it was becoming increasingly clear to everyone that the chieftain wasn't.

Kenneth was so deeply immersed in his gloomy thoughts that he was almost upon Alex before he became aware of him seated on a rock by the water's edge, arms wrapped round his lower legs, chin on his knees, gazing intently across the water to the blue mountains on the other side.

Kenneth was suddenly taken back to a very similar day nine years ago, when he had found the boy in exactly the same place, moping over not being allowed to go to battle. A lot had changed since then, not least the boy, who was hurtling towards manhood, growing at an extraordinary rate at the moment, his voice now breaking and comically unpredictable, his profile mirroring that of his father, who he resembled very closely except for the colour of his hair.

"Are ye wanting to be alone?" Kenneth asked.

"Aye, of everyone else. But ye're no' everyone else," Alex replied calmly, telling Kenneth that he'd been aware of him approaching, maybe for a few minutes. The boy was growing in other ways than just physically. "How are the weapons? Were they worth it?" he asked.

Kenneth contemplated a tactful or evasive answer, and then rejected it. Alex deserved more than that.

"No. Unless ye count the fact that none of us died, in which case, aye, I suppose so," he said.

"But Alasdair willna walk rightly again, will he? His fighting days are done."

"They were done in any case, really. He's too old now, tires too quickly," Kenneth replied, stripping off his clothes as he spoke.

"True. But he wasna a liability, and fighting gave him self-respect, a reason to live. So I'm thinking it wasna worth it," Alex said, "for he's a good man, and didna deserve to end his useful days in a pointless raid to please my da. It pleased no one else, I'm thinking. In truth it didna really please my da either, for nothing does."

Kenneth just managed to stop himself whistling through his teeth. The boy was heading towards manhood more rapidly even than he'd thought.

"He's—"

"Dinna tell me he's grieving Ma," Alex interrupted. "Everyone tells me that, as though it's a good reason for the way he is. But it isna. When Ma died we all grieved her terrible, and I miss her every day. I'll always miss her, as I'll miss Morag and ye'll miss

Alpin. But the hard grieving, the grieving that means ye dinna care for anything else, that lessens in time. It's lessened for you, for your ma and da and Flora, has it no'?"

Kenneth pulled his shirt over his head and dropped it on his *féileadh mór,* then looked up to see Alex watching him intently, his slate-blue eyes dark with misery. Kenneth bent to pick up his shirt again, not wanting to leave the boy alone when he was so desperately unhappy.

"No," Alex said. "Away and wash yoursel'. I'm no' going anywhere for a wee while."

Kenneth straightened again and walked into the water, which was icy cold. He swam up and down for a few minutes to rid himself of the dirt and sweat from the hot forge, and to clear his mind, for he needed to speak honestly but carefully when he rejoined the chieftain's son. Alex was maturing quickly, but he *was* only twelve, and prone to all the insecurities and impulses of that difficult age which straddled childhood and adulthood.

When the cold threatened to seep even his formidable strength away, he walked back to the little pile of clothing, dried himself briskly with his kilt to warm his limbs, then dressed, wringing the water out of his long hair before sitting on a fallen log close to Alex. They sat together in silence for a while, both staring across the water, and then Kenneth sighed.

"The grieving's different for your da than it is for you, Duncan and Angus," he said.

"Angus doesna grieve Ma. He canna remember her much, for he wasna even two when she died, so we talk about her when Da's no' there, for he willna let us mention her when he is. Susan talks about her as well when she's doing the household tasks for us, for I think if she didna he'd think *she* was his ma. How is it different for him?"

"It's hard to explain," Kenneth replied, "for ye havena been in love with a lassie yet."

"Can ye try? For right now I canna understand at all. But I need to," Alex pleaded.

Kenneth sat for a while longer, thinking.

"People marry for different reasons," he began finally. "Some do it because their parents are wanting them to, some because they think they should when all their friends are, and some because they fall in love with each other."

"And some because they find themselves having a bairn and have to," Alex added.

Kenneth laughed.

"Aye, and some marry for that reason, and so the priest willna make his sermon about their sin every Sunday."

Alex snorted at that.

"The ones who fall in love, after they've been married a while often find they dinna love each other any more, but they make the best of it and find a way to live well together, for the most part," Kenneth continued. "But your ma and da were different, they fell in love and then the love became stronger and stronger, until it was everything, until they became like two pieces of one person. And you four bairns were a part of that as well. It doesna happen often, I'm thinking, but I ken about it for my ma and da are the same, though ye wouldna think that maybe, to look at them."

Alex thought for a minute, as he was now trying to make a habit of doing, having learnt it from Duncan.

"So ye're saying that when Ma died, we lost our ma, but he lost half of himself?" he asked finally.

"Aye. A half of him has died wi' her, and he canna find the way back without her, I'm thinking," Kenneth agreed. Alex shuddered.

"I dinna ever want to love like that. It seems a terrible thing to me, to need another person so much that ye dinna care about anything once they die," he said.

"Aye, well, I doubt ye will. It's a rare thing to love that deeply, I'm thinking," Kenneth said.

"So if your ma died, are ye thinking your da would grow to hate ye, wouldna be able to look at ye, and wish ye'd died too?" Alex asked. "Maybe wish the whole clan had died, so he could spend all his time alone grieving for your ma?"

Kenneth looked at him in shock then.

"Your da doesna hate ye, Alex," he said.

"Aye, he does. He doesna talk to me, except to tell me what I should do. He canna even *look* at Duncan. I'm thinking, after what ye've said, it's maybe because Duncan looks like Ma; I must tell him that, for it'll maybe comfort him. And Da ignores Angus entirely. When he's home he goes directly to bed or he sits staring into the fire, and if we speak to him he doesna answer, or if he does it's clear he hasna even listened to what we've asked him. He doesna care about anything I do…anything any of us do. And he doesna care about the clan, for if he did he wouldna risk ye all wi' these stupid raids, for we dinna need a few apples and some bent, rusty blades."

Kenneth sat for a minute, having no idea how to answer this heartbreakingly honest outpouring of feeling from the boy. He could not utter a platitude, for it was not his way, and Alex would only think less of him if he did. He did not want Alex to think less of him, he realised suddenly, because he loved this boy who would one day be his chieftain, and right now, the sooner the better.

He sent up a silent prayer to God to forgive him for that wicked thought, and pondered instead how to answer, honestly but tactfully.

"I was trying to think of something that would comfort ye," he said finally, "but the only thing I can honestly tell ye is that I dinna believe your da hates ye. I'm thinking he's trapped in his grieving and canna find a way out, and canna find a way to show that he loves ye. But he doesna hate ye."

"How d'ye ken that? For Duncan and I both feel it, only Duncan doesna…never mind," he finished, clearly not wanting to tell a secret that wasn't his to tell. "Angus doesna ken any different. He thinks that's just how a da is, so it's easier for him."

"I just remember how he was with ye before your ma died," Kenneth said. "He loved ye completely – that's why he wants ye to do the learning so hard, for he's proud of ye and thinks ye can be a great man one day. Duncan too. And I think he's right in that. He talked of ye all the time, and when we were on a raid or away when ye were wee, he missed ye all fierce and wasna ashamed to say it."

"He doesna say it now though, does he?"

Kenneth cursed inwardly.

"No, for as I said, he's lost his way. For a long time. But he'll come back to ye. To us. We just have to wait for him to do it, for we canna do otherwise," Kenneth said simply. "He's our chieftain, and we have no other."

Alex smiled bitterly.

"Aye, he is. And he taught me how to be a good one when I

grow, or he started to. Ye're right. I'm sorry, Kenneth. I didna mean to burden ye."

"Ye're no' a burden. Ye never have been and never will be. Ye shouldna carry such weight yourself, no' at twelve - no' at any age. I'm here for ye and I always will be, laddie."

Alex turned to him then, and this time the smile lit up his eyes, just a little, but it was something.

"I ken that, Kenneth, and ye canna imagine what it means to me," he said simply. "I'd best away home now, for Susan'll leave soon, and we'll be eating before Da gets home. We all sleep up in the roof space now, and we go there after dark, for it's warmer up there. Da believes that or doesna care, but it's the same thing, for we can play wi' Angus easier if Da isna in the room wi' us. It was awfu hard, losing Ma, ye ken. We didna think we'd lost Da too. But we have, and I'm no' so sure he'll come back to us, though I pray ye're right. I'll wish ye a good night."

He stood then, in a flurry of long coltish arms and legs, combed his hands through his hair, a habit he'd unconsciously learned from Alexander, which, if nothing else, always betrayed his emotional turmoil, and ran off through the trees.

Kenneth stayed where he was, while a range of emotions from frustration to anger to sorrow washed through him, finally being replaced by helplessness. For short of being there for the boys to confide in, there was nothing he could do. He had sworn an oath of loyalty to Alexander as his chieftain, had sworn it on iron, which was sacred, and he could not break that oath without imperilling his immortal soul and becoming an outcast from the clan.

He sat until the stars were sparkling in the dark blue sky over the loch, the frost sparkling over the ground, and finally, when he realised no solution was going to come to him, for there *was* no solution but to wait and hope for Alexander to find his way back to them, he stood and made his way home.

* * *

"Er…p-please away hame, and…um…do your own…t-tasks, distaff and loom, ah…and make the lassies…work f-fierce as well. Er…" Jeannie paused for a moment, breathing heavily, her brow furrowed deeply, her face scarlet. "As f-f-for the f-f-fighting…"

"Oh, for pity's sake, lassie!" Father Gordon shouted. "'As f-f-f-f-f-f-f-for the f-f-f-f-f-f-fighting," he continued in mockery of her attempt. "Homer would turn in his grave if he heard such brutal massacring of his beautiful poetry, and into such poor English too! I can bear no more of it. Duncan, please continue."

"Jeannie kens the Latin as well as I, Father," Duncan replied calmly. "Maybe better. If ye give her a wee moment to calm herself, I'm sure she'll be able to continue."

"Are you the tutor or am I?" Father Gordon raged. "I havena the time for more ridiculous stuttering. Continue!"

Alex looked up from the copy of *The Iliad* that he was sharing with Duncan, then saw Jeannie's desperate shake of the head out of the corner of his eye. He turned to glance at her, saw her lovely grey eyes pleading with him, and looked back down at the book, kicking Duncan under the table as he did.

Tight-lipped, Duncan paid heed, and took over from where Jeannie had been halted.

"*Agus an t-sabaid — gabhaidh fir gnothach ri sin, a h-uile neach a rugadh taobh Thròidh, ach mis' air thoiseach orra uile,*" he said, then looked up at the priest with an expression of pure innocence. "Ye canna fault the English at least, I'm sure of that. Are ye wanting me to continue, Father, or is it Alex translating the next lines?"

Ten minutes later the pupils, having been thrown out of class for laughing, were all taking a somewhat premature break from lessons, sitting near the loch as was their custom and sharing whatever foodstuffs they'd brought with them for lunch.

Jeannie, still a little flushed from her humiliation but otherwise recovered, threw her arms around Duncan and gave him a hug.

"Thank ye, Duncan," she said. "It was kind of ye to stand up for me. And Alex, for I ken ye were going to."

"Aye, well, it isna right, the way he speaks to ye," Alex said.

"I thought I was going to die trying no' to laugh when ye gave him Homer in the Gaelic!" Alasdair Og said, grinning. "Ye near gave him an apoplexy, I'm thinking."

Duncan grinned.

"I didna want to give him a 'poor English' translation, so I had no choice in the matter," he said.

"I didna understand that," Dougal commented. "What was

poor about Jeannie's English?"

"Nothing," Alex said. "He just doesna like lassies. He always makes her translate the verses about Helen being the cause of the war, or about women doing what he sees as 'womanly tasks', instead of the ones about the goddesses armed for war, for he takes the view of St Paul, that women should keep silent."

"He shouldna be living in Scotland then," Alasdair Og commented, making them all laugh.

"Or wi' the MacGregors," Simon added. "For there isna a woman in the clan who he could better."

"He isna so nasty wi' me," Peigi pointed out.

"No, that's because ye're still a bairn," Duncan said. "But Jeannie's a wee bit older, and he was hoping to be able to dismiss all the lassies once they could read and sign their name, for he thinks education for lassies is a dangerous thing and will lead them to Hell."

"Ye'll take us with ye, too, for we're all too stupid to think for ourselves, but will just follow ye," Alex said.

"If the Father believes that, then I canna think why laddies are better than lassies," Jeannie said.

"They're no'," Duncan said. "Ye're just different, that's all. Dinna let him stop ye learning, Jeannie, for that's what he's wanting."

"I willna, although I've thought on it, for I dinna enjoy his lessons, though I did when he didna make fun of me all the time. But Ma and Da dinna mind me still learning as long as I do my tasks at home, and I willna let him win."

"Ma and Da want her to learn until she marries, for it's lovely and peaceful when she's no' in the house," her brother Dougal said.

Jeannie punched him on the arm and they all laughed, then, selecting something from the pile of food laid out between them, they started eating.

"What did yon mannie St Paul say about the lassies, then, Alex?" Alasdair Og asked, his bread and cheese finished.

Alex didn't reply for a moment, having a mouth full of food. He chewed, swallowed, then took a drink from the flask of water they'd filled from the loch. Then he stood, stepped up onto the rock he'd been sitting on, adopted an expression of benevolent superiority, looked around his congregation, and nodded.

"A reading," he began sonorously, "from the First Epistle of St Paul, to the Corinthians." He stopped then, smacked his lips together loudly and looked around his congregation again to make sure they were listening.

They were not listening, but instead were giggling, every one of them, for this was an exact copy of Father Gordon standing in the cave on Sundays, from his expressions to his gestures, the droning tone he adopted when reading biblical verses and the supremely annoying lip-smacking. Alex waited with a look of condescending toleration for them all to quieten, which, with great difficulty, they did.

"Let your women keep silence in the churches: for it is not permitted unto them to speak; but they are *commanded* to be under obedience, as also saith the *law*."

He stopped again and looked around at his red-faced companions, tears of mirth streaming down their cheeks.

"The law doesna say women canna speak in church, does it?" Peigi asked, between giggles.

"Silence, woman!" Alex bellowed, his voice rising to a sudden squeak at the end of 'woman' as his changing larynx and vocal cords betrayed him. "*A dhiabhail!*" he said in an equally squeaky voice, upon which everyone collapsed in hysterics.

He waited until they'd calmed a little then continued, his voice deep once more.

"And, if they will learn anything, let them ask their husbands at home: for it is a shame for women to—"

The blow to the side of his head took him by surprise and knocked him sideways off the rock, sprawling onto the floor. In a second he was back on his feet in a fighting stance, dirk drawn. Father Gordon stood behind the rock, his face almost purple with rage, but even so he had to stop himself from stepping back instinctively when he saw Alex's expression and the razor-sharp blade in his hand.

Alex stood for a moment facing the priest, dirk in hand, breathing heavily as he mastered the instinctive fighting rage which threatened to overwhelm him, while the laughter stopped abruptly. Then, slowly, Alex sheathed his dirk, and the priest let out the breath he hadn't realised he'd been holding.

"How dare ye mock the apostle of Christ!" he yelled, confident again, taking the sheathing of the weapon as submission. "Ye blasphemous wee loon!"

"I wasna mocking St Paul," Alex said icily, although his face was scarlet. "I was mocking you, as ye mocked wee Jeannie."

"By God, I will not tolerate this!" Father Gordon raged, then turning, marched off in the direction of the village, leaving the children sitting, stunned and silent.

"Christ, I'm sorry, Alex," Simon said, who had been directly facing him, and, if he hadn't been laughing so hard, would probably have seen the priest approaching through the dense woodland behind him.

"It wasna your fault," Alex said, taking another drink of water and shaking his head to clear it, for the blow had made him dizzy. Then he got up.

"Where are ye going?" Jeannie asked.

"I'm thinking he's gone to tell my da," Alex said, "so I'd as soon face him now, instead of hiding here like a coward."

At that all the other children jumped up immediately and accompanied him, Duncan walking with him, the others just behind.

"What d'ye think your da'll do?" Alasdair Og asked fearfully.

"I havena a notion," Alex replied honestly, "but whatever it is, I'd rather have it done with."

Alexander was standing at the edge of the clearing where many of the clan's houses were, staring up at the roof of one, on which several men were working securing the ropes that would keep the heather thatch they'd just replaced from blowing away in the next gale.

"Aye, that's it," he called, shading his eyes with one hand, for the sun was directly above the cottage. "Just a wee bit tighter wi' the rope there."

"MacGregor, I need a word with ye," Father Gordon said from behind him.

Alexander turned.

"I thought ye'd be teaching, Father," he said. "Can it no' wait until I'm finished here?"

"No, it canna. Your son has committed a most disrespectful

act, both against myself and the gospel of the Lord!"

Alexander sighed and turned away from the roof, but did not, as the priest had hoped, move away from the group of clanspeople who were standing observing the repairs.

"Which son, and what did he do?" he asked.

"Your eldest, although I have to say the attitude of your younger son leaves much to be desired as well," Father Gordon raged.

"What did they do?"

"I translated Homer into Gaelic, and the Father didna like it," Duncan called across, arriving in time to hear the priest's last sentence.

Alexander glanced in the children's direction, nodded, then turned his attention back to the fuming priest.

"Aye, well, as I'm sure ye're aware, Father, the Gaelic is our first language, but we speak the English wi' you for Gaelic isna your first tongue. And it's important for the bairns to learn the English well, for it's the language spoken by the authorities." He turned then to look at Duncan, who wore an expression of shock, not only because his da had not immediately taken the priest's side, but because he actually *looked* at him directly. Only for a second, but it was something. "Ye'll remember to speak the English in the class, Duncan, for it isna hospitable to speak a tongue your tutor doesna ken as well as you."

"Aye, Da, I will, in future," Duncan said, surreptitiously gripping Alex's hand in a gesture of unity, while Alex's heart soared, for although he had little expression in his voice, Alexander's words were more like those his da would have spoken than those of the grim stranger who'd replaced him in the last years.

"It was Alex who I really wished to speak to you about," Father Gordon continued, "for I'm sure ye'll agree that blasphemy and disrespect cannot be tolerated!"

"No, indeed they canna," Alexander agreed.

"So, I came upon the bairns at their meal, to find this one," he cast a contemptuous glance at Alex, who flushed, "ridiculing myself and St Paul, and encouraging the other bairns into sin!"

The other bairns all gasped at this, and Alexander looked at his son, his face hard.

"Is this true?" he asked.

"I didna ridicule St Paul," Alex replied hotly. "I only quoted part of his letter to the Corinthians. I didna express any opinion about the verse or the saint."

"Does he speak the truth, Father?"

"He is being sly. It was not the actual *words* he used, but the manner in which he spoke them which was unforgivable. He made a mockery of the Church!"

"I didna make a mockery of the Church!" Alex cried, trying and failing not to lose his temper at this injustice. "I wouldna do that! I made a mockery of the Father, I'll no' deny that, for he made Jeannie cry by mocking her cruelly in the class! Her Latin is good, but he always mocks her, for he doesna like lassies, and it makes her stammer, which isna right. He's wanting to drive her from the class, as he's done wi' all the other lassies, and will do wi' Peigi in time, no doubt. So I mocked him, and he doesna like it, so I'm hoping he'll no' do it to Jeannie again now he kens how cruel it is!"

He stopped then, for his father was observing him with that cool detachment that he'd come to dread more than anything.

"Is that true, Jeannie?" Alexander asked the little girl standing in the background with the group of other children.

"Aye, it is," she answered, biting her lip with nerves. "He does it a lot, for he thinks I should be preparing to be a wife and mother now, no' learning unsuitable things."

These words were so obviously repeated straight from the mouth of the priest, that Father Gordon was unable to deny them.

"Ye're thinking the lassie fit to marry and have bairns, Father, at twelve years of age?" Alexander asked.

"No, of course not! But it isna right for her to be learning the reading and writing, which will make her unfit for her future role," Father Gordon spluttered.

"My wife could read and write. I was teaching her the Latin—" He broke off suddenly. All the clansfolk witnessing this exchange had frozen on hearing their chieftain's words, for he never spoke of Moira, had not since she died. "The bargain we made, Father, was that I would give ye a house, warmth, food and protect ye, and in return ye'd say Mass and teach the bairns. All the bairns, for as long as they or their parents wanted them to learn. Jeannie, do your ma and da want ye to stop the learning?"

She shook her head.

"Well, then. Ye'll keep to your part of the bargain, Father, and I'll keep to mine, and ye'll treat her as ye do the laddies, in the classroom."

He turned to look up at the roof then, and for a moment everyone thought the interaction was over.

"How did Alex mock ye, Father?" Alexander said softly.

"He behaved abominably!"

"Aye, but what did he do?"

"He…he tried to make a laughing-stock of me in front of the other bairns! I canna teach them if they dinna respect me, unless ye give me permission to beat respect and obedience into them!"

"What did ye do, Alex?" Alexander said.

Now it was Alex's turn to flush.

"I…er…I mocked him as he mocked Jeannie, for she was awfu' upset and I wanted to cheer her a wee bit," Alex said.

"Did he cheer ye, Jeannie?" Alexander asked.

Jeannie nodded, looking at the ground, but an involuntary giggle ran around the group of children. Alexander nodded.

"Right, then. I'll need to hear what ye said, and how ye said it, to judge the matter, for I wasna there to hear it the first time. When ye're ready."

"I dinna think there's any need to—" Father Gordon began, but the chieftain raised his hand and the priest fell silent, his face burning.

Oh God. Alex tore his hand through his hair, wondering if he should just apologise to the priest and have done with it, although he never apologised if he was not sorry. But then he looked at his da's implacable expression and realised that it was too late for that. Perhaps he should have stayed where he was after all, rather than being so eager to embrace trouble. But as it was here, he would face it.

There was no rock to stand on, but after taking a couple of breaths to steady his nerves he stood as he had earlier, when it had been fun rather than torture, looking around at his enlarged audience with that expression of benevolent superiority that so irritated many of the clanspeople every Sunday.

"A reading," he began in a droning tone, "from the First Epistle of St Paul to the Corinthians…"

By the time he'd finished, everyone watching, with the exception of Alex, Duncan, Alexander and Father Gordon were convulsed with laughter, for this was the funniest thing they'd seen in a long time. His utterly perfect mimicking of the priest was absolutely uncanny, and absolutely hysterical.

Alexander waited until the laughter died down.

"I see," he said. "Father, would ye like to tell me what *ye* said to mock Jeannie? So I might compare?"

"Certainly not!" said the priest, his face as purple with humiliation as it had been with rage when he had knocked Alex off the rock earlier. "Ye'll agree, I'm sure, that such behaviour canna go unpunished!"

I do agree indeed," Alexander said. "But before I do, I must ask if ye agree to being punished as well, Father."

"What?"

"Well, it seems to me that Alex mocked you, which was childish and disrespectful, because you mocked Jeannie, which was childish and disrespectful. Ye're both at fault. In fact I'm thinking ye're more at fault, Father, for ye should be setting a good example to the bairns, as an adult and a man of God. Whereas Alex is still a bairn. I canna in justice punish him for learning his lesson from the tutor so well. No' unless I punish the tutor for teaching it too. So, it's your choice, Father."

Father Gordon looked at the chieftain in horror, realising that the man was absolutely serious. And absolutely capable, for looking at the red-faced grinning audience it was clear whose side they were on. This was unbearable. He could not stay here another minute.

He could not leave. Not now, in February, in the bitter cold, with nowhere to go. Even if he could evade capture as a Catholic priest, he could not survive without shelter, fire and food for the next two months until the weather improved. It would be suicidal.

He turned abruptly and walked away from the clanspeople, giving Alexander his answer. *They will forget,* the priest told himself. *They're simple people. As soon as something else happens, they'll forget the boy's disrespectful actions.*

"I'm thinking the man will no' be wanting to teach ye any more the day," Alexander remarked to the children. "Away hame."

The children separated, started to make their way to their

houses, but then Alex, emboldened by the fact that the chieftain had, for the first time since Moira died, showed an inkling of the man he had been, had taken his side even, and seeing that hope reflected on the faces around him, turned back to his father.

"Thank ye, Da," he said softly.

His da moved forward then, taking Alex's arm in a painful grip before bending to speak directly into his ear.

"Dinna thank me, ye wee shit," he hissed. "The priest did a shameful thing in mocking wee Jeannie, but so did you, to mock a man of God so. Ye've shamed me, and shamed your clan. Go home." He released his son then, pushing him away from him in a gesture of rejection, leaving Alex to stagger away white-faced, his arm and his heart throbbing with pain.

"Da didna mean it," Duncan said on seeing Alex's distressed face when he came into the house.

"Aye, he did," Alex said, his mouth twisting as he fought the urge to cry.

"What did he do?" Angus asked from the corner of the room, where he was busily, if inexpertly sweeping the floor.

"Nothing. Ye're making a good job of that," Duncan said, making Angus beam with delight.

"I wanted to help Susan. I was going to cut the vegetables but she tellt me I canna use the knife when she's no' here," he said.

"No, ye mustna, no' for a while yet. Where is she?"

"She had to go see Alasdair, for his leg's paining him dreadful, she tellt me. She said I had to be good while she was gone, so I thought I'd sweep the floor. That's good, is it no'?"

"It's awfu' good, Angus," Alex said, having mastered his urge to weep. The little boy smiled and continued sweeping, no easy task for the broom was much bigger than he was. His tongue protruded from the corner of his mouth as it always did when he was concentrating, making his brothers smile.

"Teach me how to do it," Alex said, when Angus had moved through the partition to sweep the bedroom.

"How to do what?"

"How no' to care what he thinks of me."

Duncan sat looking into the fire, and was silent for so long that Alex thought he wasn't going to answer.

"I canna," he said finally, making Alex jump. "I still care about him, but I dinna care what anyone thinks of me, unless I've done something to justify their ill opinion."

"But he isna anyone, he's our da," Alex said.

"Aye, he is. And no, for he isna behaving like Da did, hasna for a long time now. But I canna teach ye no' to care, for I didna learn it, it's just who I am. And you're just who you are, Alex. Ye wouldna be you if ye didna care."

"I dinna want to be me if it hurts this much," Alex said fervently, then glanced towards the other room, hoping Angus hadn't heard.

Duncan, who had been about to say something else, saw Alex's glance and stood instead.

"Right then," he said. "I'll start the cooking if you go and fetch the water, Alex, for I'm thinking Susan'll no' come back once she kens we're here to watch Angus." Angus, hearing his name, appeared in the doorway. "When we've eaten, Angus, shall we away upstairs and have a wee game wi' the letter dice before ye sleep?"

"Aye!" Angus said. "I can read…" he thought for a moment, "ten letters now!"

"Ye can! And ye can count too!" Alex agreed.

"I can count to more than ten," Angus said proudly.

"Ye'll ken the rest of your letters soon," Duncan said, "and then I'll teach ye to write your name."

"Have ye no' got Latin to do?" Angus asked, leaning the brush against the wall in the corner.

"No," Alex said firmly. "Are ye wanting to fetch the water wi' me?"

Angus had no need to answer this, for he always wanted to do whatever Alex was doing, so the two boys walked down to the loch together, Alex carrying the water pail and Angus showing how far he could count, stopping when they reached the water. Alex walked in a few steps then bent to scoop water into the bucket, nearly falling face-first into the loch as Angus suddenly and unexpectedly ran up to him, heedless of the icy water, and threw his arms around his brother's legs.

"I care about ye," he said, his voice slightly muffled by Alex's kilt. "I'll always care about ye."

Alex smiled sadly then, and a lump rose in his throat at the sincerity in his little brother's tone. He *had* heard them talking then and had understood, in part at least. He stood the half-full bucket up at the edge of the loch, then bent and scooped his brother up into his arms before walking out of the water.

"Ah, ye're growing fast now, Angus," he said, kissing him on his little snub nose. "I'll no' be able to lift ye soon!"

Angus grinned and threw his arms around Alex's neck, squeezing.

"I needed a wee hug, Angus. I care about ye, too. And Duncan. Ye're the world to me," Alex said.

Ye need to be, he thought, *for ye canna remember your ma, and ye havena had a da since she died.*

The thought made him sad, so he brushed it away, and with some difficulty disentangled Angus from his neck before setting him on the ground.

"I canna carry both you and the water," he explained. "Ye'll have to walk. Shall we take our food up the stair when it's ready, as Susan isna here, and I'll read ye a wee bit more of yon *Robinson Crusoe* book?"

Angus jumped up and down with excitement, giving Alex his answer.

"Will Da no' mind us eating upstairs though?" he asked.

Da wouldna care if we vanished off the face of the earth, Alex thought bitterly.

"No, I dinna think so. He'll no' be home yet a while, anyway."

They made their way home, Angus incandescent with happiness at having unexpected extra time with his beloved brothers, Alex determining not to let his father's cruel words ruin his evening.

The three brothers spent a pleasant evening together, eating their broth by candlelight, then teaching Angus some more letters using the dice they'd learnt with at his age, another thing their father could not bear to hear them doing, because of the memories it brought. But he was not in the house, not even downstairs, and he didn't matter, Alex told himself fiercely.

Finally Duncan read a chapter of Robinson Crusoe, while Alex mimed appropriate and amusing actions about the various events in the novel, making Angus crow with laughter, his face glowing with happiness.

Then, as they heard their father coming in, they blew out the candle and settled down to sleep. Silence reigned for a while, during which Angus's breathing became heavy and regular and small domestic noises came from downstairs as Alexander ate his solitary supper.

"Ye did well tonight. No one would have kent how sad ye are. Ye do the actions to the book wonderfully. If ye werena destined to be chieftain one day, ye'd be an awfu' good actor, like in the play we saw," Duncan whispered.

You kent how sad I am," Alex replied softly, "*and* that I wasna asleep."

"Aye, well. No one else, then," Duncan said. "Try no' to think more on it. Da did the right thing wi' the Father, but he didna have to be so cruel to ye. He's no better than the Father was wi' Jeannie. I'm ashamed of him, no' you."

"I thought…just for one minute, I thought he loved me again. But he doesna. I dinna think he ever will," Alex admitted sadly.

"It doesna signify," Duncan said. "He doesna love anybody, no' you, no' me, no' Angus, no' even himself. Ye need to stop hoping for him to come back to us, and just go on wi' becoming the man ye can be, as I'm doing. We have each other, at least," Duncan added. "He doesna have anyone. It makes me sad, but I dinna pity him, for it's his own doing."

"Aye. Ye've the right of it. I'll try no' to think on it. I dinna find it easy as you do, but I'll try."

But in spite of his resolution Alex lay awake for a long time after both his brothers were fast asleep, for he could not accept, as the others could, that his father would never love him again. Even *thinking* that it might be possible made the panic rise up in him, choking off his breath, driving all reason from his mind. Da must be lonely, even if it *was* his own doing. Surely he would come back to them, surely there was a way to make him see what he was doing?

His father *had* to love him again. For without Da's approval, what was the point in all the reading, the writing, the Latin, the wrestling and swordplay?

All of it, all those years of learning had been for one purpose only; to make his father proud of him, to make him happy that one day his son would become the chieftain he wanted him to be. He was not like Duncan, he realised now, as he heard his father go to bed and silence settle on the house. He would try, but deep inside he knew he could never accept something which rendered his whole life meaningless.

He would find a way to make his father love him again. Whatever it took. There must be a way, and if there was, he would find it.

* * *

On Sunday as he walked up to the cave in which he said Mass, Father Gordon was feeling reasonably confident that the incident earlier in the week had been forgotten. After all, since then no one had treated him any differently, the children had all been particularly well behaved in class, and they'd had a few days of very heavy snowfall accompanied by high winds which had damaged the rooves of several houses, leading to a lot of difficult and tiring work to repair them, in which virtually the whole clan had taken part. No doubt that had supplanted the minor incident, which only a few members of the clan had seen anyway.

Virtually the whole clan was in the cave, staring at him as he stepped up onto the flat-topped rock that served as his pulpit. Although the placement of the candles meant that the congregation could see him, for him the assembled clan was in the main a blur of shapes.

"A good morning to all of you!" he began, as he always did.

Silence.

That was unusual, for people usually responded in kind. But perhaps they were all exhausted; many of them had certainly been working until very late last night, battling the wind to ensure the cottages were weatherproof.

By the end of the Mass however, which seemed to the priest to be the longest one he had ever conducted, although in fact it took up no more clock time than any other service he'd taken, Father Gordon was absolutely certain that the congregation had not forgotten the incident earlier in the week.

It was true that they had given all the responses as normal, had come forward to take the Eucharist and drink the wine, but as their faces came into view he could see that all of them wore a stony, implacable expression. This confused him, as the reaction he had feared was derision, maybe stifled giggling as he'd read the lesson, not stony silence and contempt.

The clanspeople left the cave the second the Mass was over, another unheard of thing, for normally they would all sit for a time chatting together before making their way home. In the summer they would sit in the bowl-shaped area outside the cave; in the winter inside it. But today they just walked back down the slope to the settlement, leaving him alone and unsettled.

Or not quite alone. For as he left the cave a few minutes later, wondering why they seemed so hostile, a figure stepped out from the side of the cave mouth, clearly wishing to speak of some private matter with him.

Father Gordon stopped.

"Kenneth," he said. "I see you did not take communion today. Are ye wanting me to hear your confession?"

The red-haired giant grinned as though this sentence had been a joke of some kind, rather than a gentle admonition.

"No, Father. I'm wanting to tell ye a wee thing, but it isna a confession, although it *is* related, in a sense."

The priest took a couple of steps backward, not from fear but because it was disconcerting for someone who was tall enough to look down at many people to find himself addressing his parishioner's chest, as he did with Kenneth. In fact most people addressed Kenneth's chest, but unlike with the others it undermined the priest, who needed above all to feel superior to these simple, rural folk.

"What is it you wish to tell me, my child?"

"I wasna at the wee stramash between yourself and the chieftain last week," Kenneth began.

"It wasna a stramash—" Father Gordon put in.

"But of course I heard of it," Kenneth continued, as though the priest hadn't spoken at all, "and I thought to find out the truth of the matter, for ye'll maybe ken that I've a great fondness for bairns myself. Aye, well, maybe ye didna ken that, by your face, but ye do now," he added, apparently misinterpreting the priest's expression on being ignored. "And in their turn, the bairns have a great fondness for me. Which means that they tell me all their wee troubles and joys, for they ken I willna tell a soul – much as people tell ye things in confession, so I'm thinking ye'll understand what I'm saying."

"Of course I understand ye, but I fail to see the relevance—"

"They tell me these things, even if they've been tellt no' to by someone else," Kenneth said, interrupting the priest for the second time, "which is a good thing, for it means that if one bairn – or anyone else, is in the way of bullying another, then I'll be sure to hear of it. And if that bairn, for one reason or another, canna defend themselves, then ye can be sure that I'll do it for them." He smiled coldly at the priest, whose face grew suddenly pale. "Ah, I can see that ye've understood me entirely," Kenneth added sociably, "so I'll no' trouble ye further. I wish ye a good day, Father," he said, laying his hand on the priest's shoulder and squeezing it gently, before releasing him and making his way down the hill, whistling merrily as he did so.

The priest had indeed understood Kenneth entirely. If he had not known about his relationship with the children of the clan, he *did* know that when enraged or in battle the man was like the *berserkir* a Scandinavian student of divinity had told him about when in university. He went home, determined to put the unpleasant incident to the back of his mind, for indeed he could do nothing else. He could not fight Kenneth; he could not leave Loch Lomond while the weather was so horrendous; and he could not refuse to take any more lessons or any more Masses without evoking the anger of the previously reasonable but now unknown quantity that was the chieftain.

The priest, however, found it impossible to put the incident to the back of his mind. For Kenneth's 'gentle squeeze' had rendered Father Gordon's shoulder black with bruising, damaging something inside, for every time he moved his arm for the next two weeks he was reminded, like it or not, of Kenneth's friendly warning.

Lessons for wee Jeannie suddenly became much more pleasant.

Until May, at any rate. For after that lessons became non-existent for all the children, as Father Gordon, having headed off on his second excursion of the spring to other clans to preach the word of God, did not return. After a few days the clanspeople, concerned, went to his home to see if he had left any indication of where he'd gone, so that they could go to his assistance if necessary.

He had not. In fact he had left nothing at all, which made it abundantly clear that he had no intention of returning.

If most of the clan were reasonably indifferent to the priest's departure, Alexander was not, for this meant that unless he could find another tutor, which was highly unlikely, Alex at least would no longer be able to learn Greek, which he had only just started and which, in the chieftain's mind, was the final jewel he would need to acquire if he were to be successful at university.

If Kenneth suspected he was responsible for Father Gordon's departure and the subsequent religious and educational void, he kept it to himself, having no wish to enrage the all-powerful but unknown quantity that Alexander MacGregor now was.

CHAPTER SEVENTEEN

As Alex no longer had to attend lessons for three days a week, he decided to spend at least part of that time learning things that he hoped would enable him to be a worthy chieftain when the time came. If he would one day be the father of the clan, he supposed that learning at least a little of everything the clanspeople did would be useful for the time when he had to make decisions himself. As the clanspeople did a great variety of things this ensured that he was kept busy all the time, to the amusement of the MacGregors, who watched this frenetic activity of the chieftain's son with interest and good-humoured ribbing.

The exceptions to this rule were Duncan, who did not comment on his brother's decision but was painfully aware of the deeper, unspoken motivation for it; and Alexander, who appeared neither to notice nor care what either of his sons were doing in what had been their lesson times.

On discovering the priest's sudden departure, Alexander's first comment had been that he would now have to try to find another tutor to teach Alex Greek at the very least, for he did not have enough education yet to be able to go to university. This comment had been accompanied by a thunderous expression, and as Alex was aware that at least part of the reason for the priest's departure was due to him, he had wisely refrained from saying anything about not wanting to go to university anyway.

Instead he had added teaching himself Greek to his list of necessary tasks, although how he was going to do that he had no idea, as he had only learnt the first five letters, α, β, γ, δ, and ε before Father Gordon had left, and as there were twenty-seven letters in the alphabet, he doubted he would be able to learn the rest alone, not without a Greek primer, which he didn't have.

So instead over the next months, as well as taking part in the tasks all children helped with, such as planting, weeding, helping with repairs to the houses and domestic chores etc, he also began going to see various clan members who did specific tasks. This included accompanying Kenneth and Alasdair when they went to cut the peat. This had become a tradition since the '19 rather than each man cutting his own, for Kenneth could cut twice as fast as any other man and keep going twice as long, and it was one of the ways in which, although now infirm, Alasdair could still feel useful. To that end, after watching Kenneth and trying his hand at the cutting so as to know how to do it, Alex spent much of his time helping Alasdair to load the heavy peats onto the cart whilst trying to look as though he was not doing the majority of the work.

"That was a kindness ye did today with Alasdair," Kenneth remarked later as they walked down the hill together, Alasdair having gone ahead with the heavily laden peat cart.

"He was kind to me too, teaching me a lot of things that will be useful in the future," Alex said.

"Even so," Kenneth replied, but did not elaborate. "Ma said ye were asking about the dyeing of the wool, the plants used and so on, and Da said ye wanted to ken how he weaves the tartan. Are ye thinking of becoming a maker of cloth, then?"

For a second Alex thought this was a serious question, until he looked at Kenneth's face and saw the twinkle in the pale blue eyes. He laughed.

"No," he said. "No more than I'm wanting to become a maker of creels and baskets, or a fisherman. I'm thinking that if one day I've to make decisions about such things, I'd as well ken what it's like for the people who need to follow my orders. After watching ye both today for example, and trying the cutting myself, I understand now what hard work it is, and that it takes a lot of time. So if I'm telling people to cut the peat one day, I'll ken how many people are needed, how long it should take, and to give them more than the usual food and drink, for it's hungry work. I couldna make a good decision if I hadna done the work myself."

Kenneth smiled.

"Your da was like that once too. I dinna remember it, for I

was too young, but Da tellt me that Alexander was interested in everything once, just as you are. It's a pity…ye'll make a fine chieftain when the time comes, I'm thinking," Kenneth said.

Alex did not ask what was a pity, for he already knew, and did not want to embarrass Kenneth by making him finish what he'd decided not to say.

"I've likely plenty of time to learn everything, for Da's a young man yet," he said instead.

"He is. But we both ken better than others that death doesna always come when ye're old," Kenneth replied. "And a chieftain doesna always have to die before he's replaced."

Alex looked at Kenneth in shock then, expecting him to be horrified by what he'd just implied. But Kenneth merely returned his look calmly for a moment, then nodded to himself. "Are ye wanting to learn another sword move this evening? I've an hour before my bed," he continued evenly.

"Er…aye. I'd like that," Alex answered after a long moment in which he gathered his wits together.

No more was said on the subject, and lying awake in bed that evening, as he often did now, Alex decided not to repeat what Kenneth had said to anyone, not even Duncan. For he had certainly misunderstood what the other man seemed to be implying. After all, Kenneth was a straight-talking man, not given to implications. He had merely been stating a fact. No doubt some chieftains did have to be replaced, due to terrible injury, extreme age, mental feebleness…yes, it had been an innocent statement, Alex decided, ignoring the expression that had been on Kenneth's face as he'd stared at him.

In the summer Alex went up to the shielings and spent time learning about the care of the cattle, and the making of butter and cheese. He sheared the sheep, collected medicinal plants with Susan, and learnt what she knew about giving first aid in battle injuries. He learnt about bees from Barbara, how to collect the honey, and different uses for the beeswax, including waterproofing leather and cloth, now it was no longer used exclusively to make candles for Mass.

In the autumn he helped James in the forge, learning how he repaired tools and sharpened swords and dirks. He learnt to repair rooves, swarming on the top of the cottages with the other men, while Alexander, or more frequently now another clansman passed tools and heather up to them, advising them if the ropes were evenly stretched.

In the winter he learnt to cook; not just the basic oatmeal and water or a makeshift bannock cooked on a heated flat stone as men did when on campaign, but also how to make honey cakes, and was given the recipe for the rare treat cranachan by Barbara, which he wrote down for the following summer when there would be raspberries to make it. And in the evenings he learnt to knit, a skill most of the boys learnt, including Duncan. Angus tried to copy them for a short time, but soon gave up as his five-year-old fingers were not yet dexterous enough to master it.

One thing Angus *was* mastering, if Allan was to be believed, was the basics of wood carving. He had accompanied Alex one January day, Alexander being away on a raid with several members of the clan. The men had raised objections, saying that nobody raided in the winter for a number of good reasons, both practical and considerate, but Alexander had brushed them aside, saying that would give them the advantage of surprise, and at his insistence the disgruntled men had reluctantly trooped out after him.

When Alex and Angus arrived at Allan's cottage Angus was given a present of a small carved animal to his utter delight, although he had no idea what manner of creature it was.

"It's a wee lion," Allan told him. "For Alex tellt me ye liked it when Robinson Crusoe shot the lion in the book he was reading to ye."

"I did! They're awfu' fierce! Lions growl!" Angus said. "Show him how they growl, Alex!"

Alex dutifully let out an almighty roar, which, whilst sounding nothing like a lion, which he'd never heard, was certainly frightening. In fact the little wooden lion looked nothing like a lion either, as Allan had never seen one. It resembled instead the lion rampant of the Royal Arms of Scotland, which he'd seen when in Edinburgh.

Alex had asked Allan to show him how he made basic furniture – tables, stools and so on, and how long it took to repair them, but Angus was so entranced with the lion and so eager to learn how Allan had carved it, that he'd ended up watching as Allan had shown his little brother how to pick the right piece of wood, and had told him that he had to really know every angle of what it was he was going to carve before he started.

This had resulted in the two of them standing outside the sheepcote in a howling icy wind while Angus closely observed the sheep within, having decided that was what he wanted to carve.

"I'm thinking if ye're wanting to ken about the furniture, ye'll have to do it another day," Allan observed as they crouched down at the side of the building out of the wind, passing a whisky flask between them.

"I dinna mind. It's good to see him so happy," Alex said. "It was kind of ye to make the lion for him."

"He's a bonny laddie. Looks exactly as you did at his age, excepting the golden hair," Allan commented. "A sheep's a good first choice, for we can carve it wi' the fleece on, so there'll no' be as much knife work. I'll no' let him come to harm wi' the knife," he added. "I can teach him the smoothing wi' the horsetail reed first."

"If he keeps the interest that long, for he finds it hard to sit down and focus on anything for more than a few minutes. Duncan and I are having a difficult time trying to teach him his letters, although when he does concentrate, he's a quick learner," Alex said.

"Ah. He's like you in more than just looks then," Allan replied, grinning. "Though ye can sit still now. But ye've usually a look about ye, as though ye're about to jump up and run off somewhere."

Alex laughed.

"Kenneth tellt me ye're doing this, learning all these things for when ye become the chieftain," Allan continued.

Alex nodded, having just taken a nip of whisky, which was warming him nicely. Just as well, for it was very cold and Angus was certainly taking his time observing the sheep.

"That's a good thing then. Ye'll be needing them," Allan said, but when Alex looked at him, he was staring off into the distance. "Shall we away and see if the wee gomerel's fallen asleep in there?" he said, and the moment passed.

Angus did not lose interest in the idea of carving wood, and as Allan was happy to teach him, it gave Alex, Duncan and Susan more time, Susan being able to do the household chores faster without Angus under her feet asking her a million questions, while Alex and Duncan were able to continue their education as best they could alone through the short winter days.

* * *

They were reading *The Iliad* out loud together one rainy day in March, each of them taking it in turn to translate a verse from Latin to English, when Alexander suddenly and unexpectedly came in, soaking wet and cursing. He ignored the two boys sitting by the window and instead went to sit by the fire.

It would have been too obvious if the boys had stopped mid-verse and left the room, so they continued reading, self-consciously now, surreptitiously turning their stools so they could no longer see their father sitting brooding at the fireside. As Alexander made no noise, after a while they all but forgot he was there.

"'*Agamemnon cried out too, calling men to arms*
And harnessed up in gleaming bronze himself.
First he wrapped his legs with well-made greaves,
Fastening behind the heels with silver ankle-clasps,
And next he strapped the breastplate round his chest'," Alex read. "Oh, can ye imagine an army dressed all in bronze, wi' yon wondrous helmets, running wi' their spears! I'd love to see such a fearsome sight," he added dreamily.

A snort of derision came from the fireplace, where Alexander, having examined the injury to his leg that had brought him home, was now finishing eating a bowl of broth.

"No man wearing all that armour could run about as they do in Homer," Alexander said scathingly. "The man Homer wasna a warrior, that's certain, any more than you are. If ye're wanting a fearsome sight, there's nothing to match the Highland charge."

"If ye'd take me with ye on your raids as I've asked ye, I'd maybe see one," Alex shot back.

"Aye, well, I will when ye're a man, and no' spending your time reading poetry and believing it's real," Alexander said.

Alex was stunned into silence for a moment by the utter unfairness of this comment.

"You wanted me to learn the Latin, to read Homer, and

Virgil!" he cried after a minute. "It wasna me who wanted that!"

"Aye, but it's all useless now in any case, for ye canna go to university if ye havena learnt the Greek as well, can ye? Ye should have waited longer before ye drove the priest away."

He wiped his mouth, then, having finished eating, put the bowl down on the hearth and stood.

"When ye've both finished your poetry, ye can come out and help repair one of the boats," he said before opening the door and walking out.

After he'd gone the two boys sat silently for a minute, Duncan staring out of the window, Alex trying to deal with the cruelty of his father's words.

"All this reading, all this learning to work wi' metal, wood, what the lassies do wi' the cows, all that. If ye're doing it to impress him, to make him praise ye, ye're wasting your time," Duncan said bitterly, his grey eyes dark with anger. "Ye do ken that, d'ye no'? Nothing ye do, nothing any of us do will satisfy him, for he's determined to be angry and miserable for the rest of his life."

Alex coloured, which told Duncan that he knew exactly what he was referring to, and that his observation was correct.

"I'm no' doing it for that," Alex retorted instinctively, then sighed as he caught Duncan's sceptical glance. "I'm no' doing it *just* for that," he amended. "I really will need to ken everything if I'm to be a good chieftain one day. And it keeps me busy, stops me thinking about…things."

"Ye will need it. I will too, for if ye're away off doing some stupid raid in January as he does, I'll need to ken all those things as well," Duncan agreed. "I havena asked if I could come wi' ye sometimes, for if ye were doing it only to make him love ye again, ye wouldna have wanted me to."

God, it was hard sometimes, having a brother who knew you better than you knew yourself.

"Ye dinna care if he loves ye or no' though, do ye?" Alex said.

"Aye, I care, but no' as you do, for it isna going to happen. It's four years he's been gone. He isna coming back. He's found a new way to keep going. It isna living, but he canna see that. I've just accepted that we have no da any more. If ye can find a way to do that, it'll be easier for ye. But ye need to find your own way."

"I will," Alex promised, knowing Duncan was right, but no closer to knowing how to do it himself.

* * *

For the next six months Alex tried. He really tried. He cut back on the reading, stopped trying to learn Greek and told himself that he was focussing solely on learning practical activities because they would be of more use to him, not because he hoped to regain his father's respect and affection. If Duncan knew the truth behind his change of focus he said nothing, although he did start accompanying Alex to learn what the various clan craftsmen did.

Angus tagged along with them when he was not learning the carving with Allan, helping with chores suitable for a five-year-old, or being taken care of by various female members of the clan, all of whom were aware that the child had no adult to guide him and was effectively being brought up by his brothers.

Early in September Alexander called a clan meeting to announce that he needed all the capable male members of the clan to come on the raids and annual cattle sale at Crieff this year, because he was thinking to sell a larger number of cows than usual.

"I'm wanting to be sure we'll get through the winter without hunger, and without having to make any forays out, so if I make a good sum, I can buy everything we'll need. And yon laddie," he nodded in Alex's direction, "is growing fast now, and should be away to university soon. But he canna because he didna respect his tutor for long enough to learn the Greek."

"Most of us didna respect the tutor," Susan retorted.

"Aye. We shed no tears when the bastard left," Kenneth added.

Alexander scowled at them both for a moment but they returned his look levelly, although they made no further comment. The tension in the room heightened, and then Alexander continued talking as though nothing had happened. He was so distant from the clan now that he seemed unaware that everyone else had half-expected Kenneth to challenge him openly.

"So I'm also needing money to either send the boy away to school to learn Greek, maybe in Aberdeen, or to university in

Paris earlier than I was thinking I'd have to, if I can find one that will take him as he is," Alexander said. "We'll be leaving in two weeks. I'll leave a couple of ye behind, for there are jobs to do that the women canna do alone. Alasdair of course will be one."

"I'll stay behind as well," Kenneth said.

The tension heightened again, for it was not Kenneth's place but the chieftain's to say who stayed and who went. The two men locked gazes for a moment.

"Aye," Alexander replied. "I'm thinking that'll be best."

After a little more discussion about the organisation of the extended raids, the meeting broke up. At one time they would have made a night of it, with music, storytelling, drinking and laughter. But that was a thing of the past, so instead the clanspeople returned to their cottages to discuss the important thing that had almost just happened, which had nothing to do with cattle raiding.

"Let me come with you," Alex said early the next morning as Aleaxnder sat staring into the fire, his favourite occupation nowadays. He had risen as soon as he'd heard his father moving about below, having not slept at all following the meeting.

"I'm no' going anywhere the day," Alexander replied.

"On the raid. Let me come with ye."

"No."

"Why no'? All the other men are going with ye!"

"Ye're no' a man yet. Have ye no' noticed that?" Alexander remarked coldly.

"It isna right. Ye've tellt me ye're going on these raids so ye can get the money to send me away, but ye willna even let me help to earn it! It's no' right to risk the lives of the other men, while I have to stay at home wi' the lassies!" Alex cried.

"I said no. When ye're a man grown, I'll think again on it," Alexander replied.

"If ye've your way, ye'll be rid of me before I'm a man grown," his son said, swallowing back the lump of emotion which rose in his throat, threatening to choke him. "Ye took the both of us once, Duncan and me, when we were a lot younger! Why will ye no'—"

"Aye, and ye both nearly got yourselves killed, for ye didna obey my orders to hide in the forest!" Alexander shouted, losing his temper now.

"We did! Ye tellt us to hide, no' to go into the forest!" Alex cried.

"Well, ye'll obey my order now, or by Christ, ye'll regret it!" Alexander raged, jumping to his feet. "I said no, and I mean no. There's an end of it. Now get out of my sight."

Alex turned and walked out of the house, tears of rage and disappointment blurring his vision so much that he had to fumble to find the door handle. Once outside he ran full-tilt into the trees, stopping only when he was far enough away that no one was likely to either see or hear him. Then he sat on the ground at the foot of a tree and burst into tears, sobbing out his frustration, his grief, his pain at being so rejected by the man he loved more than anyone in the world.

No, he told himself later, when the outburst of desperate emotion had ebbed a little. He did not love his father more than anyone in the world. He loved Duncan and Angus much more. In fact right now he loved everyone in the clan much more than his father.

He *hated* his father. Duncan was right. Nothing he did would ever impress him, unless he could become a man immediately. Which was impossible.

He closed his eyes as a wave of fatigue and misery washed over him, crushing him completely. Then he lay down at the side of the tree, falling at once into a deep, exhausted sleep.

"Ye're wanting to fight? Now?" Kenneth asked, eyeing the wild-eyed boy standing before him dressed only in his shirt, barefoot, hair tangled on his shoulders decorated with dead leaves and bits of twig.

"Aye. Ye said ye'd teach me any time I wanted to learn," Alex said. "I'm wanting to learn."

"I did. But I was about to help Ma wi' the dyeing work, for Flora doesna feel too well. And ye havena your sword in any case," Kenneth added.

Alex looked down, as though expecting to find one suspended in air at his side.

"I need to fight," he said desperately, and Kenneth,

recognising desolation when it was staring at him, gave in.

"Ye can borrow Alpin's," he said. "Just dinna tell Ma or Da I let ye use it. Come on then."

Once armed with sword and targe they went down to the lochside, their habitual place to practice, where they both knew the ground and so could focus on technique without worrying about stumbling over anything.

"What moves are ye wanting to practice?" Kenneth asked when they arrived.

"I'm just wanting to fight, the way ye would really, no' to learn a particular move," Alex admitted. "I want ye to tell me how good or bad I am at what I've learnt, and where I can do things better than I am."

"Right, then," Kenneth said. "We'll just fight, but no' at full speed, ye ken. For I have to hold back, no' because ye're no' good at fighting now, for ye are, but because in a real fight I'd have the advantage of my strength and my size."

"Ye've a longer reach than me too," Alex said.

"Aye, but no' as long as it was, for ye're growing fast. But it'll be a wee while before your muscle catches up wi' the length of your arms and legs. It's the same for every boy of your age." He swung his targe off his shoulder and onto his left arm, then drew his sword. "Just come at me, then. I'll no' use a move ye havena learnt yet, to keep it fair," Kenneth added.

When Alex attacked, Kenneth knew he was right. Something, or more likely someone had upset the boy terribly, and he desperately needed to burn off his rage and misery somewhere, for he could not attack the person who had upset him. Which told Kenneth who had upset him.

So he let Alex just attack him for a time without commenting on his ability or his faults, parrying the blows as they came and noting with genuine pleasure just how light on his feet the boy was, and how fluid and natural the movements he'd learnt now were to him.

Although he'd said that he wouldn't use any moves he hadn't taught Alex, the boy was fighting so well overall that once Kenneth sensed Alex's emotions were stabilising a little, he began to parry the blows in more unusual ways, observing how he responded and adapted to the unknown.

"Stop for a wee minute," Kenneth said finally, when Alex's

blows weakened. "Ye've been fighting a good while now. Let's take a drink."

They sat down together on a fallen tree, both of them covered in sweat from the exertion, Kenneth relaxing while Alex, though tired, exhausted even, was still as tense as a spring.

"Ye did well," Kenneth said. "Ye could give many a grown man a good fight now. Ye just gave me a good fight."

"Aye, but ye ignored my mistakes. I've no doubt ye could have killed me a hundred times."

Kenneth grinned.

"No' that many. In the main it's because ye're focussing so much on your sword arm, ye forget to use your targe to best effect sometimes. No' often now, though. Ye've come a long way."

"Ye're no' tired though, are ye?" Alex replied. "Ye stopped out of kindness. A real enemy wouldna do that."

"No, but in a real battle ye dinna feel the tiredness until it's over, no matter how long ye have to fight for," Kenneth said.

"Aye, well, I'll never ken that, for Da willna take me wi' him on raids, and I'll no' have to fight when I'm learning shite in Paris," Alex answered bitterly.

"Dinna be so sure of that," Kenneth said, but did not elaborate on whether he was referring to Alexander's decision or the peacefulness of Paris. "One reason I'm no' as tired as you was because ye were emotional. Ye canna let your emotions rule ye."

"I thought it was good to be angry in battle," Alex said.

"Aye, it is, for it stops the fear. But ye canna let it take over your reason, for if ye do ye'll make mistakes."

"What mistakes did I make? Apart from the targe?"

"Ye didna always keep your movements tight, so ye used a lot more energy than ye needed to, which tires ye faster."

Alex nodded.

"And that also tellt ye what I was thinking to do before I did it," he added.

"Aye. Ye remember what I taught ye, at least," Kenneth said.

"It isna any good if I dinna *do* it, though. Can we try again?" Alex asked, springing off the log.

Alexander had *really* upset him, then. Kenneth resigned himself to a whole afternoon of helping Alex deal with his emotional turmoil.

He stood and they continued, Alex trying to remember to use his targe to protect his body while making a complex movement which, when mastered, would allow him to defend against an attack and then get past his enemy to strike him a killing blow on the side of the neck.

"Almost," Kenneth said. "Dinna forget ye can use your targe as a weapon too. If ye've just crushed your enemy's nose wi' it, he'll no' be able to see ye driving past him, and it makes your job easier."

"Aye, but I've to make sure he canna stab me while I've got it raised to hit him," Alex said.

"When ye raise it ye drop down though, like this," Kenneth explained, squatting and raising his targe diagonally up into an imaginary face, while Alex watched intently, "then he'll no' be able to stab ye, for ye're still protected."

"Look!" a small excited voice called from the side of them. Kenneth and Alex both turned to see Angus running toward them, brandishing a beautifully carved wooden sword. "I made a sword!" he said breathlessly as he reached them, his eyes sparkling. "Can ye teach me to fight, Alex?"

"No the now, Angus," Alex replied impatiently. "I'm learning a new move. Maybe later."

He turned back to Kenneth, already squatting and raising his targe, then saw the look on the man's face and realised in an instant what he'd just done.

He straightened and turned to see Angus already walking away, small shoulders slumped, sword trailing by his side, the point dragging on the ground, and the pain of it took his breath away.

"Christ," he said under his breath, then putting down his borrowed weaponry he ran across to his little brother, dropping to the ground as he reached him and seizing him in an embrace which startled the child.

"God, I'm sorry. I'm so sorry," Alex cried, bursting into tears and inadvertently frightening Angus, whose face was uncomfortably squashed against his older brother's chest.

"That's a wondrous sword, Angus," a deep voice came from above them, bringing Alex to his senses. "Did ye make it all yourself?"

Alex released his brother and let Kenneth take over for a

moment, who listened to Angus enthuse about how he'd made it and which parts Allan had helped him with, tactfully giving Alex the time he needed to master himself, which, with a great effort, he did.

"Are ye wanting to try it out, wi' Kenneth?" he asked finally, his voice still trembling from the surge of emotions raging through him.

Angus looked at Alex and smiled, blue eyes sparkling again.

"Can I try it out wi' you, instead?" he asked, and the uncertainty in his voice nearly broke Alex once more.

What the hell's wrong wi' me? he asked himself fiercely.

"Aye, of course ye can," he said with artificial cheer. "But we'll need Kenneth to watch us, for he's taught me everything I ken, and will no doubt teach you too."

"Aye, I will that," Kenneth agreed. "Come on then and I'll cut your brother a branch to fight wi', for we canna spoil your perfect sword on its first day, can we?"

"No. Steel is harder than wood," Angus said. "Allan said all the boys learn with wooden swords first."

"They do. I did," Alex agreed. "But I didna have such a fine one as yours."

Angus smiled happily now, relaxing completely as the Alex he adored was restored to him.

Alex spent the next hour letting Angus rush about joyously with his sword whilst avoiding being hit by the excited child, after which Susan appeared and tempted him away with the promise of a bannock with honey.

Once he'd gone, Kenneth and Alex sat silently for a while on the fallen tree.

"Are ye wanting to talk about it?" Kenneth ventured finally.

Alex shook his head.

"I need to work it out for myself," he said. "Can I learn the move another day? I'm no' in the way of it, now."

"Aye, of course. We can try again tomorrow if Flora's well, and Ma doesna need me."

Alex had stood, but stopped now.

"Oh, God, I'm sorry, Kenneth. I forgot entirely about Flora. What's amiss wi' her?"

"She just drank a wee bit too much o' the whisky last night,

I'm thinking," Kenneth replied, grinning. "Come to the house in the afternoon."

Alex took a step, then turned back.

"Will ye promise me something, Kenneth?" he asked, his eyes earnest, pleading even.

"Aye, if I can. What is it?"

"Dinna let me ever become like him. Angus deserves better than that. All of ye deserve better than that. Kill me if I ever do, for I wouldna want to live in such a way."

Kenneth considered for a minute.

"I canna promise to kill ye, laddie," he said finally. "But if it's in my power, I'll no' let ye become like him. I dinna think ye will, though. Ye're like him in some ways, but no' entirely."

"I was like him – in that way, today, wi' Angus, and about Flora," Alex said sadly.

"No. I didna need to tell ye. Ye saw it the second ye hurt him," Kenneth said. "Ye still care, deeply. It's who ye are. It's who ye always will be, I'm sure of that. Ye just need to learn when it's worth caring about someone and when it isna, and I canna help ye wi' that." He stood then, picking up the two swords and targes. "Now, away wi' ye! I'm thinking Ma'll have given Susan enough honey for all of ye to have a bannock wi' it, if ye get there before the bairn eats it all!"

"Ye're a good man, Kenneth," Alex said.

"Aye. Dinna tell the others though. I've a reputation to maintain," Kenneth answered, winking.

Alex laughed then and ran off toward home, a boy again. Kenneth watched him go, his face troubled again now no one was watching him. Then he sat down, wondering what, if anything he could do to avert what appeared to be an impending crisis between the chieftain and his son.

Nothing, he decided after a deal of thought. He had almost challenged Alexander yesterday, and in doing so had realised that he had no wish to. Alexander was a fearsome, ruthless fighter when roused, and although Kenneth knew that he was the only clansman who had a chance of beating him, in truth he had absolutely no desire to be the chieftain.

If he lost he would be killed, which would destroy his ma and da. And if he won it would split the clan. In any case, he would be a terrible chieftain. Much worse than the one Alexander now was, for Kenneth did not have the ability to lead and he knew that.

Alexander still ensured the clan had everything it needed to survive, still held the land they lived on. That was more than some chieftains did. If he was otherwise uncaring and reckless, both with his own life and others, that also was no worse than many other chieftains were.

The sadness of it was that he *had* been so much better. Still could be so much better. But the more time passed, the less likely it was that he would come back to them. Pre-empting the situation by challenging him would not help, though.

Either Alexander would pull out of his unremitting grief, or Alex would grow up and decide whether to challenge his father or not. All Kenneth could do, he realised, was try to stop Alex challenging his father before he was able to, if that was what was building in him now. Certainly something was. He had never seen the boy so unstable.

Duncan would help with that, for Duncan was a natural peacemaker. And all the rest of them could do then was wait, and choose their side when it came to it. If it came to it.

Kenneth stood, and made his way home. He would not have to choose a side. That decision had already been made, at least.

* * *

Alex sat staring into the fire in unconscious imitation of his father, deep in thought. Duncan, who had borne the brunt of his brother's constantly changing moods for a few days now, left him to it, taking Angus to Susan's, where he was going to help her prepare medicine from the bunches of leaves and flowers which had been drying all over her home for the last weeks. The rest of the women were washing every item of clothing and bedding they had, as it was now September and soon there would be few, if any opportunities to dry washing. The men had all gone up to the bowl-shaped crater outside the cave to plan the numerous raids Alexander had in mind for the following week.

Having dropped Angus off Duncan was tempted to go fishing, not because he either needed or desired a fish, but because he really wanted to be away from his brother for a while. Not from Angus; he had never known a child who was so easily pleased, so eager to learn *anything*, as long as it did not involve him having to sit still for a long time. It was virtually impossible to be unhappy when Angus was around, although Alex was managing to achieve it.

Duncan sighed. He could not go fishing and leave his older brother alone when he was so very unhappy. He took a final longing look at the sun shining on the loch, heard the women already laughing and singing at their work, then headed back to the cottage, his stomach like lead.

When he walked through the door Alex was no longer sitting brooding by the fire, but instead was in the process of drawing their grandfather's claymore out of the leather sheath it was kept in. He looked round guiltily on hearing the door open, then relaxed when he saw who it was.

"What are ye doing?" Duncan asked. "Da tellt us we're no' allowed to touch that."

"When I was a wee bairn," Alex replied, "I wanted to go wi' Da to fight for King James, but he wouldna let me, for I was only three. I was awfu' insistent, so he drew this and tellt me to lift it." He drew the sword, putting the scabbard on the table, and held it up in his right hand, looking up at the tip. "I couldna, of course. I couldna even lift the tip off the ground. So then he tellt me that when I could hold it like this, and then swing it like this," he demonstrated, narrowly missing cleaving the chair as he did, "for an hour, then he might take me wi' him to battle. I'm thinking I can do it now, and I'm going to find out."

"Alex," Duncan said as Alex sheathed the blade again, then fastened the swordbelt round his waist. "He'll no' take ye wi' him. Ye could go out now and swing it about all day and he wouldna take ye, for he doesna want to. But if he finds out ye've used his da's sword, he'll be awfu' angry."

"I mean to try. He'll no' ken, for he's up at the cave planning the raids, and everyone's either with him or down at the loch. I'll go into the trees at the far end of the settlement. No one'll see us there. Ye'll no' tell him, will ye?"

"No, of course I willna. But I'll have nothing to do with it, either." Duncan sat firmly down on the *seise,* to make his point. Alex shrugged.

"As ye please. I was hoping to practice a wee bit with ye. But

I can do it alone." He finished buckling the belt, and then walked out of the door.

Duncan sat there for a minute and then sighed, which he seemed to be doing a lot recently. Then he stood up and contemplated taking his own sword before deciding against it, not wanting to encourage Alex in this pointless escapade. Their da had not used the sword since the '19, had said he would not use it again until he fought for James once more. Even so he kept it in perfect condition, as it was the only thing he had of his father, who he had adored in the same way his sons had once adored him.

Before Ma had died.

Duncan sent up a silent prayer that no one would see Alex heading into the trees wearing the sword, and then he left, running to catch up with his idiot brother.

Once hidden in the woodland, and having found a small heather-covered clearing, Alex drew the sword again, holding it high in the air triumphantly.

"I canna believe I was ever so wee that I couldna even lift it off the ground, wi' two hands," he said joyously.

"I can. Angus would find it difficult now, and we were both his size once," Duncan said.

"Aye. Did ye bring your sword?" Alex asked.

"No. I've got my dirk, but I'm no' encouraging ye by fighting wi' ye."

"D'ye want to hold it though?"

"No."

"Ye do. I can see it in your face. Go on. Ye canna do any harm by holding it," Alex said.

Duncan gave in, for he did indeed want to hold an adult's sword, and not just an adult's, but the sword that the grandfather neither of them had ever known had fought in the '15 with. The sword he had died holding, according to Alexander, who had fought at his side.

He took the weapon from Alex reverently, raising it and then swinging it from side to side, before thrusting it at an imaginary enemy. He swung around then thrust again, and this time Alex leapt forward, blocking the strike with his dirk and sending a shock wave up Duncan's arm, who had not been expecting resistance to the thrust and was not braced for it.

Alex laughed delightedly at his brother's expression, the first time he'd truly laughed in a while, and Duncan felt the recklessness flood him. To hell with their da. He didn't care about them, about what they thought; why should they care about him?

He raised the sword again, cutting at his brother, but in slow motion and keeping a reasonable distance from him, letting Alex make the forward step to block him. They continued in this way for a few minutes, then stopped, panting and sweating with the exertion.

"We shouldna be doing this," Duncan said in a half-hearted attempt to remain the level-headed sensible one, as they both sat down next to a tree to get their breath back.

"No, but it's awfu' fun, is it no'?" Alex replied. "I'm glad ye came too. It wouldna be the same without ye."

"It's awfu' heavy," Duncan said. "No' to lift, but when ye've been using it for a wee while."

"Aye. It's because the swords we've got are still boys' swords, no' the right weight to take a man's head off wi' one swing," Alex said. "I kent that a few days ago when I was fighting wi' Kenneth, for I didna have my sword, so he let me use Alpin's. It was very different. Dinna tell Barbara or Gregor, though."

"Was that after ye had the stramash wi' Da? He didna tell me, I heard some of it."

"Aye. I used Alpin's sword for a good while, and that made me think that I could swing Da's sword for an hour now."

"Did ye use Alpin's for an hour?"

"I dinna ken. How long's an hour?"

"Well, there's twenty-four in a day, and the sun's just coming over that tree now," Duncan said, looking up at the sky and mentally dividing a circle into twenty-four segments, "so I should think in an hour the sun'll be about there." He pointed at another spot to the right, in the direction of the loch.

Alex nodded.

"Come on then," he said. "I'll practice some of yon moves Kenneth taught me, and ye can watch. And ye can block me like I did you, if ye want. I'll go slowly, as ye did."

They both stood, everything forgotten now except the

excitement of the moment, of discovering whether Alex truly was a man now.

"When ye've done your hour, can we see how long I can swing it for?" Duncan said.

"Aye, of course! I dinna think ye'll make the hour, though."

"No, but I'd like to ken if I'm half a man, at least," Duncan replied.

"Oh, ye are. I'm thinking three-quarters!" Alex replied generously, although Duncan, being only eleven, had not had the growth spurts he had yet, so at the moment there was a good difference in both height and strength between them.

They made a start, Alex leaping about, vigorously fighting an imaginary enemy with far more enthusiasm than skill, as he did not have to worry about Kenneth observing his technique and could enjoy making wildly imaginative thrusts and cuts, swinging the blade above his head, in the process accidentally shearing a low branch off a tree, which hit him on the back, making him stagger forward and nearly impale his brother, who was in the process of advancing with his dirk to block the swing.

Enervated by the sheer freedom of being able to act as warriors with no restrictions, heightened by the utter misery and gloom of the last months, years even, the two boys were giddy with excitement, feeling again the pure carefree joy of living that all children do, even while they tried to prove themselves men. This was wonderful!

Alex had been right, Duncan thought, glad that he'd accompanied him now. He glanced up. The sun had advanced a good way toward the spot they'd estimated as an hour.

"No' long now," he said. "Are ye hurting yet?"

"No," Alex replied, too fired up to feel anything except exhilaration. "Come on then. After the hour, we'll have a wee rest, and then ye can try. Da'll be gone all day, I'm thinking. We'll be home and in bed before he gets back."

They moved the fallen branch out of the way and continued, Alex twirling about like a dervish, Duncan leaping forward and backward, slashing at the sword with his dirk, laughing as they became more and more daring, Alex thrusting within inches of Duncan, Duncan ducking and running in to hit further along the blade.

Alex felt the shock of the dirk stopping the sword mid-flow as Duncan had earlier, running up his arm and making all his nerves tingle, but he was having so much fun he paid no heed to it, bringing the sword over his head and then down, a powerful strike which in battle would have cleaved his enemy in half had it landed. As it was thankfully not stopped by Duncan's head, the blade impaled itself in the ground instead, Duncan leaping forward, dirk raised, bringing it down to stop the sword as Alex lifted it from the ground.

Except Alex did not lift it straight out of the ground as Duncan expected, partly because his arm was trembling with fatigue, and partly because the point of the sword had caught in a rotten branch just under the heather, with the result that Duncan brought his dirk down onto Alex's hand as he was struggling to pull the blade free.

He realised what was happening mid-flow, and desperately tried to rein in the blow, stepping back as he did, with the result that the dirk hit Alex with far less force than it would have otherwise, slicing into his hand rather than his arm.

There followed a hideous moment when time seemed to stop. And then Alex's hand was suddenly bright red. He let go of the sword, which remained lodged in the branch, and shook his hand, causing a rain of scarlet drops to spatter the earth. And then the pain hit and he gasped, gripping his right hand with his left in an attempt to stop the bleeding.

"Oh God, I'm sorry," Duncan cried, dropping his dirk and running forward to help his brother, who had now doubled over, his face white. He sat down suddenly, pulling his hand into his chest.

Duncan knelt down in front of him, grey eyes huge and panicked.

"Christ, I havena cut your hand off, have I?" he said.

"No," Alex managed through gritted teeth. "No, but it hurts."

"Let me see," Duncan said. He had no wish to see what terrible injury he'd dealt his brother but knew he had to, for there was no one else to help. No one else *could* help, for if anyone did, their da would surely find out what they'd done.

Very gingerly Alex unclenched his hand, and Duncan looked at it. He certainly still *had* a hand, but the blood was flowing too fast for him to see the actual wound. It seemed very bad to him though. Quickly he pulled his shirt out of his kilt and over his head.

"Here," he said, "Wrap this round it, tightly, and that might stop the bleeding. Then we need to go to Susan, for we canna mend this ourselves."

"We canna go to Susan," Alex said frantically. "If we do, Da'll find out!"

"Susan willna tell him. She doesna like Da much at the minute. No one does," Duncan said. "But I'm thinking we canna hide this unless we *do* go to her, for she might be able to stop the bleeding and make it well again." He just stopped himself from saying, *so ye'll be able to fight again,* realising that it would not help Alex right now to realise that his warrior days might be over before they'd begun. A wave of guilt and horror washed through Duncan, which he firmly thrust to one side. There was no time for that now, he knew.

"Come on," he said. "Can ye walk?"

"Aye, I can walk," Alex replied. "I walk on my feet, no' my hands. Have ye no' noticed that?"

Ridiculously they began to giggle as though this was the funniest thing ever, their giggles turning to laughter, then edging towards hysteria. They both stood.

"Ye have to bring the sword," Alex said, still giggling. "We canna leave it here." They looked back at the sword, still upright in the heather, and suddenly all the mirth drained from them both, replaced by despair.

Duncan went across to it, and with strength born of desperation tugged it out of the ground. He wiped the dirt off with the upper part of his *fèileadh mór* before putting it in the scabbard at Alex's side. Then he picked up his dirk and sheathed it.

"Are ye wanting me to carry it?" he asked, but Alex shook his head.

"I'm thinking we should get to Susan now," he said, watching as the blood blossomed across the linen binding it with worrying speed.

Luckily Susan's cottage was not far from the woodland they'd been practising in as she lived at that end of the settlement, so it didn't take too long for them to get there. When they arrived Angus was standing on a stool at the table, using a pestle and mortar to grind some aromatic leaves to powder, while Susan stood watching him.

"Aye, ye're doing well, laddie," she was saying as his two brothers suddenly appeared in the open doorway. Susan looked up, Angus being too engrossed in what he was doing to notice the visitors immediately. Then she saw the way Alex was standing, the pallor of his face and the reddening cloth, and moved toward them, blocking Angus's view as she did.

"What's happened?" she asked.

"We had a wee accident wi' a knife," Alex said, hearing the sound of the pestle stop.

"Did ye now?" Susan replied, taking in the sword at Alex's waist, the look of intense distress on Duncan's face and making a reasonably accurate assumption of what had happened. "Come on then. Sit down and I'll look at it. Duncan, are ye wanting to take Angus somewhere for a wee while?"

"No," Duncan replied, "I canna—"

"Can ye take this back to the house?" Alex interrupted, instinctively moving to unbuckle the swordbelt, then grimacing.

"Ah. Aye. I'll do it," Duncan said, leaning down to undo the belt and take the sword.

"What happened?" Angus asked, looking at the scarlet cloth that had been Duncan's shirt.

"It's nothing," Alex told him. "Just a wee cut, that's all."

"Knives are very dangerous. Allan tellt me that," Angus said. "He says he'll let me carve a wee bit of my next sheep, though, if I'm careful."

"Aye, ye have to be very careful," Duncan told him, "for we're much older than you, but we can still cut ourselves. Are ye wanting to come with me? We'll come back when I've put this away," he added, seeing Angus look anxiously at Alex.

"Aye, go on," Alex said. "When ye get back Susan will be finished, and ye can show me what ye're doing wi' yon leaves."

"It's called yarrow," Angus said proudly.

"It is," Susan replied. "And I'm thinking I might be needing some of it for your brother."

"I can stay and help," Angus suggested.

"No," Duncan said. "I need ye to help me carry this, for it's heavy."

They left, Angus carefully holding one end of the sheathed sword, while Duncan prayed that everyone, but most especially Alexander was still up at the cave, or down by the loch, for they made a strange sight as they were.

Susan waited until they were gone and then shut the door, before coming back and gently unwrapping Alex's hand. Then she whistled through her teeth.

"Can ye heal it?" Alex asked anxiously, looking at the gaping wound which ran from his wrist to his fingers, still seeping blood.

Susan didn't answer at first, instead getting a cloth and a bowl of warm water from the pot hanging over the fire.

"Let me wash it, and then I'll see better what ye've done," she commented. She wet the cloth then squeezed the water out over his hand, before carefully washing it. "I'm sorry, but I canna do this without hurting ye," she said.

"It doesna hurt much," Alex lied bravely, although the pallor of his face and the involuntary spasms that twisted his mouth told a different story. Finally, the wound clean, she gently laid his hand on the table.

She looked at it, deliberating.

"Did ye do it wi' that sword Duncan's taken home?" she asked. "I need to ken. Was the blade sharp, clean, dirty, rusty?"

"Ah." Alex relaxed a little now he realised there was a practical reason for her questions, rather than mere idle curiosity. Even so… "Promise ye'll no' tell our da, if I tell ye the truth," he pleaded.

"Ye'll no be able to hide this from him, whether I tell him or no'," she said.

"I dinna think he'll care. He doesna notice I'm even there, much of the time," Alex answered, then bit his lip.

"He'll notice this," she told him. "Ye need to move it, so I can see what ye've damaged. It'll hurt ye bad, but I need to ken if ye can move your fingers."

"Why would I no' be able to move my fingers?" Alex asked. "He…I didna cut them off!"

"Because ye've got tendons, like wee strings, that run along the back of your hand, and they allow ye to move your fingers. If ye've cut the tendon, then ye may no' be able to do that. I'm sorry," she added, seeing that he'd suddenly realised this could be more serious than just getting into trouble with his father. For this was his right hand, his sword hand, and he could not be chieftain if he could not use a sword. "I have to tell ye the truth. Ye need to try to bend your fingers, but *very* slowly. Stop when I tell ye."

He looked at his hand, his whole body tense, clearly dreading trying in case he couldn't move them.

"Can ye fix the tendons, if I canna?" he asked, suddenly a small boy again, in spite of his deep voice.

"Just try," Susan answered.

He braced himself, then very slowly he curled his fingers on the table, just a little.

"Stop, and straighten them again," Susan said, watching intently as he did. "Good. Could ye feel those two fingers on the table when ye bent them, the same as the others?"

"Aye, I think so, but my whole hand's hurting, so it's hard to tell," Alex said.

She trickled water over the wound again to wash the blood away.

"Can ye feel the table under your fingers now? Try to ignore the pain, as though ye're in a battle and have to."

He focussed intently, and she saw the slight pressure of his knuckles as he pressed his fingers against the table, and because she'd just washed the blood off the wound, she also saw the tendons move. She smiled.

"Good," she said, then stood again. "Ye havena cut the tendons. Which is good, for, to answer your question, no, I couldna fix them if ye had. But ye still might have damaged them, so ye'll no' be able to use your hand rightly until it's healed, for if ye do ye could snap the tendon anyway, which ye really dinna want to do. And I'll have to sew the wound, for although yarrow's wonderful for healing, it doesna perform miracles. So your hand will swell up a lot. And your da will notice it, whether he pays attention to ye or no', for I'll have to bind it, and the rest of the clan will see it even if he doesna. So ye'll need to think of what ye'll tell them all when they ask."

Alex said something very rude in Gaelic under his breath, which Susan decided not to hear.

"What happened?" she asked again as she moved around the room getting what she needed, and cursing because she had no curved needles to stitch the wound neatly with, which meant that not only would it hurt like the devil when she did, but he would likely have a terrible scar to remind him for the rest of his life of what he'd done. Whatever that was. "I'll no' tell your da, I promise. Wait until I sit down, and then tell me."

So he told her the truth while she stitched the wound, which had the dual purpose of helping her to understand what had happened and helping him not to faint with the pain, which would have embarrassed him terribly. When she'd done the best she could, although it looked dreadful, she put a thick paste of yarrow over it and a piece of wood under his fingers before carefully wrapping it with clean bandages.

"I want ye to come back every day, for I dinna think ye'll be wanting me to come to you, if your da's there," she said. "And ye mustna use it at all until I tell ye. So your brothers will have to help ye wi' your tasks. Ye can use the time to think of a gentler story for your da. Then tell me what it is, for he'll maybe ask me what ye said."

"Ye'd do that for us?" Alex asked, looking up at her in amazement.

"Aye, I would. I was young once. But ye must promise me ye'll no' do something so stupid again. For I ken ye're no' telling me everything, and if ye were waving a sword around and Duncan was blocking it wi' just a dirk, then ye're fortunate one of ye's no' bleeding to death on my table. At the least he could have cut your hand clean off. It's a miracle he didna."

"He thought he had," Alex admitted. "That's an easy promise to make, for I can see now how stupid we were. It felt so good, though, to laugh again, to do something I really wanted to do," he added sadly.

"Aye, it did," said Duncan from the door. "I dinna think anyone saw me," he added, realising from the sentence he'd just heard that Alex had confided in Susan.

"Are ye healed now?" Angus asked, running to his brother to give him a hug, for being a very affectionate child he was convinced that hugs cured most things.

"He will be, but he isna yet," Susan replied. "And he mustna use his hand at all for some days, so he'll need you to help him a lot."

"I can do that!" Angus said.

"I'm sure ye can." Alex smiled.

After Susan had put her medical things away and they'd all had a hot whisky with water to revive them, she stated that she'd go back to the house with them.

"Angus willna stay with me now anyway," she said. This was obvious, for since he'd returned he'd been stuck to Alex like glue, and was currently sitting on his knee, leaning against his chest, taking great care not to touch his brother's wounded hand. "I can do some of the chores at home, for you mustna, Alex. Ye need to rest a little."

"I can do them," Duncan said.

"I can too!" piped up Angus.

"No, ye canna. Ye both need to rest, for Alex is wounded, and you've had a shock, Duncan, and will feel that later. Angus, ye can help me though, by sweeping the floor."

"I'm very good at that now," he said. "I do it nearly every day."

"It's one of the chores I gave him," Alex explained. "We find it easier if we each do the same chores every day, do we no', Angus?"

"Aye. I wash the table too, but I'm no' allowed to use a knife yet, no' a very sharp one."

"And now ye can see why," Alex told him, "so when ye *do* get your first sharp knife, ye must be awfu' careful wi' it, and no' use it at first unless me or Duncan are there."

"I willna," Angus promised, while Susan, listening to this, realised that the two boys had completely taken over the role of parent to their younger brother. A surge of conflicting emotions washed through her, wanting to adopt the three boys and give them at least one parent figure, and also wanting to go and hit Alexander, make him see what he was missing while sunk in his selfish grief.

As she could do neither of those things, instead she walked back with Angus, allowing Duncan and Alex to walk ahead together, aware they needed to get their story straight for when their father came home. While Angus chatted happily about every plant they saw, from grass to gorse to heather, asking Susan what ailments they cured, his two brothers discussed their options.

"We should tell Da the truth, if he asks," Duncan suggested.

"When he asks," Alex said ruefully, for Susan had said it would be best if he kept his arm in a sling for a while, as it would stop him instinctively trying to use it or banging it on something. In any other case he would have refused, but this was his right hand, his sword hand, and he was acutely aware that his whole future depended on it healing properly.

"When he asks, then."

"Why? He'll be awfu' angry if he kens the truth, and ye'll get a beating, I'm thinking."

"I deserve it, if I do," Duncan replied.

"No, ye dinna. I'm the eldest. I shouldna have been so stupid. And ye didna want to come wi' me. It's no' your fault."

"Aye, it is. For I'm the sensible one, we both ken that. I went with ye to stop ye doing anything wild, but I ended in being wild myself. I could have killed ye."

Alex moved to his brother's right side, so he could put his left arm round his waist.

"But ye didna. And ye didna cut my hand off. And we learnt from it. Dinna feel guilty, for we're both at fault. I could have killed ye too, swinging the sword over my head like I did."

"Aye, maybe. But we should tell the truth, for it seems a coward's way to lie to him."

Alex thought about this for a minute.

"If he was the da we had before Ma died, I'd agree. But we dinna ken what he'll do. And I'll no' have him be wi' you as he is wi' me since I tellt him the truth about mocking the priest. He mentions it all the time, blaming me for having to go on raids, for no' learning Greek, for the clan no' being able to take the sacrament."

"He blames ye for that?" Duncan said. "That isna true. The priest didna leave because ye mocked him, Alex. He left because the whole clan turned against him for the way he treated wee Jeannie. What ye did just made them aware of how he was behaving. Ye did right."

"Da doesna see it that way. I dinna want you to spend the rest of your life having this thrown at ye by him," Alex said, automatically raising his arm to make his point, then remembering and lowering it again before Susan saw. "For ye feel guilty anyway, and I dinna want ye to."

"I dinna care what Da thinks," Duncan said. "I care what you think. It's you I wounded. If ye forgive me, then that's all that matters."

"I forgive ye, of course I do. It was an accident. But I dinna want him to hate ye as he does me. I thought he might love me again, if I proved I was a man," Alex admitted as they came within sight of home. "But he'll hate me even more now."

"He doesna hate ye," Duncan remarked. "He's afraid."

Alex looked at his brother in shock, for his words made no sense. Their father was *never* afraid! What was there for him to be afraid of?

He was about to ask that when Alexander appeared in the doorway, and the expression on his face, combined with the fact that in his right hand he held his father's sword, drove both his unspoken question and Duncan's remark from Alex's mind.

CHAPTER EIGHTEEN

Susan, walking a few steps behind Alex and Duncan, saw Alexander's face and that his ferocious look was directed primarily at Alex, which told her that he'd already judged him without knowing the facts, something he would never have done in the past. She watched as both boys unconsciously braced themselves to receive their father's ire. Indignation at his unfair attitude towards his eldest son, towards his whole clan, rose in her. Dropping Angus's hand she moved forward past the two older boys and up to their father.

"Alex has had an accident," she said. "He came to me and I've stitched the wound and bound it. It should heal, but he mustna use it for several days and I'll need to tend it each day. He lost a lot of blood, so he'll likely need to rest now," she added, hoping that would give Alex a reprieve from any punishment and Alexander time to calm down.

"Will he keep the use of his hand?" asked Alexander, still looking at his son.

"Aye, if he doesna use it at all. I've bound it to a piece of wood so he canna bend his fingers, for if he does before it heals he could damage the tendon, which means he'll never be able to move his fingers rightly."

"It wasna his fault," Duncan put in as soon as Susan finished, aware that the da of the past, who would have understood youthful exuberance, who would have listened to reason, who would probably have recognised that there was no need for further punishment as they'd learnt their lesson comprehensively, was dead.

"Was it no'?" Alexander replied. "Whose fault was it, then?"

"Mine," Duncan said firmly. "I cut him wi' my dirk. It still has his blood on it," he added, drawing it to prove his point.

Alexander glanced at it, then back at Alex.

"And whose idea was it to steal your grandda's sword?"

"Mine," Alex said, before Duncan could accept responsibility for that too. "It was an accident. Duncan didna mean to cut me. He tellt me no' to take the sword, but—"

"Alex," Duncan interrupted, but Alex ignored him completely, ignored Susan, who had opened her mouth to speak, even ignored Angus, who was now clinging to his side. His whole focus was on his father, and their eyes clashed in an unspoken battle of wills.

"I took it because I wanted to see if I could hold it straight up, if I could swing it for an hour, for ye tellt me that when I could ye might take me wi' ye to battle. Ye'll likely no' remember," he continued, seeing his father's expression change, "for ye did it as ye rode off to fight for James when I was a wee bairn, when ye cared. I'm no' a wee bairn now, but I felt I had to prove it. I was wrong, I see that now."

Alexander broke his gaze with his oldest son for a moment to look at his second.

"Aye, well, ye may have stopped your brother becoming a man altogether, if he was ever going to be one. I couldna see any sign of that happening, and I still canna," he stated coldly, ignoring Duncan's sudden pallor. "He'll be no use at all if he canna fight, and all that education'll be wasted too, for he canna be a chieftain if he's crippled. Are ye hoping to take his place, then?" he asked.

Susan had never seen anyone's face turn from chalky white to blood red as quickly as Duncan's did at these words.

"Alexander, it—" she began.

"Ye dinna need to be so cruel to him, Da," Alex interrupted coldly. "It's me ye hate, and it's me ye're wanting to beat. I'll no' try to prove I'm a man to ye again, no' in such a way, at least. Shall we get on wi' it?"

"No!" Susan cried, seeing Alexander's hand move to his belt. "If ye beat him now and he clenches his hand in pain, as he will, then ye'll cripple him yourself, and the whole clan will ken ye did it."

"Are ye threatening me?" Alexander said incredulously, and in spite of her anger she shivered at his tone.

"No, she isna. She's telling ye the truth," Alex said. "She came back wi' us to do the household chores, for I canna."

Alexander nodded curtly in a gesture for them to go inside, and moved to the side of the door to allow his sons to walk past him. But when Susan tried to follow he stepped back, blocking her way.

"No," he said. "This canna go unpunished. Come back tomorrow. I'll no' beat him until his hand's healed. Go."

"I'll cook the meal, then," she offered, not wanting to leave them alone with him.

"Go," he repeated, and she realised that he was not going to let her stay, no matter what.

"I'll come back tomorrow to check him," she said, frustrated.

"Aye," Alexander replied, then turned and went in, closing the door behind him.

Susan stood for a moment outside, then walked away. She had never felt so helpless in her life. But he was the chieftain, and his word was law. She *was* helpless.

Inside the house Alexander observed his three sons, two of them standing shoulder to shoulder, united in their hostility towards him, the third clinging to Alex's leg, blue eyes huge with fear and misery. Just for a moment he saw the yawning chasm between them and suddenly felt unutterably lonely, assailed by a desperate longing for things to be as they'd been before. Then he shook himself inwardly and the feeling dissipated, replaced by anger that his own sons would defy him so openly.

"Ye canna beat Alex, but I'm no' injured. Shall we have it over with?" Duncan said coldly. "I'd ask that ye dinna let the bairn see, for he's unhappy enough, and he at least has done nothing to deserve your anger." Without waiting for his father to agree he turned and walked into the bedroom, knowing instinctively that Alexander would not want to administer this punishment outside, in front of the clan. And knowing why, even if his father didn't.

At first Alex stayed in the next room, not wanting to leave his brother to be flogged alone, aware that the whole incident was his fault, not Duncan's. A range of ugly emotions warred within him, and then he felt Angus shaking like a leaf next to him, wincing as he heard the sound of leather hitting skin coming from the next room, although Duncan did not cry out.

Aware that Angus would not leave the house without him, Alex stood, taking him outside and shutting the door so the sounds would not reach them. Then he sat on the bench, consoling his little brother while listening to the singing of the women as they finished the laundry, their voices carrying across to him on the breeze. As he did his feelings for his father shifted in him, settling into an altogether different pattern, although he did not realise it then, in his guilt and distress.

After what seemed to be an interminably long time the door opened and Alexander came out, buckling his belt round his waist. He clearly intended to go somewhere, but on seeing the two figures on the bench, came over to them. Alex felt Angus cringe into his side, and if he'd been whole at that point, he may well have challenged his father immediately, as reckless as that would have been.

"Ye've proved one thing to me today," Alexander spat, "that in spite of all your learning ye're a disobedient wee gomerel. If I'd been thinking to take ye wi' me I'd change my mind, even if ye werena injured, for a clansman who canna obey orders from his chieftain is no use to me at all. I'm disappointed in ye."

With that he marched off, heading towards the track that ran along the lochside. Alex closed his eyes for a moment, feeling utterly weary, then he stood.

"Let's away inside," he said, and together they went back into the cottage.

* * *

For the next week either Susan came to visit Alex or he went to her each day. She unbound his wound, checked it for infection and swelling, making him move it just a little, then cleaned and bound it up again.

"You're doing very well," she told him on the fourth day. "I ken it must be hurting ye to keep it so still, but it's healing well now." She'd written to Francis, asking if he could buy some of the curved needles used for stitching wounds and send them to her, as she had no wish to put anyone else through the pain Alex had dealt with when she'd stitched his hand with an altogether unsuitable needle.

They were a brave pair of boys, that was certain. Having seen the very careful way Duncan was moving, she'd asked him if he wanted her to look at his back, but he'd told her that he'd be healed in a few days, and had politely refused to take his shirt off for her to look at him.

"He'd be more comfortable if he didna wear a shirt for a few days," she said to Alex one day, Duncan having gone to fetch water in spite of Alex telling him one of the other clan members could do it.

"He willna even let me look at it," Alex said. "And he wears a shirt even in bed, for he doesna want Angus to see it, which tells me that it must be bad. But he hasna said a word about it, about anything to do wi' the whole affair," he finished sadly.

"It wasna your fault, Alex," Susan said.

"Aye, it was. It was my idea to try to prove I was a man. Duncan tried to stop me. He's always been the sensible one, but I wouldna heed him. I was so determined to prove myself to Da." He laughed without humour. "I canna do it. I ken that now."

"Maybe ye canna prove yourself to your father, but ye're both proving yourselves to the clan," Susan told him.

Alex looked at her, his face troubled.

"They ken what happened?" he asked.

"No. No' exactly, for I havena tellt them, but they ken ye were practising fighting in the woods and had a wee accident, and that your da beat Duncan for it. And they dinna approve of it."

"Aye, well, they've kent us both for a long time, and they'll ken who was behind the whole thing. Is my hand healed enough for me to tell Da he can beat me now?"

"I said a week," Susan answered.

"Aye. But is it healing faster? I'm thinking they'll no' disapprove of me when I've had my punishment too. Or no' so much, anyway."

Susan looked at him incredulously.

"Alex, it's no' you they disapprove of, but your da," she said. "It's clear that he beat Duncan badly for what they see as something most boys might do, which went wrong. They also ken the love the two of ye have for each other, and that he didna need to beat him, nor does he need to beat you. He wouldna have done, before…"

She bit back the end of her sentence, as no one mentioned Moira any more.

"Before Ma died," Alex finished for her. "Aye, well, if they ask tell them I deserve a beating, and I'd have it over if ye say my hand's ready. And tell them that Da's gone, and he isna coming back. We ken that, for we have to live with him, even if they dinna. But they should."

Susan nodded, wondering if she should also tell the clan how rapidly this boy was becoming an adult, not so much in body, although he was developing quickly there too, but in mind. But in truth she didn't need to tell them that, for they already knew.

"Aye," she said. "Ye're about ready. But dinna clench your fist. Ye're no' healed yet."

"Thank ye," he said. "I willna."

* * *

He did not clench his fist. Nor did he cry out, nor even moan, although it cost him dearly not to. He was determined not to give his father the satisfaction, even though Duncan had told him to, had said that he thought he'd received a worse beating than he would have had he cried.

In Alexander's view their silence denoted defiance, and the mood in the house after that was even more unbearable than it had been.

To the boys' relief, a week later Alexander, along with the rest of the clansmen except for Kenneth and Alasdair, went on the raids, which would keep them away from home for several weeks.

Alex did not ask to go with him. In fact he did not even go outside to watch the clansmen leave as the rest of the clan did. Once they'd gone he walked down to the loch, where he sat in his favourite spot, staring across the water and thinking.

He sat there for several hours each day for a week, although he did not tell anyone what he was thinking about. By then his hand was healing rapidly, and Susan had removed the block of wood and his stitches, telling him he could bend his fingers now, but must not do any heavy lifting, or any sword fighting until the wound was fully healed.

"You're young, and so ye're healing fast," she told him, "but ye're going to have a terrible scar, I'm thinking, for I didna have the right needle to stitch it."

"What are the right needles?" he asked. He'd assumed a needle was a needle, and hadn't realised there was any difference between them except in length, until she showed him the package of surgical needles that had arrived from Edinburgh.

"I'd broken my last one, and had meant to write to Francis asking him to send more. I'm sorry I didna."

"Dinna be sorry. Ye saved my hand. I can move it as normal, will be able to fight again, that's all that matters. I'm sure I'll win more scars in time," he said matter-of-factly. "And it's a good reminder," he added, looking at it ruefully, although he did not say what it was a good reminder of.

At home the boys did their tasks as usual, cooked, ate together, taught Angus more letters and numbers, played a lot of games with him, and read to him before he went to bed. The current book was *Travels into Several Remote Nations of the World* by Lemuel Gulliver, a copy of which Francis had enclosed with the curved needles, and which Susan lent to the boys, as they had finished *Robinson Crusoe* and wanted something Angus could enjoy too. Mr Gulliver's book would please a small child, although in reality it was a brutal political satire, if you were reading it as an adult.

When Angus had finally fallen asleep Duncan and Alex would lie together in bed, talking about the affairs of the day, about what they had to do tomorrow, about anything pleasant. What they did not mention was that they both knew the current happiness in the house, which had seen Angus become his normal happy self again instead of the anxious subdued boy he'd been since the sword incident, was temporary. For in a few weeks their father would return and life would once again become unbearable.

So it was, that one day in the second week after the clansmen's departure, Alex, sitting on his rock at the water's edge, finally came to his decision, one he'd been pondering since Duncan's beating. He'd gone over and over every possible alternative, but now realised that there was really only one thing he could do, and that was to leave, and to do it while his father was away.

He could no longer continue living with his father. Every morning he woke up to a black pit of despair, and it took all his energy just to drag himself out of bed. Watching Duncan become brooding instead of thoughtful, and the happy outgoing Angus become tense and silent was killing him, especially as he was sure much of his father's enduring bad mood was because he wanted rid of his eldest son.

Alex had no idea what he'd done to make his father hate him so, but he could bear it no more. Equally, watching the clan become grim and morose, dreading every meeting their chieftain called, was horrible. Maybe once he'd left his father would be happier, would become the man he had been before Ma died.

If all else failed, one day *he* would be chieftain, and when he was he would restore the trust and loyalty that bound the clan together, the joy in every small thing that made their otherwise precarious lives bearable.

But he had no idea how long it would be until that day came, and if he waited here, by the time it did his spirit would be too crushed to restore anything. If he went away for a time he might be able to think clearly again, and would gain experience of a different way of life. His father would no doubt be relieved to be rid of him, as he would no longer have to go on these dangerous raids to pay for his education. He would probably be kinder to Duncan and Angus too once the main reason for his hatred was gone.

Now certain that he was making the right decision, Alex leapt up from the rock and ran home. He would pack what he needed and then leave immediately, for if he didn't he might lose his resolve. Duncan had gone fishing on the loch, taking Angus with him for the first time. They would not be back for hours, and he would be long gone by then. It would be better that way, for if he had to say goodbye to them he might not feel able to leave. He would write a note explaining what he was doing and why. Duncan, who knew him so well, would understand.

Once home he immediately set to packing the basic things he would need for a three-day walk, and then, remembering, rummaged in the chest at the foot of his father's bed, pulling out the outfit he had worn when he'd visited Edinburgh with his father. Holding it up, he realised immediately that there was no point in trying it on – it was far too small. He would have to enter the city as a Highlander, and deal with the consequences.

He was putting it back when he saw his father's costume neatly folded at the bottom. He took it out, unfolded it and held the coat up against him. Then he took off his belt, let his *féileadh mór* drop to the ground, and put on the breeches, stockings and waistcoat. He had to roll the breeches up slightly so that they were not too long, and use his belt to stop them falling over his hips, but otherwise they almost fitted him. The waistcoat was loose in the body, but that would not be obvious when he wore the coat.

The frockcoat was a different matter though, designed as it was to fit tightly across Alexander's shoulders and arms, which were broad and heavily muscled from years of physical labour and weapons use. It hung on Alex like a sack, but even so, he had not realised just how much he had grown in the last four years until this moment. It was too big, but he would grow into it, and would be less conspicuous walking round the streets in that than in clothing that marked him out as a savage Highlander. He had no wish to attract attention in the city. He wanted to blend in, rent a room, hopefully find work and then learn about life in a city at his own pace, rather than being thrown into a foreign city in a country with different customs and a different language, as his father wished.

He was just unfastening the frockcoat when the door opened and Duncan walked in. Alex jumped guiltily and then turned, watching as Duncan stood in the doorway taking in the clothes his brother was wearing and the look of extreme guilt on his face.

"Ye're leaving, then," he said, and Alex flushed.

"I thought ye were out fishing wi' Angus," Alex replied, gazing past Duncan as he did.

"He's wi' Alasdair, learning about music," Duncan said. "He had a strange turn in the boat. He's good now," he added, seeing the look of concern on his brother's face. "We'd only been on the loch a few minutes when he got awfu' sick of a sudden. I didna ken anyone could really turn green, but he did. He was sick the whole time we were on the boat, so I took him back to land, for he couldna do anything but vomit and moan. I was going to take him to Susan, for he couldna even walk, but then Alasdair came by and tellt us that he'd seen it before, but only on a sea voyage. He said it's called seasickness. I didna believe him at first, but after a wee while Angus stopped vomiting. He was still a bit shaky and pale, but he asked to go to hear the fiddle. So he went wi' Alasdair, and I came back here. I was going to ask if ye wanted to go fishing instead, but I can see ye dinna."

Alex sighed.

"I canna stay, Duncan," he said. "I…I canna rightly explain how I feel, but—"

"Ye dinna need to. I ken how ye feel, and I dinna blame ye. But I didna think ye'd leave without saying goodbye at least. He'll be heartbroken if ye do, ye ken that?"

"Aye, I do. I didna think I'd be able to leave if I had to say goodbye to him, or to you. I was going to leave a wee letter explaining. I thought it would be easier, but I see now it's a coward's trick."

"No it isna, for ye're right, there's no way ye could explain that he'd understand," Duncan said, relenting at the sight of his brother's face. "He'd want to go with ye, and he canna do that if ye've already gone. I'll explain it to him. Where are ye going?"

When Alex didn't answer, Duncan laughed bitterly.

"Ye dinna trust me, even?" he said.

"I trust ye, of course I do!" Alex retorted immediately. "But if ye dinna ken, then Da canna command ye to tell him where I am."

"I wouldna tell him if he did," Duncan replied, causing Alex to stare at him wide-eyed.

"But ye'd have to! He's your chieftain!"

"No, he isna," Duncan said, deadly serious now. "Ye're my chieftain, or ye will be. I've always kent that. One day ye'll be chieftain and I'll be your right-hand man, and chieftain in your name if ye're away. My loyalty's to you, no' him. He doesna deserve my loyalty. Ye're going to Edinburgh?"

"Aye," Alex admitted, touched beyond words by what his brother had just said.

Duncan nodded.

"Will ye be coming back?"

"I was hoping to send for you and Angus to join me, once I've found a place to live and some way to support myself. I couldna expect Angus to live as we might have to at first, or I'd take ye with me now. Would ye come?" Alex asked.

"For you I would, although I canna imagine living in such a place as that," Duncan said, shuddering even at the thought of living in the city.

"I canna think where else to go, except another town. I canna go to another clan, for I'll always be a MacGregor, and their chieftain may be as bad as Da is, or worse. I'd stay here rather than do that. And in the city I'll learn things that might be useful."

"How to talk wi' those nobles Da used to say ye'd meet one day."

Alex laughed.

"Aye, like yon baronet mannie wi' all the paint." He bowed elaborately then, and held his arm up, limp-wristed. "Good Lord, what on earth are you doing, sir?" he simpered in perfect imitation of the baronet they'd encountered when Alexander had been teaching them how to fight on a spiral stair. They both giggled, and the mood lightened somewhat. "I dinna think yon baronet could lift the proscription though," he added.

"Ye'll need money to go through the Netherbow Port," Duncan said, "and to rent a room and buy food, until ye can find work. Take some of Da's."

"I canna do that!" Alex said. "I willna steal from him."

"Ye're taking his suit," Duncan pointed out logically. "And the money's for your education anyway. He's tellt ye that many times. Send it back to him, along wi' his clothes, once ye can," he added, seeing Alex still hesitate. "Then ye're only borrowing it. Write to Susan when ye're ready for us to come to ye."

"To Susan?" Alex said.

"Aye. She's trustworthy, and she's the only member of the clan who receives letters from Edinburgh, from Dr Ogilvy, so no one will think on it if she gets another one. This is why ye need me as your right-hand man," Duncan said dryly. "One of us has to be able to think before acting."

Alex laughed, then turned suddenly and took his brother in a bearhug, clinging to him.

"Christ, I'll miss ye," he said, his voice trembling. "I canna imagine living without ye by my side."

"Ye'd have to anyway if Da sent ye to Paris, for he canna afford to send me too, and I wouldna leave Angus here alone wi' him. We'll come to ye, when ye ask." He pulled himself from Alex's grip then, though it cost him to do so, recognising that his brother was on the point of changing his mind. "Go," he said, "before Angus comes back. I dinna ken how long he'll stay at Alasdair's."

Alex swallowed back the tears that threatened and smiled weakly.

"I'll no' make ye and Angus wait long," he said, folding the suit and wrapping it in a blanket along with his food and the money that Duncan now handed to him. He reached for his sword, then left it, remembering the Disarming Act, and that a boy of his age would not be allowed to wear a sword in Edinburgh in any case.

Then he went to the door, glancing out to see if anyone was around to see him go, half-hoping they would be so he could see them one last time, half-dreading it, knowing his resolve to go was trickling away fast.

"The whole clan's waiting, Alex," Duncan said. "Ye ken that, d'ye no'?"

Alex looked back at him.

"Tell them they're wasting their time. Da's no' coming back to us. No' after four years," he said. He clasped his brother's hand tightly, then releasing it walked away quickly, before his resolve crumbled. It would be easier when he was out of the settlement, he told himself.

Duncan watched him until he'd disappeared into the September mist shrouding the lochside. If he did not already know that the clan were not waiting for Alexander to come back to them, but for Alex to grow up, then Duncan knew it was not for him to explain it.

When he realised that for himself, he would grow up. And then he would come home. Or they would come home, if they'd already joined him in Edinburgh.

Duncan turned and went into the house, already feeling unutterably lonely, both wanting Angus to come home to fill the silence with chatter, and dreading it, because he had no idea of how to tell him that the brother he worshipped above all others had gone, and he did not know when they would see him again.

* * *

Edinburgh, September 1729

Alex arrived in Edinburgh three days later, the sentry allowing him through the Netherbow Port without comment, for although his clothes were a little too big for him they were clean, as was he, having washed himself thoroughly in a burn before changing out of his dirty *fèileadh mòr* and shirt into his father's outfit.

On the journey from Loch Lomond he had decided it would be safer to walk by night and sleep by day, hiding in the heather or woodlands, but in fact he had hardly slept at all, aware as he was of his vulnerability to attack by anyone passing if he did. On the final day he had dozed a little, but had woken up at every sound, with the result that although the icy water of the burn had woken him up a bit, as he walked past the Tron Kirk he felt the heavy lethargy of exhaustion slowing both his mind and body.

Realising that he needed to sleep more than anything else right now, and that he would be even more unsafe doing so on the streets of the city than he had been in the mountains and glens, his first priority was to obtain a room. He was hungry and cold too, but these were very minor issues, things he lived with on a daily basis. His exhaustion was not, for he knew he had to keep his wits about him until he understood how life worked here, and could not afford to have them as dull as they were right now.

The question was, how? On the way here he had rejected the idea of going to Mrs Grant, the woman who had rented his father a room last time, as it was clear she was a busybody and would no doubt inform Alexander that his son was here at the earliest opportunity. She must have a means of corresponding with him, as she'd been expecting them to arrive, and Allan had known exactly where they'd be staying when he came with the news of Ma's illness.

He rejected the idea of going to ask a church minister, as all the churches here were either Episcopalian or Presbyterian as far as he knew, and if they asked questions to determine his faith they'd no doubt know him for a Catholic immediately, something his da had said he must never reveal.

In the end he went to Jenny Ha's, the little tavern his da had had the meeting with the Jacobites at, even though it meant going back out of the Netherbow Port. Maybe they would know of a place he could stay, and he would feel safer asking at an inn that welcomed Jacobites.

When he walked into the tavern the main room was crowded with people, many of them already well in their cups, having indulged freely in the claret the tavern was famous for. Alex made his way to the counter through the rowdy crowd with some difficulty, refusing a drink as he knew it would make him even more sleepy, and asked the friendly looking if busy barmaid if she knew of a room to let.

"How much are ye thinking to pay, laddie?" she asked.

"I dinna ken," Alex replied honestly. "How much does a room cost? I dinna want anything fancy – just a place to sleep. But I'm wanting it for a week, maybe more."

She stopped then, assessing him.

"Ye're new in the town, are ye, hoping to find work?"

"I am," he said, warming to her friendly attitude.

"Ye've the money to pay, then? Or are ye expecting to live free until ye've found employment?"

"No, I have the money to pay, if it's no' a costly room," he assured her, wishing he knew how much his father had paid for the four nights they'd stayed.

"Right then. I'm busy now, as ye can see, but if ye wait until nine when I finish work, I'll take ye to someone who might have a place for ye. I canna swear to it, mind," she added.

He thanked her, and then she disappeared into the crowd, leaving him feeling awkward and out of place amidst the bustle of people who seemed to all know each other. He supposed that he'd be expected to buy a drink if he stayed, so instead he went outside again, thinking to wait in the street for her to finish her work. He had no idea what time it was now, or when nine would be, but assumed that on finishing work she would leave the building and he would see her.

He sat down on the street near the door, his back against the wall, intending to observe the street life while he waited. But after a short time he found his eyes closing, so decided to stand up rather than risk falling asleep on the street. As he stood two men came out of the tavern, and seeing him, walked over.

"Begging your pardon sir, but Isobel, the barmaid ye were asking about a room," one of the men said as they reached him, "she sent us out to tell ye that she'll most likely be late finishing work tonight, but didna want to keep ye waiting, so asked us to take ye to her friend wi' the room to let. She thinks there'll be no problem finding ye a bed for the night."

"Oh, that's awfu' kind of her," Alex said.

"Aye, she's a kind wee lassie, renowned for it, ye might say," the second man commented, and they both grinned as though that was a joke, although Alex failed to comprehend it.

The men looked respectable enough to him, one tall but very thin, with pale ginger hair tied in a neat ponytail at the nape of his neck, the other shorter than Alex but stocky, with dark hair. They were both as neatly dressed as he was, except their clothes fitted them.

Realising that he was probably feeling more cautious than was called for due to his unfamiliarity with the territory, he decided to trust them, to a point at least. After all, the tavern was near to the palace, and the king would not have lived in a squalid part of the town. And the men were polite enough, walking ahead of him rather than behind as he'd expect them to do if they were footpads. Even so, he reached inside his shirt and palmed the small knife he was carrying under his armpit in his left hand, while undoing the button on the special pocket his father had had made in the breeches to hold his dirk.

They passed through the Netherbow Port, the two men paying for themselves then waiting for Alex to pay his way, which reassured him a little. If they'd been trying to rob him, surely they would have asked him to pay for them, as they were doing him a favour? He relaxed a little, and felt the tiredness wash through him, intensified by the knowledge that in a few minutes he would be able to lie down and sleep for as long as he wanted to.

After a minute they turned down one of the dark and gloomy narrow wynds, close to where Alex had lodged with his da last time. Alex hoped that Isobel's friend wasn't Mrs Grant, as that would be a problem. They turned left and then right, and then suddenly the two men stopped, stepping apart then backwards as though performing a dance step of some kind, and in noting their strange movement Alex was instantly fully awake. He took in the fact that the wynd appeared to be uninhabited, that ahead of him was a dead end, and that the two men were stepping backward so as to be on each side of him, which could only mean one thing.

As they stepped backward a second time he exploded into action, drawing his dirk as he leapt forward between them, before turning to face them, letting the palmed knife slide from his sleeve into his hand, although he did not show he was armed.

The two men glanced at each other, and then the ginger-haired one smiled, holding his hand up in a conciliatory gesture.

"Now, laddie, be sensible," he said, "for ye're raw here, that's clear, and ye've no friends, or ye wouldna be asking strangers for a room. Just give us your coin and we'll leave ye unharmed, but wiser for meeting us."

When Alex didn't reply to this, instead weighing up his options, whether he could knock them apart and make a run for it, reason with them maybe, they exchanged another glance.

We dinna want to harm ye," the ginger-haired man continued, "for we ken ye're young, and we wouldna—"

In that moment, clearly hoping Alex would be distracted by the speaker, the dark-haired man moved toward him and Alex saw the blade glitter in his hand. Instinct, helped by years of practice with Kenneth took over, and Alex stepped forward and to the left of the man to keep away from his weapon, drawing his left hand up and across the man's neck as he did before leaping sideways to avoid any sudden thrust. Then he ran forward, taking the speaker by surprise and driving his dirk into the man's chest before he had time to unsheathe his own knife from his belt.

Alex pulled his dirk from the man's body, watching as he dropped to the ground like a stone, and then turned to see the other man writhing in the filth of the wynd, clutching his throat, blood pouring through his fingers. He looked along the wynd, saw it was deserted, and then up at the tall buildings to either side of him. No candles were burning in any of the windows, and there was no sound of life at all. Even if someone was looking down, it would be too dark in the street for them to identify him.

And then he ran full tilt back down the wynd, turning left and then right, before stopping in a doorway to conceal his weapons and fasten his coat, after which he took a few deep breaths to steady himself before walking casually back out on to the High Street, which was thronged with people about their business, none of whom paid any attention to him. Even so he knew it could not be long before the bodies were found. This was a city after all, not a lonely glen. There were people *everywhere*.

He walked resolutely as though he had a clear destination in mind, his thoughts racing. If nothing else, this incident had taught him that he absolutely could not sleep on the street. And he absolutely could not ask any more strangers about rooms.

He was about to give in and head to Mrs Grant's anyway, reasoning that even if she did write to him, his da was unlikely to travel all the way to Edinburgh for a son he wanted rid of, when he passed by a close which made him hesitate, for the name was familiar to him.

Niddry's Row.

And then he remembered, and sent up a silent prayer of thanks before turning into the street. Stopping at a house halfway down it he rang the brass bell outside, remembering the last time he'd been here, four years ago, although in many ways it seemed so much longer.

The door opened and for a moment Alex was nonplussed, having expected to need to reason with the suspicious maid. Instead he looked into the green eyes of the man who had accompanied them from this house all the way to Loch Lomond, to try to save his mother. With an effort he managed to stop himself falling into the man's arms in relief, not least because by the look on his face it was clear that though Alex MacGregor had recognised Francis Ogilvy immediately, the reverse was not the case.

"Oh, my dear boy, you are injured!" Dr Ogilvy cried, his gaze having passed professionally over his visitor, stopping at the sight of the blood staining his sleeve and hand. "Come in. You have come to the right place. Margaret!" he called, and a young woman appeared almost immediately through a door to the right of the hallway. "Fetch hot water and my bag, immediately. Come sir, and I'm sure we will have you well again in no time." As he was saying all this, he moved across to a door on the left, leading Alex into a sumptuous room then indicating he should sit at a table to the right, on which an oil lamp burned, its light illuminating an open book which Dr Ogilvy had presumably been reading before being interrupted.

Alex followed the man, not attempting to interrupt him until the door was safely shut and they were alone. Then he raised his left arm, saw the spatter of blood up the sleeve and the already crusting spots on his hands.

"Dr Ogilvy, sir, d'ye no' recognise me?" he asked.

Dr Ogilvy, in the process of moving the book from the table, intending to treat his visitor's wound there, stopped and looked across at Alex.

"My apologies. I see so many people, as I'm sure you'll understand, that I cannot remember all of them. But I'm certain I've not *treated* you before, for I always remember my patients. Did I perhaps help a relative of yours?"

The warmth of the fire, the utter luxury of the room he was in, with its rich red patterned carpet, mahogany chairs and tables, and bookshelves full of more books than Alex had dreamed existed in the world, coupled with fatigue and delayed shock, suddenly rendered him dizzy, and he sat down heavily on a chair, not wanting to humiliate himself by fainting.

"Put your head between your legs," Dr Ogilvy said at once. "Shock can make the strongest man faint, as can blood loss."

"No," said Alex, as the doctor moved forward to assist him. "I'm only tired, sir. Ye treated my mother, or would have done if she'd lived long enough. In Loch Lomond. I see ye remember now." He smiled grimly, seeing the recognition flare in Francis's eyes. "I dinna blame ye for no' remembering me, for I was a boy then, and now…" His voice trailed off as he realised he was no longer sure what he was. Not a boy, that was certain, not after tonight. But a man would surely not feel the utter desolation he felt right now, accompanied by the relief at seeing a vaguely familiar face.

"Alex MacGregor," Francis Ogilvy said.

The woman Margaret came in with a porcelain bowl and a jug of hot water, while another girl followed with the doctor's bag. He thanked them, then waited until they'd gone, and the door was closed again, which told Alex he could trust the man. He smiled wearily.

"I'm Alex Drummond here, no' MacGregor. I'm sorry to come to ye, sir, but I didna ken where else to go. Ye dinna need the bag, for I'm no' injured, although I can use the water to wash off the blood, if ye'll let me," Alex said, standing again now the momentary weakness had passed, taking off the offending coat and scrutinising the bloodstains. "I'm thinking it'll wash out, for the blood hasna dried yet," he said matter-of-factly.

"I see," Francis said, making Alex look up. Tired as he was, he recognised the change in tone, and what it signified.

"If ye'll let me just wash my sleeve and my hand, sir, I'll leave directly. I wasna thinking rightly, for I havena slept in three days, but I've no wish to bring trouble to you. You were very kind when Ma died, and I'm grateful for that." He picked up the cloth that was in the bowl, poured some water onto it, quickly washed his hands and then started dabbing at the blood on the coat.

"You said you didn't know where else to go. I take it you have no lodging for the night then?" Francis asked.

"No. It's due to that that this…never mind, sir. Better ye dinna ken what happened."

"Alex," Francis said firmly, causing Alex to stop spreading the blood around and look at him again. "Your father treated me very well, as did your clan, and both you and your brother took good care of me on the journey. I'm truly sorry that I couldn't save your mother, for it was clear to me that she was very dearly loved."

"Aye, she was indeed, sir. But ye couldna have saved her, even had we arrived earlier. Susan tellt me that."

"That's true. But now I have another opportunity, I think. You can stay here for the night, and sleep safely. I'll ask Elspeth to prepare a cold collation for you."

Alex had no idea what a cold collation was, but if it was either edible or a place to lie down in it would be welcome.

"No, wait," he said, as Francis moved to the door to call for Elspeth. "Before ye agree to let me sleep here, I must in fairness repay the trust you're showing me and tell ye something, and if ye ask me to leave, I'll understand and go immediately."

Francis continued to the door, ordered the food and then came back, sitting down opposite Alex.

"Tell me then," he said. "I doubt you'll shock me, for I've not lived a sheltered life."

Nevertheless after Alex had finished his story it was clear that he *had* succeeded in shocking the doctor, who sat back in the chair and passed his hand across his eyes.

"Both of them? On your own?" he asked disbelievingly.

"Aye. They thought I was some feeble-minded farm boy from the Lowlands, I'm thinking," Alex said. "They didna see me as a danger, or they'd no' have acted as they did. Da tellt me the city people think the Highlanders all to be savages."

"Some of them do, certainly," Francis agreed.

"Well, if these did, they certainly didna think *I* was a Highlander, or I'm thinking they'd have killed me directly, no' have talked wi' me first."

"Do you really think they'd have killed you anyway, if you'd given them your money?" Francis asked.

Alex pondered this, clearly having not thought about it before.

"I dinna ken," he admitted after a minute. "But it doesna signify, for I wasna giving them my money, in any case. And they didna need to take me to such a lonely place if they werena thinking on violence. I'm glad of that, for no one saw me, and they'll no' try to rob another young laddie."

A maid appeared with the cold collation, which turned out to be food, so once again conversation stopped while she laid the tray on the table, arranged everything, then left. While Alex ate, Francis moved to a chair by the fireplace, to allow his guest to enjoy the food and to give himself time to think.

On one level he was very aware of what he, as a respected Edinburgh citizen, should do, which was to call on the authorities and tell them where the apparently cold-blooded killer of two men in a nearby alley could be found. If he did that he would be congratulated and the killer arrested. Then Alex would be held in jail for a lengthy amount of time, after which, if he hadn't already died of jail fever or some other disease, he would be tried, and most likely hung. If he was discovered to be a MacGregor, he would definitely be hung. And Francis would be able to rest assured that he had done the right thing.

Francis snorted to himself at this thought, causing the subject of his ruminations to look across at him.

"I'm sorry. I'm just thinking out loud. Enjoy your meal. We can talk again afterwards," he said, noting how quickly Alex focussed back on the cold meats and cheeses laid before him. He had not lied about being hungry, that was certain.

In fact, having spent several days with the MacGregors four years ago, he doubted that the boy was lying about anything. He observed him now, remembering the helplessness he'd felt as he'd watched the woman's fingers relax in this boy's small hand as she died, remembering how hospitable the whole clan had been, remembering the clean clear Highland air, a pair of warm brown eyes, and the peaty taste of the whisky in his mouth. And he knew then exactly what he was going to do.

The boy he remembered was now almost a man, as tall as him, coltish but already powerful, the childish hands now large, with long strong fingers. Hands that had just killed two human beings, and a mind that seemed to accept that completely. If he had walked for three days alone to arrive in Edinburgh with nowhere to stay, then there was something very wrong at Loch Lomond. Susan lived at Loch Lomond.

"What has happened to bring you here?" Francis blurted out.

Alex stopped eating and looked across at his host.

"It's a personal matter, sir, between myself and my father. I can tell ye the part of it, if ye need to ken," he said uneasily.

Did he need to ken? No, Francis thought. Not immediately, at any rate.

"No. I'm sorry. You're very tired. You can stay here tonight. In fact Elspeth has arranged for a fire to be lit in one of the bedrooms for you. You'll be safe here, so sleep as long as you want. In the morning we can discuss what to do next."

Alex looked out of the window at the now completely dark street.

"Are ye sure? For I wouldna want to cause ye problems, if the men are found. In the morning I'll away to the chieftain, or whoever acts as chieftain in a city, and explain what happened. I'll no' mention I stayed here. But I'll leave directly, if you're no' happy," Alex said.

To his surprise, Francis laughed, at the pure innocence of that remark.

"No. I'm very sure. But I would ask you to promise me one thing," Francis said. Alex waited. "When you wake up, whatever time that is, come in here and have breakfast, and do not leave to go to the authorities – the chieftain, if you will. You must speak with me first, for you need to learn things about the city before you make your decision. Indeed your life will depend on it. I won't tell you now, for it's plain that you're reeling with fatigue. Do you agree?"

Alex smiled.

"I do, sir, for I think it's a kindness you're doing."

Once in bed, in a room containing more furniture than was in his father's whole house, Alex lay for a minute, looking at the ceiling and marvelling that he felt no guilt at all at taking the lives of the two would-be thieves. They had threatened his life and he had defended himself, and there was an end of it. If they had succeeded in killing him, they would certainly have thought no more of it either. This must be what it was like to be a man.

Or to be tired to the point of collapse.

He closed his eyes, and collapsed.

* * *

"Ah! Good morning!" Francis said by way of greeting when his visitor finally appeared in the library as promised the next day, although in truth it was close to noon. "I normally eat in the breakfast room, or dining room, but we will be more private in here," he said. Observing his visitor's bemused look, he added, "The servants are more likely to overhear what we say if we're in a different room. How is your hand? I noticed you flexing your fingers last night, and saw the scar. It's a recent wound, is it not?"

"It is, sir. Susan treated it for me. She tellt me she'd asked ye for special needles, afterwards. It's a wee bit stiff, but she did tell me no' to practice swordfighting until it was completely healed." His mouth twisted wryly.

"Well, it seems you had no choice in the matter. I can look at it later, if you wish."

Alex nodded and sat down opposite the doctor, in a chair near the fire.

"Ye have a different room to eat every meal in?" he asked, not wanting to talk further about the scar and how he got it.

"Not *every* meal. Just breakfast and dinner. Supper I usually have in here, as a matter of fact. I spend a lot of time in this room."

"Why?" Alex asked. "Why do ye need two rooms to eat in? Can ye no' eat dinner in the same room as breakfast? I would spend a lot of time in this room too, if I lived here," he added, looking round in wonder. "Are all these books yours, or d'ye have a bookshop?"

Francis leaned forward, putting his elbows on his knees and his chin in his cupped hands.

"They're all mine," he said. "But if you stay here, you may read any book you wish."

Alex stopped looking round the room at this, focussing on his visitor instead.

"I canna stay here, sir," he said. "Ye've been very kind, but I ken there's no need here of the custom Highlanders have of giving shelter to anyone who asks, for ye willna die in a street as ye might on a mountain or glen in winter. Da tellt me that."

"And yet you nearly did die last night," Francis observed.

"Well, aye," Alex agreed, not having thought of it that way. "But I dinna want to inconvenience ye, so if ye can introduce me to someone who has a room I can rent, and ye ken anyone who might have work for me, I would be very grateful."

"What kind of work can you do?" Francis asked, remembering that Susan had told him how prickly Highlanders were about matters of pride. He would have to approach this carefully.

"I dinna ken. I havena lived in a city. I was thinking to maybe work on one of yon farms outside, but this isna the season for such work. It's no' the time I'd have chosen to come here. But I'm strong for my age, and I learn fast. I'm intending to spend my evenings in my room teaching myself Greek, if I can buy a primer, so work labouring or lifting would be good, for I need to build my strength and I willna do that learning Greek."

"Why did you choose to come here, Alex?" Francis asked, picking one of the numerous questions this little speech had raised in his mind.

Alex thought for a minute, sifting through what he could and could not tell this man, before launching into a basic explanation of his father's grief, which had made him more distant from everyone, and which had caused the two of them to argue more and more as time went on.

"And so when Father Gordon, ye'll remember him, I'm thinking, sir, left, Da was awfu' angry, for he was set on sending me to university, but I didna have the Greek, and so he's away doing all these awfu' dangerous…er…things, so he can send me away as quickly as possible. We canna live together any more, for he hates me and I dinna ken why, so canna do anything about it. I thought if I left it might be easier for Duncan and Angus, and I can learn about the city, for I'll need to, if I'm to talk wi' nobles and persuade them to have the proscription lifted," he finished.

Francis sorted through this, realising that it had raised far more questions than it had answered. So, then. The bones of it were that Alexander had become subsumed in grief, something Francis had seen before, although more usually in an old person with no kin who had lived with their spouse for many years. And then it seemed that he and his son had clashed as the boy became a youth, which was normal in families where both father and son were natural leaders. That was enough to know for now.

"Very well, then," he said. "I won't ask you more for I have no wish to pry, and I don't need to know more. I would still like you to stay here. I have plenty of room, and I live alone, apart from the servants, and my evenings can be lonely. A little company would be very refreshing. So I would not be doing a duty, it would be a pleasure. As for work, I know a lot of people in the town, and can ask. I'm sure someone will have work for an honest, strong boy such as yourself.

"For your part, you will be completely safe here, and I know Greek, although I am very out of practice, so teaching you will be just the thing for me to brush up my knowledge. I'm sure I have a primer here somewhere, which I can give…loan you, until you have earned the money to buy your own. Really, that would give me the greatest pleasure." He saw Alex hesitating, still undecided, wanting to stay, but not wanting to be a burden. "When I came to Loch Lomond, your clan made me very welcome, even though I was unable to save your mother. I know I don't have to repay that hospitality, but I would very much like to, as I now have the opportunity," he added.

He had clearly said something right, for the boy relaxed visibly and then smiled at him, his slate-blue eyes smiling too for the first time. By God, but he was going to be a handsome man, Francis thought. He would not want for a wife, in time.

"Then I'll gladly accept your kindness, sir," Alex said. "Ye must tell me if ye want me to leave, for I wouldna want to impose on your goodness. But first I must go to the authorities, as ye tellt me the chief was called. If ye'll tell me where he lives, I'll go directly."

"Ah. About that," Francis said. "Let me call for breakfast for you, and then I need to give you your first lesson about the city."

The following hour ended with Alex having a stomach full of wonderful food and a head full of knowledge about the basics of the legal system in Lowland Scotland, which seemed to him a strange, complicated and profoundly unfair proceeding.

But he had decided three things: he would stay with this kind, trustworthy man, who was so clearly very lonely, as lonely as he himself was, just in a different way. And he absolutely would not go to the authorities, but would simply put the incident in the dark wynd out of his mind completely. Finally, he would keep well away from Jenny Ha's, as he now realised that the barmaid Isobel had most likely been in league with the thieves, and would probably recognise him again.

He now knew enough about the legal system to realise she would be no more likely to call on it than he was. But she no doubt had a clan, or what passed for a clan in cities, which he did not. He had been lucky to kill the two men, but he had no wish to face a whole clan alone. He had been very naïve yesterday, he realised now, but he was a very fast learner. Even his father, who saw no good in him, could not dispute that.

Whilst in Edinburgh, he would stay within the Netherbow Port.

CHAPTER NINETEEN

Edinburgh, October 1729

Alex and Francis had been sitting in the library at a table, on which was a lamp and a small pile of books, for a good two hours. Outside the rain pattered on the window and the wind howled down the close, but inside it was warm and cosy.

Finally Alex leaned back in the chair, yawned, and stretched his arms above his head, rotating his shoulders and feeling the muscles, tense from hours of hard physical work followed by hours of sitting still, start to release.

"Greek is much harder to learn than Latin," he observed, looking at the open book on the table with loathing.

"It is," Francis agreed. "Which is why you don't learn it until later in your education." He stood and walked across the room to a cabinet and took out a decanter of wine, pouring two glasses before coming back to the table and putting one down in front of his companion. "Shall we stop? We've both been working all day, and it's growing late."

"I'm sorry," Alex said at once. "It must be awfu' vexing for ye to treat patients all day, and then have to teach me in the evening too. Ye should have tellt me ye were tired."

"I'm not tired, and in truth it's a pleasure teaching you. I was thinking of you, for it's clear you're not enamoured with the language."

"No, I'm no', but I'm thinking it'll be more interesting once I can read it well," Alex said.

"Why are you so determined to learn it? It's not something you're likely to need if you're not thinking to go to university any more. You'll not need it to become a chieftain."

Alex combed his fingers through his hair and sighed.

"Aye, I ken that. My father was a good chieftain, and he didna have the Greek."

"So why bother? You're young, you should relax a little, maybe meet some boys of your own age, instead of learning ancient languages with an old man in the evenings," Francis suggested.

Alex's expression clearly expressed his view of that idea, even before he opened his mouth.

"I meet them when I'm working, and I've no wish to spend any more time wi' them than I have to," he said. "I've better things to spend my money on than whores and strong drink. I dinna think of ye as an old man at all. Ye're interesting to be with, unlike the wee gomerels at The White Horse."

"Are you not enjoying the work?" Francis asked.

"Oh, the work is easy enough, and it's interesting to be paid in money, to learn the cost of things. That's no' something I'm accustomed to, but it's the way of the world, is it no'? All things have their price," Alex replied.

Alex had only agreed to take up Francis's offer to stay with him if he could find work and pay his way. Francis had been going to suggest that Alex could work as his assistant, but that would not help to build his muscles. Within a week he had managed to get him the perfect job, by calling in a favour, although he did not tell Alex that.

The White Horse called itself an inn, serving food and drink and offering accommodation to anyone entering the city from the south, but only a desperate traveller would stay in its dingy rooms. It did, however, provide good stabling for horses, and adequate meals for strangers to recuperate a little before going about their business in the city. For four days a week Alex unsaddled horses, mucked out the stables, carried sacks of foodstuff about, and did any other necessary menial tasks. Which suited him perfectly, as it gave him plenty of physical exercise, left him tired enough in the evenings that he usually fell asleep quickly, and kept him too busy to think about how much he was missing home.

The problem was occupying the three days he was not working. After three weeks of staying with Francis, he had settled into a pattern of reading as many books as he could, borrowed from his host's wonderful library, practicing his fighting skills out in the small garden at the rear of the house, and exploring the city. He now knew every wynd and close, the price of most things in the Luckenbooths, was on friendly terms with a good number of tradesmen, and had speculated on the weak points of the castle before climbing up the castle rock one evening on impulse and discovering that it was not as difficult to do as he'd expected. There were a good number of sentries patrolling the wall though, and as he had no wish to be arrested Alex had silently climbed back down, which had been a much more difficult endeavour. He was becoming accustomed to the stench and the constant sound of people, too. In fact very few people would have known now that he was a relative newcomer to the city, a state he'd worked hard to attain.

It was the nights that were the hardest part of living here. Because once in bed, unless he was totally exhausted he would be immediately transported back to the banks of Loch Lomond, and would yearn to be there in reality with an intensity that was physically painful. He missed his brothers terribly, missed speaking the Gaelic, missed the laughter, the good-natured camaraderie that comes from living with a small group of people who know each other intimately. He missed the soft feel of grass and the springy feel of the heather under his feet, the caress of the icy waters of the loch against his body, and the sound of the women singing as they worked.

In the days he could tell himself he was on an adventure, was learning about life, was enjoying the many new experiences. But in the long dark nights, tossing and turning in his luxurious feather bed, he knew he was fooling himself, for he was so homesick he thought he might die of it.

"I have to go home," he said now, impulsively, then blushed. "I'm sorry," he added. "I dinna mean right now. I'm truly grateful for what ye've done for me. But one day I have to go home."

Francis sat back in his chair. He had thought Alex was settling in well, but having watched him lost in thought for a few minutes, a myriad of expressions crossing his face, he now realised that the boy was just accomplished at hiding his feelings.

"Alex, you don't need to pretend you love Edinburgh when you're with me," he said. "I don't own the town, and I have no loyalty to it. I'm not offended if you hate the place."

Alex looked at him in shock.

"But…were ye no' born here?" he asked.

"No, although I've lived here since I was very young, younger than you are now. I know that the Highlanders are bound to their land. Susan told me that. And I'm sure many of the Lowlanders are too. But I'm not. I've shocked you."

"Aye. I canna imagine no' having a place that's home, a place where ye feel ye truly belong," Alex replied.

"I belong here. But I could belong in another city, I think, as long as there were people who needed my help. It's my profession that is my home, if you like. If I couldn't practice medicine, I would be desperately unhappy."

Alex sat for a minute thinking this through, as he made a point of doing nowadays, instead of just rushing on to the next thing as he'd done in the past.

"I hadna thought about it in that way," he said after a time. "But I'm thinking now that if I was to go home and discover that the whole clan had moved to another glen, then I'd no' just live at Loch Lomond alone, but would follow the clan. So it's no' just the land, but the people too. I miss them, dreadfully," he admitted softly.

"Why do you not go home, then? You're welcome to stay here as long as you like," Francis added quickly, in case Alex thought he was trying to get rid of him, "but if you're so homesick, why not go back?"

"No," Alex said, with certainty. "I'll no' go back until I can…until it's the right time."

"Do you know when that will be?"

When I can challenge my father for the chieftainship, and have a chance of beating him.

But he would not say that. Even *thinking* it seemed disloyal at the moment. He hoped that was because the thought was relatively new to him. He had come here initially because he could no longer live with a father who so clearly found him a disappointment, who hated him, and he was saving money so that one day he could bring his brothers here too, make a new life with them in the city and eventually forget about Loch Lomond.

And then, three nights ago, while lying in bed staring at the ceiling and listening to the faint sounds of people talking as they passed beneath his window, he had remembered Duncan's final words to him. And then he'd remembered Allan's comment outside the sheep byre, when Alex had admitted he was learning everything for when he became chieftain - *That's a good thing then. Ye'll be needing them;* and Kenneth's comment down by the loch – *a chieftain doesna always have to die before he's replaced.* And suddenly it hit him. Rather than the clan waiting for Alexander to come to his senses, had Duncan meant that the whole clan was waiting for *him* to be old enough to take over as chieftain, because they no longer wanted Alexander to lead them?

He had lain there into the small hours, going over all the times in the last years, since Ma had died, when the clansfolk had seemed less than happy with Da's commands, and there were a lot of them. Times when people had exchanged disbelieving looks, had risen from a clan meeting silently, resigned rather than enthusiastic about participating in whatever raid he'd decided they were going on.

The clan system was wonderful if the chieftain was a fair and responsible man, as his father had been. Everyone stood together, supported each other, which they did not do in the town, not as a matter of course. But when the chieftain was unfair and irresponsible, it could be hell. Because the only way to remove such a chieftain was for someone to challenge him, and not only win, but have the clan behind him when he did.

It was clear now that the whole clan *was* behind him and was waiting, and that Duncan knew that and had been waiting for Alex to know that too. Now, in the middle of an Edinburgh night, he did, and because of that everything had changed. It was exhilarating; it was terrifying. But now he knew it, he could not ignore it. He had to grow up, and fast, become the chieftain the clan deserved, because his father was lost to them, and it seemed he was not coming back.

In that moment his reason for growing muscle, for improving his sword skills, even for learning Greek, had changed. He was no longer doing it in order to return home like the Prodigal Son, so accomplished that his father would realise what a perfect son he was and would love him again. That was a ridiculous, childish dream, he realised now

The following morning he had risen, tired, but determined now to become such an exemplary man that even Alexander could not deny he would lead the MacGregors better than anyone else, better than him. For Alex did not wish to fight his father. Not unless he had absolutely no alternative.

He started, coming back to the present moment, and was just about to say that he could manage another hour of Greek, when Francis closed the book, placing it on top of the pile on the table, picked up his wine glass, and moved to the chaise longue by the fireplace.

"I've been thinking," he said, beckoning Alex to join him, "if you're wanting to be accepted by the nobility, maybe to one day meet the king and have him treat you with respect, you need more than Greek, you know."

"Aye, I ken that," Alex said, moving across the room and sitting opposite Francis. "My Latin is good now, and I ken about all manner of things, history, geography, and Father Gordon taught me Cicero, so I ken how to speak persuasively, in theory at least. I'm thinking that if I read all your books, I'll be able to talk about any subject."

"You could do that now," Francis told him, "for most nobles, in my experience, are far less intelligent than you. Indeed the king is far less intelligent than you."

"Ye've met the *king?*" Alex said excitedly.

"I have. Not the current one, but his father."

"What manner of man was he?"

"A very tedious one. He couldn't speak English well, which made things very difficult, for I couldn't speak German, and had no wish to learn."

"Ah," said Alex, a world of disappointment in that one syllable. Francis looked up.

"Oh. You thought I meant James?"

"Aye. I would love to meet him, although I dinna expect I ever will."

"Of course. You are a Jacobite," Francis said.

"I am. You're for the Elector then?" Alex answered, tense now.

"No. In truth, it makes little difference to me who is on the throne, although I would prefer a good man who cares for the countries he rules, which George – the previous George – did not. It's a little early to know whether his son will be a better man. You can relax. I knew the MacGregors were for James. It had slipped my mind, that's all. I think no differently towards you, nor will I run about telling the world you are a traitor! I have better ways of occupying my time. Although I would advise you not to tell anyone else of your allegiance."

Alex smiled then, because although he had only known Francis for a few weeks, he thought highly of the man and could not imagine him running around spreading malicious gossip.

"But I digress. What I am trying to say is that the nobility is much like an exclusive club. And to keep it exclusive they have a lot of rules, which they teach to their members but no one else. Their children are brought up with them, just as you are brought up to learn the clan ways. If you try to join their club, or to sneak in, and you don't know the rules, it becomes very obvious very quickly, and you will be rejected, or mocked. And that will not help you to become accepted enough to influence those who are able to lift the proscription on your clan."

"Do ye ken the rules?" Alex asked.

"I do indeed."

"How do ye ken them, if they dinna teach anyone except their members?"

"Because my father was a lord. And now my brother is, because my father is dead," Francis said.

"So are ye a lord too, then?"

"No. Nor do I wish to be. I will only be a lord if my brother and his two sons die. I wish them a long and healthy life. But I was taught all the rules as a child, and if you wish, I can teach them to you, or some of them at least, so that even if you have no title, you will not stand out if in company with them. It's possible to be accepted up to a point, if you know the rules and are an interesting person."

"What manner of rules are they?" Alex asked, intrigued.

"Stupid ones, for the most part," Francis replied with honesty. "How to eat. How to stand, walk, bow, enter a room, leave a room, greet people…there are a great many of them."

"I can understand having to learn to bow, for we dinna do that in the clan. But do the nobles no' just stand and walk and eat like everyone else?"

"No. For if they did, then they would be just like you, only with finer clothes. And that would never do!"

Alex sighed.

"Christ," he said. "Da never tellt me I'd need to learn how to walk again."

"He likely doesn't know, if he hasn't been in the company of nobles. And even if he has been, they would never *tell* him if he was behaving in an uncouth manner. They would behave politely toward him, and only mock him after he'd gone. But he would not be invited to visit them again."

"I dinna think I want to meet nobles, if they havena got the courage to be honest with me," Alex said contemptuously.

"Well, some of them at least are very courageous. But it's one of the rules, not to mock people to their face."

"It seems dishonest to me. I'd rather ye were straight wi' me, than insulting me behind my back."

"I agree. It's one reason why I'm a physician, and why my family have all but disowned me. And in fairness there is good and bad amongst the nobility, as there is in every group of people. But if you're wanting to help to influence those in power in favour of the MacGregors, then you'll need to feel at home with them, I'm afraid."

Alex thought for a minute.

"Are ye *supposed* to teach people such as me the rules?" he asked.

"Dear God, no. Which will make it all the more fun to do so. If you want to learn."

"No, I dinna. But I'm thinking I'll need to," Alex said wearily.

"Very well. We'll make a start tomorrow," Francis said. "Don't be sad. I'll try to make it an amusing experience for you."

* * *

Alex could not imagine how learning to do such things as standing and walking again could ever be an amusing experience, but it was clearly something that might be useful one day, and Francis was a very pleasant companion, so he threw himself into the idea, as he did with all new experiences.

"So am I needing to paint myself and stand like this to be accepted?" he asked at the start of his first lesson, which was on how to stand properly and to walk. He stood, one hand on his hip, the other waving airily about in space.

"No," Francis replied, laughing. "Why would you think that?"

"When I came here wi' my da and Duncan, Da was teaching us how to fight on the stairway, and a wee mannie living below asked us what we were doing. He stood like this watching us, and tellt us he was a baronet. I didna think baronets lived in such places. I'd thought they must all live in grand houses like this one," Alex explained.

"Oh, this house isn't grand, not by noble standards," Francis said. "And only in Edinburgh will you have a titled person living in the same building as tradesmen and other people. You'll not see that in other cities."

"If I'm no' likely to meet any nobles in any case then," Alex said. "Why do I need to learn to bow and walk, and such nonsense?"

"You might meet them. You certainly have a way with people. James in the bookshop today told me that you were a fine young man, very interested in animals and birds. He's looking for a good book about them for you," Francis commented. "He's normally a most curmudgeonly man, but you've charmed him, it seems."

"Ah. It's no' me but Duncan who's interested. I thought to maybe send him a book, but I canna think of a way to do it without Da finding out where I am," Alex said.

"I could send it to Susan," Francis offered, "and she could give it to him. I write to her often, and she to me."

"You would do that?"

"Of course. But let us stay with the lesson. So, it's entirely possible that you'll meet someone who can introduce you to a titled man. And then if you know how to behave, that will allow you to work your charm on them. In addition, if you find a way to be of use to them then that would be helpful too. But you will need to impress them to do that, which is why you need to learn to walk, etc. And if you can be at home with the clan chiefs, the wealthy ones who live in fine castles, who will not look down on you for being a Highlander, then you might gain access to the English nobles too."

"Who *will* look down on me for being a Highlander, and more so as a MacGregor."

"If they know you are, maybe. But you are a Drummond here. I think you could be anyone you wanted to be. Yesterday I was in The White Horse, and I knew the names of all the people working there, and even of some of the customers, although I have never met them before."

"How did ye ken them, then?"

"I recognised their voices and mannerisms. Until yesterday I thought you invented your own voices, which was impressive enough, but when I was there I realised that you copy the people exactly. That is a rare talent."

"Ah." Alex laughed. "I used to do it to amuse Angus when I was reading a wee book to him before sleep, that was all. Da doesna think it's a talent, for it was me copying the priest that made the man leave."

"Well, you could certainly be an actor, if you wished. Or anyone you wanted to be, if you put your mind to it. Your education will help with that. Knowing the rules of genteel behaviour will help too. So, let us start. Stand, in a relaxed manner."

Alex obliged, feeling a little self-conscious and far from relaxed, particularly as he was wearing stockings, shoes, a waistcoat and Francis's sword and hat, none of which he normally wore in the house, and the sword not at all in Edinburgh. Francis observed him closely.

"Hmm. Now, you are standing in a good posture, with your shoulders relaxed and not pulled back. Excellent. But you cannot stand with your arms just hanging by your side like that. You must bend your right elbow, and place your hand in your waistcoat. Good, but try not to look as though you're reaching for your dirk."

"If I did this, I'd likely be reaching for the blade under my oxter, no' my dirk," Alex commented.

"You wear a knife under your armpit?" Francis asked, shocked.

"Aye. No' the day, for I'm at home wi' you. But normally. I used it to kill one of yon footpads."

"I see. Well, stabbing a noble would not endear you to them, so your hand should rest casually in the waistcoat. Good. Now, your hat should be under the left arm. No, leave your right hand there, that's perfect." Quickly he removed Alex's hat and placed it under his left arm, just above the elbow. "Press it against your side. Good.

Now, your left hand should support itself just above the hilt of your sword. Not *on* the hilt, that appears threatening. Your weight should be on your right foot, and the left leg should be a little in front of the right, with your feet turned outwards, like so."

He demonstrated, and Alex watched, then copied him.

"Perfect!" Francis said, smiling. "You look like a lord indeed."

"I feel like a loon," Alex commented. "If rich men stand about like this, it's a miracle that they're all alive, for they're awfu' open to anyone who has a mind to rob them. Is that what they're wanting to show, that they're so rich they dinna care if ye steal from them?"

"Good God, no. Why would you think that?"

"Well, because the sword's in a place where I couldna draw it easily, even if I had the time to disentangle my hand from my waistcoat before the thief dirked me. And if my left leg is stuck out like that, wi' the feet so far out, it means I've to reach further round my body to draw it, too. It'd be easier to draw it from the back. I canna understand why ye'd wear a sword at all, if ye stand so ye canna draw it."

"Nevertheless," said Francis, trying not to laugh, "this is how nobles stand, and you will need to practice this at every opportunity until it becomes natural to you."

"I canna imagine this ever becoming natural to me," Alex observed. "Ye're no' jesting wi' me, are ye?" he added suspiciously.

"Why would I do that?"

"I dinna ken. It's the kind of thing that Kenneth would do, or Alpin would *definitely* have done. And when ye'd spent days standing around like an idiot, wi' everyone laughing at ye, then they'd tell ye it was a jest."

"Ah, so a joke between friends, not malicious?"

"Oh, of course. If Kenneth was feeling malicious, then ye'd no' be standing around wi' your feet turned out, ye'd be running as fast as ye could. He's a braw fighter."

"Kenneth was the giant, yes?"

"He was. Still is. Alpin was his brother. He was killed by broken men. Christ, I miss him. I miss all of them," he burst out suddenly. "I'm sorry. Let's try the walking, then."

Over the next few days every time Alex saw someone who was wearing very fine clothes, he would stop and observe them as they walked along or greeted someone of their acquaintance then stopped to talk. And he realised that as ridiculous as they looked to him, it was clear that Francis was not inventing the rules of standing and walking for amusement. He decided then to stand and walk like a nobleman whenever he was at home alone, or with Francis. For he could not do it outside.

Even if the wealthy men on the other side of the road were oblivious to danger, Alex was not. The people of Edinburgh might think of the clansmen as savage barbarians, but in his mind city people were worse, for although there were a lot of kind, gentle people, those who were cruel had loyalty only to themselves, which made their violence far more vicious and unpredictable than a Highlander's generally was.

When in the streets he would not be putting his hand in his waistcoat, unless he was indeed reaching for the knife strapped under his armpit.

* * *

Loch Lomond, October 1729

Alexander and the rest of the men arrived home late one evening at the end of October, to the relief of the whole clan, as there was already snow on the mountains and the sky was heavy with more to come.

Or at least most of the clan was relieved, Duncan being one exception, having dreaded his father's return. Due to that, although he and Angus were sitting by the hearth when they heard the sound of the clansmen arriving, when Alexander came into the house a short while later, they were both upstairs in bed. Duncan had expected his happy, gregarious little brother to want to go out and see the long-awaited return, to share in the communal happiness, but he made no objections to Duncan's suggestion, instead heading straight to bed.

"Can ye finish the chapter of Gulliver's book?" he whispered, once they were settled down together in the box bed.

"I canna, for I canna see to read without a candle," Duncan whispered back. "I'll finish it tomorrow for ye."

Angus nodded his head against Duncan's chest.

"Will Da be angry that Alex isna here?" he asked.

"I dinna ken. We'll no' say anything until he asks about him."

The head nodded again, and then two thin arms snaked around his chest.

"I love ye," Angus said. "Ye'll never leave me, will ye?"

Duncan hugged his brother back.

"No. I'll never leave ye. Alex hasna left ye either. He's just gone to make a good place for us to live in, and when he has we'll go to him. Would ye like that?"

"Aye. I miss him awfu' bad. It makes me sad. D'ye miss him too?"

"I do. And he misses us. But he had to go, ye ken that," Duncan said softly, listening as their father moved around downstairs.

"Aye. Because Da doesna want us, and so Alex had to find a new home because he's the biggest, so we can all be happy."

As much as Duncan wanted to reassure his little brother that this was not the case, he could not lie to him. But he could not bear to confirm it either, so instead he said nothing, and after a few moments Angus relaxed, his limbs heavy as he fell asleep. Duncan waited a while, then carefully disentangled himself from his brother's uncomfortable embrace and turned over. Then he lay awake a while longer, wondering what he was going to say tomorrow morning, when his da asked where Alex was.

His da did not ask where Alex was the following morning. Instead he was up early and out of the house before his sons rose. In the afternoon he called a clan meeting, which all of the adults and some of the children attended, and after that he helped to make sure that all the provisions were stored properly or shared between the households. And then he came home and ate the broth in the cauldron over the fire, which Duncan had made as Susan was away visiting a relative on the other side of Loch Katrine. Then he sat by the hearth staring into the fire as had been his custom for the last four years, seeming not to notice as his sons passed him silently and went to bed.

The house had been happy for the last six weeks, once Angus had recovered from his heartbroken sobbing at the departure of his favourite brother. Susan had called in most days to do chores, prepare food and chat, and various other clanswomen had also come by with food or just to see how the boys were doing. Angus had spent a good deal of time with Kenneth at Gregor and Barbara's house, with the result that his fighting skills were coming along well, and he was learning the basics of weaving too. But he'd returned home every evening, saying that he would not leave Duncan to sleep alone. Instead he had chattered happily about the events of the day, and Duncan had shared his day's experiences too.

They had also tried to imagine what Alex might be doing. These possible events, which had begun with the mundane, such as him building a wee hut to live in and catching rabbits, had rapidly progressed to him becoming a great warrior with bronze armour and a spear (thanks to Homer's *Iliad*) who had travelled to Rome, having many adventures along the way and was now King James's personal hero. Soon he would call them to his side, and they would all be King James's heroes and live in a palace together, and would go to London to kill the Elector.

But now they were just two unwanted boys again, living in a gloomy house with a man who was a stranger to them, at the start of a long Scottish winter.

In fact it was three days before Alexander finally came home in the middle of the afternoon and noticed for the first time that his eldest son was not at the table, teaching Angus to read or do numbers.

"Where's your brother?" he asked casually, picking up a freshly cooked bannock from the stone by the fire and tossing it from one hand to another until it was cool enough to eat.

Duncan's stomach felt as though it had migrated to his feet, though he showed no visible sign of it.

"He's gone," he replied, just as casually.

"Gone where?"

"He's gone to live in a palace wi' King J—" Angus began excitedly, stopping abruptly when he caught Duncan's warning expression and shake of the head. He bit his lip and fell silent, looking at the table.

"He's gone away, Da. He left over a month ago," Duncan said, opting to get it over with.

Alexander stopped tossing the bannock from hand to hand

and stared at his son in shock.

"Over a *month* ago? Why did ye no' tell me the moment I got back?" he said.

"Why? What would ye have done if I had?" Duncan asked.

"I'd have…where is he?"

"It doesna signify. Ye made it clear ye didna want him any more, so he left. I thought ye'd have noticed yourself when ye got back, but when ye didna ask, I thought ye were glad of it. So there was no reason to tell ye."

"Does the whole clan ken he's gone?"

"I havena a notion. I didna run round telling them," Duncan said evasively. Surely Da knew that *everyone* would know about something so significant, whether he'd told them or not? Or at least something significant to them, if not to their chieftain.

Alexander's face darkened.

"Ye ken where he is, do ye no'?" he said.

Duncan stood then, feeling at a disadvantage sitting down while his father loomed over him, although even when standing his father still loomed over him, as he was growing steadily rather than having Alex's growth spurts, and was still much shorter than Alexander.

"Aye," he said simply. From the corner of his eye he saw Angus staring at him in shock, because he had not told his brother where Alex was. He would explain why later. Right now he kept his focus concentrated on his father, watching as his anger rose.

"Tell me where he is," Alexander commanded.

Duncan swallowed nervously, but did not answer.

"Tell me where he is. I'll no' ask a third time," Alexander said ominously.

"No. I swore that I wouldna, and I'll no' break my oath to him," Duncan replied.

"Ye swore an *oath* to him, ye wee shit?" Alexander shouted. "Ye're my son! Ye obey *me,* no your damn brother! Where is he?" He glanced at Angus then, who shrank visibly, blue eyes huge in his pallid face.

"He doesna ken," Duncan said immediately. "I havena tellt him. Nor did Alex. Leave him be."

Looking at his father's expression, he'd half-expected the blow, but when it came it still took him by surprise, partly because of the speed with which Alexander's control snapped and partly because it was not the open-handed slap he'd anticipated, but a blow from his fist, albeit reined in a little, which knocked him flat on the floor.

Duncan lay for a few seconds, hearing Angus's cry of distress as if from a long way away, and focussing every fibre of his being on not losing consciousness. Once he knew he'd succeeded in that at least, he sat up, leaning against the table leg, the side of his face throbbing. Angus knelt down next to him, crying, and with a huge effort Duncan lifted his arm and wrapped it round his brother, pulling him into his side.

Alexander bent over them, no sign of remorse on his face, and Duncan felt the rage rise in him, although he did not recognise it as such at the time.

"I'm no' your son," he said thickly, then paused, spitting a mouthful of blood onto the floor. "For a man to have a son, he has to be a father to them. Ye've no' been a father to us, no' since Ma died. Ye're no' a chieftain either, for a chieftain's father to his clan. Ye taught me that. Ye're no more a father to the clan that ye are to us. I havena sworn an oath to you, and I never will. Ye dinna deserve it."

"Ye dare speak to—" Alexander began.

"D'ye ken, this is the first time ye've looked at me, really looked at me, since Ma died?" Duncan interrupted, anger obliterating the last waves of dizziness, although he did not attempt to stand, unsure whether his legs would take his weight, unsure whether his father would hit him again if he did. "It isna my fault I look like her. It isna Alex's fault that she squeezed his hand instead of yours before she died. She likely didna ken whose hand it was. But ye canna forgive him for it, can ye? And ye canna forgive me for looking like her. I dinna ken what ye canna forgive Angus for, for he's done nothing to ye.

"At first I understood. I thought that ye loved her, as we loved her, as we all loved Morag. But ye dinna. Ye dinna love anyone, no' even yourself, for if ye did ye wouldna be like this. Ye'd have grieved with us, wi' all of us, and then ye'd have carried on, as she'd want ye to. Ma wouldna want ye if she saw ye now, for ye think of no one but yourself. She wouldna recognise ye. Ye're no' my da and ye're no' my chieftain."

He stopped talking then, and closed his eyes, suddenly very tired. He hadn't meant to say all that, but he was not sorry he had. His da would probably kill him now, and really, he did not care, except for Angus.

Susan would take Angus. Or Gregor and Barbara. It didn't matter.

His da did not kill him. Instead he stood there for a full minute, mouth working, but no sound coming out. And then he turned abruptly and walked out of the house, leaving the door swinging open, the wind blowing flurries of snow and dead leaves into the room.

Duncan sat for a few minutes cradling Angus in his arms, murmuring comforting endearments to him, until the sobbing subsided. This was wrong. Angus cried too much. No bairn deserved to be as unhappy as he was so much of the time, such a happy, loving child by nature.

"Come on then," he said, his voice still thick, his face burning. It was swelling too; he could feel the skin tightening across his cheek.

Very slowly he pulled himself up, leaning on the table until he was sure his legs would support him. The cold air was helping to clear his head.

"Shall I close the door and build the fire?" Angus asked. "I can make ye a nice drink too!"

"No. I'm thinking we should leave. Are ye wanting to?"

"Are we going to Alex?" Angus asked hopefully.

"No' yet. I'm thinking to go to Susan's, for she's away at the minute, and she wouldna mind us staying there. Then we can be as we were before Da came home," Duncan said.

Angus nodded.

"Will we have to come back?" he asked nervously.

"I dinna think so. No, we willna," he said, seeing Angus's face.

Very slowly, hand in hand, they left the house, looking neither right nor left, and made their way across the settlement, paying no attention to the various clan members who stood by their windows or doors, having heard part of the argument but not knowing what to do, as although Duncan had rejected Alexander as his chieftain, the rest of the clan had not. And it was a father's right to discipline his children, whether they agreed with it or not. They did not approve, but they dared not interfere.

The one person who might well have interfered did not see Duncan and Angus making their painful way to Susan's, because he was down by the loch side, teaching Alasdair Og and Simon some wrestling moves.

"Aye, that's good, but if ye'd hooked your leg round his knee, Simon, ye could have brought him down," Kenneth observed from the rock where he was sitting. The rock that Alex had customarily sat on to think, when he'd been here.

The rock that Alexander was heading towards, intending to burn off the emotions raging through him now with a dip in the icy waters of the loch.

Kenneth saw him before the boys did, as focussed as they were on trying to topple each other, and seeing his face, guessed that Alexander knew his son had left. He stood then, and pulled the boys apart.

"Away hame," he said, and they looked up at him in surprise, and then across to where his gaze was resting. And then they were gone, melting away silently into the trees.

Kenneth turned then to face Alexander, who, his intention interrupted, stopped in front of his clansman.

"Ye must have kent that Alex had gone," Alexander said. "Ye've been here all along."

"Aye," Kenneth replied simply.

"Why did ye no' tell me the minute I returned?"

"I didna think I needed to. I thought ye'd have kent it immediately yourself, him being your son."

Alexander blinked, absorbing the blow of Kenneth's words, too angry to deal with them now.

"Where's he gone?" he asked instead.

"I dinna ken."

"Would ye tell me if ye did?" Alexander asked hotly.

Kenneth thought for a moment, then made his decision.

"Well, that doesna signify, does it, for I dinna ken, as I said. Why d'ye care, man? Ye've made it clear ye dinna care any more, no' just for him, but for anyone. Leave him be, wherever he is. Let him be happy, for Christ knows he canna be here. None of us can be."

Alexander bristled, his hand moving to the hilt of his dirk. Instinctively Kenneth did the same.

"Are ye challenging me?" Alexander said menacingly.

Kenneth smiled then, coldly, and removed his hand from his weapon, turning his palm towards his chieftain in the universal sign of truce, although his expression was anything but conciliatory.

"No, I'm no' challenging ye," he said. "I've no desire to be chieftain. We had a braw chieftain once, by the name of Alexander," he continued conversationally. "He's been gone a long time now, and we're waiting for him to come back. We'll no' wait forever, mind, but we havena given up on him yet, so we'll wait a wee while longer."

He lowered his palm then, but kept his eyes on Alexander as he bent to pick up his leather flask of water from the rock he'd been sitting on. Then he nodded.

"I'll leave ye to your thoughts, then," he said and walked away, keeping his body relaxed with a huge effort, half-expecting the chieftain to stab him in the back, something that would never have occurred to him prior to Moira's death.

Alexander did not stab him in the back. For a while in fact, he did nothing at all. And then, very slowly he released the grip on his dirk and walked straight into the water, without even undoing his swordbelt.

He stayed in the water for as long as he could bear the temperature. And then he came out, slowly, and sat down on the rock, his limbs leaden with cold, his mind burning, as all the emotions he'd shut down so ruthlessly for so many years roared back to life, overwhelming him; grief, despair, helplessness, love, hatred, and above all, self-loathing.

They were unbearable, but they would not be silent. He could face them, or he could walk into the loch and keep walking, but he could not shut them down any more.

His sons hated him. His clan hated him. And Duncan was right, Moira would hate him, were she here. He hated himself. He could not bear it, but he could not kill himself so he had to bear it, somehow.

* * *

When Duncan and Angus drew close to Susan's house, they noticed that smoke was seeping out through the heather thatch of the roof. Duncan stopped, undecided now he realised that Susan must have returned, not wanting to have to explain what had happened to anyone right now.

What he wanted more than anything was to lie down, close his eyes and go to sleep, to forget the look on his father's face as all the things he'd wanted to say for years but had not been able to had spilled from his lips. It was done now and he could not take them back, but it would be wonderful to just let go for a while.

But he could not, because Angus needed him, and of all of them Angus deserved most to be loved. He had not left home; he had not told his father the unforgivable; and he had never known what it was like to be loved by both his parents. Duncan and Alex had at least had that, knew it was possible. Angus did not, and so Duncan had to somehow provide enough love to replace that of both parents, to replace that of his brother, until they could be reunited at least. Because of all of them, Angus was the most affectionate, the most loving, and the most in need of love.

So Duncan did not lie down and go to sleep. Nor did he go home, because that was not an option. And while he was contemplating what to do, the decision was taken away from him as the door of Susan's house opened and a stranger walked out, took one look at the two boys standing hand in hand on the track, then turned and said something to someone in the house.

Susan appeared then in the doorway, wiping her hands on her apron. She took one look at them and then ran across to them.

"What happened?" she asked, looking at Duncan's face, then, seeing his mouth twist in an effort not to break down, she put her hand on his back and ushered him towards the house. "We've only been back a few minutes," she said, "but ye're both most welcome, and we'll soon have the house warm. Ye can be the first to meet my niece, Màiri. Her parents have both died, so she'll be staying with me now."

"Is she an orphan then?" Angus asked.

"Aye, I am," Màiri said as they reached the door. "I'm pleased to meet you."

"*Halo, a Mhàiri,*" Duncan said. "I'm Duncan, and this is my brother, Angus. We're orphans too."

As Susan had seen Alexander going home less than half an hour ago in fine health, his words told her all she needed to know, for now.

"Right then," she said. "Let me look at your face while Màiri makes the food, and then we'll finish unpacking. Are ye wanting to stay tonight?"

"Aye, if we can," Duncan said uncertainly.

"Ye most certainly can."

She moved across the room to where her bags were and rummaged in one, producing a parcel from it. "Ye've saved me a task," she added, handing the parcel to Duncan, "for your brother sent a wee package to ye. I havena opened it, for there was a message for me from…someone else," she said, glancing at Angus, "which tellt me it wasna for me. I'm thinking there might be a letter from your brother in there too. You open them, while we make things cosy here."

Angus beamed, his eyes sparkling with happiness, all the events of the day erased by the joy of the first news from his brother. He looked expectantly at Duncan, who took the parcel, looked at it for a moment in disbelief, then clutched it to his chest, curled over it and burst into tears.

Angus's smile dissolved, and Susan abandoned what she'd been about to do, instead taking Duncan in her arms.

"Ah, Duncan, *a ghràidh*," she said softly. "Let it out, for ye'll feel better when ye have. Ye shouldna be carrying such a burden, no' at your age."

"Angus, would ye help me wi' the fire?" Màiri asked, appraising the situation correctly, "for I'm thinking ye'll make a better job of it than I will. I'm no' accustomed to the peat. We burnt the wood where I lived."

"Did ye?" Angus said, wanting to be helpful, recognising that he could be more use to Màiri than Duncan right now.

"Aye. How old is your brother, then?"

"Duncan's twelve. And I'm five, but I'll be six in the spring!"

"Will ye now? Ye're tall for five. I'd have thought ye older than that."

Angus beamed again, although he cast an anxious look at his brother, who was still wrapped in Susan's arms, and still sobbing as though his heart would break.

"How old are you?" he asked.

"I'm eleven, nearly the same age as your brother there," Màiri said. "So we've much in common, I'm thinking."

"Aye. Ye've got the same colour of hair, too. He's the best

brother in the world. Except for Alex, who's my other brother. He's older than us, and he's gone to live in a palace with King James, and soon he'll send for us to go and live with him!"

"Has he now?" Màiri asked in amazement.

"Well, we're thinking he might have done. We dinna ken *exactly* where he is. That's why Da hit Duncan, for he doesna ken either, but he thinks Duncan does."

"When ye've helped Màiri build the fire Angus, could ye lay out the bowls on the table?" Susan put in, casting her niece a look that she hoped would convey the message to change the subject.

"Aye! I ken how to do that. I ken how to do a lot of things now," Angus said, obligingly changing the subject anyway while Màiri was trying to work out what her aunt's weird grimace meant. "I'm learning to carve wee animals too. Or I was, but then Allan went away wi' the men, but now he's back, so I can carve one for you if ye like, so ye'll no' be sad that your ma and da are dead."

"Oh, that's very kind of ye," Màiri answered, warming to this friendly boy with the face of an angel. "Can ye carve cats?"

"I can try. Allan can carve anything, so I'm sure he'll teach me. Ye like cats?"

"I do. We had one at home, but he got very old and died. I'm hoping I might have another one one day."

Duncan was recovering from his emotional outburst now, but Susan still held him, rocking backwards and forwards to comfort him until he pulled away from her of his own accord, by which time the room was warming nicely and the bowls were set on the table. She got up then, and set about pouring Arssmart juice from a jar onto a cloth to help with the swelling and bruising to his face, while he wiped his eyes and nose and composed himself.

The food ready, Màiri came over to him.

"I'm sorry," he said, deeply embarrassed. "I canna imagine what ye think."

"I think ye've been doing more than ye should for a long time, and just needed to stop doing it for a wee while," she said softly. "I ken what that's like, and there's no shame in it."

He looked at her properly then for the first time, his grey eyes red-rimmed from weeping, the left one half-closed from the swelling, and she smiled at him with understanding, not the pity that he'd dreaded.

He smiled back then, even though it hurt him to do it, feeling a glimmer of hope blossom inside him, although at that point he could not understand why, because everything was hopeless.

He looked down at the package, still cradled to his chest.

"I'm thinking ye should eat first, and open that when ye feel a wee bit better, if Angus will wait," she said.

Duncan laughed then. This girl had already got the measure of his brother, at least.

"If he'll wait, I will," he agreed. And then he stood and moved to sit at the table, relaxing for the first time since his father had come home, while Susan bustled about putting daisy leaves in a pot of water and hanging it over the fire to boil, and Màiri brought the food and a candle to the table, because it was now growing dark.

While his sons ate, and later opened the package Alex had sent, which did indeed contain a letter as well as a book about animals, Alexander sat on the rock, lonelier than he had ever been in his life. The hours passed, night fell, and the moon rose over the loch, bathing it in a silver light, diamonds sparkling in the heavy frost that lay on the ground. No one came to see how he was, although Alasdair Og and Simon at least would certainly have told their parents, even if Kenneth had not. Alexander did not expect them to care. He did not deserve their care.

Later still, while Màiri sat on the *seise* next to Duncan, who held the soothing poultice to his cheek, Angus curled up by his side, Susan reading aloud from the animal book in a room made warm by the fire and cosy by the company, Alexander stayed on the rock, unable to bring himself to go back to the house, unable to face his sons, unable to face his clan, and because he had no alternative, could hide from them no longer, he let the emotions come, overwhelming him, while the moon travelled slowly over the loch.

The boys slept in a makeshift bed on the floor near the hearth, while Susan and Màiri shared the box bed. They were all up shortly after dawn. It was lovely not to have to lie in bed waiting for Da to leave the house before they got up, Duncan thought. It was also lovely to have happy faces to share a breakfast of porridge with, delicious porridge too, sprinkled with tiny cubes of apple, and to watch Angus become his normal happy self again.

"So how did your ma and da die?" he asked Màiri innocently as he waited for the oatmeal to be cool enough to eat.

Duncan blushed.

"Angus, it isna—" he began.

"No, I dinna mind. It happened a while ago. They were both killed in a raid, Angus," Màiri explained.

"In a raid? So your ma went on a raid? I thought only men did that," Angus said.

"No' a cattle raid," Susan told him. "They were killed in the night, in their cottage, by some bad men."

"Oh, that's awfu' sad," Duncan said. "Have the clan avenged ye yet?"

"They canna, for we dinna ken who killed them," Màiri said. "In truth Da had a lot of enemies, for when he was in drink he was awfu' fierce and said terrible things to people. He caused a lot of trouble for us, so no one was sorry when he died."

"Were you sorry?" Duncan asked. Màiri looked at him then, for he was the first person to ask that. Everyone else had just assumed she would be.

"No. I hated him," she said. "He was awfu' fierce wi' us too. I was sorry Ma died though, but she would have tried to stop whoever killed him. She always defended him, even though he didna thank her for it."

"Did you and your brothers and sisters no' wake up when the bad men came?" Angus asked.

"I wasna there. I was staying wi' Isobel. I havena got any brothers and sisters."

"Oh! Ye must be awfu' lonely then," Angus said. "Ye can be our sister if ye like! Can she no', Duncan? We had a sister once, but I dinna remember her."

"Morag. She died before Angus was born," Duncan explained. "Aye, ye can be our sister, if ye want. I'd like that."

"I'd like that too," Màiri said shyly. "I'm sorry about your sister. And your ma and da, too."

Duncan sighed.

"Our da isna really dead," he told her. "I shouldna have said that. I wasna thinking right last night. Ma died when Angus was a baby, but Da's still alive. He's the chieftain. I dinna want him for my da any more, that's all."

"Nor do I," Angus said cheerfully. "Alex and Duncan are my ma and da as well as my brothers. They teach me things like letters and numbers, and they're kind to me when I'm sad. But I only have Duncan now, until Alex sends for us."

"Is Duncan your ma or your da, then?" Màiri said mischievously. Angus thought for a minute.

"I dinna ken," he said finally. "For I canna remember my ma, and Da ignores me. He doesna like bairns, I'm thinking. I dinna like him, either."

Susan closed her eyes for a minute at this, which was one of the saddest things she'd heard a child say, although Angus was quite matter-of-fact about it. But then he didn't remember the father Alexander *had* been. Duncan did, as was quite clear from the expression that crossed his face. And then it was gone, and he was composed again.

"Well, shall we be about our business? Angus and Duncan, ye can go and collect heather to fill your mattress, for I willna have ye sleeping on the floor every night. Are ye feeling well enough to do that?" she asked Duncan, whose face was a mess.

"Aye," said Duncan. "Yon poultice helped. It's awfu sore and I canna see right at the minute though. Does it look bad?"

"It looks terrible," Màiri said with brutal honesty. "It's black and puffy, and your nose is swollen."

"It'll look better in a few days though," Susan said. "Ye've broken no bones. Away up the mountain and cut some heather, before the snow starts again."

Just before dawn Alexander had finally gone home, reasoning that the boys would be in bed and he wouldn't have to face them, for he did not feel able to do so at the moment, which shamed him. But as soon as he walked into the house he knew they were gone, Not just from the fact that the fire had gone out completely and the house was very cold, but because it felt profoundly empty, barren. He almost believed that if he spoke, the words would come echoing back at him from the walls. They had no doubt been taken in by someone, Gregor and Barbara most likely.

He went to the hearth and sat down, making no attempt to

light the fire. His wife was gone, his children were gone, and soon, unless he did something, his clan would be gone too.

And he deserved that. He realised that now, as he never had before. He had not believed he could feel lonelier than he had sitting by the loch, but in this house, which had once been such a happy place, the truth of what he had lost hit him so hard he thought he might die of it.

But no one dies from realising unpleasant truths about themselves. While two of his sons were laughing together as they cut heather on the mountain, and his third was observing the way an expensively dressed man walked down the Canongate, Alexander sat bereft in his cottage.

No one came to make a friendly call as they would have done in the past. No one came to ask him a question or seek his advice, as they would have done even recently.

He sat, and he thought. And finally, after day had turned to night and then to day again, he made his decision.

CHAPTER TWENTY

Edinburgh, November 1729

When the servant came to inform his master that he had a visitor, Francis, having finished treating patients for the day, was standing in the shadows of his upstairs covered balcony, which faced the garden rather than the street. He was both enjoying the peace after a frenetic and somewhat stressful day, and watching the absorbing scene below.

"Ah. Yes, I will see the gentleman, but don't bring him up here, Hector. I'll come down in a moment. Show him into the library, will you? Don't bring refreshments, not unless I call you."

After the servant had gone to do his master's bidding Francis stood for a moment longer, deliberating. Clearly the stressful day was not over, for this was not likely to be a pleasant visit. *I'll see what humour he's in before I decide what to do,* he thought, and made his way downstairs.

When he entered the library his visitor, dressed in full Highland garb, who had been examining the bookshelves, turned to face him.

"Mr MacGregor," Francis said, moving forward to greet him. "Or is it Mr Drummond here?"

"Drummond's the name I usually use in Edinburgh, Dr Ogilvy," Alexander replied. "It's been a long time. Ye're looking well, sir."

As Francis could not return the compliment without lying, he merely nodded his head.

"Is one of your acquaintance in need of my services, Mr Drummond?" he asked.

"No," Alexander replied. "I'm sorry to disturb ye, but I'm newly arrived in the city, and am anxious to get home again before the snow makes that difficult or even impossible. So I'll come straight to the matter, if ye'll forgive me, sir. D'ye ken where my son is?"

"Which son? And why should you think I would know?" Francis asked, unwilling to answer until he knew the purpose of the man's visit.

"Alex, my eldest. He left Loch Lomond while I was away selling cattle for the winter. I saw that my city outfit was missing, which is why I'm dressed as I am, but it also made me think that he'd come to Edinburgh, for he's clearly taken it with a purpose. And he kens no one else here, so I thought ye might have news of him at least."

"Why do you wish to see him, if you don't mind me asking, sir?" Francis said.

Alexander smiled then, sadly.

"Ah, I see ye *do* ken something then. I'm no' here to cause trouble, for you or for him. I give my oath on that. I wish only to speak with him, to try to put something right between us. And then I'll leave."

The man Francis remembered from four years ago had done many things, but he had not told a lie in the whole time they'd spent together. He had treated Francis with consideration, and had kept his promise to ensure he returned home safely. However, Alex had told Francis that his father had changed so much he could no longer stay with the clan. Observing him now, it was clear that Alexander had changed. He was thinner and looked much older than he had before, careworn. And there was a desperation about him too, all of which led Francis to think he might be better denying all knowledge of his son's whereabouts, and asking him to leave.

But then he looked directly into Alexander's slate-blue eyes, saw the misery and pleading in them. The man was a Highlander; hospitality was always given, on the understanding that all parties would remain amicable whilst under the host's roof. Surely he had not changed so much that he would betray that sacred trust? Francis decided to take the chance.

"Come with me," he said then, and leading his visitor across the hall he went upstairs and to the doors of the balcony. "I would advise you to stay in the shadows for a moment and watch, before you announce your presence."

He opened the doors quietly and the two men stepped outside, keeping to the rear part of the area. Alexander looked down, and caught his breath.

His son, naked but for a pair of dark green breeches which ended at the knee, was practicing his sword skills with an older man, who was not only fully dressed but had the pinched look of someone who wished he'd donned even more clothes before engaging with his pupil. Although who was pupil and who was tutor seemed uncertain at the moment as Alex flicked the older man's sword out of his grip and it went spinning across the grass.

Alexander watched, stunned, as Alex waited for the man to retrieve it, seeing his oldest son properly for the first time in over four years, wondering when he had become a man.

Almost a man. He estimated that if they stood face-to-face there would be only a few inches difference in height between them now. His shoulders were broad, his waist slim, and the muscular definition on his arms and legs was developing, although it would be some years yet before he reached his full strength. How had he not noticed that before? For Alex had certainly not transformed from a small boy into a man in just six weeks.

The other man returned, having picked up his sword, and said something that Alexander could not catch, to which Alex replied with a laugh and an obviously witty retort. Alexander could not remember the last time he had heard his son laugh, but he realised now how much he had missed it.

The two of them bowed to each other, then continued fencing. Now it was clear that the man was a good fighter, although not in the same way that Alex was. The older man was elegant, his moves beautifully light and graceful, almost as though he was dancing rather than fighting.

Alex was faster, more grounded, but still incredibly fluid and light on his feet, striking and parrying with ease, his left arm instinctively raised as though holding a targe.

Kenneth's taught him well, Alexander thought. *But it should have been me teaching him.*

The combat continued for a short while, a delight to watch,

until Alex parried the other man's strike then leapt nimbly behind him, patting him playfully on the top of his head with the flat of his sword as he did. The man laughed somewhat ruefully.

"I should point out," Francis said, who had been observing Alexander's reaction to his son, and now felt a little happier, "that Monsieur Giraud is one of the finest fencing masters in Edinburgh. You have a remarkable son, Mr Drummond."

Alexander closed his eyes for a moment as the full realisation of how blind he'd been to what he had hit him; he had *three* remarkable sons, not one, all of them with their own qualities, all boys that any father would be proud of. And he had driven them all away from him with his ridiculous inability to let Moira go.

Impulsively he moved out of the shadows, and applauded his son.

Alex, assuming it was Francis, stepped forward on his right leg, left bent behind him, eyes downcast, and bowed elaborately in immaculate court fashion. Then straightening, he looked up at the balcony. And froze.

"I apologise, Monsieur," he said, "but I must leave. Please pardon me." He bowed far more sketchily to the fencing master than he had to the balcony, and then ran barefoot across the frosty grass, disappearing into the house.

A few moments later he opened the doors and stepped out onto the balcony. Father and son stood facing each other for a moment, and Francis felt like an interloper. But he would not leave them together yet.

"I dinna ken how ye discovered where I am, Da, but I'd ask ye no' to bring anger to this house. Dr Ogilvy has been nothing but kind to me, and I'd no' have that repaid with violence."

Alexander flushed then, and Francis saw Alex tense, clearly expecting his father to attack him. But then the man held his hand up in truce.

"I'm no' here to fight wi' ye. I'm just wanting to talk. And Duncan didna tell me where ye were, if that's what you're thinking," he said.

"It wasna. I ken Duncan wouldna tell ye. I'd trust him with my life," Alex replied coolly. "What d'ye wish to talk about?"

"I've no notion how many ken where ye are, but no one tellt me. I saw the outfit was missing and guessed ye might be in

Edinburgh, and came to Dr Ogilvy hoping he could tell me where ye were lodging," Alexander continued, thinking Alex needed to know that no one had betrayed him.

"I meant to send it back to ye, wi' the money I took, but it wasna in a condition to, so a tailor's making a new suit for ye. I'll send it to ye when it's finished."

"I dinna want a new suit, or the money," Alexander said.

"Aye, well, I'll pay back what I took. I want no debt to ye, Da."

Alexander sighed. This had not started well. He glanced at Francis, who stood awkwardly in the background.

"Are you happy for me to leave you both together?" he asked Alex.

Alex looked at his father.

"Am I, Da?" he asked.

"Aye, ye are. I'll no' break the peace."

Francis accepted this, and quietly left the two of them. In truth he could do nothing to stop them, should they decide to fight – he was a healer, not a soldier. And he would not eavesdrop, which would be unforgivably rude. So instead he went downstairs and sat in the library, leaving the door open so that he would hear when they came down.

When he'd gone Alexander remained silent for a moment, trying to work out how to phrase what he wanted to say.

"Ye fought very well down there," he began.

"Kenneth is a good teacher. And so is Monsieur Giraud. He's teaching me how the noblemen fence. No' the day, though. That was just a wee bit of fun."

"So ye're learning how to be noble," Alexander said.

"No. I'm learning how to be *accepted* by nobles. Francis is teaching me Greek, and how to behave genteelly, to bow, as ye saw, and other things. He's a good man. I owe him a lot."

Alexander nodded.

"Are ye still hoping to go to university, then?"

"What have ye come to say, Da?" Alex said then. "Ye didna converse wi' me when I was living with ye, and I'm sure ye didna come all the way to Edinburgh at the start of winter only to make polite conversation."

Alexander took a deep breath.

"No, I didna. I came to apologise to ye. To tell ye I'm sorry for no' being the father to ye I should have been, since your ma died."

"Have ye apologised to Duncan and Angus too? For ye havena been any sort of father at all in the last four years, to any of us. Angus thinks of me as his da, for Christ's sake!"

"Aye. I ken that, now. I lost my way after your ma died, and I'm sorry for that."

"We all did, Da," Alex replied coldly. "We were heartbroken, all of us, and we needed you to help us get through it. But ye werena there, no' then, and no' now. And now we dinna need ye, for we learned to carry on without ye. Maybe Angus does, for he's just a bairn at the minute, but he's doing well even so."

"He is. You and Duncan have done a fine job. I…when I came home and found ye'd gone, Duncan tellt me some things, things that the whole clan must have been thinking, but no one else would tell me. That was awfu' brave of him. And then Kenneth tellt me some more things I didna want to hear. And then I sat by the loch for a long time, and it was as if…as if I'd had a spell cast on me and it was suddenly broken."

"Ye're no' going to blame this on the *sìth*?" Alex said disbelievingly.

"No. I'm to blame, no one else. I was grieving, but I was selfish, couldna think of anyone except myself. And then it became easier to just stay there, instead of having to face the world alone."

"Ye werena alone! Ye had three sons! Ye had the whole clan!" Alex cried. "*We* were the ones who were alone, for we lost our ma *and* da on the same day! It would have been easier if ye had died, in truth. But ye didna. Ye just hated us instead. How d'ye think it felt for us, to lose our ma and have to live wi' a da who hated us? It was hell. Ye canna just say ye're sorry and expect it all to be forgotten."

If he was worried that his father might now hit him, he certainly didn't show any sign of it. Alexander revised his opinion of his son slightly. Muscles or no, he *was* an adult now. And independent. Maybe Angus needed a father, but Alex certainly neither needed nor wanted one. And Duncan almost certainly felt the same way. He was too late.

He could *not* be too late.

"Alex, I dinna expect ye to forget. I'm asking ye to give me another chance, for I've been lost, and I can give ye no excuse for it. I was wrong. I've wronged ye, and Duncan, and Angus, and the whole clan, for that matter. But I ken that now. I see what I've done and I'm truly sorry, and I'm asking ye to let me make it up to ye."

"I'm no' coming home wi' ye, Da," Alex said. "I've got work here and a place to live, and I'm learning things, no' to impress ye as I used to, for ye've made your opinion of me clear, and in truth I dinna care what ye think any more. But ye were right that it doesna seem likely James'll take the throne back now, and if we're to lift the prohibition, I *will* need to learn to talk wi' the nobility. I'm doing it for the clan, no' for you."

"D'ye no' miss home at all?" Alexander asked.

"Aye, of course I do. I'll no' lie to ye. I miss Duncan and Angus dreadful. And I miss the rest of the clansfolk, the loch, the sweet air…I miss *everything*. But I'm no' coming home. No' yet, at any rate."

"When, then?"

Alex looked at his father. He seemed truly distraught, as though at any moment he would drop to his knees and beg his son to come home. Alex did not think he could bear to see his proud father do that, which made him realise that he did still care, after all. Not enough to comfort him, though. Or to lie to him.

"When one of two things happens. When I ken ye can be trusted, for one. I canna take your word ye'll change. I need to see ye *do* it. I've lost faith in ye, Da, and if ye've come to yourself, ye'll ken that's no' unreasonable of me."

Alexander nodded.

"And what's the second thing?"

"When I'm old enough to challenge ye as chieftain if I need to. I'm no' ready yet. I'm too young, for one thing, and I havena your strength, yet. In truth, I've no desire ever to fight ye. But the clan deserve a good chieftain, the chieftain ye were before Ma died. He was a good man, a better man than I'll ever be. If he's gone forever, then I owe it to the clan to wait until I have a chance of beating ye, for they deserve a better chieftain than ye are right now, and I hope to be that for them, in time," Alex said brutally. "Your word isna law in Edinburgh, but it is in Loch Lomond. So I'll no' come home and put myself in your power until I ken ye're truly back, or I can take your place. I'm thinking ye'll no' wish to wait until your outfit's finished," he added now, looking at the overcast sky, "so ye can leave as soon as ye want, for I've heard all I need to."

He turned then and left, and Alexander was so stunned by this curt dismissal that he stood rigid with shock for a minute. Then he came to himself and shot through the doors, catching up with Alex as he got to the bottom of the stairs. He gripped his son's shoulder, felt him stiffen, and let him go.

"How will ye ken I'm truly back, if ye're living in Edinburgh?" he asked.

Alex thought for a second.

"It's no' a secret where I am any more," he said. "Tell the clansmen, when they're ready, to send Kenneth to tell me. Wi' Duncan and Angus. And then I'll decide. I've no wish to be cruel, Da," he added, watching his father's shoulders slump in defeat, "but I'll no' tell ye a lie to cheer ye. Ye'd no' respect me if I did, I'm thinking. If ye can find your way back to who ye were four years ago, I'll be glad to come home, and glad to call ye my chieftain and my father. Are ye wanting refreshments before ye go?" he added politely.

Alexander declined, wanting nothing more than to be away from this house, from his cold, implacable son as quickly as possible. Because he did not know how much longer he could refrain from crying, from begging Alex to forgive him. And he could not do that, not because he didn't want to but because if he did Alex would see it as emotional blackmail rather than the despair it was. And although he had seen a lot of emotions in his son's eyes in the course of their conversation, contempt had not been one of them, and he did not think he could bear to see that.

So he turned and left, went back to the tiny room he'd rented for the night and spent the evening replaying the terrible conversation in his mind, realising as he did that if his own father had rejected him as comprehensively as he had rejected Alex for the last four years, he might not have responded in such a level-headed, honest way.

He had not achieved what he wanted. But nevertheless, as he headed out of the city the following morning he felt more cheerful, for he knew he had done something right after all. He had reared a man worthy to be chieftain of the MacGregors, even if he had completed the task brutally rather than kindly.

Once in the countryside he started running, at a steady pace he could keep up for hours. For he had a sense of purpose now, and had come to another decision. He just needed to get home before the snow came.

* * *

"So are ye wanting to go home, now your da's left?" Susan asked, having heard the news from Fiona while getting water from the loch.

Duncan looked at Angus, giving the decision to him.

"No," Angus said immediately. "I like living here. It's warm and friendly, and I dinna want to leave my new sister."

"Ye wouldna be leaving me, for I can call on ye, or you can come to see me," Màiri pointed out. Angus looked anxiously at Duncan.

"I'm thinking we'd rather stay, if it's no' a problem," Duncan said. "For we dinna ken where Da's gone. He could be back at any time, and I dinna want to be having to spend most of the time upstairs. It's too dark to read up there even in the day, without a candle."

"Is that what ye did? Lived upstairs?" Màiri asked.

Duncan flushed, for he hadn't meant to reveal so much. But it was done now, and Màiri seemed trustworthy. Susan certainly was.

"We sleep upstairs, always have done. So we'd try to be in bed before Da got home. No' because he hit us," he added quickly, seeing Màiri's gaze move to his cheek. "He did this because I said a lot of things he didna want to hear. I didna mean to say them but I'm no' sorry I did, for they were the truth. No, we just couldna relax when he was there. He was so unhappy all the time, and he seemed to hate anyone else being happy. So we were happier upstairs."

"But I'm even happier here!" Angus added. "Can we stay?"

"Ye can stay as long as ye want to," Susan said. "I'm happy ye're here, too."

So they stayed, even though Alexander did not come home.

After a week the clan were becoming worried. After all, good or bad, he *was* their chieftain, and he had never gone away for more than a day without *someone* knowing where he'd gone.

Kenneth, recalling his last conversation with Alexander, was particularly worried. Surely the man wouldn't have done away with himself because of a few home truths? The old Alexander would not, but this new one was already dead in many ways. Kenneth had hoped to bring him back, not finish the job Moira had started by dying. He said nothing to anyone, but asked God several times a day to keep Alexander safe and bring him home.

So when, on the ninth day after leaving Alexander returned home, immediately calling a clan meeting, everyone, Kenneth especially, was hugely relieved.

They all assembled in the cave, as he'd asked everyone to be there, and the byre was full of livestock at this time of year. To their surprise the cave was blazing with light when they arrived, it seeming that Alexander had lit every candle they owned.

He waited until they were all sitting, then looked around.

"Where's Susan, and Duncan and Angus?" he asked. "Are they on their way here?"

"Susan said they couldna come, for they're doing a task that they canna leave," Barbara explained. "I said I'd go directly after and tell them what ye said."

"No. Tell them I'm sorry, but they need to be here. Duncan and Angus especially," Alexander said.

Barbara nodded, and slipped quietly out again. Everyone waited nervously, watching Alexander as he sat in front of them staring fixedly at the floor. Whatever it was must be very serious. Or had he decided to go to war with another clan, for no good reason? It was impossible to tell nowadays.

The silence stretched out oppressively for what seemed like hours, so everyone was deeply relieved when the three missing clan members appeared, Màiri having stayed at home, as Barbara had said the chieftain appeared very serious, and it did not seem a good meeting at which to introduce a new clan member. Once they'd found a place to sit, Alexander stood.

"I'm sorry to have pulled ye all away from your work at short notice, but I've something I need to say, and if I dinna say it now, I'll maybe no' have the courage to say it later," he began.

A murmur of disbelief ran through the assembled clan. A chieftain *never* admitted to a lack of courage, in *any* situation. And yet those sitting nearest to him could see that he was indeed trembling slightly. It could be that he was cold, and shivering, but Alexander had never seemed to feel the cold at all before today. Everyone was listening intently now.

"I wanted to apologise, to Duncan and Angus, and to every one of ye. Ye all ken how much Moira and I loved each other. It was never a secret. And when she died, I lost my way. I fell into a dark place, as I'm sure the bairns did, and maybe others of ye too, for she was loved by all of ye, I ken that. But instead of doing as I should, and thinking of my responsibilities as a father and a chieftain, and making the effort to drag myself out of the dark place for ye all, I didna. Instead I just stayed there.

"For the last four years I havena been worthy to be your chieftain. I see that now. I've risked your lives unnecessarily, because I was angry wi' everyone that she'd died, and I didna much care if I lived or died either. But it was unforgiveable of me to risk all of you, too. Ye'd have been better wi' no chieftain at all, rather than the one I've been."

He paused for a minute then, noting the deathly silence in the room, the shocked faces of his clansmen as they took in his words. But no one disputed that what he'd said was the truth.

"Duncan, Angus," he continued, looking at his sons, and flinching slightly at the deep bruising on his middle son's face. "I havena been any kind of father to ye since your ma died. Ye were right in that. And I canna bring back the lost years. I want to tell ye all, if ye dinna already ken, that ye have Duncan to thank for making me realise what I've been these last years, for he said things to me that no son should ever have to say to his da, and I hit him for it, for I didna want to believe them. I'll never forgive myself for that."

"Da, ye dinna need to—" Duncan began.

"Aye I do. For it was a brave thing ye did, and I want the clan to ken that, for they should. Kenneth, I'm wanting to thank ye as well, man, for ye tellt me the truth too, and I've never wanted to kill a man as much as I did you then for doing it. But I'm glad I didna, for ye're a better man than I've been. Duncan's a better man than I've been, for he and Alex have raised my youngest son, while I wasna fit to. I'm hoping to take that burden away from ye now, and let ye be a brother to him instead of a parent."

He looked around at his clan now, gauging their reaction to what he'd said, for it was costing him dearly to show his vulnerability to them. He'd been taught by his father that no chieftain could ever show weakness to his clan, for if he did they'd lose respect for him, and that would invite challenges. But he reasoned that it would be difficult to lose more respect than he likely already had, so really, he had little to lose. Either they'd give him a chance or they wouldn't, and there was an end of it. But he would not let them choose the next chieftain, if they rejected him. Right now everyone seemed too stunned to think of challenging him.

"Ye'll all maybe be wondering where I've been the last days," he continued. "I went to Edinburgh, for I guessed that Alex might have gone there. Ye'll all be happy to ken that he's well, and safe, and staying wi' the doctor I brought here when Moira took ill. He tellt me he misses ye all, but when I asked him to come back wi' me, he refused."

His voice broke then, and he stopped for a minute, then he swiped his hand through his hair and with a visible effort pulled himself together.

"He tellt me that he wouldna come home wi' me because he doesna trust me when I say I've come back to myself. And that was a hard thing for me to hear, all the more because I canna say he isna justified. He *did* tell me that he'll come home in two cases; either when ye all confirm to him that I'm the chieftain I was before Moira died, or when he's old enough to challenge me for the chieftainship."

This produced a gasp of shock, which ran through the clan. They all looked up at him anxiously then, knowing that he would be quite within his rights if he'd killed Alex there and then.

"No, I didna kill him," he assured them immediately, thinking now that the blaze of candles had been worth it, for he'd needed to see their reactions to his extreme statements. "How could I? For I could see then that although he's just fourteen, he's exceptional. Dr Ogilvy said as much, and he was right. One day he'll make the best chieftain this clan's ever seen. He tellt me he had no wish to ever fight me, but that the clan deserved a better chieftain than I was, that it deserved the chieftain I *had* been. And he was right. He tellt me to send Kenneth, Duncan and Angus to

Edinburgh once I've proved myself to ye, and then he'll come home. And if I dinna, he'll wait until he's old enough to challenge me. I dinna want him to have to do that.

"So I'll say this to ye now, and then I'll leave ye to discuss what I've said. I'm asking ye to give me until next summer to prove to ye that the Alexander ye kent once is back. I'll have my bad days, I'm sure, but I've woken up now, and I want to prove to ye I'm worthy of ye, as I once was. At the end of that time I'll call another meeting, for everyone, and ye can make your decision, which I'll abide by. Whatever that is, Kenneth and my sons can go to Edinburgh and tell Alex to come home. For if I havena proved myself, and ye dinna want me, then I'll hand over the chieftainship to Alex myself. For if I canna lead ye, I ken no other who can do it as well as my eldest, young as he is. Especially if he's got Duncan by his side, for Duncan has all the qualities Alex is lacking, and between them they'll be formidable.

"That's my final word regarding the chieftainship, for I'll no' have ye all challenging Alex, wanting to take his place. It'll be either myself or him. And now I'll leave ye to talk on it, and when ye've decided I'll be at home to hear what ye have to say."

And then he turned and walked out of the cave, leaving his whole clan thunderstruck by what had just occurred.

It was three hours before a knock came on the door. Alexander opened it to find Kenneth standing there, his hair and kilt covered in snow, which was falling thickly now. Alexander beckoned him in, but he remained at the door.

"As it's me ye're wanting to go to Edinburgh, the clan thought I should be the one to tell ye our decision," Kenneth said. "They're all wanting to give ye the chance, for they remember well what manner of chieftain ye were, and they want that man back. They ken well what manner of boy Alex is too, and Duncan for that matter, but they think they're a wee bit too young yet to take your place. So we're all hoping ye're speaking true, and are back wi' us. For if ye're no', then we'll have a fourteen-year-old chieftain, and fine as he is, we'd no' see him, or Duncan either, take on such a burden yet awhile. They've had enough to deal wi' since Moira died."

Kenneth watched Alexander closely as he spoke Moira's name,

and was relieved to see no reaction to it. Nor was there any sign of anger at his words, which boded well.

"Aye, then. I agree wi' ye, and I ken Alex would too. He tellt me he wasna old enough to fight me yet. But before I spoke to him I watched him practice in the garden wi' some French fencing master, and he's a fearsome fighter now. Ye've taught him well, Kenneth, and I'm sorry ye had to do it alone."

"Aye, well, Duncan's a bonny fighter too. But as long as I dinna have to teach Angus alone, I'll be happy. That bairn needs a father badly, and we've all tried to help in the raising of him, for it wasna Alex and Duncan's job to do that. If ye're afeart ye may be too late, I can tell ye ye're no', for he's the most loving, cheerful bairn I've ever met. Ye go to him gently and he'll respond, quicker than ye're expecting. I'm no' so sure about Duncan, for ye've wounded him bad and he takes things deeply, even if he doesna always seem to."

"I'll no' make them come back to me if they dinna want to. But ye're right. Ye ken the bairns better than anyone, I'm thinking. Ye'll make a wonderful da when ye marry wee Jeannie," Alexander said.

Kenneth laughed then, and relaxed a little.

"I'm no' marrying wee Jeannie," he began.

"Aye, because she's a bairn. She's growing fast though, and she's set on ye."

"Well she can unset, for I'll no' marry her, if it's only to prove ye all wrong," Kenneth said. "I'm glad ye didna take it badly, me telling ye how to behave wi' your sons."

"How could I? Ye've been there for them the last years, when I wasna," Alexander replied. "I'm glad ye all want me back. I'll no' let ye down, I swear it."

Kenneth nodded then, and turning, headed home, feeling lighter of heart than he had in years. Alexander had not flinched when he'd mentioned Moira, had not been angry in the slightest when he'd told him how to approach his sons, and had joked with him about Jeannie, which the whole clan did on a regular basis, finding the lassie's continuing infatuation with the giant and Kenneth's embarrassment at it, hilarious.

It was a good start. Maybe Alexander really *was* back. Only time would tell for sure though.

* * *

Duncan and Angus stayed at Susan's for another two weeks, during which time Angus had tried and failed to carve his first attempt at a little cat for Màiri, and had now started on a second one, on which he spent endless hours working, his tongue protruding from the corner of his mouth, his brow furrowed.

"It's awfu' difficult," he told his brother. "But at least I dinna have to carve the whiskers. Allan said we can make wee holes in the face and put bristles in."

"Would it no' be easier to carve it lying down asleep than standing wi' its tail in the air?" Duncan asked, observing the somewhat oddly proportioned figure. Màiri had already told him privately that she'd treasure it no matter what it looked like, for no one had ever worked so hard to please her before.

Which had made Duncan sad, in some strange way he couldn't understand.

"I went to see Catriona's cat, for I wanted to watch one, but she's got kittens right now, so most of the time she's lying there wi' them suckling on her, and I'll no' carve her like that, for I canna do kittens too. And then when Catriona comes in, she stands up and goes to her, wi' her tail up, and Catriona said cats do that when they're happy to see ye. I want Màiri's cat to be happy to see her."

Duncan gave up. Angus was every bit as stubborn as Alex when he had his mind set on something.

The next day he went to Catriona's and had a private word with her, which he asked her to keep secret. Two days later Angus presented Màiri with his carving. And although the ears were crooked and the tail very short, it *was* just about recognisable as a cat. Màiri was ecstatic, and insisted on placing it on the centre of the table every day when they ate or studied and on taking it with her to bed, so that it would be the first thing she saw when she woke up in the morning.

"And that will make me think of ye, and how kind ye are, which is a bonny way to start the day," she said.

Angus had almost glowed with happiness at her reaction, which made the whole household seem brighter somehow. He had that effect on people, as did Alex. Duncan prayed every night that their father really was back, for he felt sick at the thought of living in Edinburgh, and almost as sick at the thought of having to be Alex's right hand man at the age of thirteen. He wasn't ready, he knew that, and neither was Alex. He didn't *want* to be ready, not for a long, long time.

He wasn't really ready to move back in with his father either, but he knew that he had to, and so did Angus. For only that way would he know whether or not Da was truly back with them. If he was, then the sooner they moved home the better, for it would be wonderful for Angus to experience the father he and Alex had both adored.

And it would be wonderful to have him back. He had missed his da, very badly.

So, two weeks later the boys made their way through the settlement and back to their home, Angus agreeing only when Duncan promised that if Da hadn't changed they would return to Susan's.

Just before they were due to leave Duncan had gone outside on the pretext of needing to relieve himself, and then had hared off to Catriona's, returning just as Susan was contemplating going out to see if he had dysentery, he'd been so long.

When he dashed in they all looked at him, for he was breathless from running, but clearly very excited. He reached inside his shirt and produced a tiny ball of hissing, spitting orange fur, which he held out to Màiri.

"I asked Catriona if she'd keep him for you. She tellt me he was the most affectionate of the litter," he said a little uncertainly, not least because the kitten, having shredded the skin on his stomach on the way back with its tiny claws, was now making a mess of his hand, too.

Undeterred, Màiri plucked the kitten from Duncan's hand, to his relief, kissed it on top of its head, then laid it against the side of her neck, where, to his utter disbelief, it curled up immediately and went to sleep, while she stroked it gently with one finger.

"He's just afeart, that's all," Màiri said, her eyes sparkling. "He's awfu' bonny. What a kind thing to think of, Duncan. Can I keep him, Aunt?"

Duncan flushed then, because he hadn't thought that Susan might object to having a cat in her house.

"Aye. I'm sure he'll be a grand mouser, when he grows," Susan said.

"What will ye call him?" Duncan asked.

"Well, I called the cat Angus gave me Cameron, for my ma was a Cameron. So I think I'll call this one MacGregor," she said.

"Was yer da a MacGregor then?" Angus asked.

"Aye. But I wouldna call shite after him," Màiri said vehemently. "I'm naming him for my aunt, and my new brothers, who've made me feel good to be a MacGregor after all."

"Alex will be your brother too," Angus said happily. "He'll be coming home soon, will he no'?" he added, looking up at his brother.

"Aye, I hope so," Duncan said. *That's why we're away hame now, to find out.* "We'll see him anyway, for we'll be going to Edinburgh wi' Kenneth."

They said their goodbyes then and left, Angus skipping happily, not at all worried that Màiri might prefer Duncan's present to his. She was happy and that was all that mattered to him. It was really impossible not to love Angus. The fact that his father had managed not to for four years did not inspire Duncan with confidence that he *could* come back.

After all, he had been so very far away, for such a long time.

As the house came into view, Duncan vowed that he would leave at the first sign that Da was still the surly hostile figure Angus had always known, rather than the loving, perfect father he and Alex had known when they were Angus's age, so long ago. He would rather live in Edinburgh than watch his brother become a timid, miserable child again.

CHAPTER TWENTY-ONE

Edinburgh, June 1730

When the doorbell rang, Elspeth, who was coming down the stairs at the time, continued across the entrance hall to answer it. The master was not one to be particular about *who* answered the door, being more concerned that it was answered quickly, as for some callers the speed with which they received attention could mean the difference between life and death.

Once the door was open however, she gave an involuntary shriek of horror and stepped back, wishing profoundly that she had called for someone else to do it. Preferably a regiment of soldiers.

Standing on the step was a man...no, more accurately a monster, for surely no human being in the world could be so enormous, or so savage in appearance. He would have to stoop to get through the door, although she prayed he would not attempt to cross the threshold. He was massively built, with a riot of long, tangled red hair, and half-naked too, dressed as he was in the primitive Highland garb. In his left arm he carried a small, very beautiful child that looked like an angel from heaven, with golden hair and huge blue eyes. At his side stood an older, solemn, dark-haired child, watching her with an intense long-lashed grey gaze which made her feel as though he was looking into her soul, and did not like what he saw there.

"A good morning to ye, mistress," the monster said in a deep, aggressive tone.

In fact, in spite of Dr Ogilvy's instructions to admit *anyone,* she most certainly would have slammed the door shut immediately, but for the angelic child. For she had heard that these Highlanders loved the taste of children, so she hesitated, wondering if she could snatch it from the monster's arms without being slaughtered immediately. She certainly could not leave it to be devoured.

"Ah! Kenneth!" the master's voice came from behind her. "It's quite all right, Mrs Ferguson. I am acquainted with this gentleman. "Come in! Would you be so kind as to tell Alex his visitors are here?"

She looked at Francis with absolute disbelief and horror.

"You want it...him to *come in*?" she asked.

"Indeed. That is what we usually do with friends who have travelled a long way to see us. Now, if you please. And arrange for refreshments to be sent to the library," Francis told her, somewhat frostily.

She subsided, and watched as the three visitors followed the master into the library. Then, reversing the order of Francis's instructions, she shot off to the kitchen, partly to tell everyone that the master had surely lost his mind this time, and partly to arrange for the refreshments to be delivered by someone who might have a chance of stopping the monster when it decided to lay waste to the household.

Oblivious to all this, Francis waited until his three guests were seated, and then smiled at them.

"Alex will be so pleased to see you all, as am I. He's been anticipating you coming for a long time. Was the journey uneventful?"

"Aye, very pleasant," Kenneth replied. "The midges were the worst foe we had."

"And they let you through the Netherbow Port, armed like that?" Francis asked.

Kenneth looked down then, as though just noticing that he carried a sword at his hip. And a dirk and pistol. *And no doubt a knife strapped to his armpit,* Francis thought.

"Why would they no'?" he asked.

Why would they no' indeed? Francis realised, watching as Kenneth swept his tangled hair back from his face with a hand that could crush a man's skull, his forearm thicker than Francis's calf. The guards had opted for survival over orders, then.

"Ye're no' allowed to carry swords in Edinburgh, Kenneth," Duncan explained. "Unless ye're a gentleman."

"I *am* a gentleman," Kenneth replied.

"Aye, but I mean one that wears breeches, and a lot of lace and such stuff," Duncan added.

"Ah. Well, I'm no' intending ever to wear yon ridiculous things, and I'm no' giving up my only means of defence, so it's as well they didna ask me to," Kenneth announced.

Angus noticed the brimming laughter in Francis's eyes, although he did not know the reason for his humour, and responded, smiling broadly at him.

"Ye have a lot of books," he said. "Are they all yours?"

"They are indeed. You must be Angus," Francis replied. "D'ye like reading?"

"I do. I like it better when Duncan reads to me, though. And even better still when Alex does, for he does all the voices, and the movements too."

"I canna do all the voices," Duncan explained.

"You can look at the books if you want to, see if there's one you might like," Francis said, watching the child squirming on the chair he'd been placed on. When Angus shot off it as though fired from a cannon, Francis smiled. This was a child full of interest in everything, and full of energy. His older copy should be here any time now.

"I'd like to ask you if the news is good, but that would be impolite of me," Francis said.

"Ye ken why we've come then?" Kenneth said.

"I know the bones of it, aye. Alex told me a little of the conversation between him and his father, and that he'd told him to send the three of you when you knew if he could go home or not."

Kenneth nodded.

"Aye, that's it. And it's why we're here."

"Look, Duncan, he's got *Don Quixote!*" Angus said excitedly from the corner of the room.

"I'm reading that to him at the minute," Duncan said. "I'm trying to do different voices, but I canna manage them. Alex—"

"Will read some more of it to ye tonight, Angus, if ye want.

Where have ye read to?" came a voice from the doorway.

Everyone turned and looked at the young man in the doorway, and for a moment the three Highlanders hardly recognised him, dressed as he was in blue velvet breeches, white stockings and silver-buckled shoes, with a matching blue waistcoat and silk shirt. His hair was brushed immaculately and tied back with a ribbon that matched his outfit. He looked like the sort of young man who would be allowed through the Netherbow Port with a sword, not because he was a terrifying giant, but because of his apparent status.

"Alex!" cried Angus, breaking the spell by tripping on the carpet as he dashed across the room, with the result that Alex ran forward to catch him as he sprawled on the floor. Alex dropped to his knees and Angus gripped him round the neck in a choking hug, which he returned. And then Duncan, forgetting everything except that the brother he had missed so dreadfully was here and real, no matter how different he looked, stood and walked across to them, before kneeling as well and joining in the group embrace.

Kenneth and Francis exchanged a warm look, and smiled.

"They've been needing that a long time, I'm thinking," Kenneth said softly.

They waited, until Alex turned to look at Kenneth questioningly, his eyes brimming with unshed tears, full of hope, full of dread.

"Ye can come home now, Alex," Kenneth said simply, and at that the tears spilled over, pouring down Alex's cheeks, then he buried his face in his youngest brother's soft blond hair, and cried like the small child he no longer was.

Once the boys had recovered, and Francis had explained to the array of burly male servants who appeared in the room, which even included his two gardeners, all of whom carried one small plate of food, that Kenneth was a *friend* and that he was in no danger whatsoever, and would have a word with his housekeeper later, the group set to eating and discussing the events of the last six months.

"I really do have a lot of business to deal with this evening," Francis said, once he'd eaten a pastry, "so I'll leave you together. Or would you rather repair to the sitting-room?"

"No, we wouldna. This is my favourite room, and Angus hasna finished looking at the books. And ye dinna need to leave. I ken ye havena got any business, for we were going out to an eating house until Kenneth came. It's why I'm dressed like this," Alex explained to the others. "Francis, I trust ye, and without ye I'd have been lost. Ye'll be interested to ken what's happened, for Susan will be affected too."

Francis blushed scarlet at that, but did not make any further attempts to leave the room.

"Ye have a room just for sitting in?" Kenneth asked incredulously. "Can ye no' sit in this room well enough?"

Alex laughed.

"That's what I said when I arrived," he said, "about the breakfast room and dining room. Rich people have all manner of rooms. It's all part of showing how wealthy they are to their neighbours. No' that Francis does that," he added. "So tell me about Da. He really has come back to us then?"

"Aye. I didna believe he could at first," Duncan replied. "No one did. After the clan meeting we stayed at Susan's for a while longer, for I thought it was easier to do that than go home and then leave again."

"And we've a new sister, called Màiri," Angus added. "She's awfu' nice, and Duncan didna want to leave her. But it didna signify, for they're together every day anyway."

Duncan blushed crimson, to Alex's amusement.

"Ye didna write to me about this new sister," he said.

"Ah, well, I had other things to write about," Duncan said, uncharacteristically discombobulated. "She's Susan's niece. She came to live wi' her when her parents were killed, and Angus asked if she'd like to be our sister, as she hasna any real brothers or sisters of her own."

Alex grinned knowingly.

"Ye're a wee bit young for the lassies, are ye no'?" he said, watching with amusement as Duncan's face reddened even more.

"She's no' a 'lassie'. Well, she is, but no' in the way ye're meaning. I like her, that's all. She's a friend."

"No' like wee Jeannie wi' Kenneth then?" Alex persisted, grinning.

"Ye need to remember it's me who's seeing ye home safe,"

Kenneth cut in threateningly, "or no', as the case may be."

Even joking the man was terrifying, Francis thought. But Alex just shrugged, still grinning.

"Tell me about Da, then," he said, changing the subject.

"He's nice," Angus told him. "He smiles, and he asks me what I'm doing, and plays wi' me. And he thinks my animals are very good. He isna like the other da, but he looks the same."

"Angus is learning to carve wooden animals," Alex explained to Francis, who was looking increasingly confused, having no idea who wee Jeannie or Màiri were. Susan hadn't mentioned Màiri in the letters she'd written. Clearly she was still keeping her distance from him. He wished with all his heart that he had never declared his love for her, for it had put a wall between them that he doubted he would ever breach.

"At the beginning ye could see that he was really trying," Duncan said, "for he'd come home and sit in front of the fire and stare at it for a minute, and then he'd shake himself, as if he was remembering that he mustna do that any more. Then he'd come and sit wi' us, or ask us questions about our day. But he wasna really interested. Ye could hear that in his voice. I was waiting for him to just go back to how he was, for he was…" Duncan paused then, looking into the distance as he tried to think of the best way to describe it. "It was as though he was walking on a ridge, a very high ridge, wi' a steep fall on one side, and if he didna think about every step he'd stumble, and then ye'd expect him to fall off it. Sometimes ye were *sure* he would, for he leaned so far over it seemed he couldna come back. But he did, and then it was like he kent the path now and didna have to think about balancing on it, so he was steadier. And then, about three months ago he just came down from the ridge altogether, when he realised he didna need to walk that path any more. And then we were all sure he was truly back."

"Three *months* ago?" Alex said while Francis was marvelling at the complex metaphor the boy had used to explain his father recovering from prolonged grief. "Why did ye no' come earlier then?"

"We all wanted to be sure, before we had the meeting to decide," Kenneth said.

"To decide what?"

"Did ye no' tell him that, either?" Kenneth asked Duncan.

"No. For I hoped it wouldna happen, and I didna want to worry him when he was alone." Duncan glanced at Francis then. "I'm sorry, Dr Ogilvy. I realise now that he wasna alone, for he had you, but I didna ken that then."

"Worry me wi' what?" Alex asked.

"When your da called the clan meeting to apologise for the last years, and to tell us what happened between ye in Edinburgh," Kenneth said, "he also said that we had to make the decision, when we were ready, as to whether we thought he was the man he had been, and if we wanted him as chieftain or no'. He said he'd abide by our decision."

"Ah, so ye all decided he's back wi' us then," Alex said, relieved. "That'll help him a lot, I'm thinking. But I wouldna have been worried about that."

"We kent that. But your da also said that if we didna want him as chieftain we had to choose you, and that he would only relinquish the chieftainship if we agreed to that. He said ye were ready, young as ye were, especially if ye had Duncan with ye, and he wouldna have anyone else challenging ye. And we all agreed wi' him, for he was right."

Alex sat there, staring at Kenneth in shock, eyes wide, mouth open. Duncan placed his hand on his brother's arm, squeezing it.

"He truly said that?" Alex asked after a minute.

"Aye, he did," Duncan confirmed. "Kenneth wouldna lie to ye. The whole clan heard him, and the whole clan agreed wi' him. When they voted Da wasna there, but I was. No one objected. A good number thought ye needed more experience, but no one thought they could do a better job than you, if Da couldna find his way back to us."

"Holy Mother of God," Alex murmured.

Duncan glanced across the room, seeing that Angus had now taken a book down from a shelf and was absorbed in it, leafing through the pages carefully.

"He never did hate ye, Alex," he said now, softly. "I'm thinking he saw the man ye were becoming, and kent that he'd been such a man, but wasna any more. And that's why he was so cruel to ye, for ye reminded him of what he should be. He couldna blame himself, so he blamed you."

"Ye really believe that?" Alex said.

"Aye. I really believe that. I'm sure of it. I was the day I tellt him he wasna my chieftain and I wouldna swear an oath to him. I saw the shame in his eyes then. At first I thought it was because he'd hit me, but later I realised it wasna that. It was because he kent that he didna deserve to be my chieftain, but that you did. And he hated me for it then."

"Aye, for ye made him face the truth. He tellt us that at the meeting too," Kenneth added. "But ye dinna need to be chieftain now, maybe no' for a long time. So ye can get the experience ye're lacking. Your da tellt me ye're a fearsome swordsman now, but I'm thinking your wrestling still needs some work."

Alex laughed then, which released some of the emotion he was feeling. Because it was a huge thing his father had done. No chieftain relinquished his leadership of the clan, unless he was utterly incapable, and often not even then. For the chief of a clan was the next thing to God to his clanspeople, and no one gave up that sort of power without a fight.

But his father had offered to, and to relinquish that power to him. Which meant his father *did* love him after all.

He could not think of that now, or he would break down. Again. And Angus would not understand that, and he could not explain just how important it was to him that his father approved of him. Because Angus was presumably only just starting to see the man Alexander had been, and hopefully would be again, for many, many years.

"Aye, ye're right. For there isna a man in Edinburgh that can wrestle like you. We can practice later, if ye want. Have ye a room for the night?" Alex said.

"No," replied Kenneth, as though this was the first time it had occurred to him that he might need one. "But if ye're no' wanting to leave directly, then I'll away and look for one."

"I'm no' wanting to leave directly," Alex said. "For I've lived here for nearly a year now, and I've people to say goodbye to. And I wouldna leave Francis without a proper farewell. Maybe Mrs Grant has a room. She's no' so far away from here."

"You'll do nothing of the sort!" Francis cried. "You'll all stay here, for as long as you want to."

"I'm thinking your wife willna be happy about that," Kenneth said uncertainly, "for she didna seem to like me, though I canna think why, for I didna say anything she could take amiss."

"My…? Oh! Good God, no, Mrs Ferguson is my housekeeper, not my wife!"

"She's a servant, Kenneth," Alex supplied helpfully, knowing Kenneth would have no understanding of the difference, for wives kept houses, among other things. "I'm thinking if ye stay for a few days, we can maybe show Angus a wee bit of the town, and you too. The castle is a mighty building, but it's my view ye could take it easier than it seems. I'd appreciate your thoughts on that, though. And we can show Francis some wrestling moves, for he's taught me a lot of things, and I'd like to teach him something."

"I would like that very much," Francis said, smiling. "I'll call for rooms to be made ready. You can stay as long as you like."

"Just the one room, for Kenneth," Alex said. "I'm thinking we'll sleep together the night."

"Aye. Angus willna let ye out of his sight anyway, in case ye disappear again. And I've missed ye tossing and turning all night, keeping me awake," Duncan added dryly, but his eyes were warm.

"Christ, I've missed ye entirely, and I'm no' ashamed to say it," Alex said with feeling, and then remembered he had no wish to cry again. Although he might later, when alone with his brothers. "But I'll no' say it again."

"No more would I expect ye to, even if we have walked through endless midges for four days to reach ye, ye ungrateful wee gomerel," Duncan retorted.

"Yon Susan woman gave us some lotion to use, wi' lavender and some lemon plant. Made us smell like lassies, but it stopped the wee beasties biting," Kenneth said. "Are ye wanting to come back wi' us, and visit her? If ye are, I'll see ye home safe, as Allan did last time."

For a second Francis was tempted, desperately tempted. But he knew that if he did, he would be unable to resist making a fool of himself again, embarrassing them both. For he loved her now as much as he had over four years ago, as he always would.

"No," he said reluctantly. "But I would very much like to see you wrestle, for I've heard much of the Highlanders' fighting skills, and seen how adept Alex is with a sword. It's a joy to watch.

He's told me that you taught him, so I'd love to see you fight. I'll go and arrange the room for you, Kenneth," he said then, and getting up, left the room abruptly before he could change his mind and risk losing Susan's friendship altogether.

* * *

When they finally walked into Alex's bedroom after saying goodnight to Kenneth, whose room was next door, Angus was reeling with exhaustion, but was also so stimulated by the many new experiences of the day that he was wound up like a watch spring. He ran to the window to look at the view, although it was almost dark outside, then examined every item of furniture in the room before finally landing on the bed, bouncing up and down joyfully and exclaiming that it was the biggest bed in the world. In the meantime Duncan and Alex, grinning at their little brother's exuberance, were undressing, which in Duncan's case, dressed as he was in the *féileadh mór,* took seconds, and in Alex's much longer.

Having scrutinised everything in the room to his satisfaction, Angus sat on the bed and observed his brother.

"Why are ye wearing those stupid clothes?" he asked, watching as Alex carefully rolled his stocking down his calf before placing it on the chair with its companion. "It must take ye an awfu' long time to dress of a morning. Do they no' make ye itch? They look very uncomfortable."

"Aye, they were at first, but I've grown accustomed to them now. Everyone wears them in Edinburgh. In most of the towns, and the Lowlands," Alex said. "If ye want to fit in, ye need to look like everyone else."

"Ye dinna need to fit in now, for ye're coming home wi' us," Angus said gleefully. Then his brow furrowed. "Ye *are* coming home wi' us, are ye no'?" he added anxiously.

Alex, now undressed, abandoned the idea of wearing his nightshirt, which would attract more comment, and lifting Angus off the bed gave him a quick hug before putting him down and pulling back the covers.

"Of course I'm coming home wi' ye!" he said. "Get yourself undressed now, before ye fall asleep."

As it was Duncan had to unbuckle his brother's belt to let the miniature kilt fall, and then pull the filthy shirt over the yawning boy's head, after which they both joined Alex.

"There's enough room in here for the whole clan to sleep!" Angus cried. Even so, although Alex and Duncan lay next to each other, a few inches between them, Angus threw himself on top of Alex, head on his chest, his arms wrapped round his brother's torso.

"I can hear your heart beating," he said drowsily, and then fell immediately asleep.

Alex and Duncan waited silently for a few minutes, listening as Angus's breathing became deep and regular, his limp body growing heavy. Then Alex lifted his head and kissed the thick mass of golden hair tickling his chin, before very carefully disentangling himself from his little brother, moving him to his left side. Angus moaned in his sleep, sighed, nestled into Alex's side, then stilled.

"Will I blow the candle out?" Duncan asked, who as the last in bed was next to the little bedside table on which it stood.

"No, no' yet," Alex said. "Or are ye wanting to sleep immediately?"

"I'm tired, but I can wait. He's afraid ye'll disappear while he's asleep if he lets go of ye," Duncan said. "He's missed ye terribly. We both have, in truth."

Alex reached across the tiny space between them and found Duncan's hand. They lay there for a minute, just enjoying being together again, the rightness of it all.

"I've no intention of disappearing again, if Da really *has* changed," he said.

"Aye, he has. He's still missing Ma badly, ye can see that, but when it's too much for him to be normal, he tells us he's no' feeling well, and he'll go to his bed so we dinna have to hide upstairs. Or sometimes he goes to sit down by the loch, as you used to do, and no one disturbs him."

"Aye, it's a good place to think, to see yourself properly, and what ye need to do," Alex said. "I miss that place too. I never did find one here."

"But those times are further apart now. I think your leaving really shocked him."

"I'm thinking that ye telling him the truth shocked him more, most likely," Alex said. "Ye're braver than I am, doing that. I left, but you had the courage to stay and face him. Ye'd be a better chieftain than I would."

Duncan turned his head to gauge if Alex was joking with him.

"No, I wouldna," he said upon realising he was serious. "Remember the snow battle? I havena the ability you've got to rouse the clan, make them see things your way, make them want to follow ye. I dinna want to be chieftain either. You do."

"Aye, I do," Alex admitted. "But no' yet. No' for a long time. And when I do, I'll need ye with me. I canna see all sides of a thing as ye can. I canna imagine being chieftain without ye by my side."

"I'm no' planning on going anywhere," Duncan reassured him. "Ye'll have to though, if ye're thinking to go to university. Or are ye no' planning on that now? Da hasna mentioned it in a while."

Alex sighed deeply.

"I want to stay home, and if Da wants me to as well, I will. But I've thought a lot while I've been here, and I've learned a lot too. Francis has taught me Greek, enough for me to carry on without a tutor, and he's taught me some of the ways that nobles have too – ways they teach their bairns so they can see just by looking at a man whether he's one of them."

"Ye can tell that by their clothing, can ye no'?"

"No. A thief could steal or buy himself fine clothes, but the nobles would ken, because they stand in a different way, walk differently, have hundreds of different ways of greeting each other. It's like a code that only they ken, and Francis has taught me some of it. But he also tellt me that it would be awfu' difficult for me to fit in wi' them if I hadna been abroad. No' to university, although that would be a big thing, but because young nobles do this thing called a 'Grand Tour'."

Angus shifted then, murmuring some incoherent words in his sleep, and both boys fell silent until he'd settled again. Then Duncan blew the candle out, because it was probably disturbing Angus, and they didn't need to see each other to converse.

"What's a Grand Tour?" he said softly, once he'd settled again.

"It's a stupid thing they do after university, I'm thinking because they havena got anything useful to do wi' their time, no' needing to grow crops or tend cattle. So they travel to France and

Italy, especially Paris, Rome and Venice, to look at paintings and statues and such things. They spend years doing it sometimes. It's supposed to make them into adults, but Francis says it more often teaches them to gamble and drink too much."

"Christ. Nobles are awfu' stupid," Duncan commented. "Why do they no' send them out on raids? I aged years on that cattle raid wi' Da, especially when yon raiders came out of the trees and saw ye behind that rock."

Alex let out a whoop of laughter, then put his hand over his mouth to stifle it, not wanting to rouse Angus.

"I canna imagine some of the youths I've seen in Edinburgh ever doing that," he said. "They'd freeze in horror and be cut to pieces. I've watched them a lot, to learn how they move. The point is, though, that they all go off and do this silly tour, and so when they come home, they can all talk about the places they've been to wi' each other. It's a bonding, a wee bit like members of a clan have wi' each other."

"Bonding about statues and paintings, and losing all your money at cards," Duncan said dryly.

"Aye. But it isna something I could read about and then pretend I've done, as I can learn to bow in the right way. I'd need to actually *go* there, if I want to fit in and be accepted by noblemen."

There was a silence while Duncan pondered this.

"*Do* ye want to fit in and be accepted by noblemen?" he asked finally.

"Christ, no. I want to fit in and be accepted by the MacGregors, go home, and never leave Loch Lomond again," Alex said passionately. "But I also want the proscription to be lifted, for if it isna, we'll never be able to walk out openly, to wear our weapons, own our land from the crown, no' just from the sword. I hate calling myself Drummond as though I'm ashamed of my name. I hate that every other clan is recognised, and that they all look on us as being useful in a fight, for we've a fearsome reputation, but otherwise we're like vermin, to be killed at will, wi' no consequences."

"I wouldna say there'd be no consequences, unless they killed every MacGregor, but aye, I agree with ye. It would be awfu' good to just tell people my name's Duncan MacGregor, and be respected for it."

"It would. And although I dinna give a fig for yon German lairdie in London, if he gave us our land wi' a piece of paper to it, then it couldna just be taken from us by the first larger clan. We could wear our weapons openly, no' have the law changed against us for no good reason as happens now. And I'm thinking now that Da was right. James Stuart isna going to come back to Britain. And by the time his sons are old enough, even if they *want* to, it'll be too late. Hanover's been on the throne for fifteen years, and even before that when it *was* a Stuart, it wasna the rightful one. Most people who remember James's da on the throne are old, or dead.

"So the only chance I have to lift the proscription is to be able to fit in wi' yon silly fools in their silk and lace, by bowing and using the right knife to cut my food wi', for they have a different one for every meat."

"And to do that, ye'll need to go to Paris," Duncan finished.

"Aye. And if I have to go, I might as well go to university and learn things to talk about. I can run round the place and see things then, without spending years looking at paintings and getting drunk. I've seen most of Edinburgh since I've been here. I'm sure I can do the same in Paris."

"If Da still wants ye to go," Duncan said.

"Aye. If he doesna, then I'll be relieved, for although I want the proscription to be lifted, I dinna see how I can do it, no matter *how* much shite I learn about etiquette and art. I'd rather fight to lift the proscription. I'm growing good at that now, and I enjoy it. It's more useful, too."

"I'm looking forward to see ye fight tomorrow, see how ye've come along," Duncan said.

"Wi' the sword I have. No' wi' the wrestling though. Kenneth's the right of it there."

"Ah, well, I'm sure the nobles dinna want to crease their fine lace by actually *touching* their opponent," Duncan commented in his best version of a lordly accent.

Alex giggled.

"They do fight, though. Dundee was a viscount, and he was a good friend of King James, but he was killed at Killiecrankie, leading the men. Alasdair tellt me he looked awfu' bonny, but he was a fearsome fighter. And a Lowlander, too. I'm thinking he kent all the etiquette, if he was a friend of the king, but he was still a brave man." He sighed again. "What I'd really like though, is to forget all that, come home and just be Alex MacGregor again, forever."

This last sentence was uttered so wearily, so plaintively that Duncan's heart clenched in his chest.

"Whatever ye have to do, whatever ye achieve or dinna achieve, I'll be with ye. Even if ye become the King of Scots, I'll still treat ye the same. Ye're my brother, and ye'll always be my brother," he said.

"That's all I want to be, in truth," Alex replied. "Thank ye. Whatever I do, I want ye with me. And this wee gomerel too," he added, nodding his head towards his little brother, who was now curled like a comma into his side, snoring softly. "We should sleep."

"Can I ask ye a question before we do?"

"Aye, of course ye can."

"Why did ye tell Da to send Kenneth, me and Angus to tell ye if he'd changed or no? Or rather, me and Angus. I ken ye trust Kenneth to tell ye the truth no matter what Da says. He's loyal to you before Da, I'm thinking ye realise that now."

Alex's eyes widened.

"What? No, I didna realise that! I kent he'd tell me the truth, for I canna remember him ever telling a lie. But Da's the chieftain! The whole clan owe him their loyalty."

"Aye, he is now. But he wasna for a long time, as ye ken. And a man canna help how he feels. Kenneth will be loyal to Da now, for he deserves it. But I'm thinking if he ever had to choose between the two of ye, he'd choose you. As would I. It's something ye should ken. I thought ye did."

The silence went on so long that Duncan thought Alex had maybe gone to sleep after all.

"Ye didna answer my question," he said softly. If Alex didn't respond he'd ask again tomorrow.

"If Da hadna changed, then I wanted ye both with me. Francis is a good man, he would have let ye stay here. I was going to wait until I could rent a room for the three of us, although I'm no' earning enough for that yet. But then I thought that if Da was still the same after six months, then ye'd be better living here wi' me than wi' him. And it was only my pride stopping me asking Francis to let ye stay, for he'd do it happily. I kent ye'd be safe coming wi' Kenneth now, but if ye didna it might be a long time before ye could come on your own, Angus being so young. I wanted ye to have the choice, to stay here or go home."

"I see."

"Would ye have stayed here? If Da hadna changed?"

"Angus certainly would. I would have too, to be with ye and away from Da as he was. But I'm awfu' glad I dinna have to, for I canna abide the town."

"No' even here? The air isna so bad here, when ye sit in the garden. It's no' like that room we had wi' Da."

"Aye, but the garden isna real. The grass is cut so it looks like a carpet, and the bushes are all stupid shapes. The fountain thing in the middle isna real either. I'm thinking it's meant to sound like a river flowing, but it doesna. Even the flowers dinna look real. They're too big and bright, and all in perfect rows. I canna understand why city people canna just let things grow as they want to. They need to control *everything*."

Alex smiled in the darkness.

"Aye, well, ye dinna have to choose between the land and me now, and I'm glad of it, for I wouldna have ye be unhappy," he said. "I dinna feel as you do about it, but I dinna like the city. It's interesting for a wee while, but after that it's relentless. I'm thinking if I *had* to live here, then I'd need to go out into the mountains regularly, to remember who I was."

"At least it's Scotland, though," Duncan said. "I canna imagine why King James went to live in England when yon Elizabeth lassie died. I canna think of anything worse than living in a big city in a foreign country!" Alex felt him shudder. "Ah, Christ, I'm sorry, Alex," Duncan added immediately.

"Why?"

"Well, if ye go to university, ye'll be doing that."

"No, I willna. I'll no' be *living* there. I'll just be staying there for a wee while, to learn things. And then I'll come home. I can do it, if I remember that. Let's sleep now. It must be awfu' late, and Angus willna let us rest once he wakes."

Duncan sent up a silent prayer that Alex would *not* need to go abroad, or to take on the huge responsibility that their da seemed to think he should, that even Alex now seemed to think he should. Duncan did *not* think he should have to take on such a burden. He wanted his brother, both his brothers, to be happy. He wanted them to grow up together in their homeland, where they belonged. And one day, far off in the future, he wanted Alex to be chieftain, and he would be his right-hand man.

And then they would marry and have children who would love them and each other, and would bring them up to be proud of being MacGregors. And they would all live at Loch Lomond for the rest of their lives, and be happy to do so, and to hell with the rest of the world.

To hell with nobles and princes in their stupid palaces with different rooms for eating every meal in, no matter where they lived, no matter what their name, no matter what bits of silly paper they could or could not give or take away. To hell with them all.

Just let us be left alone to be happy, he prayed fervently.

And then he turned over, away from Alex but edging backwards until their bodies were touching. They were together again, the three of them, as it was meant to be. That at least felt right, if nothing else about this place did.

That at least he would fight to keep, no matter what he had to do. If Alex had to go to Paris, then so be it. But he would come home, and then they would not be separated again, no matter what. They were strong together. They could do *anything* together.

And let us stay together, the three of us, and be left alone to be happy, he amended. Then he crossed himself, and closed his eyes.

CHAPTER TWENTY-TWO

Late summer, 1732

As it was raining heavily the passengers sought shelter the moment the ship had cast off from Leith, only Alex remaining at the ship's rail, listening to the mournful cries of the gulls and the more cheerful cries of the sailors calling to one another as they did incomprehensible things in the rigging, presumably to ensure the ship sailed in the right direction.

When he could no longer see even the slightest trace of land Alex stared down at the grey sea, glad of the inclement weather, for his tears were washed away by the rain and if anyone commented later he could blame the redness of his eyes on the salt wind.

Before sailing he had travelled to Edinburgh, spending a week with Francis, who, once he'd heard that Alexander was still set on sending his son to university, had offered to help to sponsor him. He had appeased Alexander's pride by writing to tell him that this was a common thing for noblemen to do for promising young men, and that he would be delighted to help.

Alexander, encouraged by Susan, had reluctantly agreed, in part because he wanted his brilliant son to have the best chance in life he could, and in part because he'd realised that the chances of him ever being able to pay both the university fees and five years of bed and board in France, were very slim.

Time had also been of the essence. Alex was sixteen, would be seventeen in November, and would certainly need a year of learning the trivium before he could progress to the quadrivium, which would take another four years to complete. Alexander wanted his son to be educated whilst he was a similar age to the other students, not when he was a man grown and likely more set in his ways.

Now it was actually happening and no longer just a dream of his father's, even the *thought* of spending five years away from home made Alex profoundly depressed. Nine months in Edinburgh when he was fourteen had been more than enough for him. He was not comforted by the fact that there would be other students from Scotland at the university. They would not be his clansfolk. They would not be his brothers. Duncan would be an adult by the time he returned, and he would have missed the end of Angus's childhood.

He would be lonely. He was already lonely, unspeakably lonely, although Scotland was only just out of sight. Right now he did not care about lifting the proscription, about being a hero to the MacGregor clan, about his name going down in history. He cared only about the fact that he felt very young, very lost, and desperately unhappy. A wild, compelling urge came over him to jump over the ship's rail and swim back to shore. He was a strong swimmer and the sea was calm; it was doable.

He shook his head to clear his thoughts.

This was no way to think. He could not go home, so he had to accept his imminent future and make the best of it. He would learn as much as he could, as quickly as he could. After all, he did not need to actually *pass* his examinations – he did not need to even *take* them. He just needed to acquire the information necessary to be recognised as a learned man, as a man of culture, as a man who could hold his own with any level of society. Who could fit in with a ridiculous set of people he felt contempt for, who had too much money, too much time on their hands. Too much power. And that was the crux of it all. He needed to use their power for his own ends. For his clan's ends.

So, he would put aside his childish wishes and would throw himself into his new life. His new *temporary* life. As long as he remembered that, he would survive. He had survived four years of his father's unreasonable grief. Paris could not be as bad as that!

He turned from the rail then, intending to make his way to the cabin which he shared with the other male passengers. Then he stopped. No, he was not in the mood for conversation, could still feel the tendrils of melancholy swirling through his mind, trying to get a hold, to drag him down into self-pity and despair. He needed to overcome them before he attempted to engage with others.

He sat down on a coil of rope instead, watching the motion of the ship as it carved its way across the sea, thinking of Angus, who had tried to go fishing on Loch Lomond three times now and had been brought back pale and clammy every time. He would probably die if he had to cross the whole ocean!

Alex laughed, then looked around. No one was listening. The sailors were all busy about their duties, and the passengers were all below.

It had been wonderful to arrive home from Edinburgh with Kenneth, Duncan and Angus, and see the joy on the MacGregors' faces as they welcomed him back. It had been even more wonderful to see his da again, his real da rather than the grim uncaring stranger he'd been since Ma died.

Once settled in, Alex had told him about Francis and about the nobleman's code, and had showed Alexander what he'd learned; how to walk, stand, bow, eat as they did.

"There's a whole lot more to learn as well," he'd said. "I'm thinking I might need to spend more time wi' Francis at some point, if I'm to fit in wi' the people who can lift our proscription. Maybe he could come here."

He did not need to be Duncan to realise that Francis was in love with Susan; every time her name was mentioned he'd reddened and his eyes had taken on a distant look. Duncan had said that it didn't signify, because Susan was *not* in love with Francis, and you couldn't make a person love someone if they didn't.

Alex was not so sure about this. Maybe if Francis came to stay with them for a while, to teach him more etiquette, Susan would discover that she was in love with him after all. But then they would move back to Edinburgh, and Màiri would no doubt go with them, for Susan was the only blood relative she had now.

Alex had liked Màiri as soon as he met her. It was impossible not to. She was so open, so kind and friendly. And she made

Duncan smile every time he saw her. She was not Morag, but she was a wonderful adopted sister to have. He did not want her to go to Edinburgh. He did not want Susan to go to Edinburgh either.

They did not go to Edinburgh, because his father had shot his suggestion down, saying that it would be very unfair to drag the man away from his lovely house and all the patients who needed him, just so he could teach Alex how to appear noble. The very least Alex could do would be to go to Edinburgh and repay the man in a small way by helping him in any way he could while he was there. In any case that could wait until he returned from Paris, so was not worth thinking about now.

"In five years all manner of things might have changed," Alexander had said. "And ye might have learned all the etiquette ye need in France. Ye'll certainly be fluent in the language, and in Latin, for all your lectures will be in Latin."

Once Alexander had known that Alex could definitely go to university, he had been very happy. The whole clan had been very happy too. After that everything had moved quickly and in no time, it seemed, he was preparing to leave.

Barbara and Gregor had presented him with a new *féileadh mór,* in a scarlet and black tartan, along with five linen shirts.

"For ye'll be at a Scots college, so ye'll no' need to wear they stupid breeches," Gregor had said. "And ye can wear a bright colour, for I'm thinking ye'll no' be needing to blend in wi' the heather and suchlike."

Alex didn't know whether there *was* heather in France, but he was touched to have such a beautiful outfit. It must have taken them a great deal of time to dye and weave the wool. He had tried it on and paraded himself before the clan, knowing that Gregor and Barbara would bask in their appreciative comments. In truth it had made him feel very fine too, very adult.

In spite of that his father had sent his measurements to Edinburgh, and had two formal outfits made for him. Francis had added in three silk shirts and several pairs of fine silk stockings. Susan had given him a number of remedies for common ailments he might suffer from, along with carefully written instructions on how to use them. Duncan had given him a copy of *Don Quixote,* saying it would last him a good long time, it being so weighty, and he could practice the voices and amuse them all by reading it when he came home. Angus had made a carving of two boys holding hands, which he told Alex were him and Duncan.

"So ye willna forget us, while ye're away," he'd said, his blue eyes filling with tears.

That had nearly undone Alex, but he had not wanted Angus to see how miserable he was, so he'd smiled, given his little brother a hug and told him he could never forget him, no matter how long he was away, and that he would be back as soon as he could.

Kenneth had given him a sword, with the instructions to keep practising at every opportunity.

"For when ye're back ye'll be a MacGregor again, no matter how many fancy French ways ye have, and ye'll be needing to fight," he'd said. "I dinna want to have to teach ye everything again."

"I'll always be a MacGregor, wherever I am," Alex had replied, swinging the sword back and forth. It was perfect, his first brand new adult sword, and he could not imagine how Kenneth had managed to pay for it.

"I dinna want to go, Kenneth," Alex had said impetuously, because, apart from his brothers and Màiri, Kenneth had been the only member of the clan who had seemed sad that Alex was leaving, the only one who he felt he could be honest with. "I'm no' sure I can be the man ye all want me to be."

Kenneth had looked at him then and smiled, although his eyes were sad.

"Ye're already the man we all want ye to be, laddie," he'd said. "If ye come back exactly the same as ye are right now, we'll no' be disappointed."

"Da will be," Alex replied.

"No' if he's got sense, and he has. This is an opportunity for ye to learn new things, things which might help ye in the future, no' for ye to become a different person. Ye're clever enough to learn them, and to make the most of the opportunity. It might be that ye come home and never need them, but that doesna matter. At the least ye'll have stories to tell us through the winters, and one day ye can teach your bairns what ye've learnt, as your da's taught you. But if something happens and ye *can* use the new things, then ye'll be glad ye ken them. The clan will be behind ye whatever ye do. We dinna expect ye to restore the Stuarts and break the Union. Just be yourself, and come back to us. That's enough."

He thought of that now, sitting on the coil of rope, then shivered suddenly, although he was not cold. He had been reassured by Kenneth's comment at the time, realising that he was right. Alex did not need to become a different person; he just needed to learn enough information to be able to *pretend* he was a different person successfully enough to fool people. Behind all the bowing and silly walking, the Latin and Greek, he would still be Alex MacGregor. He would always be Alex MacGregor, and he would always belong by Loch Lomond.

He had changed enough in the last years, and had no wish to change any more. He was no longer the boy he had been before Edinburgh. Before Edinburgh many of the things he had done had been with the aim of pleasing his father, of earning his praise and approval. He had learnt Latin, rhetoric, mathematics and even Greek, not because he'd really wanted to, but to please his father, to be told that he was a worthy heir to the chieftainship. For a long time he had thought to go to Paris to please his father too.

Now his motivation for doing so was different. He still *wanted* his father's approval, but he no longer *needed it*. He was not going to Paris for Alexander, but for himself. Right now he wanted nothing more than to return home, but deep inside he knew it was fear that was driving that desire. Fear of change. Fear of the unknown, and of the great effort it would take to profit from it.

And he knew that if he gave into that fear, he would never amount to anything. And one day in the distant future, as he lay on his deathbed, he would bitterly regret not having seized the opportunity to change his future and the future of his clan, and would wonder what would have happened if he'd had the courage to go.

At least now, whatever happened, he would not berate himself for his cowardice.

He recognised too that there was a difference between the despair he felt now and the despair he had felt when he'd gone to Edinburgh. At that time he had thought he might never be able to go home, and if he did, it would be to challenge his father for the chieftainship, maybe to kill him. Even the thought of that made his blood run cold.

But when he returned from France he would be welcomed with open arms, by his da and by all the clan. He had no need to keep his address a secret either, which meant his brothers could write to him. And he knew they were both happy at home now, so had no need to worry about them every day.

He smiled, and turned his gaze away from the west and his vanished homeland, looking instead east across the waves to where his immediate future lay. He would make the most of it, he swore now, hand instinctively moving to his dirk to bind the oath with iron, feeling the enthusiasm energising him, banishing the melancholic tendrils for now at least.

He uncurled himself from the coil of rope and stood, resolved now, then walked across the deck, making his way below to become acquainted with his fellow passengers.

To embark on his new life.

HISTORICAL NOTE

Once again I thought I'd write a historical note to explain a bit more about some of the events that take place in this book. I hope you enjoy them!

I've scattered a good bit of information about Clan Gregor throughout the book, and am also in the process of writing some blogs about the convoluted and fascinating background of the clan, which will appear on my website www.juliabrannan.com from November 2021 onwards, so I'll just look at a little of the clan history mentioned in this book. When I started writing the Jacobite Chronicles, I decided to have Alex be a MacGregor partly because I've visited Loch Lomond on numerous occasions and so am familiar with the area, and partly because I discovered that members of the clan fought for the Stuarts at every opportunity, and that they were renowned for their ferocity. If you read the history of the Highland clans, you'll quickly realise that to have a reputation for ferocity amongst them, the MacGregors must have been formidable indeed.

Although declared illegal for over a hundred years, and in spite of attempts by both the authorities and various larger clans to eradicate them, the MacGregors survived, which is pretty admirable in my view. The account of the Battle of Glenfruin in 1603, told by Alexander during the cattle raid, is taken directly from history, and did indeed lead to them being proscribed by King James VI and I. The betrayal of Glenstrae by the Campbell chief was also taken from history, as are the accounts scattered throughout the book of various injustices and attempts to terrorise clan members. The negotiations between Clans Gregor and Grant to combine also took place, but came to nothing.

In Chapters One and Two I give Alexander's view of Rob Roy MacGregor, especially with regard to his conduct during the 1715 and 1719 Jacobite Risings. Until now I've resisted writing about possibly the most famous member of the clan, not least because there are so many contradictory accounts of his life, and it can be really difficult to establish what really happened. Added to that, Sir Walter Scott turned Rob Roy into a great Highland hero in his wonderful novels, which have influenced just about every other depiction of him since.

However, whatever the truth, he was certainly regarded with suspicion by the supporters of the Stuarts, not least because he was sheltered for a time by the Campbell chief, who was a Hanoverian. I've read a few accounts of the 1715 rising, all of which state that Rob Roy did not actually fight in the battle of Sheriffmuir, having arrived too late to do so, which many Jacobites thought deliberate. Whatever else Rob Roy was, he was a survivor, and from a personal point of view this action would make sense. In fact, although he took no part in the battle, he was attainted and his house burnt down, but later 'surrendered' to Campbell of Fonab and, under his protection, suffered no further consequences.

So Alexander's suspicion of Rob Roy was reasonable, and would have been shared by many of his contemporaries, who did not have the privilege of reading Sir Walter Scott's romanticised accounts!

I also mention the secret election of Balhaldie, so I'll elaborate a little on that here, as Balhaldie features in the Jacobite Chronicles, as the man who gives Prince Charles such a favourable view of how many clans will rise for him, to Alex's disgust.

It appears that the last of the descendants of the reputed chief of Clan Gregor, Archibald MacGregor of Kilmanan, died between 1707 and 1714. His ancestors had been chiefs for nearly two hundred years, and this ending of the line caused a problem, partly because Queen Anne's government offered a pension to various clan chiefs, aimed at buying their support against a

Jacobite rising. (In fact various clan chiefs happily accepted this pension, but then rose for James anyway!)

So, in order to obtain the pension, a new chief had to be found. In 1714 a number of prominent MacGregors (no more than sixteen of them) held an election and declared Alexander MacGregor of Balhaldie to be the new chief of Clan Gregor, and signed a bond to that effect. However, this bond was kept a secret from many branches of the clan, who took no part in the election, and in fact didn't even know it was taking place.

Needless to say, given the ferocity and rebellious nature of the clan members, Balhaldie was by no means universally accepted as the leader of Clan Gregor, regardless of any written bonds.

In honesty it's incredibly difficult to keep track of the history of ANY clan, for a multitude of reasons that I won't go into here, and the MacGregors are particularly difficult, not least due to the fact that they had to adopt other names and do an awful lot in secret during the time of their proscription.

On to other things! In Chapter Two I talk about the *clach cuid fir*. This was a tradition amongst both the Celtic and Norse cultures, and involved lifting a very heavy stone to waist height and then placing it on a wall or ledge. It was a way of proving that you were now a man. Of course Kenneth, being not only a giant, but possessing abnormal strength (I've based his strength as well as his hair colour on my grandfather, who performed some incredible feats in his day), not only lifts it, but throws it as well. Each clan would have its own stone or stones, and the weights of them varied.

This tradition in Scotland goes back to the eleventh century, and was included in early versions of the Highland games. Some clan stones have allegedly survived, including the Inver stone at 268lbs (121kg), and the Dinnie stones, the heaviest of which is 413lbs (187kg).

This feat is now incorporated into some 'strongest men' competitions, and often includes walking with the stones and other variations.

Chapter Eight has Alexander taking Duncan and Alex off to learn how to reive and sell cattle. The cattle sales did indeed take place in

Crieff and Falkirk in October (for many years Crieff held the largest sale, attracting buyers from all over Britain), and drovers on three different routes did congregate at the head of Loch Lomond before continuing to Crieff, or to (at the time of this book) the smaller tryst at Falkirk, which later took over from Crieff to become the main place to sell cattle. The drovers were effectively the forerunners of cowboys, being very skilled in moving cattle through hostile country, sleeping outside in all weathers. Many drovers would visit farmers, collect their cattle and take them to market, returning later with the payment. Obviously this was open to abuse, as I mention in the book, but most of the drovers were honest, in a rough way that was often incomprehensible to outsiders.

Cattle reiving seems for hundreds of years to have virtually been a pastime between the clans, and in any research into legal issues the theft of cattle, from a few to hundreds, will crop up with regularity. Although it was an acceptable way of behaving to the clans, where other theft was not – any person claiming hospitality could stay in a home with no fear of being either molested or having anything whatsoever stolen from them – this did not mean that clans would not fight to the death to stop their cows being stolen, or to retrieve them if they had been. Cattle could mean the difference between surviving and starving in the long dark winters, so battles over their theft could be extremely ferocious.

Over the centuries various measures were put in place to try to stop this happy Highland (and Border) custom, with what appears to have been little success. It was therefore crucial for any boy, particularly one who aspired to leadership, to be very familiar with how to steal and drive cattle. It's really a fascinating topic, and one I knew little about before researching for this book.

Incidentally, the description of Crieff and of Alexander's outfit as a dealer has been taken directly from an eye-witness account by Macky, who (happily for me), wrote his description in 1723, the year in which Alex and Duncan accompanied Alexander! Cattle drovers were exempt from the various Disarming Acts imposed on Highlanders, although the MacGregors, being proscribed, would have been a different matter.

In Chapter Eleven I describe the birth of Angus, who is born face-first. I found the research into this absorbing, not least because I too was born face-first, and at home, and my mother went through hell and nearly died having me. I didn't really know a lot about it until I decided to have Angus be born the same way, but now have great admiration for the doctor and midwife who brought me into the world.

The horrendous description of the delivery of a breech baby has been taken from real accounts of the time. In the days before anaesthetics and comprehensive medical knowledge, a breech birth could be virtually impossible to deliver safely, and often guaranteed death for both mother and child. One way that midwives would attempt to save the mother was to literally pull the baby out piece by piece, cutting off each part as it was brought out. Obviously this would be at the least intensely traumatic for everyone concerned, and often fatal for the mother anyway. But it was at least worth a try.

Caesarian operations were also sometimes performed (although not by midwives), if the mother died in childbirth, in a desperate attempt to at least save the baby. Childbirth could be an extremely dangerous procedure, and was the leading cause of death for women for many centuries.

On to the trip to Edinburgh. The Netherbow Port was the main entrance into Edinburgh from mediaeval times. It's mentioned as early as 1369, but after the disastrous Battle of Flodden Field in 1513 it was redesigned as part of the Flodden Wall, which attempted to make the city impregnable to attack. Flodden Wall, along with the earlier King's Wall, effectively surrounded the old town of Edinburgh, and the Netherbow Port, approximately halfway along today's Royal Mile, was an impressive building, with conical turreted towers. Anyone entering had to pay a fee, which meant that the poorest people, who could not afford it, might spend their entire lives within the old city walls. Consequently the Port was known as 'World's End', commemorated now by a pub of that name. The Netherbow Port that Alexander and his sons go through would have been relatively new, as following an attack in 1544, the Port was remodelled and moved further down the street, becoming even more elaborate and elegant, but still a formidable entranceway. The heads of notable criminals were indeed hung on the Port, to hopefully deter visitors from committing crimes.

The Port was demolished post-Culloden, in 1764, but many parts of the Flodden Wall survive.

Surprisingly there weren't a lot of theatres in Edinburgh, mainly due to the influence of Presbyterianism on the population, which regarded such entertainments as being immoral. However plays were put on at times in the former Tennis Court Hall at Holyrood Palace, and Allan Ramsay's *The Gentle Shepherd* may well have been shown there. I've taken a few minor liberties in this chapter, which I discovered on being contacted by Dr Brianna Robertson-Kirkland, an extremely helpful music historian, who sent me a good deal of information about the play. It was initially performed minus the popular songs, but I really wanted to include them! The play was out by 1725, but the first known performances were in 1729, although there may have been private performances before that. The songs were added in 1729 too, after the runaway success of Gay's *The Beggars Opera*. It's a lovely gentle play and would have been perfect for children and adults to watch, and the music would have made it entrancing. I've read it, and it's beautiful indeed, a gentle play.

Allan Ramsay, the playwright, also seems to have been a gentle and kind man. I have every intention of writing a blog about this interesting man, so won't go into too much detail here. He was a poet and playwright, born in Lanarkshire in 1684. As an adult he became a wigmaker and moved to Edinburgh. Later he became a bookseller in the Luckenbooths, and ran the country's first circulating library, as I mention in the book. He published an extremely popular book of songs, entitled *The Tea-Table Miscellany,* and opened a theatre for a short period. He was also a closet Jacobite and allowed Bonnie Prince Charlie and his entourage to use his house when they took Edinburgh in 1745, although he ensured that he was away visiting friends at the time!

And finally, the Punch and Joan show. Yes, I also thought that the two main characters in this ancient and traditional puppet show had always been called Punch and Judy, but it seems this was not the case. Again I'll get into the details of the history of the show in a future blog, as it's fascinating, and although I'm not sure Punch and Judy shows still go on (if they do, I can't imagine them being like the violent shows of the past, one of which I remember seeing at the seaside as a child), they're a real tradition in Britain, as much so as pantomimes.

Punch came into England from Italy in the mid-seventeenth century with the puppeteer Pietro Gimonde, after the restoration of the monarchy. Initially Punch at this time was a marionette rather than a hand puppet, and was called Pulcinella or Pulliciniello, which gradually became anglicised to Punch. King Charles II loved the performance, giving Signor Gimonde a handsome reward. Samuel Pepys mentions seeing a performance in 1662 in his diary, the first recorded mention of it.

Punch was always a violent thug and always had a high-pitched voice, and by the eighteenth century he was hugely popular throughout Britain, being used to disrupt various puppet shows, although he did not have a show of his own initially. Very often he would fight the Devil, and usually, but not always, win.

By 1709 he'd acquired a wife, who at that point was called Joan, and their marital discord was highly amusing to both children and adults at the time, but they did not become glove puppets until the end of the eighteenth century, as glove puppet shows were much cheaper to put on than marionette shows were, and could be set up even in very small towns.

In the nineteenth century Joan became Judy, and they acquired a baby and a dog, Toby, often played by a real dog. In this century Punch and Judy booths became a standard feature in seaside resorts (which is where I saw my Punch and Judy show), and would attract enormous audiences.

If you'd like to read further historical blogs and other information about the period my books are set in, and also learn about future book releases, please subscribe to my monthly newsletter (no spam, guaranteed) here:

http://eepurl.com/bSNLHD

I also post a historical blog on my website every month:

www.juliabrannan.com

You can also follow me on Twitter:

https://twitter.com/BrannanJulia

Or on Facebook:

www.facebook.com/pages/Julia-Brannan/727743920650760